Library of Congress Cataloging in Publication Data

Tanner, Janet.
  The hours of light.
  I. Title.
PR6070.A545H6   1981   823'.914   80-29074
ISBN 0-312-39252-4

THE
HOURS
OF LIGHT

JANET TANNER

ST. MARTIN'S PRESS · NEW YORK

THE HOURS OF LIGHT

For my Father, Gerald Young,
1897–1973

'Who was a "carting" boy in the pits of the Somerset coal-field for ten years, and a collier in Somerset and South Wales for several more.

The stories he told me inspired this book. The
plot and the characters are fictional, but the way
of life is as he described it to me, and I believe
that he, and others like him, helped to write *The
Hours of Light* with their lives.'

BOOK ONE
CHARLOTTE

1

BENEATH a hot June sun, the coal cart rolled and ground its way through the centre of Hillsbridge.

Down the steep curving hill it came, with every turn of the wheels jarring the man who lay on the filthy wood-plank floor, covered by a threadbare working coat. Past the Rectory, whose shady trees overhung the road it rolled, past the hoop-shaped block of shops where the doors stood open to the drowsing afternoon. In the station yard the parcel-deliveries horse, standing patiently between the shafts of its baize covered wagon, stopped flicking its ears at the troublesome flies to watch with mild interest, and a group of back-shift miners squatting on their haunches against the railings spat in a studied nonchalance that was belied by the grim narrowing of their eyes.

As the cart jolted across the first of the two sets of railway lines that severed the main street, the low moans of the injured man became a shriek of agony.

"Go bloody careful, mate. He's got a broken back!" his companion called roughly to the driver.

On the wide pavement that bordered the road between the two sets of railway lines, two women broke off in their conversation to watch the cart's uneven progress.

The one, plump and fair, looked only interested. Her men were not miners, but colliery carpenters who worked in safety above ground level.

But the other stood tight-drawn, her whole body frozen into an attitude of waiting. Charlotte Hall had three sons and a husband underground at South Hill Pit. The injured man in the coal cart could be any one of them.

As the cart approached her eyes followed it, blue and anxious in her pale face, and when it drew level she set her shopping bag down on the pavement abruptly. Peggy Yelling, her companion, touched her arm sympathetically, but she brushed her aside and hurried to the roadside.

"Who is it?" she called to the haulier. "Who's been hurt?"

The haulier shrugged bad-temperedly and ignored her. He was still cursing his luck for having been at the head of the queue waiting at the pithead for his load of coal when the injured man had been brought to the surface.

"Who have you got there?" she called again, her voice rising.

The second miner in the back of the cart straightened from tending his workmate.

"It's all right, Mrs Hall. It's not one of yours. No need for you to worry."

The cart ground on its way, but still she stood on the pavement's edge staring after it as if she had seen a ghost.

This time they were safe. This time it was not James, her husband, who was being jolted through the streets in agony, nor Jim or Fred, her sons. This time it was not Ted, just thirteen years old, whose future had been ruined with a broken back. But how long could their luck hold? How long before it was a Hall in the coal cart that served for an ambulance?

"Lotty, are you feeling all right?" Peggy Yelling's anxious voice seemed to be coming at her through a haze, and she drew a deep, trembling breath.

"Yes, I'm all right, Peggy. It's just that I thought . . . oh, you know what I thought. I don't have to tell you, do I?"

"No, Lotty, I know." Peggy nodded sympathetically. "I'd never get used to it, if my men were underground. But you shouldn't be upsetting yourself. Not in your condition."

Charlotte laughed briefly and glanced down at her stomach. Not even her loose black gabardine coat could hide the large bulge.

"You'd think I'd have had more sense at my age, wouldn't you?" she laughed. "Still, it's only another month to go now. You haven't forgot I shall be wanting you when the time comes?"

"I haven't forgot," Peggy assured her. "I wrote it in my almanac as soon as you told me. I've seen all the others come into the world, and I don't intend to miss this one. Though I'm warning you, it's eight years since you had Amy. This one might not be so easy, Lotty."

Charlotte shrugged impatiently and retrieved her bag from where she had left it. "I'd have another dozen if it ended with bringing

4

them into the world," she said shortly. "It's the worry that comes after that gets me down. Now take our Jack. He's going to start work now, down the pit like the others—as if I hadn't got enough of them underground already."

Peggy Yelling looked surprised. "He's going underground straight away, your Jack?"

"No, he's going on the screens first, sorting coal," Charlotte told her. "But how long will that last? He took his labour exam this March, and passed, so he can leave school any time. A few weeks back he went to see O'Halloran about a job, and he'd have started by now, I reckon, if it hadn't been for getting the chicken pox. Chicken pox at twelve—I ask you!"

For a moment Peggy was silent, her round, pleasant face thoughtful.

"You've never thought about him going into a shop, I suppose," she asked presently.

"A shop?"

Peggy nodded. "When I went to the chemist's just now for some Liquafruta I noticed a card in the window, advertising for an assistant. I don't suppose . . . "

"The chemist's?" Charlotte repeated sharply. "Our chemist?"

"Well, yes, of course. Now I would have thought that might suit your Jack. But if he's going after it, he ought to make haste. He won't be the only one, by a long chalk."

"The chemist. I'll go home and tell him about it right away." Charlotte hitched her bag up on her arm. "You don't mind if I don't wait for you, Peggy?"

"Well, no, if you want to go on. But don't you go hurrying up the hill in this heat!" Peggy cautioned her.

Charlotte shrugged impatiently. "I shall be all right. I'll see you again, Peg. Toodle-oo for now. And thanks!"

She turned and started along the street in the direction the coal cart had gone. Over the second pair of railway lines she went, crossing the road when she reached the market place and passing through the forecourt of the George Hotel that faced its rival Miners Arms on the opposite side of the street.

Here the way branched, the main road going straight on through rolling green countryside towards Bath, but Charlotte turned to her right, passing the forge and livery stables at the foot of the hill, and beginning the steep climb that would take her home.

5

The town of Hillsbridge was set in a valley bowl, there was no way out of it except up a hill. She had never minded much in the past. While others complained of being 'done up,' Charlotte reckoned the exercise kept her healthy. But today the heat and the weight of the baby in her belly combined to exhaust her. By the time she reached the wooden bench, set into the grass verge and half-way up the steepest part, her breath was ragged and her legs felt unsafe. She paused for a moment, resting her bag on the seat and wishing she could go and get a drink of water from the spring that ran out of the hill on the opposite side of the road, as the children did.

But the memory of the coal cart was too fresh in her mind, her own fear still too real. It was too late now to stop the older boys going down the pit. She'd tried, God knew, but she'd failed, and she'd had to watch them in their turn go down the hill with their cans of cold tea, their tin of sandwiches, and the half-dozen tallow candles that would light their way underground through a day's shift.

But if she could stop Jack, it would be something.

He was still at home, getting over the chicken pox, but the spots had all gone now, and he'd been given a clean bill of health only this morning. If he could get down to the chemist's straight away, maybe they'd take him on. Jack was a smart boy, who would be a credit to any shop, and if he did well, they might even encourage him to train as a dispenser.

Hitching her bag up on her hip, Charlotte set off again. Today the hill seemed to go on forever, past cottages whose gardens were ablaze with roses, snap dragons and night-scented stocks, past the walled grounds that sloped down from the big houses on the hill-top. Hardly a breeze stirred the snow-on-the-mountain that hung in pendulous white drifts over the wall of Miss Emery's cottage, and Charlotte thought it was almost impossible to believe that only last week she had been complaining that summer was never going to arrive.

Determinedly she set her gaze on the break in the houses that would mean the end of her climb, and at last she reached it, a narrow track branching away from the hill and following the curve of the valley bowl.

From here it was plain that the town had been built around the railway lines that would carry the coal out of the valley. They ran arrow-straight through the untidy jumble of dust-blackened buildings. The strong sunlight had made a silver ribbon of the river, and pointed up the tower of the church, away beyond the shops and chapels, while on the opposite hillside, the terraced houses, with their strips of garden, looked cool and shady by comparison.

Into the track Charlotte turned. It was rough underfoot at first. Then, as it passed the allotments and reached the houses on the one side and the blocks of privies, wash-houses and bake-ovens on the other, the road was better made. To the rest of Hillsbridge it was known as Greenslade Terrace, one of the rows of cottages built across the hillside to accommodate the miners and their families. But to the inhabitants of its twenty houses, it was simply 'the rank'.

The door of number eleven, like most of the others, stood ajar. Charlotte pushed it open and walked through the small scullery to the kitchen.

Even at this time of year a fire had to be kept burning under the hob for cooking and boiling a kettle, and its heat, reaching out to meet the warmth of the summer afternoon, made the room oppressive.

She put her bag down against the settle and crossed to the door in the far corner of the kitchen. Behind it, the stairs rose, steep, scrubbed wood.

"Jack!" she called. "Are you up there?"

He came down the stairs and into the kitchen, a slightly-built boy with fair hair that grew thick and springy away from his forehead, and eyes as blue as Charlotte's own.

"I didn't expect you home yet, Mam," he said. "I was reading."

She nodded abruptly. Jack did far too much reading for his own good. Far better if he'd only get out in the fresh air more often. But she'd had it over with him a good many times, and he never took any notice of her.

"Jack, about this job of yours," she began shortly. "I want to talk to you."

He turned away, crossing to the window and looking out across the yard.

"What's there to talk about? I'm going to start at South Hill Pit now my chicken pox is cleared up."

"No, Jack." She followed him. "I don't want you going down that pit."

The boy pushed his hands into his pockets, still staring out unseeingly at the blank wash-house wall on the other side of the path.

"What else is there for me to do?" he asked flatly.

"There's a job going at the chemist's," she told him. "Peggy Yelling saw the card in the window. Now if you went down straight away, you might get it."

He half-turned, frowning and biting his lip, and she caught at his arm.

"Jack, you don't *want* to work in that filthy hole, do you?"

He shook his head. "No, but . . . "

"But what?"

"I don't want to work in a chemist's shop, either."

Her expression softened.

"You mean there's something else you'd like to do that you've been keeping quiet about?" she asked.

He hesitated, his face brightening momentarily. Then he turned away.

"It wouldn't do any good if I told you. If you live in Hillsbridge, there are two jobs you can do. You can go down the pit, or you can work on the land. A farm labourer earns even less than a miner, and at least a miner gets Sundays off."

The bitterness in his voice surprised her.

"But you'd get time off in the chemist's shop, Jack," she said. "It would be a nice, clean job."

"I don't want to work in a shop," he said mulishly. "I might as well be on the screens. And there's no money for what I want to do, so it's pointless going on about it."

"Well, what is it you want?" she asked in exasperation.

For a moment the silence hung between them, as hot and heavy as the afternoon air. Then he raised his eyes to meet hers squarely.

"I should like to be a teacher. Mr Davies wanted me to sit a scholarship, but I knew we couldn't afford it. There'd be books to pay for, and all the travelling, even if I got a free place. Mr Davies was going to come and see you and Dad, and I had to stop him. So I took the labour exam instead, and got the job at South Hill Pit."

"Why ever didn't you say?" she asked.

"I didn't want to worry you," he said simply.

She pulled a chair from beneath the red chenille folds of the table cover and sat down, easing her shoulders out of her coat. Her mind was flitting back across the years to a half-forgotten love, and a young man with gentle hands and a white body that was not blue-veined like a miner's. He had been secretive, too, and sensitive, and clever . . .

"Chemist shop, screens, I should have known none of them were for you, Jack," she said softly.

For a moment they were silent. Then the mantel clock chimed the hour and she came out of her reverie abruptly. "Jack, I wish you'd go up the hill and meet Amy for me. We'll talk about this again."

He paused in the doorway. "Are you going to tell Dad?"

"I'll have to tell him, won't I? You've taken me aback a bit, though, and I want to think about it first." She smiled briefly and encouragingly. Then, when he made no move, she went towards him, giving him a little push. "Don't look so worried. We'll sort something out. Now off you go and meet Amy for me, there's a good lad. It'll be all right, you'll see."

But as the door closed after him, she wished she could feel as confident as she had sounded.

BENEATH the black mountains, the town of Hillsbridge was sleeping.

The last customers had rolled unwillingly from the bars of the George Hotel and the Miners Arms, already dreading the hooters that would shatter their peace before dawn had broken. The tenors, baritones and basses of the male voice choir had whistled snatches of 'Song of the North Men' and 'The Teddy-bears' Picnic' as they climbed one of the inevitable hills home and fallen into bed to dream of the reception they would get next week at their annual concert.

In one or two houses, lamps burned late as men discussed ways of raising money to help the Whitehaven disaster fund, set up to help the dependants of those who had recently died in a pit explosion in far-off Cumberland.

But to Charlotte Hall, sitting beneath the stars on the doorstep of her house in Greenslade Terrace, it seemed as if she might be the only person in the world still awake.

The pits would be resting now. The great wheels that raised and lowered the cages would be still, and no steam would be belching from the chimney above the winding house. Maybe the odd maintenance man would still be at work, but by now the shot-firers who worked the backshifts would have finished blasting, and the yards that were alive throughout the daylight hours with busy men calling to one another, with hauliers' horses and carts queuing at the screens for their loads of coal and tubs shunting on the sidings, would be silent and ghost-like in the white light of the moon.

This, she recalled, was almost exactly the way she remembered first seeing Hillsbridge, and to her it had seemed to be endowed with a special kind of romance.

She had been seventeen years old, and too much in love to feel outrage at the cancerous black growth on the green Somerset countryside. Twenty-five pits, the coal veins had thrown up, and around them had grown the mining villages, clusters of small, grimy houses obtruding into rich, undulating farmland and overlooked by those mountainous mounds of coal waste, the batches.

Hillsbridge was the largest of these villages, centre of the coal-field and even dirtier than the rest. But to her it had been a magic place.

The batches had looked like black mountains, girdled with fir trees on their lower slopes and rising round and sombre or long and ridge-like against the violet sky. They were, she had thought, like guardian hills of an enchanted valley, and a trickle of warm excitement had made her tighten her grip on the arm of the young man beside her.

"Oh, James," she said. "I think it's wonderful!"

Charlotte Morris was the daughter of a regular soldier, but Hillsbridge was quite unlike any other place she had known. Since her mother had died, three years earlier, she had lived with an elderly aunt in Bath. But nine miles of open countryside separated the city from Hillsbridge, which had a bad name with the people of Bath. The miners, they reckoned, were a 'rough lot'. And they kept as far away from them as possible.

One night in the autumn of 1891, Charlotte had to stay later than usual at the draper's shop where she worked. They had been stock-taking, and it was past nine when she finally escaped, tired and footsore. But her relief was short-lived. As the door closed after her, she saw a gang of youths coming up the street towards her, and from the way they were dressed and their rowdy milling about, she recognized them instantly as Hillsbridge miners.

Alarmed, she drew back into the shop doorway, but it had been locked behind her, and offered no escape.

The gang of youths was getting closer, shouting and singing ribald songs. A nauseous knot of panic formed in her throat, but she knew that to show fear was the worst thing she could do, and she made herself leave the trap of the doorway and walk firmly towards them.

The first group parted to let her through, and, heart thumping, she passed them. But the following group fanned out across the pavement, blocking her way, and as she moved to one side they moved too, cheering and jeering.

"Hey-ey! Look what we've got here, lads!"

"Not bad, eh?"

"Don't be in such a hurry, sweetheart!"

Charlotte drew herself up tight. Fear was making her tremble, but the last thing she wanted was for them to see it.

"Let me pass!" she said.

But they only laughed, closing in around her. Even the first group had come back now to join in the fun.

"I like your hair, sweetheart. That's all right, that is!" The tallest of the lads made a grab for one of her combs, and before she could stop them, thick honey-coloured curls had tumbled down one side of her head.

"How dare you!" she cried, angry now as well as frightened. "If you don't leave me alone, I'll call a policeman!"

The lads laughed in delight.

"That won't do you much good. They're all in a fight down by the railway station," one told her, and the tall lad who had pulled out her comb reached down to tweak at her skirt.

"Got pretty ankles, too, have you?" he leered.

Tears of panic pricked at Charlotte's eyes.

"Stop it!" she cried, her control gone. "Leave me alone, d'you hear?"

"Yes. Leave her alone!" A young man elbowed his way to the front of the group. "Can't you see she's a decent girl?"

"Oh, sod off, Hall," the tall lad told him. "I like a bit of class myself."

But the other raised his fist threateningly.

"Leave her. I'm warning you!"

For a moment they squared up, surly and determined, and Charlotte held her breath. Then the taller lad relaxed, sticking his hands into his pockets and laughing.

"All right, Hall, you can have her. Come on, lads, let's see what else we can find."

Laughing and calling, they rolled off down the street; and when they had gone Charlotte turned to look at the young man who had rescued her. He was no taller than she, wiry, with hair that looked fair in the light of the gas lamp, but he was older than she had

11

first thought—twenty-four, maybe, or twenty-five.

"Thank you, I'm all right now," she said, but her voice was still uneven.

He stood looking at her, summing her up.

"I'll see you home," he said after a moment. "You shouldn't be out on your own at this time of night."

"I've been at work," she protested. "We're not allowed to close the doors while there's a customer anywhere to be seen, and tonight we had stock-taking as well."

"Then your father ought to come and meet you," he told her.

"My father's a soldier. He doesn't live with us," she replied abruptly. She was still upset by her encounter with the youths, and there was something disconcerting in the way this young man was looking at her. "I'll be all right. You need not trouble yourself any more."

She turned and began to walk, but he fell into step beside her.

"You might meet more trouble yet. There's been a rumpus at the pit today, and a lot of lads have come in on the train looking for mischief. They don't mean any harm, but when they've had a drink, well, they get stupid."

She cast a sidelong look at him.

"Are you a miner, too?"

He laughed. "Course, I am. Why?"

She bit her lip, embarrassed. "You don't seem like the others. I've heard terrible stories about miners, how they're always fighting and that. Don't you know about the notices they put up in Bath when they're advertising for servants? "Hillsbridge girls need not apply." That's because they're supposed to be so rough."

He laughed again. "They're no different to you. Except . . . " He paused, eyeing her appreciatively. "I haven't seen any as pretty."

"Oh!" she said, pleased.

She'd never considered herself pretty. Her mouth was, she thought, too wide, dominating her small, straight nose, and although her eyes were a good, clear blue, the lashes around them were stubby and too light in colour. She'd tried to darken them once with the black-lead her aunt used on the grate but a fine mess she'd made, for it had been days before she'd been able to wash away the last traces of the dark smudges under her eyes.

"I'd like to see you again," he said.

Beneath her tight-laced stays her heart began to beat very fast, and she began to feel a little sick again.

12

"I don't know your name," she said.

"I don't know yours either," he teased. Then, taking pity on her, he added, "I'm James Hall. Does that make it all right?"

"I don't know," she confessed. "And I'm not sure I should tell you my name. You might be up to something."

"I am. I want to make sure I can find you again," he told her honestly.

They turned a corner and came upon a row of small houses whose doors opened directly on to the steep street.

"This is it," she said, excitement making her bold. "This is where you can find me."

"Then I can see you again?"

"If my aunt allows it. But I expect I can get round her," she added.

"I should do something about this if I were you." He pointed to the hair she had quite forgotten to re-pin. "I don't want to get the blame for something that isn't my fault. And no more wandering about the streets on your own, do you hear? From now on, I'll take care of you, all right?"

He had been as good as his word. He had courted her with a gentleness that had surprised her, and when he proposed marriage, her father had reluctantly agreed. He hadn't much cared for the idea of his only daughter becoming the wife of a miner, but for all that, he liked the quiet pitman well enough.

So Charlotte and James were married, and she moved into a world that seemed to have a romance of its own. She was fascinated by the dark and dusty workings that were reached by means of leafy lanes, and the black batches rising out of the green fields had, she thought, a regal dignity. As for the men who worked in the unknown places beneath the earth, they were her heroes, and when she watched them walk in twos and threes across the colliery yard, sinews hard and taut beneath their working shirts and rushyduck trousers, she was proud to be the wife of one of them.

She had closed her eyes to the bent shoulders and stooping posture of the older men, ignored their phlegmy coughs and turned her head as they spat into the gutter. To her, the lung disease meant nothing. Even the pit accidents she heard about seemed more romantic than tragic, on a par with soldiers' lives lost in battle.

When she first began to learn of the indignities a miner could suffer, she had refused to believe. She had actually laughed when James told her about the duties of a carting boy, for it was beyond her comprehension that anyone could expect a lad to pull a sleigh full of coal by means of a circle of tarred rope around his waist, while crawling on his hands and knees along the narrow and sometimes steep seams.

"Just because I don't know anything about it, you think you can make a fool of me," she had said, and to convince her, James had called in a young lad from further down the rank who had recently started work as a carting boy.

She had stared in horror when he had pulled up his shirt to reveal a raw and bleeding band of flesh around his waist where the rope had cut into it.

"That's terrible!" she cried, outraged. "They shouldn't allow it! If the roadways aren't big enough for tubs, then they should make them big enough!"

But to her surprise, James had merely shrugged.

"If they spent too much money, the pit wouldn't pay, and we'd all be out of a job," he told her calmly. "Besides, the lads soon get used to it."

"I don't believe it!" she said harshly, sickened, yet unable to tear her eyes away from the red raw flesh. "Look at his poor back! You can't tell me he'll ever get used to that!"

"It'll harden. We've all been through it." James turned to the lad, pulling his shirt across the sore. "Bathing it with urine, are you, son? That's the best way. But I expect your father has already told you that."

Charlotte had been as shocked by James' easy acceptance as she had been by the boy's raw back, and that night as they prepared for bed in the small room above the parlour, she found herself looking closely at James' waist. To her surprise, she saw that there was no circular scar. But for the first time she took notice of the blue veinings that stood out in places, one short, thick and ridged along-side his left shoulder blade, one longer and shaped like a curled rope just above his buttock, and instead of the usual fierce pride, she felt the beginnings of anger and disgust.

During the busy years that followed, however, she had no time to think about the pits and what they did to the men who worked in them.

The children came, one after the other: first Jim, then Dolly, her older daughter, Fred, Ted, Jack and Amy. And between them, the two children who had not survived, but were still as real to her as

14

those who had lived: Wilfred, whose sickly little body gave up its unequal struggle after only a few days, and Florrie, fifteen months old, and beginning to talk and take a tottering step or two when whooping cough claimed her. When they died, a little of herself died with them, but there was precious little time for grief. The endless round of washing, scrubbing and baking saw to that.

When the time came for Jim, her eldest, to leave school, however, and James took him proudly down the hill for his first day underground, all her anger came flooding back. That night she had looked at his bloodied back and relived the horror she had felt so many years before, only multiplied a hundredfold, for it was her own son's body that had been used in this brutal way, a body on which she had lavished tenderness and care.

She had wanted to cry, but she was beyond tears, and to relieve her feelings she had taken down every pair of curtains in the house and washed them, working until almost midnight, while the children, half-afraid, peeped at her from behind the wash-house door. When she'd finished, she was exhausted, her eyes great dark pools, her hair hanging damply from its pins, but she felt herself washed as clean as the curtains, and as thoroughly wrung out.

"What the devil are you doing?" James had asked, crossing the yard. "Leave it and come to bed, do, or you'll kill yourself."

She laughed, and her tired, singing ears recognized the note of determination and piercing despair.

"Don't worry, James, I'm not going to die yet," she told him. "I'm going to make sure I live to see at least one of my sons in a decent job where people respect him—and his body. I'll see that, if it's the last thing I do!"

He had put his arm around her then, wondering what had happened to the naïve girl he had brought to Hillsbridge as his wife. Life hadn't been easy for her. But for all that, she was still the handsomest woman in the rank. Her neck had not turned scrawny, and her body was still straight and supple, though thickened at the waist from repeated childbearing. As for her hair, most of the curl had gone when Jack was born, and she had almost lost her life, but thirteen years had done nothing to dim its rich honeyed colour.

He moved his hand to her head, pulling it against his in a rare gesture of affection.

"Better times are on the way," he told her. "Amy is three now. In no time at all, she'll be off your hands. And with the boys earning, there'll be a bit extra money about, and with any luck we'll fix Dolly up in service where she can live-in. It'll be all right, sweetheart, you'll see."

She did not answer, for she knew that she could never make him understand, and she let him take her back across the yard to the scullery door. There, for just a moment she paused, looking towards the batches: black mounds on the skyline, trapping them all.

Now, five years later, Charlotte sat in the doorway, remembering that other night. Since then, she had seen two more sons go down the hill to the pit, and each loss had only strengthened her resolve. The coal masters would not have Jack, and they would not have her unborn child either if she could help it.

All evening, as she sat sewing moleskin patches on the threadbare knees of three pairs of pit trousers, she had been busy formulating her plans. Her hands and face had been black with the dust that spewed out from the cloth in clouds as she sewed, but she hardly noticed. Finally, when she put away her needle, she knew that in spite of being tired, she was far too excited to sleep. So she had taken her chair to the doorway where the heat that still sang in the air was less oppressive, and sat for a while turning over her memories and her plans.

A small breeze stirred the hem of her skirt, and she smiled gently to herself. Tomorrow, perhaps, it would be cooler. She hoped so, for tomorrow she had a great deal to do.

THE NEXT DAY, she went to see William Davies, the schoolmaster at the board school where Jack had gone since he was three years old.

There was no time for making appointments, so at the end of the day she stood at the school gates, waiting for Jack and Amy, turning over in her mind what she would say.

She would have liked to be able to talk it over with Dolly, she thought. Since Dolly had grown up, Charlotte had found she could discuss things with her more as a friend than a daughter. But Dolly was in service with Captain Fish in the big house at the top of the hill, living in, and would not be home until her day off, the day after tomorrow.

The bell rang to signal the end of school, and as the children began pouring out, Charlotte watched them closely. Amy was among the first. She came skipping across the yard, a small, round figure in pinafore and petticoats, with honey-coloured hair as bright as Charlotte's once had been.

"Mam! Mammy! Why are you here? I was coming home with Jack!"

Jack had returned to school that day for the first time since his bout of chicken pox.

"I've come to have a word with Mr Davies," Charlotte told her, bending to retie a hair ribbon that had been pulled into a tight, crumpled knot. "You go home with Jack like you always do."

Amy looked up at her, round-eyed.

"What do you want to see Mr Davies for, Mammy? Is it about me?"

Charlotte smiled. It was just like Amy to assume she must be the central character in any drama. It came from being the youngest child of the family for so long, she supposed, loved and fussed over by older brothers and sister. When the new baby arrived, Amy was going to have some adjusting to do.

"No, Amy, it's nothing to do with you," she told her. "Look, here's your brother coming now. He'll see to you. And if you're good, he'll take you to get an ounce of mint shrimps, won't you, Jack?"

"If you like . . . " Jack's eyes were on her best coat, and she knew he'd guessed the reason she was here. His face was pale—from spending too much time indoors, she told herself—but she knew it was not only that. "Mam, couldn't I come with you?" he said hesitantly. "I'd like to hear what he has to say."

But Charlotte shook her head decisively.

"No. It's better if you're not there. He can be frank with me then, without hurting your feelings—or making you conceited, if that's the way it goes. You take Amy home, and you'll hear soon enough what Mr Davies has to say."

Jack's face fell, and Amy looked from one to the other, hopping up and down with impatience.

"Go on now, the pair of you," Charlotte instructed.

Then, without another word, she crossed the school yard and entered the cloakroom.

After the sunshine outside, the long narrow room, ventilated only by a small window above the two little sinks, was dim, and the distinctive smell of carbolic soap and chalk tickled her nostrils.

She rounded the peg stands and mounted the two stone steps, to

17

tap on the closed door. A voice from within bade her enter, and she pushed it open and went into the classroom.

At his desk, William Davies was piling slates one on top of the other.

He was a portly little man with a fringe of dark hair around an almost-bald head, smart still in his stiff white collar, although his chalk-marked suit had seen better days. He peered short-sightedly in Charlotte's direction, searched for his spectacles amongst the welter of papers and inkpots on his desk, and settled them on his nose.

"Mrs Hall!" Able to see her at last, he sounded faintly surprised. "What brings you here?"

"I want to talk about Jack," she said.

Behind his spectacles, his eyes became brighter and his tired expression seemed to lighten.

"About Jack," he repeated cautiously.

"That's right. As you know, Mr Davies, he took his knowledge test before he had the chicken pox, and he's fixed himself up with a job on the screens at South Hill Pit." She raised her chin, looking at him squarely. "I don't think he's cut out for that. I want to know what you think."

William Davies nodded, and the joy that was swelling inside him showed in his face.

Jack Hall was one of the best pupils he had ever had, and he had thought it a tragedy that he would be wasted in the dark, soulless warrens beneath the ground. From the time Jack had come to him, he had worked with him, fostering his love of learning, helping and encouraging him.

Sometimes he had stayed late and they had read together, and talked about books. Often Jack had asked to borrow the tattered school copies of the classics so that he could take them home to study. And once or twice, William Davies had found himself talking to Jack as an equal instead of a pupil, discussing current affairs and politics and everyday things, like the changing pattern of the countryside around Hillsbridge—and even the butterflies that were William Davies's secret passion.

"Watch them, Jack," he had told him. "See how they rise and float! The most fragile things on God's earth, but they can do what we cannot."

Then, seeing his pupil's thoughtful expression, he had gone on: "Not only that, they're free. Their lives may be short, but at least they spend them doing what they want."

Now, to Charlotte, he said, "I think that if Jack goes into the pit, you'll all regret it. I've seen a lot of boys wasted who would have been capable of much, much more. But I've never seen one I felt it so strongly about. He's different, Mrs Hall. How, I don't know, but . . ."

"Yes," she said sharply. He was different, of course, and she knew the reason. But she had no intention of going into that now. "He tells me he wants to teach, Mr Davies, and I think that may be your doing. But I haven't any idea how he should set about it, and that's why I'm here."

Beneath his stiff-fronted shirt, William Davies' chest swelled with pride. The things he had said hadn't been in vain, then. The seeds he had sown were putting out roots . . .

"I think we should have a talk, Mrs Hall," he suggested. "If you'd care to come through into my house, we could talk it over with a cup of tea in our hand."

"That's kind of you, Mr Davies, but I'd rather talk here if it's all the same to you," Charlotte returned.

William Davies flushed slightly. "Of course . . . I only thought . . . but never mind." His busy hands restacked the slates yet again as he spoke, then he looked at her over the rim of his spectacles.

"I don't know if Jack has told you, but I've had this over with him. I tried to talk him into continuing with his education, and suggested I should see you and his father. But he was adamant I should do nothing of the sort."

"Why?" Charlotte asked, but she already knew the answer.

"He thought the expense would be beyond you," he told her.

She drew herself up, lifting her chin proudly.

"He had no business saying that. It's not for him at his age to judge what we can and can't do."

Again William Davies flushed slightly. It had been wrong of him, perhaps, to let the matter rest with Jack, but the boy had been adamant, and he had not wanted to embarrass the family.

"You're right, of course," he agreed. "I should have taken no notice. But for a boy of his age, he's very mature, and I tend, foolishly, to feel he's older than he is. However, you're here now. And if we can do something for him, pulling together, it would please me no end."

"What would it entail?" Charlotte asked.

The schoolmaster settled himself against the edge of his desk.

"There are various ways he could go about it," he told her, more comfortable now that he was on familiar ground. "But in Jack's case, I think it might be best if he stayed on here for a time. He'd be what's called a monitor, helping me with the general discipline, passing out pencils and collecting slates, and I might even get him to hear the younger ones read—that sort of thing. In return, I'd give him extra lessons. Then, later on, we could get him into one of the good schools as a pupil/teacher. A boy with a brain like his shouldn't be difficult to place, and he'd most likely live in with the headmaster. He might even be paid a small wage. I'd have to arrange the details later, of course, but I reckon that by the time he's seventeen, we could have made an uncertificated teacher of him. What do you say, Mrs Hall?"

He paused expectantly, but it was a moment before Charlotte could reply. The jumble of facts and unfamiliar titles were spinning round in her head, but one kept coming to the fore, and it made her glow with pride.

A teacher—Jack!

"Well, Mrs Hall?" William Davies pressed her, and she nodded, returning abruptly to reality.

"I think it's best to leave the details to you, Mr Davies. You know far more about these things than we do. As for the money, don't let that stop you. We've always managed so far, and I expect we'll manage again. Now, I shall have to talk this over with my husband, of course, but you can take it from me, Jack'll be back with you next year."

"Oh, Mrs Hall, you've no idea how delighted I am!" Unable to contain himself, William Davies reached over and gripped her hand, pumping it vigorously, and the warmth of his enthusiasm remained with Charlotte even when she had left him and set out for home.

In the kitchen she found Jack cutting thick slices of bread and dripping for Amy. He questioned her with his eyes and she nodded, beaming.

"Mr Davies says you'll do, Jack. I'll tell you all about it later when we're on our own."

It was only after she had finished explaining to him, however, that she realized she was as yet only half-way to arranging things. If it was to be feasible, extra money was needed. Already the wages that James and the older boys earned barely went round, and they had all been looking forward to Jack providing a little extra. If he stayed on at school, not only would there be no more money coming in, there would be additional expense too—books, decent clothes, a hundred and one things she was sure she hadn't even thought of yet. And very soon the baby would be another mouth to feed.

But Charlotte was determined not to let that stand in her way. If money was needed, then she would earn it. And she knew exactly where, and how.

They needed a cleaning woman at the Rectory. The one who 'did for them' had given notice, or so she had heard. It would be hard work, caring for her own home as well, but she didn't mind that, and anything would be better than taking in washing, like Ada Clements next door. Although she knew she was in no condition to go out looking for work, Charlotte felt sure she could persuade the Rector that she would be a suitable applicant for the job. If there were difficulties, she had a trump card, and she would not be afraid to play it. To keep Jack at school, there were no lengths to which she was not prepared to go.

The next morning, however, as she walked down the hill to the Rectory, it was all she could do to keep from turning back. All night, she had been thinking of the interview ahead, and dreading it more and more. She did not even like the Archers very much, she told herself. She never had done. They were a pompous and hypocritical pair, the Rector kindly enough, but full of his own self-importance and a good deal too fond of the sound of his own voice, and Caroline, his wife, the sort who might very well gloat in secret over the troubles of her husband's parishioners. If only there were some other way!

The gates were closed on the Great Western Railway line for an approaching train. As Charlotte stood on the wide pavement waiting for it to pass, she felt the same choking fear as she had felt watching the coal cart a few days ago, and her determination grew again. However difficult the interview, it would be worth it if she could make sure Jack, at least, was never jolted home that way.

When at last the train had filled its water tank and puffed away, she crossed the lines and walked up the pavement to the rectory gates, going through them and down the drive to the grey stone house.

Caroline Archer herself answered her ring, a tall, gaunt woman, who looked as if she thought enjoyment was the same as sin. Her eyes narrowed when she saw Charlotte, and her aquiline nose twitched in annoyance. "Good day, Mrs Hall, isn't it?"

Charlotte nodded. "That's right. I hear you need some help in the house, Mrs Archer. I've come to offer my services."

An expression of distaste flickered across Caroline Archer's face. "My dear Mrs Hall, you don't appear in any condition . . . "

Charlotte raised her chin. "I've never let it stop me working yet, and it won't stop me now. I can still scrub and polish and make a better job of it than some of these young flibbertigibbets who call themselves housemaids. I admit there'll be a couple of weeks when I shall be laid up, but after that I could come right back."

"And what about the baby?"

"I could easy enough get a neighbour to look after the baby for the few hours I was here."

The Rector's wife smoothed her skirt. "It doesn't sound a very satisfactory arrangement to me, Mrs Hall. In any case, we have had several other applicants who are really most suitable."

"You mean the job has gone?" Charlotte asked sharply.

"We haven't yet decided, but I'm sure when we do . . . "

"Then let me see the Rector," Charlotte interrupted her. "I'd like to tell him myself just why I want the job."

"Mrs Hall, I usually attend to the engagement of staff."

"Just the same, I'd like to see the Rector."

Caroline Archer compressed her narrow lips. "Very well. Come this way, Mrs Hall. But I assure you, the Rector will tell you exactly what I've told you."

She led the way, her gaunt body rigid with annoyance beneath the stiff violet silk of her dress, and Charlotte followed.

But in spite of her composed manner, her mind was churning. Supposing she had been wrong about Mr Archer? Supposing when she told him what she had to say, he simply ordered her to get out? It had hardly seemed a possibility before; now it seemed almost a certainty.

In the study, the Reverend Archer was poring over notes for his Sunday sermon. When the two women entered, he straightened his tall, spare frame, grateful for the interruption. The sermon had not been going very well.

"Mrs Hall!" he said with a surprised but welcoming smile. "What brings you here?"

"Mrs Hall has offered to come and clean for us," Caroline said swiftly. "I told her that in her condition I didn't think it wise, but she insisted on seeing you."

The Rector buried his hands in his pockets, smiling apologetically. "I'm grateful to you, Mrs Hall. But I do think on this occasion I agree with my wife . . . "

"I'd appreciate a word with you alone, Rector," Charlotte said, the hard edge in her voice taking them both by surprise. They exchanged glances, and Caroline moved reluctantly to the door.

Charlotte waited until she had gone, then turned to face the Rector.

"I have a reason for wanting this job," she said directly. "Our Jack is going to stay on at school and train to be a teacher, and money is short. If I don't earn some, I don't know how we'll manage."

Andrew Archer regarded her sadly.

"An admirable sentiment, Mrs Hall. But everyone has their own reason for wanting to earn a little extra money. I can't possibly accommodate you all. Your other boys have jobs, don't they, with the colliery companies? And Jack . . . "

"Jack is different," she said fiercely.

"I'm sure you think so, Mrs Hall, but . . . "

"I know so."

Something in her tone made him look at her curiously.

"Jack isn't made to be a miner," she went on. "He never was."

The Rector raised his hands helplessly. "I'm sorry, Mrs Hall, I don't understand. In mining families, a son follows in his father's footsteps. That's the way it's always been."

She swallowed painfully at the lump that had risen in her throat. A scent of roses, wafting in through the Rectory window, was evoking too clearly that other, long-gone summer's day. She felt again the potent drug of grief mingled with desire and saw once more the young man with the earnest face and the gentle hands who had seemed to her to belong to another world, where despair and hopelessness were only meaningless words.

The memory lasted unsullied for only a moment before she added to it a hundred more—choking guilt and regret, anxiety akin to panic, a body that swelled with the passing months, a child born into a family in which he had no place. Although she had tried to hide it even from herself, from the time he had begun to walk and talk she had known he was different, gentler, more vulnerable, and now she could keep her secret no longer. Now, for his sake, she had to break the silence of the years.

"James is not his father," she said.

She sensed the Rector's withdrawal, saw the embarrassment shutter his face.

"I . . . I don't see . . . " he began after a moment.

"His father was clever," she cut in. "When I knew him, he was a student. Jack takes after him. In every way. Don't you see, Rector, I can't let him waste all that. And that's the reason I've come to you."

"But why to me?" the Rector asked.

She raised her head, her eyes, clear and blue, giving no hint of the turmoil she was feeling.

"Because his father was John," she said.

For a moment the Rector stood immobile, his features so frozen by shock that they might have been carved out of alabaster.

"John? My nephew?" he repeated. Then, with a swift laugh: "Mrs Hall, you can't expect me to believe this!"

"It's the truth," she said quietly. "I wish it weren't, but it is, all the same. If you doubt it, you only have to look at Jack."

"But he was just a boy!" the Rector protested. "You must have been a grown woman!"

She did not reply, and with an effort he gathered himself together.

"I shall write to John at once. As you know, he went to Australia . . . "

For the first time her composure wavered.

"Why does he have to know?" she asked sharply. "What good would that do? I'm not asking for anything except the chance to work. I don't want charity. Only to give him the chance in life he deserves, that's all."

"But Mrs Hall . . . " the Rector began helplessly. Then, as a new thought struck him: "Does your husband know about this?"

"No." She drew herself up, feeling naked suddenly, and afraid. "No one knows, and I'll thank you to tell no one, Rector. What I've said to you, I've said in confidence. And you're a man of God. That means you're honour bound to keep it, doesn't it?"

He nodded. "If you say so, Mrs Hall. But I can't accept what you say. You must see that . . . "

"Oh, for the Lord's sake!" Suddenly his patronizing disbelief was more than she could bear. Her face contorted with the years of hidden pain, and her voice rose, shrill and entreating. "Don't you think I'd sell my soul if I could change it? Don't you think I've wished every moment of his life that he was James's son like the others? But he's not. He's not. And it's no good trying to pretend he is . . . "

She broke off, covering her mouth with her trembling hands. But still the ragged sound of her breathing escaped, rasping into the stunned silence.

At last the Rector spoke, his voice a pitiful parody of normality. "If I were to offer you the job, when could you begin?"

With a visible effort, she regained control. "As soon as you like, Rector."

"Then perhaps we could agree upon that. Without prejudice, you understand."

She nodded. The phrase meant nothing to her. She only knew that the job—and the wage that went with it—was hers.

The Rector opened the study door, and Caroline Archer appeared as if from nowhere.

Charlotte, trembling still from reaction, felt a swift shaft of fear. Was it possible Mrs Archer had been listening?

"I have offered the job to Mrs Hall," Andrew Archer said smoothly. Charlotte's fear deepened as she noticed the angry narrowing of the other woman's eyes, above her falsely smiling mouth.

She had beaten the Rector's wife, and she would not easily forgive. If she had overheard, her knowledge would be her weapon of revenge. But Charlotte was sure she was not a woman to show her hand too soon. It could be that she would prefer to keep her on pins for years with a hint here, a veiled threat there, knowing always she had the power to destroy in the end.

Charlotte shivered. But as she emerged into the June sunshine, she tried to console herself that it was a chance she had had to take. And besides, the study doors were thick. God willing, Caroline Archer would have heard nothing.

As for herself, she must push the things of which she had just spoken to the deepest recesses of her mind. For twelve years she had told no one, had not even allowed herself to think about them. She must not break the habit now. What was done was done. It was the only way.

THE WEATHER broke that afternoon with a sky-rending crack of thunder and bright vertical forks of lightning as the day-shift miners from South Hill Pit were making their way home.

Charlotte, standing at the window to watch the storm, saw them turn along the rank, too weary to hurry themselves though the rain was soaking their shirts and dripping from the brims of their cloth caps. She opened the door for them, laughing at their faces, striped black and white where rivers of rain had washed away the coal-dust.

"Come on in, you poor things. You look like drowned rats!"

They came, their boots leaving black puddles on the strip of lino that covered the scullery floor: a small, compactly-built man of around forty, and two youths whose bright hair was thick with coal-dust.

Jim was seventeen, the oldest of the family, and the image of his father. Fred, two years younger, was the quiet one. Nothing ever perturbed him, and it showed in the set of his face.

"Where's Ted?" Charlotte asked as they took off their caps. "Hadn't he finished when you came up?"

James Hall unbuttoned his shirt with wet, grimy hands. "He had a few more loads to cart. He won't be much longer, unless he starts playing the fool again."

"I thought you were supposed to be keeping an eye on him."

"So I do. But you don't expect me to stay down there with him when I've finished for the day, do you? Give over worrying, Lotty. He's all right."

Charlotte turned away, wondering how it was that Jim and Fred always managed to be ready to come home when their father did although they too were carting boys.

"As long as he's not up to mischief," she said briskly. "Get out of those wet things now, and I'll have your bath ready in two ticks."

She hurried ahead of them into the kitchen. The tin bath already stood in front of the fire and she lifted the pans of boiling water from the hob, pouring them in until the bath was more than half full. The boys followed her in, stripping off their shirts and loosening the waists of their rushyduck trousers.

"Out of the way while your father washes," she told them, and obediently they moved to one side to let James through.

This was the accepted daily ritual, and they followed it religiously. First James would wash the upper part of his body in the fresh hot water, then the boys, in order of their age, would follow. Then the same performance would be gone through for the lower part of their bodies, while the water grew steadily blacker and thicker.

Today, however, with Ted not yet home, the rota was completed more quickly than usual, and when Charlotte bustled in with clean towels and clothes, she found James and Jim already waiting for her and Fred bent double over the tub.

She handed James the towel and glanced at Fred's bare back. Around his waist, the hated ring of hard skin stood out brown and ridged, reminding her once again of the news she had to break to the family this evening—that Jack was not going to join them down the pit, but train as a teacher.

She'd have to tell James first, of course, and there would be no better time than after dinner when he was full of his favourite eye-piece stew. But she wasn't looking forward to it, and she knew she'd have to choose her moment with care. In the cramped house, it was not easy to talk without letting the rest of the family in on the conversation. Only in the bedroom at night were she and James alone, and these days he was usually asleep and snoring by the time she was ready to blow out the lamp and climb the stairs. Still, she'd find a way. She'd have to—or someone else would.

The men were deep in a discussion on Jeffries and Johnson, the two adversaries in The Great Glove Fight that was going to take place in Reno on the fourth of July, and Charlotte drew the eye-piece stew back onto the hob, skimming it absently.

The baby had begun pressing on a nerve, and the discomfort gave her yet another reason for breaking the news as soon as possible. If the baby came early, she'd be at a real disadvantage. And besides . . .

Charlotte remembered Peggy Yelling's warning and shivered. It was eight years since Amy had been born, and she was no longer as young as she had been. She knew of more than one, as healthy as she, who had haemorrhaged and died, and there was one poor soul in Glebe Terrace who had never walked since twins had completed her family in the spring.

Putting the unwelcome thoughts aside, Charlotte set the lid back on the stew pan with a clatter. It was no good to meet trouble half-way. But she'd be glad when it was over and done with.

James and the boys were upstairs dressing when the sound of boots being kicked off in the scullery told Charlotte that Ted was safely home. She replaced the cover on the stewpan and crossed the kitchen to meet him.

"You're late, my son," she greeted him. "What have you been up to?"

Ted grinned, irrepressible as always. In build, he was like the others, with the same fair hair and blue eyes. But just as Fred's nature showed in his face, so did Ted's. As a child he had been known as the scamp of the family, and he had not changed much since. Now, he met her stern question with a twinkle. "Never mind about *me*, Mam. What have *you* been up to?"

"Me? What do you mean?" she demanded.

"Come on," he teased. "You know what I'm on about."

"I do not. Get on with your wash, and don't be so cheeky."

He grinned. "It's you with the cheek, Mam, the way I heard it."

Her cheeks flamed suddenly. "Look here, Ted, just because you're at work now doesn't mean you can talk to me as if I were one of your mates," she admonished him. "Now mind your manners, do you hear?"

He took off his jacket and laid it across the back of the settle.

"All right. But I'd give a week's wages to know what our Dad's going to say when he gets to hear about it."

Too late the creak of the stairs warned him of his father's approach. He just had time to see Charlotte's agonized expression before the door opened and James emerged, buckling a belt at the waist of his clean trousers and looking from one to the other curiously.

"What's our Dad going to say about what?" he enquired.

Ted looked sheepish, and Charlotte flustered, but neither replied.

"Well? Won't somebody tell me what's going on?" James demanded.

Unnoticed, Ted slipped away, and Charlotte wiped her hands in her apron and turned to face James. "Since the subject's come up, I might as well confess," she said evenly. "What Ted has heard, I expect, is that I've got myself a job, cleaning, at the Rectory. I went down to see them this morning, and I'm starting right away."

For a moment there was no sound in the small room but the bubbling of the stew on the hob and the low chesty rattle of James' breath. "Have you taken leave of your senses?" he asked at last. "Haven't you got enough to do here? And with another baby coming too?"

"It's the money . . . " she protested.

"We manage, don't we?" he interrupted her. "God knows, you get my wages with little enough taken out of 'em—not like some women who only see what their men are too drunk to spend! And with Dolly and the boys working, and Jack starting too . . . "

"That's just it," she cut in. "Jack isn't starting work yet a while. He's stopping on at school. That's why I want the money—to keep him there."

"Stopping on at school?" James repeated incredulously. "Whatever for? He's passed his labour exam last March."

"Labour exam!" she snorted. "A bit of paper that's no good to anybody! It's a disgrace, that labour exam, pushing the bright children out before the dull ones. Well, I've made up my mind, no more of my sons are going to suffer through it. Jack's going to stop on at school and train to be a teacher. I've been to see Mr Davies, and . . . "

"You've done what?" James thundered, angry now.

"Been to see Mr Davies, and he says . . . "

"I heard you first time and I can't believe my ears! Oh, I know you've got a bee in your bonnet about the pits—you always have had. And you've always tried to make a big softy out of our Jack, too. But to do all this behind my back! Going to Davies—getting yourself a job! I won't have it, Lotty!"

Her chin came up. "You don't own me, James Hall!" she cried. "And you don't own Jack either!" Then, as if afraid of what she was about to say, she turned away, pressing her hands over her mouth.

Involuntarily, James raised his hand. In all their married lives he had never struck her, but in that moment he was closer to it than ever before. But as he realized what he was doing, his anger died as quickly as it had come. His hand fell limply to his side, and he shook his head sadly. "Oh, Lotty!"

She swung round then, and her eyes were bright with unexpected tears. "I'm sorry, James," she said quietly. "Perhaps I did wrong, not talking it over with you. But I was afraid you'd put a spoke in it. You've had your way with the others, and . . . "

"For the likes of us, there's no other way," James told her with patient conviction. "There's security for a miner. People are always going to want coal, and the stuff we bring up here in Somerset is good quality, even if the seams are narrower than most. As long as a man doesn't get himself blacklisted as a trouble-maker, there's no reason why he shouldn't stay in the pits all his working life."

"And how long is that?" Charlotte snorted. "Till his lungs are so clogged up with dust he can't breathe any more, or till he gets brought home in a coal cart with his back broke? And what sort of a life do you call it anyway, shut away hundreds of feet under the earth."

"Our Jack isn't going underground. He's going on the screens."

"And how long would that last?" she demanded. "Just a few months, and then he'd be carting like the others—a human donkey in harness. He's not cut out for it, James. I don't like the idea of any of them doing it, but if you force our Jack down the pit, it'll break my heart."

Some of her desperation reached him, and he rubbed a blue-veined hand across his chin.

"Does it really mean that much to you, Lotty?"

"Yes, James, it does."

"Even if it means nothing but hard work and disappointment."

"I'm willing to take that chance."

Rain beat a steady rhythm on the window. With the sun still covered by thunderclouds, the little room was dim, but the glow from the fire showed Charlotte's face in a soft relief of light and shadow: chin raised, eyes afraid, mouth determined.

Looking at her, James was reminded of the shop assistant he had rescued from the gang of rowdies almost twenty years ago. She hadn't changed, he thought. She was still the same Lotty, spirited, stubborn, and, in spite of her practicality, a bit of a romantic at heart. Life had dealt harshly with her, but it had not cowed her, and in this light it was almost impossible to see the passage of time in her face.

Unexpected tenderness flooded through him and he shook his head, smiling suddenly. "If it weren't for your condition, Lotty, I'd put you across my knee," he said.

A muscle moved in her cheek. "You mean . . . you'll let Jack stay on at school?"

He nodded. "When you're this set on something, it would be a brave man—and a daft one—who tried to stop you. I'll give it six months, Lotty. I don't think you'll keep it up longer than that. All I hope is, you don't kill yourself in the meantime."

She smiled, the fear leaving her eyes, and replied as she had that night in the wash-house: "Don't worry, James. I don't intend to die yet. I'll see my son a schoolmaster first, if that's what he wants. And I'll have enough life in me to be real proud of him."

30

2

THE BABY came on the first Saturday in August, on the day of the annual Foresters Fête.

It was always an occasion in the town—the procession led by the men of the Ancient Order of Foresters with their banners and regalia, winding its way to the Glebe Field for a full afternoon's programme of sports, followed by dancing in the evening, and although she was a week overdue, Charlotte went far enough down the hill to watch them pass.

Afterwards, she always maintained that it was the cornets and drums of the town band that 'started her off', and whether or not that was true, by the time the last carriage-load of children in fancy dress had passed, the first uncomfortable twinges had become recognizable pains, and as the last men on horseback disappeared from view, Charlotte knew it was time to head for home and send for Peggy Yelling.

Peggy arrived and immediately set about organizing the household. The boys had already left for the fête, planning to get their names down early for the hundred-yard and the egg-and-spoon races. So Rosa, the eldest of the Clements children from next door, was called in to take Amy to look for them. As for James, Peggy pushed him out to sit in the yard.

"It's a fine day, so you won't come to any harm," she told him with midwifely authority. "You'll be out of the way there, but on hand if we should need you to go for the doctor."

At first James protested, wanting to call the doctor straight away. But the women overruled him.

"Doctors mean bills," Charlotte told him, breaking off to catch her breath sharply as a pain spread through her like a crushing steel band, and Peggy, helping her friend up the stairs, agreed.

"I've brought more babies into the world than that Oliver Scott, in any case," she said comfortingly. "He's only a bit of a lad. Lotty'll be all right, you'll see."

Neither of them mentioned her earlier prediction that the birth might prove difficult. To Peggy's experienced eye, everything seemed to be going well, and she was right. It was all over by the time the boys returned home with Amy for a late tea.

Peggy had collected her dues and gone, and Dolly, fetched down from the big house, had arrived to take charge. Charlotte was sitting up in bed and in the cradle behind the bedroom door was the newest and smallest Hall—a red-faced creature almost hidden in a bonnet and gown several sizes too big for him.

The boys stood looking down at him, curious, but not wanting to show their curiosity; Amy, however, bobbed up and down with excitement.

"Oh, Mammy, can I hold him? Oh, isn't he pretty? What are we going to call him, Mammy?"

"I don't know yet," Charlotte said. "I haven't thought."

They all began to speak at once, piling suggestion upon suggestion until the baby began to cry. Dolly looked at her mother's tired face and pushed her brothers out, telling them to go downstairs and keep quiet.

But in the silence that followed, Ted, as always, had to have his say. Until a few moments earlier he had never given a single thought to the baby, beyond being embarrassed by his mother's swelling body, and the occasional uncomfortable pondering on how such an enormous lump could ever get out.

Now, however, he looked at the crying red face beneath the white bonnet, and for no reason that he could think of, said, "I think he looks like a Harry."

"Harry! Harry Lauder Hall!" Jim jeered, but Charlotte only smiled.

"That's a good name, Ted. I like it. I think that's what we'll have."

And Ted, more used to scoldings than praise, flushed with pride to think that it was his suggestion that had found favour and determined to be quiet and not disturb his mother for that evening at least.

FOR AS LONG as he could remember, Ted had been branded as the scallywag of the rank. He fell out of one scrape and into another with artless ease, never giving a thought to the consequences.

It just didn't occur to him that if he gave Amy a ride in the trucks used to collect horse-manure for the gardens, she would go home with her dress and knickers stinking to high heaven. And when he got his Sunday suit muddy one day going across the fields to play truant from chapel, he was surprised that washing it in the river made it worse, not better.

He felt it wasn't his fault that everything he did seemed to turn out that way, and he couldn't work out why his shirt should always be hanging out when everyone else's was tucked in, his knees far dirtier than theirs, and the toes of his boots, mended in exactly the same way, kicked through in half the time. But he enjoyed his reputation.

It was fun to lead a game of knock-out ginger even if he was caught in the end and got his ears boxed. And if he was the one who got the blame every time an unexpected parcel was found on someone's doorstep, only to be jerked away on a long string before it could be picked up, he decided he might as well have the fun of actually doing it.

As for the apples on the tree at the end of Captain Fish's garden, they were just asking to be picked, and the previous autumn Ted and Redvers Brixey had helped themselves to far more of the sharp green fruit than they could eat at one sitting. They had buried the rest in James's potato patch for safe keeping, but the tale was still told in the Hall household of how James had come in, straight-faced, and reported to Charlotte: "Well, Mother, that's the first time I've planted potatoes and dug up apples!"

But for all his mischief, Ted chose his victims with care. The old and infirm were left alone, and instead it was people like Martha Durrant, his pious and much-hated neighbour from number ten, who were singled out for his tricks.

Of all those in the rank who complained about Ted and his high spirits, it was Martha who complained the loudest and the longest, believing as she did that it was 'only for his own good'. She was a strict chapel woman, who would not even have a pack of cards in the house. If she was not airing her views on Ada Clements at number twelve, who often did the washing for her tribe of children on a Sunday, and sometimes even dared to hang it out to dry, she was thumping the tub about moral decline among the young. And on the fateful day when Ted had skipped chapel and muddied his suit, his mother had been ready and waiting for him when he got home, informed by Martha that he had been missing from his pew.

"Old busy-body," Ted had muttered shamefacedly, but Charlotte, angrier than he had ever seen her, had taken her neighbour's side.

"It's a good thing she's there to keep an eye on you!" she told Ted.

"I can't be everywhere at once, and it seems I can't even trust you to go to chapel now. Well, you may be sure if you think of doing such a thing again, Mrs Durrant will be in here to tell me about it before you can say Jack Robinson!"

Ted had wriggled away, subdued, and since that day had sat obediently each Sunday with the other boys in the hard, ricketty pew, enduring the agonies of a stiff collar. But he had not listened to the service, for he was too busy dreaming of ways to get his own back on Martha, who sat directly behind him and reminded him all the while of her presence by her daunting soprano voice and her irritating habit of holding the notes a beat or two longer than anyone else.

Yes, if Martha was good, Ted decided, she was a living reminder of how much more fun it was to be bad. For all the goodness in the world didn't seem to have made her very happy—or persuaded others to like her!

On the last Sunday in August 1911, however, as he lay in bed luxuriating in the glorious knowledge that this morning, at least, Charlotte would not be after him to get up or be late for work, Martha Durrant was far from his thoughts. The baby, crying for his early feed, had woken him, and unlike his brothers, he had not gone back to sleep. Carefully he raised himself on one elbow and looked at them.

Beside him in the narrow bed they had shared since they were children, Fred was snoring peacefully, while in the second bed, set at right angles to theirs, Jack and Jim lay side by side. Of Jim, there was nothing to be seen but a lump under the blankets, but the sunlight that streamed through the window in broad bands made Jack's sleeping face look younger and more childish than ever.

It was probably just as well he was going back to school, thought Ted; Jack wasn't really cut out for working at the pit. Mam had been right about that. And Ted wasn't even sure he wanted him there. The men could be very crude sometimes, and although he was less than two years older than his brother, he felt oddly protective of him.

Ted lay back, pillowing his head on his arms, and thinking back to the day he had started work at South Hill Pit. He'd been proud, so proud, swinging down the hill with his father and brothers, his sandwiches tied in a clean red handkerchief and his can of cold tea banging against his thigh.

He hadn't minded the ribbing he'd taken from the men. He

hadn't even minded at first that he was only working on the screens, sorting coal, hour after tedious hour. It was enough that he could no longer be termed a schoolboy, and that at the end of the week he would collect his first wages. But soon boredom set in, and Ted was looking for ways to make the day pass more quickly and raise a laugh.

Before long he had a reputation not unlike the one he had in the rank. And one day he had played a prank that made him chuckle even now to think of it.

On his way to work, he found a pair of pink flannel bloomers in a bush. How they had got there, he could not imagine, but Ted did not stop to investigate. Seeing the fun to be had, he rolled them up and took them to the pit with him. During a lull in the morning's work, he pulled them on over his pit trousers and pranced about, pretending to be the bow-legged wife of the gaffer. The other lads fell about laughing, until the gaffer came over to investigate.

He had no way of proving that the caricature was of his wife, but Ted knew he suspected and should have been warned. But typically, he took little notice. He stuffed the bloomers under a tub, until later in the day he managed to get behind one of the hauliers who was waiting for a load of coal, and then pinned them to his jacket.

The haulier was blissfully unaware of what had happened. He strutted about the yard, only mildly puzzled by the hoots of laughter that followed him. Then, when his cart was loaded, he drove off, the bloomers blowing behind him. Ted and the other lads thought it so funny they hardly took gaffer seriously when he came over and told Ted furiously that was the last trick he would play under his control.

Just how serious he was, however, Ted learned that evening when James got home.

He came in, white with anger, and called Ted into the kitchen.

"I've never been so ashamed in all my life!" he told him. "O'Halloran himself sent for me when I came up this afternoon, and told me the gaffer can't do a thing with you. He was all for getting rid of you there and then as a trouble-maker, but as a favour to me, you're getting another chance. You're starting underground tomorrow, as my carting boy, but if you don't behave yourself, that'll be it."

Ted said nothing. He was sorry his father had taken a carpeting over something that was not his fault, but he was not sorry to be going underground—he had been looking forward to it. And he knew, from the very first moment when the cage began its descent through the dank earth, taking him to the seams where coal was hewed, that he would never regret pinning the bloomers on the haulier and getting on the wrong side of the gaffer.

Carting was painful, he soon discovered. It was hot, sweaty work, and there were times when so many parts of his body ached that he could hardly separate one from the other. But it had its compensations. Scraped knees and a raw waist were a small price to pay for the privilege of squatting alongside the colliers, tea can between knees, munching cogknockers of bread and tossing crumbs to the mice that scuttled up from everywhere as soon as they smelled food. And who wouldn't drag a little extra coal in their putt if it also meant a little extra pay at the end of the week? Ted soon realized how much he liked money when he discovered how the thought of it could ease the sting of a raw wound in the middle of the night.

As for the other things he learned, some of them could still make him blush, especially when his father was in earshot. But he listened with open-mouthed interest as the older lads swopped tales of their conquests among women, and discussed the prices of the local whores, who, it seemed, demanded anything from a glass of cider to a whole week's wages for their favours.

He learned too to gamble, on 'anything that moved,' from the twist of a playing card to the speed of a cockroach, and he watched betting slips change hands well out of reach of the law. His vocabulary grew to include the sort of words he would never be able to use at the Sunday dinner table, and he tasted his first Gold Flake, walking across the pit yard after a long day's shift.

All this before he was fourteen years old. Fourteen.

The thought reminded him that next month would bring his birthday. Suddenly restless, he pushed back the bed-clothes and swung his bare feet onto the rag rug.

The trouble with his birthday was that it heralded the beginning of the winter, and the endless weeks when he saw daylight only on a Sunday. That was no fun. Just give him mornings like this one, he thought.

Quietly he padded over to the window and pulled back the curtain to look out.

Not a soul in the rank was stirring yet. On the opposite side of the yard, the doors of the privies and wash-houses were firmly closed, the only sound being the patient clucking of the Clements's hens in their pen in the gardens beyond.

Ted leaned on his elbows, letting his gaze run idly over the wash-house blocks and the bits of gardens he could see between them—small segments of rich, brown earth broken up by potato haulms, cabbages and runner beans.

Then he stiffened suddenly, his eyes narrowing. What was that down at the end of the Durrants' garden, moving slowly among the feathery green parsnip tops?

A fat, muddy-pink pig moved lazily and methodically through the parsnip patch.

The Durrants' neighbours all complained about the pig, but Martha had always overruled them. She was very partial to home-cured pork and bacon, and one pig had succeeded another in the wooden sty at the end of the garden.

Now, the current one had got out, and was having the time of her life, turning the vegetable patch into a sea of mud.

Unable to contain his delight, Ted snorted with laughter. There was no need to worry that the pig might get into their garden for Martha had persuaded her poor hen-pecked husband to surround their ground with chicken wire, believing her neighbours at number nine to be encroaching on her vegetable plot. Now, that was serving as a barrier to keep the pig in!

Ted's laughter disturbed Fred.

"What the devil's going on?" he muttered, raising his head from the pillow, and Jack, too, opened his eyes and kept them open to see his brother hanging out of the window.

"Is there a fire?" he asked eagerly.

Ted began to laugh again.

"Better than that. Come over here, boys, and see what I can see!"

They came, clambering over the beds and a sleepy Jim.

"It's old Mother Durrant's porker!" Fred said unnecessarily. "He's having a go at her parsnips!"

"He'll have the lot up in a minute," Jack commented anxiously, and Ted laughed again.

"Pigs do. They'll root up anything. Serve her right, I say, the old misery!"

"Didn't we ought to tell somebody?" Jack asked, worried, but before the others could shout him down, a sudden commotion disturbed the Sunday-morning calm.

From almost immediately below their window came the sound of agitated cries and a door banging. Charlie Durrant appeared, clad only in a pair of long woolen underpants, whose baggy seat drooped three-quarters of the way down his thin thighs, and a shirt with the tails flapping just above the seat of the underpants. Behind him, her night-gown billowing from beneath a hastily pulled-on coat, came Martha, waving her arms wildly to urge her husband on. Curling rags were still wound in her thin hair, and her plump feet were pushed into a pair of fashionable high-cut shoes.

Across the yard they ran, one behind the other, and down the path between the wash-houses. They reached the pig and began chasing it back to its sty, looking like two animated scarecrows, and the boys' merriment overflowed. Holding on to one another and to the window-sill, they roared and roared, the tears rolling down their cheeks.

"I bet there'll be pork for dinner next Sunday!" Fred chortled.

And Jim added drily, "Pork, but no parsnips, by the look on it!"

That set them off again and they were still laughing when their oddly dressed neighbours came back up the path, both red in the face, Martha's high-heeled shoes caked with mud, and Charlie's white underpants dirt-streaked on the back where he had wiped his hands. And when Martha glanced up and saw the four delighted faces looking down at her from the bedroom window, her anger only amused the boys the more.

"I thought she was going to have a stroke," Ted said afterwards. "That's just how she looked—sort of red and popping, and her mouth going, but no words coming out."

But Martha did not have a stroke. After shaking her fist at the boys, she dragged Charlie into the kitchen and out of sight, and with a sense of anticlimax they realized the free show was over.

They were still chuckling about it, however, when Charlotte called them to breakfast, half an hour later, and they told the story yet again as they watched her turn fried potatoes and rashers of streaky bacon in the pan. But their amusement was not to last much longer.

Just as Charlotte had finished dishing up, they heard someone knocking on the back door.

"What a time to choose!" Charlotte said, annoyed. "Jack, go and see who it is, there's a good boy. And the rest of you get on with your breakfast while it's hot."

They began to eat, casting curious glances in the direction of the scullery, but when Jack appeared in the doorway followed by Charlie Durrant, knives and forks dropped and six pairs of eyes were fixed on the hesitant and distinctly unhappy figure, whose woollen under-pants were now covered by a pair of trousers.

Charlie Durrant drove the winding engine at Grieve Bottom Pit, and enjoyed the freedom of being more or less his own master. It was a pleasure he certainly did not enjoy at home. Martha hounded him mercilessly, and none of the Halls had any doubt that it was Martha who had sent him on this errand.

"Well, Charlie," Charlotte said, putting down her fork. "What can we do for you?"

For a moment Charlie did not reply. He pulled a handkerchief from his pocket and stood mopping nervously at a dewdrop that had caught in his stringy moustache.

"You had a bit of trouble earlier on, didn't you?" James prompted him.

"That's right." With an effort Charlie gathered his courage to begin. "Our pig got out and a fair mess she's made of the garden, too. There's not a parsnip not damaged, and the swedes look as if they've had their lot, an' all."

Charlotte clucked sympathetically, and encouraged, Charlie went on: "Martha's had to go back to bed, she's so upset. I reckon it'll bring on one of her heads."

The boys, who knew Martha's 'heads' could keep her in bed for a day and sometimes more, exchanged glances of suppressed delight, and Charlotte gave them a warning glance.

"I'm sorry to hear that, Charlie," she said. "But what can we do for you?"

Charlie carefully folded his handkerchief and replaced it in his pocket, but before he could reply, Amy asked, "How did the pig get out, Mr Durrant?"

The innocent question brought Charlie to life like a dummy in a pier peep-show when the penny dropped. His head came up with a jerk, a muscle in his left eyelid twitched violently, and he whirled around to point an accusing finger at Ted.

"You'd better ask your brother that question!" he cried, his voice trembling and high with indignation.

They all stared blankly, but Charlotte was the first to recover her wits.

"What do you mean by that?" she demanded.

Intoxicated by his own daring, Charlie rushed on.

"You know as well as I do that your Ted's a proper varmint. He's got a name round here that I should think you're ashamed of."

"Just a minute!" James began warningly, but Charlie, in full spate for the first time in twenty years, was not to be interrupted.

"He's a bad boy," he went on. "He's plagued the life out of Martha, and led others to do the same, and if she wasn't such a good woman, you'd have heard about it before now. But this time, he's gone too far. Letting out our pig is beyond a joke, and . . . "

"I never!" Ted cried indignantly. "I never did!"

Charlotte silenced him with a look.

"What proof have you got of this, Charlie?"

"Martha saw them boys down the garden last night when it was getting dusk. Now I know for a fact that I put the catch on the pigsty after I went in to see to the porker. This morning, it were off, and you don't need to be no politician to know how it got undone. As Martha always says when they've been aplaguin' her, boys will be boys. But when it comes to letting out folks' pigs and the like, that's when it's time something were done, I reckon."

"Just a minute, Charlie," James was on his feet now, his face like thunder. "What have you got to say to this, Ted? Is there any truth in what Mr Durrant says?"

"No, Dad, there's not!" Ted asserted, and James turned back to Charlie.

"You'd better go on home, then, Charlie. And I'm warning you, there'll be trouble if you go saying things like that with no proof."

"I don't need no proof! I knows what I knows!" Charlie began, and James wagged a threatening finger at him.

"I mean it, Charlie. I won't have it, not in my own home."

His temper, slow to rise, was up now, and Charlotte intervened hastily.

"Off you go, Charlie, I'll get to the bottom of this. And I promise if Ted or any of the others are to blame, we'll see your parsnips are replaced out of our garden. I can't say fairer than that. Go on now!" She shooed him to the door, and behind her the stunned silence fragmented as the boys all began talking at once, and Amy burst into noisy tears. James scraped aside his chair to follow Charlie out, but Charlotte laid a restraining hand on his arm.

"No, James," she warned. "We don't want brawling on a Sunday."

"But I didn't do it, Mam, honest I didn't!" Ted protested.

"Didn't you?" Charlotte was annoyed at the sight of the bacon congealing on the plates, and took out her annoyance on Ted. "I'm fed up to the teeth with getting complaints about you, my lad."

"You were up early this morning, Ted. I saw you looking out of the window ages ago," Amy put in. Then her lip wobbled and her eyes filled with tears. "Oh, Mam, what will happen? Will they put Ted in prison?"

"Not this time," Charlotte said heavily. "Though the way he's going on, it's only a matter of time, Amy. But I'll tell you what's going to happen, all right. First thing tomorrow morning, we're going to dig out half our parsnips and take them round next door. I know they're better left till the frost's been on them, but I can't stand Martha Durrant's long face looking at me till then. We'll help her put them back in the ground. It's the least we can do."

"But our Ted says he didn't let the pig out," James objected.

"I'm not so sure about that," Charlotte argued. "Between these four walls, I agree with the Durrants. Our Ted is a pickle, and it's time he was taught a lesson. Shifting him off the screens and underground was just water off a duck's back. Well, if he misses his parsnips this winter, maybe he'll think twice before he gets up to his tricks again."

"But what about the rest of us?" Jim asked. "Do we have to go hungry too?"

"We'll starve!" Amy cried, dramatically bursting into a fresh spasm of weeping. "And I'll faint in class like Edie Presley did."

"You'll faint in chapel if you don't eat your bacon," her mother told her, and, realizing the futility of arguing with Charlotte when her mind was made up, the family resumed their breakfast. Even James sat down again, muttering, "Your mother's right, you know. We can't see neighbours lose all their vegetables and do nothing about it." Then, picking up his knife and fork, he began his breakfast once more.

Only Ted pushed his plate away defiantly.

"I told you I didn't do it, Mam!" he cried.

"Sit down, Ted," Charlotte warned him, but he shook his head.

"It'd choke me," he said, pushing past her chair. "I never let that pig out. But I'll tell you something. I bloomin' well wish I had!"

Outside it was pleasantly warm, the air singing with the promise of another good day, but Ted scarcely noticed.

He crossed the yard, cutting down through the gardens, and the gardens of the rank below theirs, his feet slithering as the ground

41

grew steeper. At the bottom he scrambled through the hedge and on to the road, crossing the first railway lines by means of the foot-bridge and the second by a narrow subway. Then, skirting the town centre, he headed for the part of the river that lay beyond the churchyard and in the shelter of the grassy slopes that formed yet another side of the valley bowl.

The river here moved slowly through deeps and shallows overhung with trees and bushes. In places it widened to form natural pools where the young men swam when the weather was warm enough. Ted had heard talk of making a proper swimming pool here, and forming a club, but this morning he was fairly sure he would be alone. It was early yet for a Sunday, and most people who were already up would be going to church or chapel.

As he waded through the waist-high grass, his bad humour fell away. Here, with the constant soft cooing of the wood-pigeons and the soothing murmur of the brook, it was impossible to be anything but happy. It was the place of a thousand dreams, where he and Redvers Brixey had spent so many happy hours.

Here, they had fished, lying flat on their stomachs on the bank, a makeshift oven of an old toffee tin with a couple of rusty stair-rods laid across it all ready to cook a delicious supper. But they had never actually caught anything.

Here, they had watched the placid moorhens and seen them scuttle fearfully when they clapped their hands.

And here, they had learned to swim, holding one another up with shrieking, splashing merriment, and swallowing a great deal of river water in the process.

But this morning, not a sound disturbed the peace.

With a quick look round, Ted stripped off his clothes and dropped them into an untidy heap under a bush. Then, when he was quite naked, he waded into the water.

It was cold, so cold he let out a yell, but as the first sharp shock gave way to a pleasurable tingling Ted glowed with exuberance.

So much for wasting a morning like this in chapel! he thought. And why did he need to go anyway? Here, with the sky high and blue above the tracery of green, he was closer to God than he could ever be there.

After a while, he began to feel the coldness of the water once more. He turned for the bank, and saw something move among the trees. Automatically he stopped, treading water. All was peace, and he was just beginning to think he had imagined it when a twig cracked sharply, and turning towards the sound he saw a flash of white amid the green.

"Who's there?" he called.

For a moment there was silence, then the branches parted to reveal a girl—a skinny child of ten or eleven. Her black hair was knotty and unbrushed, and her stockings and smock were stuck with burrs, but in her narrow face her dark eyes sparkled behind thick lashes, and her lips were parted to reveal teeth that were white and perfect.

"Rosa Clements!" Ted said, annoyed. "What are you doing here?"

She came to the edge of the bank, guilty but defiant.

"You followed me!" he accused. "You're always following me. Why can't you leave me alone?"

Her guilt was spiked by a look of sudden pain, so transparent he felt almost sorry for her.

She was a strange child, very much one on her own, and quite different from the rest of the Clements children, with their pale, freckled complexions and gingery curls. He'd even heard talk that her father was not Walter Clements at all, but one of the travelling fair folk who wintered each year in the market yard, and certainly she was as dark and lithe as any gypsy—and as wild. But he'd never learned the truth of it. Charlotte refused to have the subject talked about, saying there was 'none of us so lilly white we can afford to gossip about others.'

Rosa never played with the other children, either. While they drew hopscotch squares on the path with chalky stones, and ran shrieking round the rank, she went off by herself, sitting in the hen-pen for hours, or going off across the fields. But lately Ted had noticed that, wherever he was, Rosa was likely to turn up too, and it was beginning to annoy him.

"Haven't you got anything better to do?" he said now, less unkindly, as he trod water amongst the rushes.

She shrugged without replying, and he was just about to swim to the bank and get out when he remembered he wasn't wearing a bathing costume.

A fierce panic ran through him as he automatically glanced towards the untidy pile of discarded clothes. She followed his gaze and, seeing his reason for hesitation, a slow smile lit up her sallow features.

"Ted Hall, I don't believe you've got anything on!" she exclaimed.

Hot colour flooded his cheeks and, as if blushing had taken every bit of warm blood from the rest of his body, he was suddenly achingly cold.

"Go on home, Rosa!" he yelled at her, but this time she had the upper hand, and she knew it.

Laughing, she danced her way through the brambles to where the clothes lay, and he could only watch, agonized, as she picked them up, a garment at a time, waving them tauntingly at him.

"If you want your drawers, come and get them! Come and get them—I dare you!"

"Rosa!" he pleaded. "Give them back! Just wait till I get out of here!"

But she only laughed again.

Then, without warning, the quiet erupted. The undergrowth rustled, and out bounded a small black-and-white dog, barking furiously and intent on joining in the fun. It dived at Rosa, jumping up at the trousers she was waving. Screaming, she dropped them on to the bank. For one ghastly moment Ted thought the dog would take them and run off with them. But Rosa, squealing with fear, turned to flee, and the dog realized she was a better bet for a little sport. As she ran, in a flurry of petticoats, so the dog went after her, yapping round her heels.

The long grass parted and closed behind them, and Ted made the bank with a few frenzied strokes. He climbed out of the water, grabbing up the trousers that Rosa had dropped and pulling them over his wet legs. Only when he had buckled his belt around his waist did he give a thought to the girl, and with the rest of his clothes under his arm he set off across the field in the direction she had gone.

A few yards away he saw her, spread-eagled against a tree, and gazing in mesmerized horror at the dog, who stood guard over her, still barking excitedly.

"Serves you right, Rosa!" he laughed, but her terror was so apparent that he knew he could not leave her there.

"All right, I'm coming," he called.

As he approached the dog's barking lessened, and he cocked an ear in Ted's direction.

"Here, boy, leave, leave!" Ted commanded, and to his surprise the dog turned to look at him, head on one side.

"He won't hurt you," Ted said to the terrified Rosa, and to the dog, "Here, boy! Come on, here!"

The dog stood undecided, then as Ted ran a short distance and stopped, looking back, the dog made up his mind. A moving object was more fun than a still one. With one last longing look at Rosa, he galloped over to Ted and the boy patted his head affectionately.

"See?" he said to Rosa, who cautiously left her place by the tree and edged around behind him. "He only wants a bit of fun."

She watched, still nervous, but beginning to be ashamed of her fear.

"Dogs don't like me," she said after a moment. "They always go for me."

"He wasn't going for you, he was just playing."

"He was going for me," she said stubbornly. "And I know why, too. It's because I'm a witch."

"What?" He laughed out loud before he could stop himself. "You, a witch? Oh, Rosa!"

"I am too!" She drew herself up, a skinny child in a torn, grass-stained smock. "Don't you laugh at me, or I'll make you sorry. I know spells that could make your hair stand on end or your teeth drop out. I know . . . "

"Why don't you try them then?" he asked, rolling the dog over to rub its stomach.

"Because!"

"Because what?"

"Because if I did, you'd be sorry. But I do know them, all the same. I know everything." She paused, then her eyes, deep and tantalizing, held his. "I even know who let out the Durrants' pig."

"You do?" he repeated with a start.

She nodded. "I was down in the hen-pen, and I saw. 'Twas Tommy Bryant. And I know why. Old Ma Durrant had been after him for shooting peas at her from behind the wall. Mr Davies caned him for it—three strokes on Friday afternoon."

"Are you sure?" Ted asked, and when she nodded again, he got up, pulling on his shirt. "Will you come home with me, Rosa, and tell our Mam what you just told me?"

Still wary of the dog, she hung back, and Ted gave him a friendly push.

"Go on now, go on home, wherever you come from, you scamp. You've had your fun."

But the dog did not go. It stood and watched, head on one side, while Ted and Rosa started back across the field, then began to follow at a distance.

Rosa, fearful it might 'go for her' again, kept looking anxiously over her shoulder, in the hope that it would tire of the game and go home, but Ted could not help feeling gratified. He rather liked the little beast.

When they reached the corner of the rank it was still there, hanging back uncertainly, but he forgot it in the anticipation of relaying to Charlotte what Rosa had just told him.

Charlotte was out in the yard, talking to Peggy Yelling, as Ted hurried up to her with Rosa.

"Mam, Mam, I've got something to tell you!"

She turned and saw him. "Ted! Where do you think you've been? The others are at chapel. You're a bad boy, going off like that . . . "

"Wait, Mam!" he interrupted her. "Rosa knows who let the pig out. She saw."

"It was Tommy Bryant," Rosa put in importantly.

"Are you sure?" Charlotte drew herself up. "Well, in that case, I'm going to see Mr Durrant and tell him what I think of him, coming in like that, spoiling our breakfast!"

"Won't they be at chapel?" Peggy asked.

Charlotte shook her head. "They haven't gone this morning. Martha's got one of her heads, all on account of the pig. But they aren't going to get away with this, Peggy. And to think I was going to let them have half our parsnips!"

Wiping her hands in her apron, she crossed to the Durrants' door, rapping on it loudly and motioning Ted and Rosa to stay close beside her.

After a moment, Charlie appeared. He looked anxiously from one to the other and then indicated the bedroom window.

"Martha's in bed," he said jerkily. "She's bad."

"It's you I wanted to see, Charlie," Charlotte told him. "You're the one who was throwing accusations around. Now I've got a witness here who saw who let your pig out, and it wasn't our Ted. Tell him, Rosa!"

With the safe distance of half the yard between them, Rosa glowered balefully at Charlie and repeated her story.

"You see?" Charlotte attacked him triumphantly when she had finished. "What have you got to say to that, Charlie?"

46

But Charlie in defeat was even more tenacious than Charlie on the attack.

"I still say your Ted's no good!" he maintained. "He causes more trouble than enough."

"And you think that gives you the right to burst into my kitchen, accusing him of all kinds of things he had nothing to do with," Charlotte cried, really angry now. "I warn you—any more, and I'll have you up for libel."

"But our pig *were* let out!" Charlie quivered.

"Yes, and that's another thing!" Charlotte snorted. "That pig of yours is nothing but a nuisance. It shouldn't be there at all. It stinks! We say nothing because we like to be neighbourly, but when it comes to this . . . Aren't I right, Peggy?" she asked, turning to her friend. "I bet you can smell it right down your end of the rank!"

Peggy held back, reluctant to be involved in the argument, but just then the upper window of the Durrants' house was thrown open, and Martha's head appeared. Beneath her nightcap her face was pale, and she was clutching a flannel to her forehead.

"Can't you keep quiet down there, all of you?" she wailed. "And, Charlie, that dog—look what he's doing!"

They turned to see the little black-and-white dog idly cocking a leg against the post which fenced in the Durrants' garden. Charlie, already incensed, aimed a kick at the dog, and it was Ted's turn to lose his temper.

"Don't take it out on him! Here, boy, come here!"

The dog, who had nimbly avoided Charlie's threatening boot, cowered away. But when Ted called to him again, he came forwards warily. Ted rubbed the dog's nose, and in return was licked with a rough wet tongue.

"I reckon he's hungry, Mam," he said. "Have we got any scraps we could give him?"

"Ah, we have. A whole lot of cold, wasted bacon!" Charlotte said loudly. "Give him that, Ted. It's all it's good for since Charlie made a muck-up of our breakfast."

The Durrants' window banged angrily, and suppressing a grin, Ted went into the house. When he came out again, Charlie had disappeared and Charlotte and Peggy were going over the whole incident again. But the dog was still there, and as soon as Ted put the scraps down he gobbled them up, wagging his tail excitedly, then jumping up to look for more.

"Can he have the bone from the meat at dinner-time?" he asked Charlotte, and she sighed resignedly, shaking her head and smiling.

"If he's still here, I dare say he can. But he'll be gone by then, I expect. He knows where his home is if you don't."

"I suppose so," Ted said, realizing he was quite fond of the creature. "But if he is a stray—do you think I could keep him?" he ventured.

Charlotte laughed shortly, looking at the Durrants' closed door.

"I should think so. But if he's a rover, you won't have him long. He'll stay just as long as he feels like it, and one day he'll disappear just like he came. So don't get too attached to him, son."

Ted said nothing. He liked the idea of the dog being a rover. There was a free feel to the word that excited him deep down.

But he hoped the dog *would* stay, anyway.

3

I N SPITE OF Charlotte's prediction that the dog would disappear as suddenly as he had come, Nipper, as Ted named him, was still around the next day—and the day after that.

"I think you ought to put a card down in the paper-shop window," Jack suggested. "Somebody might be worried about him."

Charlotte laughed shortly. She was of the opinion that if the dog had a good home to go back to, he'd go—and in any case, Ted was so attached to the little mongrel that she couldn't help hoping he would stay. It was good to see Ted caring about something.

But Jack couldn't bear the thought that somewhere the dog's owner might be wretched with anxiety, and he insisted a card in the paper-shop window was the right thing to do. Although he and Ted almost came to blows about it, he wrote it out and took it down, and for a week or two Charlotte—and Ted—lived in fear of someone knocking on the door to claim Nipper.

But no one did.

When the weather grew colder, Ted made up a bed for him in the wash-house, and he was even sometimes allowed into the kitchen.

Christmas came and went, and Nipper was still around, and he was there the following June for the street party the rank held to celebrate the coronation of King George and Queen Mary. This promised to be the biggest and the best ever held in the rank. From the moment the coronation date was public, there had been talk of a party, but it had taken Peggy Yelling to organize it.

"She's got more time than most of us with her family all grown-up," Charlotte said, and James knew she would have loved to organize the party herself, in honour of the occasion. He was quietly amused by the way that Charlotte idolized the Royal Family and all they did. Her military background had given her a liking for ceremonial, and she avidly read every newspaper account she could lay her hands on, snipping out the pictures and getting Jack to paste them into a scrapbook for her.

But arranging a party of this size was not a job for a woman with a demanding family, a baby and a cleaning post. It needed someone like Peggy, enthusiastic, efficient and cheerfully bossy, who could shoulder the responsibility and enjoy it. She attacked the task with the same vigour she brought to delivering babies, and before long the plans had grown to take in some of the people who lived in the cottages on the hill as well as the twenty houses in the rank.

"Oh, let them come—they've nowhere to have a party of their own. And it's the more the merrier as far as I'm concerned," she said, cheerfully overruling those who thought the rank should keep itself to itself.

Soon everyone had their own special responsibility. Some of the men were detailed to collect trestle tables from the Co-operative rooms in one of the carts from Bristow's Livery Stables at the bottom of the hill, and rotas were arranged among the women for baking and jelly-making. Peggy made a collection to buy a big ham, which she cooked in her copper one warm evening when all the windows were open, and the smell wafted out to make everyone's mouth water in anticipation.

The children had their jobs, too—there were balloons to be blown up, red, white and blue bunting to be hung from the back bedroom windows to the wash-houses opposite, and the rank to be swept clean of every bit of muck and dirt that might have been left by the delivery horses.

Even Martha Durrant was roped in to man the tea-urn, a task which would keep her at a safe distance from the merry-making.

"Just pray for a fine day tomorrow, that's all," Peggy said to Charlotte as they counted through a pile of white, starched tablecloths the night before. "What we'll do if it rains, I just don't know."

"It won't rain," Charlotte replied confidently, flicking at the air in front of her face. "The gnats are flying tonight."

"Yes, and that's not all that's flying, by all accounts," Peggy told her. "Have you heard the latest? They're going to deliver letters in one of those flying machines in honour of the coronation."

Charlotte nodded. Jack was enthralled by every new development of the aeroplane, following the thrills and spills of Bleriot and the other pilots as eagerly as she followed news of the Royal Family. He had taken up a whole tea time telling the family about the mail that was going to be flown from Hendon to Windsor in September, but Charlotte thought it was a crazy idea.

"As far as I'm concerned, the postman comes around seven days a week, and he comes on foot," she said. "Now, are you sure there's nothing we've forgot, Peg?"

"Well, let's think," Peggy said, and the newfangled aeroplanes were forgotten as yet again they went through the list of things they needed for the party.

The next day the rank was a hive of activity. Although the party would not really start until mid-afternoon, a great many things had had to be left until the last minute, and people bustled about, calling to one another above the sounds of hammering and bumping.

The men caused a slight hold-up. Most of them had to work until midday, and it was pay-day too. Each Saturday, the colliers, or getters as they were called, would queue at the pithead to be paid for the coal their team had brought out that week, and it was up to them to pay the carting boys their share. This was usually done over a pint in the George or the Miners Arms, but today the men from the rank rushed through the ritual as quickly as they could so as to get the cart and pick up the trestles.

At last it was all ready and, leaving Ted, Redvers and the Brimble boys to keep an eye on things, the rest of the rank disappeared into their houses to get dressed for the occasion.

Charlotte, who expected to be working as much as playing, put on a clean apron, and at her insistence James and the boys buttoned on their clean, starched collars instead of wearing their shirts open as they usually did. Amy had to be squeezed into the party dress she was fast out-growing, and a new ribbon was tied in her hair.

They were all ready when Dolly arrived, pink and flustered from running down the hill from Captain Fish's. She had managed to rearrange things so that this was her afternoon off, but there had been a last-minute crisis in the kitchen, and now she was late.

"Oh, Mam, can you do up my buttons?" she begged, coming into Charlotte's room with her best blouse still undone. "I'm shaking so much I'm all fingers and thumbs."

"What kept you?" Charlotte asked.

"The stove was too hot, and Cook burnt the scones. We had to do them all again. She blamed everybody but herself, of course. But never mind, it's all done now," Dolly added with a return to her usual placid acceptance.

"You don't mean she blamed *you?*" Charlotte said sharply. Although Dolly had started at Captain Fish's as a housemaid, they thought highly of her, and Cook was training her so that Dolly would be able to step into her shoes when she retired in a few years' time.

"Oh, I don't think so," Dolly replied. "You know how it is. She'll have forgotten all about it in five minutes. It's just that I didn't want to be late, Mam, because I've got something to tell you."

"Now?" Charlotte asked.

From the buzz of voices outside she knew the party was beginning, and Harry would need washing and changing when he woke from his afternoon nap. But Dolly nodded eagerly, and Charlotte saw that her cheeks were pinker than they would normally have been merely from running down the hill.

"Go on down, Amy, and see if Harry's awake," she said to her younger daughter, who was waiting in the doorway and dancing with impatience. "I'll be down directly to see to him."

Then she turned back to Dolly, smiling indulgently.

"What is it, then? Something to do with a boy, I'll be bound."

"How did you know?" Dolly asked, surprised.

"It's written all over you. Who is he then?"

"Evan Comer. He comes from Purldown," Dolly said, naming the next village on the way to Bath.

"Oh, yes, and how did you meet him?"

"He delivers for the Co-op, and he comes to Captain Fish's. Only I had to tell you, Mam, because I asked him to the party." Dolly's eyes were blue and untroubled now that she had broken her news, and Charlotte laughed shortly, shaking her head.

"Oh, well, it had to come, I suppose. You're seventeen after all. But it makes me feel my age!"

"Oh, Mam!" Dolly dimpled. "It was all right, was it, me inviting him to the party?"

"Of course, it was," Charlotte told her. "You're not a child now, Dolly. But the most important thing is, do you like him? He's a nice boy, is he?"

"Oh, Mam, I hardly know him." Dolly laughed. "I'll tell you that when I've been going out with him a bit longer. But the boys'll like him, that's for sure. He's a really good footballer. He plays for Hillsbridge Reserves, and he thinks he'll be in the proper team this year."

"That's all right then," Charlotte said, not really knowing what she meant, but aware that Amy was calling to say that Harry was awake.

"Shall I do him?" Dolly offered, but Charlotte shook her head.

"It's your afternoon off, my girl. You go on down and enjoy yourself."

Dolly went, full of excitement, and Charlotte followed her down into the kitchen where Harry was sitting wedged on the settle. With all the excitement he had refused to go upstairs in his cot for his rest, but exhaustion had got the better of him, and he had put his head down and fallen asleep where he was.

Amy bobbed up and down with impatience as she saw Charlotte enter the room.

"Can I go out, Mammy? They've started! Everybody's there but us."

"Yes, go on Amy," Charlotte said.

Picking Harry up, Charlotte inspected the state of his napkin, and he stared at her with unwinking blue eyes. At eleven months, he was heavier than the other children had been, and she thought it was probably because he was less active.

Sometimes she worried about it, wondering why he was making no attempt to walk or pull himself up on the furniture. Abnormality terrified her, and the thought of something being wrong with Harry seemed to haunt her. But pushing her morbid thoughts aside, she brushed Harry's curls and changed him into a clean dress.

Outside the children were playing games. Walter Clements had produced a tin plate and organized a game of twirl-the-trencher to keep them out of the way of the food. On the cobbles it didn't work very well. Each time a number was called there was a mad scramble while the child involved dived to catch the plate, and mostly they didn't make it. But they were enjoying it anyway.

Charlotte, carrying Harry, went down the rank to Peggy's house to see what needed to be done.

On the way she passed James and the other men already congregating outside the Presleys' wash-house, which was being used as a bar, and looking longingly at the beer barrels and the crate of home-brewed that had been brought in for the occasion.

"You don't want to start on that yet," she told them sternly. "There's tea to come first."

"Let's get on with it then," Moses Brimble said with a laugh. "We've been starving ourselves for this all day."

Walter Clements kept the children occupied with yet another game of twirl-the-trencher, while Charlotte, Peggy, Ada Clements and the other women carried out the food and set it on the white-covered trestles: fresh baked bread and butter, pickled onions and chutney, cheese, brawn—and the ham. They placed the jellies at intervals down the tables, and the children's eyes grew round at the sight of them.

When it was all ready, Ted was asked to lead a chorus of *God Save the King*, and Jacob Cottle from number eight said grace. Then, they all tucked in and for a while all was quiet, but it did not last long for as the plates emptied chatter began to break out again.

Tea over, the trestles were cleared away, and there were more games, in which many adults joined their children. Then Moses Brimble got out his fiddle and began to play, and soon the more energetic among them were dancing.

Now the excitement that had sung in the air earlier in the day had mellowed to enjoyment, and neighbours forgot their differences as they twirled around to a waltz or a raucous Gay Gordon.

"See me dance the polka, see me touch the ground / See my coat-tails flying as I swizz my partner round!" sang Jacob Cottle as he and his plump little wife made breathless circles on the cobbles, and the younger ones stopped dancing to watch them.

Even Martha Durrant looked almost cheerful, presiding over her tea-urn and managing to ignore the men with their mugs of home-brewed. No one felt like telling her that Charlie had slipped into the Presleys' wash-house, and was quietly supping away well out of her view.

The younger children became wild and silly, racing about and falling over themselves, and they had to be taken away, protesting, to bed. Babies, like Harry, fell asleep in their mothers' arms while they sat watching the dancing. And still Moses Brimble's fiddle scraped on.

Charlotte, sitting in her doorway with Harry, was feeling tired but contented. It had been worth all the effort, she thought, to have everyone together and enjoying themselves. Why, King George himself couldn't have enjoyed his coronation more. And in those hot, ermine-trimmed robes, with a heavy crown on his head, he'd probably enjoyed it a great deal less.

She tucked a strand of hair behind her ear, looking up and down the rank. Dolly she had seen just now, dancing by with a well-built, dark-haired boy she'd introduced to Charlotte as Evan. Ted and Fred were over by the wash-houses with Redvers and the Brimble boys, waiting their chance to slip in and help themselves to a glass of beer. And Amy was being whirled around in a barn dance by Colwyn Yelling, Peggy's grown-up son, who was almost two feet taller than she was.

But it was some time since she had seen either Jim or Jack, and she looked for them now, narrowing her eyes against the glare of the setting sun.

Jim she saw first, though he had his back to her. He was leaning against the wall with an air of nonchalance that she knew was far from being anything of the kind, and talking to Sarah Brimble, Moses' daughter.

Charlotte smiled to herself. She'd heard the other boys teasing Jim about Sarah and saying he was 'sweet on her,' but that was as far as it had gone. Now, it looked as if Jim had broken the ice at last—and from the way Sarah was dimpling up at him, he wasn't doing too badly, either.

Feeling like an interloper, she turned away, and as she did so she saw Jack standing alone under the wash-house wall. His hands were deep in his pockets, and there was a dreaming expression on his face, an acute contrast to the obvious enjoyment of the others.

A deep, sad ache knotted inside her and the guilt that was never far away twisted sharply. There was a gentle, dreaming quality about his face that had come from neither her nor James, and another year at school seemed only to have intensified it. His eyes were blue, it was true, as clear as her own, but they seemed too often to be looking at some far-off vision that only he could see. And he was doing it now.

Or was he?

The first cold breeze of evening shivered over her, and she wondered why she was suddenly so aware that this time Jack was *not* simply staring into space. She shifted her position, trying to follow his gaze, and found herself looking straight at Rosa, the oldest of the Clements children.

Shock brought her upright. Rosa? Surely Jack could not actually be watching Rosa, the gypsy-like urchin who spent more time than was good for her alone in the woods? She was only a child, and he was not much more. And besides . . .

"If it was Ted I could understand it," thought Charlotte. "She seems to follow him everywhere, and child or not, she looks like a girl with a strong, passionate nature. But not Jack—never Jack."

"Lotty?"

She almost jumped at the mention of her name and, looking up, saw James in the doorway beside her. His shirt was undone at the neck now, his spotted handkerchief knotted inside it.

"Put Harry to bed and come out and have a bit of a dance," he said fondly to her. "It isn't every day we have a coronation, Lotty."

And pulling herself up, she smiled at him.

"You're right, James, it's not," she agreed.

NIPPER was missing, and had been since the night of the street party, three days ago.

That night, when the food had been cleared away, Ted untied him, and he wandered about, sniffing at the dancers and watching the merry-making with a puzzled air. But later on, when it got dark, some of the boys started letting off firecrackers and when the first one exploded close behind him, he took to his heels and rushed down across the gardens, paying no heed to Ted's callings.

"Don't worry, he'll be back as soon as it's quiet," Redvers assured him. But Nipper did not come back, and Ted was frantic with worry.

"I warned him not to get too attached to the thing," Charlotte said, but despite her cross tone she was sorry for Ted.

Every morning he came down early and went straight to the back door, his face a mixture of hope and apprehension. And when there was no sign of Nipper, the hope died like a light going out.

Every night, as soon as he had changed out of his pit clothes, he was off across the fields looking for the little dog, but although he called himself hoarse Nipper did not come.

For the first two nights Redvers went with him. But by the third night he was tired of the excursions, and made the excuse that he had to help his father in the garden.

Ted, setting out alone, decided he would try a different way. Up the hill he went, past Captain Fish's, and along Ridge Road which followed the line of the hillside as far as the eye could see in the direction of the down and beneath it to the village of Purldown.

From here the view was magnificent, a spread of countryside reaching clear to the Mendips, with only a sprinkling of cottages and the occasional church tower. Not a batch could be seen, not a pit wheel, and even the chimneys and yards in the valley below were hidden by the curve of the hillside.

Ted, however, was not concerned with the view. When he had left the houses behind, he crossed the road and climbed the gate that gave on to the first of the sloping fields, and beyond it 'the wood,' as the children called it.

In reality it was more a thicket than a wood, several acres of trees and undergrowth that lay between the fields and the main road to Bath as it curved upwards from the valley. But it was a place they loved, with the bushes that provided a dozen different dens, the abandoned fox holes and badger setts, and the blackberries and nuts that could be gathered in autumn. The only nightingale in Hillsbridge lived here, and on clear nights, when her hauntingly sweet song pierced the silent dark, people looked towards the wood, and nodded their pleasure.

But it was of the rabbit holes that Ted was thinking as he crossed the field that night. It was a constant dread in his mind—that Nipper had chased a white bobtail too far and got himself stuck. He was small enough to get into a large rabbit hole, and there was enough of the terrier in him to do so. But supposing he could not get out again? The thought of Nipper wriggling and pulling until he was frantic was almost more than Ted could bear, even worse was the prospect of him starving to death in some dark warren beneath the ground.

He began whistling and calling Nipper's name even before he reached the wood, stopping every few moments to listen intently for any answering sound. But except for the wood-pigeons, everything was quiet. Once he heard a rustling in the undergrowth and ran in the direction of the sound, but there was nothing to be seen.

He stopped where he was, disappointment welling up and setting off a feeling of despair. He'd never find Nipper. How could he hope to? He'd been all along the river where he'd first found the dog, and the fields where he most often took him. But there were so many, many more places he could be—across the older, grass-covered batches, the woods, the inclines—and the whole of the down. If he had nothing to do all day it would still be a mammoth task. But all he had was a few short hours in the evenings. If Nipper was trapped, he would never find him before it was too late.

A sudden unfamiliar ache constricted his throat, and with a shock he realized he was going to cry. He couldn't remember the last time he had cried, so long ago was it, and now he battled against the tears that seemed to be choking him. But the thought of never seeing Nipper again—of never even knowing what had become of him—was more than he could bear.

The first hot tear slid down his cheek, and he leaned back against the trunk of an elm tree, pressing his knuckles into his face as the dam crumbled.

How long he stood there, sobbing as he relived the raised hopes and bitter disappointments of the last three days, he did not know, but it was an unexpected sound in the branches of the elm tree that brought him suddenly upright. He jerked around only to see a booted foot protruding from the foliage just above him.

Guilt and shame momentarily dispelled his grief, and as a black stocking and the hem of a petticoat came into view above the boot, Ted swallowed his tears and hastily drew his shirt sleeve across his face.

"I know you're up there, Rosa!" he accused. "You've been following me again!"

She shinned down the tree without a thought for her clothes; there were twigs in her black hair and a tear in her pinafore. When she reached the ground she stood, looking at him with frank interest, and he realized, to his shame, that she would know he'd been crying.

"Your mother would kill you if she knew you were climbing trees," he told her, deciding that the best form of defence must be attack.

Rosa's eyes, dark as sloes, held his with tantalizing directness.

"If you don't tell her, she won't know."

"Why do you keep following me everywhere?" he asked furiously.

She ignored his question, countering with one of her own.

"Are you looking for Nipper?"

He nodded, blinking at the tears that were threatening again. "I'm afraid he might be stuck somewhere," he said roughly. "Mam thinks he's gone off after a bitch, but I'm not so sure."

Unwavering, her black eyes held his.

"I could help you, Ted."

"Oh yes, and how? You don't even like Nipper."

"I like him better than I did. He's all right. And you want him back, don't you?"

He swallowed. Slowly he was regaining control of himself.

"Course I do. But what can you do that I haven't?"

"I can do anything. I told you, I'm a witch."

He laughed, an explosion of humourless mirth. That was the second time she'd said that. It was a pretty strange thing to have in her head—but then, Rosa was a strange girl.

"A witch, eh? Oh, Rosa!" he jeered.

The smile left her eyes and her expression became intense.

"Don't you laugh at me, Ted, or I won't do it!"

"Do *what?*"

"Get Nipper back for you."

He almost said scornfully, "As if you could!" But for some reason he did not. He clamped his teeth over the words, desperately groping for the straw she was offering him. A moment ago he had thought it was hopeless, and so it was. But supposing there was something in what Rosa said . . . She wasn't a witch, that was nonsense, but there was something about her that was different from other folk . . .

She smiled, looking suddenly older than her eleven years.

"Go on home," she said. "Don't worry no more."

He went, glad to get away from the scrutiny of her gaze, and ashamed still that she had seen him cry. When Charlotte asked if he'd had any luck, he simply shook his head, but said nothing about Rosa. He was already full of scorn for himself for even thinking there was anything she could do. But deep down, there was a spark of renewed hope that he could not explain.

Another day passed, and a night, and the hope began to fade. Nipper had gone, and there was nothing that anyone could do.

Then, on the morning of the fifth day, he was awakened by sounds coming from beneath the bedroom window. For a moment he lay thinking he was still dreaming, then he identified the sounds as scratching and a thin, intermittent whining.

He leapt out of bed and rushed to the window, pushing up the sash far enough to lean out. And there, below him on the cobbles, was Nipper.

Joy exploded through his veins, and without stopping to close the window he dashed across the bedroom and clattered down the stairs. The latch was still on the back door; he thought it would never open. But it did, and the dog came bounding into the kitchen, leaping at Ted with the last of his strength. He looked poor and bedraggled, thinner than ever, and half the hair had gone from his back. But he was here.

"You're starving, boy!" Ted said, when he could bring himself to stop fondling him. "I'll get you something to eat."

Each day since Nipper had gone he had saved him a plate of bones and scraps, throwing out the stale ones and replacing them with fresh. But even if he had not done so, he would willingly have parted with his own breakfast at that moment for the dog.

"Well, well, he's back then!" Charlotte said, coming into the scullery to get the breakfast pans. "Looks as if he's been fighting over a bitch, like I said."

Ted nodded, and said nothing. She could be right, of course. There was dried blood on his face and on his back. But privately he could not help thinking that Nipper's injuries could have been caused as he tried to struggle out of a fox-hole or from the enmeshing roots of a tree. Of course it was nonsense to suppose that Rosa had had anything to do with the dog's return—and yet . . .

When he took Nipper over to the wash-house to bathe his sores, he glanced at the upper windows of the Clements's house and saw Rosa looking out. Triumphantly he held the dog up for her to see. But she only smiled, slowly, enigmatically, then turned away. And Ted, too happy to puzzle for long about things he did not understand, only shrugged and turned his attention to Nipper's sore back.

CHARLOTTE was as delighted over Nipper's return as Ted, although she hid her feelings behind a smoke-screen of impatience.

With all the everyday ups and downs of a family, it didn't do to attach too much importance to one particular incident, but she had missed Nipper, and missed him mostly for the things that usually made her consider him a nuisance, like having to keep the dinner plates out of his reach when she was dishing up.

She had been worried, too, about the effect of his disappearance on Ted. He was usually so happy-go-lucky he drove her crazy. But where the dog was concerned, it was a different story—as if all the love he had never bothered to show for anything else was centred on this one creature. The intensity of his despair had almost frightened Charlotte, making her see him in a new light, and now she said a prayer of thankfulness as she watched him fussing over the dog's sore patches, his face glowing as it had not been since Nipper's disappearance.

Yet later in the morning, as she went down the hill to the Rectory to do her daily cleaning stint, Charlotte was still aware of an indefinable knot of disquiet deep within her.

Perhaps it was that she couldn't believe the dog had returned. It certainly could not be anything else. James and the boys were at the pit, but there was nothing new in that. Amy and Jack had both broken up from school for the long summer holiday and were at home to keep an eye on Harry. So why did she feel that something dreadful was going to happen? Yet she did—and the feeling persisted as she went about her work: scrubbing the flagstoned passages in the Rectory, cleaning the mats with the newfangled carpet sweeper Caroline Archer had provided.

The only other possibility was that it had something to do with a remark Mrs Archer had made yesterday, a nasty, sly comment that Jack was doing exceptionally well at school considering the status of his parents. On the one hand, it had made her go hot with indignation, but as it had been cunningly phrased as a compliment rather than an insult, it was difficult to know how to take it. Perhaps Mrs Archer did know what she had said to the Rector in the study that day a year ago, and was no longer able to resist letting Charlotte know.

It had bothered her at the time, and it still did so, yet the foreboding she was feeling was different somehow, even more insistent and chilling.

She had to wait to clean the Rector's study that morning as she usually did. It was her least favourite job, for the desk was always lost under piles of papers, and the carpet around the fire grate was full of burn holes from the bits of coal that rolled on to it unheeded when the Rector lit a fire in winter.

Now, while she waited for the Rector to vacate the room, she took the pail of water she had used for the hall to the front door, sloshing it over the step and brushing it well down into the peony bushes.

Then she took the polish, working away on the bootscrapers until her arm ached.

While she was doing this, a movement by the gates caught her eye. She looked up casually, then stiffened. It was Jack, coming up the drive! But what was he doing here?

At once, the sense of foreboding returned, thickened to a choking apprehension. She straightened up, still holding the polish and cloth. At the same moment, he saw her and began to run, and as he drew closer she saw that his face was the colour of putty.

"Jack, whatever's the matter?" she asked harshly.

For a moment he looked at her helplessly, without speaking, his breath ragged, tears glistening in his eyes.

"Jack!" she said again, a note of panic creeping into her voice as a dozen nightmarish fears flashed through her mind.

"Oh, Mam, can you come home?" he gasped at last. "Amy's fallen in the tub."

"The tub?" Charlotte repeated. "What tub? What are you talking about?"

"The Clements's tub, the one they bathe the baby in. It was boiling water. Oh, Mam, it's awful . . . awful . . . "

Automatically she put a steadying hand on his arm though she had begun to shake from head to foot.

"You mean she's scalded?"

Jack bowed his head, nodding with his face screwed up against the tears. But he could not answer.

"All right, I'll come." She was untying her pinafore as she spoke. "Now you go round to the back and get my bag and coat—you know where I put them. I'll tell the Rector I'm going."

He ran off around the side of the house, glad to have Charlotte to tell him what to do. She went back into the hall and knocked on the door of the Rector's study, not waiting for an answer, but opening the door and looking in.

"I won't be long now, Mrs Hall," he began, then, as he saw her face, his irritation changed to concern. "What is it, my dear woman, is something wrong?"

She nodded, tight-lipped. "I won't be able to finish, Rector. I've got to go. Amy's had some sort of accident. Jack's come to fetch me."

"Oh yes, yes, of course. It's not bad, I hope?"

She half-closed her eyes against the word, then recovered herself.

"I don't know, Rector. I think it might be. Look, I must go now."

"Would you like me to come with you, Mrs Hall?" he asked.

"No, it's all right, Rector." Jack appeared again, running around the corner past the study window, carrying her bag and coat. "I don't know when I'll be back."

"Don't worry about that, Mrs Hall," he said, following her out. "Don't worry about anything."

"No," she said. "Come on, Jack." And then, as the thought struck her, "Where's Harry while you're down here?"

"Mrs Brixey's got him," he said.

She nodded, satisfied. Mrs Brixey was Redvers's mother, and Harry knew her well.

Together, mother and son half-ran down the drive and into the street.

"I knew something was going to happen!" Charlotte muttered. "Something told me it was. I should have stayed home today."

"Oh, Mam!" Jack groaned, and she caught at his arm.

"Now, try to tell me again what's happened."

"Amy went to the Clements' house to help bath the baby," Jack said tearfully. "I don't know what happened. They were playing around, I suppose, and she must have fallen. The first I knew was when she started screaming. I ran out and I met Mrs Clements, and she was screaming, too. But it was our Amy. . . . Oh, Mam, oh, Mam!"

"All right," Charlotte said.

They were on the hill now, and hurrying, with no breath left for talking.

Never had the climb seemed so long. Charlotte's trembling legs felt as soft as marshmallow—and as useless. But at last they turned the corner of the rank. And there, stopped outside number eleven, was a horse and trap.

"Doctor's here then," Charlotte said unevenly.

Jack did not reply. He trotted along beside her, filled with dread at the thought of going home again, but Charlotte did not notice, any more than she noticed the neighbours standing silently in their open doorways. A moment ago, they had been all agog with curiosity, now, sick with horror and oddly embarrassed, they shrank into their sculleries, holding their own children close into their skirts.

Outside her own door, Charlotte paused to touch Jack's arm.

"You stay here."

Gratefully he hung back and she went through the scullery and into the kitchen, her heart in her mouth.

The first person she saw was Dr Oliver Scott. He was standing in front of the fireplace, rolling down his sleeves, pain and pity clearly written in his pleasant face. Beside him stood Ada Clements. Her thin, veined hands covered her mouth, and above them her eyes were red from weeping. But of Amy there was no sign.

Fear seemed to explode in Charlotte, driving like white-hot fire through her bones. She sucked her breath in on a sob.

"Amy!"

A head bobbed up from behind the sofa, which was turned three-quarters away from the door. It was Peggy, hidden by the back of the sofa.

"Lotty, she's here."

"Oh, my life!" Charlotte ran towards the sofa, but Dr Scott intercepted her.

"No, Mrs Hall!" he said sharply. "Don't touch her!"

"No? But . . ."

"Don't try to touch her," he repeated more gently.

Amy lay face down on the sofa, her honey-coloured hair tumbling down over the white bandages that swathed her back. A cushion muffled her whimpers so that she sounded like a small, pitiful kitten.

For a moment Charlotte gazed at her in helpless horror, then she fell to her knees beside her. "Amy, love, it's all right now. Mammy's here. Mammy's here."

"Oh, Mammy!" The child tried to turn her head and the movement made her scream again. Shocked, Charlotte pushed a shaking fist into her mouth, her agonized eyes pleading mutely with Dr Scott.

"She's as comfortable as I can make her," he said grimly. "But her back is as raw as a skinned rabbit. Any movement is very painful indeed."

Charlotte laid a trembling hand on Amy's head, stroking the twisted curls gently.

"Now lie still, there's a good girl," she said evenly. "I'll be back in a minute, and Mrs Yelling's here with you. I'm just going to have a talk to the doctor about what we have to do to make you better."

"Mammy, don't go!" Amy pleaded.

"I won't be a minute, Amy. I'm right here in the house." She got up, nodding to Dr Scott, and led the way to another door in the corner of the kitchen. This one gave on to a narrow, linoleum-covered hall, and beyond it was the front room.

In contrast to the rest of the house, the front room was the epitome of Victorian tidiness. Around a central carpet square, the floor was of tiled Italian mosaic, and on the tightly stuffed armchairs were cream, lace-edged antimacassars. The fire-irons and fender were polished, and gleaming family likenesses stood in their frames on the top of the piano that had once belonged to Charlotte's mother, and a magnificent aspidistra on a wooden stand took pride of place beside the window.

It was a room used only for special occasions—family gatherings, christenings, funerals and weddings, and for entertaining special visitors. Now Charlotte led the doctor in, and closing the door behind him, faced him squarely.

"Well?"

"She's in a bad way, Mrs Hall," he said bluntly.

"You mean she's scalded bad?"

"Not so much scalded—more parboiled, I'd say." Then, seeing her expression, he said, "Her buttocks took the worst of it. She must have more or less sat down in the tub. But luckily the kidney area's not too bad. If it was . . . "

"But, as it is," Charlotte interrupted, "she will be all right, won't she, Doctor?"

For a moment he did not answer, and nausea rose in her throat, making her go hot and cold.

"There are two main dangers, Mrs Hall," he said at last. "One is the possibility of infection. A large part of Amy's body is without its protective covering of skin. You understand?"

She nodded. "And the other thing?"

"Shock. It's bound to be severe. I wouldn't really like to commit myself as to the outcome of this, but a week should give us some indication as to whether or not . . . "

His voice tailed away and Charlotte put all her weight on to the back of the chair.

"You mean she might not get over this, Doctor?" she asked.

His eyes dropped from hers, and he thrust his hands deep into his pockets.

"I'm afraid that is what I mean," he said.

"Oh, my God," Charlotte said quietly, but inside she felt as if she were screaming.

Not Amy! Oh, no, not Amy! Not my little girl! Dear God, what has she ever done . . .

Dr Scott seemed a long way off now, separated from her by swirling mists of unreality. Death of her babies she had accepted—many people lost their babies, and, although that did not lessen her grief, at least it eased the shock. Danger to her men she lived with —the danger of them meeting a violent end was built into her like a defence system. But Amy . . . Amy was past the age when she was in most danger from the illnesses that killed little ones—she had had whooping cough and measles, and even scarlet fever. It was years now since her health had given Charlotte more than a moment's worry.

And besides . . . Amy was sunshine and showers, precocity and innocence, laughter and tears. Although not as pretty as the round and rosy Dolly, there was something about her sharp little features that could stir feelings of tenderness and love, and her personality could fill a room.

If Amy died, nothing would ever be the same again. I couldn't bear it, thought Charlotte.

She lifted her head, and Oliver Scott's face came into focus, full of pity, concern and strength. Since he had come to Hillsbridge to join Dr Froster's practice two years ago, she had been one of the many people who had treated him with suspicion. He hardly seemed older than Jim or Fred, too young to be a doctor and entrusted with the family's health, and certainly too young to advise on personal matters.

Now, however, she found herself looking at him through new eyes: he was someone she could lean on, and on whose wisdom and courage she could draw. She swallowed the nervous lump rising in her throat, and lifted her chin.

"Just tell me what to do, Doctor," she said.

He nodded, relieved. "You'll need dressings—plenty of white dressings. Torn up sheets would probably be the best as long as they've been washed at least once. No new cloth. We'll treat the scalded area with carron oil. There must be as little movement as possible, so she'd better have a bed made up downstairs. It would be nice and quiet on the sofa in here . . . "

"No," Charlotte said sharply, and then, seeing his look, added, "Out there, Doctor, if she must, but not in here. This is where . . . I lost two other children, you know, and they were laid out in here. I suppose it's stupid, but it wouldn't seem right."

He nodded. "That's understandable. Well, I'll leave it to you, Mrs Hall. I'm sure you can arrange something. But you do realize she'll need attention night and day."

"She'll get it, Doctor," Charlotte said. "And if you're thinking I might leave her, I assure you, you need have no worries on that score. I shouldn't have left her this morning, but Jack was here, and I was only down at the Rectory. But I'll never forgive myself as long as I live. It's my fault she's lying there."

"You mustn't blame yourself, Mrs Hall," Dr Scott said gravely. "I suppose it's no good telling you that, but you can't be watching children all the time. If you did, you'd make them bundles of nerves. From what I gather, she'd gone in to help Mrs Clements bath the baby, and the foolish woman put the boiling water into the tub first and left the children in the room while she went to fetch the cold. They were playing around, and somehow Amy fell into the water. It was an accident, pure and simple, and if anyone is to blame, it's Mrs Clements. But she's probably suffering as much as you are. Guilt is a very hard cross to bear."

"She should be bloody suffering," Charlotte spat harshly. "I'd like to push *her* into a tub of boiling water, and if there was one handy now, I swear I'd do it!"

The doctor did not answer. It was easy to feel that way. He had been visiting the Presleys at number fifteen when Ada had come screaming out into the rank, and when he had run into her kitchen and seen what had happened, his reaction had been much the same. It was criminally stupid to leave children alone in a room with a bathful of boiling water.

But Ada was an object of pity herself—a lank-haired, consumptive-looking woman whose frail body had been worn out by repeated child-bearing and grinding hard work, and whose head was full of worries as to how to make ends meet and how to avoid becoming pregnant yet again. Given the circumstances, it was only surprising that something of the kind had not happened before.

"About paying you, Doctor," Charlotte said abruptly.

He looked away, embarrassed. "Don't worry about it, Mrs Hall."

"It's all right. Since I had Harry, we've joined the Doctor's Institute, thank God. And we don't let the payments lapse through the summer as some do. So you can send your bills in and know they'll be met."

He nodded. "We'd have looked after her in any case," he said gently. "You need have no fears about that. Now, I dare say Amy will be wanting you."

"Yes." She opened the door for him to pass into the hall. "And you'll look in again, Doctor?"

"As often as I can."

Jack had got up the courage to come into the kitchen now. He stood beside the sofa where Peggy was comforting Amy, biting his lip and looking the picture of misery. But of Ada Clements, there was no sign.

"She said she had to go," Peggy told Charlotte as the doctor's pony and trap made its way down the rank.

"Just as well," Charlotte retorted. "If she'd stayed here I'd have murdered her, and that's the truth, Peggy."

Peggy nodded. "I can't say I blame you, Lotty. But what's done's done, and it won't help Amy to have you like this."

"No, Peg, but I can tell you, it'll help me!" Charlotte returned, and as she knelt beside the small figure on the sofa, her helpless anger swelled into a great bubble of hatred for Ada Clements and the irresponsible stupidity that might cost Amy her life.

THROUGH the long days and nights that followed, it was the anger that kept Charlotte going.

Dolly came home as often as possible to help nurse her sister and Peggy looked in too, but it was on Charlotte that the brunt of the load fell. She made up a bed for herself on the settle so that Amy would not be left alone at night, but the sleep she was able to snatch was often broken by Amy's crying. After she had sung her back to sleep she would lie fuming with helpless agony, quite unable to sleep again. The days were even worse. The usual tasks of cooking, cleaning and washing seemed interminable, for she could only leave Amy for a few minutes at a time. And twice each day Dr Scott or his senior partner Dr Froster, came to change the dressings.

This was the time Charlotte dreaded most of all, holding Amy down while she screamed and Dr Scott eased the saturated cloth away from the raw scarlet of her back. But with every day that passed, Amy's chances of surviving became a little better. In the dead of night, Charlotte worried about the effect the accident would have on Amy—scarred, perhaps with some permanent disability—but she tried not to think beyond the next day and the next, and thanked God the child was still alive.

So preoccupied was Charlotte, she did not even realize that she

67

had not seen Ada Clements since the day of the accident. She had no way of knowing the torment the other woman was enduring.

On her side of the dividing wall, Ada also found sleep elusive. Over and over again she kept reliving the awful moment when the splash and the scream had reached her in the scullery and she had rushed into the kitchen to find Amy, half-sitting, half-lying, in the bath of boiling water.

Every time she thought of it she turned so cold and weak she thought she was going to faint, and she was so ashamed she could not bring herself to face Lotty. As the schools were on holiday, she was able to send Rosa for what groceries she needed, but in the blazing summer weather, the Hall's scullery door was left open most of the day, and Ada was afraid even to go across the yard to the privy in case she bumped into Charlotte. This added to her wretchedness, for she had to resort to relieving herself on the white china chamber-pot that was usually reserved for the night time use of Walter and the children. With the rim biting into her scrawny buttocks she sat and wept, thin, helpless sobs taking the place of tears. Why Lotty's child? she asked herself. If it had to happen at all, why had it happened to Amy, when Lotty was one of the few people who found it in her to be kind to her.

Lurking wretchedly one morning behind her curtain net, Ada noticed Peggy Yelling come down the rank carrying a folded sheet. The sight made her go cold, for besides being the local midwife, Peggy was also the one sent for by bereaved families to lay out their dead, and Ada assumed the worst.

Weeping again, she sent Wally, the eldest of her boys, to see what he could find out. To her relief, he came back with the news that the sheet was not for a shroud but bandages.

"It's only used sheet that will do," he reported. "Mrs Hall's torn up all her'n already, so the neighbours are chipping in with what they can spare."

The sense of this escaped Ada, but she thought about it as she went on with her work, and by late afternoon her desire to make amends was almost equal to her fear of facing Charlotte. She went to the bedroom, pulled out the tin trunk where she stored her meagre stock of bed-linen, and chose two sheets. Turned and patched though they were, they were precious to her, but she hesitated for only a moment. If she was unable to replace them and had to spend uncomfortable nights with the rough blanket next to her skin, it was too bad. It would be her own personal hair shirt, and it worried her less than the prospect of delivering the sheets to Charlotte. Momentarily she toyed with the idea of sending Wally or Rosa as carrier, but they had both gone across the fields and would not be home much before dusk. So, taking her courage in both hands, she went round to the Halls' house and knocked on the half-open backdoor.

Charlotte was in the scullery, spreading beef dripping on chunks of bread for tea, but when she saw Ada standing in the doorway, she put down the knife and wiped her hands in her apron.

"Well?" she demanded shortly, glaring at Ada.

The other woman took a hesitant step forward, holding the white bundle towards Charlotte.

"I hear you need sheets, for Amy. I looked these out for you . . . "

Charlotte struggled with an overwhelming desire to tell Ada to take her sheets and herself as far as possible from Greenslade Terrace, but Ada, shaking yet determined, pushed the sheets into Charlotte's arms.

"Please, Lotty, I want you to have them. I know there's nothing I can do to make amends for what happened in my house, but God strike me dead if I don't regret it with every bone in me body. I tell you, I wouldn't have that lamb hurt for all the world, especially after all your kindness to me."

Charlotte stiffened. "Kindness?"

"Yes. You've always been good to me, Lotty. There's people around here that have looked down on me because o' what I done all them years ago, when our Rosa was born. Because I married Walter carrying another man's babe, they called me all kinds of dirty names—and they still do. It's not the sort o' thing you can live down hereabouts. But you've never been like that with me. I've never felt you were judging me, or talking about me behind my back, and I've been grateful. That's why I'm so upset to think that such a thing as this should happen now . . . "

Ada paused for breath, drawing a scrawny hand across her mouth, and Charlotte felt the anger instantly desert her. Who was she to blame Ada for Amy's accident? She was just as guilty herself. If she had not been at the Rectory, Amy would not have been next door helping to bath the Clements' baby.

"There's none of us fit to cast the first stone," she said sharply.

"If there's one thing I can't abide, it's gossip, specially when them as do the gossiping are no more than hypocrites. It's my belief there's a skeleton behind most doors if folk were honest enough to admit it—or unlucky enough to get found out. And as for this other business, well, I'll tell you straight, if I'd laid hands on you when Dr Scott was changing our Amy's dressing this morning, there'd have been murder done. But accidents will happen, I suppose."

"That's right," Ada said eagerly. "They should have known better than to fool around with a bath of hot water there. One slip . . . "

And you should have known better than to put it there, Charlotte thought, but to her own surprise she did not say it. What was done was done. Rows and recriminations would not help Amy. The clean white sheets would.

"God bless you, Lotty," Ada went on, folding her skinny arms around her ribs, trembling now with relief. "And if there's anything I can do—anything at all—just let me know. My kids could do a bit of shopping for you, or I could sit with Amy while you went down to the Rectory, or anything like that. I know you need the money to keep your Jack at school."

Charlotte drew in her breath sharply. "I wouldn't leave our Amy with anybody, not even her own brothers," she said roundly. "Don't think you're the only one who feels guilty over this, Ada. How do you think *I* feel? But thanks again for the sheets."

Turning, she went back into the kitchen. Amy was dozing, and Jack was at the table, poring over his aeroplane cuttings, while little Harry sat on the floor catching any pieces that came his way. As she looked at them, her heart came into her mouth and the hopelessness of it all descended on her like a thick black cloud.

Amy was in this state because of her ambition for Jack. But now all that might come to nothing because she could no longer go out and earn the extra money. Perhaps she could manage to make ends meet if she economized even more than usual. But there were still Jack's books to think of, and the expense of sending him on to another school if he passed the Oxford Junior. It wasn't fair to expect the others to go without so that he could have more and more.

For the first time, Charlotte wondered if she had taken on more than she could cope with in falling in with Mr Davies' plans. Perhaps he should leave school and get a job. It would be so much easier for all of them, and she was so tired, so terribly tired . . .

He looked up and saw her in the doorway.

"Who was that at the door, Mam?"

"Oh, just Mrs Clements with some sheets for Amy."

He nodded and bent over his cuttings again, his face so serious that it tore at her heart. He'd been in a terrible state over what had happened, blaming himself because he'd been in charge, and he'd hardly left Amy's side since. On top of all that, how could she tell him now that he had to leave school and give up everything he'd worked for? She couldn't. She just couldn't.

With a sigh, she put the sheets down on the table and turned away. Worrying would do no good. She'd manage somehow. She'd have to. And maybe if the good Lord was on her side, something would turn up.

TWO DAYS later her determined optimism was rewarded when Mr Archer came knocking on the door.

Jack was out—Charlotte had persuaded him to take Harry and Nipper across the fields—and she had snatched a moment to doze on the settle to make up for the previous night's lack of sleep. The knocking awoke her, and she came to abruptly, wondering for the moment where she was. Then smoothing her hair and apron she hurried to the door.

"Rector, what are you doing here?" she said, surprised to see him.

"I should have come before," he apologized. "I've been meaning to, but I haven't quite been myself, and I didn't think I could do the hill."

"I'm sorry to hear that," Charlotte said. It was true his breathing was ragged and his colour rather high, but apart from that he looked much as usual. "It's nothing much, I hope?"

"I doubt it, though I must admit the pins and needles I keep getting in my hand can be quite irritating." He rubbed at his left wrist, then smiled blandly. "That's not why I'm here, though, to talk about myself. I've come to ask after Amy."

"That's kind of you, Rector," Charlotte said. "She's been in a bad way, but every day's a step in the right direction. You'd better come in and see her."

"Yes, of course." The Rector, never completely relaxed with children, looked less than pleased at the prospect, and Charlotte's eyes narrowed.

"You did come to see Amy? Or was it to find out about me working?"

"Both really," the Rector confessed. "Now you're not to think I'm chasing you, Mrs Hall. Nothing could be further from my mind. In fact, I'm sure it will be some long time before you could even think of leaving your daughter, and that's what's been worrying me."

"Worrying you?" she repeated.

"I know you're somewhat dependent on what you earn from me," he continued. "But while you are unable to come in and clean, I shall have to find someone else who can, and much as I would like to, I simply cannot afford to pay two wages."

"I understand that," she said stiffly. "We'll manage."

"Mrs Hall," he said, almost severely. "Won't you listen to me for a moment? I've been turning the problem over in my mind, and I think I've come up with the answer—the Hardlake Trust. You may not have heard of it, but it is a trust fund set up in memory of one of my predecessors. The idea was that the proceeds should be used to help local children make a start in the world—buy a bag of tools for a boy wanting to become a carpenter, for instance, or a cap, apron and print dress for a girl going into service."

"When Dolly went into service no one offered to buy her dress," Charlotte said shortly.

The Rector smiled. "It has rather fallen into disuse, I'm afraid," he said gently. "And I can't help feeling it's rather outdated in its concept. It should be extended to help boys like Jack, in my opinion —if there's any money left, and I'm sure there must be. If I speak to the trustees . . . "

"No!" Charlotte said. "No, thank you, Rector. I've never taken charity yet, and I'm not beginning now."

The Rector looked at her sadly, still rubbing his left arm, which had begun to ache.

"You came to me for help once before, Mrs Hall," he said at last. "We didn't call it charity then."

"And neither was it," Charlotte told him. "I've worked hard for every penny I've brought home with me."

"But now you're in no position to work," the Rector said in a slightly exasperated tone. "You must stay with Amy for as long as she needs you, but you mustn't forget Jack. He's worked as hard as you have this last year. Is it fair to him, or even good sense, to let all that be wasted because of pride? I don't believe God would want that to happen."

"Wouldn't he? Then why did he let our Amy fall in the tub?" As he opened his mouth to answer, she waved her hand impatiently. "Oh, never mind. What does it matter? What does anything matter but health and strength?"

He looked at her gravely and in his face she caught a glimpse of sincerity beneath his somewhat pompous manner.

"Love matters, Mrs Hall. And a dream, such as you have for Jack. It's important to both of you. You can't give up now. You'd never forgive yourself, and neither would he."

Charlotte stood staring with sleep-starved eyes at the sweep of blue sky above the wash-houses. Was there a God out there somewhere, a God as unlike the white-bearded father figure portrayed for her in her youth as reality is to dreams? Was there a scheme of things, a master plan, with one infinite deity manipulating it to fit his pattern? Perhaps there was. Certainly during the last few days she had often found herself praying that Amy would be spared. And more than once, when she had felt ready to drop herself, from somewhere had come the strength and the will to carry on.

"Don't turn down my offer out of hand," the Rector said, interrupting her thoughts. "Sleep on it, and I'm sure you'll see the sense in what I'm saying. The Hardlake Trust is there to be used, after all, and when the trustees know the circumstances . . . "

She moved abruptly, a sense of danger piercing the tiredness.

"You wouldn't tell them . . . "

He smiled wryly. "Oh, Mrs Hall, do you really think I would?"

Hot colour flooded her cheeks as she realized he was even more anxious to keep the secret than she was. Of course he would not tell them that his own nephew had gone with the wife of a miner! God forbid!

"It will give me a great deal of satisfaction to feel I have helped the boy get on in the world," the Rector said, smoothing over the awkward moment. Then, nodding towards the kitchen: "And I shall pray for Amy, you may be sure of that."

She nodded. "I wish you would, Rector," she said with a touch of her old, dry humour. "He's more likely to listen to you than to me."

The Rector looked at her, seeing a woman who was handsome still despite the lines that lack of sleep had etched on her face, and whose spirit and determination might sometimes be dimmed by despair, but never quenched. He saw a woman who would fight for her own with every last ounce of her strength, and he was filled with an admiration that momentarily humbled him.

THREE WEEKS LATER, Hillsbridge was buzzing with news of another accident.

"You'll never guess who's dead!" Peggy Yelling said, coming into Charlotte's kitchen.

Charlotte, who was just sponging Amy's face and hands, looked up and smiled briefly.

"Oh, hello, Peg. Who is it then?"

"The Rector!" Peggy told her. "And quite a to-do it's caused too!"

"Oh, my Lord! Was it his heart?" Charlotte asked, remembering the Rector's complaints about his health when he had visited her earlier.

"Oh, it sounds like it." Peggy bent to restrain Harry from tipping the contents of her bag on to the floor. "But wait till you hear the story. There was a horse and trap stopped up in the hill by Fords the drapers, and one of those newfangled motors came through. You know the noise they make, spluttering away, especially on the hills! Well, it frightened the horse and it ran away."

Charlotte patted Amy's face dry. "Oh, I say! Blooming motors! But where does the Rector come in?"

"He was down on the pavement outside the Rectory when he heard it coming," Peggy went on, full of her story. "From what I hear, he went to try and stop it. But it was too much for his heart. He collapsed, right there in the street. And by the time they got a doctor to him, he was gone."

"Poor man," Charlotte said. "Whatever will his wife do?"

Peggy sniffed loudly. "She'll have to leave the Rectory, of course. But I can't see her leaving Hillsbridge, can you? She enjoys her little bit of power too much. While she's here, she's still the Rector's wife."

Charlotte nodded, her heart sinking. For a glorious moment she had seen herself free from the fear that haunted her, of Caroline Archer telling what she knew—or might know.

"What happened to the horse, Mrs Yelling?" Amy asked.

Peggy smiled at the honey-coloured curls, which was all she could see now Amy was lying down again.

"Oh, it kept going until it got tired, I reckon. And with having to go up a hill again, it wouldn't be long, would it, my lamb?"

"Well, well, poor man," Charlotte said again.

And it was only after Peggy had gone that she realized just what his death would mean to her—no more wages, and, after all, no Hardlake Trust. Unless he had already done something about it. But the Reverend Andrew Archer, whatever his good intentions, had always been one for putting things off to the last possible moment. Only his death, it seemed, had been premature.

4

THROUGH the autumn and winter the Hall household seemed to revolve around Amy.

For thirteen weeks she had to lie on her stomach, although when the crisis point had passed, Dr Scott agreed that James could carry her upstairs to her own bed at night and down again in the morning. Her sofa became the focal point for the family, who never left her side for more than a few minutes.

Dolly came down from Captain Fish's whenever she could to sit with her sister, and the older boys saved all their loose change to buy small presents to cheer her up—a jar of bull's-eyes, a book of rhymes, a small china figurine of a shepherdess. James set aside an hour every night to sit with her, holding her hand and telling her the stories she loved to hear of when he had been a boy; even Harry and Nipper came to see her often, Harry pulling himself up to look at her over the arm of the sofa and Nipper licking her hand.

As for Jack, no matter how many times Charlotte told him he was not to blame for what had happened, he was still wretched with guilt, and every moment he could spare from his studying he spent with her, reading to her and letting her help him sort out the cuttings for his scrap book on aeroplanes and Charlotte's on the Royal Family. Then, when she was well enough, he took her out every afternoon in Harry's push-chair. She would have to be taught to walk again, Dr Scott had said, but for the moment the push-chair was the best way to get her out of the house and put some colour in her cheeks.

"Give it a miss today. She's already been out with me this morning," Charlotte said to Jack on more than one occasion, but he only smiled.

"Amy wants to go again, don't you?" he said, and Amy nodded, looking at him with such adoration in her eyes that Charlotte was both touched and amused. Amy idolized Jack. She always had done. But he was no longer her only hero. The other was Dr Scott.

From the beginning Oliver Scott had talked to her in the same serious way he talked to adults, and that had made her feel very grown-up. But more importantly, he winked at her and chucked her under the chin with a "That's my girl!" when he finished changing her dressings. Soon she had begun to look forward to his visits, even if they did mean a few minutes' agony, and lying on her stomach, her eyes tightly closed, she imagined what it would be like to one day be his wife.

"He'll wait for me, I know he will!" she thought, choosing to ignore the fact that as she was only nine years old and he would have to wait a very long time.

By Christmas she was so much better that he only visited once or twice a week, and Amy missed him. She was bored and miserable, and she cried a lot, losing her patience with everything and everyone, even Jack.

"I wish my back was really bad again—you were all much nicer to me then," she grizzled one dark, December day.

"Don't be so silly. You've forgot just what it was like or you wouldn't say that," Charlotte told her sharply.

"I haven't. At least Dr Scott used to come and see me," she went on, her voice muffled by the cushion. "He's forgot all about me now. He doesn't care any more."

Charlotte stood for a moment, hesitating. What Amy did not know was that last time he had come, Oliver Scott had brought with him a large brown paper parcel and asked her to give it to Amy at Christmas. At this very moment it was hidden away in her 'corner' —the magical place behind her dressing-table which was always reserved for surprises. To give it to Amy now would be to cheat, but Charlotte could not help thinking it might be just the thing to cheer her up. And this Christmas there would most likely be quite a few treats for her over and above the usual oranges, apples, and a small toy, even though money was tighter than usual.

"Dr Scott hasn't forgot you at all," she said, making up her mind. "I've got something upstairs that he brought for you."

Amy's face brightened. "Oh, what is it? Can I have it?"

"I'll get it," Charlotte said. "But don't think I'm going to make a habit of giving you Christmas presents early. And what Dr Scott's going to say, I don't know."

She went up and got the parcel and gave it to Amy, smiling at the child's delight. It was good to see her happy—and she sent up a prayer of thankfulness that Amy was alive and able to share Christmas with them.

"Can I open it, Mammy?" she asked, wide-eyed.

"Yes, go on," Charlotte told her, and then watched, pleased, as Amy unwrapped the parcel to disclose a large, cuddly toy bear.

"Oh, it's a Teddy!" she cried. "And look, here's some butterscotch, too! A whole pound!"

It was almost too much to believe. Teddy bears were the most up-to-date of toys, and sweets generally came in ounces, not *pounds*.

"If you aren't a lucky girl, then tell me!" Charlotte said. "And look, he's put a card in with it. Shall I read you what it says? "For the bravest little girl I ever met." That's you, Amy."

"Yes," she said, laying back down to rest, the Teddy bear tucked under one arm and the butterscotch clasped in her other hand.

Through the long weeks that followed, they were her special treasures. The bear was not to be removed from her sight, and the butterscotch was nibbled at, only as a treat.

"I want it to last forever," she said, when Harry came bothering her for a piece. "He can have anything else, I don't mind what it is, but not my butterscotch."

And Charlotte, smiling, understood.

CAROLINE ARCHER moved out of the Rectory at the beginning of March.

Although a new Rector had arrived in the autumn—a pleasant-faced bachelor named Reuben Clarke—she had persuaded him to let her remain in residence until she had completed negotiations for a pretty, honeysuckle-covered cottage in the shadow of the church.

On the day she moved, Charlotte had let Amy walk down to the shops for the first time, taking Harry's push-chair to bring her back up the hill again. They stood talking to Mercy Brixey, Redvers' mother, while idly watching the crates and boxes coming down the drive to be stacked in the waiting removal wagon.

"Poor soul, she's going to miss it all, isn't she?" Mercy said sympathetically, but Charlotte did not agree. She thought it would be a miracle if Caroline Archer gave up anything but the house. Already she had made it plain she intended to continue running the Mothers Union, the Christmas Bazaar and the summer garden party, and as long as she stayed in the town, she would be 'the Rector's wife' to the people of Hillsbridge.

It was her good fortune that Mr Clarke was a single man, and Charlotte wondered with some amusement what would have happened if he had had a wife. But instead he had a housekeeper, young and pretty enough to make tongues wag behind his back. And what went on behind closed doors at the Rectory was a subject for ribald speculation amongst the men at the Miners Arms.

A few weeks after Caroline Archer moved out of the Rectory, however, the people of Hillsbridge had other, more important things on their minds than the morals of their new spiritual leader. The pits came out on strike for better wages, and soon it was affecting them all.

The Halls, of course, already missing Charlotte's money from the Rectory, felt the pinch almost at once. Although James was a full union member and able to draw ten shillings a week strike pay, the boys were only half members, which meant they only got five shillings each. With the town strangely silent, the peace disturbed only by school bells instead of the usual orchestra of sirens and hooters, the miners gathered on the County Bridge between the railway lines to chat, and played endless games of billiards in the games room at the Victoria Hall, the town's magnificent community centre.

But by the time the third week of the strike came and went with no sign of a settlement, tempers were beginning to fray.

"'Tis all very well, but we don't seem to be getting nowhere," Moses Brimble remarked one day to a crowd of his companions as they squatted against the wall outside the Miners Arms. "Here we are, not asking for half nor quarter what they'm asking for in Yorkshire and South Wales, and yet they won't settle with us."

"Well, we'm sticking together now, ain't we?" Walter Clements said.

Moses snorted. "*Sinking* together if you ask me. It's getting like that now we can't even afford a pint of beer or a bit of baccy. And there's nothing much in the gardens this time of year, neither."

"That's true enough," Walter agreed. "But you must admit, the Co-op have been pretty good to us."

There was a murmur of general agreement. The Co-operative Society was strong in Hillsbridge—it owned a bakery, a dairy and a farm as well as a shop that sold everything from hardware to fresh fish—and in this time of trouble it was taking its responsibilities seriously, reducing the price of bread to fourpence for a large loaf and planning to provide free dinners for the school children.

"It's the young'uns I can't understand," Moses went on, changing the subject. "They'm treating it like a holiday, most on 'em. Even fixing up football matches against those ruddy policemen they've sent in case of trouble."

"Well, you can't blame them," James Hall put in. "Lads stuck around with nothing to do day after day. It's a darn sight better than getting up to mischief if you ask me. It's what our union is about that I can't understand."

The others turned to look at him. James was a hard-working and respected man in Hillsbridge, and he had been in the pits longer than many of them.

"What do you mean?" Walter Clements asked.

"Change for the sake of it," James said vehemently. "To get away from this strike for a moment, take the way we'm paid. We've always done our sharing out in the pub, haven't we. Always. Now what have they done? Brought out a law to stop it. I can't see no sense in it." He paused, and the others nodded their agreement.

"Then getting back to this strike," James went on. "Danger money they say we'm after. Well, we'm in no more danger now than we ever was. We've got no wages coming in, we'm having to take charity to put bread in our children's mouths, and go out on the batch picking coal to keep a fire going in our grates. And for what? The bosses'll have us in the end. They'm bound to."

The miners grunted and spat, but they did not argue. Most of them agreed with him, particularly the older ones. They were a peace-loving bunch, apart from a few hotheads like young Ewart Brixey, Redvers's older brother, who was forever trying to stir them up to fight for a better deal and would, some said, end up working for the union instead of Sir Richard Spindler, the owner of Hillsbridge Collieries. But in general they echoed his sentiments—that what had been good enough for their fathers was good enough for them. All they wanted was to be allowed to get back to work. The fun of idleness had palled now. The Hillsbridge miners were not enjoying the strike.

THERE WERE THOSE, however, for whom the strike was an eventful time, and Dolly Hall was one of them.

Although she had brought Evan Comer, the Co-op delivery boy, to the coronation street party with her, things were far from serious between them, and Dolly sometimes wondered if she was doing the right thing in continuing to walk out with him.

He was good to her, there was no denying that—almost too good. All their outings were arranged to please her, and she was afraid to admit she liked or wanted something because, almost inevitably, it would turn up as a present next time he came to see her.

"I wish you wouldn't, Evan," she told him time and again, but he did not seem to realize she meant it.

"I'd do anything for you, Dolly," he said. But instead of being pleased by his adoration, she found it made her nervous. He was so intense! And she couldn't help it if she didn't feel the same way. She liked him, yes, but that was all. And she would have liked him a great deal better if he hadn't made her feel so trapped.

But Dolly was only human, and she was flattered by Evan's attentions. He was a really promising footballer, the rising star of Hillsbridge Town, admired by her brothers for his skill, and by all the girls for his dark good looks. It was nice to feel that when he could have taken his pick of the girls, he had not only chosen her, but put her on a pedestal. And so, against her better judgment, Dolly let the affair rumble on.

One mild March evening, however, things came to a head. They were out for a stroll when they heard music coming from the town square in front of the Victoria Hall, and when they went to investigate, they found a Band of Hope temperance meeting in full swing.

They stopped to listen, and Dolly made fun of the speakers, teasing Evan that she was going to sign the pledge.

"You wouldn't really, would you, Dolly?" he asked seriously.

"Of course, I would!" she affirmed, biting her lip to stop herself from laughing. "Drink is the instrument of the devil. Mrs Durrant next-door says so."

"Instrument of the devil!" he retorted. "Don't talk so silly! It's the working man's pleasure."

"Well, I think it's wicked!" Dolly said airily, but at the sight of his face she couldn't hold the laughter back any longer. It came out in a loud explosion, and she stood with her hands pressed over her mouth.

Evan's face darkened. "You've been having me on," he accused.
"Yes," she admitted, through her giggles.

"Don't you try to make a fool out of me, Dolly," he said, and his tone abruptly stopped her laughter.

"What do you mean? It was only a joke!" she told him, but he did not answer, and a chill ran up her spine.

They walked on in silence, following the main street away from the square and past the church. Here, under the churchyard wall, a path branched away to the fields and the river where Ted had swum on the Sunday morning he had first found Nipper, and Evan turned Dolly along this path.

"I don't think I want to go that way," she said, nervous suddenly. "Let's stick to the main road."

But Evan's fingers tightened on hers, and he leaned back against the wall, pulling her towards him.

"I'm sorry, Dolly," he said.

He sounded so miserable, her soft heart went out to him.

"I'm sorry, too. I shouldn't have teased you."

"No, you shouldn't," he agreed, "not the way I feel about you, Dolly."

He pulled her close then, kissing her as he had never kissed her before. His mouth moved on hers with rhythmic insistence, and his hand slid over her back to squeeze her hips closer to his. Dolly, off balance, let herself lean against him and felt something within her respond to his maleness and his desire. But as his free hand began to fumble with the buttons on her blouse, she tried to push herself away.

"Evan, no! Stop it, please."

"But why?" He held her firm, his breath hot on her face. "You're mine, Dolly. I wouldn't hurt you. I only want to feel you, that's all. Just for a minute."

It was something in his attitude that frightened her more than what he was trying to do. All boys tried. She'd known that since she was fourteen. But this was no light-hearted raid for what he could get. There was more to it than that.

"Evan, don't!" she said again, but he took no notice, stopping her protests by kissing her again and again until she could hardly breathe. His hands seemed to be everywhere now, on her breasts, her bottom, hoisting up her skirt, fumbling and groping, and with a shock she realized his trouser buttons were undone.

81

"Evan Comer, will you behave yourself!" she cried sharply.

His hands stopped their probing and she pushed herself away, straightening her clothes.

"What do you think you're up to?" she asked indignantly. "And put yourself straight, do! You look disgusting!"

Her tone sobered him, and shamefaced he buttoned his trousers.

"I'm sorry, Dolly . . . " He reached out to put his arm around her again, but she stepped away. "I couldn't help myself, Dolly. You know how I feel about you."

"That's no excuse," she said.

But she was weakening now, and he rushed on, "Do you think we've known one another long enough to get married?"

"Oh!" she said, surprised. "Are you . . . are you asking, Evan?"

"I suppose I am." He patted his hair tidy with an unsteady hand. "I've been thinking about it a long while, but I've been putting off saying anything. I was so afraid you'd say "no".'

"Oh, Evan!" Dolly said, confused. The trapped feeling was back, stronger than ever, and she didn't know what to say to him. It would be foolish to turn him down out of hand. He was a good-looking boy with a steady job, and all her friends would regard him as quite a catch. And just now, when he'd kissed her so masterfully, it had been quite nice until he'd gone too far.

But she didn't love him, not the way she wanted to love the man she married. And she was scared of his odd, intense ways.

"I don't know, I'll have to think," she said, hesitantly.

They walked in silence back to the town square where the Band of Hope temperance meeting was just breaking up. Evan had to go to the public convenience on the corner of the Victoria Hall to relieve himself, and while Dolly was standing on the pavement waiting for him, she noticed a young policeman on duty at the back of the crowd giving her sidelong glances.

She guessed he was one of those drafted in to deal with the strike, and in his uniform he made an impressive figure. Dolly always enjoyed the fact that boys found her attractive, and immediately found herself flirting discreetly. She felt he might be about to come over to speak to her, when Martha Durrant, an enthusiastic supporter of the Band of Hope, descended on her, saying how pleased she was to see that young people were interested in temperance. Mrs Durrant had barely finished when Evan was back.

By the time she reached home, Dolly had almost forgotten the young policeman again. But he had not forgotten her, for the next day he came rapping at the backdoor of the house. Cook was severely startled to find a policeman standing on the other side of the door and was heartily relieved to discover that the purpose of his visit was to ask Dolly if she would walk out with him.

Dolly had been thinking about Evan all night, and had decided that she did not want to marry him, but telling him so was going to be difficult. She reasoned that, perhaps if she went out with someone else once or twice, he would begin to understand that she simply didn't feel as he did, and not pursue the matter.

Dolly accepted the young policeman's invitation, and on her next night off they went to listen to a Welsh male voice choir who were giving a concert in Victoria Hall in aid of the striking miners.

The next morning when Evan arrived with Captain Fish's groceries, he was in a furious temper. Dolly, who was cleaning the silver on the kitchen table, realized as soon as she saw his thunderous expression that he knew of her outing the previous evening. Despite her protestations that they were *not* engaged, Evan's temper flared, until Dolly finally fled from the kitchen, her eyes spilling with tears.

It wasn't until five minutes later, when she heard his horse clip-clop away, that she dared return to the kitchen. The room was empty —Cook had gone to the shops for some good beefsteak for the evening meal—and the door was still flapping open as Dolly had left it. She sat down, her mind in a turmoil, and endeavoured to resume her cleaning. It was then that she noticed the captain's heavy silver cigarette box was missing.

At first she could not believe it. She looked again and again through the silver on the table as if it might miraculously appear. But it was gone!

It had been there, of that she was sure. Tears began to gather behind her eyes, but this time they were tears of outrage. Evan must have taken the box! It couldn't have been anyone else! But why should he do such a thing—and what was she going to do about it?

For a moment she stood undecided, but the thought of telling Captain Fish and having him send a bobby after Evan was not a very pleasant one. In an odd way she felt guilty for even having been mixed up with someone who would resort to stealing, and she shrank from admitting it.

"I'll go after Evan myself!" she said aloud.

Without even stopping to take off her cap and apron, she hurried out. She knew the way Evan went from here—to the two or three other big houses on Ridge Road, then back again and over the brow of the hill to the cottages on the other side. For a moment she stood in the road, looking up and down, wondering which way to go. A child was kicking stones into a hopscotch on the opposite pavement, and she called out to her, "Has the Co-op cart gone back yet?"

The child shook her head and Dolly started off up the road. Just as she reached the drive of the last of the big houses, she saw his cart coming out. At the same moment he saw her, and flushed scarlet.

"Just a minute, Evan, I want you!" Dolly called.

He reined in the horse, his guilt plainly written all over his face.

"Where's that cigarette box?" she shouted at him. "Come on now, I know you've got it."

He looked around embarrassed, trying to shut her up. "Dolly, I . . ."

"Are you going to give it back, or am I going to call a bobby?"

He jumped down from the cart on to the road beside her. "For goodness sake, keep your voice down! The whole road can hear you."

"I don't care if the whole of Hillsbridge can hear me!" she shouted. "How could you, Evan? Stealing while my back was turned . . ."

"I didn't!"

"You did, too. Don't tell me you're a liar as well as a thief."

He was really flustered now.

"All right, all right, I took it," he conceded. "But I only did it for you."

"For *me?*" she spat.

"To get some money to buy you something nice. I thought maybe if I got you that brooch you've had your eye on in the jeweller's window, you might change your mind."

"Evan Comer! If that's not the most insulting thing I've ever heard! You think you can buy me with a brooch!"

"No, Dolly, you've got it all wrong . . ."

"Wrong, is it? And what about all those other things you've given me? Did you get them with stolen money, too?"

"No, of course not," he protested. "I don't know what came over me. It was thinking you'd finished with me, like—and then there was the cigarette box right there on the table. I took it without thinking."

"And you can put it back the same way," Dolly ordered. "I'll have it this very minute, Evan, if you don't mind."

Shamefaced, he reached under the seat of the cart and got out the cigarette box. She took it from him and hid it under her apron.

"I'm glad you've seen sense, Evan."

She turned away, but he called after her: "Dolly, just a minute! When will I see you?"

Her chin went up, and her lips set in a determined line. "I'm sorry, Evan, but I don't want to see you any more. Not now."

"But, Dolly . . ."

He looked so wretched she almost weakened again, but making up her mind, she said decisively, "I'm sorry, Evan. Mammy wouldn't like me getting involved with someone who could steal. She's very particular about us only ever having what belongs to us."

Then, before he could say anything else, she turned and hurried back down the road. The cart still had not passed her when she reached the gates of the house, and looking over her shoulder, she saw it pulled into the side of the road. Evan was recovering himself, she supposed, but she did not wait. She wanted to get the cigarette box back inside the house before Cook came back and missed it— and her.

Luck was on her side. Cook was still out, and she was able to replace the box with no one any the wiser. But she did not change her mind about Evan. A man who could steal was not the man for her, even if he had done it on the spur of the moment. And somehow she felt it was probably not the first time. Dolly knew she would never be able to trust him again.

She told nobody of the incident with Evan, not even Charlotte, who was somewhat dubious about her giving up a local boy for one of the policemen who would be gone when the strike ended.

"Nothing will come of it, you know," Charlotte warned her.

"Oh, Mam, I don't want anything to come of it!" Dolly replied impatiently. "I don't want to get married yet. There's a lot of things I want to do first—like learning to be a cook. And I don't see why I shouldn't have a bit of fun while I'm young."

Charlotte nodded. She would like to see Dolly settled, but let her have a good time first, as long as she knew where to stop.

"Just as long as you don't get too attached to this bobby, that's all," she said.

It was much the same thing as she had said to Ted about Nipper, but this time her advice was heeded. When on Easter Eve the miners voted to accept the pay and settlement terms offered them, and the police were marched out of Hillsbridge for the last time, Dolly's heart was still intact, though she promised to write to her policeman boyfriend if he wrote to her.

It was Evan who was unable to forget, Evan who brooded while love turned to hate, and plotted his revenge on the girl who had spurned him.

THE PIT WHEELS were turning again, and the men were back at work, but in the Hall household things were not easy, for the six-week strike had left them in severe financial difficulties.

Although Charlotte had scrimped and saved wherever she could, the list of things for which money was needed had grown and grown. All the men's boots were in desperate need of repair. Amy needed new clothes for she was getting up and about now, and nothing she had worn before the accident would fit her. As for Jack, he needed school books.

During the strike, William Davies had been very kind, providing what Jack needed out of his own pocket because, he said, he did not want Jack's chances to suffer. But he could not afford to do so for ever. A schoolmaster's salary did not allow for it, and Charlotte had begun to think Jack would have to leave school after all.

To her surprise, however, James did not leap at the idea as she had expected.

"There's not much work going at the moment anyway," he said philosophically. "If you ask me, he might as well bide where he is."

"Well, I shall have to start looking around myself," Charlotte said. "Maybe there's something I could do in the evenings when you're home to look after Amy and little Harry."

But although she made inquiries she could find no work. Too many other women had the same thing in mind.

"I believe it's going to come down to taking in washing like Ada Clements," Charlotte said. But there, James drew the line.

"That's one thing I'm not having," he told her firmly. "Wet washing about the place all the time isn't healthy, and our boys are too big now to want to be running about fetching the baskets of dirty stuff and taking back the clean like the Clements boys. And besides," he added, "if you want to finish up with hands like Ada, I suppose that's up to you, but I shouldn't like it, I can tell you."

Charlotte only smiled. Ada's hands were not a pretty sight—red and scrawny as the rest of her, but with the amount of washing she had to do for the family, hers were often almost as bad. But if James hadn't noticed, she wasn't going to tell him. It pleased her that he thought her hands were still nice enough to be worth saving. And that night, as well as preparing an extra batch of dumplings to conceal the absence of meat in the supper-time stew pot, she found the energy to turn an old petticoat of her own into a pretty new pinafore for Amy.

Early in July Charlotte heard that the manager of the Palace Picture House was looking for another cleaning woman. At present it was taken care of by Bertha Yelling, Peggy's sister-in-law, but it was such a popular place for all kinds of entertainment that it was more than one person's work to keep it clean, and now there was talk of opening the room beneath the picture palace for dancing classes, too.

It was Peggy who told her—she had got to hear about it through Bertha—and without wasting any time, Charlotte put on her hat and went to see about it. The result was that she was taken on and was able to start right away. It was a day-time job whereas she had really wanted an evening one, but it would have to do.

Peggy agreed to look after Harry for the hour or so she would be gone, and Jack, who was breaking up now for the summer holiday, would be at home with Amy. By the time he went back to school in September, Amy would be well enough to return also—or so Charlotte hoped. Already she had missed a whole year's schooling!

Charlotte started the job with her usual vigour, but her enthusiasm did not last long. The picture palace was a dirty, unpleasant place, dim and dusty, and the rows of red plush seats were impregnated with stale cigarette smoke. Charlotte, who had never seen a moving picture in her life, soon knew every inch of the place, from the projection box to the upright piano that provided the stirring accompaniment.

The picture palace was situated in Glebe Bottoms, a narrow lane that dipped away from the main street on the north side of the Miners Arms, and one morning as Charlotte plodded up to cross the road and climb the hill for home she was surprised to see Dolly coming down, a basket on her arm.

"Where are you going to, then?" she asked, stopping and resting her own bag against her legs.

Dolly indicated the shop at the foot of the hill where the roads joined.

"Cook asked me to come down to the County Stores for some things she wants for a special cake."

Charlotte nodded. Although they bought the bulk of their groceries from the Co-op, who delivered, none of the 'nobs' would be seen on their premises, nor allow their servants to be seen there either. The 'posh' shop was the County Stores.

"Mam, I'm ever so glad I've seen you," Dolly said suddenly.

"Why's that then, Dolly?" Charlotte asked, noticing that her daughter's usually tranquil blue eyes were troubled.

"It's Evan, Mam. I don't know what to make of him."

"Evan? But I thought you finished with him back in the spring."

"I did. But I don't think he's taken it even now," Dolly said. "I wasn't there yesterday when he came with the groceries, but he asked Cook to give me a message. He wants to meet me tonight. He said he's going to call for me."

"Why?" Charlotte asked.

Dolly shook her head. "That's what's worrying me. It seems so funny after I told him definite I didn't want to see him any more."

"If you take my advice, you won't go—unless you *want* to take up with him again, that is," Charlotte said. "I must say he seemed a nice boy to me, but if your mind's made up, it wouldn't be right to build up his hopes for nothing, would it?"

"You're probably right, Mam. Anyway," Dolly hitched her basket up on her arm, "I'd better be going, or Cook'll be after me for these things. Captain Fish is having visitors this afternoon, and it's all a go, I can tell you."

She went across the road to the shop, and Charlotte stood waiting. For some reason she felt uneasy about Dolly.

As they walked back up the hill together, the talk turned to other things. Captain Fish had recently bought a gramophone, and Dolly was so entranced by the music of Harry Lauder and Marie Lloyd that could be heard almost as clearly in the servants quarters as in the drawing-room that she forgot Evan long enough to tell her mother all about it.

"It's wonderful really," she enthused. "And since it came, Cook and me have been singing "Stop your tickling, Jock" all day long."

"Cook has?" Charlotte asked, surprised.

Dolly giggled. "She says it takes her mind off her bunions."

88

"Well there is that to it I suppose," Charlotte conceded.

But when they reached the point where the roads branched, Evan sprang to Charlotte's mind once again.

"When he calls for you, Dolly, I should just send a message down that you don't want to see him," she said.

"P'raps I will, Mam," Dolly replied. "I'll have to think."

ALTHOUGH it was officially Dolly's evening off, Captain Fish's visitors had stayed later than he expected, and she was still in the throes of clearing up when Evan came knocking on the door.

"I'm sorry, Evan, but I'm nowhere near finished," she told him. "And I can't stand here dripping soap-suds all over the mat, either."

His eyes narrowed, giving his handsome face a hostile expression. "I'll wait."

"Well, you can't come in here, and I'll be ages yet," Dolly said, hoping he would give up. But he didn't.

"That's all right. It's a nice evening. I'll stop outside," he said.

It was another hour before Dolly had finished clearing up and changed out of her print working frock. But Evan was still sitting outside the backdoor on the low wall that bordered the vegetable garden.

"What is it you want to see me about?" she asked, shaking off the hand he tried to put on her arm. "I haven't changed my mind, you know."

"I just want to talk to you," he wheedled. "Can't we go for a walk? I don't want everybody listening," he said insistently.

"Oh, all right. Just up the road and no further."

They walked up Ridge Road beyond the houses and stopped in the gateway leading down to the woods. Dusk was falling already, and a chilly breeze was springing up.

"This is far enough," she said. "What is it you want, Evan?"

He turned towards her suddenly, so that she was forced back against the gate. "I want you, Dolly. You know how I feel about you."

Her mouth tightened. "Evan, how many times do I have to tell you? I don't want you. Not in that way."

"But it used to be so good. I'd do anything for you, Dolly, anything!" he begged.

"No, Evan, I'm sorry," she said. "Now, let's go back, shall we?"

"No!" His voice was so strange it frightened her, and she tried to move away. But his hand was on her arm, the fingers biting into her flesh.

"Let me go!" she cried. Then she felt something sharp pricking into her stomach. Quite suddenly she was overcome with fear. "Evan, what . . . ?"

"You're mine, Dolly, and if I can't have you, no one else will!"

"Evan, stop it! You're hurting me!"

His fingers bit harder into her arm; the pressure on her stomach increasing. "I'm going to kill you, Dolly," he said.

"Evan!" she sobbed, looking around wildly. But the lane was deserted.

"You shouldn't have left me, Dolly," he said. "I love you. I want to marry you."

"Oh, God, Evan!" she cried.

Slowly his fingers relaxed their hold on her arm, sliding up across her shoulder and around her throat. Dolly was mesmerized by fear, her breath coming in shallow sobs.

"He's going to strangle me," she thought, but she could not move.

His fingers were rough against her throat, moving upwards with a steady pressure. Then they fanned out beneath her chin, holding it in the same iron grip he had held her arm. Slowly he brought his face towards hers. Holding her head steady he kissed her so hard she cried out, but the sound was lost.

The world seemed to stand still, frozen by fear. Then, suddenly, across the quiet hillside the first owl hooted. Dolly jumped violently; so did Evan. His hold on her slackened, and with presence of mind born of terror, she pushed hard at him with both hands. Caught off balance, he stumbled. She twisted away and ran, sobbing with fear, her heart beating wildly, her legs unsteady. Along Ridge Road she fled, and it was only when she reached the entrance to the house that she realized there was no one following. She stopped and looked round. There was no sign of Evan.

Sobbing and frightened, she stood there in the drive. But she didn't go in. She didn't want Cook to see her like this. She couldn't face her questions. She wanted Mam!

With another look back up the road to make sure Evan was not following, she started to run again, on down the hill. Several times her ankle twisted on the steep ground, almost throwing her down. But she kept going, and turned into the rank. Past the first ten houses she ran, past a startled Moses Brimble, still cleaning the fork and spade he had been using on his garden that evening.

The door of number eleven was ajar. She pushed it open and half fell in, the tears spilling again from her eyes, coursing down her face.

"Dolly, whatever are you doing here?" Charlotte asked, startled.

But for a moment Dolly could say nothing but: "Oh, Mam! Oh, Mam!"

EVERYONE was present in the kitchen when Dolly came bursting in. Only Amy and Harry were in bed. For a moment there was complete silence, but for Dolly's sobbing. Then suddenly they all began talking at once.

"What's happened?"

"Dolly, whatever is the matter?"

"What's going on?"

"Leave her alone for a minute!" Charlotte ordered, leaping up from her sewing and running across to Dolly. "Go and fetch the brandy, one of you. You know where it is—in the chiffonier in the front room."

Jack went, and when he returned with it, Charlotte forced a drop or two between Dolly's trembling lips while James supported her.

"Now tell us what's up, Dolly," he said when she seemed a little better.

Dolly did not answer.

"It's that Evan Comer, isn't it?" Charlotte said savagely. "What did he do to you, Dolly?"

Dolly covered her face with her hands. "Oh, Mam, he said he was going to kill me," she sobbed.

"*What?*" they all chorused, again shocked into silence.

"Kill you?" Charlotte repeated. "Whatever do you mean—kill you?"

She was interrupted by the stair door opening. It was Amy, wakened by the commotion and wanting to know what was going on. Sharply, Charlotte told her to go back to bed, but she only retreated a fraction, standing round-eyed behind the half-open door while Dolly poured out her story, none of them noticing she was still there.

"Oh, it was awful—awful! He had a knife! He said he was going to kill me!"

James stood up, reaching for his jacket that hung behind the door.

"This is a job for the police. I'm going down to get Sergeant Eyles."

"No, Dad, no!" Dolly began weeping wildly again. "Not the police—no, don't!"

"If he thinks he's going to get away with this . . . "

"No, Dad, please! I couldn't bear it . . . "

"Threatening you with a knife . . . "

"No, Dad!"

Charlotte put a restraining hand on his arm, speaking over Dolly's bowed and shaking head. "Don't upset her any more."

"But if he had a knife, Lotty . . . "

"I didn't see it!" Dolly said wildly. "I didn't actually see a knife, Dad!"

"But you said . . . "

"I know. I felt it. But it mightn't have been, might it? I could have been wrong. I was so frightened. I didn't know what to think."

"And he's going to have the police on him for it!" James thundered, his voice filling every corner of the kitchen. He moved towards the door, and Dolly became almost hysterical.

"I don't want to get him in trouble with the police! Oh, Mam, stop him can't you? Oh, please!"

"Dad!" Jim said. "Wait. We'll sort the bugger out."

James stopped, and Fred and Ted both stood up, closing ranks with Jim.

"Leave him to us, Dad."

"We'll make him sorrier for what he's done than any policeman."

For a moment James looked at them, then his lips curled upwards in a satisfied, mirthless smile. "All right, boys, I'll leave it to you. But if I was a bit younger, I'd come myself, and that's straight up."

Without another word they put on their jackets. Jack went to get his too, and Charlotte put a hand on his arm.

"Not you, Jack. Leave it to your brothers."

He hesitated. He hated violence, but he too wanted to extract his revenge for what Evan had done to Dolly. Sensing his dilemma, and seeing the stair door moving slightly, Charlotte said to him, "Go and put your sister to bed. She shouldn't be hearing this, but I don't want to leave Dolly."

Jack nodded, relieved, and went to escort a highly excited Amy upstairs. When the door had closed after the three older boys, Charlotte turned back to Dolly.

"I told you not to go," she admonished gently. "I knew something would happen if you did."

Dolly snuffled softly into one of the large handkerchiefs Charlotte had given her. "I know, but I didn't like to upset him, Mam."

James and Charlotte exchanged looks. Her soft heart would be her undoing if she was not careful. But neither of them wanted to upset her any more now.

"Your father will go up to the house and tell them you're taken poorly," Charlotte said. "And your brothers are going to take care of Evan Comer, so you haven't a thing to worry about, have you?"

Dolly shook her head. Her trembling was subsiding, and her eyelids drooped as if she might fall asleep any moment. Charlotte stroked her hair protectively—the boys would sort Evan Comer out, of that she was sure.

THEY MARCHED up the hill side by side, Jim and Ted on the pavement and Fred walking in the gutter. Into Ridge Road they turned, past Captain Fish's house and the other big houses. They knew that Evan could get home to Purldown by following this road until it met up again with the main road to Bath, and if they did not catch up with him before he got there they intended to knock him out of his house. Evan Comer would not be allowed to threaten their sister and get away with it.

When the gateway leading to the woods came into sight, however, they were all surprised to see a figure standing there. It was too dark to see at a distance who it was, but as they got closer, they exchanged glances.

It was Evan. He had not moved from where Dolly had left him. He was leaning over the gate, his head bowed like a drunk.

As they approached, he looked up and saw them. A look of surprise and fear crossed his handsome face, and without a word they closed in around him. Fred took one of his arms and Ted the other, pinning them behind him, and as they did so, something fell out of his hand and lay shining on the ground.

Jim bent to pick it up. It was a knife, the blade still extended from the fancy handle. So Dolly had been right. He straightened, pointing the sharp blade at Evan's throat.

Evan winced away from the sharp point, but Jim let the knife rest there while Ted and Fred held him fast.

"You little bugger!" He spat the words at him. "You do that to my sister, and you've got us to deal with!"

"I didn't . . . hurt her . . . " Evan spluttered, almost choking with fear. "I didn't touch her . . . I wouldn't!"

"Well, I think you did. She wouldn't be in the state she's in for nothing." Jim pressed the knife point further against Evan's throat.

"Don't . . . don't hurt me . . . I didn't . . . I wouldn't . . . "

Jim brought his face close to Evan's, and saw the fear glittering like tears in his eyes.

"You leave her alone then. If you go near her again, you know what you'll get—all right?"

"Yes . . . yes . . . " Evan sobbed.

With one movement Jim lowered the knife and brought his knee up into Evan's groin. He heard, and felt, the breath come out of him in a choking explosion. Then, as his body jerked convulsively Ted and Fred let go of his arms, and he folded up on to his knees, retching.

For just a moment the three of them stood over him, watching with satisfaction, but they did not touch him again. They were not bullies.

Leaving Evan retching on the ground they turned and walked back down the hill, and when they came to the thickest part of the hedge, Jim thrust the knife deep into it.

5

I T WAS summer, 1913, and the Hall household was busy with preparations for a wedding. Jim had asked Sarah Brimble to marry him, and Charlotte was only surprised that it had taken him so long.

Sarah was a pretty girl, with soft brown curls and eyes to match, and she would have been a very willing bride. But Jim had hesitated over settling down. He had seen too many of his friends rush into marriage, only to lose their enthusiasm when the responsibilities began piling up—wailing babies, a complaining wife if they spent too long over a pint or a game of quoits at the Miners Arms, and wages they were no longer able to call their own.

One warm evening in June, however, he and Sarah went for a walk up to the down. On the way back, they found a field gate that was easy enough to climb, and sat down under the hedge for a rest. It was pleasant there, and soon they were kissing and cuddling.

"I never met a girl who likes to be kissed as much as Sarah does," Jim had confided to Fred. "Though she won't let me go any further. If I so much as try, she goes into a mood and tells me, if I don't watch myself, she won't go out with me any more."

Today, however, Sarah seemed different. When Jim pushed her back into the long grass, she went on kissing him, her body soft and yielding. Even when she felt him bunching up her skirt, she made no protest. The scent of the grass was around her, and the desire she had resisted for so long ached within her. He parted her legs with his hands, and she let him, afraid, yet mesmerized by her own longing, and there beneath the violet evening sky they made love.

Afterwards Sarah cried; she lay with her head turned away from him, the tears sliding down her cheeks.

"What's the matter?" he asked, raising himself on one elbow, looking down at her. "Did I hurt you?"

She shook her head, but went on sobbing.

"What then?" he asked. "I love you, Sarah, there's nothing to cry about."

Still she did not answer, and he moved away a little impatiently.

"Oh, well, if you won't tell me."

She twisted her head then, looking at him with eyes brimming with tears.

"Don't you realize what we've done? I could be going to have a baby!"

The shock of it made him go cold. Stupid as it seemed, he just hadn't thought of it. He was so used to her stopping him just when he most wanted to go on that he simply had not thought beyond the yielding beauty of her body and the all-consuming fire in his own. Now, he looked down at her, shaken but still trying to retain a masterful air.

"It'll be all right. It was the first time. It couldn't happen the first time."

"It could. I know girls it's happened to. Oh, Jim, I don't know what I'd do! The disgrace . . ."

She began to cry again, and feeling guilty, he said, "We could always get married."

Her tears stopped as if by magic. "Oh, Jim, could we? Really?"

"Course we could. We'd have to get your father's permission— mine, too, come to that. I shan't be twenty-one until next year. But they wouldn't object, would they?"

She shook her head. "No, I know they wouldn't. Oh, d'you think we could make it soon? Just in case? Then we could always make out the baby was early."

"Well . . ." He experienced a moment's panic, but Sarah was smiling at him with eyes that were still bright with tears and already he was beginning to think he'd like to make love to her again. "I'll see O'Halloran and find out if there are any houses going," he promised.

CHARLES O'HALLORAN was the general manager of Hillsbridge Colliery Companies, a bluff north-countryman with a reputation for fairness, although he was a hard taskmaster.

Jim went to see him the next day, and Hal, as he was popularly known, told him there was a cottage he could have right away, provided he was prepared to put it in order. Cockahoop, he called in at the Miners Arms, where Sarah worked, to tell her they could begin to make their plans, and then went home to break the news to the family.

The announcement, naturally, was greeted with great excitement. James smiled and nodded to himself as if he could not believe it. The boys teased Jim and called him a fool, and Amy bobbed up and down demanding to know if she could be a bridesmaid. Only Charlotte gave him a narrow, probing look, and Jim had the uncomfortable feeling that she had seen through his sudden decision and knew the reason behind it.

"Have you got anywhere to live?" she asked shortly.

Jim nodded. "There's a house empty in Pit Cottages, along under South Hill Batch," he told her. "It's been empty some time, Hal said, and it'll need a bit of doing to, but it will be very handy for me getting to work. Just up the pit path and I'll be there."

"Whose place can that be?" Charlotte asked, puzzling. Pit Cottages was a line of houses sandwiched between the long, ridged batch and the railway line on the south-west side of the valley, and far enough from Greenslade Terrace for her not to be acquainted with the people who lived there.

"Well, whoever it was, they bain't there now," James said reasonably, and Charlotte turned back to Jim with characteristic briskness.

"If it's empty it'll be damp and dirty," she told him. "You'd better ask Sarah if she'd like me to help her get it cleaned up. With two buckets and scrubbing brushes, it'll be ready in half the time."

The date had been set for six weeks time. Besides helping Jim and Sarah at the cottage, Charlotte found herself caught up in the wedding arrangements, for although they were primarily the responsibility of the Brimbles, living next-door-but-one it was inevitable that she should find herself almost as involved as they were. There were guest lists to be planned and food to be organized. The chapel service had to be decided upon, and Stanley Bristow's wagonette booked. Charlotte also had to arrange her family's outfits. Amy and Dolly were taken care of. Sarah had asked them to be her bridesmaids, along with her own sister, Queenie, and she was having their dresses made for them—an expense Charlotte could hardly credit. But the boys' best suits had to be cleaned and pressed, and Charlotte treated herself to a new flower at Fords draper's shop to put in the lapel of the good silk coat she always wore on special occasions. For Harry, Charlotte went to great lengths to save on her housekeeping and managed to run up a neat little sailor suit for him.

At last the great day arrived. Some of the rank walked down to the chapel for the service, and the rest stood in their doorways to watch the families leave.

Charlotte, James and the boys set out first, though Charlotte was certain something would go wrong the moment her back was turned. Then just before noon, Dolly, Amy, and Queenie Brimble emerged, dressed in pink with daisy wreaths in their hair, and climbed into Stanley Bristow's wagonette, which had been especially decorated for the occasion.

A few moments later, Sarah herself came out of the house with her father, and the watching neighbours gasped in awe. She looked beautiful in her simple, cream-silk dress, with a circlet of orange blossom in her hair. Stanley shook the reins and as the pony trotted off, the occasional tear formed in the spectators' eyes.

As Sarah walked into chapel the same breathless hush hung in the air while the organ poured forth its melodious song. Down the aisle she went, on Moses' arm, and stood where Jim was waiting for her.

Charlotte looked with pride at her eldest son standing at the altar —once he had been her baby. Twenty years ago it might have been, but to her it seemed like only yesterday that she had looked at him, her first-born.

Of course, he hadn't been the only one for long, and he'd had to adjust his ways and become independent. She remembered the day when he'd started school, three years old and yet somehow appearing so grown-up in comparison with Dolly and Fred. Her heart had been in her mouth that day, just as it was now, because although it was a beginning, it was also an end.

Soon all her children would go their own ways, and the house would be empty instead of full of banter and quarrels and laughter. The time would come when she would be old and useless, no longer needed by any of them . . .

When the ring was on Sarah's finger, though, and she walked down the aisle on Jim's arm, the moment for tears had gone. Instead there were congratulations and laughter and a great show of seriousness, while Peggy's son, Colwyn, who was trying to set himself up in business as a photographer, disappeared with his camera under an absurd black sheet and was gone for so long that Ted started tapping on his back to ask if he were still there.

At last Colwyn was satisfied, and the wedding party climbed into Stanley Bristow's wagonette for the journey home. In the street, people stopped to watch them pass and wave. But none watched with such round-eyed wonder as the small figure who knelt in the bedroom window of number twelve Greenslade Terrace.

Rosa had watched them go, and waited patiently for their return. She would have liked to go down to the service, but the Brimbles, who had never cared for the Clements family, had not invited them to the wedding breakfast, and Ada had too much pride to allow Rosa to go when she hadn't been asked.

So Rosa had to content herself with watching from the window, and when she heard the clip-clop of the horse's hooves, she pressed forward eagerly, with her nose close to the pane. Her eyes slid quickly over Dolly, Queenie, and Amy, whom she hated, and came to rest on Sarah, and as they did so, they grew dark with longing.

Perhaps one day that would be her, riding in a wagonette with orange blossom in her hair. People wouldn't snigger then, or point their fingers at her. They wouldn't say all the nasty things that made her feel lonely and hurt. They'd be admiring, smiling, wishing her well. Especially if . . .

Her gaze took in the Hall family, sitting together on one bench of the wagonette, and as she concentrated on Ted, the breath caught in her throat and her heart swelled within her.

How handsome he was. A warm, excited feeling grew deep within her. From the time she had been able to walk she had adored him and not really understood her feelings, except that she wanted to be with him all the time, to see him if not to speak to him, and simply know he was there.

Now, still without really understanding, she knew the way she felt was bound up with Sarah and her wedding dress and the wagonette ride to the chapel, and she stood at the window savouring every detail, storing it away in her memory.

"Get away from that window! Don't let them know you're looking!" Ada's shrill voice brought her sharply back to reality, but for a moment, Rosa defied her mother, craning out of the window and trying to recapture the magic of the moment. But it was too late. The dream had shattered, the moment was gone forever.

Rosa's mouth puckered tight with disappointment.

"Come away from that window, do!" Ada repeated, and Rosa swallowed at the knot of tears that gathered in her throat.

Disappointed she might be, at losing the precious illusion. Left out she might be, but even at twelve, she was too proud to let anyone know just how much she cared.

A WEEK after the wedding, Sarah was able to tell Jim he was not to be a father just yet.

She had known before that, but wondered if the good news would make Jim change his mind about the wedding. It was a short respite. By the end of the summer she was pregnant, and Charlotte, not quite certain whether to be pleased or horrified, was looking forward to the arrival of her first grandchild.

The boys teased Jim, of course, but he seemed not to mind. Married life was suiting him, and he looked so well that Fred thought that if he could find the right girl he might follow his example.

Ted, however, did not envy him at all. At seventeen, he liked girls well enough, but only as a passing fancy. There were too many other things to interest him.

He had always had a good voice, and when Stanley Bristow from the livery stables invited him to join his concert party, he soon discovered he enjoyed entertaining, too. The concert party was fun —besides singing some solos, he was expected to join with the rest of the company for comic and musical sketches, and the rehearsals and the shows themselves added spice to the long winter evenings.

Then, in the summer, there were the horses. It had only taken one visit to Bath Races with his mates to get him hooked. There was something electric about the atmosphere. He placed a bet or two himself, and was lucky enough to win a few shillings, but it wasn't the money that attracted him. It was the way the adrenaline flowed as the horses galloped past the rails, the feeling of being perched on the very edge of a precipice with the difference between winning and losing finely balanced, the sensation of leaving the real world behind for an hour or two.

So entranced was he, Ted made it his business to get to know Joe Chivers, the local bookmaker, and when his regular 'runner' was laid up with a broken leg, Ted was employed to carry the bets, which he collected from the other men in the George and the Miners Arms. It was against the law, of course, but Ted didn't let that worry him. It wasn't as if he was doing anything really wrong. Slipping the bets out under the very nose of the local bobby was all part of the fun, and when he took them up Westbury Hill to Joe's house, he always had the excuse of taking Nipper for a walk if anyone asked him awkward questions.

But these things were all welcome distractions from the pit, and the carting which he had grown to hate. How he had ever found it satisfying, he could not imagine. He had now had four years of crawling on his hands and knees with the putt of coal attached to his waist, and he was bored and frustrated. Sometimes he thought of looking for a different job, but thinking was as far as it went. He wasn't trained for anything, and the few jobs in Hillsbridge he might have had a chance of getting were just as boring as carting, and some of them less well-paid. He could go to South Wales, he supposed, as some of the older lads had done. The seams there were thicker, so that a man could walk upright instead of crawling on all fours, and the money that could be made was much better than here in the Somerset coal-field. But moving to South Wales would mean leaving home and Charlotte's cooking, and Ted didn't bother to give it much serious consideration.

Most other men, after all, continued working in the pits week after week, year after year, his father included. It was not so much what you did to earn a living that mattered; how you spent your free time was far more important, and the two were hardly connected.

At least, so Ted thought, until in October of 1913, something happened to change his mind.

It was a wet and wild Friday afternoon. Above ground, the weather had turned cold so suddenly that the leaves had fallen from the trees with almost indecent haste, covering the lanes and pathways with a carpet of dull brown, but in the warren of black passages beneath Hillsbridge, it was as muggy as ever, and Ted was feeling wretched.

He was suffering from a heavy cold, partly caused by the change of temperature when the cage emerged from the bowels of the earth into the chill October air, and partly by the succession of late nights he'd had lately. His eyes were streaming, so was his nose, and he'd had no appetite at all for his cogknocker—the huge hunk of bread and cheese Charlotte had packed for him. Most of that he'd thrown to the mice. But he'd drunk every drop of his cold tea, and his throat still felt like a piece of sandpaper.

As the day wore on, he grew steadily worse, and each putt of coal felt like a ton weight as he dragged it on hands and knees along the narrow way towards the topple—the steep incline that led from the seam to the road below. Here it was his job to walk down the incline, fetch a tub, and bring it back to the top. Then, when he had filled it with two or three putts of coal, he had to take it back down the incline again, using an iron sprag between the spokes of the wheel as a brake.

It was a tortuous exercise and a dangerous one, though the carting boys took it cheerfully for granted, and Ted was no different. Like them, he accepted the fact that the tub would run away each time the sprag was removed unless he did something to stop it, and the obvious way to do that was to hook the crook that was fastened around his waist into an eye on the tub, to enable him to use the weight of his own body to hold on to it. The fact that the tub weighed five hundred weight or so when it was full did not worry him unduly, and he had become adept at running the tubs down the incline in a series of stops and starts, releasing the sprag, letting the tub run down a few feet, and driving the sprag back into the wheel before it gained too much speed.

So good at it was he that he did not stop to wonder what would happen if the sprag missed the wheel for some reason. It didn't do to worry about things like that.

That afternoon, however, Ted was tempted to take the tub down with two putts of coal in it instead of three. Twice as he was pushing the tub up the incline he had to stop to blow his nose into the soaking rag he had tucked into the waistband of his trousers, standing with his back against the tub to stop it from running away, and it all seemed too much effort. But coal left at the top would mean an extra journey, and he didn't care for the thought of that either. So into the tub went the usual three loads, and Ted hooked himself to it and released the sprag.

At first it seemed like an ordinary run. Down the incline he inched, with the tarred rope biting into the flesh around his waist each time he released the sprag and took the strain for a second or two. A couple of stumbling steps, braced against the weight of the tub, a quick lunge forward, and the relief as the sprag bit into the wheel and held. Pull it out, be hauled a step, push it in, stop. Pull it out, be hauled a step, push it in, stop. It was a relentless, beating rhythm, and it came to him as automatically as breathing.

But today something went wrong.

A third of the way down the incline, with the wheel free and the tub straining at the rope, he drove the sprag back and waited for the jerk and the skid that should follow. But it never came. Perhaps because of his feverishness, he had missed the all important gap in the wheel. The sprag struck a spoke, and was catapulted out again. The wheels took another turn, gathering speed already, and Ted, still attached to the tub by the rope around his waist, was jerked roughly forward.

For a split second in time, he wondered stupidly what had happened. Then, as the tub surged forward, he knew. He dug his heels into the rough, dust-covered floor and pressed his hands against the topple walls, bracing himself until he thought his spine would snap. But his feet slithered over the stony incline, and the skin hung in ribbons on the palms of his hands. On the steep gradient it was hopeless. The tub gathered momentum, the rope jerked painfully around his waist, and he lost his footing and fell face down on the track. Faster and faster the tub rolled on, dragging him behind it. His eyes and nose were full of coal-dust.

Oddly, in spite of the rough ground, he felt no pain. Reality no longer existed, and he was only aware of a strong feeling of indignation.

"I'm going to die, and I'm not ready," he thought. "I'm too young."

The black walls of the topple rushed past him and Ted had the vague yet unmistakable impression of being pulled through a dark tunnel at great speed. Then there was a crash so loud that it reverberated through his body, and he felt himself being thrown up like a rag doll by the rope around his waist. For a moment it felt as if the world were turning over, then, with the clarity that comes when the happenings of a split second seem stretched into eternity, he believed he was flying. The roof of the passage skimmed past. He felt it brush his leg, a kiss of searing pain. The earth rushed up to meet him, and in the blackness he was surprised to see his mother's face, clear, radiant, and oddly untroubled. His body thudded down on dust-covered rock, knocking the breath from his lungs. He was aware of nothing but a bright light coming closer and closer until it enveloped him in its intensity and the world about him was still.

They told him afterwards that less than a minute had passed between the sprag missing the wheel and the tub becoming derailed at the foot of the topple, catapulting him in a full arc so that he landed on a heap of coal in front of it. But to Ted it seemed as if he had lived his life and gone beyond in those moments. He regained consciousness as the cage jolted him to the surface, but his first impression was not of pain or discomfort or the streaming walls of the shaft, but rather of coming back, somewhat unwillingly, from a great distance.

The grey October light filtered into the cage and with it the chill, damp air. Someone threw a coat across him. And the pain began, like the first waves of a rising tide that lapped at him gently but remorselessly, with the promise of the swirling flood to follow. He gritted his teeth against the searing agony of flesh scraped raw, and nothing seemed important beyond living through the next moment —and the next.

Dimly, he was aware of voices and people scurrying to and fro. Then, as the fog that seemed to blanket his senses lifted for a second or two, he realized what they were saying. There was no cart waiting at the pithead for coal. They had nothing in which to take him home.

Above him, the great wheel turned and the cage descended once more. The rhythmic grinding sounded both loud and distant at one and the same time. Moments later a familiar voice penetrated his brain, and he opened his eyes to see his father and Fred standing beside him, their faces pale beneath the thick layer of black dust.

"What are you doing here?" Ted croaked.

Fred leaned over, sliding his arm under his neck and raising him. "I'm going to get you home, mate."

"There's no cart. I heard them say."

"I know. I'm going to have to carry you on my back."

Fred stood up, flexing his knees and standing ready. James and the other men lifted Ted on to his brother's back, so that his arms were around Fred's neck and his legs about his waist. Then, with James walking beside them, they started across the colliery yard.

Down South Hill they went, through the centre of town and into Conygre Hill which led to Greenslade Terrace. Never had it seemed longer or more steep. With every step Fred took, fresh waves of pain flooded through Ted's body. Before they had passed the seat that marked the half-distance, sweat was pouring off the older boy in black rivers. But he plodded on, his breath rasping harshly while beside him James swore helplessly at his own inability to help. His back might still be strong enough, but the effort would be too much for his chest, constricted as it was by coal and stone dust. There was nothing he could do but walk beside them and watch Ted's blood mingle with Fred's sweat.

"This'll do it," James said to Fred. "This'll start your mother off again."

But in spite of Ted's wounds, he felt no animosity towards the pit. Accidents happened often. They were a way of life. And Ted was alive. That was all that mattered.

TED LAY on the sofa where Amy had lain, fighting the same battle that she had fought.

But as the pain and memory of the accident receded, Ted began to feel sorry for himself. His gratitude at being alive turned to resentment that the accident should have happened at all, and he was particularly angry that it should have been the result of his own carelessness.

Lying on the sofa was such a waste of time. He'd missed out on the concert party rehearsals and one concert, and lost his chance of being permanent bookie's runner for Joe Chivers.

"He's like a bear with a sore head," Charlotte told Redvers when he came in to see him. "He'll snap your nose off as soon as look at you."

"Is that right?" Redvers asked, poking his grinning face round the kitchen door. "Is it safe to come in?"

"Yes, come on," Ted said. "Come and tell me what's been going on at work, and I might even be glad I'm here."

Redvers sat down on the settle, stretching his legs out to the fire. "There's nothing much to tell."

"No, I don't suppose there is," Ted grumbled. "That's it really, isn't it. Day after day—nothing. Just grinding on, and for what? We haven't got a chance of making colliers. There's plenty of them. It's carting boys they're short of, and that's what we'll still be doing in ten years' time, if you ask me."

Redvers stretched out a lazy hand to scratch Nipper's ear.

"You're probably right. But there's nothing we can do about it."

"We could go to Wales," Ted said. "There's several gone over there, and they're doing very well. They earn twice what we do. It makes you think, Redvers."

"I s'pose it does," Redvers said affably, and there the conversation ended. Charlotte came in with Harry, and they both sat down to look at a picture book. The two boys went off at a tangent, discussing the fortunes of Hillsbridge Town Football Team, and even touching on Evan Comer, who was now playing a wing position for them.

"After what we did to him, it's a wonder he can still play," Ted said, smiling with satisfaction at the memory. Already he had forgotten what he had said about going to Wales. It wasn't, after all, a serious plan, just an idea that provided an escape route from the prospect of carting year after year at South Hill Pit. In reality he knew he would be returning once he was well enough.

It was one November afternoon that Ted took his first walk since the accident. He decided to call into the pit and have a chat with the lads on the screens, but not long after he had arrived he was surprised to be summoned to the manager's office, a small, spartan room in the corner of one of the smith's shops, and the domain of Herbert Gait.

Gait was O'Halloran's under-manager, and responsible for the day-to-day running of South Hill Pit. He was an untidy, red-faced man, whose waistcoat was always covered by a dusting of ash from his cigarette, and whose baggy suit had seen better days. But in spite of his slovenly appearance he was an ambitious man, with an eye on the general managership when O'Halloran retired.

"And God help us all if he gets it," Ted thought. For where O'Halloran was generous, Gait was mean, and while O'Halloran put a good deal of thought into improving conditions for the men, Gait thought of no one but himself.

When Ted entered the office, he found Gait sprawled in the round-backed chair behind the desk, hat perched on the back of his head, a cigarette stuck to his lower lip.

"You wanted to see me?" Ted said.

Gait shifted in his chair, peering at Ted through the screen of cigarette smoke.

"Yes, lad, I've been hearing stories about you—that you're thinking of leaving us and going over the water to Wales. I hope there's no truth in that."

His tone put Ted on the defensive. "And what if there is?" he asked.

Gait rolled his cigarette along his lip, looking at Ted steadily.

"Well, if you were to go off anywhere like that, you'd have to take your father with you, you know, and it might not be so easy for him to get a job at his age," he said slyly. "Oh, I know what you're thinking—that he's pretty well settled here. But things aren't what they used to be. I've got plenty of good men waiting for your father's job, men that are sound in wind and limb. But a well-trained carting boy like you, Ted, that's something else again. I don't like to lose a carting boy."

Ted looked at him in disbelief. "Are you trying to tell me . . . "

"That if you go, there'd be no work here for your father. Yes, that's about the size of it. But it won't come to that, will it, lad? I'd stake my last ha'penny it won't come to that."

For a moment, Ted did not answer. Anger was boiling up inside him. With a contemptuous movement he unrolled the cap he had kept in his hand throughout the interview as a mark of respect and rammed it on to his head.

"I'd hate to see you lose your last ha'penny, Mr Gait," he said.

Then he turned and walked out of the office.

Outside, the pale November sunshine was warming the rough-hewn lias stone of the row of cottages, the saw-pit shed and the frame house on the opposite side of the yard, and glancing dully off the grey slate roofs. It was a scene he had come to take for granted over the years, but now he stood staring at it through different eyes.

Until Gait had threatened him, he had given no serious thought to leaving the pit, but now, suddenly, he felt trapped and desperate. He'd been half joking when he'd said to Redvers that they would still be carting in ten years' time—but now it was no joke. All his youth the pit would take from him, and maybe his life, too, and what would it give him in return? A bare living wage, blue veins all over his body, and a bad chest—if he was lucky. And the prospect of being on the scrap-heap by the time he was forty-five, as was his father.

But the door had been closed on his escape. Gait was not the one to make idle threats, and he had the trump card. He knew Ted would never go if he thought it would mean his father losing his job.

"Blackmailing bastard!" Ted muttered over his shoulder. "You'd do it, too, wouldn't you?"

He'd do it, and it would be the end of James. Ever since he had left school, he'd been in the pits, and it was life and breath to him. Perhaps there was unemployment benefit now for those who found themselves without work, but that wasn't enough. They couldn't dole out self-respect, or a purpose for living.

Restlessness stirred in him and the desire to escape. His flesh crawled with it, and his stomach twisted in anticipation of the sight and smell of new places, where there was no coal-dust. They were out there, somewhere, beyond the black mountains, and he wanted to see them.

What he would do for a living if he escaped he didn't know, and it didn't matter much. He would take whatever came—and it was bound to be better than crawling along dark and narrow passages, steadying tubs down steep topples. Anything must be better than that.

But for the present, escape was out of his reach, thrust away by a vindictive under-manager.

"One of these days," Ted said to himself, "Gaity will get what's coming to him."

6

JIM'S BABY was born in May—"Taurus the Bull," said Dolly, who read the horoscopes with Cook every morning when they had cleared away the breakfast things. "He'll be just as stubborn as our Jim, wait and see if he's not."

"That's a lot of nonsense," Charlotte said shortly. "But you really will be seeing stars, my girl, if you don't get back to service quick sharp!"

Dolly got up, collecting her things. Like the rest of the family, she was mesmerized by the baby. It was strange in a way, for there had never been a shortage of babies in Greenslade Terrace, and it was only four years since Harry had been in the cradle. But there was something special about a first grandchild—or nephew—and Alex, as they were calling him, was a beautiful baby, not wrinkled at all, but pink and placid.

Sarah was not well, though. There had been some trouble with the afterbirth, and Dr Scott had said she mustn't set a foot to the ground just yet. So Charlotte and Sarah's own mother took turns at going over to the cottage to look after things—the rest of the family making that an excuse to call in often.

It was just down the pit path for James, Ted, and Fred, of course. They walked down with Jim in the evenings, and collected Charlotte. Then they all went home together, although sometimes Charlotte left them at the County Stores where she now worked, the men returning home to an empty house and a somewhat inadequate tea that Amy had been left to organize.

Those days they disliked intensely, and for the first time they realized how much they took Charlotte for granted. But there was no way it could be avoided. Sarah had to be looked after, and the job at the County Stores was far too good to risk losing through bad time-keeping or unreliability.

Charlotte had started the job in the spring, taken on when a new manager came from London. It made a welcome change from the dim and dusty Palace Picture House, for although on wet days the floor got filthy, it was a different sort of dirt to the Palace—good, wholesome mud and coal-dust. She was left alone, too, which she liked, for she had soon discovered at the Palace that, if she worked while Bertha gossiped, in the end she usually did Bertha's share as well as her own. And there was another attraction to the County Stores, one which made it different from any of her previous jobs. When the regular counter assistant was indisposed, Algie Smith, the manager, would ask her to help out.

To Charlotte, this was more like a game than work. When she had been in the draper's shop in Bath before she was married, she had always enjoyed serving, and the County Stores presented even more delights. There was the sharp wire for cutting cheese, the big scales for weighing up sugar, biscuits, tea and dried fruit, and the small ones for doing paper twists full of mint shrimps or bull's-eyes for the children. And best of all was the cash railway that whisked the takings to the central till and returned the change—a strange contraption of wooden cups screwed to a system of overhead wires and sent into action by means of a sharp pull on a dangling chain. Charlotte never tired of using it, and while pretending to serve the next customer, she would watch the wooden cup skim along the wire to the cage-like office in the centre of the shop where Christine, Algie Smith's Dutch-born wife, sat in solitary splendour.

Even Harry enjoyed the days when his mother helped in the shop. He was at school in the mornings, but, if Charlotte was working in the afternoon, he could go with her and root around among the boxes and biscuit tins in the small rear yard to his heart's content.

The money was better, too, and that was a great consideration. For Jack was going to take his Oxford Junior Examination in the summer, and, if he passed, he would be going to the grammar school at Wells one week out of two.

"I'm afraid it's going to mean extra expense," William Davies told Charlotte and James when he called them up to the school to talk to them about it. "If Jack does as well as I expect him to in the exam, there should be a scholarship for him. But that's not going to cover everything."

"What do you mean?" Charlotte asked with a sidelong look at James.

"Do you remember me explaining how the pupil/teacher system works when you first decided to let Jack go on with this?" William Davies asked. "Half the time, Jack will be here with me, helping to teach here, in our school. The rest of the time he will be learning himself, at the grammar school. I've already spoken to the headmaster about it, and he's prepared to let Jack live in with him during the week. Unless you want him to travel daily. But it's an awkward journey and means changing trains."

"If the headmaster says he can live with him, I should think that would be a very good idea," Charlotte said. "We'd have to pay his board and lodge, of course."

"Yes. And there'll be books and equipment to find—pens, pencils, an unspillable inkpot, that sort of thing. And a school uniform, too. To set against that, I may be able to get him a small wage for the work he does here with me. But it's still going to be an expensive business, I'm afraid."

"We'll manage," Charlotte said quickly. She was anxious to clinch things before James could ask too many questions. He was not as enthusiastic as she was, she knew, and why should he be? To his way of thinking, all this education was above their station.

"You know I'll do all I can to help, too," William Davies said, smiling. "I'm so proud of Jack. My butterfly really is finding his wings, isn't he?"

James grunted, looking at him suspiciously, and he laughed, a small, nervous sound. "Have you any idea what this means to me, Mr Hall?" he asked. "To see one of my pupils really making a success of an academic career? I've been here in Hillsbridge for nearly twenty years, so you can imagine how many children have been through my hands. They come to me at three or four, bright as buttons, like Harry is now, and so eager to learn it does your heart good. But what happens? By the time they're twelve or thirteen, all they can think about is leaving and getting a job. Some soul-destroying grind that will extinguish all spark. It's sad. Very sad."

"There's nothing wrong with an honest day's work, Mr Davies," James said.

William Davies, realizing he was criticizing the system that had moulded James and three of his sons, coloured slightly.

"Not a thing. But it should be each to his own, Mr Hall, the way it is in the world of nature. And that's why I think of Jack as a butterfly," he said with almost childlike simplicity. "He won't be caught under the ground. He'll be soaring, free, wherever the fancy takes him!"

"He's cracked," James said to Charlotte when they left William Davies. "He's got a screw loose. Butterfly, indeed!"

"It's just the way he talks," Charlotte argued. "He's a clever man, and I don't know where our Jack would be without him."

"Butterfly!" James snorted again.

"Well, he's keen on them, isn't he?" Charlotte explained. "Our Jack was telling me he's got cases of them in his house, all stuck on pins. I shouldn't like it myself, but there's no accounting for taste."

James did not reply, and she took his arm affectionately. "Cheer up, now. I know you worry about what your mates think, but I'm sure they don't take nearly as much notice as you imagine. Jack will pass his scholarship with flying colours, and you'll be as proud of him as me."

James gave her a slow, sidelong look while he took two or three long, rattling breaths.

"And have you thought what'll happen if he doesn't pass?" he asked at last.

Charlotte's fingers tightened on his arm. It hadn't even crossed her mind that Jack might fail. She'd taken it for granted that, clever as he was, success was assured. Now, she felt sick, as if James had knocked the ground out from under her.

"He'll pass," she said. "Mr Davies says . . . "

"Mr Davies isn't going to mark his paper, is he? And Jack's worried about it himself."

"He never said anything to me!" Charlotte said indignantly.

"Well, you aren't very often there when he is, are you?" James remarked. "Oh, I know it's no good talking to you, Lotty. That's why I haven't said anything before. But I don't like what all this studying is doing to him. He's as pale as skimmed milk, and heavy-eyed. Now if he was to go out a bit more . . . "

"But he wouldn't be happy," Charlotte argued. "He's not the type."

"No, I can't understand him," James said heavily. "He's not much like me, I can tell you."

Again her stomach knotted inside, the sudden chill, the wondering: How can I explain without telling him? Will he ever credit Jack with being an individual, or always compare him with his brothers?

Aloud, she said, "There's no explaining these things. And he'll pass the exam. I know he will!"

"I hope so."

"He will."

"Well, I shouldn't like to be around either of you if he doesn't," James commented drily.

THROUGHOUT the early summer months, Jack hardly left his books. Often, he was late home from school because William Davies had given him extra tuition after the others had gone, and when he did arrive, he would take his work upstairs the minute he finished his tea. On fine days, at Charlotte's suggestion, he took a chair down to the end of the garden, beyond the beansticks, but the neighbours were all out working in their own gardens, and the small children running up and down the rank to play made such a noise that he found it difficult to concentrate.

"Go across the fields," Charlotte suggested. She had taken seriously James's remarks about the pallor of Jack's face.

Jack did as she said, and found it worked quite well. It was pleasant, sitting in the long grass with a book—as pleasant as any of his studying could be now that the pressure was on.

As he had confided to James, he was nervous about the examination. So much depended on it! From the moment he woke in the morning, he thought of nothing else, and even when he was asleep it must have been on his mind, for he became restless, tossing and turning and waking before dawn. His brothers ignored him, Amy did her best to distract him, and even Sarah complained that he hardly ever seemed to visit her and the baby. Sarah was particularly fond of Jack, and always had been. But finally the day to sit the exam arrived and there was nothing more anyone could do but pray.

All the family had become so engrossed in Jack's future that they hardly gave a thought to the events stirring in Europe. The newspapers were shouting the most alarming headlines, but Sarajevo was just a foreign name they couldn't pronounce, and the Austrian Archduke who had been murdered there seemed as remote as Father Christmas. Even when ultimatums began to be bandied about between countries, they refused to take it seriously, even Charlotte, who had seen her father go off to fight the Boers. It was said that there couldn't be a war, that the weapons were too terrible and the losses would be too high on all sides. In any case, it had nothing to do with miners and farm workers, except perhaps a few reservists like Frank and Ern Eyles, the police sergeant's sons, who had gone marching off in uniform, with their kit-bags on their backs.

So, while Churchill talked of mobilizing the fleet, Charlotte set her mind to cleaning up a second-hand leather satchel Mr Davies had offered Jack, and when the Germans were marching into Luxemburg, and France was demanding to know if Britain would stand by her, the Halls were more concerned with counting the days until the exam results were announced.

But at last, at the beginning of August, the result came through, and they all went wild with joy. A pass!

"I knew he'd do it," Charlotte said, conveniently forgetting the doubts that had been plaguing her, and James shook his head slowly from side to side as if he could hardly believe it.

Even the neighbours came in to congratulate him—Peggy, beaming and asking Jack if he'd still pass the time of day with her when he was at the grammar school, Walter Clements and Ada, muttering and nodding their pride at living next door to such a successful scholar, and the Brixeys, promising to buy him a pint next time they saw him in the Miners Arms.

"There'll be moths in their wallets if they wait till then!" James commented drily, for Jack was no drinking man, and never would be.

As for William Davies, he was thrilled—'like a dog with two tails,' as Charlotte put it. When he'd finished patting Jack on the head and congratulating him, he turned to Amy.

"You'll be the next, miss. You could do well, too, you know, if you put your mind to it."

"Oh, one at a time, Mr Davies!" Charlotte pleaded.

And James said, with a snort, "A girl? It would never be worth it, even if we could manage it."

Amy looked hurt, and William Davies ruffled her hair affectionately.

"Ah well, she's got this year to make up for the one she missed. There's time yet, plenty of time."

Only Jack said nothing. Relief was so enormous he wanted to shout with it, or soar and fly like one of William Davies's butterflies. But he kept it inside himself, so that it ran through his veins like warm, bubbly treacle. He was going to be a pupil/teacher. And nothing could stop him now.

Afterwards, history would record third August as the day when Sir Edward Grey made his important speech to the House of Commons and the machinery for the Great War was set in motion. But to Jack, it would always be the day he learned he had passed his Oxford Junior.

And although, as Sir Edward had said, "The lamps were going out all over Europe," for Jack, one small lamp had brightened his life, and it would never go out again.

CHARLOTTE heard the news of war as she raked the hot embers out of the bake-oven next morning, and prepared to stack the loaves of bread for baking in its warm interior.

Charlie Durrant rounded the corner of the rank at a run, waving a newspaper and shouting at the top of his voice. At first, Charlotte, who could not hear what he was saying, thought he had taken leave of his senses. She had pushed the last loaf into the oven and slammed the door when he ran up to her, moustache quivering with excitement.

"Whatever is it, Charlie?" she asked.

He pushed the newspaper towards her, stabbing at it with an eager

113

finger. "Haven't you heard, then? We're at war! Twelve o'clock last night we declared war on Germany!"

7

W AR FEVER gripped Hillsbridge as it gripped the rest of England.

The Mothers Union, under the guidance of Caroline Archer, started a sewing circle to make warm clothing for 'our brave soldiers,' and not to be outdone, Martha Durrant and the stalwarts of the chapel organized knitting bees.

As for the men, they were wildly jubilant, treating the war as a glorified glove fight or football match, and cheering from the sidelines.

"Kaiser Bill's in for a shock if you ask me," Moses Brimble remarked to a group of regulars in the Miners Arms one evening towards the end of August. "If he thinks he's going to eat his next Christmas dinner in Buckingham Palace, he's got another think coming!"

"We'll soon show him what's what," Hubert Freke, long past being able to show anyone anything, predicted confidently.

"Well, now Kitchener's in charge of the War Office, we will." James Hall put in.

There were murmurs of agreement from the other men sitting in a loose circle around the tables. Lord Kitchener was a popular figure, whose name still held magic, and already Colwyn Yelling, Evan Comer and Jacob Cottle's son, Bert, had responded to his first appeal for 100,000 men. In spite of fierce opposition from their parents, they had been among the first to join the queues at the recruiting office, and were now drilling on Salisbury Plain.

"It'll all be over by Christmas, anyway," Hubert Freke went on. "The boys won't see nothing of no fighting, if you ask me. The Navy will take care of it all—see if I'm not right."

There were a few mutterings of dissent from the other men. As an old naval man who had seen service in the Boer Wars and actually sailed on the *Bacchante* with the King when he was still Prince

George, Hubert was known to favour the Navy as the answer to everything. But to most of them, the big ships were slow, unwieldy instruments of war compared to the guns of the modern army. If it came to a real dogfight, with Kaiser Bill trying to get into Britain by the back door, maybe it would be useful to have a few gunboats in the channel to send him off with a flea in his ear. But for fighting and winning, the English Tommy would take some beating.

"You know they're having Stanley Bristow's horses?" Jim Hall said. Since the baby had been born, he had become a regular in the Miners Arms along with his father, for although Alex was a good baby most of the day, he seemed too fond of crying in the evening, for Jim's liking.

"Stanley Bristow's horses!" Moses exclaimed.

"I bet he's in a way about that. He looks after those horses like his children. Still, like I say, 'twon't be for long," persisted Hubert Freke.

"Let's hope not, anyway," Reuben Tapper, porter on the Somerset and Dorset railway, remarked. "The government are supposed to have taken us over, but they don't know what they'm doing, and that's a fact. If we don't soon get back to normal, there won't be a railway left—not one that's worth having, anyway."

The men continued to drink their beer, pushing all harbingers of doom and destruction to the back of their minds. They did not want to think about the uncomfortable change in the pattern of their lives. They discounted it, as they had discounted the threat of a food shortage. They had no way of knowing that the German Army was swarming up over the flat Belgian countryside, sweeping everything before it.

So they drank and laughed, not realizing that the bitter struggle ahead would affect each and every one of them, and mean the end of a whole way of life.

THEIR jubilation did not last long. It was shattered with the news of the first Hillsbridge casualty—Jacob Cottle's son, Bert.

Charlotte was in the County Stores when she heard of it. It was her afternoon for serving behind the counter, and she was weighing up dried fruit for Martha Durrant and trying to avoid being talked into knitting socks for the soldiers.

"I've got enough work of my own to do, Martha," she was saying, when Amy came bursting in, breathless with the news.

"Mammy, what do you think? Mrs Cottle's had a telegram—Bert's been killed!"

Charlotte went cold. She stood, paper bag in one hand, scoop of sultanas in the other, and felt for a moment as if the ground had rocked beneath her.

Bert Cottle—young Bert? Killed? It couldn't be true!

On the other side of the counter, Martha Durrant had gone white, and Charlotte knew she was experiencing the same feeling of disbelief.

"Why? How?" she asked foolishly.

"Oh, Mammy, I don't know," Amy's voice was impatient. "It was only a telegram."

"Then how d'you know it's right?" Charlotte asked.

"Because Mr Cottle said. I heard him tell Mr Brimble. And he looked really strange. I think he'd been crying."

"Dear Lord," Charlotte said. "Bert Cottle. Well, well, our Jim's going to be upset about that."

They stood in silence for a moment, still stunned by the news. Then, with a quick, determined movement, Charlotte folded down the top of the sultana bag.

"How many pairs of socks did you want me to knit, Martha?" she asked, matter-of-factly.

They continued discussing the knitting circle then, and when Charlotte had finished serving Martha, she suggested to Amy that she might as well take Harry home with her. But when they had gone, she lost all concentration. It was incredible. Bert Cottle dead! She could remember the last time she had seen him, swinging along the rank and whistling 'Meet Me Tonight in Dreamland.' Well, he was in dreamland now, poor lad.

Everyone in the town was shocked by Bert Cottle's death, even those who did not know him. The *Hillsbridge Mercury* carried a full report, under a banner headline: LOCAL MAN DIES AT YPRES. And there was a photograph of Bert, smiling proudly under his military cap.

The town read the report with growing dismay. Bert's unit, the North Somerset Yeomanry, had been sent to Ypres, or 'Wipers' as they called it, and after two days and two nights in the trenches, Bert had been killed by a coal-box shell. Five other men had been hit by the same coal-box.

The horror of it was almost beyond belief, but there was more to come. Within a matter of days, news was received that Colwyn Yelling had been wounded, with shrapnel in his shoulder and a badly damaged arm, and was being shipped back to hospital in Portsmouth.

As soon as Peggy heard he had arrived, she arranged to go down to see him, and when she returned to Hillsbridge, with his terrible stories of the fighting in France fresh in her mind, she was almost beside herself with worry.

"He saw Bert Cottle killed," she told Charlotte, sitting white-faced in the Halls' kitchen. "He says it's sheer hell out there. The Germans have got some sort of guns—Jack Johnsons he called them —that'll make a hole twenty feet deep and thirty feet across. You can't imagine it, can you? That's bigger than your kitchen and mine put together! And the towns, he says, are smashed to matchboxes. People are having to leave while their homes burn and take to the roads with all they can carry in carts and wheelbarrows. He says it's like being in heaven just to be in hospital."

"I don't know what to say, Peg." Charlotte was worried to see the usually strong and capable Peggy so upset. "You stay there, and I'll put the kettle on for a cup of tea."

But even then, horrified though she was, the war did not seem real to her. For life in England was much the same as it had ever been.

Autumn had turned to winter beneath rain-heavy grey skies, the leaves had fallen from the trees to lie in sodden heaps in the gutters. In spite of the knitting bees and the newspaper reports of fighting and the fund that Jack's school at Wells had set up to send plum puddings for Christmas to the boys at the Front, she found it hard to imagine that beneath the same grey skies a land across the Channel was ravaged and desolate, tramped over, burnt and blown-up, and she did not have the time or energy to try.

So when the stories began to circulate about the German spies infiltrating the country, she dismissed them as fanciful and foolish. And when James came home one evening and told her the latest suspect was Algie Smith, the manager at the County Stores, she almost laughed in his face.

"What are you on about?" she demanded, looking up incredulously from the boiled bacon she was slicing. "Mr Smith, a German spy? He comes from London."

"So he says," James said cryptically. "But the story as I've heard it is that his name isn't Smith at all. It's Schmitt. And his wife's foreign. You can't deny that."

"She's Dutch," Charlotte said. "She comes from Holland."

"She's not likely to admit being a German, if she's here to spy," James argued.

"But they were here before the war started!"

James wagged his head knowingly. "Planted here, in good time, so that when it all started, nobody'd think it were funny, them coming."

"Well, I think it's the silliest thing I ever heard," Charlotte said, resuming her slicing of the bacon. "Mr Smith's no more a German than you or I."

"I don't know so much," James reiterated stubbornly. "And I think you ought to stop going down there to work, Lotty."

She set the knife down with a clatter. "Whatever for?"

"Because whether it's right or not, it's what people are saying. You'll get a bad name for yourself. They'll call you a German lover."

"That's nonsense!" Charlotte said.

But James went on: "I want you to give notice. If you write it out, one of the boys can take it down to him."

"Now?" Charlotte exclaimed. "You mean today?"

"There's no time like the present," James said. "I don't want you associating with Germans, Lotty. Nothing's too bad for them. One of the blokes at work was only saying today, his wife's nephew has been hit in the face and lost the sight of both his eyes. And he's just twenty-one. It's terrible, what they'm doing."

She nodded. "I won't argue with that. But it's got nothing to do with Mr Smith. It's a good job I've got there, and good money. And goodness knows, we can do with it, with all our Jack needs."

She saw James's face tighten and knew that she had said the wrong thing. Only last week, Jack had come home needing a new cap, because the other boys had taken his while fooling about on the railway station, and somehow it had been lost. James had been furious, saying boys like them should know better.

"I don't care, Lotty," he said firmly. "There's not much I put my foot down over, but this is one time when I'm going to. Now, write out that notice, or I shall."

She could see his mind was made up, and she knew it was no good to argue any more. Much as she loved the job, it would have to go, or there'd be more trouble than it was worth. And besides, if this rumour gathered strength, there wouldn't be a job for her to go to much longer. People wouldn't shop at the County Stores if they thought Mr Smith was a German. In fact, there didn't seem to have been as many customers as usual this afternoon.

"All right," she said. "But I'm finishing the week out, James. There's a floor down there that wants washing, and I'm not leaving Mr Smith in the lurch."

James, knowing this was the best he could hope for, remained silent, but there was a strained atmosphere around the table as they ate their evening meal, which the boys didn't help by harking back to the subject of Mrs Smith again.

"I reckon she's got a wireless set in that box thing she sits in," Ted speculated.

"She could hide earphones in those coils round her ears," Fred added.

"And what do you think she'd hear in Hillsbridge worth passing on?" Charlotte asked crossly.

What was this war doing to people? she wondered later as she set out down the hill, her notice in an envelope in her pocket. As if it wasn't bad enough that Bert Cottle had been killed, Colwyn Yelling wounded, and the unknown boy blinded, now people were beginning to turn against one another, making mischief where there should be none.

It was a dark night, but fine, and a light in the room above the shop told Charlotte that the Smiths were at home. She did not need to disturb them, however. She let herself in through the backdoor with her own key, took off her coat in the small stock room, and set about filling a pail with water.

As yet she had not decided the best way of giving her notice to Mr Smith, and she thought about it again as she carried the steaming pail into the shop and went back for her broom and scrubbing brush. Under normal circumstances, she would have come out with it straight, but these were not normal circumstances.

"Drat the war!" she said loudly. Why had it had to come along and make complications just when everything had been sailing along so nicely?

When she had swept the floor, she took her pail of water and scrubbing brush and went down on her hands and knees behind the counter.

She began to scrub vigorously, venting her anger on the floor. So

119

engrossed was she, she did not notice the voices outside, or if she did, she thought nothing of them. And when the first explosive crash came, it made her jump so much that her heart seemed to stop beating.

Automatically she leaped up, but the edge of the counter caught her shoulder, knocking her down again and half-stunning her with shock and pain. She felt water slopping from the bucket around her knees, and still she didn't know what was happening until there was another crash and another, and an awful, nerve-jarring rumble like thunder right beside her. As it died away, she realized it was glass breaking and tins tumbling down.

She struggled to her feet again, and the sound of voices came at her through the broken window—not one voice, or two, but a cacophony of noise rising like an angry tide. As she stood, frozen, gripping the counter with shaking hands, there was another crash and the glass door shattered. At once, the black baize blind billowed out alarmingly. A stone, flying into the shop through the broken window, hit a pile of Quaker Oats boxes and brought them tumbling down. Then the lamp went out.

Shaking like a leaf, Charlotte edged along the counter. In the glow of the street-lamp she could see a dozen or more men, brandishing sticks, stones and bottles. She drew back, but too late. They had seen her.

"There he is, the German bugger!" someone yelled. "Let's get him, boys!"

Another stone came hurtling through the window, showering her with fragments of glass, and as she backed away into the dark interior she realized what was happening. The story of Algie Smith being a spy must have spread, and these men had come after him!

Panic flooded through her then, making her go first hot, then cold. They were like madmen—madmen! But she could still get out through the back door if she was quick.

She turned wildly, but her elbow caught the scale and pile of weights, knocking them over, so that they crashed to the floor. She stopped again, a sob catching in her throat. But at that same moment another kind of dread swamped her.

Algie Smith and his wife were upstairs, trapped, and these men were in murderous mood. If someone didn't stop them, heaven only knew what they would do.

Undecided, she stood her ground, as other men followed the first through the window. Tins of treacle, bottles of gripewater and a display of Lux wafers went everywhere, as the men barged their way in.

Then one of the men saw her standing there and stopped in his tracks.

"Mrs Hall, what are you doing here?"

The men behind him were too drunk, or too enraged, to care.

"Come on, out of the bloody way! We want the German bastard. We're going to make him bloody suffer!"

Charlotte took a step backwards and almost tripped over the broom she had left propped against the counter. Automatically she caught at it, holding it out in front of her threateningly.

"You keep away from me!" she cried.

To her surprise, the men stopped, looking at her uncertainly, but at that moment she caught sight of a youth climbing on to the counter and reaching up to swing on the overhead cash railway. Without even stopping to think, she rushed across to him.

"Get down from there!" she shouted, outrage lending her courage. "Get down before I knock you down!"

He backed away from her threshing broom, and, still holding on to the wire railway and its pulley, he fell backwards to the floor. As he fell, there was a sickening sound of tearing plaster and splintering wood, and slowly the cash railway separated itself from the ceiling. One by one its wires fell, draping themselves around the men in the shop and dangling drunkenly from the corners of the wooden cage that was Mrs Smith's lofty office.

Charlotte watched in horror and disbelief. Her beloved cash railway was ruined! Ruined! Never again would the wooden cups hum along the wire. Never again would it return exactly the right amount of change for her to hand to a waiting customer.

"You ought to be ashamed of yourselves, the lot of you!" she cried. "Grown men, are you? Well, if you want to fight Germans, go and join the army. Or does it take twenty of you to get one man and his wife? Get out! Get out before the bobbies get here and arrest the lot of you!"

And to her amazement, they went. Ashamed, suddenly, they turned and shuffled away, some through the window, stuffing their pockets with tins and bottles as they went, some through the shattered glass door. Sergeant Eyles, who had rushed to the scene with as many burly constables as he could muster as soon as he heard the disturbance, arrived at just the right moment. He was able to round them up, and take them back to the police station.

When he heard the police outside, Algie Smith, who had been hiding with his wife in the stoutest wardrobe they owned, braved it down the stairs, and found Charlotte sitting on an overturned box in the wrecked shop. She was shaking from head to foot, perspiration dripping down her face and into the hands that were pressed tight against her mouth. Beside her lay the broom, its head nestling against her soaking feet.

"Are you all right, Mrs Hall?" he asked anxiously. "I didn't dare come down. I thought they wouldn't hurt you . . . "

She brought her face out of her hands with a jerk, looking at the wreckage all around her, the scattered tins and boxes, all awash in the water that had spilled from her pail, and the broken glass. Then she drew her breath in sharply.

"They swung on the cash railway!" she said, her eyes dark and brooding. "They've broken the cash railway!"

NEXT MORNING, the men who had been caught leaving the shop were brought up before the magistrates and sentenced to seven days' hard labour. Half the town were incensed by this, and the Smiths, fearing another attack, stayed only long enough to do an inventory on the stock left in the shop before getting on a train back to London, never to be seen in Hillsbridge again.

Charlotte, although shaken, would have defied James and insisted on going down to help them clean up the mess, but next morning her ankle was so swollen she could not get her shoe on, and she guessed she must have twisted it during the confrontation without even realizing it.

By the time she was able to hobble down the hill, the windows of the County Stores had been boarded up, and the flat above remained unoccupied. She stood on the pavement outside for a moment, and there was an ache of emptiness inside her. The loss of the cash railway had got through to her as nothing else had. Trivial, it might be, compared with the terrible things that were happening in France.

But for Charlotte, involvement in the war had begun.

BOOK TWO
TED

8

ONE EVENING in early December, a concert party was in full swing on the rickety wooden stage in the Victoria Hall. Horace Parfitt, whose antics had kept the people of Hillsbridge entertained for twenty years and more, had already performed his country-yokel act in battered hat and smock, and been rewarded by enthusiastic cheers from the audience, and now Grace O'Halloran was charming them with a selection of music hall favourites, her sweet, clear voice carrying easily through the vaulted windows to the square below.

"She's a cracker and no mistake!" Horace commented as he changed his smock for the Victorian lady's evening dress he needed to wear for his next act. "I'm surprised you haven't been after her, young Ted me lad."

Ted Hall laughed, but before he could reply, Stanley Bristow, who ran the concert party, had spoken for him.

"If I know you, you're after her yourself, you wicked old goat! I heard about the extra practice you wanted to put into that turn you're going to do with her. "A Hole In My Bucket", indeed! It's a hole in something else, if you ask me!"

"You'm jealous, Stanley. Jealous, that's what you be!" Horace returned good-naturedly, and Ted chortled quietly to himself as he left them and crept out into the corridor that led around to the back of the stage. Horace and Stanley never stopped teasing one another. Their banter went on backstage at every concert party and every rehearsal, and occasionally Ted suspected there might a touch of irritation behind their chaff. But since Horace and Stanley had been together in concert parties since before he was born, he didn't suppose it was likely to blow up now. Whatever their differences, the two men had certainly been right about one thing. Grace O'Halloran was a very attractive girl.

He climbed the two steps to the stage and craned his neck to

125

watch her. He wasn't sure why he hadn't made a play for Grace. Besides her looks, being O'Halloran's daughter, she had a sort of class about her—an aura of remoteness and self-assurance that made her different from any of the other girls he knew. But he was sure he could win her heart if he really tried. More than once she had looked at him in a way that had seemed to tell him so, her lips slightly parted, head tilted to one side, while her eyes narrowed tantalizingly behind the sweep of long lashes. But something had always held him back from taking up the invitation. Perhaps it was knowing he could have her for the asking that deterred him; perhaps it was a secret fear that Grace, with her teasing ways, might discover that he was less experienced with women than he liked to pretend. But when she looked as delectable as she did this evening, he considered it a chance almost worth taking.

A burst of clapping interrupted his thoughts, and Ted realized that Grace had finished her turn.

"You're on, sir," she whispered as she passed him, and he tipped his black topper on to the back of his head, waiting for the pianist to bang out the introductory notes of 'Burlington Bertie'.

For twenty years, Stanley Bristow's concert party had been the favourite entertainment in Hillsbridge. Not even the coming of the picture house had affected its popularity, and now that the proceeds were going to the war effort, the crowds flocked in more eagerly than ever. They cheered Ted's 'Burlington Bertie' just as they cheered all the acts, stamping their feet, whistling and calling for more, and Ted felt on top of the world. Nothing, not even the thrill of watching a horse win when you'd staked your last pound on it, could beat this intoxicating moment. He took his last bow and came off stage to find Grace watching him from the top of the steps.

"That was first-class, Ted," she whispered, and her educated voice and the way she was looking at him stirred something inside him.

"Are you staying for a drink after the concert tonight?" he asked casually.

She looked at him through her lashes. "I might do."

"I'll have one ready for you then."

"You take a lot for granted," she said, but her eyes were still teasing, and, as she turned away to go into the ladies' dressing-room, she brushed against him so that for a moment he felt the pressure of her breast on his arm.

That wasn't accidental, he thought. The invitation was there, just as he'd known it would be. Excitement stirred, and he smiled to himself as he pushed open the door to the men's dressing-room.

As the concert rolled on, Ted sat in the dressing-room smoking and thinking about the O'Hallorans. There were two daughters, although the younger one, Stella, was so plain it was difficult to realize that she was Grace's sister. She'd come to the concert parties a few times, a round-faced girl, too plump to be attractive, with thick, reddish hair. Mrs O'Halloran, Hal's wife, was a nervous woman who had met Hal when he was still a miner himself, and when he had studied and worked his way up to manager, she had been dragged along with him. Even Ted had noticed, when he had been to their grand house at the top of South Hill for a concert party rehearsal, how ill at ease she had seemed amongst the grandeur. But Grace, Grace was something different again. She'd been born to it, and it had enhanced all the charm, the flirtatiousness that would have been there anyway, making her twice as desirable.

And if he played his cards right, who knew what would happen? The concert party members always stayed behind afterwards for a drink, and when she was mellowed a little, perhaps he would ask if he could see her home. He might even get to kiss her . . .

At last it was over, even the finale that took the form of a wedding procession with Grace as the bride, and Stanley, who had directed it, as the groom. Then, back in the dressing-room, the men took welcome swigs from Horace Parfitt's hip flask, while changing into their everyday clothes.

"There's a bottle in the cupboard for when the ladies come to join us," Stanley said, and Ted's heart thudded with uncomfortable anticipation.

To steady his nerves, he lit another Gold Flake, but it was the last in the packet.

"I'll have to run over to the Working Men's Club for some more cigarettes, Stanley," he said, crumpling the empty packet and throwing it into the waste bin. "I won't be a minute."

Stanley clicked his teeth disapprovingly.

"You smoke too much. You'll ruin that good voice of yours," he warned, but Ted ignored him, left the dressing-room and ran down the stone stairs to the street, taking them two at a time in his haste.

While the concert party had been in progress, the dank December air had thickened to fog. It clung in suffocating clouds around the street-lamps and swirled damply about the town square. Ted picked his way between the folk who were streaming out of the main doors of the Hall, calling a greeting here and there, but stopping to chat with no one. He crossed the square at a run, turning up the collar of his jacket and heading for the subway that crossed beneath the railway lines, and in the fog he almost collided with someone who was standing in the narrow dip of pavement.

He muttered an apology, noticing to his surprise that it was a girl, but not a girl whom he immediately recognized. He wondered what she was doing, standing in the shadows at the entrance to the subway. She must be waiting for someone. But it was a rotten night, all the same, for a girl to be out on her own.

He went under the subway, crossed the main road, and walked along to the Working Men's Club. As he opened the door, he was greeted by tobacco smoke, warmth and laughter, and the cheerful tinkle of the piano.

"It's Ted Hall! Come on, Ted, give us a song!" someone called, above the general chit-chat, and although he protested that he'd only called in for a packet of Gold Flake, Ted allowed himself to be steered towards the piano, where a pint mug was pushed into his hand, and the half-blind Welsh pianist tinkled expectantly, waiting for Ted to tell him what to play.

It would mean an extra ten minutes before he got back to Grace, Ted knew, but he decided not to worry about that. Better not seem too keen, he reasoned. He whispered something to the pianist, took a long drink from the foaming glass of bitter, and broke into the opening bars of 'Little Grey Home in the West'.

It was almost a quarter of an hour later when Ted passed under the subway again on his way back to the Victoria Hall, and as he emerged from the tunnel, he was surprised to notice that the girl he'd almost collided with was still there. As she heard his footsteps, she moved out of the shadows, peering anxiously into the murky darkness, then shrank back again.

He looked at her curiously. From her appearance, it was clear she was no common woman waiting to be picked up. Her coat, high-buttoned at the neck, and her hat, pulled well down on to her upswept hair, suggested she was a very respectable girl.

Disturbed, Ted hesitated.

"Are you waiting for somebody?" he asked.

To his surprise, she shrank even further back into the shadows until her shoulders came into contact with the rough stone wall behind her, and regarded him with big, frightened eyes.

"It's all right. I'm not going to hurt you," he said, half-amused. "I'm only asking. If you're waiting for somebody in the Hall, I could always tell them to hurry up for you."

She shook her head silently and with a shrug he turned away. If that was the way she wanted it, he wasn't going to bother himself unduly. But before he had gone more than a step, her voice arrested him.

"Please . . . just a minute."

He turned again.

"Yeah?"

"You . . . you didn't see a boy and girl the other side of the subway, did you? Coming along from the railway lines, or down by the river?"

He shook his head.

"No. It's not courting weather."

"No, but . . . I don't know where they can be."

He looked at her, puzzled. In the light of the street-lamp, he could see she was close to tears.

"Who is it you're looking for?"

"My friend, Marjorie Downs. We went to the concert in the Hall —at least Marjorie and I did—and Billy, her young man, happened to be there. They went off out before the end. She said they wouldn't be long—just go up the road to say goodnight—and she'd be back again. But I haven't seen her since and I don't know whether to wait for her or go on home, or what . . . "

"Oh, I'd go on home if I were you," Ted said. The girl was so close to tears, Ted was beginning to feel slightly uncomfortable, and he was also impatient to be with Grace.

"Well, I would, only . . . " The girl broke off, pressing one small gloved hand over her mouth.

"Only what?"

"We came together. My father wouldn't have let me come at all otherwise. And if I go home on my own . . . "

"Well, you can't stay here all night," Ted said matter-of-factly. "She's forgotten all about you, I shouldn't wonder. Go on home. She'll be all right."

"Yes, I suppose so," the girl said uncertainly. She took a step or two along the path into the thick swirling fog, and Ted felt a pang of something like irritation. Why did she have to look so vulnerable, damn it? If she chose to come to the concert with some flirty friend who buggered off and left her at the first opportunity, that was her funeral, surely, and nothing to do with him. Yet, as the fog closed in around her small figure, he found himself remembering how close she'd been to tears, and he called after her.

"Where do you live? Have you got far to go?"

"Eastlands. Waterley Lane."

"Waterley Lane? Hey, wait a minute. That's out in the wilds."

"Yes, that's why Marjorie and I came together. But I'll be all right." Her voice was tight now.

Ted swore softly to himself. The heck she'd be all right! It was a terrible night—and late, too—for a girl to be out alone. And once past the church and the farm opposite, the road to Eastlands was just a lane, with hedges on both sides all the way.

"Look, perhaps you had better wait a bit longer for your friend," he said, but she shook her head, a small quick movement that reminded him fleetingly of someone, although the impression came and went before he had time to think about it.

"No, you're right. I can't stay here any longer. I'm late as it is, and my father is going to be furious."

She turned again, walking away across the square in the direction of the church, and Ted made for the lights of the Hall and Grace, who would be wondering where he was. But at the foot of the steps he hesitated, the girl still very much on his mind. He looked around, but she had disappeared into the swirling fog, and he climbed a couple of the stone steps before stopping again.

Above him in the Hall, he could hear the sounds of merriment as the concert party rode out the wave of exhilarating success that came from a show well done. But to his own exasperation he found himself thinking about the strange girl walking, alone and frightened, along the deserted lane where the hedges grew out over the bank.

She wouldn't come to any harm, he told himself. It was another half-an-hour before the pubs turned out. And there was no need for him to get involved. Why, he wasn't even sure who she was! But the voice of conscience was louder than the voice of reason. Cursing her silently, he went back down the steps and crossed the square with quick strides. Damn girl, why did she have to get herself into a pickle like this tonight of all nights? He must be mad to bother about her with Grace waiting for him.

Although he broke into a trot, he was past the church before he saw her again. As the mist parted to reveal her small, hurrying figure, he called out to her, but she gave no sign of hearing, hastening her step if anything. As he drew level with her, he realized from the quick, defensive start she gave that his footsteps had frightened her into thinking she was being followed.

"Hey, steady up a bit!" he said.

"Oh, it's you!" She was breathless with relief.

"Yes, it's me. You can't go gallivanting about on your own on a night like this. I'll see you home."

"Oh . . . oh, will you really?"

"Look, I've got sisters of my own. I'd like to think somebody'd do the same for them," he said, but resentment at what he was missing with Grace made his tone sharp. "Who are you, anyway?"

"Rebecca Church. My father's secretary of the Co-op."

"Oh, him!" Ted said rudely, picturing the bewhiskered, overbearing man he'd seen about the town. "Well, he ought to make sure you're better looked after."

"He does look after me. He thought I'd be with Marjorie, I told you. And if you only knew the trouble I had getting out at all—and the trouble I'll have getting out again . . . "

"That's all right then. I shouldn't want to have to make a habit of this . . . "

She stopped walking and turned to look at him.

"You don't have to see me home if it's such a nuisance. I didn't ask you to."

Ted was immediately ashamed. It was, after all, his doing and not hers that he was walking along a foggy lane instead of enjoying himself in the dressing-rooms at the Victoria Hall.

"It's all right," he said, but still she faced him.

"I mean it. I don't want to put you out. I'll be all right on my own." Her look of bewildered fear had been replaced by one of defiance and oddly enough it made her appear more vulnerable than ever.

"Come on, don't be daft." Ted said sharply. "I said I'd see you home, and I will."

Without a word she turned and walked on, her head held high, her ridiculous hat bobbing, and he measured his step to hers. The lane began to slope upwards, gently at first and then more and more steeply, so that they had no breath left for talking, and Ted was glad. They reached the top of the hill and turned into an even narrower lane that was little more than a dirt track. The fog shifted slightly, and he saw a pair of houses, square and ugly behind large gardens.

"There's my house—and Marjorie's next door to it," she said. "But don't come any further. I'll be all right now."

"I'll come to the door with you."

"No. Please. I'll be all right." To his surprise, he noticed the frightened look was back on her face. "Thanks, anyway. Thanks very much."

Then, before he could stop her, she had taken to her heels, running along the dirt track towards the house. He watched her go, bewildered by her behaviour and his own reaction to it, for just a moment he had felt he wanted to keep her with him a little longer. The cottage door opened before she reached it, and he had a brief impression of the large frame of the Co-operative Society secretary standing there, an oil lamp held high. Then the fog closed in again and only the dark outline of the houses was visible.

He shrugged, and made his way back down the hill. It took him less than half the time that the climb had taken, but when he reached the square, the Victoria Hall was in darkness.

So much for that, he thought. Grace would have gone home alone —or in the company of one of the other men. Curiously, the thought did not disturb him overmuch. His thoughts instead were with a pretty, solemn-faced girl in a ridiculous hat.

ALFRED CHURCH, secretary of Hillsbridge Co-operative Society, was a big man. He stood more than six feet from the ground, and his gold watch chain strained across an expansive barrel chest. Even his voice had a deep, stentorian ring, and Alfred had long since learned how to use all these characteristics to their best advantage.

Since taking office at the Co-op a year before, he had bullied his entire staff into the sort of grudging respect he reckoned to be his due, carefully controlling the temper his family believed to be uncontrollable. Alfred ruled his household with a rod of iron, upholding all the Victorian standards that had been instilled in him by his own father, and punishing misdemeanours with the harshest justice.

Rebecca was his only child, but she was far from spoiled. At mealtimes, she was not allowed to speak, and if she dared to slouch, a board was strapped to her back for the next week or so, to "make her sit up straight." Each morning and evening she had to recite the catechism, and on Sundays she and her mother were marched to the village church at Withydown, half a mile further along the winding lanes, for both matins and evensong. In addition, Alfred made use of the Sabbath afternoons to preach hell fire and damnation while Rebecca sat meekly in front of him, hands folded, eyes downcast, wondering when he would ever stop.

As for moral standards, Alfred Church was quite fanatical. As a young man he had seen a servant girl who had disgraced herself by becoming pregnant, bundled unceremoniously from his father's house, and he had found it a curiously satisfying experience. First, he had allowed himself to dwell on the sinful behaviour that had brought her to her present predicament, relishing every detail with righteous disgust until he had almost begun to feel that he himself had had a part in it. Then, as an exorcism for the lust that had begun to swell in him, he had stoked up a rage that a servant girl could so degrade his father's house. Lastly, he had taken an unhealthy pleasure in contemplating the forms of punishment his vengeful God would mete out to her, an exercise which usually ended with a vision of the wretched girl giving birth to her child in a ditch.

For years the memory had fed Alfred's imagination, a treasure to be taken out and examined in the dark of his bedroom at night, a dart to titillate interest when he looked at a lovely woman, and as a young man, he had done plenty of looking, if nothing more. But growing older, he had begun to feel a certain guilt at his own lustful imaginings, and a terrible fear that fate would wreak some suitable vengeance on him.

His wife was timid and cowed; he did not think she would do anything to bring about his downfall. But of Rebecca, his daughter, he was less sure.

She was a pretty, solemn-faced girl with her mother's soft brown hair and hazel eyes. But even as a child she had shown a sense of mischief and fun that she had certainly not inherited from her mother, and occasionally Alfred saw a forewarning of rebellion in the toss of her head or the flash of her eyes.

Remembering the maid who had been thrown out of his father's house brought no pleasure to him now. As he watched Rebecca grow into an attractive young woman, he grew more and more afraid that the punishment inflicted on him for his secret lusts would come through his daughter. Through downcast eyes he saw her body fill out to the soft curves of womanhood, and the anxiety that nagged him became an obsession.

When she was fifteen years old, he insisted that the showering brown hair should be pinned up in a "seemly" fashion, and he kept a stern eye on the modesty of her clothes.

When he had been offered the position of Co-operative Society secretary, he had almost refused, for he realized it would mean moving to Hillsbridge, the notorious centre of the coal-field, but eventually desire for advancement had overcome him. He had settled for a house as far out of town as was practicable and forbidden Rebecca to associate with the local riff-raff, but so far had failed to find suitable employment for her. In Bath, where they had lived before, Rebecca had helped out at a small private nursery school. Now, she stayed at home all day, sharing the chores with her mother, cooking and sewing.

And that was as it should be, Alfred thought, until he could arrange a satisfactory marriage for her. He had a young man in mind —the son of a distant cousin who was at present articled to a solicitor in Bristol. Rebecca was a pretty girl, too pretty for her own good, and when the family had gathered for a reunion at Christmas-time, he'd noticed young Rupert watching her with an approving glint in his eye. A word or two from him outlining the advantages of marriage to Rebecca, and he felt sure Rupert would jump at the chance. As for Rebecca, she would do as she was told.

Although she was now almost seventeen, Rebecca was scarcely allowed out of his sight, and when she was, she was always threatened with "harsh strap" punishment if she misbehaved. That meant, as she knew only too well, the strap that hung on a peg behind the wash-house door. Once, when she was a little girl, he had used it on her for telling a lie—some silly, childish thing about a disappearing rock-cake—and she had never forgotten. The deep, burning pain, the weals on her back, the sickening sense of shame and degradation had lived on in her nightmares, and even now, years later, it was as real a threat to her as it had ever been.

And so, as she ran up the path that foggy December night, Rebecca's legs trembled beneath her, and sick apprehension turned her stomach over. Father was bound to be angry. She had been hoping desperately she might be able to slip in quietly so that he would not realize she had come home without Marjorie. But as he was waiting for her, there was no chance of that. Even on a night like this, he would hardly have been able to miss Marjorie running up the adjoining path to her own front door and calling her good-nights. That in itself would arouse his temper, for it was Marjorie who had talked him into allowing her to go to the concert, with her engaging persuasion and her assurance that: "We'll be together, Mr Church."

Lantern-light flared in the porch, and Rebecca cast a quick, fearful glance over her shoulder. If her father should see Ted, there would be hell to pay. But to her relief, he had gone, and she tried to compose herself as she ran towards the door.

"I'm sorry, Father, I know I'm late, but Marjorie and I lost one another in the fog . . . " Her voice died away as she saw his thunderous expression, and she tried to slip past him to her mother, who was standing hesitantly in the kitchen doorway. But he caught her arm, stopping her and swinging her round to face him.

"How dare you behave like a common slut?" he demanded, his voice shaking with anger.

"But, Father, I haven't," she pleaded.

"My God, that my daughter should come to this!"

"But, Father . . . "

"Silence! Don't dare answer me back. A girl brought up to fear the Lord, deceiving her father and mother as you have done—oh, you'll be punished, make no mistake of it!"

"I haven't done anything wrong!" Although trembling with fear, there was a trace of defiance in her voice, and he advanced on her, seeming to grow taller as his fury heightened.

"Nothing wrong, you say? Nothing wrong? That was a boy I saw you with in the lane. No! Don't deny it. Don't add lies to your wickedness. You see—here on your coat is proof of your sin!"

He pulled her towards him, wrenching at her coat. "There, you see?" He jabbed an accusing finger at the dusting of damp plaster that clung to the shoulder. "How did you come by that, you wretched girl?"

For the moment, the memory of shrinking back against the wall beside the subway escaped Rebecca.

"I—I don't know," she whispered.

"Well, I do!" he thundered. "It's from some dark yard where you've been with that boy. Who is he, Rebecca? Answer me now!"

"I don't know," she whispered again through chattering teeth. "I only met him tonight. But he was in the concert."

Her words rendered Alfred speechless for a moment.

Then he raised his hand, a paroxysm of rage distorting his face.

135

"You don't know? You've gone with the first lout who picked you up?"

"No . . . no . . . it wasn't like that . . ."

"It wasn't, eh? We'll see about that. Well, you know what you've got coming, my girl. I've promised you long enough. Winifred!" He turned to the doorway where Rebecca's mother cringed. "Fetch my strap!"

Fear widened the girl's eyes, but she stood motionless, her lip rucked between her teeth. She was past arguing now, past trying to explain. Whatever she said to him, her father would hear only what he wished to hear.

"Not the strap, Alfred!" Winifred Church spoke for the first time since her daughter's return, creeping along the passage to catch at her husband's arm imploringly. "Don't beat her, please!"

"Why not?" he snarled. "Answer me that!"

"Because . . . we don't know she's done anything wrong . . ."

"We know Marjorie came home an hour ago, like a decent girl should. And I saw that . . . that boy with my own eyes. Now, will you get that strap, or shall I?"

"No, Alfred!" She clung to his arm, her small cowed face more determined than he had ever seen it. "No, I won't let you. She's an innocent. You only have to look at her to know no boy has laid a finger on her. Do this, Alfred, and Lord knows where it will end."

He raised his arm to throw her aside, then, as his eye fell on the two cowering women, a feeling of power swelled inside him. His breath rasped unevenly in his throat, and he drew himself up to his full height, elated by his own supremacy. He could crush them both if he had a mind to, stupid, sinful daughters of Eve. He could throw them out into the street as his father had thrown out a fornicating housemaid. Lust, unleashed by fury, began to burn in his belly, and he caught at his daughter's arm so savagely that his fingers bit into her flesh.

"All right, I'll let you off this time, my lady. But next time I won't be so lenient. And if you ever do anything to bring disgrace on this house, I swear I'll beat you till the skin's clean off your back, and no boy will want to look at you again. Now, get upstairs to your room before I change my mind. I've business with your mother."

He threw her towards the stairs with such force that she stumbled against the bottom step and fell. Behind her she heard the uneven rasp of his breath, and ignoring her stinging hands and knees she scrambled to her feet and ran hurriedly up the stairs.

The blackness at the top of the stairs enveloped her, and she barked her skin on the corner of the marble topped washstand as she ran into her room. Shivering with cold now as well as fear, she tore off her clothes and pulled her nightgown over her head. Then, acting automatically from long habit, she fell to her knees beside her bed, stumbling into the Lord's Prayer. After a few phrases, however, her voice died away, and her indrawn breath came out on a long, strangled sob. Tears drenched her cheeks, and she covered her face with her hands.

She was still bent double against the iron frame of the bed, the eiderdown stuffed into her mouth, her belly aching with the depth of her sobs when she heard the footsteps on the stairs. She froze, fear choking her. Had her father changed his mind? Was he going to beat her after all? She thought she heard the thud of the strap swinging against his side, and her heart seemed to stop beating. Then she realized it was the sound of light, faltering steps beside his heavy ones. Paralysed by fear, she waited. But the steps went past her door and into the next room. Then she heard the low growl of her father's voice and the frightened, whining protests of her mother, and sick with dread, she knew what was to come.

She leaped to her feet, throwing herself into her bed and dragging the covers over her head. But nothing could shut out the sounds of lust coming from the next room, the grunts and cries and the rhythmic creaking of the bedsprings. Curled like a foetus in the womb, she heard it all, cringing away from the sounds and sobbing silently and helplessly while her stomach churned.

Dear God, how could you let it happen? He's an animal—an animal!

For what seemed a lifetime it went on, and when at last it was over, she could hardly believe it. Her agony was spent, like Alfred's passion, and into the great, aching void that was left, came guilt.

It had been her fault, all of it. Because of what she had done, her mother had been subjected to the ordeal she dreaded most—being used not just as a wife, but as a plaything for a sick man. Without being told, Rebecca knew it was so.

Tears gathered again in her throat. She could never go out again, never again see the young man with golden hair. And she would have nothing to look forward to but marriage to a man of her father's

137

choosing, a man who would bully her and drag her to bed as her father dragged her mother.

Despair gnawed like hunger inside her, and the tears began once more. They were still wet on her cheeks when she fell asleep.

BLISSFULLY unaware of the scene he had left behind him, Ted climbed the hill on the other side of the valley. The fog was thicker than ever now, and he regretted having left his muffler behind in the Victoria Hall. But it wouldn't hurt him the way it would hurt the older men. There'd be a lot of sickness among them if this weather kept up—bronchitis, pneumonia and the like. His own father hadn't been at all well the last few weeks. But as Mam said, it was no good worrying about things before they happened.

Ted pushed his hands into his pockets, and thought of the recent reports of the war in the *Hillsbridge Mercury*. Letters had been reprinted from soldiers in the British Expeditionary Force, describing conditions bad beyond belief: units retiring under terrible fire, doing their best to take their guns with them; coal-boxes falling into squads of infantry; shells dropping into piles of ammunition left behind by fleeing troops.

What was more, the Germans were trying to bring the war to Britain, and battle cruisers had actually tried to attack Great Yarmouth! They hadn't succeeded, but the cheek of it astounded Ted. It looked as if those who had predicted the war would be over by Christmas were going to be wrong. Kaiser Bill was putting up more of a fight than anyone had expected.

Ted reached the top of the hill and turned along the rank. The fog was less dense here, and with the valley below completely hidden, he felt as if he were standing on the edge of a bank of cloud. As he gazed along the line of houses he noticed a light giving the swarming mist a pinkish glow. Puzzled, he hurried towards it. That lighted window looked to be just about the right distance along the rank to be his own kitchen. Surely the family would be in bed by now!

A few more steps, and he could see he was right. His heart came into his mouth with a jolt. Something must be wrong! Remembering his fleeting anxiety for his father, he began to run.

Urgently he flung the door wide, to find the family in the kitchen. Mam was standing in front of the fire, her skirts catching the warmth of the dying embers: Jack was on the settle; and Fred leaned

138

against the table. They all looked so serious that Ted, already half-expecting the worst, asked in a low voice, "Dad?"

They stared at him blankly.

"He's not . . . " He broke off, unable to form the words, and Charlotte shook her head impatiently.

"What's your Dad got to do with it? He's gone to bed as if nothing had happened. It's our Fred, causing all the trouble."

"Fred?" he repeated, not understanding.

"Yes. Your brother here. He's just told us he wants to go and join the army. He thinks he's going off to fight in this bloody war!"

Ted stared, and the room seemed to sway around him. Rebecca was forgotten now as he looked at his brother, the most peace-loving one of the family.

"*Fred* does?" he repeated.

And their silence told him it was true.

9

D URING the night the fog turned to rain. Charlotte, lying awake, heard the first soft flurry against the window, and felt her anger dissolve into despair.

Rain. It rained ceaselessly in Flanders, so they said. It rained day after day until the battlefields were seas of mud and the trenches were awash. And the men and boys fought and died thigh-deep in the sort of mess in which you wouldn't leave a dog—if you had an ounce of humanity in you . . .

She rolled over, staring into the darkness and seeing in her mind's eye a composite picture of all the stories she'd heard of the Front rolled into one.

No Man's Land seemed to her to be an extension of Farmer Bert's ploughfield in November—dark, bumpy, barren and wet as far as the eye could see. The trenches were the ditches at the side of the lanes where she'd taken the children for afternoon walks, deeper, perhaps, and more roughly dug, but cleared of dead leaves and branches as they were when they'd been prepared for February Fill-Dyke. The barbed wire would look much the same as the makeshift barrier they put up to keep the cows out of the allotments; the poppies would be the same vermilion silk as those that dotted the railway embankment in high summer. And the makeshift ambulances taking the wounded away to field hospitals would be not unlike the coal carts that jolted injured miners from pithead to home along rutted roads.

The guns, she found more difficult to imagine, though recalling a firework display she'd seen during the coronation celebrations, she wondered if they lit the sky in the same way, accompanied, perhaps, by a tearing, echoing crash like the thunderclap that ended a summer heat-wave, and smaller, more distant explosions like the crackers they put on the railway lines in foggy weather. But from the reports that came back, France was worse, much worse, than she could ever imagine.

And it was to this living nightmare that Fred, her son, was going, to this hell that was painted not in the scarlets and golds of eternal flame, but in the mud-browns of trampled earth and the greys of a rain-heavy sky, a purgatory permeated by the damp cold that chilled bone deep and scattered with the the mutilated bodies of the wounded and the dying.

Pain rose in her throat like bile, bitter and sickening.

Why? she asked herself. Why, when men were coming in droves to look for jobs in the coal-field and so avoid the conscription that everyone said would be made compulsory if the war didn't end soon, should Fred want to volunteer? It didn't make sense. If he was out of work, it would have been different. If he was doing a job that had nothing to offer the war effort, perhaps she could have understood. But in times of strife even more than in times of peace everyone knew coal was vitally important to keep things moving, and the well-known poster with Kitchener pointing his finger and proclaiming "Your Country Needs You" might apply as much to a miner as to a soldier. In Fred's case, it might be even more apt to think of it that way, for he was a good carting boy and knew nothing of soldiering.

She'd tell him that in the morning, she thought, but even as she grasped at the straw of hope, in her heart she knew it would do no good. Already she'd tried every argument she could think of, since Fred had come home with this tomfool notion in his head, but they'd all gone in one ear and out the other. He'd simply leaned against the table, shaking his head in disagreement, steadfastly refusing to be drawn into a heated argument. That was Fred all over, of course, quiet, slow to anger, immovable almost, but it made it all the more ludicrous somehow that he should be the one who wanted to go and fight the Hun.

She had put that to him, pointing out how he hated fights and quarrelling and how, even as a little boy, he'd tried to keep the peace between his brothers.

"But that don't mean I can't do what I think is right," he had replied evenly. "Besides, I don't know why you'm so keen to keep me down the pit. It don't seem long ago you was keen to keep me out of it!"

Charlotte had been unable to answer. To her, it seemed a lifetime ago, something she had worried about in another world. For what was a chafed back and raw knees compared to limbs blown off by shell-fire?

Now, her thoughts aching in her like physical pain, she shifted restlessly, and the movement disturbed James. He turned over, coughing in his sleep, and a new wave of helpless anger swept over her.

How could he sleep at a time like this? Didn't he care? When Fred had come in and told them what he planned to do, James had seemed unmoved. And when she'd begged him to reason with Fred, he had only said that the boy must do as he thought fit.

But even as she silently accused him, she knew it was not true, and she found herself wishing she could be more like him, accepting things instead of fighting them, being resigned to what could not be changed.

Impulsively she turned to him, curling herself around his back. Although he was asleep, she seemed to feel his quiet strength, and there was comfort in the warmth of his body. She lay her face against him, wishing he would wake and hold her. But he did not, and she closed her eyes, willing herself to be as calm as he was.

Tomorrow was another day. In the morning everything would seem different.

But in the morning, nothing had changed. Fred was still determined to join the army.

Just to make things worse, later in the day she heard news of two more Hillsbridge casualties—Ern Eyles, one of Sergeant Eyles' sons, who had died of wounds received in the last days of the Battle of Ypres, and Evan Comer, who had lost an arm and a leg in an explosion at an ammunitions dump.

Ern Eyles she heard about while she was shopping, but it was Dolly who told her about Evan. She arrived at the kitchen door in a terrible state, having just heard the news from Evan's sister, who had made it her business to call on Dolly up at the house and imply that it was all her fault.

"It was terrible, Mam," Dolly said, her lip quivering. "She said if I hadn't finished with Evan, he'd never have thought of volunteering."

"That's nonsense, Dolly!" Charlotte said sharply, shooing Harry out to play in the rank with his hoop and stick. "You can't live your life worrying about what other people will do. You didn't want him, and that's all there is to it."

"But she said . . ."

"Never mind what she said. Nobody made him go off to war, least of all you."

"But she's right, Mam, don't you see?" Dolly said miserably. "If I was still going with him, he'd have stayed here. Now he's lost an arm and a leg. He'll never play football again. And whatever you say, it is my fault."

"Then why is your brother going—he hasn't been let down by anybody," Charlotte remarked harshly, and this upset Dolly even more.

But when the boys came home, Dolly's tears worked where Charlotte's plans had failed, and Fred agreed to leave signing on until after Christmas, although he refused to be put off altogether.

"Oh well, maybe the war'll be over by then," Charlotte said. "It's going a bit quieter, according to the newspapers."

BUT SHE was wrong. Any lessening of activity was only the lull before the storm, and ten days before Christmas, the war came to England. The German battle cruisers that had carried out the abortive raid on Great Yarmouth six weeks earlier came back to the attack, and more than a hundred civilians were killed in Scarborough, Whitby and Hartlepool.

"I've never heard the like!" Peggy said, coming in to talk to Charlotte about it. "In one place, a family of eight was completely wiped out—their dog and canary as well!"

"I read about it," Charlotte said. "Was that the house where they found the cat asleep and unharmed under the washing copper?"

Peggy nodded. "I think it was. But think of it, it could have been you, and the children, and Nipper, all gone, just like that!"

When Peggy had left, Charlotte kept thinking about it. If innocent people were being killed in their own homes, perhaps there *was* a point to the boys going to fight. She just wished it weren't Fred, and she knew Peggy felt the same. Colwyn was almost recovered by now, and would be home for Christmas, but after that he would be sent back to France. No one knew where it would end.

It was then that Charlotte decided this Christmas, at least, would be one her family would remember.

HILLSBRIDGE MARKET was usually held on a Saturday, and it brought the town to life from early in the morning until late at night.

Inside the big, stone-built market hall were three avenues of wooden-wheeled stalls selling everything from cabbages to cockles, ribbons to bird-seed. There were some stalls outside too, in front of the George, and on the other side of the road on the forecourt of the Miners Arms, but they were outshone by the wagons that never missed a market day—Dr Quilley, the Indian Quack, selling pills, potions and cure-alls in a jar, and Dr Rainbow, his partner, pulling teeth in full view of the appreciative on-lookers. Then there was Smasher, the chinaware man, throwing cups and saucers into the air so that they smashed to smithereens on the pavement. People clustered round, laughing and cheering, calling him mad, but Charlotte always doubted whether he was as silly as they thought. The tea-sets he disposed of in this way were only "seconds," she suspected, and he always did a roaring trade as a result of his antics.

Later in the day, with shoppers still thronging around the stalls, the Salvation Army band would arrive and form a circle outside the George to play their rousing music and roar out the hymns, while Leah, a small, stout woman in bonnet and tunic, tried to persuade reluctant shoppers to put a copper or two into her collecting bag.

At teatime, the fair that wintered each year in the yard behind the market house would open, and the young people would troop along to ride on the roundabouts and the cake-walk, throw rings at the hoop-la, or try their luck at the coconut shy. On quiet afternoons, the fair folk would let the children ride free on the amusements, and one afternoon Amy had come home with her gloves worn out because she had stayed so long on the cake-walk, holding on to the rail while the floor bucked beneath her.

When darkness fell, the yards would be lit by carbide lamps and gas flares, and it was usually ten or eleven o'clock before the stalls were wheeled away and the last shoppers drifted homeward.

This week, however, with Christmas Day falling on the Friday, market day had been brought forward to Christmas Eve.

Understandably, it was busier than ever, with gypsies selling holly and mistletoe and a queue at Farmer Brent's stall for butter and cheese that wound half-way down the market hall.

As she pushed her way through the crowds Charlotte was glad she had been able to bribe Amy and Harry into staying at home, promising them a bag of bulls-eyes on her return. She could understand them wanting to come, but they would have delayed her dreadfully, hanging on to her bag, insisting that they stop and look at everything. Besides, she had a few things to get for their stockings.

Money was tighter than ever this year since her job at the County Stores had come to an end, but she managed to run to some small sweet oranges and a bag of nuts for each of them, and some teething rings for Alex, her grandson.

She had just finished her shopping and was crossing the forecourt of the George when she became aware of a commotion behind her. She half-turned, but as she did so someone cannoned into her, almost knocking her over, and making her spill fruit and nuts from her laden bag all over the pavement.

It was a hobbledehoy who had been stealing apples from one of the greengrocery stalls as a decoy—now, while the angry trader chased him, his friends were filling their pockets from the unattended stall.

"Ruffian!" Charlotte shouted after him, but no one was taking any notice, and fuming with annoyance, she stopped to retrieve her scattered shopping from the pavement.

"Here, I'll help you."

To Charlotte's surprise a girl stopped and croupied down beside her. She was young and pretty, but Charlotte did not know her.

"Those boys want their backsides tanning!" Charlotte said tartly. "I'd do it, too, if they were mine. Big as they are it's the only way to teach them respect for law and order."

"That's right, Mam, you tell 'em!"

It was Ted's voice. Charlotte straightened up, and as she did so she caught sight of the girl's face. Surprise was written all over it, and recognition. The young girl had turned pink from the neck of her high-buttoned coat to the sweep of her brown hair!

So she knew Ted! Well that wasn't surprising, and she wouldn't be the first girl to have fallen in love with the good-looking boy in the concert party. But as she turned to Ted, Charlotte saw the girl's expression mirrored in his own. Clearly he hadn't realized who she was until she looked up, and now they were staring at each other in a way that made her feel like an intruder.

"Well, I've finished my shopping, Ted," she said with a briskness that disguised her true feelings. But he seemed almost unaware of her.

"You go on home, Mam. Leave your bag with me, and I'll catch you up."

She hesitated, not knowing why she felt so uncomfortable. Ted was growing up, and she might as well accept it. Then she sighed.

"All right," she said. "But don't be too long, will you?"

WHEN SHE had gone, Ted quickly recovered his usual irrepressible confidence and smiled at the girl.

She looked different in daylight, still serious but no longer frightened. Her eyes were hazel and dark-fringed in her heart-shaped face, her mouth delicate and childish. But there was a hint of determination in the tilt of her chin, and he found himself remembering the way she'd flown at him for his rudeness the night he'd seen her home.

Beneath his gaze, her flush deepened. "I must go. I've got a lot of shopping to do."

"Don't be in such a hurry," he urged her. "You're always running away from me."

She bit her lip. "Am I? My father doesn't like me out on my own. And if he thought I was talking to a boy . . . " Her voice tailed away and the frightened look returned.

"You won't come to any harm with me," Ted said. But he could see she was about to go, and he didn't want her to. "Would he let you come out with me if I asked his permission?" he went on.

"No!" Her voice was sharp, and he stared at her in bewilderment. "It wouldn't be a very good idea," she added lamely.

Automatically he shrugged. She was turning him down, and he wouldn't ask twice, however much he wanted to. But as if she knew what he was thinking, she said, all of a rush, "If I went out with you, he wouldn't have to know."

"Wouldn't he? Oh, all right then," Ted said casually. It seemed funny, but the morals of it didn't matter much to him. All he wanted was to see her again, with or without her father's consent. "When could you get out?"

Uncertainty flickered across her face.

"I don't know . . . "

"Boxing Day?"

"Oh, I don't think so."

"Monday, then."

"Say Tuesday. Wait for me here. Then if I can't get out it won't matter so much."

"But you will try?"

"Yes, I'll try. Now you'd better go. Your mother will have got a long way ahead."

"How did you know she was my mother?"

"I didn't know until you called her "Mam." But she's nice, isn't she? Straight, somehow. You must always know where you are with her," she said wistfully.

He nodded. "You're right there. So I'll see you on Tuesday—here. At about half past seven."

"If I can. Happy Christmas."

"Happy Christmas."

He set off up the hill in pursuit of Charlotte, whistling again, and wondering why he suddenly felt on top of the world. She was only a girl, after all. He'd had girls before. He could think of a dozen who were prettier than she was, and most of them wouldn't have this habit of running away from him, let alone a frightening father-figure at home. But it didn't matter. None of it mattered. He was going to see her again. And he was glad.

CHARLOTTE awoke early on Christmas morning, because she had so much on her mind, she supposed. Certainly it was not through a surfeit of sleep! By the time all the preparations had been finished the night before and Amy and Harry sleeping soundly enough to enable her to creep in and fill their stockings it had been nearly midnight. But now here she was wide awake before six, thinking of all the things she had to do. And as if that wasn't enough, she couldn't get the image of Ted's face looking at that strange girl out of her mind.

"He's really taken with her," she had said to James when she had got home. "I hope she won't let him down."

146

But James had only smiled. "You worry too much. Our Ted can look after himself as well as any of them—better, if you ask me."

Charlotte had said nothing, but privately she wondered whether Ted's carefree attitude in fact made him more vulnerable than the others.

It's like Nipper all over again, she thought now, lying awake in the frosty darkness. Look what he was like that time the dog was lost! And that's nothing to the way he'll be when it comes to a girl he cares about.

A board creaked, bringing her back to awareness, and the bedroom door opened a fraction.

"Mammy, are you awake?" Harry asked in a loud excited whisper.

Charlotte smiled to herself. That was the end of any hope of going back to sleep. "Yes, Harry, you can come in," she whispered back.

James grunted and grumbled at being disturbed, but he moved over to make room for Harry and Amy, who came in too as soon as she heard voices, and the children began turning out their stockings on to the counterpane. Amy was too old, really, to be still having a stocking, let alone coming into their bed to open it, but she still enjoyed it and Charlotte was happy for her to remain a child as long as possible.

The stocking ritual over, it was time to get up—for Charlotte at any rate. Although she had singed the cockerel the night before and peeled the potatoes, there was still a great deal to be done if dinner was not to be delayed until half-way through the afternoon.

When breakfast was finished they started getting ready for chapel, the boys grumbling all the while, but for once it was James who was insistent.

"It's only about the once a year we go all together," he told them. "That pleases your mother. It's like a Christmas present for her, and she doesn't get many of those."

The boys began laughing and nudging one another.

"What's the matter with you all?" Charlotte asked in exasperation.

"Shall we give it to her now, or keep it for after?" Jack asked the others.

"Give me what?"

"If we give it to her now p'raps she'll let us off going to chapel," Ted suggested.

"I shall not!" she told them roundly. "What are you on about anyway?"

Amid more laughter they brought out a bulky parcel and gave it to her.

"Happy Christmas, Mam. From all of us."

Still pretending to be impatient, she pulled at the paper and they watched her, smiling in anticipation. She tore it away, exposing crimson flannel, and her expression changed to surprise and delight.

"It isn't . . . oh, boys, you shouldn't have!"

She shook it free of the paper and held it up, a crimson dressing-gown, creased from being folded but so obviously smart and warm.

"That's right, isn't it? That's what you wanted?" they asked.

"Always," she said, a little tremble in her voice. "I've always wanted one. But how did you . . . "

"That's our business," they scolded her. But they were delighted by her pleasure.

After chapel there was the usual rush to get the dinner on the table, and Charlotte was glad Dolly had been able to come home for the day to help her. Jim and Sarah arrived, too, with Alex. They had planned to have dinner with the Brimbles and tea with the Halls, but now they knew Fred was off to the war as soon as the festivities were over, they had changed their plans.

"I hope you're all good and hungry!" Charlotte remarked, coming in with the cockerel, resting majestically on its bed of sausages and roast parsnips.

Noisily they agreed that they were, and while James carved they struck up a chorus of We Wish You a Merry Christmas and For She's a Jolly Good Fellow.

Christmas dinner was always the highlight of the day, and when their plates were full the singing and joking stopped and they all tucked in to their food. Cockerel was a treat—there wouldn't be another one until next year—so they made the most of every mouthful, and the silence lasted until their plates were empty again. Then they sat, stretching their full bellies, while the plates were cleared and Charlotte carried in the pudding, surrounded by mince pies and topped with a sprig of holly.

"Now just go careful!" she warned them. "This is the first year I've put in sixpences since your father broke a tooth on one when we were first married."

"I've found one! I've found one!" squeaked Harry, and the boys smiled at his excitement. They knew what he did not—that later on Ted was going to dress up in a Father Christmas outfit he had borrowed from Horace Parfitt.

When no one could eat another mouthful the men sat back by the roaring fire while the women cleared away. James fell asleep in his chair and Alex in Harry's old cradle.

"The oldest and the youngest!" laughed Charlotte.

The afternoon slipped by in a pleasant aura of well-being. The Brimbles came along to join them, and everyone enjoyed Ted's Father Christmas act, although it was difficult to stop Harry from recognizing his brother. "Look, Harry, see what he's got in his sack!" Amy pleaded when Harry became too interested in Ted's false beard, and Ted managed to push it back into place again, and make a hasty exit, waving and ringing his big school bell.

"Christmas is nothing but one long feed," Dolly said as she helped Charlotte cut sandwiches for tea and put the finishing touches to the Christmas cake. "We shall all be too full to move."

Charlotte agreed. She was tired but glowing from the goodwill and the comfort that came from having her family all around her. But when tea was over and they had sung yet another chorus of We Wish You a Merry Christmas, Sarah said it was time to be getting Alex home and Charlotte felt the first chill of apprehension whisper over her skin.

"Stay a bit longer," she begged them, but Sarah remained firm.

"There's always next year," she said.

Charlotte turned away quickly.

As Jim and Sarah were leaving, Colwyn Yelling and the two Brixey boys arrived. They had heard the news about Fred volunteering, and they had come to pull his leg about it.

"We're looking for a soldier," they joked. "Name of Hall—Fred Hall."

"You'd better come in then, hadn't you?" Charlotte said tartly, but her feeling of discomfort was growing. The day that was to be so special was slipping away from her and the Lord only knew what would happen before they had the opportunity to be all together again.

The boys were teasing Fred, and it made the sick dread in Charlotte all the sharper. "Let's forget about the war—this is Christmas!" she said when she could stand it no longer. "I've got a nice fire in the front room, and we could sing some carols round the piano."

They agreed, but she felt they were only humouring her. As soon as her repertoire of carols ran out, the boys began singing marching songs.

"Come on, lads, I'll drill you!" Colwyn offered. He seemed to have forgotten his fears about going back to France for the moment, and was enjoying being the only serving soldier among them.

They lined up, using the long-handled broom and the brass fire-irons for rifles, while Colwyn bellowed orders at them. Everyone, even Dolly, who was making eyes at Colwyn, laughed and thought it a great joke. But not Charlotte. She sat on the piano stool watching them, and feeling as if the world were crumbling around her. How could they joke and laugh about it? Didn't they realize how deadly earnest it was? Colwyn at least should know better. And where would they be next year? Still laughing and playing the fool? Or would they be . . .

She stood up abruptly, cutting off her thoughts. "Supper time lads!" she called to them. To her relief they stopped their drilling and followed her. But for Charlotte the warmth and safety of her Christmas had gone, and as she carved thick slices of ham, desperately preserving the air of jollity, she could not help wondering if it would ever be the same.

10

CHRISTMAS DAY in the Church household was a family occasion too, but it was very different from the Halls' Christmas.

Every year for as long as Rebecca could remember, it had been the same—midnight mass on Christmas Eve, matins on Christmas morning, thank-you letters to be written while Winifred cooked lunch, and the afternoon spent receiving the first of the endless round of annual visitors.

There was plenty of good food and wine—Alfred made sure of that—and there was always a Christmas tree tall enough to reach to the ceiling, which it was Rebecca's job to decorate on Christmas Eve.

It was the nicest part of Christmas, she had always thought, unwrapping the baubles and the tinsel from their tissue paper and hanging them one by one on the branches until they sparkled like something from a fairy tale. But this year her hands trembled as she eased the tiny bells and globes from their wrappings, and she could not concentrate on what she was doing.

She had arranged to meet a boy—not just any boy, but Ted Hall, who had sung 'Burlington Bertie' in the concert party, and walked home with her afterwards.

Each time she thought of it she began to tremble again. Deep, deep inside she trembled, her nerves knotted and rose in her throat in little spasms, her mouth became dry in anticipation.

She had arranged to meet him, and she could think of nothing else, just as she had been able to think of nothing else but the things he had said to her and the way he had made her feel when he had seen her home after the concert party. That made her tremble again, because she knew he was very special. She hadn't known many boys. The life she had led had been manipulated to prevent her doing so, but none of the ones she had met had affected her in the same way as Ted Hall. In the past she had sometimes been glad of her father's strictness, for it had prevented her from having to get to know them better. But Ted . . .

She wanted to see him again more than she'd ever wanted anything in her whole life. But how could she? Her father would never allow it, and what excuse could she give for going out by herself? When she had been talking to Ted, she had been determined to think of something. But now, at home, in the imprisoning atmosphere, she knew it was hopeless.

Tears pricked her eyes as she imagined him waiting for her, then realizing she was not coming and going away again, despising her. It was awful, she couldn't let it happen, but how? How?

"Please, God, let me think of something!" she prayed, slipping a candle into position in its tiny basket on the tree, and she went on praying until she had finished the decorations.

Next morning at the service at St Mary's, Withydown, she still had no solution.

"Hark the Herald Angels Sing!" sang the congregation, and Rebecca's lips mouthed the words. But inside she was still whispering, "I must see him. Oh, please, let me think of something!"

It was as they left the church that she saw a notice that seemed the answer to her prayer. Hillsbridge Girls Friendly Society were giving a carol concert—and it was to be held on Tuesday! Rebecca's eyes went round with awe. Fancy God hearing her and putting an excuse in her path that way! It must mean it couldn't be so wrong to deceive her father after all. But still it was only half the battle. She would never be allowed to go on her own. If she suggested it, either Winifred or Alfred himself would take her.

No, there was only one person who could give her an alibi, and that was Marjorie Downs.

Before moving to Hillsbridge, she had never known anyone quite like Marjorie, who was gay and pretty and never seemed to worry about anything. She was a flirt, and she "told stories," embroidering her accounts of everything that happened to her to make them more interesting, but there was no malice in her.

Alfred liked her, too, and this puzzled Rebecca. She did so many things he was always ready to condemn: walking out with boys, and even letting them kiss her, going to picture shows and concerts at the Palace, and working as an apprentice at Fords, the big drapers shop in South Hill. Yet whenever she came knocking at the door, Alfred seemed pleased, smiling a strange smile that turned his mouth down at the corners instead of up, and narrowing his eyes until they were half-closed. Sometimes he patted her on the shoulder, or put his arm around her waist, his hands lingering as if he were fond of her. And when he spoke to her, his voice was low and full of hidden depths.

Yes, if there was anyone who could get around Alfred and persuade him to allow her to go to the G.F.S. concert, it was Marjorie. And after the way Marjorie had let her down and left her stranded after their last outing, perhaps she would be willing to make amends. But Rebecca knew she would have to see her and explain, and with her father home all over the Christmas it wouldn't be easy.

As they walked home along the wintry lanes, Rebecca decided to broach the subject.

"Can I go round to wish Marjie a Merry Christmas?" she asked as they reached the track leading to their two houses.

Alfred's face darkened. He had been hoping Marjorie might come around to wish Rebecca a Merry Christmas. "Your mother will need some help in the kitchen," he objected.

But Winifred patted her daughter's arm. "Not for a bit, I won't. The vegetables are all done, and the turkey's in the oven. You go and see Marjie if you like."

Rebecca nodded, her heart thudding as she ran down the path to Marjorie's house.

Marjorie was one of a big family. It seemed to spill into every room, and although she usually enjoyed their company, today Rebecca began to despair of ever getting her friend alone. At last she managed it, and she quickly outlined her plan before they were interrupted.

When she had finished, Marjorie laughed delightedly.

"Well, I am surprised at you, Becky! And I always thought you were too good to live!"

Colour flooded Rebecca's face. "Oh, please, Marjie! I don't know how I can get there if you don't help me. You know what he's like —he'd never let me go."

"You don't handle him right," Marjorie said wickedly. Then, seeing Rebecca's worried look, she laughed again. "Oh, all right, I'll help if it means that much to you. What do you want me to do?"

"Could you ask him for me?" Becky said eagerly. "He wouldn't be so likely to suspect anything if he thought it was your idea. Come back with me now—say we've been talking . . . "

"What did you say it was—a G.F.S. concert?"

"Yes. On Tuesday. Oh, please, Marjie!"

"All right. But what am I supposed to do while you go off courting?"

"Oh!" Becky's face fell. "I hadn't thought . . . "

"Never mind. I'll think of something," Marjie said impatiently. "You worry too much, Becky. You want me to come round to see him now?"

"Oh, please, Marjie."

"All right," said Marjorie, clearly enjoying the whole episode.

As Rebecca had suspected, her father was so pleased to see Marjorie he agreed to her suggestion without much ado. Though when she had gone, Alfred turned to his daughter sternly.

"You see, I am trusting you again, Rebecca—for Marjorie's sake," he told her. "It would be a pity for your friend to be penalized for your wrongdoing. But I shall not overlook another lapse. I am putting you on your word of honour not to let me—or her—down again."

Rebecca flushed slightly, guilty at her own deceit, but she said nothing, and presently the discomfort faded. The happiness, bubbling inside her, was too intoxicating to be suppressed for long.

After lunch, the visitors arrived in their brand-new, shiny black motor car—Alfred's second cousin, Kessey Thorne, her husband Donald, and their son, Rupert.

Of all the relatives who came duty-calling at Christmas, they were the ones Rebecca disliked the most. But because Winifred was still upstairs changing into her afternoon frock when the motor drew up at the gate, she had to go out with her father to greet them, and somehow, happy as she was, even they didn't seem as bad as usual.

As they sat in the living room, making polite conversation and inquiring after all the family, Rebecca stole critical looks at them, amusing herself by trying to decide what animals they reminded her of. Kessey, she thought, was like a Pekinese dog, fluffy and fluttery in scarves and feathers. Donald, with his whiskery little beard was like a billy-goat. And Rupert reminded her of a sleek, self-satisfied slug.

Finally Winifred came down, apologizing for not having been ready, and the conversation broadened, as it always did, to a catalogue of the health and fortunes of every member of the family, from Alfred's sister, Amelia, who had done very well in life and was a companion and personal maid with a titled family, the Harcourtes, in London, to a number of distant cousins who were apparently eking out their lives in genteel poverty and surviving one crisis after another. Most of them Rebecca had never met, and usually she sat stupefied with boredom, trying to avoid Rupert's leering glances in her direction. But today she was in a world of her own, glad to be able to curl up on the pouffe and think, and Alfred had to address her twice before she even realized she was being spoken to.

"Why don't you entertain Rupert with a piano solo, my dear?" he said benevolently. "There's a nice fire in the parlour, and I'm sure you two young people don't want to listen to all our family gossip."

Hot colour flooded Rebecca's cheeks. She did not want to be alone with Rupert, but she did not know how to avoid it.

"I'm not really very good," she said lamely, but Alfred could not have that.

"Not good? Why, you have a wonderful touch! You'll appreciate it, Rupert, I know you will."

He stood up, opening the door, and Rebecca had no choice but to go. She led the way to the parlour, and when she sat down on the piano stool he stationed himself in front of the fire, lifting his coat tails to warm himself as he had seen his father do. But she still felt ill at ease alone with him, and to hide her nervousness she began to sort through her music.

"What would you like to hear?"

As soon as she had said it, she realised her mistake. He crossed the room, and leant over her shoulder, his nearness making her stomach churn.

"How about this one?" she suggested, beginning to play the first tune on the page in the hope that he would go away, but he did not. He stayed beside her, so close that her fingers stumbled over the keys.

"I . . . I've gone wrong, I'm afraid," she said.

"Never mind," he simpered, his oily voice making her skin crawl. He reached over to turn the page of music, his hand lingering against hers for a moment. It was always the same with him—when they were alone together, or if he thought no one was watching, he touched her as often as he could, but always in such a way that he had an avenue of retreat should she object.

Now, as on every occasion, his hand was removed before she had any reason to complain, but it left her feeling somehow soiled.

"You don't have to be shy with me, Becky," he said, faintly reproving. "We know one another too well for that, don't we?" Then, before she could think of an answer, he had turned the page again. "How about "Drink to Me Only with Thine Eyes"? That's a nice sentiment, don't you think?"

She began to play again, willing herself to concentrate, but she could not rid herself of the unpleasant sensation Rupert's nearness had on her. There had been a time when she had thought all men would make her feel the same, but now she knew different. Ted Hall hadn't made her feel that way. He had made her warm and excited and happy. And she was going to see him again on Tuesday, whereas if she was lucky she may not have to see Rupert again until next Christmas! The thought cheered her, making her fingers light and nimble, and although he was right beside her, it was not to Rupert that she played "Drink to Me Only."

The Thornes stayed until after tea, then left abruptly when Donald looked out of the window and saw the frost shining on the paths. He did not want to risk driving his motor on slippery roads. Rebecca, watching them go, felt heady with relief. Not only had Rupert gone, but Christmas Day was nearly over, and that meant one day less until she would see Ted again.

The thought made her nervousness return, and day by day it intensified, so that by the time Tuesday came, it was almost stronger than her desire to go. What was the point? she asked herself as she tried to put up her hair with shaking hands. After tonight she wouldn't be able to see him again, even if he asked. There wouldn't be another convenient G.F.S. concert. And he probably wouldn't ask to see her again anyway. Already he might be regretting having asked her out at all, and perhaps he wouldn't come. She had heard of girls left standing—Marjorie had told her about them.

If it hadn't been for the fact that Marjorie would be calling for her, Rebecca thought she might have given up the idea of going herself! But at twenty past seven, Marjorie knocked on the door. Rebecca's excitement bubbled as she went to answer it, but her father seemed to appear from nowhere and got there first.

"Marjorie, my dear!" he greeted her warmly, and Rebecca's heart sank. A few minutes ago, she had been contemplating not going at all, now, she knew if her father kept Marjie talking, she would be late. Already it was going to be a rush to get there—the G.F.S. concert did not begin until a quarter to eight, so it would have looked odd if they had gone too early.

Rebecca put on her hat and stood buttoning her coat while her father spoke to Marjorie.

"Now, you will make sure that Rebecca stays with you, won't you? I don't want you coming home on your own, the two of you, like last time."

Rebecca's heart turned over, but Marjorie looked the picture of innocence.

"Yes, of course, Mr Church. That was all a misunderstanding. It won't happen again."

If only I could be like her! thought Rebecca.

At last they got away, and Rebecca persuaded Marjorie to trot down the hill. "If he's keen enough, he'll wait," Marjorie grumbled, but Rebecca was taking no chances.

"What are you going to do with yourself?" she asked breathlessly as they hurried past Farmer Brent's fields opposite the church and followed the road along one loop of the horseshoe of shops towards the town's centre.

Marjorie laughed. "Have you ever heard of Esperanto? It's a sort of universal language. There's a class tonight in the rooms above the bicycle shop. I thought I might go."

"Whatever for?" Rebecca asked, surprised.

"It would be nice to be able to talk to foreigners. There might not be a war going on now if we'd been able to talk to the Germans," Marjorie said seriously, then, seeing Rebecca's expression, she laughed again. "I know you're thinking that doesn't sound much like me, so I might as well tell the truth. I should like to be able to talk to those Belgian refugees that are billeted at the farm at the end of our lane. They're rather good-looking boys, aren't they?"

"You're impossible, Marjie!" Rebecca told her, shaking her head.

Marjorie added, "So if you want me to cover up for you again, make it a Tuesday or a Thursday. Then you'll be doing me a favour. My mother thinks you're learning Esperanto, too."

"Just as long as she doesn't expect me to speak it!" Rebecca said, and they both began to giggle. They were still giggling as they crossed the first set of railway lines, and the square silhouette of the George came into view. Instantly, Rebecca was sobered. Her heart thudded painfully against her ribs. Would he be there? And did she even want him to be?

Over the second set of railway lines they went. There were a few people about, but no one who looked in the least like Ted Hall.

"Can you see him?" Marjorie asked.

Rebecca shook her head, unable to find her voice for the lump in her throat. And then a figure detached itself from the doorway of the George, coming across the dark market forecourt towards them, and her nervousness disappeared. It was him. Even in the dark, even though she had seen him only twice before, she would have known him anywhere. She saw him hesitate, puzzled by the fact that there were two of them, and she turned to Marjorie catching at her arm and stopping her.

"I'll be back here at nine o'clock. All right?"

Marjorie smiled and nodded, looking at the boy who was coming towards them. "All right, Becky." Then she had gone, back across the railway lines, the heels of her boots tapping more and more faintly until they could no longer hear them.

Into the awkward silence, Ted said, "I didn't think you were coming."

"I'm sorry, I didn't mean to keep you waiting . . . "

He had been smoking. Now he threw away the cigarette butt and ground it out. Unknown to her, he was wondering how they could spend the evening. Until the moment he'd seen her come across the railway lines with her friend, he had thought she might not come. Now, he realized he couldn't ask a girl like her to have a drink, and it was too late for the picture show at the Palace.

"I don't know what we're going to do," he said. "It's not a very nice night."

She smiled, taking courage from his uncertainty.

"It's not so bad. I don't think it's as cold as it was, and at least the stars are shining."

"You mean, you wouldn't mind going for a walk?"

"As long as it's somewhere quiet, where I'm not likely to meet anyone I know."

It crossed his mind to warn her she shouldn't trust men she didn't really know, but he decided against it.

"Don't you really want anyone to know you're with me?" he asked.

Her face was very small and serious. "I told you. If my father found out, he'd kill me!"

"Well, in that case, we'd better go down to Glebe Bottoms," he said. "Once we get past the Palace and Lower Pit, we aren't likely to meet anybody, and if we do, it's dark."

She nodded agreement, and, as they crossed the road to the sloping lane that led away from the town centre, he wondered if he should take her arm. It seemed the most natural thing to do, yet he couldn't help wondering if she would think it presumptuous of him. He decided to risk it, and to his relief she did not move away. But when two men came into sight, walking up the high pavement towards them, she ducked her head, turning it so that it was almost buried in her collar, and her whole body tensed with apprehension.

She really was scared that her father might find out, Ted thought. He was surprised that in this day and age a girl should be so much under her father's thumb, yet he could understand the older man's motives. She was so vulnerable.

They drew level with the entrance to Lower Pit, and she looked with interest across the yard to the pithead buildings and the great wheels, still now, and silhouetted against the dark sky.

"Is that where you work?"

"No, I work at South Hill Pit."

"Are you a collier?"

He hesitated, torn between basic honesty and the temptation to impress. Honesty won.

"No, I'm a carting boy."

"But you're not a *boy.*"

He laughed, but it pleased him all the same.

"It's just an expression. It doesn't matter how old you are. I know carting boys in their twenties. But I would be a collier now if I'd gone to Wales."

"Wales?" she repeated, puzzled.

"I was going to. I might still one day. But I cart for my father. He couldn't manage without me." Talking to her, his awkwardness faded and his old breezy confidence returned. Being with Rebecca made him feel good, as if the world were his and anything he wanted to do was within reach. Everything looked different, somehow. He could even talk about the job he was tied to and not mind.

He released her arm, and reached instead for her hand. She gave him a quick, half-frightened glance, then her fingers curled round his.

"What about you?" he said. "I don't know anything about you."

"There's not much to tell," she said, but when he pressed her she told him about her family, and the house where they had lived before moving to Hillsbridge, and her dream of having a nursery school of her own, where she could teach and look after the small children she adored.

"You should talk to my brother—he's going to be a school-master," he said with pride, and the conversation turned to Jack, and Fred, and the rest of the family. As they talked, their steps grew slower, and so engrossed in one another were they that it was only when the first outlying cottages at the end of Glebe Bottoms came into view that they realized how far they had walked.

They stopped then, leaning against a gate that led to an isolated farm track.

"I will see you again, won't I, Rebecca?" Ted asked.

In the darkness, she flushed happily.

"Yes . . . well, I hope so. There are Esperanto classes started in the room over the bicycle shop. Marjorie's gone to one now, and I think Father would let me, too."

"Esperanto?" Ted said doubtfully. "I've never thought of learning Esperanto."

"Oh, I didn't mean that," she explained, embarrassed without knowing why. "I suppose I'd have to go once or twice, to pick up a smattering, but Father can't speak it anyway, so he wouldn't know any different . . . "

Her voice tailed away as guilt returned. Why did it have to be this way? Why couldn't she arrange to meet Ted openly? But she knew that if her father suspected for an instant that she might be interested in a boy, she would never be allowed outside the front door unaccompanied. And the thought of never seeing Ted again was unbearable.

"When are these classes, then?" Ted asked.

"Well, Tuesdays, like tonight, and Thursdays, Marjorie says."

"Could you come on Thursday?"

"I don't know," she said doubtfully. "It's a bit soon. Listen, could you see Marjie? She works at Fords, the drapers, in South Hill. I'll give her a message. Only you'll have to be careful how you do it. Mrs Ford wouldn't like to think her shop was being used for message carrying."

"She wouldn't know," Ted said with a laugh. "She'd think it was this Marjorie I was after."

"Oh!" Rebecca said, dismayed, and he realized she was wondering whether that might actually happen.

Gently he turned her towards him. "Don't worry, it's you I want to see," he said roughly. "I wouldn't go to all this trouble for anyone else, you know."

"Wouldn't you?" Her lower lip was thrust out and trembling slightly, but there was muted wonder sparkling in her eyes. The moonlight had made her skin pale and translucent; a tendril of hair had escaped and fallen on to her cheek in a loose curl.

"Rebecca," he said softly.

She did not move or answer. For a moment suspended in time they looked at one another, then he stretched out his hand, tucking the curl behind her ear and sliding his fingers around her neck.

Still she did not move. She might have been carved in alabaster. But when he leaned closer, touching her lips with his, she sighed, a tiny, whispering sigh like a summer breeze in the grass, and her lashes drooped on to her cheeks.

Across the valley, a train whistled as it shunted slowly out of the town, and in the fields that ran down to the river, a cow lowed mournfully. But they might have been in another world. To Ted and Rebecca, reality was the gentle brush of lips on lips, sending out shivers to make them ache with unbearable sweetness. There they stood, cocooned in magic, and it was only when they heard the town clock strike the hour that the spell shattered.

Rebecca twisted away, her head cocked on one side as if she could hardly believe her own ears, and her eyes had gone round with fear.

"Is that nine o'clock?" she asked. "Oh, surely it can't be!"

Ted tried to pull her back for one more kiss, but she wriggled away, tugging at his sleeve.

"There'll be other times," she promised. "But not if I miss Marjie!"

Holding each other's hands, they started back.

WHEN REBECCA had left the house with Marjorie that evening, Alfred had stood at the window, watching her go, and trying to identify the mixture of emotions he was experiencing.

Marjorie always unsettled him. There was something about her that aroused in him sensations he would rather not feel. Perhaps that was the reason for his unrest every time he looked at Rebecca. She was about the same age as Marjorie and, in her own way, just as pretty. Or perhaps it was the way Rupert had openly admired Rebecca on Christmas Day, jumping at the chance to be alone with her. Rupert he approved of, welcomed even, but if *he* found her attractive, it was not likely he would be the only one. There might be others, less suitable, who would lead her into the ways of sin.

Staring out at the clear, frosty night, Alfred thought of his plans for Rebecca. He had always hoped she and Rupert might make a match, but now he felt a sense of urgency that had not been there before. It would be some years before Rupert could seriously think of settling down. Supposing in the meantime Rebecca took up with someone else? For years Alfred had suffered the nightmare of thinking she might meet the fate of his father's servant girl, and now, inexplicably, the fear was mounting. Perhaps it was time to nudge circumstances along in the direction he desired.

Long ago he had decided how he would reward Rupert for taking responsibility for Rebecca's future. Alfred had no sons of his own, something he bitterly regretted. There was only Rebecca, and women he considered neither fit nor able to look after a family's heritage. So to Rupert he would endow everything he possessed—his nest-egg, his house, and the family treasures. He would not expect him to wait for them. He would make over a lump sum to him as soon as he had his agreement on the proposal, and a further lump sum on marriage.

Rupert would find such an inducement irresistible, Alfred was sure. The Thornes were well-to-do but not really rich. They liked to live in a style which ate up most of their income, and Rupert must be finding it difficult to survive as an articled clerk. Besides this, he wasn't the one to pass up a good opportunity when it was offered. And it wasn't as if he didn't think Rebecca attractive.

He smiled, drumming his fingers together and wishing he had broached the subject when Rupert had been here a few days ago. Still, no matter. Perhaps it would be better explained in writing. Rupert would know then that he had no intention of going back on his word.

He went to his writing desk, taking out a sheet of ivory notepaper, pen and ink. Then, in his beautiful copper plate script, he set down his proposal to Rupert. Half an hour later, when Winifred looked in, he was just setting his signature at the bottom.

"I thought you were lost," she quavered. "Whatever are you doing?"

Alfred smiled, slyly.

"Settling Rebecca's future," he told her.

I'LL NEVER forget, thought Rebecca.

She had called her good-nights to Marjorie from the front door, and paused for a moment in the frosty air to compose herself. She was so happy she felt sure it must show, and she was anxious suddenly about the glow of her cheeks and the dizzying thud of her heart. Still, she could not stay out there all night. She opened the door, taking off her coat and hat and patting at her hair in front of the mirror in the hall. Then she went into the living-room.

Both her parents were there, sitting in the old familiar way, yet somehow they were subtly different. She couldn't have explained it —she didn't try. On the chiffonier was a white envelope addressed to Rupert Thorne, and it crossed her mind to wonder idly why her father should be writing to him. But the thought was gone almost as soon as it came. It was unreal, as unreal as her parents' questions about the concert and her own evasive answers. The only reality was the happiness bubbling inside her.

It might be difficult, it might be dangerous, it might mean bribing Marjie and lying to her parents. But whatever was necessary in order to see Ted again, she would do it. Anything . . . anything . . .

Alfred boomed with unaccustomed benevolence, Winifred twittered, but almost unaware of them, Rebecca dreamed on.

I'll never forget, she thought again. As long as I live, I'll never forget.

11

IN THE New Year, Fred marched into a Bath recruiting office, just as he had promised, and signed on as a soldier, for "four years or the duration of the war."

"Well, there you are, I don't suppose it'll go on anything like that long," Ada Clements comforted Charlotte when they met in the gardens, each hanging out their washing in the wintry sunshine, but Charlotte only snorted impatiently. When this thing had started, everyone had said it would be over by Christmas, but they were wrong.

"You must feel proud of him, anyway, Lotty," Ada said. "That was a lovely photo of him in the paper."

"I'd rather it didn't have to be there, Ada," Charlotte said shortly.

As soon as he'd enlisted, the *Mercury* had printed a photograph of Fred in uniform under the headline PATRIOTIC FAMILIES. It had become a regular feature, giving news of all the local boys serving in France, but Charlotte had noticed that too often the same photographs reappeared a few months later in the ROLL OF HONOUR column for the dead and wounded.

Already, there was hardly a family in Hillsbridge who had not suffered the loss of a relative. And as the relentless winter gave way to spring, the list grew longer. Fighting had broken out fiercely again at Neuve Chapelle, the Navy were skirmishing around Gallipoli and the Dardanelles, and in every engagement, it seemed, was somebody's son, or cousin, or nephew. And the deaths of people they knew seemed to go on and on.

"Sergeant Eyles's other son has been killed now," James told them one night when he came in from work. "That's both of them gone."

Charlotte turned cold. Poor Sergeant Eyles, to lose not one boy, but two!

"That's terrible!" she said, with feeling, and to the surprise of all of them, Amy burst into tears.

"What's the matter with you? You didn't know him did you?" Ted asked her.

"No, but . . . oh, Mammy, it just reminded me, that's all," she sobbed. "Mr Davies said today he's starting a scroll at school for all those old pupils that have been killed, and I thought how awful it would be if . . . "

She broke off, covering her face with her hands, and they all knew exactly what she had been going to say.

"Oh, I don't know why he had to go!" Charlotte said, plonking the teapot down with such force that tea spurted from the spout and splashed on to the tablecloth. "There was no sense in it."

"No sense at all," James agreed, and Amy wailed again.

"Oh, Mammy, he won't be killed, will he?"

Her only answer was Harry drumming his spoon on his plate as he waited for his food, and Amy went on: "Supposing we were never to see him again—ever!"

"Oh, Amy, be quiet, do!" Charlotte snapped. "I expect they'll let him come home before they send him off to France."

Harry, thoroughly frustrated by the delay, now gave a hearty kick to the high chair standing at the corner of the table. He didn't use it any more, but Charlotte had kept it for Alex, whom Sarah had brought over that afternoon. It had spindly legs and was easily tipped, and under Harry's well-aimed onslaught it toppled over with a crash.

When Charlotte had righted it, smacked Harry, and sent Nipper out, James said thoughtfully, "How would you all like to go and see our Fred?"

"See Fred?" Charlotte repeated. "How could we?"

"Well," James said slowly, "I was thinking we could hire a motor car."

"*What?*"

Even Jack, who was home this week, and was on the settle with his nose in a book, looked up in amazement.

"Us—hire a motor?" she said again. "Oh, James, don't talk so silly."

"I'm serious," James said stoically. "Didn't I tell you young Cliff Button is setting up in business?"

Charlotte looked hard at him, still wondering if he was joking. Since most of Stanley Bristow's horses had been requisitioned for the army, there had been a shortage of transport in the town, and Cliff Button's motor would fill the gap. But it had never entered her head that they would hire it, even for short journeys. And as for going all the way to Fred's camp on Salisbury Plain — it seemed an incredible idea.

"But it's a long way." she said. "It must be fifteen or twenty miles."

"Motors can really travel. We ought to be able to get there in an hour."

"Oh, James, do you think we could?"

"It's up to you, Lotty."

"Oh, Mammy, say yes! Say yes!" Amy was hopping up and down, her tears forgotten.

"We'd have to find out what it would cost," Charlotte said cautiously, and then, abruptly, "No, why should we bother about the cost? Whatever it is, it'd be worth it to see our Fred. How many will it seat, James?"

"I wouldn't like to say for sure. I should think perhaps six of us —and the children, of course."

"That's us," said Amy, prodding Harry.

"Well, there's four of us here," Charlotte said, counting. "If the boys are able to come, that is. And then there's our Dolly, and Jim and Sarah . . . "

"When would it be?" Ted asked.

"A Sunday, I should think. We're all here on Sundays, except Dolly. And you never know, Captain Fish might give her the day off, if she explained why she wanted it. Even *you're* here on a Sunday, Ted, though it's about the only time you are."

"I don't know that I should want to go anyway," Ted said.

"Not to see our Fred?" Charlotte was indignant. "Well, that's a fine thing, I must say! The trouble is, you've got your mind on this girl of yours and nothing else."

"Oh, all right, count me in," Ted said hastily.

On the day of the trip—the last Sunday in March—Charlotte was up early, making sandwiches and packing them into a picnic box she had borrowed from Peggy. And for once it was no effort to get the family ready in time. Except for Ted who had had yet another late night with his concert party.

When the large black motor turned the corner, doors and windows opened up and down the rank. The children crowded round, eager, but afraid to get too close, and Nipper ran away down over the gardens in fright.

"Don't worry, I'll give him some scraps at dinner-time," Peggy said. "You just go off and have a good time."

While Jack and Ted climbed into the front, and the others into the back, Cliff Button put his back into cranking the starting handle and after a few vigorous turns, the engine spluttered into life, making the motor shudder as if it were about to explode. Cliff leaped back into the driver's seat, and with a crashing of gears they were off.

They passed Martha Durrant on her way to chapel and waved to her. The look of sheer amazement on her face made Charlotte and the children laugh so much that they immediately forgot their nervousness.

"I expect Martha thinks we shall go straight to the devil!" she said.

And from his lofty position in the front, Ted remarked, "I'll tell you this, Mam, I shouldn't want to go to heaven if they're all like Mrs Durrant up there!"

The car bounced over the first level crossing and turned left into Westbury Road. Between the two sets of lines and the river, the road ran past the newspaper shop that always fascinated them because the back of it was built on stilts in the river and into a hill almost as steep as their own. The car shuddered and slowed so that they thought it would never make it, but miraculously it did, and soon they were out in the open countryside, bowling along a grey ribbon of road between green fields.

When they had passed through the market town of Frome, they knew they must be almost half-way there.

"So this is Salisbury Plain," Charlotte said, taking in the avenues of trees in new and tiny leaf that gave way to grassy slopes, stretching away as far as the eye could see and broken only by clumps of stunted, windswept bushes. And in spite of the purpose behind their trip, she felt the weight in her heart lighten.

Here, on the plain, a new season's life was unfolding beneath a clean, washed-blue sky. Even in the chuntering motor, she could feel the peace of it, and the promise of the perennial rebirth of vitality and fresh, singing life, and it filled her with hope. Here, the whole of nature was proving that life rises, phoenix-like, from the ashes of the greyest December day. And in it there seemed to be a message for mortals hell-bent on destruction.

Then they rounded a corner, and suddenly the peace was no more.

The training camp had been built on the side of a hill and just outside a village, several meadows given over to hutments and bell-tents. As Cliff Button pulled into the side of the road and stopped, an army vehicle emerged from what had once been a farm track, raising a cloud of dust from the road that was more used to hay-wagons and threshing machines, drawn home from the fields by plodding shire-horses. And in a flat field nearby the road, a squad of men and boys in ill-fitting khaki uniforms was drilling untidily.

"Dear Lord," Charlotte said, her sick fear returning.

When they met Fred, it became more of a reality than ever. In uniform, with the rough khaki accentuating the fine, scrubbed fair-ness of his skin, Fred looked younger than his nineteen years. But there was a glow about him that was timeless—and terrifying.

So have they looked through the ages, young men going to war, with their thirst for adventure heightened by an illusion of gallantry and heroism. Fred's uniform was that of an English Tommy, but his proud, glowing face might have belonged to a Crusader following the Lionheart to the Holy Land, or a Highlander fighting for the Pretender at Culloden Field. The rigours of training had done noth-ing to quench his fervour. He had not even begun to question the wisdom of the war lords who would use him as a tiny weapon in their armoury, one of an expendable, nameless mass of humanity who might, if he was lucky, live long enough to kill a German or two or, if he was not, stop a bullet or a piece of shrapnel.

Men like Fred lay dead in their hundreds for mile upon mile in front of the trenches in France, their bodies heaped as they had fallen because neither side could get out to bury them, and still the war lords used the survivors like human chess pieces. Armies were marched this way and that, meaningless strategies were attempted, and games of power were played out. But Fred neither knew this, nor cared.

He held his head proudly above his scratchy collar as he told his family of the training he was undergoing, of the marches across miles of open country to the rifle ranges, and the places earmarked for practice in throwing bombs. He straightened his shoulders uncon-sciously as he described the rifle and bayonet drill, and laughed as he told of the physical jerks and fitness tests, for his life in the pits had made him strong enough to regard most of them as games. And without a thought to the perils that lay ahead he looked forward eagerly to getting his chance to take a shot at the Kaiser.

There was something precious in that day with Fred. Pride and patriotism mixed with sadness, and flavoured with the urgency of a day stolen out of time. But when they left him, Charlotte felt drained, as if there was nothing inside her but a great, yawning emptiness. She wanted to take him in her arms and hold him the way she had held him as a baby, protecting him, and showing the world that to her at least he was special and irreplaceable. But she knew that now the time for pleading was over. She could best help him by being strong for him. So she left the tears to Dolly and Amy and kept her own emotions to herself.

As they drove back over the plain, darkness fell. The fresh promise of the day was forgotten as the sun went down, pale and early, behind the curve of green, and in the half light there was a cheerlessness about the grey and empty landscape. The darkness and the loneliness were a warning for the future, unwanted and inescapable, and Charlotte shivered, staring with unseeing eyes at the tunnel of light thrown ahead of them by the lamps of the motor.

"What's wrong, Mammy?" Amy asked, but Charlotte did not answer her.

"Let's have a sing-song," she said.

Soon Ted was leading them in one music hall favourite after another, and the wind was catching the words and blowing them away, back across the plain. And if Charlotte felt she had left a part of herself behind, in the hutments under the hill, none of the others, except perhaps James, guessed it.

AS THE spring turned to summer, there was a new subject of conversation among the men in the bars of the George and the Miners Arms. Herbert Gait, the hated under-manager at South Hill Pit, was secretly calling on Molly Hamblin, the wife of one of the South Hill colliers. But as always, everyone but Wilf, the cuckolded husband, seemed to know about it.

"Ould'st think he could smell a rat," Hubie Freke observed sagely, draining his pint and looking at the other regulars with rheumy old eyes.

"Ah, but the husband's often the last to find out, 'sknow," Moses Brimble said.

"Or the wife!" Ewart Brixey put in wickedly, and the others chuckled into their pints but said nothing. It was common knowledge amongst them that Moses had had a fling with a girl at Purldown a few years earlier, but it was all over and done with now, and none of them but the hot-headed young Brixey would have been tactless enough to bring it up.

"I reckon it's scandalous," Walter Clements said. "A man in Gait's position. It's taking advantage if you ask me. He waits till he knows the man's underground and out of the way, and then off he goes for an hour. Somebody ought to tell him."

The men mumbled non-committally into their beer. Wilf Hamblin was known to have a fiery temper and no one intended to be the one to break the news to him that Gait was making a fool of him.

"If you ask me, it's a pity the army can't requisition Gaity like they did your horses, Stanley," Ewart went on with a laugh. "He could be our secret weapon. Just the stink of him'd be enough to kill off a few Germans."

"Well, you've heard they've started using gas in the trenches," James said, referring to the reports that were filtering back from the renewed fighting at Ypres, and the talk turned, as it so often did, to the war.

But the men did not forget about Gaity and Molly Hamblin. The talk spread in ever-widening circles until almost all the miners at South Hill knew what was going on. Only Wilf remained in ignorance.

"Gait's a lucky sod not to have had Wilf after him before now," James said to Charlotte when he told her about it.

But not even Gait's luck could last forever. One morning, while working underground, Wilf got his hand caught between the tubs. It was not a serious accident, but bad enough to stop him working.

He took the cage to the surface, swopped his helmet for his cloth cap, and set off for home. The men on the screens who saw him go were agog. They knew that Gaity was missing from his office, and guessed that meant he had gone to visit Mrs Hamblin.

The Hamblins lived in Pit Cottages, two doors away from Jim and Sarah, so Wilf was able to get home within a few minutes, long before anyone could warn Gaity that he was on his way. Sarah, who was in the garden, cutting a cabbage for dinner, had a grandstand view of the whole drama.

"I couldn't believe my eyes," she told Jim later. "I saw Wilf come round the corner, and I knew Mr Gait was in there with Molly. The door was closed, and the windows, and I reckon they were upstairs.

I didn't know what to do. I couldn't warn Molly. There wasn't time for anything."

"You wouldn't have done right to warn her anyway," Jim said sternly. "You're best off not meddling with other people's business, Sal."

"I know, but I was really scared," Sarah went on. "He's got such a terrible temper, I thought he might kill him. I mean, for all that he's on the stout side, Mr Gait doesn't look very strong."

"He's just a bully," Jim said. "Yes, carry on, Sarah. What happened?"

"There was all this shouting and screaming—I could hear it as clearly as if I'd been in there with them. Then the door opened and out came Gait—all of a heap, if you know what I mean. It was just as if Wilf had got hold of him and thrown him. He landed on his hands and knees, and before he could get up there was Wilf kicking him and Molly hanging on to his arm and crying and trying to stop him. And her dress was all undone, Jim. It was disgusting, really, especially when I think of that nasty, dirty-looking little man . . . "

"Money talks," Jim said darkly, and when she looked at him questioningly: "Go on, then, finish telling me what happened."

"I thought there was going to be murder done," Sarah said. "Mr Gait's face was all bleeding, and he couldn't get his breath—he was winded, I suppose. Wilf stood over him, shouting, "You leave my missus alone, you filthy swine, or you'll get what's coming to you." Gait started to pick himself up, holding his face. "You've broke my nose," he said to Wilf, all pained-like, though how he had the nerve with Wilf standing over him, I don't know. Then Wilf got hold of him round the collar. "If I catch you anywhere near my wife again, I'll break your neck, never mind your bloody nose!" he said. "And it won't be only me you'll have to reckon with. There'll be two or three of me mates as well!" Then he pushed Mr Gait over again, and went back into the house. I thought I'd seen the last of him, but a minute later, out he came again, with Mr Gait's hat—the one he's always wearing—and just threw it at him. "And take your bloody hat with you!" he shouted. Well, Jim, it couldn't have been funnier, really. The wind swept up the hat, and blew it all down the garden. And there was Mr Gait chasing after it, with blood pouring down his face!"

Jim shook his head, laughing. "I wish I'd been here. That's a sight a lot of us would have liked to see. Gaity getting his come-uppance, and not before time!"

Sarah sobered. "Oh, I know he's not liked, Jim, but surely nobody would wish that on him."

"You're wrong there," Jim told her. "All the blokes at South Hill would for a start. They aren't going to forget this in a hurry."

Jim's prediction soon proved correct, for O'Halloran got to hear of it and sent for Mr Gait to explain. What exactly went on behind the walls of his office, no one ever knew for certain, but it was widely supposed this was just the excuse O'Halloran had been waiting for. For some time he had been uneasy about Gait's way of dealing with the men, which was so different from his own, and now he had proof of Gait misusing his position, he felt the limits had been reached.

Gait did not leave immediately. O'Halloran was too shrewd for that. But the men suspected things were being made gradually more and more uncomfortable for him, until one day he announced he was leaving to work in the Yorkshire coal-field.

All the men were delighted to hear of Gait's departure, for he was a man who had long since lost the respect of the workers. A new under-manager was installed at South Hill, and soon Gaity was completely forgotten. Occasionally his name would come up over a pint, and the incident with Molly Hamblin would still raise a malicious chuckle.

That was Gait's memorial in Hillsbridge. It was not one he would have cared for.

12

JULY sunshine, streaming through a gap in the curtains, woke Rebecca Church.

Although it was still early, the air was already heavy with the promise of a scorching summer day.

It was going to be fine, she thought, relief and happiness coursing through her. It was going to be fine, and she'd be able to meet Ted at the church garden party this afternoon as they had planned.

It was more than a week now since she'd seen him, a week when she had been haunted by the constant fear that it might rain and the garden party would have to be moved indoors or cancelled altogether. That would have been a disappointment that didn't bear thinking about, for she had no idea how or when they would be able to meet for the next few weeks. The Esperanto classes had stopped for the summer holiday, and excuses to go into Hillsbridge alone or with Marjorie were hard to come by.

Each time she met Ted the difficulties and danger seemed to increase. Sometimes her nerves were stretched almost to breaking point, so that she wondered if perhaps it would be better to have a break from the scheming and the skulking and the fear of being caught.

It had been bad enough in the spring, when wet day had followed wet day and half the valley had been under water. Then there had been times when her mother had refused to let her get herself soaked through walking down the hill on a Tuesday evening and she had had to hide her disappointment and the horrid feeling that came from knowing that Ted would be waiting in vain for her. But now, with the evenings long and light, it was more difficult than ever. They could go across the fields when it was dry enough underfoot, but there was always the chance of being seen, and even the Picture House afforded less cover than it had done, for more often than not they had to queue in broad daylight while Henry Pinker, the one-time sergeant major turned commissionaire, stood at the door and shouted his almost unintelligible, "Early doors this way—three, six, nine, a shilling!" in a fair imitation of his former parade-ground bellow.

Rebecca felt the risks were greater now than they had ever been, and with each successfully conducted rendezvous it seemed to her the odds of being found out became greater too. But when she said as much to Ted, he brushed her fears aside.

"If he hasn't found out in six months, why should he find out now?" he asked with his usual confidence, and she had said no more, for although she was far from convinced, there was really nothing she could do about it. She couldn't suggest not seeing him for a few weeks. Her hunger for him was too great. And besides, there was always the nagging fear that, if she was away from him for too long, he might find someone else. So she suppressed the mounting sense of foreboding and tried to forget her doubts and the fear of what would happen if her father learned that she had been deceiving him.

Six months had done nothing to dull the magic that came from being together. There were still so many things to talk about, so many things to discover about one another.

They had watched the bare winter trees turn green for spring. They had picked the first bluebells in the woods that flanked the river. They had laughed in wonder at the spindly legged calf in Farmer Brent's yard as it took its first staggering steps, And as the earth swelled with promise and burst into new life, so their love grew from their first uncertain tender kiss until it seemed to fill the whole world.

I never knew it could be like this, Rebecca thought, drawing her knees up so that the sheets formed a cool tent around her legs. I never for one single moment imagined that this was what they meant by love—this breathless anticipation, this feeling of living in a fairy-tale world where wonderful things really happen.

A tiny breeze stirred the curtain, wafting the scent of a fresh summer morning into the room, and Rebecca let the sheets collapse around her legs, turned them back and slipped out of bed.

There was water in the jug on the wash-stand, and she poured some into the bowl, splashing it on to her face. Then she stood back, looking at her reflection in the mirror.

Her hair, falling thickly to the high collar of her cambric night-gown, framed her small heart-shaped face, and the cold water had brought a glow to her cheeks and a sparkle to her eyes. Slowly she unfastened the nightgown, slipping her arms out of the sleeves, and letting it slide down into a heap at her feet. Then she reached out and tilted the mirror so that it threw back a reflection of her body: small firm breasts, rounded hips and plump white thighs separated by a small pointed tuft of soft brown hair. For a long moment she looked, safe in the knowledge that the rest of the house was sleeping, studying every detail as she had never studied it before, and pride began to warm her. She ran her hands lightly over her belly, apprais-ing the flare of her hips and thighs, then moving up to cup her breasts. In her hands, they felt firm and full, and as she rubbed them gently she felt the soft little nipples swell and harden against her palms.

Something stirred inside her then, a shiver of excitement deep inside the most secret part of her, and a smile curved her lips so that her whole face looked somehow fuller and more mature.

Fleetingly she thought of the decorum with which she had been raised, the terrifying modesty that had led her mother to explain menstruation as a way of getting rid of blood if you make too much, the shame she had felt when first one breast and then the other had begun to grow, small, unevenly shaped swellings beneath her all-concealing camisole. They had led her to believe there was some dark secret about maturity, so that she had tried to dress and undress herself without a single moment of nudity. But now there was something in the way she felt—in the way Ted made her feel—that made her bold, and it seemed to her that she stood on the brink of something enormous and wonderful and unknown.

She moved her hands again, sliding them over her skin and feeling the small, delicious shivers that spread like ripples on a pond.

Why should she be ashamed? she asked herself. Why should she be ashamed to touch her own body, or even look at it? God had made her this way, after all, just as he'd made the trees and the flowers and that sweet, rubber-legged, little calf. He'd given her breasts and a belly and secret places between her thighs, and the Bible taught that God was pleased with his work . . .

"Rebecca!"

So lost in wonder was she that, until the thunderous voice shattered her dream world, she had no idea she was being watched, and she jumped violently, instinctively trying to hide her body.

"Rebecca, for the love of God what are you doing? Cover yourself at once!"

He stood in the doorway like an avenging angel, a robe pulled on over his nightgown, his face distorted with rage and disbelief. Beneath his furious gaze, her shock became acute embarrassment. She fumbled for her own gown with hands that shook. Why couldn't he go back to his own room while she dressed herself? Why did he have to stand there, looking?

Her legs were trembling so that she had to struggle to get the nightgown past her knees; she tried to turn away from him, and almost fell as she stepped on a fold of material. After long, agonizing moments she managed to get it up over her hips. Another wriggle, and she was able to pull it high enough to cover her breasts.

Terrified, she turned to look at him, clutching the cambric folds about her. But to her surprise he said nothing. His eyes, dark and furious, held hers for a moment, then with a tightening of his mouth, Alfred Church swung around and left her and went back along the landing to his own room.

Still shaking and still clutching her nightgown around her, Rebecca stood in the middle of the room and waited. But the sounds she dreaded to hear did not come. Soon afterwards her mother began moving about, and she knew the day had begun.

But when she reached for her camisole, which was hanging over the back of the wicker-work chair, and slipped it on, she managed to do so without baring her body for a single moment, and suddenly it seemed as if the morning sun had dimmed and everything was tinged with shadow.

THE SIGHT of Rebecca had shocked Alfred more than he would have believed possible. For the life of him he did not know what had made him cross the landing and look through her bedroom door that morning when he got out of bed to use the chamberpot, and he could only think he must have been guided by Providence. For although he had been aware for a long while now that she was growing up, what he had seen this morning made him realize that Rebecca was not only a mature young woman, but also a sensual one.

He had stood in the doorway, looking at her with fascinated disgust, and the indecent beauty of her body seemed to impress itself upon his memory, so that all day as he went about his tasks he kept seeing her. How could such a transformation have taken place under his very nose and he not have realized it? he asked himself. Not only that, how could he reconcile his shy, modest daughter with a hussy who could fondle her breasts and stand to admire her naked body in a mirror? It was what he had imagined in his worst nightmares, and it was becoming a reality. Heaven only be praised that Rupert had agreed to his proposals for a settlement on Rebecca, although he would have to wait until he had finished his articles before marrying her.

If he could have managed it without Rupert losing face, Alfred would have liked to suggest that he should finance the couple so that they could be married without delay, but it couldn't be done. He, like Rupert, would have to be patient. But the intervening years would be difficult ones, when her every move would have to be watched, for there must be no question of her letting her sexuality betray her now.

The thought reminded him that Rebecca had been going out a great deal more lately than she used to, and he wondered at the wisdom of this. She was with Marjorie, it was true, but if he was honest with himself, he was not sure that Marjorie was the best company for her, and although the things they did seemed harmless enough, there were times when he had asked himself just what it was they learned at Esperanto that had brought such a sparkle to Rebecca's eyes and made her so happy and eager to please.

All day he thought about it, aware of some sixth sense telling him all was not as it should be, and that afternoon, when Rebecca and Marjorie left for the parish garden party that was being held on the Rectory lawns, the feeling intensified. How could he know if Rebecca was behaving as she should? There was only one way to find out.

"I think I'll walk down to the garden party myself," he said to Winnie, who was hulling strawberries for jam on the lawn behind the house.

She looked up at him anxiously. "In this heat, Alfred? Why don't you wait until it's a bit cooler."

He hesitated, tempted by the thought of a pleasant half-hour's relaxation on the shady swing seat, but the memory of Rebecca's abandon this morning was too strong.

"It's a beautiful afternoon!" he told her. "It's all down hill going, and it'll be cooler by the time I come back."

As he started down the hill, however, where the cow parsley grew high in the hedges, and the banks were white with moonflowers, he realized just how hot it was. Before he had gone far, perspiration began to trickle down his neck, his waistcoat felt uncomfortably tight, and at every step his shoes stuck to the newly-tarred road. Briefly he allowed himself the luxury of toying with the idea of buying himself a horseless carriage, like Donald Thorne's, and learning to drive it. It was, he thought, the kind of status symbol a man in his position needed to keep up his standing in the town. But not even the contemplation of a motor could keep his thoughts from Rebecca for long.

He walked on, past Farmer Brent's fields, past the church and the cottages opposite, with their upstairs windows thrown open to the summer afternoon, but their doors firmly shut and their gardens deserted. The town was so quiet that, if he had not seen the preparations for the garden party from his office window, he might have thought Rebecca had invented the whole thing. But even as the thought crossed his mind he heard the strains of the town band, and as he walked on it grew louder and louder until it seemed to sit in a mushroom cloud over the Rectory lawns and spill out into the road beyond.

At the stone-pillared entrance gate, Caroline Archer sat beneath a large black umbrella, a bowl for collecting admittance charges on a card table in front of her. Alfred paid his tuppence and went in, pausing for a moment or two on the drive to look around him.

At first sight, it seemed the whole of Hillsbridge must have come to the garden party. Most of the adults were clustered around the improvised bandstand at the end of the drive, while the young ones were trying their hand at the croquet game and the other competitions. A small marquee had been set up, and there were a number of stalls selling everything from pincushions to home-made pickle. Grace O'Halloran, pretty as a picture, was running the hoop-la stall and doing a roaring trade with the men, while her younger sister Stella was in charge of a bran tub for the children.

Because of the heat, most people were trying to stay in the shade under the trees, but Alfred could not see Rebecca or Marjorie anywhere. Once, he thought he caught a glimpse of Marjorie's cream blouse and dark skirt, but before he could make his way towards her he found himself confronted by Reuben Clarke, the bachelor who had succeeded Mr Archer as Rector.

"How nice to see someone from Withydown here" he beamed, stationing himself directly in Alfred's line of vision. "And how fortunate we are with the weather, too! I think we may say the Good Lord is smiling on our effort here today."

Alfred surveyed Reuben Clarke with contempt. He had no time for a parish spiritual leader who lived in the Rectory alone with his housekeeper. But Reuben Clarke was perhaps not the most sensitive of men and seemed unaware of the expression of distaste that was fixed on Alfred's face.

"I suppose the truth is that people are glad of an excuse to enjoy themselves," he went on. "Since this war started, they've missed the flower shows and fêtes. One can understand the need for economy, of course, but it is still nice to see a garden party in full swing, even if we did need the excuse of raising funds for our boys at the Front to justify it."

"Quite . . . quite . . . " Alfred muttered impatiently. He turned away, and as he did so, he saw Marjorie among the crowd. Cutting Reuben Clarke off in mid-flow, he raised an imperious hand to her, but to his surprise and annoyance she seemed to look straight through him before turning and disappearing hastily into the crowd again.

Puzzled, he bade the Rector a curt "Good afternoon" and hurried

177

across the lawn after her. How could she have failed to see him? And, more to the point, where was Rebecca?

He pushed his way irritably between the people, searching for the two girls. Drat it, they'd both disappeared! It was just as if they were trying to avoid him.

The crowd in front of him parted slightly, and Alfred pushed forward. Then he stopped abruptly. There, in front of the bandstand, was Marjorie, and with her a young man—a young man who actually had his arm round her waist. But of Rebecca there was no sign.

Swelling with indignation, Alfred strode forward. The young man turned and saw him, and his arm dropped from Marjorie's waist. But it was at Marjorie herself that Alfred found himself looking. She had turned pale suddenly, and her eyes were startled and afraid.

"Why, Mr Church, I didn't expect to see you here . . . " she said in a desperate effort at normality. "Becky didn't say . . . "

Although he was inwardly seething, he asked stonily, "Where is Rebecca, Marjorie?"

"Becky?" There was just the smallest hesitation, then she went on smoothly, "She's just gone off to search for a . . . a privy, Mr Church. It's very hot, and we've been drinking rather a lot of lemonade."

Alfred's brows lowered, and he glared at Marjorie to express his distaste at the indelicacy. Then he let his eyes pass to the boy who stood awkwardly beside Marjorie.

"Is she alone?" he asked, his voice heavy with meaning.

"Of course." Marjorie's eyes were wide and innocent. "Who would be with her, Mr Church? I'm just . . . just talking to Billy while I wait for her. Billy's an errand boy at the shop where I work."

Alfred inclined his head majestically.

"I see. I will wait for her here with you then, shall I?"

An expression that might almost have been alarm flashed across her face and was gone, then she tucked her arm into his, smiling up at him with all her old charm.

"Oh, I wouldn't do that. She'll be ages, and it's very hot. Why don't you sit down and have a cup of tea, and I'll tell her you're here when she comes back. You really do look as if you could do with a cup of tea."

He hesitated, melting slightly. It was impossible to be angry with Marjorie for long, and the thought of a cup of tea was very tempting.

"Come on, Mr Church," She tugged at his arm, smiling up at him. "Come and sit down, and I'll tell you what I'll do. I'll go and look for Rebecca myself, in case she's stopped to talk to someone. It's so beautifully cool in the Rectory it's tempting to do just that."

"In the Rectory? She's in the Rectory?" he repeated and she laughed.

"Of course. Where did you think she'd go? They wouldn't expect young ladies to walk along to the public conveniences."

Slightly mollified by the fact that she was now completely ignoring the young man named Billy, he let her lead him across to where the tables and chairs had been set out on the grass.

"Now you sit there, Mr Church. Look, that's the best table. Take it quickly while it's empty, and I'll get your tea."

Her touch on his arm and her bobbing curls had almost restored his humour, and as he stretched his long legs he found himself wondering momentarily whether people might be deceived into thinking she was actually with him. The thought had the effect of making him feel almost young again, and he narrowed his eyes, watching her join the queue at the tea stall and then pick her way back towards him across the grass carrying the cup and saucer with the utmost care.

"There you are, Mr Church. Now I'll go and find Becky."

From the seat she had chosen for him he had a perfect view of her slim figure dancing down the drive in the direction of the Rectory, and he watched her until she had disappeared into a group of folk gathered round a stall by the front door. Then he stirred sugar into his tea and settled back to drink it.

Clearly, he thought, his suspicions had been unjustified. He should have known that Rebecca would be safe with Marjorie.

When a fly began buzzing around his table, Alfred Church was annoyed. He had always hated flies—they had gone against his code of extreme hygiene at all times. And now this fly was becoming persistent and landing on his teacup. He flapped at it aggressively with his handkerchief, but he accidentally knocked it into the tea, where it buzzed loudly in an attempt to save itself from drowning. Disgusted, he rose to get himself another cup, but as he did so, he saw a girl with bouncing curls and a cream blouse hurrying away down the drive. It was Marjorie! But where was she going? She was supposed to be fetching Rebecca from the Rectory!

The cup of tea forgotten, he stared after her, until she disappeared through the gates and into the street. Then, clumsily, he pushed the chair aside and went to follow her.

By the time he had reached the gates, she was half-way along Town Street and he hurried after her. For a few moments when she disappeared around the slow curve in the road, he was afraid of losing her, but when he rounded the curve himself and saw her still hurrying in the direction of Eastlands he slowed his pace and moved closer to the wall that bordered the road.

She was going into the churchyard, if he wasn't mistaken! Could it be that the Rector had asked her to run some errand for him? If so he was making a fool of himself by following her. And yet . . .

No, whatever errand Marjorie was on, it had nothing to do with the Rector, he was certain. If she had had nothing to hide, she would have come back and explained where she was going, not just slipped past him. In addition to all her other actions this afternoon, he realized she was behaving very oddly indeed, and his instinct, clearer now that the entrancing Marjorie was a street-length away, told him that whatever it was, it had something to do with Rebecca.

Marjorie, hurrying still, skirted the high pavement at the roadside and passed through the arched gate into the churchyard, and, puzzled, Alfred hastened his own step again.

Surely Rebecca was not in the churchyard? It was a pleasant enough spot, certainly, particularly on a hot afternoon such as this, with the broad path winding between the weathered old gravestones and the tall yew trees throwing large patches of shade, but there had been shady spots in the Rectory garden too without leaving the garden party and walking right across Hillsbridge. Unless . . .

Alfred's eyes narrowed suddenly, and his breath came faster. The only possible reason for coming to this part of town on a Saturday afternoon in summer would be to find solitude. There was no shortage of that. Beyond the churchyard, the meadows lay, green and sleeping beneath the still hot sun, stretching all the way to the river and beyond, curling around the secret places on the banks and under the trees, waist-high in purple loosestrife and yellow flags. But Rebecca would not have come to look for solitude alone. There would have been someone with her.

The memory of a December night and a boy, half seen in the fog, came to Alfred. Then, in a blinding flash of realization, a hundred other things fitted into place so completely that he marvelled at his own stupidity in not seeing the truth before. The change in Rebecca's manner, her gaiety, the number of times she had been out unescorted in the past months, and the way he had found her only this morning admiring her body in the mirror—yes, that particularly —could mean one thing and one only.

A boy! Rebecca was deceiving him with a boy, like some common, whoring slut! He had raised her with firmness and decency and the moment he allowed her a little freedom she behaved in this disgraceful, filthy manner!

Almost beside himself, he hurried on, and as he rounded the corner of the church building, he saw Marjorie again, standing beneath the yew trees at the churchyard's edge, and looking down across the low stone wall towards the farm track. Her eyes were shaded against the sun as she peered anxiously to left and right, and with her arms raised, the thin material of her blouse strained enticingly across her slender back. But for once, in his blind fury, he hardly noticed. He left the path, his boots making no sound on the soft grass, and came up behind her without Marjorie knowing he was there. Then his rage burst from him in an explosive: "So!"

She spun round, gasping with fright and turning pale as she had done at the garden party.

"Mr Church . . . " she stammered.

He towered over her, his face purple with fury.

"Where is Rebecca?"

She swallowed, recovering herself a little, though her eyes were still round with fear.

"Rebecca? I told you, she's . . . "

"Don't lie to me!" He caught her by the arms. "You've done enough lying, you brazen hussy! All this time she's been deceiving me, and you've been helping her. Don't deny it!"

"But Mr Church, I didn't mean to . . . "

"Lies! All lies! Just now you looked me in the eye and told me she was in the Rectory, while all the time . . . You're lying, cheating vipers, the pair of you!"

His fingers bit painfully into her arms, pulling her closer, and his breath came in harsh gasps. Sweat poured down his face, and his eyes were wide and crazed, the eyes of a maniac. Terrified now, she tried to break free, but he held her fast.

"Lying, whoring vipers!" he roared.

The smell of him came at her then, the camphor in his clothes, the sweat and his fetid breath, all in one nauseating cloud. She twisted her head away, retching, and he towered over her, half-lifting her off her feet and pressing her back. She struggled in blind panic, too shocked even to cry out, but he was too strong for her. For agonizing, timeless moments she pulled and wriggled and squirmed, kicking at him helplessly.

"Please!" she sobbed. "Oh, stop, please stop!"

But he was like a man possessed. Back, back, he pressed her until she thought her spine would snap.

Then, just as the edges of her consciousness began closing in like the dark, curling edges of an old photograph, the pressure seemed to lessen, and as she fought her way back through reeling senses, she became aware that he was no longer looking at her, but beyond her, towards the river. For another moment, still paralysed with fear, she dangled from his grasp like a limp rag doll. Then, with a sudden violent movement, he flung her aside. She hit the ground with a sick thud and rolled over in the long grass.

He was staring still towards the river, but Marjorie did not stop now to wonder what it was he had seen. She only knew she had to get away from him, back to the garden party and normality. Somehow, she found herself on her feet, and picking up her skirts, she fled. In the bright sunshine she was shivering violently, and her teeth were chattering. Back across the grass she ran, darting between the old stone tombstones and half-buried kerbs, and as she ran, she cried softly, "Dear God, he's mad! Mad!"

FOR REBECCA and Ted, the afternoon had been a perfect one.

In the cool places under the trees, where the heat of the sun had been unable to penetrate, they had lazed in the long dry grass, Ted sprawling full length, Rebecca sitting tidily with her knees drawn up beneath her long skirt and her hat tossed down beside her.

They had talked for a while and dreamed for a while, enjoying the sounds and the smells of a summer afternoon. Beside them, the river, still full enough from the recent rain, had gurgled over the stones, and there was the occasional splashing flurry as a moorhen scuttled for the bank.

Ted, looking up at the blue sky above the tracery of green, was reminded of another summer day, long ago, when he had come to the river to swim and been caught in the act by Rosa Clements. He chuckled to himself, on the point of relating the story to Rebecca, but at the last moment, looking up at her small dreaming face, he checked himself. She might not understand. She might even be shocked. She would know nothing of the pleasures of swimming naked in ice-cold water, that much was certain, and in spite of the desire a look or a touch from her could stir in him, he wanted, in some perverse way, to keep her as innocent as she was. Although he longed to possess her, he knew he should wait until the time was right if it meant waiting forever.

Sensing his dreaming mood, she turned to look at him, pensively. "Hello," she said.

He pulled a blade of grass, reaching out to tickle her nose, and when she tried to snatch it from him he pulled her down beside him.

"Stop it!" she whispered, laughter bubbling in her throat. "Let me go, you bully."

He held her fast, her head against his shoulder, and when her half-hearted struggles subsided he stroked her hair away from her face and kissed her eyes.

"Oh, Becky." His breath on her face was warm and soft like the summer breeze, his voice low with suppressed longing. His hand moved gently across the top of her breast, hovering on the buttons of her dress.

"Ted, you wouldn't . . . " Her hand covered his, and he felt her tense against him.

Desire flared within him so that he longed to push her down into the dry grass and feel her body, soft and yielding, beneath his. But even as the passion within him mounted, he felt her fingers cool and restricting on his and heard her whisper again urgently, "Ted, no! You mustn't! You wouldn't, would you, Ted?"

With a supreme effort he regained control of himself.

"No, love. I wouldn't. That's not to say I don't want to though."

"Oh, Ted!" She raised herself on one elbow, looking down at him, but today there was no reproach in her eyes, only tenderness. "Oh, Ted, is it very bad—wanting me?"

He felt a moment's mild surprise. She was learning, he thought. The Becky he had first met six months ago would never have said a thing like that.

"It's not so bad," he said. "Oh, in one way, maybe. It hurts, here, when I look at you. Did you know that? And when you kiss me, well, it's enough to drive a man crazy. But in another way, it's not bad

183

at all. Because one of these days you're going to belong to me, and until then I'm looking after you."

She nodded, satisfied, and snuggled down beside him again. All around them in the grass the crickets sang and the air was heavy with the scents of summer. He reached for her hand, pressing it against his mouth. It smelled of soap and of grass and that elusive, hauntingly sweet smell of sun-warmed flesh. He kissed her fingers one by one, and then he kissed her palm.

"You are going to marry me, aren't you, Becky?" he asked.

For a moment she did not reply. He looked at her sharply, afraid he had upset or offended her in some way, and to his surprise he saw that her eyes were full of tears.

"Becky?" he said tentatively, and she turned towards him, the tears spilling down her cheeks. But in spite of the tears, she was smiling.

"Oh, Ted, I'm sorry, I didn't mean to cry . . . "

"What are you crying for, then?"

"Because . . . oh, I don't know. I can't explain. I just am!"

He raised himself on one elbow above her, loosening the pins in her hair so that it spread around her face and tumbled in the grass. He traced the line of her nose and her chin and her mouth with one finger and then he kissed her. Beneath his, her mouth was soft and yielding but tight shut like a child's. She wound her arms around his neck, pressing her body to his until the blood pounded in his veins and the ache inside him became sharp and insistent. But still her mouth was closed, and the innocence of her turned his passion to tenderness.

He raised his face an inch or two, whispering at the small closed mouth, "You haven't answered my question yet."

"You mean am I going to marry you? Oh, Ted, do you need to ask?"

"Well, are you?"

"Of course! When we can. I mean, I don't know when it will be. Father . . . " She broke off, determined not to spoil the moment with thoughts of her father. "There's nothing else I really want," she added simply.

For a while they lay in each other's arms while the summer afternoon drowsed on. Her virginity seemed to him almost a holy thing, all the more special because of the more brazen girls he had known, and he felt in some strange way that his protection of her was one of the most vital parts of their love.

At last she sat up, straightening her skirt and tucking her hair into its pins once more.

"It must be getting late. We'd better go back to the Rectory."

Reluctantly he stood up, then pulled her to her feet, holding her at arm's length and looking at her. They kissed once more, then hand in hand and without a backward glance at their special place under the trees they started back towards town, following the path along the river bank until they came to the spot where the water was shallow and a row of stepping stones bridged the river.

"Come on, I'll go first," he said, going ahead of her then turning to steady her as she jumped, laughing, from one stone to the next. But on the centre stone she stopped, her face suddenly solemn, her hand going to her throat.

"Becky?" he said. "What's wrong?"

She shrugged, pushing the moment aside.

"Nothing. A goose walked over my grave, that's all."

"It's colder out here in the middle of the river," he said, but they both knew it wasn't that.

The grass on the Hillsbridge side of the river had been mown, but they stayed beneath the trees until they drew level with the small gate that led to the top end of the churchyard. Then they crossed the stubbly field and walked hand in hand along the rough lane beneath the wall that banked the higher ground of the churchyard.

They had almost reached the main road when Rebecca suddenly stopped walking, covering her mouth with her hand.

Ted glanced at her. "What's the matter?"

She did not answer. Her eyes were fixed on a tall, bearded figure who seemed to be standing on top of the churchyard wall, and the fear was naked in her face.

"Who is it?" he asked. But he already knew.

"My father." There was a catch in her voice. "Dear God, it's my father."

In spite of the heat of the afternoon sun, Ted felt a cold sweat on his forehead. The man was mountainous. Poised as he was on the high bank of the churchyard, he looked almost inhuman. For a moment Ted felt like turning to run, then he glanced at Rebecca, ashen-faced beside him, and controlled his apprehension.

"Don't worry," he told her. "This had to come, sooner or later."

"But . . ."

His fingers, holding hers, urged her on. "Don't be afraid. I'm here. I won't let him hurt you."

They walked on. Her father did not move until they were almost immediately below him. Then he turned to the flight of stone steps that were cut into the wall and came down on to the path to meet them face to face.

Even on the same level he was an awesome figure, a full head taller than either of them. Twice, his mouth opened as if he was about to speak, twice it closed, as if the words were inadequate to express his feelings.

Then, to his own surprise, Ted found himself saying, "Good afternoon, sir. Were you looking for Rebecca?"

The effect was immediate. Alfred's head came down like a bull about to charge and a pulse throbbed in his temple.

"How dare you!" he roared. "And take your hands off my daughter!"

Ted was startled, but he stood his ground and the Co-operative secretary drew a deep, shuddering breath.

"Take your hands off her before I thrash the skin off your filthy back! If you think you can defile a decent girl and . . . "

"He didn't!" Rebecca sobbed.

He turned on her, pulling her away from Ted. "As for you . . . " Words seemed to fail him and his face turned dark with rage before he recovered himself enough to go on. "As for you, when I get you home, you know what will happen to you!"

Ted took a step towards him. "She's done no wrong!"

Alfred ignored him. "You should see yourself, miss!" he bellowed at her. "Your skirt is crumpled, your hair is falling down, and full of grass. And all this on top of your lies! You've cheated and deceived your parents and dragged Marjorie down to your level. Well, I've promised you often enough to expect a thrashing if you disgraced yourself, but I never thought it would come to this."

"Now look here!" Young as he was, Ted was not unused to dealing with men. Since the age of twelve he had lived and worked amongst them on equal terms, and although he was wary of this mountainous, foul-mouthed Puritan, he was determined not to be overawed by him.

But Alfred merely brushed him aside, venting all his anger on Rebecca. To him, it seemed that she was the one who had sinned. The boy had only done what all men did given the chance, and satisfied his lust with the first girl who opened her legs to him. It was Rebecca who was to blame, and Rebecca he could castigate.

"Pray God you are not with child!" he thundered at her, excited by her fear. "If you are, I swear I'll do away with you myself before I'll allow you to bring a bastard into the world and disgrace us all before heaven and our neighbours!"

This last exhortation was too much for Ted. The man was not only a Puritan, but a religious maniac! Ignoring him, he spoke to Rebecca.

"You don't have to go with him. You can come home with me. Mam will look after you."

Hope flickered in her eyes, then died. "I can't, Ted."

"You stay away from my daughter, do you hear?" Alfred bellowed at him. Then, to Rebecca: "As for you, my girl, get up that hill before I flay you alive—and your mother, too, for bringing you to this."

Twisting Rebecca in front of him, he began to march along the path.

"Becky, don't go with him!" Ted pleaded again. "He can't make you! Don't go with him!"

She did not answer, and he saw that tears were streaming down her face.

"Becky!" he cried.

Alfred began to roar more threats, but Ted scarcely heard him. He could see only the fear in Rebecca's eyes, and it was a terrible thing. The girl who had lain beside him in the long grass was gone now. In her place was a small, cowering animal.

"Leave me, Ted," she whispered through her tears. "You'll only make it worse."

Helplessly, he watched them go away, still not really understanding what had happened. The man was mad—but he was her father, and she came from a world where his word was law. And although he was afraid for her, it was true that there was nothing he could do without making things worse for her.

They turned the corner into the hill, and when they were out of sight, Ted, angry, and sick at heart, made his own way home.

ALTHOUGH panting with exertion, Alfred propelled Rebecca up the hill remorselessly. She could visualize the belt he had sworn to thrash her with, and deliberately, so as to be prepared, she let herself think about it. Would it be as bad as it had been when she was a little girl and he had given her three stripes for telling a lie? And would he make her undress to do it? Across the years, the memory of the pain had dulled, but the shame remained as sharp as ever.

As they reached the top of the hill and the cottages came into sight, Rebecca's heart thudded painfully. Why had she not gone with Ted? she asked herself. She could have done. If she had kicked her father and run away he could not have stopped her. Even now it was not too late. She could run back down the hill and find Ted. He would look after her, perhaps take her away somewhere where her father would never find them . . .

But all the time she knew she would not do it. He was her father, and she must obey him. 'Honour thy father and thy mother that thy days may be long in the land that the Lord thy God givest thee.' For six long months she had lied to him and deceived him, and now the time had come for her punishment. If she tried to escape that, heaven only knew what would happen, but one thing was certain. It would be her mother who would bear the brunt of his wrath, her poor cringing ill-used mother.

Down the narrow lane to the cottage they went, but instead of taking the path to the front door, Alfred propelled the frightened girl around the side of the house to the kitchen entrance.

There was no doubt as to his intentions now. The strap had not been an idle threat. Again she thought of running, but he kept hold of her arm as he unlatched the wash-house door and reached one-handed for the leather belt that hung there. Then he pushed her in front of him into the kitchen.

"Alfred—what is going on? What are you doing?"

Winnie Church, who had seen them coming up the lane, appeared suddenly in the doorway, her pinched face ugly with fear.

"Your daughter is a sinner. She has been lying with a boy. She has been . . ."

"I haven't," Rebecca cried. "Oh, Mother, I haven't. We only went for a walk!"

"And now she has to pay for her lust."

Violently he tore at her dress, ripping it open, and she backed away, terrified, holding the bodice round her.

"Take it off!" he ordered.

"No, Father, please don't make me . . . "

The heat of his body beneath his heavy clothing somehow heightened his rage and his desire for retribution.

"The Lord is with me," he intoned taking a step towards her. She cowered away, mute with terror, and he raised his hand.

"The Lord will punish . . . "

But at that moment the exertions of the afternoon told on Alfred. He was a heavy man and not a very fit one, and the struggle up the hill had been more of a strain than he had realized.

As he raised his arm, a pain so sharp that it took his breath knifed through his chest, and he stopped in his tracks, his hand going to his heart, a surprised expression on his face.

"Alfred!" Winnie Church cried.

The strap fell from his hand, and he leaned heavily against the table to steady himself. His breathing had become laboured, and his eyes glazed.

"Alfred, you've done too much!" Winnie rushed forward, pulling out the hard-backed chair and placing it behind him. For the moment, her fear of illness and death had taken all thought of her daughter's punishment from her mind. But Alfred did not forget. Sitting down heavily on the chair he raised a trembling finger to point at Rebecca.

"Take that whore upstairs and lock her in her room until I can decide what to do with her." The words were stumbled and rasping as he fought for breath, but his anger was as terrible as ever.

Winnie leaned over him, loosening his collar and mopping his brow. "Never mind about Rebecca, Alfred. Don't worry about anything . . . "

But still his trembling finger pointed, and his face was suffused with colour. "Take that whore . . . " he attempted to rise, then sank back weakly. "Take that whore . . . "

"All right, Alfred, whatever you say. Don't upset yourself any more." Winnie crossed to Rebecca, but stopped short at the expression on the girl's face. Fear had gone now—her hazel eyes were clear and cool as spring pools.

"The Lord guided your hand, didn't he, Father?" she said, and the confidence in her voice brought a new frenzy of fury to his distorted features. Once more he attempted to raise himself, once more he failed, falling back into the chair with a harsh gasp, and Winnie flew at her daughter.

"How could you, Rebecca? What has got into you, making your father ill like this? We've tried to bring you up decently, and this is all the thanks we get . . . "

Rebecca said nothing. She simply turned and went up the stairs to her room. Winnie followed, wailing new accusations all the way, but Rebecca did not even look at her. Her head held high, she marched into her room, crossed the floor and sat herself down on the bed. For the moment Winnie stood in the doorway, more unsure of herself than ever in the face of her daughter's new-found dignity.

"You'll stay here until your father's well enough to decide what's to be done with you, my girl," she said almost defiantly.

Then she went out, closing the door behind her, and Rebecca heard the click as the key was turned in the lock.

13

AMY LEFT school in the summer of 1915, in spite of all William Davies' efforts to stop her.

"You're a bright girl, Amy. You could get a scholarship like your brother," he told her. "Let me have a talk with your mother and father. I'm sure they'd take notice if I explained to them."

But Amy was adamant. "I don't want you to, Mr Davies. They can't afford to keep me on at school. It's as much as they can do to keep Jack at Wells, and there's Harry, too."

"Well, it's a great pity, but I must commend you on your attitude, Amy—admirably unselfish," William Davies said.

Amy had the grace to blush. She knew that money was short, and if she allowed William Davies to talk her mother and father into letting her try for a scholarship, things would become more difficult. But that was not the whole story—far from it. Amy was bright, but she was not the dedicated scholar Jack was, and never would be. As long as learning came easily to her, she didn't mind learning. But the very thought of spending long hours shut away with a lot of dusty old books was enough to put her off any idea of further schooling. She wanted fun, freedom to go out sometimes, and a little money to spend. Nothing else was included in her scheme of things.

But of course if she was not going to stay on at school, she had to find a job. Charlotte, who still loved shops, tried to get her an apprenticeship at Fords, the drapers, but there were no vacancies, and when Dolly came home and suggested Amy might be able to work with her up at Captain Fish's, there was great relief all round.

"You'd be able to keep an eye on her, Dolly," Charlotte said.

Amy, too, liked the idea. She knew she could get around her older sister any time she liked, and there could be a lot of advantages to working under her, instead of a stranger who might work her much harder.

"I can't promise, of course," Dolly said. "But with Cook's legs getting worse, I'm having to do more of her work, and I know Captain Fish was talking of getting a new housemaid."

"If you were to put in a word for her, I should think our Amy would stand a very good chance," Charlotte said, and she was right.

Captain Fish agreed to take on Amy, starting as soon as she finished school. Amy was delighted, quite fancying the fact that she, too, was going to have to 'live in,' and she spent a lot of time neatly mending her underwear and unfolding and folding the new cambric nightgown Charlotte had bought her.

Only one thing marred her happiness—Dr Scott had become engaged to Grace O'Halloran, and although she was now old enough to realize her passion for him was quite hopeless, it didn't stop her aching inside every time she thought of it.

The news had come as quite a surprise to Hillsbridge. Dr Scott had always seemed too busy to have much social life, and a story that he had a girl at home in his native Gloucestershire had been tacitly accepted. Then, quite suddenly, Grace O'Halloran had been seen in his pony and trap, and now, almost indecently soon, his engagement had been announced.

"I heard that it's because he's going off to the war," Charlotte said.

"To the war?" Amy repeated, horrified. It was bad enough to think of Dr Scott married to someone else, but she was acutely depressed to think she would no longer see him about the town.

"He's going as a doctor, I suppose," Charlotte went on. "And goodness knows, those poor things over there need all the help they can get."

"But why Dr Scott?" Amy wailed.

"Why any of them?" Charlotte asked shortly. "Why our Fred, and Colwyn Yelling, and poor Bert Cottle? They want their heads examined, if you ask me. It's just plain daft."

"No, it's not daft, Mam," Jack said, and they all looked at him in surprise. Jack was usually so quiet, even if he wasn't upstairs studying, opinions had to be dragged out of him.

"What's that, Jack?" Charlotte asked.

"I said it's not daft," he repeated, uncurling his slender frame. "There are times when you've got to stand up and fight for what you believe in, just like our Fred said."

"Don't tell us you're going off to join the army next!" Charlotte exploded.

"No, but if I was old enough I'd join the Flying Corps," Jack said.

Charlotte raised her eyes to heaven. He'd always been too interested in flying machines for his own good. She still blamed William Davies for that—all his talk of butterflies and soaring above the ground.

"Well, all I can say is, I hope you've got more sense than that," she said. "And let's pray it's all over before you're old enough. What do you say, Dad?"

James nodded, reaching for his cigarettes and coughing as he lit one. "I bloody well hope so."

"And so say all of us!" Amy chimed in.

Only Ted said nothing. He stood by the window, hands in pockets, staring out in a dream.

"Ted, what do you think about it?" Charlotte said, trying to draw him into the conversation. It worried her to see him this way. It wasn't like him to be so wrapped up in himself. But he'd been the same ever since last Saturday when he'd come home from the parish garden party in a terrible mood, and told her how Alfred Church had marched Rebecca away.

"Well, I can't say I blame him!" she'd returned sharply. "It's asking for trouble to go across the fields on your own like that. If she was a girl of mine, I dare say I'd feel the same."

"But he's not normal, Mam, he's mad! And Becky's frightened to bloody death of him."

"There's no need to swear," she admonished him.

"No need to swear! I feel like beating the bugger's brains in, never mind swearing about him."

"That'll do, Ted!" she told him briskly. "I know you're upset, but carrying on like this won't help anybody. If Becky behaves herself and you both go about things the right way, he'll come around."

Ted had said no more, and she had hoped he would see sense. Wild as he was, he must know that if he helped a girl deceive her father, only trouble could come of it. But as the days went by his mood deepened. The only one he had any time for was Nipper, taking him off for long walks, but Charlotte was fairly sure he was not meeting Rebecca.

"Well, Ted, and what do you think about this war?" she said now.

"I think it's a pity they don't take Alfred Church and set him up in front of a firing squad," Ted said bitterly. Then, whistling to Nipper, he turned and walked out of the kitchen.

WHEN he left the house, Ted walked quickly and purposefully down the hill towards the town.

Although it was evening, there was no sign of the market packing up—the strains of the Salvation Army Band floated up the hill—and he hoped Fords, the drapers, would still be open.

For a week he'd waited, letting things settle down for Rebecca, but now his mind was made up. He was going to do something about it.

Through the market place he went, past the Rectory, and up a short, steep hill. Half-way up, in a curve in the road, Fords the drapers stood. The stone pillars outside were chipped and marked by all the carts that had collided with them, and the big double windows had been smashed more times than anyone could remember. But Fords was still the most successful shop in Hillsbridge— apart from the Co-operative—and certainly the grandest.

Ted had never been inside the shop before. Drapery was a mystery to him, he hardly knew what was sold there, and had no idea what he would ask for if Marjorie was not about. But luck was with him. Through the glass panel in the door he could see her standing on a pair of steps, reaching up to the fixtures, and he lifted the shiny brass latch and went in.

When she turned and saw him, she almost fell off the steps with surprise. Then, recovering herself, she climbed down and came over to him.

"Good evening, and what can I do for you, sir?"

He stared at her, nonplussed. "Well . . . I . . . "

"A ha' p'orth of pins? Yes, of course, sir," she said with cheerful ingenuity, then, under her breath, she added, "You're Ted Hall, aren't you? Becky's Ted?"

He nodded. "Yes. But why all the secrecy?"

"Mrs Ford's in the millinery room," she whispered, taking down the pins and weighing them up. "What did you really want?"

"Well, to know if Becky's all right, of course."

"I don't know," Marjorie said seriously. "I haven't seen her."

"What do you mean, you haven't seen her?" Ted repeated, too loudly. "You live next door to her, don't you?"

Quickly she pulled a face to quieten him. "Yes, but I haven't seen her all week," she whispered.

Ted felt the first stirrings of real anxiety as he remembered things Rebecca had said about her father.

"Where is she then?" he asked roughly. "She's not ill is she?"

"I don't know. I haven't been near the place." Marjorie shivered, but before he could ask her what she meant, the door to the millinery room opened and Mrs Ford, briskly business-like, swept into the shop. She glared at Ted and Marjorie, her sharp little eyes full of suspicion, and Ted had no option but to pay for his pins and leave.

His thoughts were churning, and outside he hesitated, wondering if he could make some excuse to go back into the shop, but common sense told him it would be pointless. Marjorie had said she hadn't seen Rebecca, and he believed her. But *why* hadn't she seen her? The weather had been good—surely she should have been in the garden if nothing else.

For a few moments he stood undecided, then he started back down the hill with the same purpose with which he had come. There was nothing for it but to go to Eastlands and see Rebecca for himself. Perhaps if he went to her house and knocked on the door, Alfred would realize his intentions were serious, and that he wanted more than just a quick roll in the grass. The thought almost made him smile—him, Ted Hall, admitting to honourable intentions! But he had never been more serious in his life.

At the bottom of the hill he turned left, along the half-horseshoe of shops that were Town Street, past the Victoria Hall and the church, scene of last week's encounter with Alfred, and into the long curving hill to Eastlands.

When he was half-way, he heard the gentle clip-clop of a horse coming towards him, and stopped for a minute, leaning on the bank to watch it pass. It was Stanley Bristow's wagonette, pulled by his last remaining horse, running his weekly service to market for the people of Eastlands. He was going home empty now, and he called out to Ted as he drew level, "Lost yer way, lad?"

Ted laughed, but the joke somehow brought a knot of suppressed nervousness into his throat. He went on, up the hill and into the narrow lane where the honeysuckle grew wild in the hedges. As he

194

reached the pair of cottages he bypassed the path to the front door, walking along under the hedge to the back of the house.

This was his best point of attack, he reckoned. Rebecca was more likely to be at the back of the house and if he knocked at the front door, it would be easier for her father to keep him there and prevent him from seeing her.

He could hear the murmur of voices and thought perhaps they were sitting outside as his mother sometimes did on a warm evening. He rounded the corner and was almost surprised to find the yard and the lawn beyond it deserted. But when he looked towards the house, there, framed in the kitchen doorway and almost filling it with his bulk, was Alfred.

He was not wearing his jacket, and beneath his waistcoat, a billowing white shirt made his shoulders and arms appear more vast than ever. A gold watch chain strained importantly across his chest, and above his stiff collar his face was mottled putty and puce. Ted, however, was determined not to be overawed. Last week, descending from the churchyard wall, he had somehow had the aura of an avenging angel. Here, in the doorway of his own kitchen, he was at least human.

"Good evening," Ted said politely. "I've come to see Rebecca."

At once, Alfred Church swelled. His watch chain strained more tightly than ever, even his height seemed to increase.

"Go!" he roared. "You're not wanted here. I thought I made myself clear!"

"Oh, yes, you did," Ted said. "But it's Rebecca I want to see, not you. And it's not what you think. I want to marry her . . . "

"Marry her?" Alfred repeated incredulously. "You think I would allow my daughter to throw herself away on the likes of you? You must have taken leave of your senses. In any case, she is betrothed. And that is the end of the matter."

He went to shut the door, but Ted moved quickly, putting his foot in the way.

"Wait a minute! What are you talking about—Rebecca betrothed?"

"Young man, remove your foot and get out of my house. Rebecca is betrothed, I tell you."

"Betrothed! She's not bloody betrothed—unless it's to me."

"To you? A filthy fornicator? I'd see her dead first!" Alfred's eyes were burning now with the righteous fury of a madman, and fear for Rebecca's safety came to Ted in a great, sickening rush. Who could tell what lengths Alfred would go to keep his daughter, in his eyes, pure? Who could tell to what lengths he had already gone?

With a desperate, mighty heave Ted pushed at the door, and Alfred, taken by surprise, gave enough ground for Ted to be able to see that the kitchen behind him was empty.

"Becky!" he shouted, through the half-open doorway. "Becky, where are you?"

Suddenly, Alfred stepped aside, and the door flew open with such force Ted almost fell. "What the hell . . . " he began, but before the words were out, he understood. Alfred had stepped into the kitchen, and now he reappeared with a studded leather strap clutched in his huge fist and dangling threateningly.

"Now will you get out?" he bellowed, raising the strap until it was level with Ted's face. "Now will you leave us alone? You will not see her again, you sinner, you defiler of innocent girls . . . "

His fury mounting, he swung his arm back across his body and the evening sun caught the metal teeth of the strap, making them gleam coldly against the dark leather. Ted's reaction was instinctive and violent. If this man thought he was going to thrash him, he had another think coming!

Before Alfred could bring the strap down on to his head, his arm shot back with the swiftness and precision of a piston, and he sank his balled fist into the soft, unprotected belly, six inches below the straining watch chain.

Alfred was a big man, but not a fit one. As Ted's fist connected, he crumpled, an expression of surprise on his face, and the belt dropped uselessly from his grasp. Then, clutching at his stomach, he sank to the floor in a gasping heap to retch over the bright rag rug.

Ted snatched up the belt and stood over him threateningly.

"Don't you ever try that again, mister! Ever!"

A small frightened sound caught his attention, and he looked up from the heaving man to see Rebecca and her mother in the kitchen doorway. The older woman pushed her way through, dropping to her knees beside her husband and trying to raise his head. But Rebecca did not move. Her face was ashen, her small, firm breasts rising and falling with her uneven breathing.

Ted took a step towards her. "Becky, you're coming with me."

Her eyes went to her father, and she covered her mouth with trembling hands. "You've killed him!" she whispered through her fingers.

"I've winded him, that's all, but I'll break his bloody ribs if he ever tries anything like that again. Now, get your things, Becky. You can't stay here."

On the floor, Alfred began to stutter a protest, and Winnie raised her eyes appealingly to her daughter.

"Becky!" Ted said sharply, but she did not move, standing as if mesmerized by the scene before her.

Alfred, wheezing and coughing, pulled himself on to his knees.

"Get out!" he gasped, and his weak voice was somehow more awe-inspiring than his stentorian roar. "Get out before I call a policeman and have you arrested." His face diffused, he clutched his chest, and gasped again. Winnie fell upon him, loosening his collar and whimpering softly, and Rebecca, pale and trembling, caught at Ted's arm.

"Please go, Ted—please. You'll only make things worse. Oh, don't you see what you're doing?" The tears filled her eyes and began to run down her cheeks, and frustration and anger rose in Ted again. He looked from the small, anguished face to the man and woman on the floor, and realized that for the moment there was nothing more that he could do.

He crossed to the doorway, towering now above the heaving body and looking with distaste at the sweat-beaded head.

"I'll go for now," he said. "But I'll be back. And don't you lay a finger on Becky, either, or I swear I'll break your bloody neck!" Then, not trusting himself to stay in the house a moment longer, he pushed open the kitchen door and went out.

Somehow he had to get Rebecca away from that madhouse, he thought as he wandered back the way he had come. And he had to do it soon, before her spirit was broken completely by her monster of a father. Somehow he had to get her far enough away from Hillsbridge so that Alfred was no longer able to reach her with his bullying and his threats. How he would do it, he didn't know. But if he thought hard enough, there had to be a way . . .

Tossing the belt into the thickly woven centre of a nearby lavender bush, Ted dug his hands into his pockets, and walked towards the scarlet sunset.

ALL NIGHT Ted lay awake, tossing and turning on his hard flock mattress as he ran over the events of the evening again and again, and searched for an answer to the seemingly insoluble problem of how to get Rebecca away from her father.

But it was the following Monday that the germ of an idea was soon in his mind. It was dinner-time, the half-hour break when the miners squatted down together along the sides of a roadway, to eat their cogknocker and cheese and drink their cold tea.

Today, James and Ted had been joined by Walter Clements and Reg Adams, a Bath-born lad who had recently begun work at the pit as a carting boy.

To Ted and to the others, Reg was something of a puzzle. In some ways, he reminded Ted of Jack, for he had the same quiet manner, and the same lack of interest in what Ted termed "the good things of life." But there the likeness ended, for Reg seemed far more knowledgeable about what was going on in the outside world than Jack had ever been, and there was a wiry strength about him that surprised everyone who saw him dragging a putt of coal.

When he had first come to apply for the job, O'Halloran had privately given him a week at the outside, and had even speculated that the lad might not come back after his first day. But the days had become weeks, and Reg was still there, working as hard as he had to and no harder, and entertaining his work-mates with his strange talk and his wild predictions about the course of the war.

That dinner-time, the talk had somehow turned to conscription.

"It's bound to come," he said in his soft, almost girlish voice. "You've only got to read the papers to know that."

In the light thrown by their candles, the others had exchanged glances. They hadn't read anything about it in their papers. There'd been talk, yes, but talk was cheap, and there still seemed to be train-loads of young men responding to Kitchener's war cry without bringing in conscription.

"You know what it's going to mean, don't you?" Reg chattered on, and Walter laughed deprecatorily.

"Oh, ah, we do. There'll be a lot more like you after nice safe jobs in the pit, while our lads are off out to fight Kaiser Bill."

"No, you don't understand," Reg said earnestly. "If they bring in conscription, it'll mean you can't go. Didn't you know that?"

"Can't go? What d'ee mean?" James asked. "How be 'em going to stop us?"

The boy threw a crumb of cheese towards a mouse who had seen the circle of light and approached it boldly.

"They've got to have coal," he explained. "And mining is one of those jobs you can't have a woman doing. Well, when all the men who don't work in the pit get called up, there won't be none to take up any vacancies down here. So they'll have to make sure there aren't any vacancies—leastways, as few as they can manage. And it'll be the same with munitions, they say."

The other three men stared at him. They hadn't thought of it that way, but now it had been pointed out to them, they could see the sense of it. Most men in Hillsbridge worked in the pits anyway, but a good few of those who didn't had joined up already, and most of the rest had professed themselves willing to "attest" since Lord Derby had called for it. And if conscription came in, there wouldn't be an able-bodied man between nineteen and forty-one left in England, let alone here in Hillsbridge.

"That's why you come here to work, isn't it, Reg?" Walter Clements asked, voicing aloud the question most of the men had muttered behind Reg's back. "You want to get out of being called up."

"That's right," the boy admitted. "They might get me anyway, of course. After all, I haven't been here all that long, and I can just imagine some red-faced pen-pusher taking a delight in sorting out those of us who ran to the coalfields after the war started. But at least it's a chance."

James, thinking suddenly of Fred, whose expected letter home was several weeks overdue, and who might, for all he knew, be wounded or dying, stabbed the air with a vehement finger.

"You'm one of them slackers they'm after, Reggie," he said bitterly. "And I hope they bloody well catch up with 'ee."

The boy chewed slowly on his cogknocker, then raised his head to look directly at James.

"I suppose that's what a lot of folk think," he said philosophically. "Well, that's just too bad."

Ted rubbed his chin.

"Why, Reg?" he asked. "Are you scared, or what?"

"Course, I'm scared. I bet they're all scared when it comes to the point. But that's not why I don't want to go."

"Why then?"

"Because it would mean leaving me mother to cope with the youngsters and my father all by herself, and she's not fit."

"What's wrong with your father, then?"

"He's a cripple. He used to drive a mail van in Bath, and he had an accident that really bad winter—1910, wasn't it? The hill was slippery, the horse couldn't stand, and the jumping van ran away with him. He tried to stop it—there was this taxi cab coming up, you see—but it went over his legs. Since then . . . well, he can't do no work, nor nothing else much, neither."

A silence fell on the little group. Accidents, men who couldn't work any more, both were too close to home for them to mock again.

"So that's it, you see," Reg went on. "I do most things me father would do if he was fit. The next two to me are girls, and they're both away in service, and then there's Bert, but he's not well. He had scarlet fever when he was a nipper, and it's left him with a dicky heart. So I'm sort of relied on, really."

James drew the back of his hand across his mouth in a gesture of embarrassment.

"Don't take no notice of what I said, Reg lad. I didn't know the half of it, did I?" he conceded, and the others muttered their agreement, made awkward suddenly by the discovery that they could know so little of the personal troubles of a boy they had worked alongside for a month and more.

For his part, Ted was horror struck by the catalogue of woes that made his own childhood seem like one long holiday. But when he returned to work, drawing the putt along the topple, it was the earlier part of the conversation that returned to his mind.

Supposing Reg was right? he thought, and conscription did mean that no one from the pits could be accepted into the military. Might that not only be a short step away from the day when miners would be obliged to stay in the pits—for the duration of the war at least? And who could say how long that would be? Why, already all the folk who had predicted it would only last a few months had been proved wrong. Already more than a year had gone by, and there was no sign of an early armistice. Good grief, if they brought in some sort of law about it, he could be stuck in the pit for years.

Ted momentarily slackened his pace, resting on his heels and letting his back support the weight of the tub, while a sinking feeling swept through his body.

Since meeting Rebecca, he'd been too preoccupied to give any more thought to leaving the pit, although he didn't suppose anyone would threaten his father's livelihood as Gait had done.

And times had changed, too. Whereas before carting boys had been hard to come by, now there were plenty of lads who, for one reason or another, were thinking on the same lines as Reg Adams and deciding that the coalfield might be as good a place as any to hide away for the duration of the war. And they, Ted realized, could be his passport out of the pit. But if Reg was right, and some kind of compulsion was going to be brought in, he'd have to do something about it—and quickly.

Ted crawled on, wishing desperately he could get out of the dark tunnels and into the green quiet of one of the woods behind his home.

He couldn't stay in the pits for years, he was certain of that much. As long as he did so, there was not much future for him, and none at all for his hopes of taking Rebecca away from her father. He couldn't ask her to live in a poky cottage, even if he could find one. She was worth more than that. And the thought of seeing her worn down by too much work and too many babies was painful to him. He wanted Becky—wanted her so much his whole body ached for her—but not on those terms.

No, he would have to try and take her away—right away—so that they could start again. But what could he do that would raise enough money to keep them both? Go to the Welsh coal-field, maybe, where seams were thick and colliers paid good wages—or even to Yorkshire. More than one lad had packed his bags and headed north. But to do either meant leaving Rebecca alone with her father, at least until he could find a home for her.

If only she'd marry me now, Ted thought. She could live with Mam for a while. There's plenty of room now with half the family gone, and she'd be company for Mam, too.

Grunting, he emptied the tub of its load and set off back to the face. Maybe he wouldn't be doing this again too many times, he thought. Maybe before Christmas there'd be some new lad carting for James, and he, Ted, would be off to make a new life.

That evening after he had washed and changed, Ted told Charlotte he had to give someone an urgent message. Then, without waiting for the question that was forming on Charlotte's lips, Ted made his way down to see Marjorie at Fords.

Tonight, he did not hesitate outside the shop, but went straight in. Marjorie was tidying fixtures, but when she saw him a strange expression crossed her face. She climbed down from the steps so rapidly that she almost fell, and he wondered briefly if she had overheard the commotion the night before.

"Ted Hall, what are you doing here again?"

He glanced around to see if Mrs Ford was in evidence. "I wanted you to give Rebecca a message for me."

"Oh Lord, you don't know then."

"Know what?" he asked, mystified.

"She's gone, Ted."

"Gone? Gone where?" he repeated stupidly.

Marjorie's face was flushed, and she patted her hair with a small, distracted movement.

"I don't know. All I know is she's gone. The car came for her first thing this morning, and I heard them say it was for the station at Bath. Then he came out—Mr Church—and Rebecca, and all her cases. He's packed her off somewhere, out of your way I should think. But I've no idea where she's gone, or when she'll be back. Knowing him, maybe she never will be."

Ted stared at her, too shocked to even begin to understand the implications of what she had told him. Then, dazed, he turned and left the shop.

14

As TED left the shop, someone watched from a window that overlooked the street.

In her starched cap and apron, Rosa Clements, the Ford's new housemaid, looked as demure as the strictest of mistresses could have wished, and only her eyes revealed the turmoil of emotion within her.

It worked! she thought, and excitement, rising inside her in a sharp, dizzying rush, made her shake so violently that she had to hold on to the cream-painted window sill for support. It worked—I got rid of her! But, oh, I wish I hadn't seen his face. I wish I hadn't seen how much he cared . . .

Rosa had been in love with Ted for as long as she could remember. It seemed there had never been a time when she had not wanted him, or when one glance, idly thrown in her direction, had not made her heart sing. As a child, she had followed him everywhere until he had told her to clear off. But that had not lessened her love. For a while it had hurt, but little by little her love had grown again, and she had gone back to sitting at the upstairs window of the little house in Greenslade Terrace to watch him go whistling up the rank, or standing with her back against the outhouse wall while the others played hopscotch, staring intently at his house, willing him to come out and speak to her.

Even in those days, she had tried to make spells or put a charm on him. She had gathered herbs and wild flowers on her lonely expeditions through the woods and mashed them into paste in her room at night when her brothers were asleep. But for all that she had believed in them, they had never worked—except for the one she'd woven the night after she'd found him crying because his dog had disappeared. Yes, she'd got it right that time, but the others, the important ones, to make him smile at her or notice her, hadn't worked at all, and Rosa had begun to doubt the thing she hoped most of all was true—that it was not Irish tinker's blood that ran in her veins, but pure Romany—the blood that carries the secrets of spells and curses handed down from generation to generation, and weaves an age-old magic, and sees the future. Above all things, Rosa wanted that, maybe even more than she wanted Ted. For if she could make spells, all things were possible. And if she were a Romany, or even a witch, she would be someone in her own right at last.

Rosa Clements had been born at the turn of the century. She drew her first breath when the trees were bursting with new green life and pink and white blossoms hung heavily upon the apple trees. Between spasms of pain as she fought to bring her daughter into the world, Ada, had looked at the apple trees through the dusty bedroom window and tried to find an omen in their beauty, or at least a reason for hope. It was less than eight months since she had wed Walter Clements, and she knew that tongues were wagging in Hillsbridge. What was more, she knew what they were saying. For there were plenty of people who had seen her creeping out of the market yard, where the fun fair wintered, on the evenings when Walter had been working a back shift that last year before their marriage. And when the fair had returned the following year, those same people watched eagerly to see if a certain swarthy young man was still amongst their number.

Ada had pictured him as she sweated and laboured that day in the spring of 1900. She closed her eyes and saw again the dark-skinned face, the thick curling hair and the deep jet eyes that could tempt and tantalize. She heard his mocking laugh, and saw the muscular, weather-tanned shoulders that were as different from Walter's fair-skinned puny frame as could be. As the pain intensified she fancied she heard the raucous music of the merry-go-round, and when it seemed that the fire deep inside her would tear her in two, some-where on the edge of her consciousness he was there, riding around and around, legs splayed to balance himself against the sway of the merry-go-round, one careless hand resting on a wooden support, the other stretched out as if to invite her once more to his caravan.

As Rosa grew, there were others, too, who remembered. When her hair grew thick and dark, and they saw the lustre of her black eyes, they nudged one another and whispered in triumph. They'd been right, then, in what they'd suspected, right when they'd speculated that Walter, simple as he was, had taken for his wife a woman who was no better than she should be. But the thing they'd all have given a good deal to learn was whether or not poor Walter knew.

Years passed. Ada bore Walter five more children, all sons, and all as pale skinned as Rosa was dark. In the process she grew thin and scrawny, and her hands, once her pride and joy, became red and knotted. She no longer went to the market yard in winter, and although no roving-eyed fair man would invite her into his bed now, she was still looked on as a common whore. As if they needed some excitement in their own drab lives, the townspeople kept alive the scarlet sceptre of a foolish girl long after she had become a haggard, rather pitiful figure who walked with a quick, nervous stoop and who would probably not survive the results of another night of abandoned love.

Rosa, too, came in for her share of notoriety. At school, the other children, who had been told without explanation to keep away from her, treated her with a mixture of fascination and fear, but none wanted to be her friend, and Rosa, who was always more at home in the woods and under the stars, kept to herself. Once, she asked Ada what it was that made people avoid her, but Ada busied herself with her washing, turning her back on Rosa and sinking her arms elbow deep in the steaming water.

"You'm different," she said shortly. "Folk are always funny with anybody a bit different."

Rosa could get no more from her, and she did not ask again. But she began listening to the talk when she could, standing so still and so silent that it was easy to forget she was there at all, and she compared the way she looked with the fairness of her parents and her brothers.

After much consideration, she came to a conclusion. She was a foundling. It was the only answer.

At first the thought frightened her, for it seemed she had suddenly lost everything that had made her feel safe—her family, her name, even her identity. Then, gradually, excitement stirred as she realized the wonderful, endless possibilities.

If she was not Rosa Clements, she could be anyone. It was like being born again, with the world to choose from.

She debated the possibilities sitting in the fork of a tree in the woods above Greenslade Terrace. She stared at her own dark-skinned reflection in the cracked mirror above her wash-stand. But it was when the black cat from along the rank had come to her one day purring and rubbing itself around her legs that she had known.

I'm a witch, she thought. I'm a witch-child, and that's why they left me. And she smiled a secret smile and laughed softly to herself because, if she was a witch, then it made her more important than any of them, and there was nothing she could not do.

For a while, she was satisfied with the knowledge, but then the desire to test her powers began to gnaw at her—and with it the problems of being a witch-child separated from all other witches. For who was there to teach her spells and magic incantations? Who could show her which herbs had special properties and which were useless to her?

She began to experiment, choosing the wild garlic that grew by the river because of its pungent smell, and the cuckoo pint and the berries she knew to be poisonous. Once she even crept from her bed to see if she could find some "flowers of the night," and in the dark fields, with only an owl hooting across the valley, she was not afraid, but alive and tingling with a strange excitement.

In the morning, however, when Ada found her stockings damp and stuck with burrs, there were questions she could not answer, and she knew her night-time expeditions would have to be kept for very special occasions.

When she was eleven years old, her world almost fell to pieces around her ears. In a rash moment, when the teasing of her school friends had become almost too much to bear, she had shouted at them that they had better beware, for she was a witch. But they only laughed at her.

"You're not a witch, you're a gypsy," one of them taunted, and Rosa recoiled as swiftly as if she had been stung.

A gypsy—no, she couldn't be! She thought of the families of poor, ingratiating tinkers who went from door to door with their baskets of clothes-pegs and paper flowers, begging from folk scarcely better off than they were, and her heart sank. Had they left her on a doorstep in a basket along with the clothes-pegs? It was a thought so awful it made her curl up inside, yet it had to be faced. They were dark-skinned as she was. Their eyes in their wizened, nut-brown faces were black, like hers. But she didn't want to be a gypsy—oh, she didn't want to be a gypsy! Unless . . .

Unless she were a Romany. Now that would be something different again. Romanies lived in bright painted caravans and burned them when the occupant died, together with everything they owned. Romanies were bold and free, spoke a language of their own, slept under the stars. Romanies could read palms and tea leaves; they knew the future—and the past. Oh, it would be good to be a Romany . . .

The thought satisfied her, and even as she grew older, she clung to it. Even when she began to realize that the foundling story was unlikely to be more than the figment of a child's imagination, she never doubted that there ran in her veins blood that was wilder and more free than that of the people she called her parents, a blood that responded with restless longing to the call of the woods and the fields, and knew truths that they would never know. Deep inside, she recognized some part of her that was at one with nature and with super-nature, and she spurned the ordinary, everyday folk in their ordinary, everyday houses, living their ordinary, everyday lives.

All except Ted. She adored him with a passion that was boundless and also irrational. For she knew that for him she would sacrifice the woods and the fields, for him she would live just as the rest of Hillsbridge lived. For him, she would cook and clean and mend, and bear and raise all the children he wanted. And she would be proud and happy to be his wife—and perhaps a little relieved, too, that she would no longer be the one on the outside—the one at whom fingers pointed and shoulders shrugged.

She first knew she wanted to marry him the day his brother Jim wed Sarah Brimble. She watched from the upstairs window as the wagonette carrying the bridal party lurched along the rank, and she dreamed of the day when she would be the one to sit proudly in a white dress with flowers in her hair. Her dark eyes grew huge in her thin face as she pictured it, and love swelled inside her until she had thought she would burst.

Two years had passed since that day, but Rosa's love for Ted had not dimmed. She was hurt when she saw him with other girls, but she had told herself her time would come. To him, she was still a child, but she would not always be a child. With pride she watched her thin body round into the curves of womanhood and the roses begin to colour her sallow cheeks. Soon, she thought, she would be ready to make him notice her. She would paint her lips scarlet and draw her thick hair away from her face so that it did nothing to hide her huge dark eyes. She had experimented secretly in the cracked mirror above the wash-stand and been pleased with the result. But she was not quite ready. She must wait for her breasts to fill out that little bit more. Then he would not doubt she was a woman. And in the meantime, what did it matter if he played around with every girl in Hillsbridge? She would soon outstrip them all.

But she reckoned without Rebecca Church.

She noticed the difference in him almost at once, and it worried her. That new buoyancy coupled with seriousness, and the way he seemed to whistle one moment and dream the next reflected her own feelings for him. Could it be that Ted had found someone who meant more to him than the casual, flirtatious encounters he had had before?

Then something else happened to add to her troubles. Since leaving school, she had worked as a maidservant to the Misses Holland, two elderly spinster sisters who lived in a grand house on South Hill. But in the spring of 1915 Florence, the younger of the two, collapsed with a massive stroke. For a week the older Miss Holland, determined her sister should not be taken into hospital, struggled to nurse her. Then, on the morning that Florence slipped away, she collapsed herself before Rosa's horrified eyes and died before the doctor could be fetched. The two sisters were buried together near the churchyard seat where they had often sat to watch the world go by, the house was put in the hands of Mr Clarence, the solicitor, and Rosa found herself out of a job.

Panic seized her. There were few enough jobs in a town like Hillsbridge for young girls, but to leave the district, as so many of her friends had done, would mean leaving Ted. Rosa, in desperation, went to the woods. There, hanging from a tree, she found a piece of rope, and her heart lifted. What the rope had been used for, or why it was there, she had no idea. But she remembered having once heard that a knot tied in rope was part of a spell, and it seemed to her that the rope had been left there for her own special purpose.

She picked some strong smelling onion flowers and lay them in a circle on the ground, then sat cross-legged in the centre, the rope between her hands. She tied three knots and whispered incantations that seemed to come from deep within her. Then she sat, her eyes narrowed against the sun that splintered through the branches of the trees, while the stillness inside her swelled and grew powerful. When at last she moved, her fingers were numb around the rope knots. As she flexed them, they tingled as if someone were driving pins and needles into them. She stood up, feeling for a fleeting moment that the world and everyone in it was under her control. Then, slowly, she folded the rope and placed it under the ivy in the crook of a nearby tree. The onion flowers she scattered, murmuring over each one. But the feeling of power did not leave her. It hung over her in a satisfying cloud, and she somehow knew that things would come right in time.

Rosa did not have long to wait. Next day, she received a message from Mrs Ford, at the draper's shop. She had been a friend of the Holland sisters, she knew Rosa from the visits she had paid them, and she realized the girl was now seeking a new position. Her own housemaid had recently left to be married, and if Rosa would care to present herself . . .

Rosa was jubilant. That night she returned to the wood, found the rope and whispered further incantations. It was necessary, she thought, to thank whatever power had helped her.

Her jubilation, however, was short-lived. For when she began work at Fords, she found she had a new and privileged window on to Ted's relationship with Rebecca, and she was not pleased by what she saw.

Rosa didn't have a great deal of contact with the girls in the shop, but she did learn from Marjorie about the serious relationship between Ted and Rebecca.

"I wish somebody thought that much of me, that's all," Marjorie had said. "Though what will happen when her father finds out, I dread to think."

Rosa was distraught. Throughout the summer she watched and waited, her body tense with concentration as she willed the affair to end. But it was only when she heard Marjorie talking of the way Alfred Church had learned the truth about his daughter's lover and the way he had reacted, that she realized the time had come for drastic measures.

That night she went to the woods again. She found the rope where she had hidden it, deep in the ivy, and she heaved a sigh of relief. If it had gone, she would have known that it was an omen of her own fallibility, and she must never again sit cross-legged in a circle of onion flowers. As it was, she was half-afraid to put the strange spell to the test again. After all, it was her own innovation, called up from the depths of her and owing little to anything she might have learned of magic. But now, so desperate was she, that she trembled as she sought for the onion flowers in the thickest, deepest places beneath the trees, and laid them in a sparser circle than before on the ground.

At first the trance was more difficult to summon. Her mind was too preoccupied for concentration. Then she set herself to dwell upon the one thing that mattered to her.

Send Rebecca away, she whispered, and the words seemed to encircle her and spiral up like chimney smoke between the overhanging branches. Send her away . . . away . . . away . . .

The sun dropped behind the hills in a blaze of scarlet and gold, and still Rosa sat. Only when the first cool breeze of night rippled over her bare arms, making her shiver, did she move, and as she stood up, she waited for the rush of power to fill her as it had done before.

It did not come. Rosa felt a rush of disappointment and a weariness. She'd tried her best. She'd done all she could do. But why should it be enough? Why should she, a fifteen-year-old girl, think she could change anything? And yet . . .

I did it before, Rosa thought. Let me be able to do it again, just this once. If she doesn't go away, I think I shall die . . .

Next day, Rosa ached from head to foot. Every muscle jarred when she moved, and there was a heaviness in her head and neck that made her wonder if she was going to be ill. Even her mother remarked on how pale she was, and when she peeped at herself in the cracked mirror, she was startled by her drained appearance. She knew, of course, that her session in the woods was to blame, but she did not tell her mother.

"You'm cracked, Rosa," she'd say in her whining voice. "Sometimes I think you bl'aint all there."

Rosa, already unsure of herself, certainly did not want her spellmaking to be reduced to that.

For the first time since she had begun working for the Fords, she was late arriving, and Mrs Ford gave her a ticking off so that she had felt obliged to work harder than she usually did, in spite of the heaviness inside her.

But when she was polishing the hall-stand in the passage that ran alongside the millinery room and gave access to the shop from the house, she had overheard Marjorie talking to the other apprentice, and their conversation had made her stop work and stand, wide-eyed, the duster still in her hand.

Could it really be Rebecca Church they were talking about—bundled into a car and driven off to the station? As she listened, Rosa began to tremble, her aching body suddenly cold with fear.

What have I done? she asked herself. What am I capable of doing? And then, through the fear, she caught the first glimpse of triumph. Rebecca had gone away. She, Rosa, had willed it, and it had happened. The feeling of power that had deserted her last night came to her now, and she closed her eyes, her fingers tightening around the crumpled duster.

"Rosa, are you feeling quite well?" She opened her eyes to see Mrs Ford regarding her suspiciously. "You really are very pale, you know."

Rosa nodded, unaware of the strange, distant expression on her narrow face.

"I'm sorry, Mrs Ford. I'm all right really." she said and returned to the polishing with new vigour.

All day, as she worked, the excitement grew in her as she thought of what she had done. Sometimes it constricted her throat so that she could scarcely breathe. It was so momentous, so enormous, she could hardly believe it. Yet it had happened.

I was right, she thought, over and over again. All along, I was right. I am a witch. I do have magic powers. This time there can't be any doubt about it.

So carried away was she that she hardly spared a thought for Ted. It was only when she glimpsed his face as he left the shop, Marjorie having told him the news, that a shadow crossed her trembling excitement.

She loved Ted. She didn't want to hurt him. She just hadn't thought about it from his point of view, that was all.

Her dark eyes grew serious as she remembered his look of disbelief and desperation. Then, determined not to let her moment of triumph be spoiled, she tossed her head, casting her doubts aside. She'd make Ted happy if it was the last thing she did. She'd show him what love was, and he'd soon forget that shy, sheltered little Rebecca Church.

She smoothed her apron over her hips, feeling the roundness where before there had only been skin and bone. The time had come, Rosa thought. With the spell, she had left behind the last of her childhood. Now, at last, she was a woman. And not even Ted Hall could fail to recognize it.

15

AS HE left the shop, unaware he was being watched, Ted fought off a feeling of utter disbelief.

Rebecca gone! It couldn't be true! But Alfred had told him he'd never see her again, and he must have meant what he'd said.

For Christ's sake, why didn't I bring her away with me? Ted thought. She was frightened, but she'd have come if I'd made her. There was no way the old bugger could have stopped her, lying there with the wind knocked out of him.

Helplessly he struck his side with his balled-up fist, wishing he'd hit Alfred harder, wishing he'd grabbed Rebecca and dragged her out of the house. He shouldn't have left her. He should have made up his own mind and done what his intuition had told him to do. But he hadn't, and now it was too late.

In a dream, he rounded the bend, but as the Co-operative store loomed up before him, all his confused thoughts and emotions crystallized into a sense of purpose. Above the Co-operative store were the Co-operative offices. And in the Co-operative offices, unless he, too, had taken a taxi and a train and disappeared, Alfred would be at work.

Ted crossed the road without looking to left or right. A bicycle, speeding down the hill, narrowly missed him and the rider yelled abusively. But Ted took no notice. He marched on, staring up at the windows that overlooked the town and wondering which was Alfred's office.

There was a passageway along the side of the ugly stone building and a flight of steep stairs leading to the offices. Ted marched up them, his boots thudding loudly on the bare boards. A cubby hole marked 'Inquiries' faced the head of the stairs, but he ignored it. He did not want Alfred warned of his arrival.

The corridor branched away to his left, and at the end of it he could see a heavy, oak-panelled door decorated with a large plaque. He turned towards it, past tall cupboards and a room full of musty ledgers where Joey Bird, one of the clerks, was huddled over his books. He looked up at the sound of Ted's approach, but Ted ignored him and marched on.

As he neared the door, he saw that he had been right. The plaque was inscribed with the word 'Secretary.' Without knocking, he turned the brass handle and pushed open the door.

Alfred Church was there, seated behind a desk impressive enough to do justice even to his majestic frame. He had been bending over a ledger, and as the door opened he looked up, startled but otherwise immobile, so that for a moment he looked oddly like a figure in the waxworks Ted had once toured on a day-trip to the seaside. But as he recognized the young man his eyes widened and he half-started to his feet.

Ted crossed the office in two strides, planting his hands on the paper-covered desk and leaning across so that his face was close to Alfred's.

"Where is she?" he demanded. "What have you done with her?"

Alfred swelled with indignation. Then, as suddenly, he relaxed, sinking back into his chair, and a small smile of satisfaction twisted his mouth.

"I don't know what you're talking about."

"Becky. What have you done with Becky?"

"My daughter? What business is that of yours?"

"You know damn well it's my business!" Ted brought his fist down hard on to the desk.

"I'm afraid that there we must agree to differ. There is no need whatever for you to concern yourself with my family. But since you are here, I will tell you Rebecca has left the district. She is staying with relatives and will remain with them until she comes to her senses. Then she will be married to Rupert Thorne, her cousin. She is betrothed to him—I believe I told you. And now, perhaps you would be so good as to remove your hand from my desk."

Ted leaned towards him, infuriated by his patronizing manner. "Where is she? In Bristol?"

Alfred smiled with smug assurance.

"Bristol? Oh, dear me no! Much farther away than Bristol. Now will you leave?"

"Not until you tell me . . . "

"Do you really expect me to do that?" Alfred's tone was sarcastic, yet utterly reasonable, the tone of a caring father trying only to protect his child.

Ted suddenly realized the hopelessness of his position and his control snapped. Furiously, he lunged across the desk at Alfred, but the older man drew back sharply. Ted's hands slipped ineffectually across his white wing collar and shirt front, and he landed in a heap on the ledger on which Alfred had been working.

"You bastard!" he muttered, levering himself up. "You bloody bastard . . . "

Alfred stood up, towering over him. The rage was naked in his eyes, yet still he controlled it.

"Get out of my office!" His voice was dangerously low. "Get out before I call a policeman and have you arrested!"

Ted lunged at him again.

"Becky . . . "

"Mr Bird!" Alfred said sharply, side-stepping, and Ted swung round to see Joey Bird standing in the doorway. "Mr Bird, would you call a policeman? I'm a reasonable man, but . . . "

"Reasonable? You?" Ted began.

"Mr Bird . . . "

"All right, all right, I'm going," Ted said. "But you haven't seen the last of me, Mr Church. I'll be back!"

With that, he turned, pushing past a startled Joey Bird. He was seething still with mingled anger and frustration, but he was as determined as ever. Alfred had sent Rebecca away against her will, and he would not get away with it.

In his office, Alfred was mopping his face with his pocket handkerchief, weak from the exertion of controlling his temper. It was enough to give him a seizure, he thought, but here, at the office, nothing was more important than preserving the image of a reasonable man.

"You shouldn't have let him get away with it, sir," Joey Bird twittered from the doorway. "The youth of today . . . well . . . "

"Disgraceful, I agree. But I see no point in making further trouble, Mr Bird," he said magnanimously.

As Joey went back to his cubby-hole of an office, Alfred found he was actually smiling to himself. This time, he was certain, he had taken the trick—and shown his staff his admirable self-control at the same time. Taken all in all, he was not displeased with his day's work.

AS THE DAYS went by, Ted, frustrated and angry, realized there was nothing he could do but wait for news of Rebecca, and Marjorie was his only contact. He hung around the drapery shop so much that Mrs Ford started complaining and Marjorie had to tell him to stay away.

"You're getting me a bad name," she complained. "I promise I'll let you know the moment I hear anything, but you can't keep waiting outside for me."

"Do you think it would do any good to go and see her mother?" Ted asked. But Marjorie shook her head.

"Not a bit. She's just a shadow of him and scared out of her wits. Leave it to me, Ted. I'll find out, but I can't rush it, or it'll look odd."

And seething though he was, he had to be content with that.

Late summer became autumn, and still there was no news. Life went on as usual, but Ted felt distant, removed from it. His only thoughts were of his sweet Rebecca.

The constant talk of war began to irritate him. Couldn't people think of anything else? Everybody seemed to have a story to tell about a relative at the Front, or if they didn't, they discussed 'slackers' and 'shortages' and the way things should be run.

It was different when it came to Fred, of course. For all his preoccupation with Rebecca, Ted always read with interest his brother's hastily scribbled letters. But although Fred wrote in general terms of days spent marching along mile after mile of dirt tracks, of nights passed in a convenient cow-shed or byre, and of the distant rumble of guns, he wrote little about his own exploits. It was Peggy who first told Charlotte about Fred's promotion to corporal in telecommunications, having heard it in a letter from Colwyn. And it was the same at the beginning of September when news got back of what the papers were later to call his "heroic exploit".

It was a Sunday morning when Peggy got Colwyn's letter, and as soon as she had read it, she ran along the rank to see Charlotte.

For a change these days, the house was full. It was Amy's weekend off, so she was at home, and Jim, Sarah and Alex had come to dinner. Sarah's second baby was due in two weeks' time, and she was glad of the chance to take things easily for once, leaving Harry to play happily with Alex and keep him quiet.

James and Jim had just put on their caps to go out for a pint when Peggy arrived, waving the letter excitedly.

"Did you know your Fred's a hero?"

"A hero—what be talking about?" James asked.

"Come and listen to this!" Peggy said importantly, and when they had clustered around, she smoothed the letter out on the table.

"Now, this is the bit about your Fred.

All the boys were talking about Fred Hall today. You know he's in telecommunications now? Well, it seems he was trying to send a message yesterday and found the lines dead. He climbed a telegraph pole to investigate and found the wires cut. Well, you know Fred. Never one to give up. Off he went and jumped on his bike to deliver the message himself. He hadn't gone far before he came under shell-fire, but he went on, with firing all around him. Of course, he couldn't get away with it. One shell exploded right over him, but he managed to jump off his bike and into a ditch just in time. The shell knocked all the spokes out of his bicycle wheel, but Fred's all right, thank God.

She stopped, looking round. Charlotte had gone chalky white, and the others were almost as shocked. Amy sat with her hands pressed over her mouth, and even the boys were quiet.

"Our Fred—under shell-fire?" Charlotte said at last. "On his bike?"

"Oh, Lotty, I'm sorry!" Peggy touched her arm. "I didn't mean to upset you—I didn't think . . . "

"That's all right, Peg," James said roughly. "It was good of you to let us know."

But Peggy was overcome with guilt. "I just thought, well, it was a heroic thing to do. And I'm always that thrilled when I get a letter from Colwyn . . ."

"I know," Charlotte said. She knew the feeling well enough, the intoxicating sense of relief that was followed too soon by the sharp realization that since the letter had been written, anything could have happened.

"Oh, I wish our Fred was here!" Amy cried, and they all started talking at once.

Only Sarah said nothing. She sat in the fireside chair, her lip caught between her teeth, hands pressed against her stomach.

"Sarah, it's all right. Fred wasn't hurt," Ted said, turning and noticing her.

Sarah nodded and gave an odd little laugh. "I know. It's not Fred. It's me. I think . . . " She broke off, looking at Jim, and he crossed the room to her, all thought of Fred forgotten.

"You don't mean—the baby! Oh, Sal, it can't be, can it?"

"I don't know," Sarah said in a frightened voice. "But it feels like it . . . "

"Well, we've got the expert here," Charlotte said. "Come on, Peg, you didn't expect to get roped in for this, I know, but all the same . . . "

Peggy smiled. "And if it is the baby, you'll all blame me, anyway. All right, you men, out you go. I'll have a look at her."

They went, but before long, the house was in uproar again. The baby certainly was on the way, and according to Peggy, it wasn't going to be long. Clearly there was no time for Sarah to get home, and her own parents, next-door-but-one, were away for the day visiting. So Sarah had to be taken upstairs and put to bed in Amy's room.

"I think somebody ought to go for the doctor," Peggy said, rolling up her sleeves and issuing instructions like a sergeant-major. "She had a bit of trouble last time, didn't she? And it might happen again, you never know."

"I'll go," Ted offered, pleased of the excuse to get out of the house. "It'll have to be Dr Froster, won't it, now that Dr Scott's gone off to France."

"Yes, more's the pity," Charlotte said. Compared with the genial younger man, Dr Froster was so abrupt.

Ted put on his cap and set off. He turned down the hill, walking briskly, but before he had gone far, he saw a familiar figure coming towards him.

Marjorie, he thought. Oh no, it couldn't be. He must have her on the brain. But as she came closer he could see he had been right. It *was* Marjorie.

His breath began to come more rapidly, and his mind churned. She couldn't be coming to see him—could she? But he'd never seen her on this side of town before—and before dinner-time, too . . .

"Hello, Marjie," he said as he reached her.

She stopped, panting with exertion. "Phew, what a climb! I'm glad I've met you so I don't have to go any further. Not that I knew where I was going, anyway."

"You mean, you were looking for me?" he asked.

She nodded. "Yes. I've got some news for you. Becky's in London."

"London?" he repeated.

"Yes. It seems her Aunt Amelia, her father's sister, is a kind of companion with a titled family who live there, and she's got Becky in as a personal maid to the daughter. From what I can gather, the aunt has been angling for her to do that for some time, but nothing had come of it because Alfred's got plans for marrying her off to some cousin or other."

Ted nodded grimly. "Yes, so he told me."

"Oh!" She looked surprised. "Well, anyway, Becky's mother told my mother that he's decided now that she would be better off well out of your way. So she's been packed off to these people—the Harcourtes, I think they're called."

"So I'm no further on then," Ted said, depression returning, but Marjorie opened her bag and pulled out a sheet of folded paper.

"I've got the address if you want it," she said.

"Marjie!" he snatched it from her eagerly. "Marjie, you're a treasure."

"I know," she said with a smile. Then: "Where were you off to in such a hurry, anyway?"

All of a rush he remembered Sarah and the coming baby.

"Oh Lord!" he said. "I shall have to go. Are you going back down the hill now?"

She nodded. "Yes. The things I do for you and Becky!"

WHEN TED got back with Dr Froster, riding in his pony and trap, the house was still in turmoil, with Peggy rushing about and Charlotte trying to cook the vegetables for dinner on the same hob as the boiling water. Although he grumbled, Dr Froster remembered the trouble Sarah had had on the last occasion and went straight to her room. Ted, his duty done, left the house and went down the garden.

It was pleasantly quiet there, with only the Clements's hens clucking in the next-door garden, and for some reason Ted found himself remembering the time the Durrants' pig had got out and rooted up the parsnips. They'd never kept one after that, and the rank had said it had done a good morning's work. But how long ago now it seemed!

He took the sheet of paper Marjorie had given him from his pocket and read it again.

Windsor Square, Belgravia. It sounded a very grand place. But what should he do about it? Should he write to her? If the aunt had been warned, her mail might be intercepted and he wouldn't know. Besides, after all this time, a letter simply was not enough . . .

I'll go and see her, he thought. I'll go and see O'Halloran tomorrow and tell him I want to take a couple of days off, and then I'll go to London myself.

Satisfied with his decision, he turned back to the house, and as he crossed the yard, he heard a thin, unmistakable wail coming from Amy's bedroom window. At the same moment the back door opened, and Jim rushed out, smiling proudly.

"The baby's come then, is it?" Ted asked.

"Yes, and it's a little girl." Jim punched him playfully on the shoulder. "A pigeon pair. Try beating that, laddie!"

"Well done, Jim. Congratulations," Ted said. And it seemed to him that the birth of a niece might be a very good omen.

TWO DAYS later Ted, squeezed into his best blue suit and clutching his new cap firmly in his hand, stepped off an omnibus on the corner of Windsor Square, W.1., and stood looking about him.

When he had told them what he planned to do, James had been scornful and Charlotte incredulous.

"Go to London? Have you taken leave of your senses?" she had asked between running upstairs to see to Sarah, who was obliged to remain in Amy's bedroom for the next week or so.

But Jack, surprisingly, had seemed to understand, and so had Hal. With his daughter Grace separated already from her newly-wed husband, Dr Scott, he was feeling sympathetic towards young lovers.

And so Ted had found out about trains, made the necessary

arrangements, and now here he was, in the capital of England for the first time in his life.

It was a bright autumn afternoon, and here in Belgravia the red and gold of the trees that lined the streets were lending bright splashes of colour to the grey of the pavements and the tall, gracious houses. What surprised Ted was that they were all identical behind their ornamental railings, and each was joined to its neighbour on both sides.

"It's just like a glorified rank," he thought, unable to suppress a feeling of disappointment. "And I'll bet they haven't got half the ground on them that the Rectory has."

For a moment it occurred to him to wonder if Marjorie might have somehow made a mistake. Then a shiny black motor car turned the corner and drew up outside one of the houses, and as he watched the lady passenger alight, cross the pavement and mount the flight of stone steps to the front door, he realized that he certainly must be in the grandest part of London. That lady was unmistakably gentry. And if she lived here, so might the family who were employing Rebecca.

Although he had already memorized it, he looked again at the sheet of paper on which Marjorie had written the address—number 114. Then, with a pulse beating beneath the tight white collar of his shirt, he started along the pavement in the direction of the Square.

It seemed he walked forever, looking at the numbers on the identical front doors, but at last he found it, and stood for a moment looking at the stuccoed pillars and the windows veiled in heavy curtain nets. A flight of stone steps led up to the front door, a second flight curved downwards, below street level, and it was to these he turned. A nerve was throbbing in his throat, and he was worried now that they might send him away without letting him see Becky. If Alfred's sister was anything like Alfred, she could be a dragon . . .

He went down the steps. The basement door was set immediately beneath the bridge leading to the front entrance, so that daylight hardly reached it, and there was a chill in the air that made him even more nervous. It seemed deserted, somehow, shut up. Conquering his anxiety, he rapped on the glass window at the top of the door. No answer. After a minute he rapped again on the wooden panelling, but there was still no reply. Desperation making him bold, he tried to peer through the window, but the heavy nets obscured his vision.

After banging once more on the door with no response, he climbed the steps and went to the front door. He hadn't wanted to disturb the butler, or whoever was in charge, but it seemed he had no choice. He found a bell in the stuccoed stonework and rang it, louder and longer than he had intended, but although it echoed through the house it called up no more response than the basement had.

Defeated, he stood back, looking up at the house. It was almost unbelievable bad luck to come all this way and find the house empty. But where could they all be—and most important, where was Rebecca?

A door banged further down the Square, and he saw a woman climbing the steps from the basement of one of the other houses. From her appearance, Ted guessed she was some kind of cook or housekeeper, and as she came nearer, he went down the steps to speak to her.

"I was looking for the people who live here. You don't know where they are, I suppose?"

For a moment he thought she was going to ignore him. She tossed her head so that the flower garden on top of her hat wobbled violently, and her face set in an expression of affront. Then, as if curiosity was too much for her, she stopped and looked him up and down suspiciously.

"What do you want with them?" she asked in a shrill Cockney voice.

Ted was tempted to tell her to mind her own business, but he knew that would help no one.

"I'm looking for a friend of mine," he said. "She's employed here as a lady's maid."

"Oh, friend is it!" she sniffed. "Well, they wouldn't thank you for calling at the front door, I can tell you that. If they was here, that is, which they ain't."

Ted ignored the criticism. "They're away then?"

"I'm not sure as I ought to answer that. You could be a messenger boy for one of them gangs of ruffians up the East End, wanting to find out how long they'll be away so you can break in and make off with their valuables."

"Do I look like a ruffian then?" Ted asked, disgusted.

"Oh, I wouldn't know. But you don't sound like one. You sound —where *do* you come from?"

"Somerset," Ted said. "Look, I've come all the way from Bath to see my friend. I'm not going to break into the house if you tell me —though I might if you don't," he added.

"You wouldn't get much anyway. Everybody's putting their valuables into safe-keeping while they're away, with things as they are."

"What do you mean?" Ted asked.

"Gorn off to their country house, they have, out of the way of the air-raids, or so their cook told me. I can't understand it meself. Not likely to harm the likes of us. And when the Zeps do come over, it's worth watching, like the fireworks they had for the coronation, you know. Nothing to get all het up about."

The Zeps, Ted thought—the German Zeppelins which were bombing London. He'd heard about it, but it hadn't even crossed his mind to think it might make any difference to him, or even to wonder if Rebecca might be in any danger. The war was in France, not here in England.

"Where have they gone, then?" he asked. "And when will they be back?"

"Oh, they won't be back till our boys put a stop to this air-raid nonsense, I shouldn't think. And it's Oxfordshire they've gone. They've got a place there that used to belong to her family—the lady's. Very pretty, so they say. But I should miss London meself. I couldn't abide all that fresh air and no decent shops."

"Where in Oxfordshire?" Ted asked.

"Oh, I'm sure I wouldn't know." And then, as if suddenly annoyed with herself for allowing the chatterbox side of her nature to get the better of her, the woman hoisted her basket on to her hip. "If you want to get on, my lad, you'll learn not to ask so many questions," she told him and she marched off along the street.

Dismayed, Ted watched her go. There was a hollow emptiness beginning to deepen inside him. He was not going to see Rebecca after all. He had come all this way for nothing. There was absolutely no chance of him finding the address of the country house. No, there was only one thing left to do—return home and try and glean some more information from Marjorie.

Taking one last look at the grand house, he walked slowly back along the street. Beneath his feet, the leaves that had already fallen from the trees rustled, and they seemed an ominous portent of the winter that lay ahead. He kicked at them, in helpless impatience, and wondered what to do. He might as well go back to Paddington and take an early train home, he thought. Yet still he hesitated, reluctant to leave the city where there was always the chance that he might still discover some clue as to Rebecca's whereabouts. As yet he was at a loss to know what he could do, but he had not planned to go home until the last train, and he had even considered taking lodgings and staying until the following day, Sunday. Perhaps if he did that, some inspiration would come to him. He was grasping at straws, he knew, but his optimism was beginning to surface once more.

He turned out of Windsor Square and walked along aimlessly. The thought of losing his way did not occur to him, and he took no notice of where he was going until he found himself standing and staring at a large building behind an impressive forecourt, with armed sentries at the gates.

Buckingham Palace, he thought, recognizing it at once from the newspaper photographs he had seen, and a small stirring of patriotic pride swelled in him. Mam would like to be here now, that was for sure. She'd followed all the news about the Royals for as long as he could remember.

He stood for a moment, taking it all in so that he could relay it to her when he got home again. Then, his spirits lifted a little, and with a sense of adventure he walked on, down the tree-lined Mall, beside the park where uniformed nannies pushed their charges in impressively large baby carriages.

At the end of the broad, straight walk, he passed beneath a stone archway, and before he knew it he stood looking at a square where fountains bubbled and the proud figure of Nelson surveyed London from his lofty plinth.

Ted crossed the road and walked towards the fountains, his anxiety for Rebecca temporarily forgotten in the feeling of pleasure and surprise. This was a far cry from Hillsbridge, he thought, and deep inside an emotion stirred that was partly a thirst for the new and exciting and partly a wonder that he, Ted Hall, should be here in the heart of London.

For a while he stood there, watching the omnibuses and the taxi-cabs, the horse-drawn carriages and the bicycles that revolved around him, and time seemed to take on a new dimension. Then he walked around the Square himself, inspecting the buildings and the roads that led off, and wondering which one to explore next. For Ted suddenly had no intention of leaving without first extracting every new experience that offered itself.

An orange-seller was sitting on the steps of St. Martin's-in-the-Fields, and Ted stopped and purchased a piece of fruit from her. But as he bit into the orange, Ted remembered that he had only eaten a piece of bread and dripping that Charlotte had packed up all day. Suddenly he was starving. He looked around him, immediately becoming aware of the tempting aroma of food that wafted from the open doors and windows of the public houses that punctuated the Strand.

In the doorway of one, a child was sitting, dress pulled down over her knees, grubby face upturned to watch him pass.

"Evenin', mister." Her voice was pert, her eyes bright, and in spite of her grimy appearance and tangled hair, she reminded him of Amy as she had been five or six years ago. "Spare a copper then, mister?"

"Haven't you got a home to go to?" he asked.

She shrugged her bony shoulders. "I'm waitin' for me Mam."

"Where is she then?"

"Oh, in the pub, I think. Or she might be wiv a man . . . "

Ted took a coin from his pocket and tossed it to the child, and although she snatched at it greedily there was something so mischievous in her manner that he was forced to smile. He didn't agree with women leaving their children on pub doorsteps while they drank away the money they should have spent on food, but there was nothing he could do about it, and this waif was a likeable little madam.

Putting her out of his mind, he went into the saloon bar and in the smoky, noisy atmosphere, he enjoyed a hearty meal of steak, kidney and oyster pudding, washed down with a pint of good strong beer.

It was as he scraped the last of the thick delicious gravy on to his knife that the murmur began to run around the bar, swelling until it was loud enough to drown all other conversation.

"The Zeps are coming, they say. That geyser over there was going by Marconi House when somebody came out and said so. Yeah, they're on their way, the swine."

Ted put down his knife and fork, and a shiver ran up his spine, not of fear, but of excitement. The Zeps coming—and he was here in the thick of it!

Remembering what the Cockney lady had said about an air-raid being a show well worth watching, he pushed back his chair and got to his feet.

The other customers in the bar seemed curiously unmoved at the prospect of a raid. They talked about it, then filled their glasses and went on drinking. As Ted left, he noticed that the child he had likened to Amy was still sitting on the doorstep, but now she was fast asleep, her head folded down into her pinafore, her knees splayed defencelessly. He took another coin from his pocket and tossed it into her lap. She did not stir, but he pictured her face when she awoke and found it there, and smiled to himself.

Outside, darkness had fallen. While he had been eating, dusk had turned to inky blackness, and as the lamps had been lit up and down the Strand, so the shutters had been put up, blotting out the shafts of brightness that would make a target for a Zeppelin.

Ted began walking, although he did not know in which direction he headed, and it was not long before he heard the first distant throb of engines in the sky. Slowly, remorselessly, they grew closer, filling the night with deep, rhythmic sound. Ted stopped to listen, taking a packet of cigarettes from his pocket and lighting one from a carefully shielded match. But before he could draw the smoke into his lungs, the quiet of the night erupted around him. Anti-aircraft fire crackled across the sky, sharp as the snapping of a twig underfoot, but a hundred times louder. The air vibrated with the throb of engines, and then, cutting across the other sounds came a mournful whine, screaming towards a high-pitched crescendo. Ted had never heard anything like it before, but he knew what it was. A bomb! And not far away—overhead, almost!

He stood, riveted by horror and fascination, as the whine grew louder and more piercing, and the bomb sliced through the air. Strangely detached, as if he was watching a picture at the Palace Picture House, Ted waited for the explosion, but when it came, a heavy, muffled thud that spread and grew into rippling echoes, it was close—much closer than he had dreamed it would be. The pavement trembled beneath his feet, the buildings around him shook, and Ted felt the first stirring of alarm.

He turned, wondering where he could run for shelter, but before he could move, the whining sound came again, closer and more penetrating even than the throbbing of the Zeppelin's engines. It was another bomb—and almost directly above him!

For one surprised second, he thought, as he had thought when the tub had dragged him down the incline: I'm going to die! Then the instinct of self-preservation galvanized his paralysed limbs into action and he hurled himself along the street away from

224

the direction of the first explosion and away from the whining crescendo.

The second bomb hit the ground with a deafening sound, the impact flinging him against the wall of a building. For a moment he lay, dazed, yet oddly certain he was unhurt. His ears felt muffled as if they had been stuffed with cotton wool. But then, as his hearing cleared, he heard the sounds of pandemonium, the crash of falling masonry, the tinkle of raining glass, the screams, the cries, the distant thud of more bombs falling. Beside him, a man's voice asked, "Are you all right, mate?" He raised his head and shoulders from the pavement, turning his heavy, numbed body with difficulty.

"Yes, I'm all right," he said, but his voice seemed to come from a long way off, and his head had begun to ache with a dull, insistent thudding.

Feeling like a drunk, he struggled to his feet. Then, as he turned round, a feeling of utter horror swamped him. The pub where he had eaten had gone! There was nothing left of it but a pile of smoking rubble!

"Good God!" he said under his breath. And in the same shocked moment he thought of the little girl. She had been in the doorway —she could be buried alive.

As he tried to walk, one of his legs gave way. It was numb, and the other one was throbbing and sore. But he hardly noticed. Like a man possessed, he picked his way across the carpet of glittering glass.

There were arms and legs sticking out of the rubble, but Ted thought only of the child. He found what had been the doorway, and miraculously part of it was still standing, and the child was still there. In the midst of all the destruction, she looked almost untouched by the blast. Perhaps the doorpost had saved her from the worst of the blast, Ted thought, and she was only stunned as he had been. He bent over and picked her up gently. Her head lolled awkwardly against his shoulder, and he looked around, wondering what to do with her.

"Up to the Lyceum, anybody that's hurt," a man shouted to him. "It's the only place left standing."

Ted had never heard of the Lyceum, but he followed him along the street, stumbling over the rubble. There was a pool of light spilling brazenly on to the glittering pavements further along, and when they reached it, he realized it was a theatre. Or was supposed to be. Just now, it was more like a battleground, with the injured lying moaning and bleeding on billboards, and people screaming and crying as they looked for their missing relatives and friends.

Ted staggered in with the child, half-blinded by the sudden blaze of light. He walked up to the man who seemed to be issuing instructions.

"Help her, for God's sake. She's only a nipper!" he pleaded.

The man looked down at her, turning her face out of Ted's shoulder and taking her limp wrist between his fingers. Then his face darkened, and he dropped her hand again.

"She's dead," he said shortly.

"No! She can't be!" Ted argued foolishly.

He looked down at her again. Her face was unmarked, except for a small cut on the temple, and she looked more childish and innocent than she had when she was asking him for money. But it was true. She was dead all right. Here, in the brightly lit foyer, there was no mistaking it.

A sudden wave of nausea enveloped him. Gently he laid her down on the floor and stood looking down at her. She was so young, so young, and there had been something so infectious about her— cheeky, irrepressible, bubbling with life although she must have spent too many nights waiting outside pubs for her drunken whore of a mother. And now one bomb dropped by a Zep had snuffed all that out like a candle.

"The murdering bloody swine!" Ted muttered.

"Hey, mate, you'd better sit down."

To Ted it seemed that the voice came from a long way off. Around him, the brightly lit foyer became a jumble of jarring sounds and disembodied faces—a magic lantern show with each facet reflecting a different, fragmented part of the whole.

Without knowing how he got there, Ted found himself lying on a bed of coats. The throbbing of his leg had increased, and when he glanced down he was surprised to see scarlet flesh beneath torn cloth.

"My best bloody suit!" he muttered foolishly.

Then the foyer seemed to go away from him, and darkness closed in from the edges of his consciousness.

FOR TWO WEEKS Ted was in hospital in London. His legs had been cut by shrapnel and flying glass, and he was suffering from delayed shock. But it was all they could do to keep him there. As he lay immobile, day after day, anger and frustration grew in him, and Jack, who came to London to visit him when the news of what happened was telegraphed to Hillsbridge, was shocked at the change in him.

"He's so bitter," he said to Charlotte when he got home. "As if he was suddenly all full of hate. And he kept going on and on about a little girl who was killed, as if he couldn't get her off his mind."

That just about summed it up. Ted's anger had centred around the two main incidents of that day when the bomb had fallen on the Strand—losing Rebecca, and the death of the unknown child. Alfred Church and the Hun seemed like one and the same—The Enemy. And Rebecca and the child—both were helpless victims.

But what could he do about it?

After all his reasoning, the answer came in a flash. He would leave the pits and enlist, and it would be a way of killing two birds with one stone.

On the one hand he would be building a future for Rebecca and himself. He would be out of the mines and the life of bondage to which they sentenced men—and their wives. And when it was all over, there would surely be employers only too willing to give a chance to young men who had done their bit for king and country.

And at the same time he would be able to help avenge the deaths of the beggar child and the seventeen others who had been killed by that one bomb in the Strand. Seeing the war at first hand had made more impression on him than all the talk in the local pub in Hillsbridge, and he was so angry at the brutal waste that, next to finding Rebecca, he was determined to seek his revenge on the faceless Hun.

Fate was a strange thing, he thought. If the bomb had dropped ten minutes earlier, he would have been in the pub bar, and he would probably have died over the remains of his steak, kidney and oyster pudding. But he had not died. He was alive. And he was young and strong, and when his legs were healed, he'd be fit too.

And so, two weeks later, when he climbed out of the train at Bath, he went off to find a recruiting office and enlist with the Somersets. Perhaps he was no closer to finding Rebecca, but he believed, fervently, it was the best thing he could do.

16

TED WAS not the only Hillsbridge boy to enlist that October. When he came home and the news spread along the rank, Redvers Brixey decided to do the same.

Mrs Brixey was as distraught as Charlotte.

"I'd go and fight the Kaiser myself if I thought I could keep him out of it!" she said.

But the boys had signed on, and that was it. Within a matter of days, they had left for Salisbury Plain, the camp where Fred had done his training, and there were two more empty places at the dinner tables in the rank.

"I can't get used to having to do so few vegetables," Charlotte said to James one morning as she peeled potatoes in the scullery. "I keep filling the saucepan up and then remembering it's only you and me and Harry to eat them."

"Well, I shan't want many, anyway," James told her.

November had arrived, dank and chill, with cold, gusting winds and rain that washed rivers of coal-dust along the gutters. James had been obliged to stay off work for over a week now due to a bad chest cold.

Charlotte cast a quick, worried glance in his direction. He *wasn't* eating as well as he used to, hadn't for weeks now, but she supposed that was hardly to be wondered at.

She knew that, as well as being ill, he also missed the boys. He didn't say much, that wasn't his way, but they'd been with him in the pits for so long now it was bound to be strange without them. There was still Jim, of course, but he was a getter in his own right, and more often than not was working in a different seam. And when he'd finished his day's shift, he was always in a hurry to get home to Sarah and the children.

"It was all over that girl, you know," she suddenly said to James, as if stating a new fact. "From the first time I saw them together, I knew no good would come of it."

James nodded, saying nothing, and she went on. "He took it too serious, that's the trouble. Now if only he could be a bit more like our Dolly . . ."

Dolly had another boyfriend, a nephew of Cook's, who was in the Marines and had come to visit her while home on leave. But although he had been all for getting engaged before he went back to the war, Dolly had refused to be tied down.

"Amy said he begged and begged her," Charlotte said. "But you know our Dolly. She won't be hurried. And I think she learned her lesson over that Evan Comer business, though she's still got him on her mind, I know. She saw him in town the other day, on his crutches, and it quite upset her."

"That girl will go all around the orchard and finish up picking a crab-apple," James said sagely. "Just see if I'm not right."

"Crab-apple—that reminds me!" Charlotte carried the pot of potatoes into the kitchen and set it down on the hob. "I promised Amy I'd get her some new ribbons to go on her petticoat."

"What have petticoats got to do with crab-apples?" James asked, puzzled.

"Nothing," Charlotte replied. "It just reminded me, that's all. Amy's petticoat is muslin, and you use muslin to strain the fruit when you're making apple jelly. Now, I wonder. Have I got time to run down to Fords before we have dinner? It's Amy's half-day, and she might come down this afternoon to see if I've got it."

"If it's her half-day, why doesn't she do her own shopping?" James grumbled.

"Because it's Wednesday, early closing," Charlotte said. "Now, if I put the potatoes on, you could watch them for me, couldn't you?"

"I could, but I don't see it's necessary for you to run about after her."

Charlotte did not reply. She did not want to have to explain that with the boys away in France, she felt she wanted to do all she could for the children who were still with her. She had thought a lot about them all lately, wishing she had had more time to spend with each of them. But there had been too many of them, too close, and she had always been kept so busy. And now they were grown up, all but Harry, and it was too late.

She put on her coat and hat and went out. Charlie Durrant was just crossing the yard to the privy, reading the pieces of torn-up newspaper that he was taking with him to go on the wire behind the door, and she thought what a shrunken old man he had become since he had retired in the summer. They passed the time of day, and she hurried on.

In the hill, she saw Edgar Hawker, the telegram boy, pushing his bicycle as he climbed the steepest part of the hill, and her heart began to thud with sick dread. She'd always had this awful feeling when she saw a telegram boy—they so often brought bad news—and since Fred had been at the Front it was a hundred times worse. But Edgar passed her without comment, and as she turned to watch him, he went through the gateway of one of the cottages in the hill.

Charlotte heaved an audible sigh of relief and went on. The town was quiet this morning. As she passed the Rectory gates, she saw Caroline Archer going up the drive, and smiled to herself. She still wasn't leaving the new Rector alone, then. But at least Charlotte felt she had little to fear from her these days.

Up the hill to the drapers she went, pushing open the door and making the bell jangle.

The girl assistant who served her was dark and pretty, but Charlotte could not help noticing the curious looks the girl gave her as she measured and cut the lengths of ribbon, and when Charlotte got out her purse to pay, she said in a low, hurried voice, "I am right, aren't I? You are Ted Hall's mother?"

Charlotte's eyes narrowed. "Yes. Why?"

"Because . . . oh, look, my name's Marjorie Downs. I live next door to Becky Church, or next door to her mother and father, anyway. Becky's not there any more. But I've found out where she is now, and I promised Ted I'd . . . "

"Ted's enlisted in the army," Charlotte said shortly. "He's in training on Salisbury Plain."

"Yes, but you must write to him. Couldn't you just pass on an address?" Marjorie said urgently. "I was going to send the message to you by Rosa Clements, the servant. But somehow I don't quite trust her. And it's very important to Becky—and Ted."

Charlotte hesitated. From the moment Marjorie had introduced herself, she knew what was coming and wished she could have avoided it. With a gut instinct she knew Rebecca could never make Ted happy, and she thought that the sooner he forgot her the better. But now the matter had been raised again. If she refused to pass on a message, Ted would never forgive her.

"All right. Tell me what it is and I'll put it in my next letter," she said.

With a quick look towards the millinery room, Marjorie wrote on the bill pad and passed it to Charlotte, who glanced at it while the young girl finished folding the ribbon.

"Wycherley Grange, Wycherley."

"Where's that?" Charlotte asked.

"Oxfordshire. Didn't I put it?"

"No, but it doesn't matter. I will," Charlotte said.

And taking the ribbons and the address, she left the shop.

TO TED and Redvers, it seemed that it had rained ever since they arrived at the camp on Salisbury Plain. Everything was grey, from the heavy skies merging on the horizon into the misty hilltops to the hastily erected hutments and tents. Underfoot was mud and sodden, squelchy turf, and even the sheets on the narrow camp beds felt clammy and damp. Ted and Redvers, billeted in one of the hutments, were lucky. The men in the tents were much worse off. The large bells were on the side of the hill, and when it rained really hard the water ran in one side and out the other.

But the sergeant-major made no allowances. He drilled them relentlessly, and when the rain dripped down his neck, or his socks were damp, he only shouted at them the louder, marching them up and down the flat valley floor until their legs ached and they thought their gun-carrying arm would drop off.

It was not all drill, of course. There was shooting out at the rifle ranges, and bayonet drill, and bomb-throwing practice which took place in an isolated spot some three miles away from the camp. The boys enjoyed that. There was something satisfying about hurling a missile and seeing it explode in a cloud of smoke. But when the weather was especially bad, three miles was a long way to march. And that particular November afternoon, when they got back from bomb-throwing, they were all exhausted and soaked to the skin.

"Why did I let you talk me into this?" Redvers asked Ted as they towelled life back into their numb bodies. "I must have been off my trolley."

"I didn't talk you into anything," Ted retorted. He sounded snappish because there was clean underwear to be put on, and he hated the scratchy tightness of it, and knew he'd be itching all night.

"Cheer up, lads, here comes t' mail!" Wally Gifford, a taciturn Geordie who shared their billet, announced.

"Shut up, Gifford, you've no business here anyway," Redvers chided him good-naturedly, and Wally laughed.

"You're right enough there, lad," he agreed in his flat tones. He had thought he had joined one of the northern regiments, and it was still a mystery to him how he had come to find himself in the Somersets.

The mail was distributed, and they all fell upon it eagerly. But Ted, seeing his letter was from Charlotte, left it on his bunk until he was properly dressed. He was as keen to get a letter from home as anyone, but Charlotte wrote regularly, and he thought the gossip from the rank and the tales of Harry's latest pranks could wait until he was warm and dry.

At last, shivering in his tight undershirt, he sat down on his bunk and slit open the envelope. It was as he had thought—all the usual family gossip. But at the bottom of the second page, almost reluctantly, Charlotte had added a postscript.

> *I saw Rebecca's friend Marjorie today, and she told me Rebecca is now at Wycherley Grange, Wycherley, Oxon. But according to Marjorie, things are as difficult as ever, so what you do is up to you.*

For a moment he stared at it, almost unable to believe his eyes, then he let out a whoop that made the others turn to look at him.

"Wha's up wi' you, lad?" Wally asked, unsmiling, and Ted could have bitten off his tongue.

"Oh, nothing, just a girl I thought I'd lost contact with," he said, but it was too late to cover up the way he felt, and besides, Redvers knew all about Rebecca.

"You don't mean the old boy's let her go, do you?" he asked.

"No," Ted said. "But now I know where she is, I can go and see her."

"I'd write first if I was you," Wally advised. "Just to make sure the coast's still clear."

Ted thought about it. "If I do that, someone might get hold of my letter and take her out of my way. No, I think it would be best to take them all by surprise."

They began to tease him then, but Ted took it all in good part. He was too relieved to care what they said. Knowing where Rebecca was made him feel great, even if he couldn't go to see her until he finished his training and got his embarkation leave in just over two weeks' time. And for the moment he didn't stop to think that after that brief leave there would be the Channel between them, if not an ocean.

As the initial excitement wore off, the two weeks stretched ahead of him endlessly. Sometimes, he passed the time by wondering what she would say when she saw him. Sometimes he tried to look further ahead, making plans as to how he could get her away and marry her. He was eager now to get to the Kaiser. The sooner the war was over, the sooner he and hundreds like him would be able to return to normal living and get on with their lives.

Redvers was going home for his embarkation leave, and the night before their passing-out parade, Ted asked him yet again to explain to Charlotte why he was not coming home, too. He had written, of course, but words on paper could not adequately express his feelings, and he knew the family would be hurt to think he was going to France without seeing them first. But it couldn't be helped. It wasn't really that Rebecca was more important to him than they were, just that when he was thinking of her anyone else ceased to exist.

On the last day he managed to save his bacon rinds at breakfast time and wrap them in his handkerchief.

"Give these to Nipper, will you?" he said, pushing them into Redvers's kit-bag. "He loves a bit of bacon, always has." But there was no time for sentiment, and even the thought of Nipper's wagging tail and rough tongue could not change his mind.

"Anybody'd think this was t'only girl in t'world," Wally remarked. "Later on, tha'll see more on her than tha' wants."

But Ted ignored him. He knew better than to try to explain he could never, if he lived to be a hundred, see too much of Rebecca. Here, with the other recruits, he was expected to behave like a man —and men were not supposed to have romantic notions.

With the others, Ted went to Westbury Station to catch a train, but he could not concentrate on their jokes or bother to join in when they started whistling after a buxom young woman in porter's uniform who was pushing a laden trolley up and down the platform. He had not realized that women really *were* doing men's jobs, but that was as far as it went. He couldn't be bothered to join in the catcalls, for his mind was too occupied.

As he stood in the corridor of the train, his kit-bag propped against his knees, watching the rolling hills of Wiltshire disappear into the December mists, his thoughts were far from the war. To him all that mattered—all that had mattered for the last year—was almost within his grasp once more. He was going to see Rebecca, and no one, not even the Kaiser himself, could stop him.

WYCHERLEY VILLAGE was set in a valley, not a steep-sided bowl like the one Hillsbridge had sprung up in and around, but a gentle fold in the Chiltern Hills. After leaving the train, Ted had begged a lift on a fruit wagon, and when it set him down outside the Crossways Tavern, dusk had already fallen. He looked around him and saw a handful of cottages, whitewashed and thatched behind their neat patches of garden, and a small all-purpose store whose window overlooked the spot where he was standing. The tavern was not yet open, but a light was burning behind the jars and bottles of sweets in the shop window, and Ted hoisted his kit-bag on to his shoulder, crossed the road and pushed open the door.

The jangling bell brought a woman into the shop. She emerged from a curtain behind the counter like a genie from a lamp.

"Yes, can I help you?" Her eyes moved over him quickly and with interest, and he guessed that this shop was the local gossip spot.

"I'm looking for somewhere to stay, just for a day or two. Does anybody here let rooms?"

Her brow creased. Wycherley had never enticed many visitors, and since the war had begun there had been none at all.

"Well, there's the pub. They might . . . "

"They aren't open yet."

"I don't know then. I can't suggest anything. Why?"

Ted decided he might as well tell the truth now as later.

"I've come to see a friend of mine—a girl—who's in service at Wycherley Grange. I'm being posted to France next week."

Quite suddenly the little woman's attitude became more cordial. "My man's in France," she said with pride. "A regular he is, of course, but when there's a war on . . . " She broke off, looking at him closely. "Where you from then?"

"I've just been training on Salisbury Plain. Left there this morning."

"And you've been travelling ever since?"

He nodded, and after a moment's thought, she seemed to make up her mind.

"I've got a spare room. It's not much, mind. But you can stay there the night if you want. It's not for bringing this lass of yours back to, of course. I wouldn't want them sort of goings on, but . . . "

"Nor me. How much will you want for it?"

She looked embarrassed. "Oh, I don't know. We can talk about that later, can't we?"

He held out his hand. "Right, it's a deal. And thanks very much. I'm Ted Hall, by the way."

She nodded, lifting the counter for him to come through. "Mrs Pledger. Now. I expect you could do with a cup of tea . . . "

The rooms behind the shop were small and cluttered. It was a tiny living room which, to Ted's bewilderment, seemed to be full of the ticking of at least a dozen clocks. He climbed the narrow wooden staircase leading to an equally narrow room beneath the eaves. Ted set down his kit-bag beside the chest of drawers, flung his greatcoat across the bed, and went back down for the promised cup of tea. He was shaking with impatience to see Rebecca, but he hoped that Mrs Pledger might be able to tell him something of the situation at The Grange.

Sure enough, over a cup of tea so strong that it seared his empty stomach, she talked of the 'gentry' from London, going into so much of their family history that Ted was soon hopelessly lost. What he did manage to learn was that The Grange was the home of Lady Harcourte's parents, and the household had moved down to the country to escape the bombing in town. After a break to make him a plateful of egg sandwiches, Mrs Pledger went on to tell him that there was a daughter, Rachel, who was about Rebecca's age.

"I should think your young lady is lady's maid to the young mistress," she told him, proud of her knowledge.

"I think I'll go up there right away," Ted said when he had finished his tea and sandwiches. "I've only got a couple of days, and they'll go by like lightning."

Mrs Pledger sighed, wiping her hands on her apron, and using the voice of experience. "You're right there. There's nothing like a leave for giving the clock wings," she said. "Well, good luck to you, my lad, that's what I say. Good luck to all of you!"

For the first time for more than a week, it was a dry night. The stars were shining, and the wind had dropped. Ted followed the road Mrs Pledger had described, turning into a lane and then into a drive.

As the house came into sight, so the drive divided, one fork leading to the high vaulted front door, the other curving around to the side of the house. He took the latter path. Every nerve in his body was taut with tension. What sort of reception would he get? If the aunt answered the door, perhaps she would not even let him see Rebecca. He climbed two stone steps, raised his hand to knock and, after the smallest hesitation, banged sharply. Almost at once he heard footsteps coming along a flagged corridor, and for the first time in years he found himself praying: "Let her be here. Oh, dear God, let her be here."

The door opened. Lamplight flooded out into the darkness, and he stood for a moment, half-blinded, half-disbelieving. It couldn't be, surely . . . She wouldn't be opening the door, would she?

"Becky," he said.

She stood with one arm raised to hold the door open, her head tilted to one side so that she looked like a small neat bird. No words passed her lips. Then, "Ted," she whispered, her voice trembling, uncertain and full of awe. "Ted . . . oh, Ted."

Time was suspended as they looked at one another, then, in a fluid movement that seemed to envelope them both, they were in each other's arms, laughing, crying and clinging to one another.

From the depths of the house, a stern voice called, "Who is it at this time of night?"

Rebecca wriggled free.

"It's all right. It's someone come to see me, Mrs Haydon."

Then, without explanation, she pressed her face to his again.

Beneath his lips, her cheeks were salt, the taste of tears mingling with the delicate perfume of her hair. Her body was smaller and firmer than he remembered it, and he moved his hands from her shoulders and breasts to her narrow waist and the curving swell of her hips, as if to remember, by touch, every inch of her.

"Oh, Becky, I want you so," he said breathlessly.

"And I want you. Oh, Ted, I've wanted you and wanted you."

He laughed then, delighted by her, and she turned to pull the door after her, shutting them out into the night.

"Won't you be missed?" he asked. "Your aunt?"

"Lady Harcourte had to go visiting for a couple of days. Aunt Amelia has gone with her. Oh, Ted, what luck that you should come just now! Look, let's go into the garden. There's so much to say . . ."

"But you'll be cold . . ."

"Oh, I don't care if I am. I don't care about anything now."

"Go back and get a coat."

"No, you might disappear again."

"Well, have mine then."

He took it off and slipped it round her shoulders, taking the opportunity to caress her again, and she leaned fondly against him.

"You came, Ted, you came," she whispered.

"Soon as I could. I've joined up."

"Yes. But why ever did you go and volunteer for a soldier?"

They were in the garden now, walking along the narrow path between the shadowy cabbages and making for the shelter of the wall that divided it from the orchard. Ted did not want to talk. He was burning with urgent desire, and he wanted only to hold her again and feel her so close to him that a single thrust could make them one. His body ached for her, his senses reeling.

"I did it for you, Becky," he said.

They passed through the stone archway, and he turned into the shadow of the wall, leaning his back against it and pulling her against him.

"For me? Why for me?"

"So we can make a new life together when it's all over. I'd take you away—I'd have done it long ago, but there's nowhere to take you."

"But to go and enlist! Supposing you're . . . " She could not bring herself to speak the word "killed". "Suppose something should happen to you?"

He laughed softly, sure in the knowledge of having faced death once before and won through.

"Nothing will happen to me. And afterwards I shan't go back to the pits, Becky. I'll make the sort of life for you that you deserve. That's a promise."

"You mean, we'll be married?"

"That's right. Oh, Becky, Becky . . . "

His coat slipped unheeded from her shoulders as he pulled her close again, and above them the fitful moon slid behind a ragged cloud. But lost in one another they noticed nothing. This was the meeting they had longed for, and too soon it would be over. They had no intention of wasting a single second.

FOR TED and Rebecca the next two days were a wonderful, stolen interlude. For the first time since they had met, they were free to be together almost as often as they wished.

Rebecca confided the whole story to Miss Rachel, her young mistress, who was enchanted by the romance and intrigue of it all. She was wildly in love with a young Grenadiers officer who was himself leading a troop into battle in France, and without hesitation she gave Rebecca all the help she needed to meet Ted secretly.

"Of course, I couldn't do it if Mother were here," she whispered. "But as it is I'm just so envious of you I can hardly bear it. And oh, he is so very handsome! You must see as much of him as you can before he goes off to war, in case he never comes back. And don't look at me like that! Facts have to be faced. We all have to face them."

Her blue eyes filled with tears, and Rebecca thought again of the dashing young Grenadier and decided that Rachel was a great deal braver than she, to talk so blithely about men who might never come back.

With Rachel's help, she met him both in the village and in the garden behind the house, and on the day before he was due to leave, her young mistress actually suggested that she should entertain him in her personal drawing room.

"Oh, I couldn't!" Rebecca had said, but Rachel quashed her arguments.

"I'll bring him up here myself," she said, with the firm decisiveness that came from a life already spent in giving orders. "Then all you have to do is slip up here yourself. Oh, Rebecca, for heavens sake remember he's going straight to hell. Be nice to him."

Her words had brought Rebecca face to face with reality. In the strange, dream-like atmosphere of the last two days, she had asked nothing more than to be with Ted, talking, laughing and kissing. There had been so much to say, so much to tell.

She chattered on and on about London and her new life, wanting to share every experience with him. And all the while there had been the excitement of his nearness, the thrill that darted inside her when he touched or kissed her, the warmth that swept through her body when their eyes met.

She knew he loved her. Perhaps, she thought, she had always known, and only been afraid to acknowledge it in case the wonder went away. For that had seemed sickeningly inevitable. Sooner or later, Ted would grow tired of waiting and scheming, of being preached at and threatened, and would forget her in the company of some other pretty girl. Now, however, for the first time, she was sure of him, and it was wonderful.

It was only when Rachel spoke to her about entertaining him in her private drawing room that she was brought back to reality. By this time tomorrow he would be gone! All she would have of him would be her memories. Life would go on as it had before he came, and soon it would seem that he had been no more than a dream.

And perhaps he would never come back.

The thought almost made her cry out, but she forced herself to face it as she knew she must. She covered her face with her hands, pressing against her eyes until the blood ran in flashes of purple and scarlet behind the closed lids. He mustn't die. I won't let him. But what can I do? Perhaps if I gave him something, as a talisman . . .

A photograph! She had gone with her father and mother to a studio in Bath just before her departure. There they had posed together in a stiff group. Alfred had dominated the photograph, standing sternly with his thumbs tucked in his watch chain, and Winnie somehow managed to look demure instead of cowed. But it was an especially good photograph of Rebecca. She had been so pleased with it she had kept a copy in her bag, and now she took it out, looking at it critically. Would Ted think it vain and presumptuous to give him a photograph of herself?

Of one thing she was very sure—he wouldn't want to take her father and mother with him too. Rebecca found a pair of scissors and carefully cut her own likeness out of the photograph in a neat oval. Then she slipped it back inside her purse. When the chance came, she would give it to him as a keepsake.

On his last evening, she was still in her room when Rachel came in to say Ted had been shown into her private drawing room. "Now off you go, and remember to treat him nicely," she told Rebecca sternly. "And don't worry, I shan't be the one to disturb you." She smiled, a knowing smile that reminded Rebecca oddly of Marjorie.

Why does she keep harping on about being nice to Ted? Rebecca wondered. How could she possibly think that in the circumstances I could be anything but nice?

She went down the carpeted stairs to the drawing room feeling hot with embarrassment. It was nice of Rachel, of course, to allow them to use it, but she wished she hadn't done it all the same. When Lady Harcourte returned at the end of the week and got to hear of it, there would be all kinds of trouble, and besides, she would have been far more at ease with Ted in the garden or going for a walk along the lanes. It was a dry night, and she rather liked the thought of snuggling under the collar of his great coat in some quiet gateway.

But Rebecca had the uncomfortable feeling that however much she had protested, Rachel would have eventually had her own way. She was paid to be her companion as well as her maid, and if arranging her private affairs amused Rachel, then arrange them she would.

Rebecca pushed open the drawing room door to find Ted standing on the hearthrug before the ornately carved mantelshelf.

"Hello," she said shyly.

He turned, and she realized he was not at all overawed by his surroundings. "Hello," he teased in return, reaching for her hand and pulling her towards him. "Now this is what I call doing it in style."

She bit her lip. "We should have gone out, Ted. I don't like using her room."

He held her at arm's length, looking at her.

"If we'd gone out, you'd have been all buttoned up in your coat, and I shouldn't have been able to see you properly—or feel you when I kiss you, either."

She looked at him, half understanding his meaning and her stomach churned relentlessly. She liked to be close to him, of course, and sometimes, when he held her, the restless excitement made her cling to him with an immodesty that made her cringe when she thought of it afterwards. She had even begun to accept the sensations his nearness excited in her as pleasurable as well as forbidden. But to hear him talk of it so openly only increased her self-consciousness.

Searching for a diversion, she put her hand into the pocket of her skirt and brought out the photograph. "Ted, I've got something for you. To take with you to France, or wherever it is you're going. It's not much, I know, and perhaps you won't want it . . . "

She held it out and saw his face soften as he looked at it.

"When did you get this done?"

"Oh, a while back. If you don't want it, you don't have to . . . "

"Don't be so silly!" He pulled her towards him, holding the photograph up in line with her face as if to compare. "Hmm, not bad," he said, mockingly critical. "Not as good as the original, of course."

Ridiculously, she felt her chin wobble.

"You don't like it?"

"Of course, I like it. If I can't have you, it's the next best thing.

But it's you I want really. A piece of paper can't be any substitute for you."

As he spoke the teasing note left his voice, and she saw the desire in his face. He laid the photograph on the mantelshelf and pulled her roughly towards him, exploring the curve of her breast with one hand while the other slid down her back to hold her hips firmly against his.

Breath caught in her throat, a tiny rasping sigh. His face was close now, so close it was out of focus, and it seemed to her that everything was happening too suddenly, too fast. Yet how could it happen too fast when there was so little time?

His body moved against hers, and she felt the first small twisting stab of answering desire making her ache for something unknown and out of reach.

"Ted!" she whispered urgently.

For answer, he covered her mouth with his own, his tongue thrusting between her lips.

For a moment she floated upwards on a wave of unimagined excitement mingled with sweet sharp fear. But as his tongue thrust deeper into her mouth, moving with rhythmic urgency, she found herself remembering fragments of conversations held over the last two days: "Be nice to him," Rachel had insisted. "I won't be the one to disturb you." Could it be that she had known what Rebecca herself was now beginning to realize—that it was physical love Ted needed to take with him?

An overwhelming desire to give him what he wanted most washed over her, drowning all her shyness and making her forget her strict upbringing. For a moment she strained against him, savouring the sharp delight, then taking his hand, she began to unfasten the bodice of her dress.

Fear and fascination sharpened all her senses, and as the buttons came undone, one by one, and his hand slipped inside her bodice, the longing to please swelled inside her. She pressed her breast into his palm. She felt her nipple rise at the touch of his work-toughened hand.

Slowly, he raised his lips from hers, running a line of kisses down her chin and neck. Easing her breast free of her bodice, he covered the nipple with his mouth. Surprise almost made her cry out, then as the pressure of his teeth shot a dart of pain through her, she arched her back, thrusting her breast harder into his mouth.

Reality took on a new dimension then, every crevice of her body coming alive beneath his touch. He kissed her mouth again, until she felt she was drowning. Then he pushed her gently back on to the sofa, and the weight of his body started a new awareness, so that nothing in the world mattered except to be closer, even closer. Every nerve in her body cried out, and the deepest parts of her were taut and yearning. She parted her thighs, and the desire rose in her like a flood so that her whole being was stretched and waiting. But the thrust she expected never came. Instead, her world jolted roughly, the weight lifted, and coming back from a long way off, she realized he was standing up, looking away from her.

The sudden loss was like falling from a pinnacle.

"Ted!" she cried, and when he didn't turn around, she leaned over to take his hand, bewildered, pleading. "Ted, what's wrong?"

He pulled away from her roughly.

"Stop it, Becky, for God's sake."

"But what's the matter? Don't you want me?"

"Of course, I do." With shaking hands, he pulled a packet of cigarettes from his pocket and lit one.

"Then why?" She was close to tears.

He drew smoke into his lungs with a long, shuddering breath.

"Another minute and I wouldn't have been able to control myself. Don't you know what I mean?"

Her mouth puckered. "Of course, I do. Don't *you* start treating me like a child, Ted."

"Well, stop talking so stupid then. And do up your bloody dress."

She glanced down and pulled the two edges of her bodice together.

"I am not talking stupid. And don't you swear at me!"

"Becky." He ran a hand through his hair, looking at her with exasperation and tenderness. "How can I make you see?"

"You don't have to. I understand." Her chin was up, her hazel eyes suspiciously bright. "You don't really want me at all."

"Becky . . . "

"You don't. I thought you did. And I wanted to make you happy. Oh, Ted, I wanted that so much. After all, you're going to France tomorrow and heaven knows when we'll see each other again . . . if we ever do . . . " Her anger was dissolving into tears, and her last words were muffled as she pressed her fist over her mouth to suppress a sob.

"Oh Becky!" he said helplessly, reaching out to touch her neck where the stray ends of hair lay in loose brown tendrils.

"Don't cry. I do love you, truly I do."

"Then why . . . "

"*Because* I love you. I want you, God knows. But not like that. How do you think I'd feel going off and leaving you and not knowing how you were? I could give you a baby like that, don't you realize? And what would you do then, eh? No, when I make love to you, it's going to be for real. I'll make love to you all bloody night when you're my wife—or when I know I'll be there to look after you. Now, dry your eyes and don't be so silly, do you hear?"

She was silent for a moment. Then she whispered, "I wanted to give you something to take with you."

"You've done that," he told her, picking up the photograph from the mantelshelf. "You've given me this. Look, I'm going to put it in my wallet, and you know where that'll be, don't you? It'll be in my pocket all the time—with me wherever I go."

She nodded, still sniffing at the tears, but managing to smile.

"I'm sorry, Ted. I didn't want to quarrel—not on our last night."

He grinned, his old composure nearly regained.

"Oh, I'd rather quarrel with you than anybody else. Now, how about a stroll to cool off?"

She nodded, smiling back.

"Rachel will be disappointed."

"Too bad," Ted replied.

AN HOUR later, they parted at the gate. For as long as she could, she clung to him, unwilling to accept that the time had really come for him to go, but at last he prized himself free, kissed her gently and put her aside with firmness.

"I have to go, Becky," he said.

She turned cold, for suddenly it felt to her as if he had gone already.

"Oh, Ted!" she whispered, a sob catching in her throat.

"I'll be back," he said.

Before he had gone more than a few steps, the darkness swallowed him up, but she stared after him, imagining she could still see the brightness of his hair and the dark bulk of his greatcoat. Tears trickled down her cheeks, and she put out her tongue to intercept them as they slid past her mouth. The salt was sharp on her lips, and it made her think of the sea that would soon be between them.

"Dear God, please take care of him," she whispered into the darkness.

Then, feeling more alone than she had ever felt before, she turned and went back to the big house.

17

REBECCA was not the only one to pray for Ted's safety. Rosa Clements was distraught when she heard that Ted was leaving for France, and not even coming home first.

What have I done? she asked herself over and over. And what can I do now?

The guilt lay so heavily on her, she could think of nothing else, and when she could bear it no more, she went to the woods.

It was a night in early January.

By the time she climbed the stile, hitching up her skirts and jumping down into the drift of dead leaves on the other side, her shoes and stockings were already soaked through, and her dark hair, peeping out from beneath her shawl, lay in dank strands across her cheeks. But undeterred, she went on with the sure-footed stealth of a cat, picking her way between the tree roots and the branches brought down by the December gales.

There was no moon, and Rosa was glad. Her eyes quickly accustomed themselves to the dark. She preferred it to those nights when the woods seemed as light as day and the trees stood like silver ghosts casting their long, shivering shadows across the paths. The dark was friendly. It hid her from curious eyes.

Here in the heart of the woods it was very still. The gentle, rustling sounds of night seemed muted by the fog. Rosa raised her head, sniffing the air so that the scent of the dank leaves tickled her nostrils like woodsmoke, and a pleasurable sensation ran through her in a bubbling tide.

This was where she belonged. Out here anything was possible. Romany, tinker, witch—what was there in a name? All that mattered was the power that was unleashed whenever she put aside the bonds of ordinary, everyday life and stepped into this other world.

It was like a religion with her now, and she was a high priestess. The woods were her cathedral, the branches of the trees forming the high vaulted roof, the mosses and dead leaves serving for kneelers. But she had no need of an altar. That was somewhere inside herself, a place so reverent and so singing with power that it almost frightened her. And she knew that wherever she went and whatever she did, if she lost that power, she would want to die. Without it, there would be no point to living.

Beneath the hollow tree she stopped for a moment, one hand resting against the gnarled trunk while she thought about what she was going to do, justifying it to herself once again.

She must not misuse the power, or cheapen it by trivial demands. It was too precious for that—a sacred trust. But Ted was precious, so dear to her that she knew she would risk everything, even the power, if there was a chance it could keep him safe. She reached up into the hollow tree until her fingers encountered the rough cable of rope. She pulled it out, then slowly sank to her knees.

With the rope between her hands, she turned her face upwards to the overcast, moonless sky, and the power warmed her through and through.

"Keep Ted safe. Keep Ted safe."

The words reverberated through her being like the echo of a great shout. But in the January woods, nothing broke the heavy silence.

THE SECOND spring of the war came slowly, refusing to be hurried even by the innovation of British Summer Time.

"Why they have to muck about with nature, I don't know," Charlotte grumbled as she rose in the dawn that had suddenly taken a pace or two back into darkness.

But when the longer evenings meant that lighting the lamps could be delayed for an hour or so, she felt a stirring of gratitude. While daylight lasted, fears and depression could be kept at bay. When the curtains were drawn and the lamps threw their long and eerie shadows, she felt somehow as if the darkness had crept inside her, and the unlit corners of the room reflected the nightmares that lurked in the corners of her mind. Two of her boys in France when there was no need of it—it was more than flesh and blood could stand.

And just to make things worse, the Derby Bill had been passed now, bringing in conscription for all unmarried men between the ages of eighteen and forty-one and ending voluntary enrollment. If it had happened just a couple of months sooner, they would have refused to take Ted.

But what was done was done. There was no way of changing it now. And early in the year, when Fred came home for a well-earned leave, she tried to forget all her worries, planning a family celebration.

They would all be eager to see him, so Charlotte invited Jim and Sarah and the children, and arranged for Jack to swop his week at Wells around so that he could be at home while Fred was there. On the day he was due, Dolly and Amy both managed to get some time off, and Peggy said she would meet Harry out of school.

Charlie Durrant soon heard of Fred's homecoming and looked out the flags they had hung out for the coronation. But when she saw them, Charlotte thought it was going too far, and asked him to take them in. With Peggy worried about Colwyn, who was in hospital in France, and the Cottles, whose boy Bert would never come back, living so close, she thought it would be salt in the wound to lay emphasis on the fact that Fred was safe and well.

By midday, everything was ready for him, and the house was spring-cleaned from top to bottom so that nothing had to be done while he was at home. James had concealed a barrel of beer—a real treat—in the wash-house. Charlotte had an enormous dinner prepared, Fred's favourite boiled beef and dumplings, with enough vegetables to feed an army, followed by boiled apple pudding with milk and sugar.

"If I know our Fred. After all this time away, there won't be much of that lot left," she said with a smile. But she was wrong.

Jack had gone down to meet the trains in, and she kept going to the end of the rank to see if there was any sign of them coming. But when at last they did turn the corner, she could hardly believe the figure in the khaki greatcoat was Fred. He looked so thin even at a distance!

Forgetting she was still wearing her pinafore, she ran down the hill to meet him. Her eyes were blurred by tears, but in her arms he felt like a bundle of bones, and she held him away, looking at him, shocked by what she saw.

There were hollows in his cheeks, and a wary, haunted look in his eyes. And as she held him, she felt his nerves twitch compulsively once or twice.

"Whatever have they done to you?" she asked.

He shifted his kit-bag, impatient to get home. "Oh, I'm all right, give or take a bug or two."

"Bugs!" Charlotte exclaimed, taking a step backwards. The boys both laughed, but the wary look did not leave Fred's eyes, and she turned away so as not to see it.

"Come on home," she said. "We'll soon have the water hot for you to have a bath, and you can get out of those clothes. They smell awful."

Fred laughed again. "I'm not surprised. You can't march half-way across France and not sweat, Mam."

She tucked her arm through his. "Jack, take that kit-bag off your brother. Can't you see how done up he is? You'll feel better with a hot meal inside you, my lad. Boiled beef and dumplings—how does that sound to you?"

"Sounds champion," he said.

But when it was on the table in front of him, there was something wrong. He ate, gobbling hungrily, but with no enjoyment. He seemed unaware of his surroundings and had no desire to talk about the war.

"Tell me what's been going on here," he said at last.

"Nothing much except that we've had to wave your brother off, too," Charlotte said shortly and was disturbed by the way Fred's eyes narrowed, one lid twitching slightly.

"You shouldn't have let him go."

"How could I stop him?" Charlotte asked. "I tried to stop you, didn't I? But you're grown men, both of you. What you do is up to you."

"I wish I was old enough," Jack said, and they both looked at him in surprise.

"Oh, Jack!" Charlotte sighed.

Fred put in, "You don't know what you're talking about, our Jack."

"I shouldn't go in the army," Jack said. "I'd join the Royal Flying Corps, or the RNAS. I've always wanted to fly, you know that."

"But this is no game, Jack," Fred said shortly, and again Charlotte was disturbed by the look in his eyes.

At that moment, however, James came home and the conversation was forgotten as father and son greeted one another. Then, when he'd had time to get changed and have something to eat, Jim came with Sarah and the children, and soon after that Dolly, Amy, and Peggy with Harry, so that the house seemed to be overflowing with people and chatter. It was rather like a party, with a lot of laughter, and the kettle sitting on the hob to keep the teapot topped up. But when Charlotte looked at Fred, she knew she had done the wrong thing in letting them all come today. She had so badly wanted to make it a celebration that she had made the mistake of thinking he would be as pleased to see them all as they were to see him. But he wasn't. Oh, he was laughing with them, and shaking hands, but all the time he was as taut as a violin string, and when he thought no one was looking, the haunted look returned to his eyes.

After tea she started dispersing them as soon as she reasonably could. Jim and Sarah took the children along to see their other grandparents, the Brimbles. James tapped the beer, and Fred seemed pleased to have a drink, but still he wasn't really relaxed, and although he went off to bed quite early with Jack, she could still hear them talking when she went up herself after midnight.

The next evening when Fred had gone down to the Miners Arms with James to see his mates and have a pint, she asked Jack what they had been talking about.

"It's not that I want to pry," she explained. "I just can't make him out, that's all, and I wondered if he said anything to you."

"Not really," Jack said. "He seemed to want to talk, and yet when it came to the point, he didn't. And he's got a wound in his shoulder, too, that he didn't mention."

"A wound? You mean . . . "

"Oh, it's not much. Nothing to worry about."

"That's all right, then," she said. But she knew it wasn't. Fred was different, and in an odd way, it frightened her. There was a hard edge to him that hadn't been there before.

When Fred and James returned from the pub, Charlotte presumed he would want another early night, but he didn't. The others went on upstairs, and Charlotte remained with Fred, but he was still restless—it was as Jack had said, he didn't seem to know what he wanted to do.

"Did you enjoy your drink, Fred?" she asked.

He shifted in his chair. "It was all right. But nothing's really like you remember it, is it?"

"How d'you mean?"

"When I was in France, I kept thinking about home, and I had this rosy picture of what it was like. I'd lie awake and picture the sun coming up so that half the valley's in light and the other half in shadow, and it all looked so clean and good . . . "

"Well?" she said gently.

"It's not like that really, is it?" He took out a cigarette and lit it. "It's all grey and dirty, and coal-dust everywhere."

"It's winter, Fred. It rains here just like anywhere else."

"I know. But still . . . " He hesitated, then went on, "And it's not only that. It's everything. The food doesn't taste right . . . "

"Oh, thank you very much!"

"Sorry, Mam, there's nothing wrong with it, I know. It's me, I expect. I've had too much stodge. I can't taste any more. In France I used to dream of your stews and boiled puddings, and now . . . "

"That'll come back," she said. "Your stomach's all upset."

"An' me mates," he went on. "I can't even talk to them any more. It's like there was a barrier between us. The blokes out there, in France, they understand. They've been through it all, too. But here —they don't know what they're on about."

Tears ached in Charlotte's throat. "Is it very bad, my son?"

He didn't answer, and she put her hand on his arm. "If only you could talk about it, tell me . . . "

"Tell you?" He jerked round suddenly, his eyes blazing. "You wouldn't want to know, Mam."

"That's not true, Fred."

"You wouldn't."

"I want to know so I can . . . oh, share it with you, I suppose."

"All right." His voice was hard. "Supposing I was to tell you I've had mates killed both sides of me, or walked over German gunners lying dead in the trenches and felt me boots sink into them. I've killed a man, Mam, as close as I am to you, putting round after round into his face until there was nothing left of it because it was either him or me. Now, do you still tell me you want to hear more?"

The ache in Charlotte's throat had become a choking knot. She thought she was going to be sick, and her whole body had turned cold.

"Oh, Fred!" she said softly.

She sat down on the arm of his chair, putting her arms around him and pulling his head into her. At first he drew back, but after a moment he relaxed, burrowing his face into the fullness of her breast. Gently she stroked his hair as she had when he was a child, and gradually she felt the tension ease out of him.

"I'm glad you told me, Fred," she said.

For how long they sat there, neither ever knew, but in the end it was James who disturbed them, poking his head around the stair door to ask if they were ever coming to bed.

"Yes, we're coming," she said. She felt heavy, now, and old—as if she had lived for a hundred years, and taken the troubles of the world on her shoulders. But she seemed to have helped Fred.

Next morning he was much more his old self, eating a good breakfast and even laughing at a photograph in the newspaper of two women humping sacks of coal in one of the big cities.

"They wanted men's work, now they've got it," he said. "But give me a woman that looks like a woman every time!"

"That reminds me, Renee Presley up the rank was asking after you the other day," Charlotte teased. "You ought to go up and see her."

"I might do that," Fred said, and Charlotte and James exchanged glances. Renee was Edie's older sister and not a bad-looking girl. Fred had known her all his life, and if anything was going to come of it, Charlotte thought it would have happened before now. But it was good to hear Fred making plans and having a joke.

Throughout the rest of his leave, things continued to improve. It was as if talking to Charlotte had cleansed him somehow, and released him from the nightmare. But all too soon it was over, and time for farewells.

They all went down to the station to see him off, hovering around him in an uncertain knot. "You might run into our Ted in France," Charlotte said foolishly, as they stood on the platform.

Fred did not snap at her as he might have done earlier in his leave that the line stretched for hundreds of miles, with back-up sectors too, and he'd have as much chance meeting a flea in the market as meeting Ted. Instead, he smiled and gave her a quick hug. "You never know."

And then the train was in, stopping to fill up with water at the tank so that it seemed to be in the station for hours and the parting was delayed until it was almost unbearable. But at last the guard waved his green flat, the driver whistled back, and they were off. Harry and Jack ran along the platform beside the carriage for as long as they could, but Charlotte stood with James, watching until Fred's head, poking out of the window, was just a faceless blur. The train rocked slowly around the bend, the signals clacked back to a neutral position, and the clouds of steam spread into the murky sky. Charlotte swallowed at the loss and despair that rose steadily in her throat.

"Come on, Harry!" she said.

Together they went down the station slope, back to the house that would seem bereft and empty, back to the waiting and the praying. There was nothing else to do.

FOR TED, the war had begun disappointingly.

When he had boarded the steamer that was seeing service as a troopship, he had been ready and eager to do his bit, but two weeks, and a good many blisters later, it seemed to him that he was no closer to having a crack at Fritz than he had ever been.

When he walked down the gang-plank on to French soil, he was told he would be among those who would go to the Front immediately, and far from frightening him, he found the prospect exciting. He said as much to Wally Gifford, the taciturn Geordie who had shared a billet with him and Redvers on Salisbury Plain.

"Ah'll save me judgement, lad," Wally replied morosely, but Ted knew that the mournful expression was only a cover-up, and Wally was in reality as eager as he was to try out their new-found skill with a gun, a bayonet or a hand grenade.

The first stage of their journey was by train, and Ted watched from the window as mile after mile of bleak and ravaged countryside unfolded before him. Then the men were set down and formed into a column for the route-march that would take them to the lines, and the anticipation of action stirred in him again. As they swung along the ribbons of dirt track or tar macadam roads, he managed to ignore the blisters that his overlarge boots had raised on his heels by leading the others in a bawdy song or two, undeterred by the rumble of the guns and the scream of shells that grew louder and more resonant as they neared the lines.

After several days' marching, they reached the valley where their unit was camped. It was nightfall when they arrived, and most of the men who had been 'over the top' that day and emerged more or less unscathed had already marched back and wearily dressed ranks outside the orderly room tent, but a few stragglers were still drifting in—men who had been separated from the rest of their company in the fighting.

While he tucked into a supper of stewed beef topped with hunks of French bread, Ted watched them with fascinated curiosity. It was hard to believe that these weary, staggering, mud-stained figures could ever have been part of a smartly turned-out and well-drilled squad. They looked shattered now, hardly able to hold their heads up under the weight of their tin hats. Their rifles slanted wearily against the uniforms that were spattered with blood and dirt.

For a moment or two their dejection sobered him, but when they had disappeared like grey shadows into their tents, his enthusiasm began to return.

"Our turn tomorrow," he said softly to Redvers, and then, while he finished his stew, he pictured what he would do—hurl a hand grenade into a Hun trench, perhaps, and then bayonet the bastards one by one as they tried to run away.

Take that—and that! he thought, stabbing at his bread with his spoon, and wishing he could have the chance of doing the same to Alfred Church.

Because they were not yet official, there were no tents for Ted and the other new men, and after they had tried, without much success, to erect a tent from ground-sheets, they were reluctantly allowed to share with the 'old sweats.'

"Not very friendly, though, are they?" Ted commented to Redvers as they got themselves undressed.

"Not that I want them too close." Redvers hissed back. "They're bloody lousy—look!"

Ted turned, startled to see that most of the men were probing the hairy parts of their bodies. "What are they doing?" he muttered softly.

"Looking for bugs. Bugs, you know—fleas!" Redvers told him, and Ted was unable to suppress a shudder. Guns he had expected. Bombs he had been prepared for. But to have bugs crawling all over you was something else again.

That night, Ted's sleep was interrupted by the mutterings and mumblings of the seasoned soldiers. Even asleep they still seemed to be fighting, their arms and legs jerking spasmodically. Ted awoke as dawn began to break, and after lying awake for a while, he decided to get up and go to the latrine.

The camp lay quiet in the cold grey dawn, but there was a great disturbance coming from the tents where the cookers were situated, and Ted, curiosity getting the better of him, went across to them and asked what was going on. At first, realizing he was one of the new draft, they were unwilling to tell him, then one of them gave him a nasty grin. "You're in luck, chum," he sneered. "They've had too many losses in this unit, and we're being pulled out until they can get it up to strength again."

"You mean, we're going out of the line again?" Ted asked, almost disbelieving.

The cook laughed. "That's about the size of it. Looks as if you're one of them that comes up smelling of violets, doesn't it? There's not many as gets here and then has a rest before he's done anything."

"Some of the blokes 'll take it out on you for that, an' all," said a plump man who looked as if he finished up every bit of uneaten food himself.

"Take it out on me? What for?" Ted asked.

"For not being through it with them. They even takes it out on us sometimes. But you can't blame the poor buggers. Just thank your lucky stars you're sound in wind and limb yourself."

From somewhere over the ridge of hills came the sound of shells exploding, and the cook pointed with his thumb.

"It's started," he said unnecessarily. "Just you think o' that, lad, when they start calling you a conchie, and remember when you're well off."

"A conchie?" Ted repeated, puzzled, and the other sniffed loudly.

"That's what you are, ain't it? One of them conscientious objectors the Derby Bill's pulling in?"

Ted was surprised the man didn't know it was much too early for the first conscripts to be in France, and that conscientious objectors were among those exempted anyway. Suddenly he felt annoyed to be classed with them when he had volunteered.

"A conchie? No, I'm not!" he retorted vehemently. "I was quite looking forward to a bit of action."

The cooks looked at one another as if they thought he was weak in the head, and he went on, "What time are we moving out of here, anyway?"

The cooks exchanged another look, and he laughed. "It's all right, I'm not a Gerry spy, either, if that's what you're thinking. I just wanted to know, that's all."

There was a stirring of movement in the officers' tents, away to their left, and the cooks busied themselves once more.

"Two o'clock, conchie. Now bugger off," the fat one hissed at him.

Feeling strangely flat, he walked back to his own tent, and by way of compensation, he allowed himself the luxury of thinking of Rebecca.

What was she doing at this moment? he wondered. Still in bed, perhaps, her face rosy and innocent above the sheets. Or scurrying about the big house, getting Miss Rachel's clothes ready for her and running her bath.

To his dismay, he found he was unable to conjure up a clear picture of her features, and he stopped outside his tent, sliding his wallet out of his pocket and opening it so that he could look at the photograph she had given him.

"Come on, lad, that's enough o' flaming that!" From behind him came the heavy tones of the sergeant-major. "There's work to be done. This is a bleeding war, you know, not a Sunday school outing."

Ted snapped his wallet shut, smarting under the sting of authority. It was what being in the army was all about, he supposed, but he didn't care for it too much.

As the wintry sun got up, the distant shelling became more intense, and again Ted found himself prickling with frustration. With no first-hand experience of fighting, he felt no fear, only impatience to join in the scrap that was going on on the other side of the hills, and earn the badge of comradeship that would make him one of the lads.

When the company assembled for roll-call, he was shocked, however, by the number of gaps in the line, and by the matter-of-fact explanations of absence that were barked out by former comrades.

"He were blown to bits. I saw it with me own eyes," a sandy-haired man explained when one name was called.

Ted listened with a sense of growing outrage. This calm acceptance of death, spiked sometimes by anger but never by grief, was something as far outside his experience as the shells that soared and whistled on the other side of the hill. How could a man talk so casually of a mate whose life had been so cruelly and wastefully wiped out?

Later, however, marching with the others of the new draft to set up a new camp a mile or two further back from the line, he began to understand.

Out here, death was so commonplace that, if you didn't treat it matter-of-factly, you would never be able to face another day. It was talked about as much as any other everyday occurrence—for that was what it was.

But the indifference was only a defence. Beneath it, blood ran icy cold, and stomachs churned. A soldier could still feel sick through and through, but he mustn't show it.

For the first time, Ted wondered if warfare in the trenches might be less of an adventure than he had imagined. But as the days passed and the noise of the guns became more distant, his impatience began to return.

The war had eased a little on the British front, it was said, although there was still fierce fighting on the French lines at Verdun. But it seemed to Ted his company was continually on the move, no sooner getting themselves established in one camp than they were moved on again.

The days were spent marching along slushy roads, heavily weighted down by kit and taking turns in pulling the gun-carts, a painful job if it ran too close to your heels, but a chance, at least, to dump heavy kit on the cart and march free for a time.

At night they slept sometimes in barns where the straw was infested with hen-fleas, or sometimes in billets in evacuated villages that reminded Ted of the 'ghost towns' he had seen portrayed in countless Western film shows at the Palace Picture House. As he looked at the gaping windows and abandoned treasures, he had the feeling of moving across time to a different world, especially when one night they billeted in a ruined chateau where the walls on three sides stood tall and elegant and on the fourth the moon illuminated their sleeping faces over a pile of snow-covered rubble.

New recruits joined them, fresh-faced lads who made Ted feel old although he had never yet seen a shot fired, and when they began to march again, a rumour rustled through the ranks that they were heading for a railhead to be entrained for the Front. But the hiatus continued, with only drill parades and practice attacks to remind Ted he was a soldier.

Wherever he went, Ted made friends. Although he had not been able to speak a word of French when he first stepped off the boat, he soon found ways of communicating, and he, Redvers and Wally often found themselves invited into a French farmer's parlour for a glass of 'vin rouge' or—if they were lucky—a tot of brandy.

"I think he had his eye on you to make an honest woman of his daughter," Redvers joked after one farmer had plied Ted with drinks.

"And she weren't too bad, neither," Wally added. "If you was to creep out of your billet tonight and round to her bedroom window, I reckon you'd be all right there, lad."

Ted laughed, but he knew, and so did they, that a bit of fun was as far as it would go. Some of the men were going overboard for every woman in sight, even leering after dowdy matrons they would never give so much as a second glance to at home, and the VAD nurses from sheltered homes were being almost eaten alive. But for him, no other woman existed but Rebecca, and he much preferred to spend his recreation time in an *estaminet*, smoking one of his precious cigarettes, drinking the local concoction of apples and potatoes that was known as 'champagne' and playing pontoon, or crown and anchor.

By the end of January, they were within reach of the lines again, billeted in a half-deserted mining village, and for the first time he felt homesick. Although the dusty buildings were brick-built, and the familiar black batches were referred to as 'slag heaps' by the other men, it gave him a strange feeling to think of the coal seams beneath his feet. He had a sudden longing to see the great wheels turning, and feel the rush of air against his face that came when a cage dropped beneath the level of the earth.

He said as much to Wally as the two of them stood in line waiting their turn for a change of shirt and underpants. "We none of us knew when we was well off, lad," he said mournfully. "But we shan't have time to think about it much from now on, if it's right what I hear. They're starting carrying parties up the line tonight, so I reckon we'll soon be seeing a bit of action."

"Carrying parties? Carrying what?" Ted asked.

"Gas cylinders. But you know what that'll mean, don't you? We'll have to wear gas-helmets, and you can't breathe in the bleeders. I hate 'em."

Ted did not answer, merely moved up in line, unbuttoning his dirty shirt and stripping it off. He didn't care for gas-helmets, either, but he was excited by the prospect of some action at last, and he hoped he would soon be detailed for one of the working parties.

That night, when darkness had fallen, he and Wally were amongst those who were sent from the billet on the three-mile march to the British trenches.

It was a bitterly cold night. As they waited to set off, they stamped their feet and sang a chorus or two of 'Mademoiselle from Armetiers,' but when they had been loaded with the poles, one between two, on which were slung the gas cylinders, they had no breath left for singing. The cylinders dragged them down so that their boots felt like lead weights in the mud, and the carrying poles cut into their shoulders.

"This is a bleedin' mug's game, in't it?" Wally grumbled, but Ted was determined not to be depressed. Hard work and discomfort had never bothered him, and he strode out as boldly as his mud-caked boots would let him, savouring every moment of the new experience.

As they approached the trenches, it was fairly quiet. Most of the men had pulled out to their dug-outs, leaving only observers and a cover of gunners, and although the occasional shell lit the sky, Ted had no real premonition of disaster. He and Wally followed the pair in front of them to the fire-trench where they were to dump their load. It startled them both to realize they were so close to the German lines that they could actually hear Gerry in his trenches.

The pair of men in front of them dumped their load and turned aside; now it was their turn. Easing the pole on his shoulder with palms that were sweaty in spite of the cold of the night, Ted followed suit.

It was as he turned away from the trench that he saw it—an elongated shell that seemed to appear from nowhere and curve with incredible grace across the sky.

For a moment he watched it, mesmerized. It looked as if it would overshoot by a mile and come to earth harmlessly somewhere in the wilds of the country behind the line. Yet even as the thought crossed his mind, some instinct of self-preservation took him in its grasp.

With a yell to Wally that was muffled hopelessly by his gas-mask, he leaped for the safety of the slit trench, tumbling on to his hands and knees and rolling over. He never saw the sausage bomb come to earth. He only heard it, and felt the earth tremble and rock as it exploded, showering him with clods of dirt and stones.

Half-stunned, he lay motionless, his face pressed into the mud.

"Christ, that was a close one," he muttered to himself, and at the same moment he thought of Wally, who had been close behind him when he had leaped for safety.

He raised his head a little, turning towards the bay, and saw to his horror that the ground where he had been standing seconds before was now a gaping crater.

Shaking, he scrambled up, holding on to the rough sides of the slit trench and steadying himself with hands that were scratched and bleeding.

A stretcher party from one of the dug-outs pushed past him, almost knocking him over. He opened his mouth to shout Wally's name, but no sound came out. Within moments he was leaning against the wall of the trench, retching. Beside him, one of the younger lads was crying softly from fear and shock.

Someone else was swearing. "The bastards. The bleeding bastards. You don't know where the sods are going to land."

Again Ted lurched forward, hitching up the khaki that he felt had been almost torn from his body, then stopped, horrified. Right in front of his eyes, the stretcher party were gently lifting the remains of what had been Wally Gifford from his muddy grave. His face was almost unrecognizable, his features blackened and bloody, and his legs had gone.

Ted took a step towards them. "Let me . . . he's my mate . . . "

But the stretcher party were in command, grimly efficient where shock had left him weak, and they brushed him aside.

"There's nothing you can do. Leave 'im . . . "

Ted, recognizing the truth, let them go. But sudden anger consumed him.

Senseless, it was, bloody senseless. What had they gained, those sodding Germans? They'd killed one bloke, one good bloke, and they weren't a fuck closer to winning the war. Let him get hold of them —just give him the chance, and he'd kill the bleeders with his bare hands . . .

"You lucky sod, Hall. How d'you do it, hey? By rights you ought to be on that stretcher an' all!"

The comment, at Ted's elbow, brought him out of his trance, and he felt his flesh crawl.

By Christ, he'd done it again—been so close to death that it had missed him only by a whisker. But missed it he had. Why, now he came to think of it, he was hardly touched.

It was almost as if something, or someone, was looking after him.

18

ONE DAY in the spring of 1916 Rupert Thorne contacted Alfred Church at the Co-operative Society offices.

"I wondered if I might come to see you, Uncle," he said in the affected drawl he liked to use on the telephone. "Under the present circumstances, I'd like to talk to you about our . . . arrangement."

"What present circumstances?" Alfred asked.

"I think it might be easier to discuss it face to face," Rupert said smoothly.

"I see," Alfred said, his mind racing.

Since the previous Christmas when he had written to Rupert, outlining his plans for his future with Rebecca, things had slipped effortlessly into gear. First, the two men had met to discuss the settlements Alfred was prepared to make if Rupert married Rebecca, and Rupert had accepted his suggestions more readily than he had dared to hope. Rupert had been so enthusiastic Alfred had realized that, quite apart from the settlement, he found the idea an attractive one.

But now, hearing the guarded note in Rupert's voice, he found himself wondering anxiously if some snag had arisen. And if Rupert, in spite of having taken his money, now wanted to back down.

"When did you want to come?" he asked. "I'm very busy at the moment. But I could spare an hour tomorrow night."

"Thank you, Uncle. That would suit me very well," Rupert said, and put the telephone down.

For a moment, Alfred sat frowning at the receiver. As he had told Rupert, he was very busy at present. He had recently bought himself a motor car, so there was no longer any need for him to live within walking distance of the Co-operative offices. Immediately he had mastered the gears and steering, he had begun looking around for a house out of Hillsbridge.

He soon found one, six miles out into the country on the Bristol road, and now he was embroiled in all the problems of buying and selling property and moving his household from one place to another.

But busy as he was, if Rupert wanted to see him, then time must be found for him. The 'arrangement' was of the utmost importance to both of them. Alfred fervently hoped the request for a meeting did not mean Rupert was getting greedy. If so, he would have to draw his attention, very gently, to the paper he had signed, and point out how awkward it could be for him—and his career—if he should become known as a man who could not be trusted to keep his word.

Rupert arrived the next evening riding a motor cycle combination.

Paid for with my money, I suppose! thought Alfred as he watched the young man come up the path looking like the grounded pilot of a flying machine. But he greeted him with just the right amount of pompous warmth, keeping his suspicions to himself.

"Come in, my boy! Take his jacket, Winnie—and his gloves. And will you have some refreshment after your journey, Rupert?"

"Thank you, Uncle. A small brandy, perhaps."

"Certainly, certainly. We'll take it into the parlour with us so we can talk."

When they were alone, he turned to Rupert expectantly.

"Well, my boy? What did you want to see me about? There's nothing wrong, I hope. I should be most disappointed if . . . "

Rupert gulped at his brandy, the only sign he was nervous.

"I'll come straight to the point, Uncle. I was wondering if you might agree to bring the date of my wedding forward."

"*Forward?*" Alfred was so surprised he almost choked on his drink.

Rupert nodded earnestly. "I know you think Rebecca is very young, and I'm not qualified yet, but . . . I don't think I can wait, Uncle."

A slight smile twisted Alfred's mouth. He remembered being young and impatient too well.

"The flesh is weak, Rupert. I understand."

Rupert looked puzzled. "The flesh? Oh, I see what you mean. But that's not the reason."

"It isn't? Then what?"

"You've heard about the Derby Bill? Conscription for men between the ages of eighteen and forty-one? I fall into that category. I think I may be liable for service in France."

Alfred set his glass down heavily. "Forgive me, Rupert, I hadn't even thought of that. Conscription. And you don't want to go."

"It would set my career back no end."

"Of course, of course."

"But if I were married, I'd be exempt. For the time being, anyway. It's only single men being pulled in at the moment."

"So you want to bring the wedding forward. Well, Rupert, I don't know. There would have to be a proper period of betrothal, and Rebecca is away at present."

"Couldn't you get her home?"

Alfred considered. "Possibly. We shall be moving soon to our new house at High Compton. Rebecca would be well away from . . . yes, perhaps it could be done."

"I do hope so, Uncle. It really is very urgent."

He nodded, and topped up both glasses from the brandy decanter.

"There is just one thing, Rupert," he said after a moment. "I have never told Rebecca about our 'arrangement'. She knows, of course, that I have always hoped you and she would one day marry, but that is all. I thought that any serious approach would be better coming from you—as a young man's natural approach to courtship. I am sure I can rely on your discretion in this matter. You do understand what I am saying, don't you?"

"Of course I do, Uncle."

"And you will treat her as a young woman should be treated if a man wishes to marry her?"

Rupert raised his glass, and above the rim, his eyes were narrow with anticipation.

"You can be sure I shall do my best to please her, Uncle," he said smoothly.

REBECCA heard the news that she was to leave Wycherley from her Aunt Amelia.

"I'm to go home? But why? Why?" she asked.

"I really couldn't say, Rebecca," Aunt Amelia snapped. After taking the trouble to arrange employment for her niece, she was annoyed that Alfred was removing her again so abruptly. "All I can gather is that your father has moved house, and wants you at home."

"But I can't go!" Rebecca wailed. "I don't want to!"

"*I* don't want you to. Lady Harcourte doesn't want you to. She is most displeased by all the inconvenience it will cause, and I can't say I blame her. But your father is adamant. You're to go home at once, and that's an end of it."

"Well, I just don't understand it," Rebecca said miserably. She was happy here, happier than she had ever been anywhere, and the thought of returning to her father's tyranny was almost unbearable. "When have I got to go?"

"At the end of the week. He's coming in his new motor car to fetch you," Amelia told her. "Now, don't look like that. You'll enjoy the ride."

"I shall not!" Rebecca retorted, and then stopped. Since she'd been away, she'd learned to speak up for herself, but if she had to go home, it would have to be controlled. Alfred would not approve and might even threaten her with the strap if she persisted . . .

"Oh!" she said, her hands flying to her mouth as the association of ideas made her think of Ted.

"What is it?" Amelia asked, but Rebecca shook her head.

"Nothing."

She couldn't tell Aunt Amelia what she had just realized, that when she left here, Ted would no longer be able to contact her. He wrote to her here, and she was able to write to him, but at home, under her parents' jurisdiction, it would not be so easy. And besides . . .

"Where exactly is our new house?" Rebecca asked.

Amelia shrugged. "I don't know. Six miles or so out of Hillsbridge, your father said, but it's not an area I know."

"But you must have the address!"

"No, I have not. But you don't need it anyway. Your father will be taking you."

Rebecca turned away, overwhelmed by a feeling of helplessness and panic. To be back under her father's thumb would be bad enough, but if she couldn't let Ted know where she was . . .

Perhaps Miss Rachel will help me, she thought in desperation. Miss Rachel had helped before. And it might appeal to her to play postman.

But when she tried to broach the subject, Miss Rachel, upset at losing her personal maid, was cold and unresponsive.

"I can't think why you want to leave me, Rebecca," she said haughtily. "I'd always thought of you more as a friend than as my maid."

"I don't want to go," Rebecca said.

"Then tell your father so."

"I can't . . . he wouldn't take any notice of me."

"That's just an excuse. I don't believe you want to stay here at all. But it was different when you wanted my drawing room to entertain your men friends, wasn't it?"

The injustice of the remark stung Rebecca hurtfully.

"I'm sorry if you think that, Miss Rachel," she said, coldly, realizing there would be no more favours she could ask of her mistress.

Three days later, Alfred arrived, chugging importantly down the drive in his silver-grey motor car and coming to rest at the fork in the paths with a crashing of gears.

"I'll run away from him," Rebecca thought as she watched him arrive. "When I get outside I'll take to my heels and run!"

But she had nowhere to go and no one to help her. Escape was just an impossible dream. And so she greeted him with the politeness born of long habit and climbed dutifully into the car beside him.

"Why are you taking me home?" she asked when they had left the house behind.

Alfred stared imperturbably at the road ahead. "You are my daughter."

"But you sent me away."

"The reasons for that no longer exist."

For a moment she turned cold. Did he know something she did not? But he went smoothly on, "It wasn't proper for you to be in that den of iniquity. Heaven only knows what would have become of you. But things are different now. You'll like the house, I know. Your mother is delighted with it."

"I liked the other one," Rebecca said, thinking of the long, overgrown garden with the gooseberry and blackcurrent bushes, and Marjorie just next door.

"There's something else I have to tell you," Alfred went on after a moment. "Rupert has been to see me, and asked my permission to come and visit you."

Rebecca said nothing. Her mouth turned dry, and the dread weighed heavily inside her. Rupert! So that was it! They'd got together, he and her father, and planned . . . what?

"Naturally I agreed to his suggestion," Alfred negotiated a bend in the road with difficulty. "As you know, I think most highly of Rupert. And he is very fond of you. In fact I have always hoped . . . "

He glanced at Rebecca, but her set expression gave nothing away. He sighed deeply, pitying himself for having been burdened with a daughter instead of a son. But Rupert would be a son to him soon.

"He's a fine young man," he went on.

Rebecca sat staring silently at the road that unfolded before them. Perhaps her father was right and she was wrong. Perhaps he was a fine young man, who would make some girl a good husband, and not a repulsive fat slug as she thought. But, oh, Father, don't try to force him on me, she prayed silently. Because I won't have him whatever you say or do. I just couldn't!

IN SPITE OF Alfred's assurances that she would like the new house, Rebecca hated it.

It was square and ugly, with only a small perimeter of garden. To the rear, it overlooked a sparse paddock, and the fourth wall, which might have given the most pleasant view over the surrounding countryside, had no windows at all.

Inside, the house was dark, the rooms small and cramped. In vain, Winnie pointed out the advantages of the spare bedrooms, the inside ones reached by way of the outside ones, like a Chinese puzzle. She sang the praises of the walk-in larder with its marble slab for keeping milk and butter cool in summer. But Rebecca hated it, and nothing would change her mind.

And when on the second evening she was home Rupert came calling, she hated it even more. She sat with him in the parlour, and from then on he became a part of the dark and ugly room with its sunless window.

He talked politely enough to begin with, asking her about Wycherley and trying to amuse her with carefully rehearsed stories of happenings in his office. But before long he began inching closer to her, letting his arm slide along the back of the sofa, then down, until it rested on her shoulders. At his touch, she squirmed inwardly, but she didn't know what to do. At least she was sure now it was intentional, but it was no good complaining to her father. He approved of Rupert. And besides, what was there to tell? He wasn't doing anything really improper, just stroking her shoulder with those soft, fleshy fingers of his. But oh! how it made her cringe.

She moved away from him, hoping he might take the hint, but he took her withdrawal for modesty, and followed her along the sofa, gradually making further advances.

"Rupert, don't, please," she said, embarrassed.

"Why not?" he asked, his voice low and silky.

"Because I don't like it."

"Oh, Rebecca!" he chided playfully, moving closer. "Don't be unkind to me. I've always liked you, you know. Even when we were children . . ."

She could feel his breath on her cheek as he turned towards her, and she knew he was going to try to kiss her. With a quick, desperate movement, she stood up, and walked over to the fire-place.

"I said no, Rupert. I don't want you to do that."

He let his arms fall back into his lap, and his small eyes were narrowed with desire above his pouchy cheeks.

"I'll show you how nice it can be, Rebecca. But don't worry, I won't take you faster than you want to go."

She stood looking down at him, her breath coming fast and ragged. She'd escaped his advances this time, but what about the next time . . . and the next?

"I'd really rather you didn't come to see me again," she said. "I don't mean to be rude, but . . ."

For a moment, she thought she had hurt him. It was there, written in his flaccid face. Then it was gone, and he was smiling at her with a sly, knowing grimace.

"I know you've led a sheltered life," he said as if he hadn't heard her. "But that just makes me like you all the more. It'll be all right, you'll see."

She turned away, tears of despair stinging her eyes. She didn't want him here, pawing her and trying to win her. She never had—and now she had Ted she wanted him even less. But with her father on his side, how could she stop him?

A few days later, however, it seemed luck was on her side. Rupert telephoned Alfred at the Co-operative offices to say he had had a spill, and broken his arm.

"I'm sorry to disappoint you, my dear," Alfred told Rebecca when he came home. "Rupert doesn't know if he'll be able to get here this week. The motor cycle isn't damaged, fortunately, but of course he can't ride it with his arm in plaster. If he can find someone to chauffeur him though, he promises he won't let you down."

"I don't really want him to come anyway," Rebecca said, but her protests fell on deaf ears.

"You don't know what's good for you," Alfred said.

And Winnie added with a simper, "He's such a well set-up boy. So handsome!"

Rebecca turned away, fervently hoping her luck would hold and

Rupert would be unable to find anyone to bring him. But to her dismay the motor cycle drew up outside two days later as arranged. The boy who was riding it she had never seen before, but when Rupert emerged from the side-car, he explained he was Ned Doughty, son of one of the clerks at Rupert's office.

"He's an enthusiast," he told Alfred. "He's willing to bring me out as long as I let him go off for a spin while I'm here. And of course I'll buy him a couple of packets of cigarettes for his trouble."

"You see how eager Rupert is to visit you, Rebecca?" Alfred said to her. "Not even a broken arm can keep him away."

"How did you do it, Rupert?" Winnie asked. "Fell off your machine, did you? You'll be safer with someone else driving, dear."

Rupert flushed. "It was just a silly spill, Aunt. One of those things." .

"But at least it means they can't send you off to the war just yet," Winnie went on, blissfully unaware of the looks both the men were giving her. "That's one blessing, isn't it?"

"I think we should leave the young people to enjoy each other's company, my dear," Alfred intervened hastily.

Once more Rebecca and Rupert were left alone. But the broken arm had given her an advantage. So long as she kept away from his uninjured arm, he was unable to get his arm around her, and he had to restrict his courting to silky, suggestive remarks.

As the weeks passed and she learned how to manipulate him, her confidence grew. He was so stupid, Rebecca thought, imagining he could win her by paying her compliments and leering at her! Didn't he know how she despised every pompous inch of him, from his slicked-down black hair to his shiny, square shoes? Didn't he realize he was wasting his time, because she would never, ever allow things to progress beyond this stage? And so she took a wry amusement in playing the piano for him and hearing him praise her as if she were a virtuoso, and bringing out her samplers and tapestry for him to admire.

As long as he kept his distance, Rupert was bearable. Once or twice he tried to kiss her, coming up behind her when she sat on the piano stool, encouraging her to face him. The very thought made her shudder, but if she was quick enough she could manage it so that his plastered arm got in the way, and she could slip away with a demure, "Oh, Rupert, your poor arm!"

But of course it couldn't last. And when the day came when the plaster was removed, and he arrived riding his own motor cycle, she knew her respite was over.

It was a Thursday evening, and Alfred was due to preside over a shareholders meeting at the Co-operative rooms. But before he left in his silver-grey motor car, he and Rupert spent a long while alone together in the hall, talking in voices too low for Rebecca to be able to hear what they were saying.

"It might be about your future, Becky," Winnie said conspiratorily.

Rebecca shuddered, but said nothing. It would be a waste of time to try to make an ally of her mother.

At last they heard the front door close and knew Alfred had left for the meeting.

"You go into the front room with Rupert, dear," Winnie said. "I shan't disturb you."

"But, Mother . . . " Rebecca protested.

Winnie only patted her arm and smiled. "I'm in the kitchen cooking. Don't worry about me."

"Come on, Becky. You're going to play that new piece for me, aren't you?" Rupert said, appearing in the doorway, and beaming falsely.

I'll have to be firm, she thought. I'll tell him I won't see him any more, and I'll do it now, before he gets any ideas.

As soon as the door closed behind them, she turned to face him, hands clasped in the folds of her skirt, chin up.

"Rupert, there's something I must say to you."

"Afterwards. Play the piano for me first." His eyes were running all over her, devouring her, and suddenly she felt uneasy.

"I'd rather say it now," she said. "I told you once before that I didn't want you coming to see me, and you said, if we gave it time, I'd feel differently. Well, I don't."

He stood with his back against the door. She had expected him to look hurt, as he had before, and perhaps for a moment he did. But the twist of his mouth was more sly than unhappy, and his eyes had narrowed into a calculating gleam.

"It's early days yet. This arm of mine hasn't helped, but things will be better now, you'll see."

"You don't understand," she said with determination. "I don't want you to call on me any more, Rupert."

"I'm sorry you feel like that," he said lightly. "But you'll get over

267

it. If you don't, it won't be much fun for either of us when we're married."

He came towards her, his hands reaching for hers. Automatically she backed away.

"But I'm not going to marry you, Rupert."

"Oh yes, you are, my dear. It's all arranged. I've promised your father."

"What do you mean?" she asked. He was close to her now. She could feel his body warmth and smell the faint odour of sweat. She tried to back away another pace, but her shoulders were pressed against the mantleshelf. "I don't want you, Rupert," she said desperately.

She didn't see him move, but suddenly she felt his hand on her waist, pulling her towards him until he towered above her.

"But I want you," he said softly.

Panic rose in her, and she pushed him away. "How dare you, Rupert!"

His breathing was ragged, and she knew she had angered him.

"Because I'm going to marry you, whatever you may say. It's what your father wants—and he's making me his heir."

"His heir?" she repeated, bewildered. "You mean he's making his will in your favour?"

"I've already had some of it, Becky," Rupert said with a smile. "So you see, I couldn't back out, even if I wanted to."

She gazed at him, horror-struck. She had been frightened before. Now she felt betrayed.

"You mean he sold me."

"Becky, don't be like that! I'd have married you anyway. I've always wanted you, much longer than you realize. Do you remember one Christmas when we played hide-and-seek all over your house? You hid in the linen chest on the landing, and I found you there. You were squashed in amongst the sheets, with your petticoats bunched up and your drawers showing. I knew then that I wanted you."

He ran his tongue over his lips, reliving the moment, and Rebecca shuddered. "But I was only a little girl then!"

"Oh, how I wanted you!" he went on softly. "I wanted to climb in with you and pull the lid down so no one would know we were there. And I wanted to kiss you—like this . . . "

Suddenly he pulled her towards him again. She gasped under the pressure of his wet lips, but it was impossible to push him away.

At last he raised his head though he did not release her, looking down at her with his curious light eyes. "You see how it can be?" he asked triumphantly. "We'll be married soon, Becky, as soon as it can be arranged. And there's another reason, too. If you don't marry me, I'll have to go to war. I've been lucky, so far. This arm of mine held things up. But now it's mended . . . "

Suddenly she found her strength, pushing him away again. She was shaking now, with outrage as well as fear. He had taken her father's money, agreed to marry her against her wishes, and all the time he was using her as an excuse to get out of going to France.

"You don't understand, Becky . . . " Rupert began, but she faced him, her eyes blazing.

"Oh, I understand all right! You're using me! You're nothing but a coward, Rupert!"

"Now wait a minute . . . "

"You filthy coward!" she flung at him.

His surprise gave way to fury; she watched it mottle his face. Fear throbbed through her, but before she could move, his hands were on her arms, gripping them so tightly she cried out.

"A coward, eh? Is that what you think? I'll show you I'm no coward!"

His mouth came down on hers again, bruising her lips and making her gasp. Helplessly she struggled, but he was like a great bear, twisting her body against his. Then, with a guttural noise deep in his throat, he lifted her bodily. Her head cracked against the edge of the marble mantleshelf, and her senses swirled. She thought she was falling, and she cried out; then, as his soft, moist hand covered her mouth, she realized she was lying on the floor and he was kneeling astride her.

Her heart was racing now, her terror so acute it almost choked her. His face was close to hers, slobbering, obscene, and she felt his weight come down on her chest. As she opened her mouth to gasp for breath, his tongue thrust deep into it, and she heaved violently. His hands were everywhere, exploring her body and forcing her legs apart, so that her drawers tore like rotten silk. Soundlessly she sobbed, clawing at him with her hands. But there was nothing, nothing but his weight, squeezing the life from her, and his body, hot and hard upon her own.

Just as she thought her lungs would burst, he arched up for a moment, and she gasped wildly. But simultaneously he forced himself deep into her, and her breath came out again in a scream. Pain throbbed through her in waves, burning with a slow fire and reaching a sharp-edged crescendo with each rhythmic thrust of his body. A sob broke in her throat, but she did not struggle any more. She lay like a rag doll, her eyes fixed on the ceiling while shame and blind terror welled up in her, but even when he had finished with her, rolling away without a word, she did not move.

She didn't want to see him, not his plump white body or his sticky, wet skin. That would just make it that much worse—if such a thing were possible.

He pulled himself up, kneeling beside her and looking down at her in a mixture of triumph and fear at what he had done. As the last dregs of his spent passion drained away, so did his bravado.

"You'll have to marry me now," he said, and when she did not answer, he stood up with an impatient movement, fastening his clothing. "Get dressed, do! You can't lie there like that, half-naked."

Bruised and stunned, she obeyed, pulling up her torn drawers and trying to tie them together across her stomach. Her eyes were wild, but she did not speak, and he had the sudden crazy notion that she might never speak again. Then she slumped back against the chair, leaving her skirts bunched up around her legs, and staring into space as if she were in a trance.

The tiny hairs on the back of Rupert's neck began to prickle. Tears he could have coped with, but this silence was unnerving.

"Becky?" he said tentatively.

For a long moment she did not answer. Then she slowly swivelled her head until her eyes rested on him.

"Becky, you'll marry me now?"

Her face was blank and expressionless, but oh, her eyes! They were like black coals, shining with hate.

"Becky?" he said for the third time, and she caught her breath in low, shallow gasps.

"No, I won't marry you."

"But . . ."

"If my father finds out about this, he'll kill us both."

"You're exaggerating!"

"No. You don't know him as I do." Her voice was flat, emotionless, matter-of-fact. "You've only seen the side of him he wanted you to see. He wouldn't stand for you doing that to me. He'll kill you, more surely than any Hun."

"But I only . . . "

"It's sin. Fornication."

"Where did you learn that word?"

"From him. He hates fornication."

"Dear heaven!" Rupert was afraid now, more afraid than he had ever been in his life. There was something so odd about Becky repeating herself in this sing-song drawl that it made him shiver, and the vision of Alfred's fury was an alarming one. As Becky had said, he thought he might prefer to look down the barrel of a German gun than face the full wrath of her father.

"You'll marry me, then everything will be all right."

"No." She shuddered, straightening her skirts in the same distant manner, as if none of this had anything to do with her any more. She did not tell him of the nights she had lain listening to Alfred using her mother as a plaything for his perverted lust. She did not tell him she would rather die than face the same fate, particularly now she knew that it was every bit as bad as she had imagined it to be. She did not tell him that, if she could not marry for love and give herself freely, she would rather stay an old maid for the rest of her life. But somehow she had no need, for the expression in her eyes said it all.

He buttoned his jacket, slapping his pockets with a pretence of normality. "Well, I'll be going then."

"Please do, Rupert."

"Next week perhaps I could take you for a spin in the side-car."

She did not answer. Her face was small and stiff.

"Well, goodbye for now then . . . "

"Goodbye."

Only when the door had closed after him did she move. She drew a deep, shuddering sigh, and the tears glittered in her eyes. The pain was still there, not so sharp, but burning still deep within her.

Never again, she thought. If I can help it, never ever again. Not with him.

One of the tears escaped and slid down her nose. "Oh Ted," she whispered, and the tears began to fall in earnest. "Ted, where are you? And would you even want me now?"

Desolation, so complete it swamped even the pain, washed over her, and sinking into the sofa, her head in her hands, she wept.

19

SUMMER came, and as France sweltered the Western Front erupted again with a new and frightening violence. On the 1st July, thirteen British divisions went 'over the top,' bayonets glinting in the sun, and the long and bloody battle for the Somme had begun.

Ted Hall was amongst those who formed the human battering ram that hot summer's day, and as he staggered wearily back to his dug-out that night, he wondered how he could ever have wanted to be part of the stinking mess that was war.

Five months of action had taken their toll. His bright gold hair was darkened now, caked with dust and sweat. His face was thinner, and his chin covered with fine, fair stubble. And if his blue eyes still blazed with defiance, it was directed now as much at Haig and the British staff officers who sent wave after wave of men to certain death, as it was against the Hun.

They were all-powerful, those staff officers who led from the rear. He had seen them at practice attacks, sitting astride their sleekly beautiful horses, and looking for all the world as if they had just turned out of a spotless barracks. Some, he supposed, weren't as black as they were painted, and he had heard grudging stories of generals who did care what their men were going through. But largely, they had no idea, and Ted reckoned they looked on the Tommies as toy soldiers on a nursery floor instead of living, thinking men. He couldn't understand why so many of the men accepted them automatically as their betters, doing as they were told without question or criticism just because they wore breeches and Sam Browne belts and had red staff-officer tabs on their collars.

As for the junior officers, they were another breed again, as stupid in their way as their seniors, but brave too, bringing the traditions of their public schools on to the battlefield. They 'played the game' at all costs, and more often than not got themselves killed in the process. Ted admired them without understanding them, for he could not share the maxims they lived by.

That night, the 1st July, as he lay sleepless, listening to the steady rumbling thunder of guns, Ted thought that never had he imagined he would see so many corpses as he had seen in the last twelve hours.

Where could they all have come from, he wondered? Battalion upon battalion had been drawn up on the lines, it was true. But those dead! All those dead!

Ted closed his eyes, then opened them again. Now that the guttering candles had been snuffed out, it was dark in the dug-out, but not so dark as when his eyes were closed. And the darkness only brought the events of the day so close that he felt he was living it all again, from the nervous, but jaunty, start, when they had sipped their rum rations before dawn to give them Dutch courage, and then set off in single file along the communications trench to the front line.

He lay remembering the way his stomach had seemed to almost fold up from a mixture of fear and anticipation, so that he had wondered for a moment if he was in for a dose of the dysentery that had gone through so many of his comrades. But as the trenches became deeper, interspersed with craters, and the shells began to burst around him, there was no time left for thinking.

The noise was deafening, and the earth shook beneath his feet. Fear and the awareness of danger honed his senses to a fine edge, but he felt a strange detachment that was almost indifference.

And yet now, lying in the dark and reliving it, all he could see was the mile upon mile of corpses . . .

Those corpses. No matter how he tried to get away, they kept drawing him back. Again and again they rose before his weary red eyes, men in both khaki and field-grey, whose bodies had fallen into the most awkward and undignified positions, some horribly distorted, some curiously unmarked. There they lay, beyond help, while the flies that were already multiplying in the oppressive heat feasted upon them.

Dawn came, creeping slowly into the dug-out and bathing it in soft pink light. The ghosts of the dead receded with the shadows, and Ted pulled himself up in the narrow, make-shift bunk, and reached into the pocket of his tunic for his cigarettes. He found them, and put one between his lips, then changed his mind and replaced it carefully in the packet. His mouth was already stale and bitter; a cigarette would not taste good. And out here, cigarettes were too precious to waste.

Instead, he fumbled for his wallet, thinking he would reread the

273

last letter he had received from Rebecca. He knew it almost by heart, but remembering it was not the same as holding the paper that she had held, and seeing her rounded, carefully formed hand.

He wished he had a more recent letter to read, though, for it was several months since the last one had reached him. He blamed the number of times his company had moved about for that—most of the men complained about the irregularity of mail which was a lifeline to them—but he had received letters from home, telling of Jack and Harry's schooling, Dolly and Amy's latest boyfriends, and the progress of Jim's children, and there had even been a parcel of cigarettes and chocolate. Only from Rebecca had there been no word.

Her last letter was from Wycherley, where she was safe and happy, well away from her father and the ravages of war. Ted consoled himself with this knowledge, telling himself that although something had prevented her letters from reaching him, they would catch up with him eventually.

He reached again for his tunic, twisting it around so that he could get at the pocket where he kept his wallet. It felt curiously flat, and when he slipped his hand inside, it was empty. He wrinkled his brow, perplexed but not worried, and lifted his tunic up on to his bunk, systematically going through the pockets. When they yielded nothing more than a handkerchief or two and a half-used packet of cough lozenges, his frown deepened. His wallet must be somewhere. He'd had it yesterday. He reached for his trousers and searched those pockets too, although he knew he never carried his wallet there, and when they, too, proved to be empty, he pulled himself up, leaning over to look on the floor of the dug-out.

"What's wrong, old son?" Redvers Brixey asked from the bunk above, and Ted swore.

"I've lost me wallet."

"Go on! How d'you manage that?"

"I don't know. It's not here, is it? I must have lost it yesterday."

"D'you reckon it's been pinched?"

Ted shook his head. It was not in his nature to think the worst of people. "I reckon I've lost it. Though it might turn up yet."

"Is there much in it?"

"Every bloody thing of value I've got with me," Ted said bitterly. "There's not much money, it's true. But it's all my personal things —letters, photographs, stuff you can't replace."

"That's hard luck," Redvers sympathized.

He watched Ted get up and search every corner of the dug-out before adding unnecessarily: "You're not going t' find it here."

"No, you're right there, Redvers," Ted said, dejected.

The sky was lightening with every passing minute, and when the dug-out was roused, Ted asked the other men if they had seen his wallet, but none of them was interested enough to give him a satisfactory answer. Out here, a lost wallet seemed of little importance. They grunted and shrugged and gulped at their rum ration, and after a while, Ted gave up, gulped his own belly-warming rum, and followed Redvers up the rough ladder from the dug-out.

The morning air was cool, and smelled of death. Ted, suppressing a shudder, thought it was an odour he would never be able to get out of his nostrils.

As they left the dug-out they swung around to the right, following one behind the other in single file. "We're pushing 'em back, you know, we're pushing the buggers back," Redvers murmured optimistically over his shoulder, and Ted nodded.

It was true, the line had moved a little further to what he supposed must be the north-east. The trench they were filing into now had been a support trench yesterday. Now, it was on the Front, and the forward trenches that angled sharply away from it were cutting into the heart of No Man's Land, their tentacles protected from attack by a wide hedge of barbed wire.

In a curve of the trench, a German soldier, bloodied, broken, and trodden over by scores of determined British boots, confirmed that the enemy attack had indeed been beaten back in this sector. Ted, following Redvers closely, side stepped hastily to avoid treading in the soft pulp that had once been a face.

"See, we've got the bastards on the run!" Redvers muttered gleefully. "They must have sent a raid over last night, and we beat 'em back!"

But where are we going now? Ted wondered. What had they to encounter today? How could he protect himself? Only by being alert and adaptable, and keeping his wits about him.

As if his thought process had triggered off the enemy reflexes, a shell exploded in the sky. It was a signal for all hell to break loose. With a roar like a wall of water breaking through a dam, the German guns opened fire; a second later the British countered with their own. Shells screamed through the still morning air, raining splinters of steel on to both men in the trenches and those who had been caught in the open. Machine guns crackled and drummed, mowing down row upon row of advancing men. Soldiers yelled and sobbed and swore, and the whole earth shook. Ted saw a shell land in the front trench, and as it exploded the air was full of flying mud and boarding, flesh and torn khaki. Then the sides caved in, concealing the destruction.

The desperate optimism had gone now, and the bravado turned to panic. A shell exploded nearby, and Ted felt a sharp pain in his foot. It quickly dulled to a burning sensation, and he dismissed it altogether. Only when he tried to take a step and the weight of his body made him scream in surprised agony did he realize that a splinter of shrapnel had pierced his boot and buried itself in his foot.

"Get back, lad, go on, get back!" the sergeant shouted at him over the cacophony of guns. "You're no good here now."

His boot was spurting blood like a geyser, but Ted burned with resentment at the sergeant's words. No good? He was more use even now than the poor devils who were falling all around him.

Gritting his teeth, he took another step forward, but as his foot touched the ground, sharp screaming pain enveloped him again. He held his breath to keep from crying out, then swore. He knew that the sergeant was right, and that he'd have to get back behind the lines until his foot was bound up, at least.

Stumbling, Ted inched his way back towards the dug-out. Men pushed past him, their voices lost in the roar of battle, yet adding oddly to the general pandemonium. They swore at him, their faces moving, gaping, meaningless, and he inched on, moving like a man in a dream, determined but unreal.

The trench was shallower here, hastily dug to consolidate ground gained, only three to four feet deep, and within a stone's throw of the barbed-wire. Above it, a cluster of shattered trees stood sentinel, their branches and trunks blasted to premature death, but their roots spreading tenaciously through the trench walls. Ted crawled along it on hands and knees while above him the storm raged on. At the intersection where the split trench curved away, he paused to get his breath.

A burst of machine-gun fire crackled, sharper and closer than before, and automatically, he ducked. Then, as it died away, something made him straighten just enough to peep warily over the rim of the trench at the narrow strip of barren earth that reached to the barbed wire.

Men, long since dead lay there, heap upon untidy heap, but now there were fresh corpses and those not yet dead who writhed and moaned. Although he knew he was in mortal danger, and although his eyes were misted from pain and loss of blood, Ted stared for a moment in horror. Then he started, tingling through and through with awareness.

Among the shattered bodies was one he thought he recognized. That boyish face, imploring heaven as he tried to drag himself across the sunbaked ground, was one he knew. Somehow he was sure it belonged to no one from his company, no one he'd met in this godforsaken hole. It came from a different place, and a different time. The khaki uniform was distracting Ted's memory, and the pain confusing him.

The small body out there in No Man's-Land flattened, the face dropped forward to bury itself in the bloodied mess of a shattered soldier, and in the same instant Ted remembered.

Reg Adams! The boy from Bath who had come to South Hill Pit to avoid conscription! Suddenly the fury of the battle seemed very far away, and Ted was back in the black passages beneath the friendly earth, chewing on a cogknocker and drinking cold tea from his stone bottle as he listened to the boy explaining his reasons for wanting to stay at home.

He hadn't made it then. He hadn't been able to escape the notice of the pen-pushers. They'd caught up with him, just as he'd been afraid they would. And he wasn't going to make it now, either, unless someone helped him, and helped him soon.

Hurriedly Ted looked around to see if anyone else had noticed the dying lad. But what was special about one boy dragging himself back to the lines when men were dying all around? He looked back at Reg. The boy's hands were stretched out before him, clawing helplessly at the earth, and Ted was suddenly reminded of Harry learning to crawl.

The pain in his foot had spread so that his whole body seemed to be encircled with it. This, for some strange reason, made it easier for him to put his weight on it. He searched the planking against the wall of the trench to find a toe-hold, and was surprised when he felt nothing. Strangely, his foot was numb from the ankle down— it was the rest of his body that was consumed in pain.

With tremendous effort, Ted found his toe-hold and hoisted himself up. It was hard going; his strong and muscular arms felt like pieces of gas-mask tubing that would not bear the weight of his body.

All around him the fury raged on; a shell fragment spattered him with earth, snipers' shots whizzed past him and the angry air sang in his ears. Behind him, another shell landed with a dull thud, and he heard the rush of soil as the trench walls caved in. But he did not look back.

Inch by inch he wormed his way forward, his injured foot dragging uselessly behind him, his eyes blurring from sweat and loss of blood.

A little more. A little more. Not much farther now.

It never occurred to Ted that he might be too weak to drag himself back to the trench, let alone a wounded boy, too. Neither did it occur to him that the lad might be beyond help. He reached the body, pulling himself along with one last, mighty effort, and spoke the boy's name with eager urgency.

"Reg, Reggie, are you all right?"

There was no answer, no answering movement. Ted raised himself on his elbows, prodding the boy.

"Reg! Come on now! It's not far. We'll make it together."

There was still no reply.

"Reg!" With a supreme effort, he lifted the lad, turning him on to his side, and two facts presented themselves simultaneously.

First, the lad was dead. The pleading gesture had been his last, and his wide and staring eyes would never see England again. But even as Ted tried to digest the fact that all his effort had been in vain, he grasped the other.

This wasn't Reg Adams. He wasn't even very like him. Only the small-boned wiriness of him was similar. And this was only a boy—one of those who'd faked his age to join up, more than likely.

Rage filled Ted, lending him new strength. He'd get the youngster back if it killed him! Somewhere, someone was worrying about him, and he wanted them to know. Besides, to leave a kid like this out here to rot was filthy—obscene—a sum total of all the obscenities.

Ted gritted his teeth, and catching the boy by the shoulders, pulled him an inch or two. But he was heavy, much heavier than he looked, heavier than any putt of coal.

The thought gave Ted an idea. From his pocket he took a length of twine which he had saved in case it came in useful. This he tied round the boy's chest, passing it under his armpits and knotting it firmly. Then he dragged himself up into a kneeling position, bringing the twine between his legs and fastening it around his waist.

278

Just like the gus and crook, he thought, and then there was no effort left to spare for thinking.

Ted was half-way when it first came to him that he might not make it. He hardly seemed to be moving, and he felt as though he were swimming against a strong tide with useless limbs, lungs that were bursting and a head that sang from weakness. The battle still raged around him, but he was no longer aware of it.

Pull, move, one knee, the other, keep your face off the ground. Why can't you see, damn it, why can't you see? Pull, move, you're not trying hard enough. It's all right, Reg, we'll make it. Not far now, see? Not far. But why the sea? How did you get into the sea? No, the beach—it's the beach, the sand. Can't you hear the breakers, you silly bugger? There, against the rocks. The tide must be coming in. Can't you hear it?

From the tumultuous cacophony, one sound isolated itself, a shrill, high-pitched whine, coming closer and closer. Ted lifted his head, puzzled. What was that? What was it?

And then he knew. For a second, his fogged brain cleared, and suddenly it was like looking through the clearest crystal. He saw the trenches, the men, the guns silhouetted against the clear, blue sky. He saw the earth beneath him, brown and ravaged, and felt again the pain in his foot.

A shell! he thought. A shell, coming this way! So it's all been for nothing. All for nothing!

20

ALMOST from the first, Rebecca knew that she was pregnant. It was a sick certainty inside her that she could not dispel however often she told herself it had been only once, and somehow she felt it was a just punishment for her sin.

I must have encouraged him, she thought. For him to do such a terrible thing, I must have been partly to blame. And now I shall have to pay.

Days passed, and the signs accumulated. There was the nausea rolling over her in waves when she got out of bed in the mornings;

then, there was the absence of 'the curse', which should have come around two weeks after Rupert's attack on her; and lastly, there was the change in her breasts—they had become firmer and engorged, the area around her nipples growing darker. But she told no one; there was no one to tell. And all the time she trembled from head to foot as she wondered what to do.

If only Ted were here! But he wasn't. He was in France. And although she managed to smuggle some writing paper and envelopes out of her father's desk when she found it unlocked one day, and scribble Ted a hastily written note, she'd had nothing in reply.

But on one thing she was determined. Whatever happened, she would not marry Rupert. Quite apart from the fact that the very thought was as repugnant to her as ever, it would be her revenge on him for what he had done to her. For, as he told her that night, he was certain to be conscripted into the army sooner or later, unless she became his wife.

"You'll have to marry me, Becky," he had said to her several times after that dreadful night when he had taken her, but she only set her mouth in a determined line and shook her head.

"I won't marry you, Rupert. And if you and my father try to make me, I'll say no at the altar."

Rupert subsided then, wretched with guilt, and for the first time since she had known him, she had felt he was actually afraid of her. She knew why, of course. He was afraid she would tell her father what he had done, and that would be the end of all Alfred's promises to set him up.

When no mention was made to him of an impending wedding, Alfred began to wonder what had happened and mentioned it to Rupert.

"You were so keen to bring the date forward, my boy," he said in puzzled tones. "Is something wrong?"

Rupert coloured, and his hands began to shake.

"Becky's so shy and inexperienced, Uncle," he said. "I don't want to hurry or frighten her."

"Would you like me to speak to her?" Alfred suggested, and was surprised by Rupert's vehement response.

"No! No, just leave it to me, Uncle. Given time, I know I can bring her round to the idea of marrying me willingly. And I wouldn't want her any other way."

"But your conscription?" Alfred said. "Men are being pulled into service in their hundreds. It can't be long before it's your turn."

"No, I've thought of that," Rupert said. "I'm making out a case for the Appeals Tribunal now, on the grounds that I shall be of more use to the community as a solicitor than a soldier."

Alfred nodded. The Appeals Tribunals had been sitting every two or three weeks since April, hearing pleas from reluctant conscriptees on every imaginable ground, from their indispensability at work to the fact that they were the last remaining son of a family not already in France.

"I still think you'd do best to set the date for the wedding," he said, blissfully ignorant of how hard Rupert was trying to do just that.

As the weeks passed, Rebecca's desperation grew. Certain now that she was going to have a baby, she was terrified of what would happen when her father found out. What he would do to Rupert she didn't know, and didn't much care either, for she was sure she would be the one to take the brunt of his anger.

Just when she reached the depths of despair, she thought of Ted's mother. Although she had only met her once, Rebecca had liked her, sensing the inner strength that made her just the person to turn to in a crisis. And it would be the next best thing to having Ted at her side. But how to get to see her? There was one way, and one way only.

"Take me to Hillsbridge, Rupert. I want to see someone there," she said the next evening when he came to visit her. "There's no reason at all why I can't ride in the side-car."

"Why do you want to go to Hillsbridge?" he asked bad-temperedly.

She lifted her chin, meeting his gaze defiantly. "That's none of your business. Now, are you going to take me, or am I going to tell my father what you have done?"

Rupert's eyes fell away and a bead or two of perspiration stood out on his forehead. Curse it, how could he have been so stupid as to get himself into a position like this? But for the moment he would play along with her.

"Where in Hillsbridge?" he asked.

"You can drop me outside the George Hotel," she said. "I'll walk from there."

"All right."

It was bumpy riding in the side-car, and before they had gone far, Rebecca began to feel sick. But she gritted her teeth and forced back the nausea, and when he stopped outside the George she climbed out.

"I won't be long," she said. Then she turned the corner into Conygre Hill, and was lost to his sight.

The sun was low in the sky now, but it was still oppressively hot, but that did not lessen her pace. If she was too long, Rupert might decide to come looking for her after all, and that was the last thing she wanted. Only when she reached the point where Greenslade Terrace angled away from the hill did she pause, the beating of her heart keeping time with her ragged breath. This was the rank. Now, she had only to find the right house. But when she did, what was she going to say? All the carefully rehearsed speech had flown from her mind, and she felt the beginnings of panic.

How could she possibly tell this woman she scarcely knew that she was going to have a baby? And why had she ever been so foolish as to think she might help?

I must have been crazy! Rebecca thought. But it was too late to turn back now, and taking her courage in both hands, she walked along the rank until she came to number eleven. Then, before it could desert her, she raised her hand and knocked on the door.

For a moment there was no sound from within and her heart fluttered somewhere between relief and despair. Then she heard footsteps and voices coming closer and the door was flung open by a little boy in short trousers and a shirt with a sailor collar. Although he could not have been more than six years old, his colouring was so like Ted's that Rebecca knew at once that this must be Harry.

"Is your mother in?" she asked.

"Yes, I'm here," Charlotte called.

Because she had bent down to speak to Harry, Rebecca had not seen Charlotte, and now she jumped self-consciously.

"Oh Mrs Hall! I didn't know you were there!"

"Rebecca! Then you've heard!"

"Heard? Heard what?" Rebecca asked, staring at Charlotte. The older woman had aged somehow since their last meeting; her eyes were hooded and tired, her face drawn and pale.

She moved Harry aside and opened the door wider. "Come in, Rebecca."

The girl followed, her nervousness growing. There was something different about Mrs Hall, and she was not certain of her welcome. And what was it that she thought Rebecca had heard?

"Harry, go out in the rank and bowl your hoop," Charlotte said, and led the way through into the kitchen.

Rebecca followed, fighting down a new wave of nausea, but Charlotte did not seem to notice. It was as if she was in a world of her own, and when she spoke, her voice was toneless.

"I never expected to see you here, Rebecca."

"No, but I had to come. Mrs Hall, have you heard from Ted?"

The tired, hooded eyes were staring into the distance, the drawn mouth twitched slightly, and Rebecca looking at her, knew. The blood left her body in a rush, and weak and trembling she grasped the back of the settle for support.

"Something has happened to him, hasn't it? That's why I haven't heard from him."

Charlotte crossed to the mantlepiece and took an envelope from behind the clock. "A telegram," she said. "It came three weeks ago. Ted is posted as missing, believed killed in action."

Rebecca felt her knees sag and only the settle prevented her from falling. Around her the room darkened, fragmented, came together again in one claustrophobic whole, and she stood with her eyes tight-closed, swaying against the settle like a young willow in a storm.

Charlotte made to go to her, but her own limbs were heavy with a grief too deep to be shared, and the reserve which rebelled against giving way to emotion held her back. She stood looking at the girl Ted had loved, perhaps too much, and knew that her own iron control would break if she so much as touched her. Charlotte wanted no mawkish, sentimental weeping in each other's arms; that would be quite unworthy of Ted. So she kept her distance, watching the spasms pass over the girl's face like the lace-edged waves washing over the beach at high tide, and trying to remain unmoved by them.

Suddenly Rebecca opened her eyes. "But he might not be dead at all!" she burst out. "It doesn't actually say he is, does it? Only that he's missing! And if he were dead, I'd know it—I know I'd know it!"

Charlotte bowed her head, wondering why the words had the power to make her feel so old, and wondering too why they had brought her closer to tears than she had been at any time in the dreadful days since the telegram arrived.

"It's true, Rebecca," she said. "You might as well accept it."

"But why should I? They could be mistaken—they could! Oh, we mustn't give up just because . . . "

"Rebecca!" Charlotte said sharply. "There's something else you don't know about. I don't suppose you saw the *News of the World,* did you? Well, last week there was something in it that we recognized—something you'll recognize too."

She pulled open a drawer in the table, taking out a newspaper that had been folded and re-folded into a small square, and handed it to Rebecca, pointing as she did so. "Look, here."

Rebecca looked, her eyes widening in surprise. "It's the photograph I gave Ted—the one he carried in his wallet!"

"Rebecca, you'd better come and sit down," Charlotte said roughly, worried by the girl's white face.

"No, tell me what it's all about!" Rebecca was trembling all over, but refusing to move or give up her hold on the high back of the settle. "How did they get my photograph?"

The need for action restored Charlotte's self-control. Firmly she levered Rebecca away from the settle, bringing her round to the deep fireside chair and pushing her down into it by the shoulders.

"It's a column all made up with details of stuff that's been found in the trenches—and photographs too. If you look at what it says, you'll see your photograph was found in the front lines on the Somme. I wrote to the *News of the World* straight away to identify it, and I got a reply with the full details yesterday. The photo was found in a soldier's pocket. But the soldier . . . " She broke off, unable to go on.

Rebecca's eyes, feverishly bright, bored into hers. "Yes? The soldier?"

Charlotte took a deep breath, determined to speak calmly. "The soldier was dead. Blown to bits. There was nothing else with which to identify him."

Rebecca sat motionless, her hands twisted tightly together in her lap. It couldn't be true. If Ted were dead, she'd have known. She'd have *known.*

"I know it's hard to accept these things." Charlotte's voice seemed to be coming from a long way off. "Especially when you're young. But who else would have had your picture in his pocket?"

"No one." It was a whisper only.

"There you are then. It's a clear proof. Ted's gone, Rebecca. Now, how about a cup of tea?"

Rebecca jerked upright. "How can you talk like that? As if this was a social visit and we were discussing the weather? Don't you realize what you're saying? That we shall never see Ted again! Doesn't that mean anything to you?"

Charlotte sighed deeply. "Is that how it seems to you? I suppose it must. I've learned to hide my feelings over the years. But it doesn't mean I don't have any."

"I don't believe you! You don't care a bit. If you did, you couldn't be this way!" The first tears had begun, thickening her throat so that her voice was loud and vehement. "It's different for you," she cried. "To you, Ted's just one of a lot. To me, he's special. There isn't anyone else."

Charlotte stopped in the doorway, her hand going to her throat. Her back was turned from Rebecca, so the girl could not see the agony of her expression, the pain, the grief, the unbearable ache that came from losing not only a son, but a part of her life, her hopes, her past and her future.

"Becky," she said quietly, "my children are all irreplaceable. That's the way it is with a mother. You'll find that out for yourself one day. Oh yes, you will. You might not think so now, but you're young. There'll be someone else for you. And when that day comes, you'll know I was right."

Rebecca stood up.

"No, never. There won't be anyone but Ted for me. If you think there could be, you don't know me, and you don't know the way it was with us, either. Now, I think I'd better be going."

"Oh, Becky, Becky!" Charlotte turned, distressed. "I don't know what to say. Let's have that cup of tea now, shall we?"

Rebecca shook her head. Somewhere in the emptiness inside her, she could feel a tiny ticking, like an irregular pulse. Could it be the baby? She didn't know, nor did she care. Everything had retreated into the distance. Nothing really mattered any more. Ted was dead, and she hadn't known. That hurt more than anything else.

"Well, Becky, you know where we are if you want us." Charlotte showed her to the door. "If there's anything I can do, you know I will."

"No, there's nothing."

High in her waist the pulse ticked again, but she knew there was no point in telling Charlotte now. How had she ever thought she could?

There was a darkness about the evening now, and for a moment Rebecca wondered if thunder was brewing up. But there were no storm clouds. The darkness was inside her head.

She walked along the rank almost as briskly as she had come, past Harry, whose hoop clattered noisily to the ground as he watched her go, past two women standing on their doorsteps gossiping, past a slight, dark-haired girl who stared at her with such hate in her eyes that even in her state of stunned shock, Rebecca could not help but notice. She turned into the steep decline of the hill in a dream, and she did not even notice the roar of the approaching motor cycle until it turned around in the road and came to a shuddering stop beside her. Then she turned indignantly. Rupert!

"You were supposed to wait for me outside the George!" she said, but while he had been waiting, Rupert had been thinking, and this time he was determined not to be bullied.

"Where have you been, Becky?" he asked.

Startled, she lifted her chin. "That's none of your business."

"I think it is. After all, I am going to be your husband. Now, get into this side-car. I'm taking you home."

"Don't think you can tell me what to do, Rupert Thorne! Remember, my father wouldn't like . . ."

"Two can play at that game," he interrupted. "You won't tell him. You'd be too afraid of what he'd do to you."

She crumpled suddenly, her face distorting into something midway between tears and laughter. There, in the road, she stood, her arms folded about herself as if awareness of a hundred truths had hit her all at once.

"Oh, Rupert, you don't know how funny that is."

"Funny? Why?" He sounded alarmed.

"Funny, because he's going to have to know anyway."

"Why? It's our secret, yours and mine."

"But how can you keep a baby a secret?" The words came out on a small, strangled sob. "Oh, don't look like that, Rupert. Don't tell me you didn't know what you were doing. I'm going to have your baby."

For a moment Rupert said nothing. He stood speechless, his jaw dropped, his eyes glazed. Then he raised one hand to mop his forehead.

"I don't believe it. You're just trying to put the wind up me. It was the first time, wasn't it, and everyone knows . . ."

She said nothing, but the expression on her face told him more than mere words could have done. He broke off, sweating, to chew at his lower lip.

"But . . . but how can you be sure?" he asked presently, all bravado gone. "You couldn't know, could you?"

She shrugged. "There are some things a woman's body tells her."

"But you're as slender as ever . . . your waist . . . "

"I won't be for much longer." At the thought, her cool mask slipped a little, and she almost sobbed. "Oh, what am I going to do?"

"We'll get married, Becky, right away. Nobody will think anything of it, with the war and everything . . . "

She stamped her foot, impatient again. "Oh, Rupert, how many times do I have to tell you I'm not going to marry you. Not even now. **Especially** not now."

Helplessly he slapped at the pockets of his motor cycling jacket. "But you'll have to!"

"I won't, I tell you. I'll kill myself first."

"For God's sake, don't talk so stupid, Becky!"

"It's not stupid. I don't care if I live or die now. I wish I *could* die, I do . . . "

The tears began as she spoke, streaming down her cheeks while her body shook. Rupert, embarrassed as well as shocked, opened up the side-car and bundled her in.

As he drove, his thoughts churned, his concentration was gone, and he found himself approaching bends so fast that he had to brake violently, making the side-car sway from side to side. With an effort, he slowed down, as he realized that if Rebecca was still in a state when he got her home, there would be questions asked. And at present he had no answers to give.

He turned the machine into the lanes. On either side, the hedges were high and sweet, and above them the sky was a perfect violet, but Rupert saw only a vision of Alfred. How would he react when he learned the truth? This wasn't like getting some whore in the family way—there were bound to be serious repercussions. One way or another, an answer had to be found, and quickly.

It came to him in a flash, and he stopped the machine in a gateway, dismounted and went around to the side-car.

Rebecca sat clutching the casing. She was deathly pale and Rupert glared at her quizzically. If she wasn't all right, then so much the better. There would be no need to put his plan into action.

"You'll have to take something to get rid of the baby," he said, suddenly.

"What do you mean?" she asked, wide-eyed.

"Oh, for God's sake!" he said impatiently. "Do you want this baby?"

"No, of course I don't! I don't want any part of you!"

He ignored the insult. "Then I'll get something for you. All you need do is take it, like medicine."

"But what will it do?"

"I don't know. Stop the baby somehow. This isn't exactly an everyday occurrence with me, whatever you might think. But I know a chap who . . . well, just leave it to me."

"Oh, Rupert, I don't know . . . "

"Well I do. If you do as I say, no one need ever know about it. I'm going to take you home now, but I'll be back just as soon as I can with the stuff. And in the meantime, don't you say a word to a soul. Do you hear now?"

She nodded. "Yes. Yes, I hear."

"Right. Let's go home then. I need a good stiff drink."

He turned, mounted the motor cycle and started the engine.

In the side-car, Rebecca sat too dazed by the evening's events to be able to string two thoughts together coherently.

Stop the baby? What did he mean? Right or wrong, it hardly seemed to matter. If Ted was dead, nothing really mattered any more.

As the side-car began to jolt and sway once more, Rebecca pressed her fist tight against her mouth and closed her eyes. All she wanted in the world at that moment was to be left alone.

RUPERT brought her the potion a week later, an evil smelling concoction in an old medicine bottle.

"Now look, Becky, all you have to do is take this before you go to bed. Two or three spoonfuls should be enough, but you'd better keep the rest just in case it doesn't work. Otherwise I shall have to take you to see this chap, and that wouldn't be much fun I can tell you."

"But what will happen?" In her small, pale face, Rebecca's eyes were huge and haunted, the legacy of a week of secret weeping and little sleep.

"It'll stop the baby. I told you."

"But how?"

"Oh, Becky, for God's sake, do I have to spell it all out for you?" he blustered, unwilling to admit to his own ignorance. "One thing, though, it'll probably be a bit painful, so be prepared. There's no point in frightening yourself when it happens. Have you got some old towels, and brown paper? You'll need both, this chap said. And some water to clean up."

She nodded, not understanding, but not caring much either.

"Where did you get it, this stuff?"

"That's my little secret. But I can tell you, it cost me, Becky. I hope you'll be grateful afterwards."

Her look withered him, and he turned away awkwardly. "Well, you know what I mean. Now, you've got to do it tomorrow. I've found out that your father will be in Bristol for some 'do'. If I can find where he parks his motor I'll fix the engine so that it won't start, then he'll most likely spend the night at our place. That'll be one less in the house for you to worry about. You'll only have your mother to contend with then, and her hearing isn't too good, is it?"

Rebecca nodded absently, and Rupert looked at her sharply. "Now you are going to do it, aren't you, Becky? You won't change your mind?"

She shook her head, but she still wasn't sure. For a week she had wondered about it, turned it over in her mind in between her grieving for Ted, but she still didn't know whether she could go through with it.

The baby was completely repugnant to her, because it was a constant reminder of Rupert, and yet she almost felt it was the only reason left for living. That her father would take his strap to her, if he found out, she had no doubt. And there would be more, horrors as yet undreamed of, humiliations too great to contemplate. She would have borne them all if the baby had been Ted's. But it was *not* Ted's.

Rupert handed her the bottle. "Put this away where nobody can see it. And remember, Becky, however much it hurts, you mustn't make a sound. You mustn't wake them up, or the whole thing will come out. I wish I could get you away, but I can't. But you can handle it. I know you can. They say there's nothing to it. And with your father out of the way, it should be a piece of cake."

Again she nodded, but said nothing. Tomorrow. Tomorrow was the night. It was all arranged. Rupert had arranged everything. The solution to everything was here in a bottle.

That night, she lay sleepless, unable to think of anything but the mysterious bottle lying hidden in her underwear drawer. The enormity of what she planned to do hung over her like a cloud, dark yet nebulous, frightening enough to make her heart pound yet unreal.

Instinctively she recoiled from the act, yet it seemed the only solution. Even if she bore her child, facing all the horrors that would come with discovery, what sort of a future would he have, branded as bastard, cut off, no doubt, from the rest of the family? She had no money, nowhere to go, except to Rupert, and she was determined she would rather die than face a life with him.

Hatred for him welled up in her, and she pressed her hands to her belly, imagining his seed growing like a cancer inside her. What would it be like, this child of his? Would it turn out to be like him? Or would it have a likeness to her father, passed down unwittingly in her own blood? Suppose—just suppose—that it might be a mixture of both of them?

The thought was so nightmarish it almost made her cry out.

I can't bear it! she thought. I can't bring a monster like that into the world! Tomorrow, I'll get rid of it. Tomorrow . . .

But why wait until tomorrow? She sat bolt upright, her body tingling with sudden anticipation as the idea suggested itself to her. If it was as easy as Rupert had said, she might as well do it now! She had no brown paper, but every drawer in her room was lined with old newspaper, and there was plenty of old linen in a chest on the landing.

Feverish now with excitement, she got out of bed and gathered the things together. When they were heaped on the bed in neat piles, she picked up the grimy bottle, holding it between her hands as if it were a precious ornament. She had no spoon, but what did that matter? If she wiped off the crusted rim, she could drink it straight from the bottle. And if she had a little more than she was supposed to, what did that matter? It would only ensure that the potion did its work.

Now that her mind was made up, she left all her doubts and agonizings behind, thinking only of the monstrous child she might bear if she did nothing to prevent it. She felt excited, yet strangely calm, as if she had already crossed the Rubicon. Carefully, as if she had all the time in the world, she unscrewed the top, wiping the neck of the bottle with her handkerchief and tipping it to her lips.

The liquid tasted foul, as foul as it smelled. It scorched her tongue and throat, but she drank deeply, afraid that if she paused she would never find the courage to begin again. She took the bottle from her stinging lips and observed that it was half empty.

Panic flooded through her then, panic at what she had done. She set down the bottle as if it were a hot coal, scrubbing at her lips with the back of her hand, and all her doubts, and a hundred more besides, rushed in to threaten her.

"Thou shalt not kill!" she thought, and the commandment repeated and repeated itself in her head.

Thou shalt not kill. Honour thy father and thy mother. Thou shalt not kill. Thou shalt not commit adultery. I didn't! I didn't! Thou shalt have no other God but me, for the Lord Thy God is a jealous God . . . Ted was my God, I made Ted my God, and now I must be punished . . .

It was unbearably hot. Although the weather had broken, it was still sultry, and Rebecca felt sick in the airless room. She stumbled across to the window, throwing it open, and the perfume of the honeysuckle and the night-scented stocks wafted up, making her retch.

What have I done? she asked herself in terror. Oh dear Lord, what have I done?

As the sickness rose in her throat, she ran to the wash-stand, leaning over the bowl. But she found she was heaving at nothing. Her mouth and throat felt parched, and her face burned hotly. She tried to pour some water into the bowl from the jug, but her hands were trembling too much to lift it and she had to content herself with dipping her handkerchief into the cool water in the jug and dabbing it on to her face.

And then the pain began, a flicker of fire in her gut that quickly fanned itself into screaming tongues of flame that licked and seared every corner, every passage.

She straightened up, eyes widening, then doubled again as another bout of sickness caught her. She clutched at her nightdress, twisting it between her hands as she fought the desperate need to cry out.

Without knowing how she got there, she felt the bed hard behind her knees, and then it came up to meet her with a rush. She lay there, writhing in fear and agony; then she began to vomit again. She was too weak to get back to the basin, but lay sobbing and retching into the counterpane.

As if from a long way off, she heard someone knocking at her door, and then a voice calling her name, but she did not answer.

The door burst open, and there Alfred stood, an enormous figure threatening even in his nightshirt and carrying a candle. Behind him, Winnie hovered, whimpering and gabbling. But Rebecca did not see them. Her world had closed in around her to a small, dark pinprick.

But somewhere, far away, like the light at the end of a tunnel, was a brightness that seemed to be coming closer, eating up the terror, taking away the pain. Without moving, she seemed to turn towards it, and suddenly the guilt had gone, too, and Rebecca felt herself overwhelmed with love. She was floating now, floating on the back of a swan towards the light, and she was happy, more happy than she could ever remember.

Briefly, she opened her eyes, and a smile curved her mouth.

"Ted," she whispered.

It was the last word she would ever speak.

21

DR FROSTER was asleep when Alfred came for him, banging on the door with the engine of his silver-grey motor car still running in the road outside.

"For God's sake come quickly, Tom!" he shouted when the doctor pushed up his sash window and looked out. "It's Rebecca. I think she's dying."

Dr Froster's head disappeared, and a few minutes later he came out of the house, still fastening the jacket and trousers he had pulled on over his nightshirt.

"What's the trouble then, Alfred?" he asked with professional calm.

"It's a mess, Tom, a mess!" Alfred was beside himself. "I think she's taken poison. There's a bottle . . . oh hurry, man, do! Get into the car—I'll drive you. From the look of her when I left, we're too late already."

"Dear God, Alfred, what are you saying?" the doctor asked, shocked. "You don't mean that Rebecca has attempted suicide?"

Alfred threw the car into gear, and it leaped forward. "It must be that, Tom. She's in agony—and there's this bottle."

"What does *she* say?"

"She couldn't say anything. She was too far gone. Except . . . "

"Yes?"

"Nothing. It was nothing," Alfred said, reluctant suddenly to tell the doctor that he had thought she had whispered the name of the pit lad with whom she had been involved.

"But this is a serious matter, Alfred," Tom Froster said, his mind racing. "If Rebecca *has* committed suicide . . . "

"I know, I know," Alfred interrupted him, not wanting to dwell on the consequences. "Pray God, we're in time. But if not . . . Tom, you will help us, won't you? If this came to light . . . "

The doctor said nothing. It was not the first time he had been asked to help in a matter of this sort; suicide was an offense against God and the law of the land, a degrading scandal.

"I can rely on you, Tom, can't I?" Alfred blustered.

The doctor nodded, drumming his fingers on his medical bag. "Of course, of course. But let us hope it doesn't come to that. We may be in time to save her."

The lights were all burning in Alfred's house, so that it stood out on the dark road like a beacon.

Alfred drew up outside, and both he and the doctor rushed in. Winnie came down the stairs to meet them, still wearing her nightgown, her hair in curling rags. Her eyes were red, and she was sobbing soundlessly.

"Winnie . . . " Alfred began.

"She's gone, Alfred," Winnie whispered. Then, her voice rising to a wail, she repeated it again and again. "She's gone!"

"Oh my God!" Alfred took the stairs two at a time, and the doctor followed. Winnie waited downstairs, twisting a sodden handkerchief between her trembling hands. After a moment, Alfred emerged once more. His head was bowed now, the shock written all over his majestic face.

"Alfred?" Winnie cried, and when Alfred shook his head slowly from side to side, she began to wail again, a thin, high sound that penetrated every corner of the silent house.

"Why?" Alfred asked in a stunned voice. "She had everything to live for. Why should she do such a thing?"

He was still repeating himself when the bedroom door opened and the doctor came out, the grimy medicine bottle in his hand, and

Winnie echoed him. "Whatever made her do it, Doctor? My lovely girl . . . "

Dr Froster looked from one to the other of them, his face very serious indeed. Then he drew Alfred to one side. "I don't know how to say this, Alfred, but I'm not absolutely certain Rebecca meant to kill herself."

Alfred's eyes narrowed. "But the bottle—I've never seen it before!"

"No, but . . . "

"What are you trying to say, Tom? Out with it!"

Dr Froster glanced at Winnie, who had collapsed, sobbing, on to the linen chest.

"Did you know she was going to have a baby?"

"*What?*" Alfred's eyes bulged. "No, no, you're wrong, Tom."

"No, Alfred. She was going to have a baby all right. And I think she was trying to get rid of it. I suspected it as soon as I smelled what was in this bottle. It's a concoction quacks make up to cause abortion. At least, that's the idea behind it. In practice, it rarely works. Too little, and all you get is an upset stomach. Too much, and . . . " He broke off, glancing towards Rebecca's room.

"Oh my God!" Alfred covered his face with his hands. "But what makes you think . . . "

"Did you look around in there?" Dr Froster asked. "There's paper, mounds of it, and linen. She was expecting to lose her baby tonight, I'm certain of it."

"But she couldn't . . . she wouldn't know . . . "

Unnoticed by them, Winnie had raised her head and was listening, round-eyed with horror. "You're wrong," she burst out suddenly. "She couldn't be having a baby, not my Becky!"

"I'm sorry, Mrs Church, there's no mistake. I've examined her," the doctor said, then turned back to Alfred, holding up the bottle. "I'm sorry to press the point, Alfred, but I must find out how she got hold of this. It's lethal stuff, and whoever gave it to her must be found."

"Oh, Doctor, it's not all going to come out, is it?" Winnie cried, "I couldn't bear it! For people to know my Becky was . . . oh, Alfred, tell me it won't come out!"

Alfred and Tom Froster exchanged glances. "Tom's already promised to issue a death certificate, haven't you, Tom?" Alfred said heavily.

The doctor hesitated. "Yes, but this is a much more serious matter. There's someone responsible for Rebecca's death . . . "

"You can leave that to me, Tom," Alfred said. "I don't know where the stuff came from, but there's only one person who could have got it for her. And he'll give me some answers, or I'll flay the hide off him."

"Oh please, Dr Froster, please!" Winnie begged. "Nothing can bring her back now."

"That's true, but we must do our best to stop others going the same way," the doctor said gravely. "Very well, Alfred, in the circumstances, I'll issue a death certificate giving a stomach disorder as the cause of death. That's near enough to the truth to salve my conscience, and it'll protect Rebecca's good name. But that is on condition that you find out the source of this evil stuff, so that I can have it dealt with."

"Discreetly," Alfred said.

"Well, of course, discreetly. Once I've signed that certificate, I'm hardly likely to admit the origin of my complaint, am I?" the doctor asked tetchily.

By the time the formalities were complied with and Alfred came to drive Dr Froster home again, the night was half gone, and above the black mountains of Hillsbridge dawn was beginning to break. Although he had had only an hour or two's sleep, he was not tired, and as yet he felt no grief, only bewilderment and anger. It had happened, the thing he had feared all these years. Rebecca had brought disgrace on him—and paid for it with her life. But that Rupert should have been involved—Rupert with whom he had trusted her future—Rupert, whom he had treated like a son . . .

The fury rose in him, making him tremble. He turned his car down the hill towards the Co-operative offices and pulled up outside. His keys were in his pocket—he carried them everywhere with him —and he unlocked the door and climbed the stairs to his office. He wouldn't be coming in today. He'd leave a note for Joey Bird explaining. But first he had to vent his anger.

The telephone was on his desk; he reached for it and cranked the handle of the generator to call the exchange. At last the operator answered and connected him with Rupert's number. For a long while it rang, and it gave him grim satisfaction to picture them waking, cursing, and wondering who could be ringing at this early hour.

It was Rupert himself who answered at last, his voice bleary from sleep. It was all Alfred could do not to shout both the news and his accusations down the telephone, but remembering the operator was probably listening in, he controlled himself and said tightly, "Rupert, I want to see you."

"Is that you, Uncle Alfred?" Rupert sounded nervous.

"Yes, it is. And I want you out at my house as soon as it's light."

"But, Uncle, I have to go to the office . . . "

"Never mind that. Just do as I say."

"But, Uncle . . . "

"I wouldn't advise you to argue, Rupert," and with that he replaced the receiver. After writing a note for Joey Bird and propping it up against his ledgers, he went back out to the car, locking the doors behind him.

As he drove home, the countryside was waking up, a fresh green August morning. Birds flew from the hedges, ducking and weaving, and sometimes a rabbit scuttled across the road, but Alfred, driving like a man in a dream, noticed nothing.

He walked into the house and found Winnie sitting at the kitchen table in her nightgown, staring into space. "Whatever shall we do, Alfred?" she asked in a trembling voice. "We shall have to send for the undertaker, I suppose, and someone to lay her out. But they mustn't know. If they found out . . . "

"You can leave the undertaker to me," Alfred said. "But you'll have to lay her out yourself."

Winnie flinched, then stood up, fluttering nervously around the kitchen. "The curtains—I ought to draw the curtains . . . "

Alfred's mouth tightened. "Not yet. There's time for that later. I've asked Rupert to come here, and I don't want him warned of what's happened."

She caught at his arm, the tears welling up again. "Oh, Alfred, don't make a scene, please! I couldn't bear it."

"You needn't be there, Winnie," he said, patting her hand. "Now, is the kettle on? What we need is a cup of tea."

Glad to have someone to tell her what to do, Winnie set the kettle on the hob and went upstairs to get dressed, hurrying past Rebecca's door with a shudder. In spite of her maternal instincts she dreaded the thought of seeing her again, let alone laying her out. But if Alfred said she must, she must.

She had just finished dressing and taken the rags out of her hair when she heard the roar of a motor cycle on the road outside. Rupert! She hurried downstairs in time to see Alfred open the door, and the sight of Rupert started her crying again. He stood on the doorstep, looking from one to the other, twisting his gloves nervously between his hands.

"You'd better come in," Alfred said. His voice had the edge of doom in it, and Rupert did as he was told.

"Uncle, Aunt, what's wrong?" he blustered.

Alfred closed the door and led him into the living room without a word. The medicine bottle was on the table; he picked it up and turned to Rupert, holding it out accusingly.

"Did you give this to Rebecca?"

A quick look of guilt crossed Rupert's face, and the colour crept up in his cheeks. "No . . . no, I've never seen it before."

"Don't lie to me, Rupert!" Alfred bellowed at him. "Don't add that to your sins."

Rupert spread his hands, still trying to bluff. "I don't know what you're talking about, Uncle. If this is some kind of joke . . . "

"Joke?" bellowed Alfred. "Joke?"

"Uncle, just tell me what all this is about . . . "

"I'll do better than that, you fornicator. I'll show you!" Furiously he took Rupert's arm and began propelling him along the hall towards the stairs. "Come with me!"

Rupert, too startled to argue, would have gone, but at that moment Winnie ran from the doorway, catching at Alfred's sleeve. "No, Alfred, you can't do this! I won't let you!"

"Out of my way, woman! He's coming upstairs with me!"

"No, Alfred, no!" she sobbed. "She's your daughter! Let her rest in peace!"

Rupert swung round abruptly, knocking Alfred's arm aside. "What's going on here?" he asked hoarsely.

"Oh, Rupert, she's dead!" sobbed Winnie. "Rebecca's dead!"

The colour drained from his cheeks. *"What?"* It was no more than a whisper. Then, as realization dawned on him, his face crumpled, little by little, and his body folded up as if someone had kicked the wind out of him. "Oh, my God, oh, my God!" he gasped. "I never thought! I never knew that would happen, I swear . . . "

"So it *was* you," Alfred spat at him. "You fornicator! You murderer! You've killed her, did you know that? You've killed her!"

"No!" Rupert sobbed. "No . . . not Becky . . . I couldn't have . . . "

"You've killed her," Alfred roared. "You gave her a child, and then, to hide your sin, you made her take this evil stuff. And I treated you like my son, thought of you as my own boy . . . "

"Uncle, for God's sake . . . "

"For *God*'s sake? I tell you, Rupert, his wrath will strike you down for this!"

"But it wasn't my fault! She must have taken too much! He said it was safe . . . he told me . . . "

"Who?" Alfred bellowed. "Who said it was safe?"

"He didn't say this could happen . . . oh, my God . . . my God!"

"Tell me, Rupert, who said it was safe?" Alfred repeated.

He shook his head, his eyes wild. "No . . . no . . . I can't . . . I don't know . . . "

"Rupert! You've got a lot of questions to answer. I intend to have the truth!" Alfred's face was purpling with fury, his eyes bulging. Rupert backed away from him, down the stairs and into the hall.

"It was you, Uncle! It was all your fault! You made me do it. You wanted me to marry her!"

"Rupert!" Alfred thundered, following him, but Rupert was not waiting for more. His hands found the heavy door knob and turned it. The door swung open and he ran out. His motor cycle was at the roadside, he leaped astride it and kicked it into life. Then before Alfred could stop him, he had roared away, leaving them staring helplessly after him.

CHARLOTTE heard the news on Saturday when she went to market.

"Rebecca Church?" she repeated, the blood seeming to drain out from her body. *"Becky?"*

Ada Clements, who had heard it from the woman who cleaned the Co-operative offices, nodded. "Yes, and they say there's more to it than meets the eye."

"More to it. What do you mean?"

"Well, it was supposed to be a stomach upset, but it sounds a bit fishy if you ask me," Ada said. "It was all done so quickly, by all accounts, with an undertaker from Bath, and her own mother laying her out. Makes you wonder, doesn't it?"

"Whatever next!" Charlotte said, shocked. "You don't think she did anything silly, do you? She came to see me just a week ago, and I had to tell her about Ted. She was in an awful way, Ada!"

"Well there you are!" Ada said triumphantly. "I knew there was something fishy—a young girl like that dying! They're keeping it very quiet, of course. It's all wheels within wheels . . . "

"Excuse me, Ada," Charlotte said. "I shall have to go." She turned away from the other woman and walked in a trance through the market. It was almost beyond belief that Rebecca was dead. But if it was true, and she *had* killed herself . . .

"Oh, my Lord, whatever will Ted say?" Charlotte wondered, and then felt the answering rush of emptiness. Ted wouldn't say anything. Ted was dead too.

When she got home, Jack was amusing Harry with the scrapbooks he'd always kept—his own on flying and the ones he'd made for Charlotte about the Royal Family. Harry loved looking through them, but he wasn't allowed to have them unattended.

At the sight of the two of them together her heart turned over again—the last two of her sons left at home. And soon Jack would be gone. He had taken his Oxford Senior at the end of the summer term, and when the results came through, if he had passed, he would be an uncertificated teacher. But he had turned eighteen in the spring, and now he had left school he was expecting his conscription papers any day.

Every time she thought of it—which was often—she went numb inside. As if it wasn't bad enough that Ted was missing, presumed dead, and Fred was out there being shunted around France, now they wanted to take Jack, too.

"Your father will go up before the local tribunal and appeal for you, won't you, James?" she had said. "I'm sure you've got a real good case."

"No, Mam," Jack said. "There's no reason at all why I shouldn't go and do my bit."

"But there's plenty appealing with less cause than you," Charlotte argued. "The butcher put up a case for that lad that works for him, saying how he's trained him up, and can't manage without him. I read it in the paper this week. And when I think how you've worked to get to be a teacher, just to see it all thrown away . . . well, it's enough to break your heart."

"I can teach when the war's over, Mam."

"If you're still alive," Charlotte said. "This isn't a glory game, Jack. With your own brother missing, I should think you ought to have realized that."

"I know that." Jack's face was serious. "Don't you realize that's one of the reasons I'm even more determined than ever to go? If Ted is dead, it mustn't have been for nothing. And besides," he added, "whatever you say, I quite fancy learning to fly."

"Oh yes, that's it, isn't it?" Charlotte flared. "You've always been mad keen on those stupid flying machines. I should think you want your head examined—getting up there in the clouds for somebody to shoot you down."

"At least he wouldn't be in the trenches," James said, joining in the conversation. "He'd be out of all the mud and mire."

"Saints preserve us!" Charlotte exclaimed. "Haven't you heard about the number that's getting killed now? They're using planes to fight with, not just go out over the lines like they used to for recog . . . oh, what's the word for it?"

"Reconnaissance," Jack supplied. "Well, of course, they're fighting, Mam. There's more uses for an aeroplane than just taking pot-shots at Gerry's observation balloons. Can't you see . . . "

"No, I can't," Charlotte said. "And I don't want to talk about it any more, either."

But they did, over and over again, and Dolly and Amy tried to dissuade him also.

"You wouldn't have to go if you were married," said Amy, who had been walking out with the local bookmaker's clerk until he had received his call to active service a few weeks earlier, and who had marriage very much on her mind.

"That's right, Jack," Dolly agreed. "Why don't you make a match of it with Edie Presley? She's been sweet on you for years."

"I don't want to marry anybody, especially not Edie Presley," Jack returned, and they pulled faces. Jack had never shown the slightest interest in girls, except perhaps to give Rosa Clements some rather long looks. And she had grown pretty enough to turn any man's head.

"You don't know what you're missing, Jack," Dolly teased, and he turned on her.

"If you think marriage is so wonderful, why don't *you* take the plunge, instead of leading all the poor chaps on!"

"Because I'm enjoying myself too much," Dolly retorted.

"Well, there you are, each to his own!" Jack told her, and Charlotte, sensing an argument brewing, stepped in quickly.

"All right, all right, you two. Don't make it worse by quarrelling.

And it's no good thinking you'll change his mind, Dolly, because you won't. Our Jack's got the same stubborn streak you all have."

"And I wonder where he got it from, eh, Mam?" Dolly asked, dimpling wickedly. But despite the light-hearted banter there was an underlying tension. Since the telegram about Ted had arrived, and the photograph seeming to confirm the worst had appeared in the *News of the World,* nothing was the same, nor ever would be again. Although they tried to hide their grief from one another under a front of cheerful normality, it was all a charade, and they knew it.

And that Saturday morning when Charlotte came in from market, the weight of it pressed down on her so that for the moment she wished she did not have to tell Jack what she had heard, because the telling would make it a reality.

But there was no avoiding it. When he looked up and saw her face, he knew at once there was something wrong. "What is it, Mam? What's happened?" he asked, getting up to take her bag from her.

Charlotte shook her head from side to side. "The most awful thing, Jack. It's Rebecca Church—Ted's Becky."

When she had finished telling him, his face was the colour of parchment. "Oh, that's just terrible! What can we do?"

"We ought to send some flowers. Ted would want that, I know. And we must find out when the funeral is, and where. I shall go. And Jack, do you think you could . . . "

"I'll come with you, Mam," he said.

She nodded, grateful to him for understanding. "Oh, Jack, I wish you would," she said.

REBECCA was buried not at St Mary's, Withydown, where the family had worshipped when they lived at Eastlands, but in Hillsbridge, and it was an impressive funeral.

There was an ornate hearse, with black-plumed horses in the shafts, the undertaker in tailcoat and *crêpe-*trimmed top hat, and as many mourners as befitted the young daughter of the Co-operative Society secretary.

Charlotte and Jack were amongst them and Marjorie Downs, who had taken time off work especially to be there.

The Thornes came from Bristol in their motor car, Donald and Kessey thoroughly upset because Alfred had not telephoned to let them know the details of the funeral, and it had been left to Rupert to find out.

"We should be going from the house with the family mourners," Kessey said in hurt tones. "We are relations, after all, and you were courting the girl."

"I still say I should have spoken to Alfred myself," Donald stated. "I know you said you and he had words, Rupert, but I don't suppose he meant whatever it was he said. He was probably in a state of grief about what had happened, that was all."

"Well, I'm sorry, Father, but as far as I'm concerned the things he said were totally unforgivable," Rupert blustered. "I have my feelings, too. And if either of you so much as mentions it to him, I shall be most upset."

"Very well, Rupert," Kessey said, although she later remarked to Donald that she would have it out with Alfred one of these days.

When the service was over, the mourners followed the coffin into the churchyard, where the sun, shining fitfully from behind heavy black storm-clouds, cast a rosy glow on the weathered old tombstones, and the mound of earth beside the newly dug grave. The tragedy of young life cut down in its prime hung over them all, and as the Vicar intoned the time-hallowed phrases, there was hardly a dry eye or a throat that did not ache with tears.

"Man that is born of woman hath but a short time to live, and is full of misery . . ."

Marjorie, looking at the elm coffin that appeared too small to hold her friend, was remembering the times they had giggled together over silly, girlish things. In spite of the life she had led, the spark of fun had never been quite extinguished in Becky. She had never been "full of misery."

"He cometh up, and is cut down, like a flower; he fleeth as it were a shadow, and never continueth in one stay . . ."

That held special meaning for Winnie, who was almost too heavy with grief to hold her head up. If only Rebecca could have remained a child, none of this would have happened! she thought.

"In the midst of life we are in death: of whom may we seek for succour, but of thee, O Lord, who for our sins art justly displeased . . ."

"Forgive her her sins," prayed Alfred. "For her sins are my sins. She could not help herself—it was born in her, with my blood. And the sins of the fathers shall be visited upon the children."

The coffin was lowered, the handful of earth scattered upon it, and as Alfred raised his head, across the open grave he saw the portly figure of Rupert. For a moment, the two men's eyes met, and their hatred sparked. Then Rupert, flushing guiltily, turned away, and went to walk back towards the path where his mother and father were waiting.

Alfred, however, was too quick for him. As the mourners moved respectfully away, he pushed through them and confronted Rupert face to face.

"How dare you come here!" His tone was low and angry. "I thought I'd seen the last of you!"

"Uncle!" Nervous and embarrassed, Rupert looked around him. Most of the mourners were out of earshot, but Rebecca's friend Marjorie Downs was uncomfortably close by. If she wanted to listen, she could do so without doubt. And by the look on her face her curiosity had obviously been aroused.

"Well, now you are here, I'll ask you the same question I asked you the other day: Where did you get that evil stuff? I shan't rest until I know, Rupert! And Dr Froster wants to know too."

"Uncle, people can hear you!" Rupert protested, and Alfred, with a quick and furious glance in Marjorie's direction, drew him to one side.

They stood between the gravestones arguing, until Winnie, who had seen what was happening, ran across the grass and caught urgently at Alfred's sleeve.

"Alfred, please!" she begged. "Don't make a scene here. I couldn't bear it, with Rebecca . . . " She broke off, her eyes going to the still-open grave, and the tears overcame her once more.

Alfred looked from one to the other, undecided, and Rupert snatched his opportunity. "She's right, Uncle, it's not decent!" he said, sliding past him.

"But don't think you've heard the last of this!" Alfred shouted after him.

Alfred and Winnie walked back towards the gate, and the waiting carriages, while Rupert and his parents, who had seen the exchange and did not want to be involved in any unpleasant scenes, took their car and drove back to Bristol. And as Rupert sweated and trembled on that homeward journey, he ironically realized that the conscription papers would be the only thing to take him from this living nightmare.

If they don't send for me soon, I'll volunteer, he said to himself.

But he knew that wherever he went, and however hard he tried to justify himself, it would not be easy to forget what he had done to Rebecca.

A WEEK LATER, while Charlotte was washing up the breakfast things, Harry came running into the scullery with a letter from the postman.

"Look, Mammy, look at the envelope! What is it?"

Charlotte looked, and caught her breath. The International Red Cross! Oh my God, not Fred too! she thought. As she hesitated, she heard the soft thud of stockinged feet running down the stairs and Jack came through the door, his face eager.

"Did I see the postman outside? Is there anything for me?"

Charlotte shook her head. She knew what it was Jack was hoping for—the results of his Oxford Senior.

"There's nothing for you today, Jack," she said, but she could not hide the nervousness that was making her heart pound and her knees feel weak.

Jack came further into the scullery, looking at her anxiously. "What's up, Mam?"

She tossed her head impatiently, attempting to adopt a casual attitude. "I don't know, Jack. There's a letter here from the Red Cross in Germany. I haven't opened it yet. It's addressed to your father, but he won't be in until dinner time, and . . . "

Jack's face grew serious and he stretched out his hand for the envelope. Mam had seemed to cope so well with the shock that Ted was missing. But since she had heard about Rebecca, it seemed to have hit her all at once. Coming home from the funeral, he'd looked at her face and seen, for the first time, an old woman. Now, as she stood uncertainly with the letter in her hand, he had the same impression.

"You want me to open it, Mam?" he said.

"Would you, Jack? I don't think I . . . "

"Give it here."

He ripped open the envelope, the tension unbearable. Then a small, guttural sound escaped him, his face creased, and softly at first, then louder and louder, he began to laugh.

"What is it?" Charlotte cried. "What does it say?"

"It's our Ted, Mam!" Somehow he controlled himself, catching at her arms and swinging her round. "He's alive!"

"What?" she gasped.

"He's alive! It says so here. Wounded in the foot, neck and shoulder, shell-shocked after being blown into a shell hole, but alive! Crikey, it's a miracle he wasn't drowned! Those shell holes are full of water, most of them, they say!"

"But where is he now?" Charlotte asked.

"He's a prisoner of war, in Germany," Jack said, studying the letter again.

Charlotte covered her face with her hands. She could not, at that moment, have sorted out her emotions one from the other, much less identify or describe them. She only knew with a soaring lightness that Ted was alive when she had thought he was dead, and that, God willing, she would see him again, touch his bright hair, laugh at his silly jokes, scold him for swearing unnecessarily.

"But the photo," she said at last. "Poor Becky's photo that was in the *News of the World*—it had to be him carrying it! Oh Jack, do you think they've made a mistake? Is it our Ted in their prisoner of war hospital?"

"Course it is, Mam. They wouldn't write to you if they weren't sure. And they never did tell you officially he was dead, after all. Missing was all they'd admit to."

"But with all the thousands that was killed . . . Jack, I can't believe it! I'm afraid to believe it!"

"Well, this is good enough for me, Mam. And you know what it means, don't you? Ted's a prisoner—he'll be out of the war until it's over. He won't have to go back in the trenches."

Charlotte nodded, her eyes filling with happy tears. It was more than she had dared hope for, and even now she was almost superstitious about giving way to too much relief. But neither did she want to think about sad things, like Rebecca, who had died for nothing, or wonder whatever Ted would say when he came home and found out what had happened. She wanted nothing to spoil her glorious relief.

Then, with a shrug, she blinked the tears away, becoming the old Charlotte once more. She went over to the mantlepiece and took her purse from where it was propped up beside the clock.

"Here," she said briskly, taking out some loose change and handing it to Jack. "Go down the shop and get some cigarettes. I'm going to get a parcel off to our Ted straight away. If I know him, he's most likely dying for a Gold Flake!"

BOOK THREE

JACK

22

AT THE end of August, Jack Hall went off to join the Royal Naval Air Service, and Hillsbridge buzzed with the news. Everyone knew plenty of boys in the trenches, and one or two sailors besides. But for a local boy to become a pilot was something worth talking about.

"He always did think he was better than anybody else," Evan Comer grumbled, using his good arm to raise his pint in the bar at the Miners Arms. He had never forgiven the Halls for the beating they had given him.

"Good luck to 'un, I say," Stanley Bristow said loudly, and then, in a whisper, "I should keep your voice down if I was you, laddy. His father's up at the bar waiting to be served."

Evan coloured, looking furtively over his shoulder, and when he saw that James *was* by the bar, he downed his beer hastily and called good-night. James probably hadn't heard him, but he didn't want any further aggravation from the Hall family.

"How's your Jack getting on?" Stanley asked James when he pulled a chair up to the table where they were sitting, but James was non-committal. Privately he was embarrassed by the fact that Jack was doing something different from the sons of all the men he knew, and Jack's talk of a course in drill and discipline, after which he would be going on to a training station, seemed all very vague to him.

"An officer, is he?" Hubert Freke pressed him, and James tried to hide his reply behind the foam on his beer.

"Well, yes, I suppose he is. But it's no good asking me about his aeroplane, or where he's supposed to be going when they've learned him the way to fly," he said flatly, and to the disappointment of the others. Stanley Bristow, sensing Jack's embarrassment, quickly changed the subject to Ted, the concert parties of the old days, and the likelihood of Ted, at this very moment, leading a sing-song in the prison camp. That was of interest, too, of course, but what they all really wanted to hear about was Jack and his aeroplanes!

It was almost as bad for Charlotte. People were always stopping her in the street to ask about it, and Martha Durrant, who had never bothered to be very friendly towards her next-door neighbours, suddenly decided they might be worth some of her attention after all.

"This war's gone to Martha Durrant's head," Charlotte said to Peggy, and it was true. Martha was always busy organizing some fund-raising event or other, or marshalling people to knit or sew for the soldiers, and lately she had been seen hob-nobbing with Caroline Archer.

The alliance made Charlotte vaguely uneasy. She had never quite been able to forget that Caroline might know her secret, and with Martha so anxious to parade her affinity with Jack and his family, there was always the awful possibility that Caroline might not keep it to herself. But it was no good to worry too much, Charlotte thought. She had enough on her mind without adding that.

But not all of her thoughts were depressing. At the beginning of September, Dolly came home pink and excited, to introduce them to her sweetheart, Cook's nephew, Eric, who was in the Marines.

"I think he wants to talk to you, Dad," she said to James, and they all made a great play of pretending not to know what she meant until the front-room door had closed behind them. Then Dolly turned to Charlotte, bubbling over. "You know what he wants, I suppose, Mam."

"I can guess," Charlotte said with a smile. "We're going to lose you, is that it?"

Dolly giggled. "Well, not just yet. I don't want to do anything in a hurry. But Eric keeps on so, and I thought it wouldn't do any harm to get engaged."

"Oh, Dolly, I am glad, truly I am!" Charlotte hugged her. "But with this war going on . . . "

"I know, Mam," Dolly said, her face going serious. "It's awful, isn't it? Sometimes I think everybody I know is going to be gone before it's over. And I don't want to be an old maid."

Charlotte said nothing. She only hoped Dolly hadn't been swept off her feet by the handsome uniform. It could happen so easily, and the boys would look quite different when they got back into their everyday working clothes. But for the moment this was to be an engagement only, with no date set for the wedding. And Dolly was a sensible girl—both her daughters were in their own way. Flighty and full of fun they might be, but when it came to making decisions about their future, both had their feet planted firmly on the ground. Amy was just the same. She could charm the birds out of the trees, but she always had an eye on the main chance, and Charlotte thought she would not hesitate to wave good-bye to her present sweetheart if someone with better prospects came on the scene.

It was strange really that, while the girls should be so level-headed, the boys should be so much at the mercy of their emotions. Not only had Ted fallen in love, body and soul, first with Nipper and then with Rebecca, she was sure that Jack could very well go the same way when at last he opened his eyes for long enough to notice a girl. And Jim, without a doubt, totally worshipped Sarah. Only Harry and Fred were different. She glanced at Harry, absorbed in building a tower with some wooden blocks Dolly and Eric had brought for him, and smiled to herself. She didn't envy the girl who tried to rule him! As for Fred, he was himself, and always would be.

"I had a letter from Fred this week," she said to Dolly.

"Oh, did you? How is he, Mam?"

"All right, I think. He said he's got a bit of a gyppy tummy, and he wondered if he might be going down with this dysentery. But if he does, at least it'll mean they'll pull him out of the lines until he's better. So I'm living in hopes."

"Oh, Mam, how can you say that?" Dolly scolded. "He joined up to fight, after all. And you know what they say out there—if a shell's got your name on it, it'll find you. I mean, look at our Ted. By rights he ought to have been killed several times over. But he wasn't. It wasn't meant to be."

"No," Charlotte said, and wondered why she was suddenly full of foreboding.

"Is there any more news, Mam?" Dolly asked, changing the subject.

Charlotte gave herself a little shake. "Well, yes, there is, Dolly. You'll never guess what Rosa Clements has done."

"No, what?"

"Gone off to Bristol to work as a conductress on the buses or the trams, I'm not sure which."

"*Rosa* has?" Dolly repeated, surprised. Rosa had always been so much a country girl, and it was difficult to imagine her in the city.

"Well, somebody's got to do it, with the men all off at the war," Charlotte said, and she didn't add that she, too, had thought it odd that Rosa, of all people, should have chosen to do her bit in Bristol.

They heard the front-room door open, and James and Dolly's Eric came out, both grinning. "Well, Dolly, it looks as if I'll be taking you up the aisle on my arm pretty soon then," James said, and Dolly ran to hug him.

"Oh, Dad, did you say yes?"

"Well, of course, I did," James said drily. "What good would it have done for me to say anything else?"

They all laughed again, Eric swung Harry up into the air, and for a few minutes, the war seemed far away. Unfortunately, at that very moment, it was a great deal nearer to touching them again than any of them realized.

WHEN Jack had finished his initial course in drill and discipline, he moved on to a training station on the south coast. And there, after less than four hours' dual instruction, he took the Longhorn into the skies for his very first solo flight.

As he climbed into the open cockpit of the flimsy little aeroplane, his heart was thumping wildly, and he was certain he would never be able to remember all he had been told.

The controls were simple enough, it was true—four or five dials on the dashboard and a joy-stick. But there were so many other things to remember—aerodynamics, meteorology, a whole new language for a whole new world.

"Watch out for the reservoir, chum!" one of the older pilots called out to him jokingly, and he knew what he meant. More than one novice had stalled his engine and ditched in the cold, grey expanse of water that lay just outside the perimeter of the airfield.

"I'll try!" he called back, sounding more cheerful than he felt.

"You'll do better than that, lad!" his instructor yelled at him over the noise of the engine. "And no silly tricks, either. This Longhorn's precious to me. I want her back in one piece!"

Jack gave him a nervous thumbs-up, and then he was off, his heart in his mouth as he gathered speed and rose slowly in the sky like a giant bird. Only when he had cleared the hangars did he relax. As they fell away beneath his wing tips, his nervousness disappeared, and in its place was a tingling exhilaration that ran through his veins like sparkling wine. Beneath him the road was a streamer of light blue-grey, around him the air was still and cold. And he was flying —flying! For all too short a time, he soared and banked, gaining confidence all the time, then it was the moment to bring her down again, and some of his apprehension returned. The landing field looked so small! But, somehow, miraculously, he did it.

"How did I do?" he called, easing himself out of the cockpit once more, and his instructor just laughed. "I wouldn't like to see you have to get away from an enemy aircraft yet, Hall. But at least you've brought her down in one piece!" he joked, and Jack knew that, for a first attempt, he was pleased with him.

"Go and have a hot drink to warm yourself up," he went on.

"Yes, it's cold up there, isn't it?" Jack said, slapping his hands around himself, and the instructor snorted.

"Cold? You don't know what cold is yet! Wait till you've flown in the winter with the drippings from your nose freezing on your lips! It's no joke up there for brass monkeys then, I'll tell you!"

Laughing, Jack went back to the mess. Perhaps it wasn't as cold yet as it would be, but that didn't alter the fact that a warm drink would be more than welcome.

As he went through the door, someone called out to him. "There's some mail here for you, Jack! A letter from home!"

"Thanks." He took it and knew from the handwriting it was from Charlotte. He was doing well for mail this week—yesterday there had been a letter from William Davies, keeping him up to date with all the news from his school and congratulating him on passing his Oxford Senior. *Although it would be more of a surprise to me if you* hadn't *passed,* Mr Davies had written.

Now, as he walked through the mess, Jack slit open the envelope from home and glanced at it idly. Then he stopped short. "Fred?" he said aloud in a stunned voice. *"Fred?"*

"What's up, then?" one of the older men asked, coming up behind him.

Jack turned, looking at him blankly. "My brother's been killed," he said in a flat, unemotional voice. Then he looked back at the letter, reading it again.

This will be a shock to you, Jack as it is to us all, Charlotte had written in her heavily rounded hand. *Fred had a bad dose of dysentery as you know and was, or so we thought, safe in hospital behind the lines. But the Germans shelled the hospital. There were twenty or thirty killed there, patients, nurses and doctors. Dr Scott was there, too, or so I heard in town today, but he was only hurt.*

But our Fred was killed instantly. I didn't telegraph you, Jack, there didn't seem any point. He's been buried out there, and I didn't want to worry you with a telegram. We're all in an awful way here, you can imagine. Our Amy is beside herself—she made herself ill with crying and had to come home from Captain Fish's. But like I told her, that won't do any good. We've got to put a brave face on it.

Take care of yourself, my son, and try not to upset yourself too much. We shall all meet again one day, I know we shall. It's just for now it's hard. Write soon. Your ever loving Mam.

He stared at the letter, seeing for the moment, only blackness. Fred dead! And Mam writing about it in this newsy way as if it had nothing much to do with any of them! That was just a cover-up, of course. Beneath all the bravado, she would be shattered. Perhaps he should go to her—ask for leave and go home for a day or two. But she had plenty of people around her. There was nothing more he could do. But he felt strangely disembodied, now. His exhilaration and sense of achievement had been crushed, the hopelessness of it all swept over him.

"There'll be no winners in this war," he thought bitterly. "By the time it's over, we'll all be losers, wait and see if we're not!"

Yet, as the numbing shock became grief, he grew more and more determined to do his bit. Every time Charlotte wrote, it seemed, there were more deaths to report, boys he had known all his life. There was Billy Beck, who had been an errand-boy at Fords before his conscription; one of Farmer Brent's boys; and a nephew of Reuben Tapper, the railway porter. And Peggy's Colwyn was in a bad way, too. He had been hit in the head, and although he was still alive, Charlotte said he would never be the same again.

Then, in the summer of 1917, with the wedding fixed for September, Dolly's Eric was killed, and for all her light-hearted approach to life, Dolly was devastated.

"She thought more of him than she ever let on," Charlotte said to James, and to Jack, she wrote: *It's just one thing on top of another. The Lord only knows where it will all end. You'd think we'd be used to bad news by now, but every time it seems to hit worse. If it goes on much longer, I think I shall be ending up in the asylum.*

As soon as he had learned to fly his aeroplane to the satisfaction of his instructor and been trained in bomb-dropping and the use of the Lewis gun, Jack had left Dover for Dunkirk, where he was flying with a force of light bombers and fighters, attacking the harbours, docks and submarine pens along the Belgian coast.

The news from home still disturbed him, but it seemed to be happening at a distance from him. As he flew dawn raids and night stunts, it was the emerald green flashes of the enemy range-finders and the following bursts of anti-aircraft fire that were real, and it was the mates that never came back to the mess who were truly dead —those who were caught in the anti-aircraft fire, or were killed by one of their own bombs that refused to be loosed in spite of frantic stunting over the sea. And the air raids, too, were real, heralded by "Wailing Winnie" and all the other sirens. Then, before their mournful sound had died away, the night would be torn apart by the exploding shells and bombs, and the answering roar of the angry air.

But for all the discomforts and dangers, a year and a half after he first took his Longhorn into the skies, Jack's love affair with flying was as fresh as ever. For him, there was nothing still to compare with the magic of cloud-land, where an aircraft could twist and weave in the banks of soft white cotton wool, nothing to compare with the throb of engine power at take-off, and certainly nothing to compare with the satisfaction of bringing a plane in, bloody but unbowed, at the end of a mission. And sometimes he wondered if, when it was all over, he might stay in the RNAS and make flying his career instead of teaching.

Charlotte would be furious, of course, but after living this way he didn't know if he could ever go back to the life of a schoolmaster, and an ordered routine. The danger and excitement had become too much a part of him—and the comradeship, too. For nothing seemed so bad when there was someone with whom to share it.

That was how it was that morning in January of 1918. There was nothing to warn him that today would be any different from any other. He had lived too long with danger, and had become hardened to it, and it seldom occurred to him now that tonight it might be his own face that was missing from the mess room.

It was a clear morning, frosty and bitterly cold—so cold that as they washed their faces the water froze on the sponges. But as the six bombers with their fighter escort of two took off in formation, everything but the mission ahead was pushed to the back of his mind.

The target this morning was an enemy aerodrome and dump. As

they neared the lines, the anti-aircraft fire began, filling the air with shrapnel puffs and scorching holes in the fabric of their fuselage and wings. But none of the de Havillands was seriously damaged, and they dropped through the patchy cloud base to their target in perfect formation.

The line of hangars was there beneath them, grey and squat from this angle, but an easy target, and Jack thought that for a job like this, it should be possible to get a perfect aim even without the guidance of the string 'reins' the gun-layers used to help them.

The first wave of bombs were loosed and fell through the air like deathly rain. Two hangars erupted into balls of flame, thick black smoke billowing up from a third.

Jack pulled up to follow the formation, but Maurice Kelly, his gun-layer, signalled two bombs left, and reluctantly he turned to go in again. He didn't want to take them home with him. Sitting in their honeycomb bomb racks beneath his wings they were potential death-traps, and there was an enemy aircraft in the middle of the tarmac runway, a sitting duck.

He swooped in, a small smile twisting the corners of his mouth as he saw black beetle-like people scuttling and diving on the ground beneath him. "I'm not after you," he whispered. "It's your Albatros I want." The enemy plane disappeared beneath his wingtips and the bombs had gone, one hitting the tarmac and sinking into it like a spoon in treacle, the other catching the Albatros smack on and shooting splintered wood and burning fabric into a hedgehog arc around the twisted frame.

As he glanced back at it, Kelly held up one thumb to him in a gesture of triumph and momentarily he released his tongue, held tight between his teeth in an effort of concentration throughout the operation. But at that very second they began firing at him from the ground, and his tongue flicked back again as he raised the nose of the de Havilland and pulled up, intent on catching the now straggled formation and tucking into position for a safe run back to base.

This, he thought, was the best part of any mission, the moment when you turned for home, relieved of your bombs, exhilarated by success, drawn by the thought of the warmth and comfort of the mess after the Arctic cold of the skies. Yet there was a tingling awareness, too, that at any moment your luck could run out. It was a thought that ran like a trickle of ice-cold water on skin clammy with sweat, and as it prickled at the back of his mind, Jack flexed his stiff fingers on the controls, consciously forcing himself to relax a little.

Ease up, ease out, and fall into formation. Stick together and you're invincible. Almost. A dark line, goose-like in the sky. Tuck in, stay vigilant. Look strong, and you'll be strong. And watch the sun. Too often they come out of the sun.

But he knew the formation was still too loose to be safe, and up ahead there was cloud that hadn't been there on the way in, high cumulus, ivory towers in the sky, and the sun coming through like arrow shafts. It worried him, and his skin prickled with an awareness that should have warned him but somehow didn't, until it was too late.

They came from nowhere, diving like hawks with folded wings, half a dozen Fokker triplanes with the vivid red fuselages of the Richthofen Circus. One moment the sky was clear, the next it seemed full of aircraft and tracers and spurts of orange flame that vied with the sun for brilliance. Two attached themselves to Jack's tail, and another came at him head on.

Startled, he made to fire his guns—the twin Vickers that he so seldom had the chance to use—but the triplane fired first and a bullet straight through the propeller arc put paid to one Vickers. Jack zoomed, but not in time to avoid another bullet that passed through the fabric of his flying jacket, scratching his skin in a long, painful tear.

Breath whistled through his teeth, and he twisted the rudder this way and that, trying to dodge the tracers of the following enemy aircraft. Up ahead, he saw one of the de Havillands begin a downward spiral, black smoke pouring from its tail. Seconds later, a triplane exploded into a ball of fire.

Sweat stood out on his face in crystal beads and rolled down the neck of his jacket, but he hardly noticed. His breathing was shallow and ragged, his heart pumping blood around his body at twice the normal rate. For long, timeless minutes he twisted, climbed and dived, doing all he could to keep the triplanes from getting beneath his tail, and giving Kelly his best chance of getting the sights of his Lewis guns lined up for a hit. But one of the Fokkers broke away from the others, coming in at him broadside, spraying the side of his fuselage with bullets and then diving away to safety.

At first, Jack was too concerned about damage to the aircraft to realize he, himself, had been hit, then, looking down, he saw to his surprise that blood was gushing in a scarlet stream from his thigh. Instantly he tried to move his foot, but the muscles refused to answer his command.

The wound was bad, he knew it instinctively without even investigating the sticky mess beneath the torn cloth. But there was no time now for speculation. Time enough for that when they had got away from the triplanes—if they ever did.

A sudden blast hit the de Havilland from beneath, tossing the aircraft like a toy and sending shock waves up Jack's spine so that the very core of him seemed to vibrate, his injured leg exploding into a furnace of pain. In that first surprised fragment of time the de Havilland's nose dropped sharply, and she went into a spin, but the air rushing past his face and the sensation of the dreaded spin brought Jack to his senses, and he went into the levelling-out procedure taught at training school and practised on numerous occasions: stick forward to gain speed, full opposite rudder—and pray!

Just when he thought the spin would never come under control, he felt the plane begin to right itself, and as sky and ground took their proper places on the horizon he realized that the shells bursting around him came not from the triplanes, but from the ground.

So that was it! The dogfight had driven them back over enemy lines, and the shell that had exploded right under the de Havilland had come from the anti-aircraft guns. Now the triplanes had left, thinking that the men on the ground could finish what they had started, and not wishing themselves to be used as target practice by their own anti-aircraft fire.

Hope leaped in Jack, firing his reflexes anew, and he pulled on the joy-stick, raising the nose and climbing once more.

Those of his formation who had escaped were away now, scampering for home, and of the fighter escort, there was no sign.

So I'm on my own, Jack thought, and by way of comfort and reassurance of at least one friendly soul in this cruelly alien wasteland, he risked a look over his shoulder to catch Maurice Kelly's eye. But what he saw horrified him. Kelly was slouched over his guns, his head lolling forward.

Sweating, he jerked his head round once more. He was alone, over enemy territory, in a damaged aircraft with a gun-layer who was either unconscious or dead, and he himself was bleeding badly. With no gun-layer to protect his vulnerable rear, he was a sitting target for any patrolling enemy aircraft who happened to spot him.

Dodging acrid bursts of high explosive and climbing higher, he tried to think.

Perhaps it would be better if he flew north to Holland rather than battle against the west wind all the way home. The people there would be friendly, he knew. But with his gun-layer unconscious, and his own leg badly injured it could be difficult for the peasants to hide them both as they had done other pilots in the past. And today, instead of friendly Dutch country people, he might find himself surrounded by German soldiers. Even leaving his wounded leg and poor old Kelly out of it, Jack had no wish to spend the rest of the war in a prison camp like Ted, and besides . . .

"I don't believe I've got any matches to set light to the aircraft," Jack said aloud, talking to himself to keep his mind off the pain. "I'm sure I didn't put any in my pocket this morning. And I'm not leaving a de Havilland there as a showpiece for every Fritz within miles. They can find someone else to make them a present of an instructor's exhibit."

He gritted his teeth against the now-excruciating pain in his leg and climbed to five thousand feet. Then he set his nose for home. "You can make it, Jack," he told himself. "Dig your heels in and keep going. Every mile is a mile nearer. Every mile is a mile you won't have to fly again."

He ran into the cumulus again over enemy lines, and blessed it. Here, in the valleys between the towering cliffs of fluffy white cloud he was quite hidden from the anti-aircraft guns on the ground, and from enemy fighters. The problem was that they would be hidden from him, too. There could be any number of them just above him, waiting to pounce, and he would never know it.

Beads of sweat rolled down his face, and he curled his hands tightly round the controls, fighting the urge to go down and get beneath the cloud bank. That would be pointless, for he would then make a perfect target for any enemy fighter who chose to sit hidden in the edges of the cloud, watching for aircraft in the sky beneath.

He checked his compass and flew on, and after a while the cloud began to thin so that beneath him he could see patches of barren winter ground. His tongue was back between his teeth, and fierce concentration drove all else from his mind. Keep going. Just keep going. Maybe you'll do it yet. Maybe . . .

The German fighter must have been hiding behind one of the last patches of cumulus. As he crossed the pool of clear sky it dived towards him, an Albatros with a tiger's head emblazoned on its fuselage. For a moment it seemed to him that his heart had ceased beating and his throat and mouth had folded inwards, choking him.

This was it then, the end, and just as he had feared. An Albatros was coming in for the kill and he was defenceless, with one of his Vickers guns out of action and the gun-layer unable to fire the twin Lewis. The Albatros closed, its guns spitting orange fire. But as the planes passed, so did Jack's moment of panic. Adrenaline burst like shell-fire in his veins, and he was filled with the fiercest determination he had ever known.

I don't want to die, he thought—not here, not like this. And while there's life in my body, I won't give up.

The Albatros came closer, the sun flashing on its wings. As it dived, Jack pushed hard on the rudder, swinging round sharply, and the Albatros fell away beneath his starboard wing, out of range. It turned to come in again and so did he, so that they faced each other head-on. It was his only chance, Jack reckoned, to keep the German from getting behind him where he could shoot at his vulnerable, exposed rear. The Albatros came in, and Jack fired at him with his one remaining Vickers gun, but the shots went wide, scorching holes in the wing fabric but doing no real damage. The German's shot was more accurate. As they swooped away from one another again, Jack saw his temperature gauge shoot up, and he knew his radiator had been holed. His heart sank, but still he refused to give up. In a situation like this, he had nothing to lose. He would probably die in the end, but at least he could try to take the German with him.

He turned again, but the Albatros was quicker. It banked hard, with full throttle, the pilot risking a spin in order to manoeuvre himself into a position behind and beneath Jack's vulnerable tail. Jack sucked in his breath, trying to squirm out of danger, but although the Albatros was unable to get under him, it was now directly behind him, the very thing he had been so desperately trying to avoid.

He glanced over his shoulder. Yes, here it came. And the pilot was grinning, damn him. As clear as if he were sitting beside him on a bus, Jack saw the satisfied curl of his lips. Already, no doubt, he had counted the de Havilland as another notch on his wings. Again, but without much hope, Jack grasped the joy-stick, pulling it hard towards him, and as he did so, he heard the sharp crackle of gun-fire.

So this was it, he thought, waiting for the inevitable sickening fall or the smell of burning. He's got me.

But instead the de Havilland rose at his bidding, coughing, protesting, but still obedient, and beneath him he saw to his amazement the spiralling wreck of the Albatros, trailing black smoke as it fell. Half bemused and weak from loss of blood, he watched it until it hit the ground and exploded into a mass of vivid flame.

What happened? he wondered senselessly. What in the world happened? Automatically he glanced over his shoulder to where the inert figure of Kelly had slumped a few moments earlier, and he was rewarded by the weak but unmistakable thumbs-up of his gun-layer.

Kelly was not dead after all! And by some miracle he had managed to shoot the enemy aircraft down in flames!

A wave of weakness threatened Jack, and looking down he saw his cockpit was awash with blood. So dizzy did he feel that now, at the very moment of triumph, it was all he could do to keep from giving up. But the knowledge that Kelly was still alive drove him to one last effort. Kelly had saved him, now it was up to him to save Kelly.

With an enormous effort he turned the nose for home once more. The temperature gauge was now showing zero and he guessed that most of his water had gone. If so, his engine would probably seize. As he flew, he listened to it knocking and groaning, and somehow the ominous noise kept him on the edge of consciousness. He began muttering to himself again.

"A little further . . . a little further. Hell, these engines are marvellous to take a hammering like this! Ease her on, ease her on. Drop a little, look around. Why is everything red, even the sky? And the mist—not mist too! Come on Jack, hold on. A little further. You can do it."

And then, beneath him, he saw the airfield, spread out like the arms of a waiting mother. He came in, almost unable to believe now that he and the de Havilland were home. His wheels skimmed the hangars, and then he was down, pancaking on to the tarmac. The nose fell forward, buried itself in the ground, and the tired tail tried to rise, then fell back. Men ran out towards the crippled aircraft, the heat from the engines scorching their faces, but mercifully there was no fire.

In the rear Maurice Kelly was unconscious once more, but alive. And in the cockpit, his leg almost severed, awash in his own blood, Jack too hung on.

321

As they approached him, he looked at them with eyes weary, but feverishly bright in his white face.

"Thank the Lord," he said.

And passed out.

JACK WAS taken to hospital first in France, then, when he was fit enough to be moved, hospital train and boat brought him to London, where the battle to save his leg continued.

At first he was too ill to know or care. As he surfaced from the black-edged hell of pain, the threat of losing a limb refused to seem real to him. It was still there, his leg, and it would mend. He was in England now, and English doctors could do anything.

But it was what went on inside his head that was the reality—the battles he still fought over and over again with the German triplanes, the bombs he had to drop, the air raids night after night on his base.

It was some time before the nightmares stayed at bay for long enough for him to notice what was going on around him. And the first person he became aware of as a flesh-and-blood reality and not a fevered hallucination was a girl.

She was tall and well-built, and her VAD uniform suited her. But there was something about her which seemed familiar—an impression he hastily dismissed as fanciful. He couldn't know her, a nurse in a London hospital. But he watched her all the same, his eyes drawn to her by the vague chord she struck somewhere deep in his memory.

After a while he asked the young, curly-haired flier in the next bed to his if he knew her name. But he shook his head.

"Sorry, can't help you. I haven't seen her much myself before. But she's got a pretty sharp tongue for all that she looks like the proverbial angel of mercy. I heard her giving that chap down at the end a piece of her mind earlier on."

Jack smiled, and the young flier, who introduced himself as Nick Morland, went on, "Just leave it to me. I'll find out for you."

This offer, Jack hastily declined. In lucid moments he had noticed Nick fancied his chances with the nurses, and he had no wish for him to begin heavy-handed advances on his behalf. If he had met the girl before, which he doubted, he'd no doubt find out all in good time. If not, well, in his present state, it didn't matter much one way or the other.

At midday, however, when lunch arrived, he was pleased to see that it was the tall, attractive nurse who came to serve him. "I hope you're going to eat this all up today, Lieutenant. I understand your appetite isn't all it should be!"

The faint burr in her voice struck another familiar chord, and he grimaced at the plate of watery tripe and onions. "The food here doesn't exactly come up to standard, does it? Now if I had a piece of nice, juicy steak . . . "

"Chance would be a fine thing. With all the rationing, you're lucky to get what you do. Now eat it up, or you'll never be fit enough to go for a run up the batches this summer."

He looked at her sharply, his eyes narrowed. First there had been a familiar look about her, then the familiar accent, and now she was talking about batches. Only local Somerset people called the slag heaps batches.

"I know you, don't I?" he said.

The generous mouth lifted, the eyes, challenging and amused, held his. "You should do. I come from Hillsbridge, too."

"I thought so! And you're . . . "

"Stella O'Halloran. You probably know Grace better than you know me."

Stella O'Halloran—Grace O'Halloran's sister—of course! He should have known. She'd been away at school, of course, and so had he, and now, seeing her more or less grown up, and in uniform, he just hadn't realized.

"Well, well, it's a small world," he said inanely.

"Isn't it? But I must get on with my work, or I shall have Sister after me."

He nodded, watching her go back down the ward. Stella O'Halloran, well, well. She wasn't as good-looking as her sister, but she was still a very pretty girl for all that, with her mischievous grey eyes and the sprinkling of freckles across her nose. And she was doing war work, too. He couldn't imagine Grace doing that—for all that she had married Dr Scott. What a coincidence that Stella should be here, in London, nursing at the very hospital he'd been brought to!

"Getting shot up has its advantages, eh, old man?" Nick Morland ventured from the next bed, and Jack grinned.

"The tripe, you mean?" he inquired wickedly.

As the days passed, Jack found that hospital life was a strange, limbo existence, unrelated to anything he had previously known. Time took on new dimensions, and the things that were important here bore no relation to the things that had been important in the world beyond the sturdy walls. Two years ago, he might almost have welcomed a stay in hospital as a golden opportunity to read all the books he never had time to read at home. But as soon as he recovered enough to begin to feel bored, he realized that in practice it didn't work out like that. Here he was surrounded by frustrated young men who had no intention of letting him keep his nose in a book when he could be talking to them, or listening to their exploits, and even when he did have a few undisturbed moments, he found it difficult to concentrate for more than a sentence or two. It was irrelevant, all of it, he thought, stupidly futile, and it set his flesh crawling with irritation. He wanted to read. He longed to lose himself in a rattling good book. But somehow he couldn't. And instead he watched for Stella.

She really was a rather remarkable girl, he thought, and more than a match for a ward full of love-starved young officers. With her engaging freckles and wide grey eyes, she was bound to be a target for their attentions, but her attraction went deeper than that. She somehow managed to be an intriguing blend of good-humoured fun and razor-sharp intelligence, a girl who had no intention of letting anyone take advantage of her, but who clearly enjoyed their trying.

They might make her blush from time to time, these frustrated young men who were emboldened by the comparative safety of their hospital beds, and who could make the most outrageous suggestions without the risk of the recipient calling their bluff, but they usually got their come-uppance. For not even the most dashing of them could maintain their dignity for long perched uncomfortably on a bedpan, or made speechless by a thermometer left too long in their mouths, and Jack was able to watch and enjoy Stella's mischievous triumph.

Although he never joined in the flippant chit-chat himself, he became obsessed by her. On nights when he could not sleep for the pain in his leg and the recurring nightmares of exploding planes, he forced himself to think of her instead, and the thoughts were balm to his jangling nerves and tortured brain. Staring at the ceiling, glow-lit behind the black-out curtains, he pictured every detail of her face, her generous body and her gentle hands with their spatulate fingers and nails cut short and straight. He wondered what her hair was like beneath that all-concealing nurse's head-dress, and whether her legs were as well-shaped as her arms. And he imagined the way she would feel in his arms, soft and warm, yielding yet firm. After all the death and destruction he had witnessed, nothing was more appealing than her vitality.

But being Jack, he did nothing. It was not in his nature to talk to her the way the other men did, nor did he want to. For him, a woman still belonged on a pedestal. One day, perhaps, when his leg was mended and the bad dreams had stopped and he could see things straight again, he'd come back and try to court her in a real, old-fashioned way, with flowers and invitations to dinner and the theatre—all the things she deserved. In the meantime, he would content himself with chatting to her about people and happenings in Hillsbridge, and confine closer contact to those waking dreams where nothing was impossible.

But had he but known it, the worst was not yet over. The thing they had feared happened. Gangrene set in, and a decision had to be made swiftly and finally. His leg, or his life—he couldn't keep both. The outcome, of course, was never in doubt. They operated late one afternoon and next day, when he came out of the anaesthetic, Jack found he had a whole new battle to fight, that of coming to terms with facing life with an artificial limb.

At first, he was too stunned to accept it. For one thing, it was hard to believe his leg was gone, except when the sheets were turned back and he could actually see the empty pyjama leg and the heavily bandaged stump, for it still felt to him as if the leg were there, nerves, bone, sinew and flesh, as painful as it had been since the day he had been wounded.

And besides, even after all he had been through, it still seemed to him that something as catastrophic as this happened only to other people. That he, Jack Hall, should find himself without one of the legs he had taken for granted since before he could walk was unthinkable. He had known, of course, that amputation was always a possibility but never did he believe it would actually happen.

Lying against the pillows, sunk in depression, he remembered all the pals who had been maimed or disfigured. How easy it had been to tell them it would all work out—and how difficult to accept when it was yourself to whom the terrible thing had happened! Around him, the world closed in, black, choking, and no longer welcome, and this time it seemed to him there was no way out of the well of pain, no chink of light to be seen.

With the darkness the nightmares began again, as vivid as ever.

325

Only now they had an added dimension—an added horror—and time after time as he saw the aircraft spiralling downwards, it seemed to him that his leg was falling too, a bloodied, disembodied mess that nevertheless still belonged to him, still hurt with the fierce, burning pain that blotted out senses. Each time the dream recurred, it was pervaded by the feeling that if only he could catch it before it reached the ground he could save it. But no matter how he tried, it was always just out of reach. Always . . .

One night the dream was more vivid than ever, so that he fancied he was standing on the wingtips, reaching out and down, but then, it seemed he had lost his balance and was falling after his leg, down towards the bleak brown fields. Head over heels he spun, his heart missing beats, his scream echoing across the barren, empty landscape. And then, suddenly, miraculously, he was no longer alone. Someone's arms were holding him. Someone was crooning to him, and he was not falling any more.

"It's all right now. You're all right. Hush now. Hush."

Consciousness returned, but he did not open his eyes. He was unwilling, as yet, to relinquish the warmth and safety of the place in which he found himself, for it was as though he were a child again, cradled in his mother's arms, not wanting to wake, nor wanting to sleep, for fear of being put down.

It was so long since she had held him this way, yet his fevered brain remembered not only the feel of babyhood, but the smell and the taste of it too. For a sweet fragment of uncounted time it lasted, then he awakened and knew grim reality had returned.

Impatient with himself, he turned his head, but his cheek encountered the cold metal of a nurse's watch.

"Don't, Jack. Just lie still. You're all right now."

Hot shame flooded through him then, driving away the last dregs of comfort. Stella! It was Stella! And he'd made the most utter fool of himself.

Angrily he wrenched himself out of her arms.

"I was dreaming."

"I know. Was it bad?" Her face in the reflected light from the ceiling lamps was not teasing now, and her grey eyes seemed to mirror his pain.

He twisted his head to avoid looking at her.

"Oh, it's the same bally thing over and over again. I expect I'll get over it."

"Yes, you will." Her hands found his and held them. "Not for a long while maybe, but eventually. When you have other things to think about, other memories to take the place of . . . of what happened."

"What other things?" His voice rose bitterly, and she touched his lips with her finger.

"Hush! You'll wake the whole ward."

He shifted angrily. His leg was throbbing unbearably.

"All right. But you tell me—what other things?" His voice was softer, but just as bitterly vehement. "My life's finished."

"Oh, don't be so silly!"

"I'm not being. Talk's cheap when you're not in the position yourself."

"Because it's possible to see things more objectively."

"Oh, yes? Well, I'm finished with flying, that's for sure. They won't want a pilot with one leg."

She settled herself. "Did you want to fly again?"

He shrugged. "I enjoyed it. Just at this moment I don't ever want to see an aeroplane again, but . . . "

"Well there you are then," she said briskly, and her matter-of-fact philosophy, along with the pain in his leg, angered him again.

"How do you know what I want from life?" he asked truculently, then, at a warning glance from her, lowered his voice to go on. "I could have wanted to make a career in flying. But there wouldn't be much chance of promotion for me now."

"You trained to be a teacher," she said reasonably. "There's no law against one-legged teachers. And you've never been a sportsman, have you? So that's no loss."

He didn't answer. She was right, of course. He'd never liked football, and if he never ran to catch another cricket ball it wouldn't be the end of the world. But she had no right to make it sound so easy.

"I'd like to have driven a car, or had a motor bike." He knew he sounded peeved, but it still hurt when she laughed.

"Poor old you! That is a bit hard. After flying great big bombers, it is a bit of a come down not to be able to manage a motor bike, I suppose."

He pulled his hands away from hers, not wanting to snap, yet unable to help himself. "You take it very lightly."

"Because I've seen too many men carried out of here stiff and cold. At least you're alive, and you've still got two arms and a leg."

His anger died, and he felt his throat thickening. Dear God, surely he wasn't going to cry in front of her.

"I thought," he said slowly, "when I was up there in the skies, trapped in a crippled aircraft, that nothing mattered except that I should get back alive. But I was wrong."

"Oh, Jack!" Her voice was soft with compassion. "Don't you see, you were right! You *were* right! Life *is* the most important thing."

"No." He couldn't meet her eyes. "The quality of life is what counts."

"Maybe. But you can still have a good life."

His throat thickened again, tears burned behind his eyes. How could he tell her what was in his mind, this pretty, earnest, innocent girl who thought she knew so much, and in reality knew nothing at all? How could he say to her: Who would want me now, an incomplete, imperfect, repulsive cripple? I was never the most handsome of men, but at least I had two good legs. Now I have only a stump, thick, squat, truncated, and covered by puckered, stitched-down folds of skin. How can anyone ever feel anything but pity or revulsion for me now? And how can I ever feel anything but embarrassment?

The words were there, churning in his head, but he knew he could never say them. So he stared down the darkened ward, using all his will to hold his chin and mouth immobile, but quite unable to stop the hot tears from running down his cheeks.

For a moment she sat motionless, her heart aching for him, and when she spoke, her voice was husky with suppressed emotion.

"Are you thinking what I think you're thinking?" she asked, and when he did not answer, she reached for his hands again. "Oh, Jack, you're so wrong."

Still he could not speak, and she turned him gently to face her.

"Jack, listen to me, if a woman loves a man, something like that makes no difference. You may think your stump is ugly, but for her, it would be part of you, just something else to love. Don't you see that?"

Unconsciously her hand had gone to his bandaged stump and inwardly he shrank.

"It's different for you. You're a nurse."

"I'm a woman, too." Her eyes held his, and in their depths was something he could not read. For a long moment they looked at one another, then she tossed her head as if throwing some unwelcome thought away.

"I'm a woman, too," she said again. "And if I loved you, Jack Hall, I'd love you leg or no leg. In fact, with no leg, I might just love you more."

"Stella . . . " he said.

A light showed at the end of the ward, and she put her finger to his lips again.

"It's time you tried to go to sleep again. And if the nightmare comes back, just yell, and I'll be here."

"Promise?"

She smiled, her mouth a generous curve in the half light.

"Promise. Now go to sleep."

And she was there, whenever he needed her. The dreams came less and less frequently, and in the end they hardly came at all, so that he felt somehow as if she had stopped them.

She had said that if she loved him, she wouldn't let it make any difference. She didn't love him, of course. She would have said the same to anyone in the same position. But her words became a talisman, a part of him not forgetting the closeness they had shared in the sleeping ward.

They talked again, often, but never on quite such a personal level. The opportunity did not often arise when she could spend more than a few minutes with him uninterrupted, and he suspected that if he had not been so ill that other night Stella would never have been allowed to stay so long with him.

For the most part, the nurses were rushed off their feet, and the VAD's fared worse than many, coming in for the most distasteful tasks and most of the criticism. As Jack grew stronger and more observant, he noticed how tired Stella often looked, her face drawn with strain, and circles deepening beneath her eyes. She still bustled and smiled, but her tongue grew sharper, and he thought she was beginning to look much older than her years.

Lying despondently against the pillows and watching her at work, he wished desperately he could talk to her again, but it was hardly possible with Nick Morland all ears in the next bed, joking and ragging every time she came near.

One day, he told himself, I'll have the courage to tell her the feeling I have for her. Until then . . .

As soon as he was allowed out of bed, Jack threw himself wholeheartedly into the business of learning to walk again, and before long he was hopping up and down the ward on his crutches. But as his new-found friends cheered his progress, they little guessed the black despair that gripped him still when the lights went out and the ward quieted down for the night.

All this, Jack kept to himself. The doubts as to his acceptability as a man and particularly as a potential husband and lover festered on in the depths of his being.

Slowly his stump healed, not sufficiently for him to be fitted for his new artificial leg, but enough for him to wear a peg-leg for short periods at a time. By the end of March, he was declared fit to go home, provided there was someone willing and able to nurse him for the rest of his convalescence.

Jack knew, without asking, that this was exactly what Charlotte had been waiting and praying for, but he wrote all the same, explaining what the doctors had told him, and waited for her answer before telling them that his bed could be used for some other wounded flier just as soon as they were prepared to boot him out.

"You're a lucky bastard. You always were," Nick Morland told him cheerfully when he heard the news. "You'll be glad to see the back of this place, I know."

Jack nodded without replying. He had no intention of telling the voluble Nick how mixed his feelings were on that score. It would be good, of course, to be able to tuck into Charlotte's home-cooking again instead of the tasteless swill that passed for food here, but the thought of leaving Stella was a lead weight on his heart. However slight their contact, it was better than nothing. And once he left London, who knew how long it would be before he saw her again?

She had been away from the ward now for several days, taking, he supposed, a well-earned rest, but her absence had already given him a foretaste of the days to come when he would no longer see her bustling figure or generously smiling mouth, and he was beginning to be afraid that he might have to leave before her return.

The day before his discharge arrived, and there was still no sign of her.

It was 1st April, the day when the Royal Naval Air Service was officially merged with the Royal Flying Corps to form a brand-new fighting force of the skies—the Royal Air Force. But even that momentous occasion was submerged by the fact that it was also All Fools Day and an excuse for every man in the ward with an ounce of fun left in his body to indulge in one April Fool joke after another, so that when Jack eventually asked one of the VAD's for news of Stella, she simply took it as another prank and gave him a tart answer before bustling away. Another nurse he asked pretended to know nothing of Stella's plans, and he abandoned the attempts as futile. The nursing fraternity were like a branch of a secret organization, he thought, tight-lipped and prepared to defend one another's secrets to the very last ditch.

By the time the lamps were lit and the black-out curtains drawn against a possible air-raid attack, he had almost given up hope. But as the night staff came on duty, he found himself holding on desperately to this one last chance. And his prayer was answered—there she was walking along the ward!

At first his relief was so great that he was content to lean back against the pillows and simply allow her presence to flow over him. Then, after a while, he wanted to speak to her. Would she never venture to his end of the ward? Would someone else put the lights out, so that he would have to try to sleep, knowing that she was in the office with the duty Sister or attending to some of the more seriously ill men in the side room and not being able to speak to her?

The thought spurred him to action. He rolled back the blankets and swung his good leg over the edge of the bed. Then he hoisted his crutches under his armpits and began to hop down the ward, hoping that the nurses and other patients would assume he was going to the W.C.

He reached the double doors at the end of the ward without being challenged, but as he pushed them open and began to steer himself through, he heard her voice behind him, brisk and good-humoured but painfully impersonal.

"And where do you think you're going, Lieutenant? Just because you're now a member of a brand-new fighting force doesn't mean you can take off too."

He swung round, smiling his surprise. He hadn't expected her to be so well-informed.

"The Royal Air Force," he said, savouring the words. "I'm sorry to see the old RNAS go, of course, but it does make you feel that you're appreciated as a separate unit with a tradition all your own, not just an appendage of the old guard."

She tutted at him and tucked her hand under his elbow.

"Well, don't let it go to your head, that's all. Now, if you're going nowhere in particular, I would get back to bed if I were you, and make the most of it while you have the chance."

Her nearness started a slow fire in him, and for a moment he forgot his disability and the shyness it had magnified a hundredfold, forgot everything except that there would be some other wounded man in his bed tomorrow, with calls on her time and attention, while he would be two hundred miles away.

"I'm going home tomorrow," he said, but he could detect no answering flicker of dismay in her attitude. She simply continued to propel him up the ward with firm good humour.

"Tomorrow, is it? I thought it must be soon."

He ached with desperation. How could he get through to her, let her know what was in his heart without messing it all up? And how could he phrase it so that there would be no embarrassment if he had misread her thoughts.

"Stella . . ."

She eased him round, her eyes wide and serious, meeting his. "Yes?"

"Will you be coming home at all?"

"Oh, sometime, I hope!"

"Maybe . . . well, when you do, I'd like to see you. It'll be a while before I'm any good on this dummy leg of mine, but . . . "

He heard the sharp intake of her breath; she was quite unable to conceal it.

"It'll be quite a while before I'm home," she said tonelessly.

A heaviness began to ache inside him which seemed to accept the inevitable without feeling any pain. That would come later, the pain. For the moment all that mattered was to keep pride flying high, to pretend that her answer didn't matter.

"Oh well, never mind, it was just a thought. Since we both come from Hillsbridge . . . "

"Yes." The expression in her grey eyes was quite unfathomable, and she settled him back against the pillows, deftly flicking the blankets across his leg. "I'll be a long way from Hillsbridge, though."

"Not that far," he said before he could stop himself. "Mam and Jim, my brother, are coming up for me tomorrow by motor car."

"Yes, but I won't be in London. I'll be in France."

"France?" His voice rose anxiously. "What do you mean, France?"

"I've volunteered," she said evenly. "They're always looking for nurses to work behind the lines, and I think I've been here long enough. I leave next week."

"Stella, you can't! For God's sake, it's hell out there . . . " He broke off, aware of the inadequacy of the clichéd expression.

There was no way he could tell her, in words she would understand, of the horror, the raw, unmitigated butchery. She was a nurse, yes, but the wounds she had seen had all been removed from their immediate savagery by two or three healing weeks. She had never seen a man with half his face blown away, moments after it had happened, or a boy still holding his guts into the cavern that had been his stomach.

There was no way he could tell her, young and confident as she was, of the effect of nightly shelling on taut, jangling nerves. Or of the other things war spawned—the nurses who had arrived as fresh and innocent girls who had fallen so quickly for the advances of desperately lonely young men so that they were sick with VD, or pregnant, almost without knowing how, in a matter of weeks.

There was no way to tell her, and no time. But as if she read his mind, her mouth curved a little, although he noticed the usual sparkle had gone from her eyes. "I'm not so green as you seem to think," she said briskly. "I've been nursing men wounded in this damned war since 1916, and I happen to think I'll be more use out there, that's all. It's not as if I've got anything to stop me. Or anyone."

He recognized the hint of challenge in her voice, and his heart leaped in him. He sat up, catching her wrist with his fingers and forcing her to go on looking at him.

"Don't go, Stella," he said. "Come home to Hillsbridge for a rest. Tell your conscience you're coming to look after me if it makes you feel better."

For long seconds she did not answer. Her eyes had gone misty, and he thought her mouth trembled slightly. Then she tightened it into its characteristic upward curve.

"Selfish bastard!" she teased. "One man on the way to recovery doesn't need a nurse all to himself."

"Don't you believe it," he heard himself say. "And the language you've picked up from all these officers is shocking, Nurse O'Halloran!"

She laughed, and for a moment it was all there again, the closeness they had shared that night. Elation lifted him. So he hadn't imagined it! They were reaching out to one another with the fingers of the mind, touching more gently and more surely than his fingers on her wrist, meeting in a fusion that seemed to him to blaze with light.

333

For timeless moments it lasted and he was unaware of anything but her face, blurred but smiling, the face of his dreams. Then, with a sense of rude awakening, he became aware of a commotion at the end of the ward. Voices called, bowls clattered, and Stella, stiffening, had wrenched her hand from his to become a nurse again.

As she bustled away, leaving him with a feeling of cheated frustration, he became aware of Nick Morland watching him from the next bed with unashamed interest.

"Inconsiderate of old Bates to take a turn for the worst just at that moment," he said good-humouredly. "Never mind, you wouldn't have got anywhere, anyway. But don't let it worry you. We all fall in love with a nurse sooner or later. Angels of mercy, you see. In our position, it's only natural. And they understand. They're used to it."

"For Christ's sake, shut up!" Jack told him, at the same time wondering if he was making a fool of himself. Was he letting his imagination run away with him? He didn't know, and only time would tell.

All night he waited, watching the figures that moved like shadows against the soft light at the end of the ward, but she did not come back to his bed. And as the hours ticked remorselessly by to that low abyss that is sleepless dawn he was forced to the conclusion that he had been wrong to think she returned his feelings in even the slightest degree. She was a nice girl, a kind girl, and she had treated him with all the compassion that was in her nature. But as soon as he overstepped the mark, she would keep her distance, because to do so was easier than to tell him the truth—that she did not really care for him, that he was only another patient.

All night he waited, while the ache inside him grew and spread. But he had no way of knowing that while he dozed and fretted, Stella had let herself out a side door as soon as the ward was quiet and stood alone in the moonlit passage, her hands tightly folded together in her apron, tears running unchecked down her cheeks.

If only I'd known! Stella O'Halloran whispered over and over again. If only I'd had some inkling of the way he felt! But he was always so indifferent, always so distant. And now it's too late. I'm committed to the thing I decided to do to forget him.

Then, almost as if she had heard Nick's words to Jack, the self-same thought repeated itself to her. But maybe it's for the best I'm going, anyway. Patients always think they are in love with their nurses—it's something for them to hold on to in an alien world. We try to be kind and understanding, and they take it to heart. But when they get back to normality, they soon forget. They want to forget. And if there was more than general sympathy behind the care we offered them, they never know it, and it is best they should not.

When morning came, an orderly brought Jack a message.

"Nurse O'Halloran says would you give her love to Hillsbridge."

At once, Jack was wide awake and sitting up.

"Nurse O'Halloran? Where is she?"

The orderly shrugged. "Gone off duty an hour ago. I came on just as the night staff was leaving."

With an effort he hid the sinking of his heart. He'd been right to think she was avoiding him. She'd left, and she hadn't even come to say goodbye.

"Thanks for the message," he said. And knew that as long as he lived, it would be a sentiment he would remember with aching poignancy.

IN THE April of 1918, Hillsbridge was buzzing with two pieces of news. The first, that Alfred Church, the Co-op secretary, had died of a stroke, was accepted philosophically enough. Mr Church was not much liked. But the second affected almost everyone, for it was a new development in conscription. With so many killed, the army was in desperate straits, and the thing that everybody had said was impossible happened—the collieries were told to send their quota of men to war.

"How will they decide who's to go?" Charlotte asked James. Nowadays only the young and foolhardy were anxious to enlist for what seemed like certain slaughter.

"They'm going to have a draw, down at the Victoria Hall," he told her. "It's the fairest way, they say—ten men to go from each pit."

"A draw for their lives, dear God!" Charlotte said, and then, as the thought struck her: "What if our Jim's name gets drawn out?"

"It won't."

"How do you know?"

"Because he won't be put in," James said calmly. "He's a married man with children. They haven't got to the stage of calling them up yet."

"That's all right, then," Charlotte said, and wondered what had happened to her that she no longer cared whose sons went to France as long as her own were safe.

On the morning of the draw, all roads led to the Victoria Hall.

Jack, who was home from London and going a little further on his crutches each day, said he would go down with James to see what happened. Harry wanted to go too, but Charlotte said it was no place for him, and they stood in the doorway watching the men go down the hill.

Over the whole of Hillsbridge there was an atmosphere of something momentous happening, and the square in front of the Victoria Hall was swarming with people. Jack wasn't sure if he could manage the steps to the upper floor where the draw was to be held, so he stayed outside, sitting on the seat, while James went up to the main hall.

It was easy to see at a glance which of the men had their names in the hat. They jostled together pretending joviality, outrage and nonchalance. But caught unawares, they looked afraid, twisting their caps between nervous hands.

The draw began, and such a hush fell on the hall that Jack could hear every word clearly through the open windows. They took Grieve Bottom Pit first, calling the numbers and names of the ten who had to go, and then continuing until every name was drawn out, so that there could be no accusations of fraud, or names left out of the draw.

Then it was the turn of South Hill Pit, and the first name out of the hat was Ewart Brixey, Redvers' older brother. One by one the other names were called, men Jack knew, all of them, and suddenly he wished he hadn't come. How many of them would never come back? How many of these familiar names and faces would pass into the realms of people he had once known?

He stood up with difficulty, swinging himself away from the open windows, the list of names echoing like some obscene roll-call, and his mind went to Stella, in France. Would she nurse any of these men? If so, even now, he would willingly change places. There were even times when he thought it had been worth being wounded to have met her. But then it seemed all so pointless—all such a waste.

Jack spoke to one of the men standing on the steps, who had been unable to get into the main hall. "Tell our Dad I've started walking home," he said, and turning his back, he swung off along the street.

NOT LONG afterwards, Jack learned that he had been awarded the DSC—"the price of a leg," Charlotte called it—but in spite of her threats to dump it in the rubbish bin, he knew she was as proud as he when he went to Buckingham Palace for his investiture by the King.

"What did he say to you?" she asked, over and over again, never tiring of Jack's anecdotes, and he knew that if he told her the truth about what he really thought—that the King must be sick to death of the endless procession of servicemen presented to him to be honoured—it would only spoil it for her.

"A son of mine at Buckingham Palace, and shaking hands with the King," she would mutter to herself. It was a supreme accolade, which she took personally and of which she never tired of thinking about. All Hillsbridge now treated Jack like a hero. The *Mercury* glowed with praise for him, and his brothers too—"this patriotic family," it called them, and there were photographs of Ted and Fred taken from earlier issues and even a rehash of Fred's exploit when he had cycled with the telegraph message under heavy fire.

"If it weren't for the Halls there wouldn't be no paper this week!" Charlie Durrant grumbled, but he was pleased too, because he had the distinction of living next door to someone who had won the Distinguished Service Cross.

But as the cheering died away, the atmosphere in the town was a sombre one. Battered and bruised by the happenings of the last four years, they had almost given up hope of it ever ending.

"It's the modern-day Armageddon," Caroline Archer said to her friends in the sewing and knitting circles, and for once, no one felt like disagreeing with her.

IT ENDED on a pale November day when the sun shining through the bare trees turned the wet streets to liquid silver. Its death warrant was signed in a railway carriage that had once rattled through Europe with the noblest of passengers. By communiqué and order, notice of its impending demise was passed from front to front across the countryside it had shattered and beaten to a bare and bloodied wasteland.

In England the news broke with surprising suddenness, bursting on tired ears like a bright mountain spring, then gathering force as it rushed and tumbled onward to become a great, joyful torrent, sweeping away doubt and despair like dead leaves caught in its foaming tide.

The war was over. The killing had stopped. At eleven o'clock the maroons had been fired. And the boys would be coming home.

337

As the whisper became a shout, people rushed into the streets, delirious with joy, waving flags, hugging one another, and dancing. Fire crackers exploded on the railway lines, bells pealed in church towers the length and breadth of the land, and in London crowds flocked to the palace in the hope of catching a glimpse of the King. They packed into motor buses and taxis and even military lorries; going nowhere in particular, they were too relieved and excited to care where they ended up.

The war was over. No more bombing raids. No more rationing. No more black-edged telegrams. The war was over, and the Kaiser had fled like the coward they had always known him to be. And the shout of triumph that went up was so infectious that even the children, too young to understand, joined in.

For too many, of course, the victory had come too late. In Hillsbridge alone, there were fifty-three men and boys who would never come home again. And there were plenty more, like Jack, and Colwyn Yelling, and Evan Comer, who would carry the scars with them to their graves.

The war was over, let it die. But never, ever, let humanity forget what suffering and slaughter it had caused, or what courage and comradeship it had revealed.

The war to end all wars, they had called it. With God's grace, it would be just that.

23

ON THE heels of the Great War came the influenza epidemic, and people went down like flies. Whole families, their resistance weakened by years of rationing, succumbed, and the Halls were no exception.

On the first Saturday in December, James, Jack and Harry were all confined to their beds. At lunchtime, Charlotte, bringing them mugs of weak tea, was taken ill almost without warning. The vague stirrings of nausea she had been trying to ignore all day suddenly overcame her, and she collapsed in the doorway at the bottom of the stairs. Roused from their sick beds by the noise, the others groped their way downstairs to find her lying in a pool of spilled tea and broken china.

They got her to bed, although she protested weakly, and one of the Clements boys was given a threepenny bit to run up to Captain Fish's and bring either Dolly or Amy home. Dolly was indispensable, so Amy came, not very pleased at the role of sick nurse.

"Hasn't anyone wondered if *I* might get the influenza, walking right into it like this?" she inquired plaintively as she filled her father's stone water bottle with hot water and placed it against his back.

"You won't get it, Amy," Charlotte said with certainty. "Apart from your accident, I don't believe you've had a day's illness in your life."

"That's because I'm like you, Mam," Amy replied, and as she hurried out of the room, Charlotte stared after her, smiling to herself. Amy like her? Yes, perhaps she was. Except that I'm getting old, thought Charlotte, and the realization chilled her in much the same way as the realization had chilled Jack that his leg had gone forever. Old age was something that happened to other people. Bones might ache, she might get tired more easily, and the face that looked back at her from the kitchen mirror might have more lines. But inside she felt like the woman she had always been.

"I'm only forty-four, and I could still have another child if I was daft enough," she told herself. But when every move was such an effort it left her dizzy, limp and shaking, Charlotte found herself more conscious of her mortality than she had been at any time since she had been expecting Harry. Her own mother, she remembered, had died when she was only thirty-two years old, and the aunt who had brought her up, and who had seemed such a very old woman to her at the time, could not have been much older than she was now.

As for James . . .

Charlotte cast a sidelong look at him, wheezing in the big double bed beside her. There was an unhealthy pallor to his skin that she did not like, and it heightened her awareness of her own age. They had been young together. Now, he was a sick and broken old man who would struggle through a few more years' work at most before succumbing to the inevitable and wheezing out his last years in his favourite chair with the open fire for a spittoon.

But what we did together, James! she thought. What we did

together! We made a home and raised a family, and none of them has done anything to disgrace themselves or us. That at least is something to be able to stand tall and say. Each one of them has done us proud, in his own way. And if I can't help feeling that Jack is mine and mine alone, you were still a father to him, James. Nothing can take that away from you, not even me and my silly notions.

She lay back against the pillows once more, drifting in the hinterland that is midway between sleeping and waking, and when the first sounds of the commotion downstairs edged into her consciousness, she thought it was part of her dream. She moved her head restlessly on the pillow, blowing the stale taste of sleep out of her mouth and wishing she could move without aching in every bone. But the noise persisted: Nipper barking, raised voices, Amy's high and hysterical tones, and another voice that if she hadn't been dreaming she would have thought . . .

"Mam, Mam, are you awake?" It was Amy in the doorway. "Mam, Dad, there's someone to see you!"

She sat up then, aches and pains forgotten. But she still thought for a moment that the figure framed in the doorway was part of a delirious imagining. Her bunched fist found her mouth and slowly opened like the petals of a sea anemone to mask her face. And only then did she speak.

"Ted!" she said, her voice muffled by her fingers. "Ted, what are you doing here?"

He came into the bedroom smiling. "What a way to greet me after all this time! Not much of a home-coming, is it?"

His voice was exactly as she remembered it and had heard it a million times in her mind while he had been away, but oh, the look of him . . . The cheekbones seemed about to protrude through the fair skin, and the eyes, blue as ever, had a haunted look about them that had not been there before. But as she stared at him above the tips of her splayed fingers, her heart seemed to burst in her throat, and weak tears rose in her eyes.

"Hey, Mam, that won't do!" he chided, laughing but embarrassed. "And, Dad, too—is he asleep or what?"

Charlotte swallowed her tears and reached over to shake James awake.

"Wake up, Dad! Our Ted's here! Look, it's our Ted home! Would you believe it!"

James, bleary and congested, rolled over to face the door, and then with an effort pulled himself up in bed as Charlotte had done.

"Our Ted?" he echoed incredulously.

Suddenly the small room was full of people. Amy, who had followed Ted upstairs, her face wreathed in smiles, Jack, who had hopped in from his room, Nipper going quite crazy despite the fact he was white around the whiskers these days and a bit stiff in his back legs, and even young Harry, still poorly but anxious not to miss a single moment of the excitement.

Ted reached out to ruffle his hair, and Charlotte noticed with a painful start that even his hands were thinner, the nails grown too long and the veins standing out in blue ridges.

"Oh, my boy, just look at you!" she said, her voice thick with emotion.

Ted pulled his cap off and tossed it on to the bed in a gesture that was almost defiant.

"Well, at least I'm alive, Mam," he said.

The statement sobered each one of them with the exception of little Harry, for it reminded them all too sharply that Fred would never be coming back. But almost as one they closed their minds to the sad thought. Fred might be gone, but Ted was here, and they were not going to let anything mar the moment of his home-coming.

"Well Ted, you've really hit us for six!" James said, his voice wheezy, and Charlotte told Amy to run downstairs and put the kettle on.

"This is a fine state of affairs," she said, wiping her eyes on one of James's large handkerchiefs. "If we'd known you were coming, we could have had something ready for you, instead of this. Why ever didn't you send a telegram or something?"

"I thought that would only frighten you," Ted said reasonably. "You never did like to see the telegram boy coming this way. And besides, I hardly had time. One minute I was a prisoner of war in a Fritzy camp, and the next I was on the boat home. I still can't believe it myself."

"Freeing prisoners is just about the first priority now an Armistice has been signed," Jack put in. "You're home a lot sooner than you would have been if you hadn't been taken, Ted, because they still need a lot of soldiers to act as policemen out there, and they will do for quite a long time yet, I should think."

Ted nodded soberly. "It's still a hell of a mess, if you ask me. But

I'm not going to worry myself about that now. I'm home. That's good enough for me. And how about the rest of you? What's up with you all?"

His words were a signal for general hubbub. The first stilted, surprised moments were over, and suddenly everyone was talking at once, half-laughing, half-crying, all contributing snippets of news that no one could properly take in. When Amy came back with the tea, she too joined in.

"Well, this is the best tonic we could have had," Charlotte said at last, setting down her cup and looking around at her assembled family. "We've all been pretty rough, but this is going to do us the world of good. Why, it's just like it used to be at Christmas when you were all little."

And so it was. Jack was sitting in the window-sill, Ted and Amy had perched themselves on the edge of the bed, and Harry had clambered in between the sheets with Charlotte and James.

The mention of Christmas reminded them of food. None of them had been able to eat a thing for almost a week, and even the thought of it had made them feel sick. But after three years of living in a prison camp, Ted did not give that a thought.

"Oh, do you remember the spread we used to have!" he said. "A nice fat cockerel from the fowlman, and a ham you could slice at for days."

"And parsnips and potatoes cooked in the oven," Jack put in. "And Mam's mince pies."

"And Christmas pudding and custard," Amy added, and suddenly, miraculously, they were all ravenously hungry.

"Things aren't what they were," Charlotte explained. "We've had food rationing here, too. There's been a shortage of some things. But we've still been able to grow our own vegetables, and there's usually a bit of a porker to be had if you keep your ears open."

"I've got a piece of bacon in the larder now," Amy told them. "It's salted, and I thought it would keep all right until you were all fit to eat it."

Charlotte nodded. "Well, make sure, Amy. We don't want to be bad again. And talking of salted, there's a stone jar in the pantry full of kidney beans I put down last August. Do some of them to go with it. Do you think you can manage, or shall I get up and come down to help you?"

"No, I can manage, Mam. You stay where you are," Amy said,

and when Charlotte had finished giving her instructions, she clattered off down the stairs to make a start on preparing the meal. Jack, that much further along the road to recovery than the others, went with her to help peel potatoes.

"Well, Ted, this is a treat," Charlotte said when the room was comparatively empty again, but Ted's face had grown serious.

"Mam, I was waiting for them to go before I ask you—have you seen anything of Becky?"

The blood seemed to leave Charlotte's body in a rush, and she felt weak and sick again. From the moment Ted had appeared in the doorway, she had known it had to come, but she had tried not to think about it, just as she had tried not to think about Fred, dead and buried in France. Ted knew about Fred, of course. She had broken the news to him in one of the scores of letters she had written while he was a prisoner of war. But she had never mentioned what had happened to Rebecca, thinking that, if he knew, he might lose the will to live, and clinging, without much hope, to the straw that by the time he returned, he might have forgotten her a little.

Now, however, seeing the anxiety and eagerness in his face, that last faint hope died. Ted still loved the girl, maybe even more than he had done when he marched away, if that were possible. And now she had to tell him Rebecca was dead. There was no escaping it any longer.

As if he had read from her expression that something was amiss, his face changed. "Why haven't you ever mentioned her in your letters, Mam? I've asked about her often enough."

Beside her, Charlotte felt Harry wriggle as if he had sensed the tension, but James lay back on the pillows, his eyes fixed on a point far outside the bedroom window, and she knew she could expect no help from him.

"Harry, I think it's time you went back to your own bed," she said, and then, as he began to protest, "No, do as you're told, there's a good boy. You can come back again when supper's ready if you're still feeling better."

A subdued Harry obeyed. As he passed Ted he looked up at him as if expecting him to ruffle his hair again, but Ted was preoccupied now.

When the door had closed after him, Ted came closer to the bed. "There's something wrong, isn't there, Mam? That's why you didn't mention her. And why she hasn't written, either." His voice was as even as ever, but Charlotte heard the suppressed fear that was in him, and her heart went out to him.

"Ted . . ." she said helplessly.

"Come on, Mam, out with it. Her father's taken her away somewhere, is that it?"

"No. Oh, Ted, it's your first day home . . ."

"Mam!" he said warningly.

"It's bad news, Ted." Unexpectedly, James spoke, swivelling his rheumy blue eyes to meet his son's. "Your mother's kept it from you because it wasn't something she could write in a letter. Not as things were."

"What do you mean, Dad?"

As Ted turned his questions to his father, Charlotte felt a glow of gratitude.

"I mean you've got to brace yourself for a shock, son," James said quietly. "Now you know what I'm going to tell you, don't you? You've seen enough of death these last years to learn you a thing or two, and . . ."

"Death?" Ted had turned chalk white. "Death? You can't mean that Becky . . ."

James nodded slowly, stifling a wheeze that rose in his throat, and Ted stood stunned and unbelieving like a boxer who has taken a knock-out blow, yet somehow, incredibly, is still on his feet.

"Becky—dead?" he repeated. "But how—why? I don't understand."

"She was taken ill, Ted," Charlotte said gently. "It was all very sudden. We never did hear the rights of it, except that it happened in the middle of the night. By the time they got the doctor to her, she was gone."

"But when did this happen?" Ted asked, and Charlotte and James exchanged glances.

"Oh, a long time ago, Ted. It must have been—yes, it was just after you were posted as missing . . ." Charlotte broke off, uncertain as to how to go on. She had told him before in her letters about Rebecca's photograph that had been in the *News of the World,* and how they had thought it was proof that he was dead, and he had replied, telling them how his wallet had been stolen or mislaid that first day on the Somme, and the mutilated body on which it had been found must have belonged to whoever had pocketed it. But she had said nothing about Rebecca's visit, and she was unwilling to mention it now. Bad enough that she should be dead, without him thinking, as she did, that perhaps she had killed herself because she could not bear to live without him.

"Dear God!" His hands closed over one of the brass knobs of the bedposts squeezing them until his knuckles turned white.

"She was at home when it happened," Charlotte told him. "They'd sold the house at Eastlands and moved out to High Compton, and her father had fetched her home."

For a moment he looked at her, puzzled, then he brought his fist down hard on the bedpost.

"That old bugger had something to do with it, I'll bet! She was frightened to death of him. I'll go and see him and find out the truth if it's the last thing I do!"

"No, Ted," Charlotte said. "He's gone, too. He had a stroke last spring. It was no surprise, by all accounts . . . "

"Well, her mother must know anyway. Is she still there?"

Charlotte shook her head. "She went funny. She's in the asylum, Ted. Now look, it's awful, I know, and it's going to take you a long while to get over it. But what's happened has happened, and there's not a thing you can do about it. They're gone, both of them, and that's the end of it."

The words seemed to penetrate Ted's brain as nothing else had. He sagged, then straightened, and the pain in his eyes was so vivid that James and Charlotte both looked away.

Without another word he turned for the door, and neither of his parents did anything to stop him. They were wise enough to know that he must endure his grief alone.

They heard his footsteps clattering down the stairs, and the surprised voices of Jack and Amy as he went through the kitchen. Then the back door slammed, and they knew he had gone out.

Charlotte, feeling sick and old once more, sank back against the crumpled pillows. "Why did I ever have children?" she asked weakly.

James wheezed into his handkerchief. "You always wanted them, Lotty."

She grimaced. "I must have been born silly. It's one long nightmare. Everything that goes wrong for them, you feel ten times more keenly than if it was yourself. I'd sell my soul for their happiness, but it's the one thing I can't give them."

James looked at her with sad but mild blue eyes.

"They'm still better off than a lot," he said prosaically, and Charlotte turned her head into his shoulder in search of a comfort that she knew, in the depths of her being, would elude her.

"I sometimes wonder what we're put in this world for," she muttered, but the words were muffled and he did not hear her.

"He'll get over it, Lotty," James said, smoothing her hair. "Just like the rest of us, he'll get over it."

THE CHURCHYARD was bare and winter-brown, and the lowering December skies seemed almost to be resting on the square, turreted church tower.

Ted, still half in a dream, followed the path around the weathered old stone walls that he and Becky had taken in that long-ago summer of 1915 and passed beneath the sun-dial carved in the South Wall with the inscription that had always intrigued him.

> When as a child I laughed and wept
> Time crept
> When as a youth I thought and talked
> Time walked
> When I became a full grown man
> Time ran
> When older still I daily grew
> Time flew
> Soon I shall find in passing on
> Time gone.

'Time gone'—that was it. For Becky and for him, time had gone. Those fleeting summer days, too perfect to last. Looking back now, they seemed like a dream. Yet once he had been the boy who had walked hand in hand with her and lain beside her in the long grass, listening to the sounds of summer, feeling the sun warm upon his face, smelling the fresh sweetness of new-mown hay. It seemed so long now since he had done any of those things. And he knew that for him they would always mean Becky.

Three years can be a lifetime or a day. Every gravestone he passed was so achingly familiar that it seemed hardly possible to him that it was not just last week when he had last walked this way. But the vast emptiness inside him told a different story.

He did not know how he knew which way to go. Perhaps she had once told him which plot her father had bought for the family. But whatever the reason, he followed the path without hesitating, climbing the steps and turning towards the newer part of the churchyard.

There were flowers on the graves here, bronze and yellow chrysanthemums, even a Christmas rose or two. These were the graves of those who had gone within living memory, those who still had relatives left to care. The stones were new, the grass between the kerbs neatly trimmed.

On, on, he walked, his steps small and quick, his eyes darting about him as he went. It must be up here somewhere if they had been buried in Hillsbridge, and somehow he was sure they had been. Hillsbridge, after all, had seen the greatest of Alfred Church's achievements. Here he was known and would be remembered. People would look at his grave and say, "Oh yes, he was the secretary of the Co-op." But where was he buried? Find Alfred, and he would find Becky . . .

When he saw it, a marble angel mounted on a pedestal and inscribed with her name, a sense of deep shock ran through him, making him tremble.

He left the path, his feet sinking into the soft turf between the graves, and stood reading the words on the gravestone beneath the angel's out-stretched arms.

> REBECCA ANNIE,
> daughter of Alfred and Winifred Church,
> died 15th August, 1916, aged 18 years.
> Sleeping in the arms of Jesus.

It was true, then. She was dead, and the pain and the despair were so intense he felt he was choking. But still his numbed brain only half-believed. Becky was sweetness and life. Becky was sunshine on early morning dew, the deep sparkle of spring water over stones, the soft green coolness of moss and dock leaves. She couldn't be there in the dank, cloying earth, under a shovelful of chipped granite—not his Becky.

He thought of the body which had been soft and rounded lying there in a cold coffin and decaying, and suddenly it was more than he could bear. The pain became a silent scream, rushing through him like an angry wind, and he clutched handfuls of empty air. Becky, oh Becky, what have they done to you? I went to war, leaving you safe, as I thought. But I am back in one piece, and you . . .

The trees at the edge of the churchyard rustled, and he looked towards them. Their bare arms reaching towards the leaden sky looked as dead as the bodies they stood guard over. But they were not dead. In the spring they would put out new green shoots. Mam would probably say there was a lesson there, but at the moment he could not see it. Becky was dead, and spring could never be the same again. Becky was dead.

"Did you know her, my son?"

At the sound of the Rector's voice, he swung around, resenting the interruption of his thoughts and feeling oddly guilty at having been caught standing here beside Becky's grave.

"She . . . I . . . " he faltered, then added, as if to explain everything, "I've just got home from Germany, sir."

The Reverend Reuben Clarke looked at him with deep compassion.

In his years in Hillsbridge, he had seen enough trouble and suffering to mellow his early zeal. He had turned more and more to his God as the weary war years passed, drawing on a spiritual strength that grew only deeper and more sure as he increased his dependence on it, and sharing it somehow with those of his parishioners who needed its healing comfort.

And the Lord knew, there had been enough of those. Sometimes Reuben Clarke had felt that the whole valley was awash with grief. But his faith never faltered. The darker the night, the brighter burns the candle.

"She lives on, you know," he said gently, aware that the baldly spoken sentiment sounded false and trite, and he saw the young man's face twist bitterly as if for a moment he had expected more, far more, than that, and had been disappointed.

"Lives, Rector? How can you say that?"

"Oh, my son, I wish I could tell you. But I can see you're not the sort to be comforted by the simple phrases we invent to cover a depth of meaning that is fathomless. To explain would take longer than either of us can spare just now. So I will have to ask you to take my word for it that I know it is so."

For a moment he thought he had caught the boy's interest. There was a sharp curiosity behind the grief, but also scepticism. Then he kicked at a sod of earth.

"You can't fool me, Rector. When you're dead, you're dead."

Sadness filled the Rector. Oh Lord, show me the way to help this young man, he prayed.

"How can you tell me different when this whole churchyard is full of dead bodies," Ted persisted.

"Bodies, yes," the Rector agreed. "But we are not talking of bodies. We are talking of spirits. Ah, yes, I can see from your face that the spirit sounds to you like more milk-sop fairy stories to fill the needs of the masses. But you and I both know there is more to us than other folk can see, and I don't mean just our brains or our bones. I mean the essential something inside us that makes us what we are."

Ted shrugged. "Maybe so. But dead is still dead."

"No. The body dies. The spirit lives on."

The wind, cutting through the tombstones, made the Rector shiver. He drew his cloak more tightly around him, and as he did so, the analogy came to him.

"You've seen plenty of dead, I dare say," he said conversationally, and Ted grimaced.

"I've seen my share, yes."

"And how did they look to you?"

"A hell of a mess, Rector. More of a mess than you've ever seen a man in."

"I expect you're right," the Rector acknowledged. "But that wasn't quite what I meant. Did they still seem like your friends lying there—or did they seem different?"

"Well, of course, they were different," Ted said impatiently. "They were dead."

The Rector smiled. "Exactly. And in dying, the essential part of them, the something inside that made them who they were went from the body, so that what was left behind was no more that person than their coat left hanging behind the door. The body is a garment for the soul. When it is no longer needed, it can be discarded like a worn-out shirt. And if the spirit is no longer in the body, then where is it? It must be somewhere, living on."

"Where?" Ted asked bluntly.

The Rector shook his head. "Ah, well, there you have it. We don't know, any of us. We can only theorize. Now, we see through a glass darkly, but one day we shall see face to face."

For a moment, Ted stood deep in thought, oblivious of the cold. If only there could be something in it. If only he could believe all that stuff about the essential part of Becky not being dead at all but still living! If only there was something that would make sense of the whole bloody mess. But if he believed in a God, it was a God of nature, who showed himself in the regeneration of the countryside, and after almost three years of looking at bomb-shattered landscapes, even that belief had been sorely tested. Ted the realist did not see how he could alter beliefs to suit his own convenience, and the talk of spirits seemed to him, even with the Rector's clever analogy, a lot of pie in the sky with no more foundation in reality than his mother's superstitious dislike of seeing the new moon through the glass.

"My brother Jack would probably agree with you," he said at last. "But I'm a man that needs proof first. I suppose I'm your modern Doubting Thomas."

The Rector sighed. Oh Lord, thy way is often hard, he thought. But how much harder for those who are denied faith!

He reached out to touch the boy's arm, painfully thin beneath his cheap demobilization suit.

"Think about it, my son," he said. "Remember that in God everything, however senseless, has its place. Go to Him, ask His help, and He will give it to you."

"And would it have helped if I'd asked Him to look after Becky?" Ted asked bitterly. "I'm sorry, Rector, I'm afraid you've got the wrong person. You're catching your death of cold and all for nothing."

The Rector inclined his head, acknowledging defeat. "If you want me, my doors are always open," he said. Then he turned as a sudden flash of inspiration showed him the boy more as a secular figure than a religious one. "Think of Danny Boy, my son. He went to war and left his love behind, just as you did. But remember what she told him."

"What?"

"Oh no, my boy. I've talked enough. Good day to you."

The Rector turned, and Ted watched his black-cloaked figure walk down the path in the direction of the church. Quite a character, he thought. He might almost have converted me. But what did he mean about Danny Boy?

He looked again at Becky's resting place, and in his head the haunting Irish tune began to run like one of the gramophone records he liked to play. He had sung the words a hundred times, and now they ran through his head, line by line, until he reached the end.

And I shall hear, though soft your tread above me
And all my grave will warmer, sweeter, be
And you will bend and tell me that you love me
And I shall sleep in peace until you come to me.

The first hot searing tears blurred his eyes. Without knowing how he got there, he was on his knees on the marble kerbstone, his head bent low, his hands spreading out over the granite chippings.

"Oh, Becky, Becky, Becky," he whispered.

There was no need for him to say more.

HIS MOOD lasted until he reached the churchyard gates once more and then, quite suddenly, his anger returned like the uprush of a rekindled forest fire licking through dry brush and fanned by the wind of his grief.

Crushing his cap between his hands he stood, while the sky above the tower deepened to violet and the hatred in his heart darkened every part of him. And there, in the shadow of the church, he swore an oath—before God.

If ever I find out that there was something sinister about her death, if ever I find out that someone was responsible for harming her, I'll kill them with my own bare hands.

By all that's Holy in this place, I swear that. And may God strike me dead if I fail.

24

IN THAT grim winter of 1918, funeral followed funeral in Hillsbridge. The town that had mourned so many sons, lost for ever on foreign soil, saw burials enough to satisfy even the most greedy of undertakers, as the effects of war, broken hearts and broken spirits made folk reel beneath the great flu epidemic.

Dr Froster was one of the first to die of it, with Charlie Durrant following not far behind. Then, before January was out Ada Clements had also died.

"You never know what you're going to hear next," Charlotte said when news of Ada's death reached her. "She's been a creaking gate for years, I know, but it's still a shock."

The people of the rank agreed. Without Ada's line of washing blowing high above the gardens day after day life would never be the same again. And what would become of the family now? Wally, the eldest boy, had faked his age to join the army and was still away. Rosa was in Bristol, and Harold had gone to Yorkshire in search of work. But there were still three boys at home, and Walter struggling as always to keep a roof over their heads. Clearly, there was only one solution.

A week after her mother was laid to rest, Rosa Clements returned home for good.

She came up the rank one cold, bright afternoon with all her worldly belongings packed into a carpet bag, wearing a new slouch hat and a skirt that Charlotte considered to be far too short to be decent. But her hair was as long, dark and lustrous as ever, her complexion as clear and fresh as a young girl's.

She walked with her head held high, her expression giving no hint as to what she might be thinking or feeling. Only someone who knew her well could have guessed at the turmoil of excitement, anticipation and awe that were within her, and there were few enough of those.

I'm home. And Ted is home too, she thought, her heady joy far outweighing her grief for the haggard and complaining woman who had been her mother.

Only one thing marred Rosa's home-coming and that she pushed aside. There had been a time when she had felt guilty about Rebecca Church. She had made one of her spells, after all, to 'send her away', and sometimes, in the dead of night, she had lain awake wondering just what it was she had done. The frightening feeling of power had been one of the reasons behind her going to Bristol. She had felt she needed to get away for a while from everything and everybody that was familiar to her, and to be out of reach of the temptation of the woods, the rope, and the circle beneath the trees. But once there, things had fallen back into perspective.

There was a pattern to life. It was as it had to be. And Ted and she were meant for one another. She was as sure of that as she was of the sequence of the seasons.

Her first thought, as she went into the scullery, was how tiny and cramped it was compared to the room she had rented in Bristol. She felt almost claustrophobic in the tiny dwelling. But she pushed that to the back of her mind. Ted was the other side of that confining wall. And if Ted was there, anything was bearable.

She thought about him all the time, as she went about the mundane chores and tried to make life as comfortable for the family as her mother had done. But the first time she saw him, she was shocked by the look of him, by his slimness turned to thinness, by the dark hollows in his once handsome face. And even more worrying was his air of detachment, of being removed from the happenings of the real world.

When she smiled at him, he smiled back. When she passed the time of day, he replied, but his mind was far away. Was it the legacy of the prison camp, she wondered, or was there more to it than that?

"I could help you, Ted, if only you'd let me," she told him silently. "I could make you forget it all if you'd just give me the chance."

But he seemed hardly to notice her, and fate was against her, too. However hard she tried to engineer things so that she would accidentally meet him, something always happened to divert his attention.

And then, late in January, the snow came.

It fell during the night, and the people of Hillsbridge woke to a white world. Beneath a leaden sky, which promised more to come, the batches rose like a range of Alps, and the squat, ugly buildings and the bare fields and allotments were all softened by a thick layer of cotton wool.

The wind had blown it against the backs of the houses in the rank, so that it lay against the windows and doors in deeply draped drifts. Families had to dig themselves out to cross the back yards to the privies. At Walter's insistence, the Clements boys had cleared the worst of the drift from directly outside the door before leaving for school and work. But there was no time to cut a proper path and salt it before it froze, and Rosa knew that if the way was to be cleared before nightfall she would have to do it herself.

From the warm comfort of her kitchen, the snowy scene outside was not inviting, and she delayed the job as long as she could. Then, mid-morning, she heard the scrape of a shovel on stone, and looking out of the scullery window she saw Ted clearing a path from his own back door.

At once, her heart began to thud so hard that it seemed to reverberate through her whole body. It was the chance she'd waited for! Ted would be in the yard for another half-hour at least, and with her own path to be cleared, she had a perfect excuse to be out there herself.

She put on her coat and hat, wound a muffler round her neck and thrust her feet into her stoutest boots. Then she went out, looking for the shovel that the boys had left standing against the back wall.

At first she thought Ted was going to ignore her. When he heard the slam of the door he half-turned, nodding briefly, then resumed his work. She hesitated, looking at his stooping back, not sure whether to go or stay, speak or keep quiet. Then, on sudden impulse, she bent down and scooped up a handful of snow, shaping it into a ball and aiming it at the patch of soft gold that showed between muffler and cap.

"Take that, Ted Hall!" she laughed.

He let out a yell as the snowball caught him right on target and small, icy rivers ran down inside his collar.

"What the . . . ?"

He spun round, and as he did so, the second snowball burst on the front of his jacket.

"Rosa Clements, I'll give you!" he yelled, but there was no mistaking the laughter in his voice, and her heart soared.

"I couldn't resist it," she began. "You made such a lovely target . . . " But she broke off in mid-sentence and watched Ted bend to grab a handful of snow.

'Right, Rosa Clements,' he called, raising his arm to hurl the snowball at her.

"No! No!" She screamed with laughter as she tried to run for safety, but she was too late. The snowball caught her on the shoulder, and the battle was on. Without another word, they began to bombard one another as they had not done since they were children, ducking, dodging, shrieking with laughter, growing sillier and wilder until they were throwing nothing but handfuls of snow. Then Rosa jumped aside too smartly, her boots slid away from her on a hard-trodden patch, and she fell with a thud into the snow.

"Hey, careful!"

Ted ran to her, slipping and sliding himself, to take her hands and pull her up. "You all right? You haven't hurt yourself?"

"No, I'm all right." She was laughing again, but as he steadied her she was aware he was looking at her differently, and the laughter died away as the muscles in her throat suddenly tightened into a choking knot.

"Ted . . . Ted, why are you looking at me like that?"

He did not answer, and she had no way of knowing the picture she made as she laughed up at him, dark eyes sparkling, sallow cheeks whipped rosy by the icy wind, hair tumbled and dusted with snow. She did not know how the breath had caught in his chest, or how he had wondered briefly how the little urchin who had lived next door for most of his life could have grown into this beautiful, tantalizing stranger. She had no way of knowing, and yet somehow she did.

"I came out to clear the path, not play the fool with you!" she said with a tartness she was far from feeling.

"I'll do it for you if you like when I finish ours . . . "

"Oh!" She didn't know whether to be pleased or not. It was nice that he should have offered, but she wanted the excuse to stay out with him in the snow.

He picked up his shovel from where it had fallen, and she stood uncertainly biting her lip.

"I can do it, really, you've got enough to do . . . "

"And all the time in the world to do it." The bitterness was back in his tone. "There won't even be any football, weather like this."

"Football?" she repeated, surprised.

He scraped another foot of path clear of snow. "Hillsbridge Town are at home on Saturday—or should be."

"Oh!" she said again. She hadn't realized he was a football supporter, though she thought she should have guessed he would be. And it explained where he went on Saturday afternoons, too.

"The team's not what it should be, with so many of the lads gone, but still it's something to do," he said, as if pleased to have something to talk about. "And they aren't doing so badly, considering. But Saturday should be their big day. It's the local derby with Purldown."

She nodded. Purldown was the next village, its boundaries running into Hillsbridge. Plenty of Purldown men worked at South Hill Pit, so Saturday's game would see mate set against mate and the rivalry would be fierce.

Rosa had never had the slightest interest in football, but at this moment it seemed to her the most fascinating subject in the world.

"I'd love to see it!" she said, truthfully. "I think I might go."

He looked at her in surprise. "It's not a place for a woman on her own. It'll come to trouble later on, more likely than not, fighting and that. They get very worked up, some of them."

"I can take care of myself," she said stubbornly.

Sadness tore at him, echoes from the past, and he seemed to hear another voice saying those words. Afraid of the reaction his memories could evoke, he pushed the thought aside.

"If you want to go, you'd better come with me. If they can get on the ground, that is. But it's going to be a cold outing."

She shrugged her shoulders.

"Oh, I don't mind that," she said truthfully.

FOR THE rest of the week she watched the weather eagerly. If there was more snow, the game would certainly be cancelled, and how long she would have to wait for another opportunity like this she didn't know. But the heavy skies lightened after unloading only a few more sparse showers, and by Saturday the roads were wet and slushy and patches of sad green grass were showing through the dirty snow that had hung on the fields.

"Will they play?" she asked her brothers anxiously at breakfast, and they looked at one another in surprise, unable to understand their sister's sudden interest in the fortunes of Hillsbridge Town.

"I'll find out for you," Percy volunteered. "I shall go up and have a look at them meself most likely if they'm playing."

A pulse jumped in Rosa's throat. Brotherly scrutiny was the last thing she wanted. But she dared not say so. And when Percy came in at dinner-time with the news the match was on, the excitement rose to almost choke her. She dished up the tripe and onions hastily, plonking the plates down in front of them and telling them, "Get going, don't wait for me." And all the time she wondered what to do.

The game would start early at this time of year, but Ted hadn't come to the door to tell her when to be ready. Supposing he hadn't meant what he said? Supposing he just went without her?

Somehow she forced down mouthfuls of the tripe, then she got up to clear the dishes while the others sat smoking and talking over the likely results of the afternoon. When she had finished she put on her outdoor things, the warmest she had. Her hands were trembling—so was her whole body. It was, it seemed to her, the most important day of her whole life.

"I'll be back in time to get the tea," she said, but even as she opened the backdoor she was unsure what she was going to do.

To her immense relief he was waiting for her, standing by his own backdoor, stamping his feet against the cold.

"Come on, I was beginning to think you'd changed your mind," he said.

It was more the greeting of one mate to another than a man to his girl, but she was determined not to let it spoil her happy mood.

"I had things to do. I'm glad you waited."

He shrugged. "I said I would. Though I still don't think it's a place for a woman."

Another stab of disappointment. Then why didn't you suggest taking me somewhere else? she wanted to say, but she knew better. Ted was still grieving for another girl. She mustn't hurry him—never that.

She hopped along beside him, her shoes sliding a little on the wet path, and he gave her his arm for support. She took it with her gloved hand, feeling tremors of excitement run through her. She had waited so long for this, and now here she was, walking down the hill with Ted Hall, her arm through his for all the world to see.

They crossed the bridge and began to climb the hill that led up to the football field. From Hillsbridge centre, the only way was up. Soon she was panting from the effort of keeping up with him, but he did not slacken his pace. There were other folk streaming up the hill too, mostly men she noticed, and they all seemed to know Ted.

At the gates there was a crowd, jostling and talking in voices that were already loud and excited.

"I'll get your ticket," Ted said, and she nodded, relieved. In all the excitement she had forgotten to bring any money!

They found a space beside the wire midway down the pitch. Even before the players had run out of the changing room, the cold had begun to seep through their shoes, and Ted stamped his feet again and blew on his fingers.

But Rosa didn't feel the cold. Her own world was warm and glowing. And although she scarcely followed the game, she joined in the excitement, cheering and shouting. At half-time she queued at the tea stall with Ted and drank a steaming cup of weak tea. Then she trooped dutifully back to her place by the wire for the second half and more of the mounting excitement.

At last it was all over and with no trouble either. Ten minutes before the end, when a Hillsbridge victory looked assured, disgruntled Purldown supporters began drifting away, and only the most hardy Hillsbridge men remained to cheer their team off the field.

As Rosa trotted along beside Ted, she began to feel anxious. It

357

was nearly over, this great occasion, and she didn't know yet if he would suggest another meeting.

"I did enjoy that," she said hopefully, and he smiled at her.

After more than two years, it was good to have a woman on his arm again, especially one as pretty as Rosa. And for the first time since he had come home, he had actually been able to forget himself for a little while.

"I'll take you again if you like," he offered, and she nodded, concealing her delight.

"Yes, all right," said Rosa.

IN THE weeks that followed, they became close companions. Besides the football matches, he took her to the pictures and to the dances that were sometimes held in the room beneath the picture house.

At first, she lived in a glowing world where anything seemed possible. She rose above the household tasks she hated, floating through them with only half her mind on what she was doing, and she did not allow the black looks she got from Ted's mother to worry her in the least. All her life, she had been used to people's scorn, and although she was surprised that Mrs Hall, who had always treated her kindly, should be against the new-found friendship she had with her son, she was determined not to let it spoil her happiness.

But as the weeks went by and the relationship did not progress beyond companionship, she began to get impatient. Under cover of darkness in the picture house, she tucked her hand into his, but although he held it dutifully, he never attempted to kiss her. When they danced a Veleta, he twirled her round, laughing, but she was left feeling he would have done the same with any pretty girl. Her happiness began to be dulled by anxiety. Surely he should be beginning to forget by now? Rebecca Church had been dead for almost three years.

Or was it that at all? Might it not be that he just didn't find her attractive as a woman, in spite of all her efforts? Or was he simply shy? It seemed unlikely, but she could not be certain. Sometimes the most outgoing people were the very ones who were inwardly unsure of themselves. If that was the case, perhaps she should take the initiative. But if she did that, and it wasn't shyness at all, she might ruin everything.

February passed, and March, and although there was not yet

much warmth in the sun, at least it was shining. The evenings too were becoming lighter. On a Saturday night, the lamps in the market place no longer had to be lit at tea time, and more and more young folk walked along the bottom road to the fair, knowing that soon the cake-walk and the chair-o-planes would be packed up and taken on to the road for another summer.

Ted and Rosa always enjoyed the fair—Ted because he liked the noise and the unabashed gaity, Rosa because the caravans and the dark-skinned people held a fascination for her that she wouldn't admit, even to herself. Whenever it was fine enough, and they had nothing more pressing to do, they would idle along in that direction to throw a handful of darts or hurl a ball at the coconut shy, and that Saturday night was no exception.

There had been another big football match that afternoon, an exciting cup match with Purldown again, and this time Hillsbridge had been the losers.

Feelings were running high. There had already been a fight or two, spilling over from the pubs into the market place, and Rosa had watched in some alarm as a man was knocked from top to bottom of the steps leading to the subway beneath the railway lines.

Just so long as Ted didn't get involved, she thought. But Ted, for once, seemed preoccupied. When she suggested going to the market yard, he agreed, but without his usual enthusiasm, and she felt a stab of disquiet.

"What's the matter with you?" she asked, but he just shook his head, taking her arm and steering her along the road towards the fair.

"Oh, nothing much. Come on, I'll see what I can win you on the darts."

But his aim was no good, his concentration elsewhere, and Rosa was not convinced by his denial. Her heart grew heavier as she watched him, and the music and noise that usually exhilarated her only pressed in on her until she was ready to scream.

"Let's go for a walk," she suggested, feeling she couldn't stand another moment of enforced jollity, and Ted followed her. But the strained atmosphere was still there. They left the market yard and struck out along the bottom road beside the stream. Finally, she stopped walking and turned to face him.

"Don't tell me there's nothing the matter," she said. "You've been as quiet as a mouse all the evening."

He sighed and pulled a face. "Oh, it's just that I've been doing a lot of thinking these last few days."

"Oh, yes, what about?" she prompted.

"The future," he said, and her heart came into her mouth.

"Your future, you mean?"

"Yes. Oh, look . . . " He glanced round, seeing they were quite close to a field gateway and pulled her into it, leaning his back against the wooden frame and holding her at arm's length to face him. "I can't go on as I am forever. I've been home going on four months, and I've got to do something about finding a job. I'm more or less fit now, and . . . "

"You could get your old job back, no trouble," she said confidently, and he grimaced.

"I don't want my old job back. That's it in a nutshell. God knows, it took me long enough to get away from carting. I don't want to walk back into it just like that."

"Maybe they'd take you as a collier now." The blood was pumping through her veins very fast and singing in her ears.

"I don't know as I want to be a collier. I don't know as I want to go back underground at all," he said.

"Well what do you want to do?" she asked, pretending exasperation.

He stared over her shoulder into the darkness. "I'm not sure. I think I might travel round a bit, doing what I can."

"Travel?" she echoed faintly, and then, grasping at straws, "But there's an awful shortage of jobs. Men are out of work all over the place."

"Maybe. But I don't know as I want regular work. I'm not ready to settle down to one thing from now till I get me gold watch. It's funny, people seem to think there's something special about staying in one place for fifty years, but I tell you, it frightens me to death."

"But what would you do?" she asked. She was shaking all over.

"Anything. Whatever was going. The summer's coming, and there'll be seasonal jobs at the resorts. Now this war is over, people are going to want to get away. Or I could go to London. There's sure to be something I could do there. I liked London. I went there once when Becky . . . "

He broke off, his eyes misting as he stared at some distant spot over Rosa's shoulder, and the name seemed to explode all around her.

Becky. All this while, and he had still not got over her. Becky. She had been there in his heart all the time that she, Rosa, had been trying to make him forget, and nothing they had shared had really meant anything to him at all. She had been a diversion, a companion, but nothing more, because he was still in love with Rebecca Church.

And why? Rosa wondered. What did she have to hold him like this? She was prim, she was colourless, not a girl you'd look at twice. Oh, I could show him a thing or two if only he'd give me the chance. I'd show him what a woman can be when she's got fire in her blood. But he's going away—he's going to leave me. Maybe this is the last time we'll be together, and all because he doesn't know . . .

She looked at his face, and at the eyes that were seeing something no one else could see. "She's dead," she wanted to say, but she knew the words would be cruel and useless. There was only one thing to do and that was to show him—make him realize once and for all that she was warm living flesh, a woman who loved him.

Without a word she moved towards him, sliding her arms about his waist and tilting her face to his. For a startled moment he held back, then with a suddenness that took her breath away, he crushed her close, leaning back against the gate and taking her with him. His lips found hers, kissing her with a hunger that both frightened and exhilarated her.

So I was right! she thought joyfully. I should have done this long ago, given him some encouragement! Then his tongue was caressing hers and probing the soft recesses of her mouth, and as the answering excitement rippled through her body, thought was drowned by emotion.

Dizzy with desire, she pressed still closer. His hands were on her breasts, stroking, kneading, fumbling with the fastening of her bodice. Passion rose in her like a warm flood-tide. She pulled away slightly, arching her back so that the muscles of her throat pulled taut, and above her the stars seemed to dance and sway in the heavens.

"Ted," she moaned softly. "Oh, Ted!"

But suddenly, with even less warning than he had taken her, she felt herself thrust away. Bewildered, still mazy from passion, she tried to slip her arms back around his neck, but he disentangled them roughly.

"Ted, what's the matter?" Shock put a sob in her voice, but the

361

tenderness had gone from him with the desire, and he shrugged almost angrily.

"I'm sorry. I shouldn't have done that."

"But why?" she cried. "Don't you know I wanted you to?"

"I'm sorry," he said again, turning away, and the sense of loss coming on top of her broken dreams was too much.

"It's her—Becky—isn't it?" she burst out. "You keep thinking about her! Oh, why can't you realize she's gone, and I'm here? I could make you forget—I could. I love you, Ted, you must know that. I've always loved you. Oh, don't turn away from me now, please don't!"

"Rosa!" His voice was harsh, his features set. "For goodness sake, leave it!"

Despair brought tears to her eyes. "But, Ted, don't you know I'd be good for you. We'd be good for each other. Oh, please . . . "

His face softened, a mirror of sadness, and he touched her arm.

"I said I was sorry, Rosa, and I am. This is all my fault, I know. I shouldn't have let it come this far. But I liked you—I liked your company—and I thought, well, I thought maybe in time I'd come to feel differently."

"And you will!" she whispered urgently. "You will, I promise you . . . "

He shook his head. "No, my dear. Don't you see? You're worth more than that. You deserve somebody to love you for yourself. Not just to pretend you're someone else . . . "

She jumped, startled and hurt. So that was it! When he'd kissed her, held her, touched her he'd been pretending she was Becky! Dear God, it was more than flesh and blood could stand!

He saw the look on her face and stepped towards her.

"Rosa, I didn't mean . . . "

But she jerked away, pride coming to her rescue. She'd thrown herself at him, and he'd just been wishing she was someone else. She'd bared her soul to him, told him she loved him even, and all she'd done was make a fool of herself. It was too late to take back any of these things, but at least she could redeem herself now.

"That's all right. You don't have to explain. I thought I could help you get over her, but I was wrong. That's all."

"Rosa . . . " he said helplessly, but her face was proud. In the moonlight, with her hair tumbling over her shoulders she looked more like a gypsy than ever, and the breath caught in his throat. With a sigh, he went to take her arm.

"Come on. I'll see you home."

But to his surprise, she shrugged away, tossing her head.

"I don't think I'm ready to go home yet."

"But . . ."

"I think I'll go back to the fair. There's sure to be somebody there I know. Don't wait for me."

"But, Rosa, I can't leave you here."

"Why not?" She laughed, a high, false sound. "I can look after myself."

For a moment longer he hesitated, then he shrugged.

"Well, I'll walk back as far as the fair with you, anyhow."

"If you like."

They walked side by side, yet a million miles apart. Ted was thinking that he'd made a mess of things and no mistake, and Rosa was concentrating on keeping the muscles in her cheeks steady. If she relaxed for a moment, she knew she would cry, and that would be the last of her pride gone.

The walk back to the market yard seemed endless, but at last they reached it.

"Are you sure you'll be all right?" Ted asked doubtfully, and she nodded, not looking at him.

"I said so, didn't I? Go on, Ted, leave me alone."

"All right, Rosa. Goodnight."

Then he had gone, disappearing into the darkness, and she was alone. She stepped into the market yard, letting the noise and the activity swallow her. So that was it, she thought. Ted had gone, and she had retained a little of her pride. But oh, the pain!

She stumbled into the yard, letting the crowd jostle her this way and that. Her throat ached, and she saw the bright lights as if through a haze. They blurred and spread and merged like a candle glow on a wet window. The music of the rides roared in her ears like the thunder of the sea, and tonight it held no magic for her. She wished she were in the woods with only the sounds of the night for company and nothing to disturb her thoughts. That was what she really wanted—to have time to think about what had happened, living it all over again—all the years of loving and waiting and hoping and . . .

A sudden commotion drew her attention, and she saw that a scuffle had broken out on the planking that surrounded the round-about. There was bumping and barging, and people were scattering in all directions.

Rosa, disgusted but not much worried, turned her back and slipped through the gathering crowd. Somebody was going to end up falling into the roundabout if they weren't careful, and she didn't want to be there to see it. Perhaps she'd go home now. Ted should be far enough away not to know she had no intention of staying to make a night of it alone. Once round the yard, then out of the gates and let the darkness hide her.

She passed the stalls, ignoring the calls of the barkers, and stopped for a moment to watch the laughing figures on the juddering cakewalk. Then she headed back towards the road.

She had to skirt the roundabout—there was no way she could avoid it—but she wasn't much worried about that. She cut through on the opposite side from where the fight had started, too deep in thought to even bother to look in that direction. But a sudden yell made her jerk her head around just in time to see a man coming head first over the wooden balustrade above her.

Startled, she skipped aside, but even so the falling body bumped into her, almost knocking her over. He landed with a sickening thud on the ground at her feet, and she stepped back, drawing her skirts away in a panic.

A movement above made her look up again, and she saw another man crouching on the wooden rail. He was grinning, his face in the carbide lights brown and leathery like a monkey, and as she watched he vaulted the rail, landing on his hands and knees beside the first man. As he got to his feet and roughly prodded his victim with the toe of his boot, Rosa tried to edge away, but a crowd of rowdies now blocked her path.

Trapped, she watched in horror as the monkey-faced man hauled his victim to his feet and knocked him down again with a heavy punch in the stomach. He stood aside then, dusting down his hands and jacket and looking around as if to dare any of the onlookers to challenge him. As he did so, his eye fell on Rosa.

"Hello, hello, hello, and what have we got here then?" he jeered. "If it's not the Hillsbridge Town mascot herself."

Rosa shrank back, apprehension making her shiver. She did not know the man, but it seemed that he knew her, and she guessed he must have been amongst the Purldown contingent at the match that afternoon. Now, full of beer, he was on the rampage. Suddenly she wished she had not been so ready to let Ted leave her alone.

"Well, well, what are you doing here, sweetheart?" The monkey-faced man came closer. "All on your own, are you? Now that's what I call the spoils of war!"

Rosa tossed her head, her eyes blazing with a confidence she was far from feeling. "Leave me alone, you ape."

A flicker of anger crossed his features, then he began to laugh.

"Oh-ho, a little fire cracker! Well, that's right up my street. But you want to support a good team, sweetheart. Now, if you come with me, I'll soon show you this Hillsbridge lot aren't worth bothering about."

His face was too close. He reeked of beer fumes and stale sweat, and she felt her gorge rise. With a quick, almost unthinking reaction, she brought her toe up and kicked him on the shin as hard as she could. She saw his rubbery features fall slack with surprise, then with a snarl he lunged at her.

With a swiftness born of fear, Rosa ducked beneath his arm, twisting out and away and dodging on to the steps of the roundabout, the only way that was clear to her. As she ran on legs that trembled she heard shouts above the deafening music, and she knew the man would come after her.

If only she could see someone she knew! She ran along the boarding, all eyes following her. Then she dived down into the crowd again, wondering wildly which way to go. Maybe if she climbed the wall at the back of the yard she could get away across the gardens. They'd be a sea of mud, but that was just too bad.

The wall was high and sheer. Cursing her skirts, she tried to find finger and toe holds, but there seemed to be none, and she realized in a flash what a picture she would make if she reached the top. There she would be, silhouetted against the darkening sky for all to see, and if anyone came after her across the gardens, there would be no escape.

A little sob escaped her, then turned to a scream as she felt a hand on her arm.

"Leave me!" she cried, spinning round.

But as she recognized Jack Hall she almost wept with relief.

"Come on, Rosa, I'm getting you out of here." His voice had a quiet authority, but she shook her head, too frightened still to trust anyone.

"Leave me, Jack. They've gone mad, those Purldown blokes. They'll lay into you especially, with your leg."

She knew at once she had said the wrong thing. "I mean, you don't want to get in a fight," she said lamely.

He took her arm. "I can take care of myself. If anyone bothers me, they'll get my walking stick across them."

There was a new hardness in his voice, and she shuddered.

"Which way, then?"

"Just follow me."

She did as she was told, trotting along behind him with quick, nervous steps. Over by the roundabout there was still a rumpus going on, and she wondered if the mates of the man who had been thrown over the rails had caught up with monkey-face. But whatever the reason, there was no sign of him now. Jack led her to the outskirts of the crowd and out on to the road, and only then did she let her breath out in a sigh of relief.

"Thanks, Jack." Of all the Halls, he was the one she was least at ease with. He was clever, he was different somehow, and she had always had the feeling that he must look down on her. She knew this was irrational, since Jack was usually in too much of a dream to look down on anyone.

Today, however, she was conscious of him looking at her differently, and she tossed her head, some of her confidence returning.

Jack's eyes passed over her, then he began to walk, pulling her with him.

"Our Ted shouldn't have left you there by yourself."

"It was nothing to do with him," she said haughtily. "I told him I didn't want him to stay."

"That doesn't make any difference. He took you out, he should look after you."

She tossed her head again. As fear ebbed, the pain began again. "I'm not his responsibility any more—if I ever was."

"What do you mean?" he asked.

"It's all over between us. His lamp's still burning for Becky Church, and I'm not taking second place to a ghost." Her voice was strong and confident, revealing nothing of the way she felt. He glanced at her, seeing the beautiful woman she had become and feeling an ache of fire within him.

"So that's what it's all about," he said, covering his feelings as well as she had covered hers. "When I met him outside the George I could see there was something up, but he wouldn't say what. But I thought it was funny he'd left you alone. That's why I came to look for you."

"You came . . . to look for me?"

He didn't answer, and suddenly she knew what she was going to do. She'd show Ted Hall once and for all! Why, she'd worshipped him since she was knee-high, and where had it got her? He'd taken her for granted, and now he'd left her all alone with the rowdies in the market yard. Perhaps it was time someone showed him he wasn't so great after all. Perhaps it was time.

Out of the corner of her eye, she looked at Jack, knowing with sudden certainty that for all his difference, he found her attractive. Supposing I was to go off with his brother, Rosa thought. Why, he's a far better catch than Ted. He's been a pilot, and he's going to be a teacher. He's even been to Buckingham Palace and been decorated by the King. And what will Ted ever be but a general dogs-body, drifting from one job to the next—if he's lucky.

Egged on by the sting of rejection, she laid her hand on Jack's arm. Looking up at him in the light of the swinging carbide lamps, she smiled—a smile that with her looks managed to be provocative in spite of the heaviness of her heart.

"Thanks for rescuing me anyway," she said, and as an afterthought, "It's easy to see why you were decorated, Jack. You're quite the hero, aren't you?"

A week later Ted left home, and Charlotte did not know whether to be glad or sorry. She would miss him terribly—after the long years when he was away, it was wonderful to have him back—but he was so changed, so restless and unhappy, and she thought it might be best for him to get right away and try to make a new life for himself, somewhere where Rebecca's ghost did not walk.

"I thought for a bit he might be going to make a go of it with Rosa Clements," she said to Dolly when she came down for one of her afternoon visits. "I don't really care for the girl, but if she could make him happy, I suppose that's all that matters."

"Rosa's all right, Mam," Dolly said, "but our Ted isn't going to forget Becky Church in a hurry."

"No, you're right there," Charlotte agreed, wishing that Ted could be more like placid Dolly. After the first terrible upset of Eric being killed just before the wedding, Dolly had accepted it as she accepted everything, and already had a new beau—a boy from Bath who had been invalided out of the army suffering from the effects of gas, and who came twice a week to do Captain Fish's garden.

"There's something else worrying me, too," Charlotte went on, changing the subject. "I may be wrong—I hope I am—but I think our Jack is seeing her."

"*Jack?*" Dolly repeated in disbelief.

"I may be wrong," Charlotte said again. "But I've seen them talking out in the yard several times this week. And he went off last night without saying where he was going."

"Oh, I can't believe that!" Dolly was scathing. "Not Jack. I've never known him take any interest in a girl—let alone Rosa."

"Well, he's older now. He wouldn't be human if he didn't look at a girl sometime," Charlotte told her, and she did not add that she was remembering a long-ago street party when she had caught Jack staring at Rosa with a very dreamy expression on his face.

"Rosa's an attractive girl, the sort men go for," she went on after a moment. "And she's sly, too. If she made up her mind to it, our Jack would be putty in her hands!"

"Oh, Mam, you are funny!" Dolly teased her.

But Charlotte did not laugh. "With our Ted gone, it wouldn't surprise me," she said grimly.

And she had no idea how close to the truth her prophesy would turn out to be.

25

IN THE spring of 1919, Jack began teaching at Hillsbridge Church of England School in the valley next to the church, but it was only a temporary measure.

"To fill in until I go to Bristol University in the autumn," he explained to William Davies when he went to see him to tell him of his plans.

"University! Well, I'm very pleased for you, Jack." William Davies smiled. "And to think I thought I'd be doing well to make an uncertificated teacher of you! You're doing it properly, and no mistake!"

"The way things are changing nowadays, I think I can make a better future if I'm properly qualified," Jack told him. "I think I can get a government grant as an ex-service student, and if I put that on top of my officer's gratuity, I should be able to manage."

William Davies nodded. Things certainly were changing in the teaching profession.

"We've got a lot to thank Fisher for," Davies said, referring to the recent education act named after H.A.L. Fisher, which had raised salaries and brought in a pension scheme for teachers among other things. "Though I'm not sure whether it's a good idea raising the leaving age to fourteen. It's not that I want to see child labour —far from it—but the classrooms are overcrowded now, and half of them don't want to be there, anyway."

Jack was surprised to hear his old mentor express this sentiment, but he could see he had a point. "They think it's a waste of time, having to stay on another year when they want to be earning their living," he agreed, "but in the end they'll come to realize it's for their own good."

William Davies sighed. "Will they? I'm not so sure. And if they want to, the local authorities can raise it by another year. You know that, do you?"

Jack nodded and admitted to himself that he really wouldn't relish the thought of having to teach unwilling fifteen-year-olds. The ones he had were bad enough, and he wasn't sure he'd made too auspicious a start. It had been different at the board school with William Davies always within earshot, and he had been only a pupil/teacher then. But now he was expected to wield his own authority, and he didn't think he was doing too well. The children called him 'Hop-a-long' and 'Peg-leg' and played him up whenever they could, and he hadn't been very proud of the fact that one day the strict and old-fashioned headmaster at the school had had to come in and lay about him with his cane to restore order.

Part of the trouble, he was sure, was that they knew him too well. He would much prefer to work further from home, and there had been a vacancy he would have liked at Sanderley, a village three miles north of Hillsbridge on the road to Bath. But he had no way of getting there each day, and walking was out of the question with his artificial leg.

He had been fitted now with what he called his 'proper one'— the leg that attached to his stump by straps, and which he would be using, if he was lucky, for a good many years to come. After his early struggles, he found it surprisingly easy to manage, and he could get around at a good speed. But if he overdid things, the stump

rubbed raw. And six miles walking a day, would certainly be overdo-
ing things!

But he would only be at the C of E for a few months, he consoled
himself, and it would be experience which would stand him in good
stead. And by the time he finished his training and came to look for
another job, he would be that much older.

"You were lucky to get into Bristol University," William Davies
said, harking back to the training that was so close to his heart.

Jack nodded. "Yes, it's good to be within striking distance of
home. And I'm looking forward to working with the university
students as well as doing my teacher training."

"And not too far away from your girl, either," William Davies
added with a smile, and Jack coloured. He wouldn't have mentioned
it, but it certainly was a consideration. He didn't want to be far away
from Rosa.

Since that night when he had rescued her in the market yard,
Jack's life had revolved round Rosa. Just how it had happened, he
could not be sure, but suddenly he had found himself thinking about
her all the time, picturing her dark eyes, her glossy hair and the curve
of her red lips when she smiled.

He'd always found her attractive. Even in the days when his world
had consisted of schoolwork and aeroplanes. But now, suddenly, she
was within his reach, and she was not only lovely and enchanting,
but there was also something of the old days about her that gave him
a warm and pleasurable feeling. She had known him when he was
whole, and she had known Fred, too, and all the others who had once
been a part of his everyday life and were gone now.

Sometimes, it was true, he still thought of Stella O'Halloran, and
blushed to remember how he had thought she might care for him.
Had she known how he had felt? He hoped not, although he thought
that after nursing as many soldiers as she had, she was probably used
to them falling in love with her, and understood, or even dismissed
it as a part of the healing process. But in spite of his embarrassment,
and the brief, warm intimacy they had shared when she had listened
to his fears and comforted him, she was unreal to him now. In fact,
had it not been for the reality of his stump, he sometimes found it
difficult to believe those months in hospital had ever happened at
all. While Rosa . . .

Rosa was beautiful and mysterious, a potent mixture of the un-
tamed and the vulnerable. And there was no doubt at all that *she*

was real, though he sometimes felt as if she had woven a spell about him.

"You're a witch," he told her one night, smiling into the dark eyes that seemed to hypnotize him, and he had no way of knowing how much the remark pleased her, even now.

"You think so?" she asked, tossing her head and looking at him narrowly, and he put his arms around her, pulling her into the gap between the coal-houses and kissing her until she was breathless.

It was a warm April evening. After the harsh winter, spring had come early and it had been just the right weather for Jack to take his 'constitutionals' as he described the slow, painful excursions when he tried to teach himself to walk without a stick. But painful or not, he did not mind, for they also provided a good excuse to be alone with Rosa in the way that both of them liked best—out in the lanes, away from distractions, where they could simply enjoy one another's company and watch the countryside wake up from its winter sleep.

Jack had never been a one for the entertainments Ted enjoyed, and Rosa was more at home under the stars, so this at least they had in common, and for Jack, just being with Rosa was a delight.

He knew Charlotte disapproved. And he would have liked her to accept Rosa as she had accepted Jim's Sarah or even Ted's Becky, but she didn't, and he was determined not to spoil things by worrying about it. She was his mother, maybe, but he had his own life to lead, and with Rosa, it promised to be very exciting.

As he felt himself rise and harden he drew her deeper into the shadow of the outbuildings, balancing himself against the wall and pulling her close. If only there was somewhere they could go for a bit of real privacy! But there wasn't, and perhaps it was just as well. If he had her on his own for too long, he didn't know how long he would be able to resist her.

He bent her head beneath his, kissing her again and feeling her lips open gently like the petals of a water lily. As the layers unfolded he tasted the sweetness of her mouth and his desire mounted, spreading from the heart of him in ever-widening circles like the molten lava that pours from a volcano. The kiss became deeper and more demanding: her arms were around his neck, her fingers playing in his hair, and her body moved against his with a sensuous insistence that brought him to a pitch of desire. He moved his body against hers and felt her thighs yield beneath the pressure. One of her hands left his neck and moved slowly down his back, setting every nerve alight, and each time he raised his head, her mouth sought his again, drawing it down until he felt he was drowning in her.

It was sweet torture. Part of him wanted to stay locked in the embrace forever, part demanded the release of passion in an earth-shattering climax. But this was far too public a place, and even if it wasn't . . .

There was only one way he could have her, without guilt. It had occurred to him before, when he had lain awake aching to have her with him, but he had dismissed it, telling himself it was too soon. Now, however, it was there again, and he knew that where Rosa was concerned, it could never be too soon.

He held her away from him so that he felt her warm breath slide over his cheek. "Rosa, I want you to marry me," he said.

The ripple of breath against his face stopped, so did her hands and the gentle, sensuous movement of her hips. She looked at him, her eyes wide with surprise, then he felt a shudder run through her body. It stirred a new depth in him, and he shifted himself awkwardly, aware suddenly of the importance of her answer.

Time seemed suspended, the sounds of the night very far away. In the kitchen of one of the houses along the rank, someone was whistling tunelessly. From a nearby coal-house came the sound of a scraping shovel and the thud of falling coal, and far out over the valley an owl hooted its low, mournful call. Jack shifted again so that Rosa's profile came into focus, the clearly defined line of nose and chin, the slender throat, the rounded thrust of breast.

"Rosa . . . " he said again, but she interrupted him, as if the sound of his voice had broken the spell.

"Yes," she said, and he wasn't sure if he imagined the slight harshness in her tone.

He swallowed at the lump of nervousness that seemed to be choking him. "You mean . . . "

"I mean, yes, all right, I'll marry you." There was no mistaking it now, that edge that shouldn't have been there. He shuddered slightly, then pushed the unwelcome thought away. Rosa was accepting his proposal. It didn't matter that she wasn't blushing and whispering shyly as all the girls in the music-hall songs did. She was no retiring maiden left behind by the Victorian era. Nor was she a modern miss either. She was a free spirit, as wild as the vixen who came down to the gardens at night to steal a hen to feed her cubs. She would never give herself lightly—if she gave herself at all! He must never, ever, expect too much of her, or try to cage her. He knew that with certainty. But it did not stop him from pulling her close again, his body on fire with joy.

"Rosa, you've just made me the happiest man alive! Come here."

But she pushed herself free, all the passion she had displayed a few moments ago gone now.

"Not here, Jack Hall! What ever are you thinking of? Someone might come by and see us . . . "

He laughed, kissing the top of her head and taking her hand.

"All right. Let's go and tell them we're going to be married. Then if they see me kissing you, perhaps they'll have the decency to look the other way!"

She hung back.

"Tell who?"

"Well, your father might be a good start. I ought to ask him properly if it's all right, I suppose. And then there'll be a dickens of a lot to talk about—like where we're going to live for a start."

"With us," she said promptly. "I'll have to stay home to look after the boys."

His face fell.

"Well, I hadn't thought of it that way. And I'll be in Bristol after the summer anyway. I couldn't travel every day. We'll have to work something out."

She didn't answer. There was the strangest expression on her face, and he gave her hand a tug.

"Never mind about it now, anyway. For tonight, let's just think about celebrating. Tomorrow will be time enough for problems, eh?"

She nodded, and they left the shadow of the coal-houses and crossed the yard to the back door. With her hand on the latch she paused, looking up at him.

"Jack, you are sure, aren't you?"

In the moonlight her face was a pale oval beneath her heavy dark hair.

"I wouldn't have asked you if I hadn't been sure."

"No, but . . . " Again the hesitation, then her eyes met his, challenging him. "You haven't said you love me."

"Haven't I?" he asked, melting inside. "Well, in that case, I love you. Will that do? Or do you want me to say it again?"

She shook her head, a faint smile lifting the corners of her mouth.

"No, that'll do nicely. Let's go and see Dad, shall we?"

And as he followed her into the scullery, it did not occur to him that he hadn't asked whether she loved him too. And Rosa had certainly no intention of telling him.

WALTER CLEMENTS received the news of his daughter's engagement quietly and without surprise. He had known for some time which way the wind was blowing, and although he had expected it to be Ted who would take her down the aisle, he thought Jack would do almost as well, even if he did have a few ideas above his station.

There were, of course, certain things that would have to be sorted out, but he didn't expect any serious problems. The last few weeks he'd been chatting to Molly Hamblin, whose husband, Wilf, had been killed on the Somme, and he thought that he would be able to persuade her to come in and 'do' for him and the boys, if nothing else. With Rosa at home, he had had no excuse to ask her, but if she was going to get married, that was rather different. Why, he might even think of getting married again himself. For all that Ada had been a poor, skinny creature and about as responsive to his love-making as a lump of best lard, his bed was cold on winter nights without her, and he was still barely middle-aged. Yes, maybe it wasn't such a bad stroke of fortune, Rosa wanting to get married.

On the other side of the dividing wall, however, at number eleven, Charlotte Hall was taking a less tolerant view.

When Jack came in and announced his intention of marrying Rosa Clements, she was both amazed and furious. "You must have taken leave of your senses!" she declared, her voice rising so loudly that he was afraid that, in spite of the thickness of the wall, Rosa might hear her. "You're just starting a job that's taken us all our time for the last ten years to get you into, and you talk about saddling yourself with a wife. Have you thought what it's going to mean to you, son?"

"I know it's come as a bit of a surprise to you, Mam," he said, trying to pacify her. "But we can work something out, I know. I'm not hard up. I've got my gratuity put by, and the ex-serviceman's grant to come. We'll find somewhere in Bristol to live and . . ."

"Hah!" Charlotte exclaimed shortly. "Finding somewhere to live isn't so easy these days. Don't you know there's a housing shortage on? Or haven't you heard about the people building themselves shacks to live in out of any old oddments they can find? Disgusting, I call it!"

"Look, Mam, I've got no intentions of doing anything so daft," Jack said. "There must be places to rent if you can pay. And when I've finished training and get a job, there might be a house to go with it."

"And what if babies come along, have you thought of that?" Charlotte asked him. "They do, you know, once you start your goings-on."

Jack coloured. At heart he was still quite reserved, and the subject of contraception was not one he felt ready to discuss with his mother.

"There's no need to start a family until you want to nowadays," he said quietly. "There's ways and means, you know."

"Ah, and so there always has been for those in the know," Charlotte informed him. "But all it takes is a drop too much to drink and a bit of carelessness, and all the ways and means in the world won't do you any good."

"I don't drink, Mam," Jack snapped, growing a little tired of the opposition. "And nothing you can say is going to make me change my mind, so you might as well accept it. I'm going to marry Rosa."

Charlotte turned away, slicing bread ready for supper with a ferocity that alarmed him.

"Mam . . . " he said, still hoping for her approval, and after a moment her rigid back slumped, and she turned back to face him, the breadknife still in her hand.

"You'll regret it, Jack, I'm telling you. When you get to college, you'll meet girls more like yourself . . . "

Jack's temper, slow to rise, was up now. Offended by her words, he sprang to Rosa's defence. "So that's it! I wondered how long it would be before you started telling me she wasn't good enough for me, Mam."

Charlotte recoiled a little at his tone, then returned to the attack.

"She's a nice enough girl, Jack, I'll give you that. And she's got the looks as well. It's not that I'm blaming you. It's just that I know, if you wait, you can do better for yourself."

He shook his head.

"I don't understand you, Mam. Just who do you think we are, that she's not good enough? You always stood up for her when people pointed the finger at her. But when it comes to welcoming her into your own family, it's a different story. And I call that hypocritical."

"Oh, maybe, Jack." She brandished the breadknife helplessly.

"It's just that I don't want to see you throw yourself away. If you marry her, you'll live to regret it. It's as simple as that. Maybe she and Ted could have made a go of it. I don't know. But in the end, when those looks of hers have gone, or when you come to wanting more than love morning, noon and night, you'll get tired of her. You need your own kind, Jack, that's what it boils down to. And she's not your kind."

He stared at her, not understanding the certainty in her tone, but shaken by it all the same. Then he straightened his shoulders.

"I think you've said enough, Mam," he said coldly. "I'd hoped you would be pleased for me, but as you're not, it would be better for all of us in the long run if you were to keep your thoughts to yourself. And you might as well make up your mind to it. I'm going to marry Rosa, and nothing you can say is going to alter that."

"I see. Well . . . " Charlotte stopped suddenly mid-sentence, biting on the words that had flown to her lips, then turning away. "Well, if that's the way you feel, I dare say there's no more to be said. But I hope you won't rush into this just to prove me wrong. I hope you'll take your time and sort things out properly."

He nodded.

"I'm not the fool you seem to take me for, Mam. When I marry Rosa, it'll be all done properly, with a chapel service and a reception and a few days away. It's what she wants, and I owe that to her. And I only hope that by then you'll see things differently." His voice softened. "I'm grateful to you, Mam, for all you've done for me. Don't think I don't know the sacrifices you made. But that doesn't give you the right to choose my wife for me. Never that."

She inclined her head abruptly. The years passed before her eyes, from the day when he had told her he wanted to become a teacher and proved what she had always known—that he was different from the others. She saw herself calling on Rector Archer, humbling herself for Jack's sake, baring her soul as she had never bared it in her life. She felt again the pain in her hands when they had cracked and bled from too many hours in a pail of hot, soapy water on a winter-cold doorstep, and the tiredness she had fought and conquered so as to keep going to earn the money to keep him at school. Through it all, she had kept her eyes fixed firmly to a star—Jack's star—and her determination to help him win the position in life that was his birthright. Now he was going to throw it all away by marrying Rosa Clements.

It would be a mistake, she knew it in her bones. And it wasn't just a matter of snobbery. Charlotte was a realist, not a snob. She knew that Rosa, daughter of a washerwoman and a fairground man, could never fit into the life that Jack would want. If she had been clever, as he was clever, she could have made the jump, but she wasn't. No, as she had told him, once the physical attraction wore off, there would be nothing left.

But how to make him see it? How to stop him making such a terrible mistake? He was twenty-one now, so he could marry whom he pleased. And in any case, withholding consent often did more harm than good. She'd seen it happen.

There has to be a way, Charlotte thought, and whatever it is, I'll find it. I'll not stand by and see him throw it all away now. Not after all we've been through.

But to Jack, she nodded her head, so that the strand of greying hair escaped from her bun and fell down her cheek.

"Oh, well, I dare say in the end you'll do whatever you think," she said. And went back to slicing bread.

"MRS HALL, excuse me, it is Mrs Hall, isn't it?"

Charlotte, who had been looking in the window of the butcher's shop, passing the time of day with Mercy Brixey and wondering what to get for a change for dinner, turned sharply at the sound of the unfamiliar voice speaking her name.

She saw a tall, well-built girl with a mop of reddish hair, and a smiling, good-natured face, not exactly pretty, but pleasant and full of character. She recognized her at once as O'Halloran's younger daughter, Stella.

Taken by surprise, she looked her up and down and the girl put a hand on her arm. "I'm sorry. I hope you don't mind me speaking to you like this, but I thought I'd ask after Jack. I nursed him, you know, in London, when he had his leg amputated."

"That's right, you did. I remember him saying. Full of praise for you, he was."

Slight colour suffused the girl's freckled face and she smiled, looking both pleased and embarrassed.

"Oh, well, I . . . How is he, anyway?"

Charlotte's eyes narrowed, her shrewd brain taking in more of the situation than the girl realized.

"Oh, he's not doing so badly at all. He's off to Bristol to the university after the summer, going to do the teacher training course so as to be properly qualified."

"I'm so glad," the girl said, smiling. "I knew he'd make it. I told him so."

Charlotte nodded.

"And how about you? Stella, isn't it? I know he'd want me to ask."

"Me? Oh, I'm still nursing. I went to France from London, and the demobilization is taking so long they still need medical attention for the troops even though the fighting is over, thank God. But I'd thought of coming back this way eventually, to Bath maybe—or Bristol . . . " The colour rose in her cheeks again, and Charlotte was quick to notice it.

"Bristol! Well I never! You might run into our Jack . . . "

"Yes . . . "

"But I thought . . . " Mercy Brixey, who had been listening with unashamed interest to the conversation, could keep silent no longer, and both women turned towards her rather strident voice. "But I thought your Jack was getting married, Mrs Hall."

"Yes, well . . . " Charlotte blustered, but Mercy was not to be done out of her moment of glory.

"Engaged to Rosa Clements, isn't he? Going to be married before he goes to college, surely."

Charlotte, flustered as she was, could not help seeing the dismay on the girl's open face before she hastily covered it with a forced smile.

"Engaged to be married? Jack? Goodness, what a surprise!"

"Yes, to all of us," Charlotte said drily. "Now look . . . "

But before she could go any further, the girl interrupted her, touching her arm again with a quick, awkward movement.

"I must go, Mrs Hall. I'm so pleased to have seen you. Give my regards to Jack, won't you? And my congratulations."

Then, before Charlotte could recover herself, she had gone, hurrying off down the street.

"Well, well, fancy Hal's daughter talking to you!" Mercy remarked in awe, but Charlotte cut her short.

"And what's so funny about that? She's flesh and blood like you and me. And not so stuck-up as some. Now, I've got my shopping to do, Mercy. You won't mind if I get on."

As she marched into the butcher's and joined the queue, her heart was thumping so hard she had to loosen the neck of her blouse, and she felt on fire with exhilaration, disappointment and indignation.

Why in the world had Mercy Brixey had to poke her nose in and say about Jack being engaged to be married? The fact that it was true was beside the point. That girl was interested in Jack, not a doubt of it, and from what Charlotte could remember, Jack had been interested in her too.

Not that he'd actually said much, of course. That wasn't Jack's way. But there'd been a look about him when he'd mentioned her name that had told her more than any words could have done.

She'd be just right for him, too—a nice girl with a thousand times more in her than Rosa Clements, and a touch of class into the bargain. If she could have got them together maybe he would have seen that.

Charlotte shook her head impatiently. Why couldn't he see it for himself? How was it he could be so clever about some things and so stupid about others? Well, she wasn't going to give up this easily. If anything, she was more determined than ever to stop the match.

She stood in the butcher's queue, waiting while he gossiped to his customers about everything from the shortage of meat to the new motor ambulance that had been placed at the town's disposal by the War Office now that it was no longer needed for wounded troops, but Charlotte heard not a word. Instead, she planned the next stage in her campaign to put an end to Jack's ridiculous plan to marry Rosa Clements . . .

THE OPPORTUNITY arose a week or so later. It was a cold May afternoon when the wintry weather made a marked contrast to the warm spring sunshine of a few weeks earlier. Charlotte was alone in the house, and so, she supposed, was Rosa. The youngest Clements boy, who had been away from school with whooping cough, had now returned.

When she finished clearing up her baking things, Charlotte set the kettle on the hob, and went around to tap on the Clements' door. "Rosa, I'm just making a pot of tea. You're welcome to come in for a cup if you've got a minute."

Rosa was surprised. She was used to hostility from Charlotte these days, and her first reaction was one of caution. Then she pushed it aside. Jack wanted her to get on with his mother. However much he might try to pretend it made no difference to him, she knew it did. And she owed Jack his happiness, at least.

"All right, Mrs Hall," she said. "I'll be round in a moment."

Charlotte nodded, a little frightened by the way everything about

Rosa grated on her nowadays, but only the more determined to do what had to be done. She got out cups, milk and sugar, and waited. A few moments later, Rosa came in, Charlotte poured the tea, and they began to make small talk. Then, as if she could keep up the pretence no longer, Charlotte set down her cup with a clatter.

"Why do you want to marry our Jack?" she asked directly.

Rosa, taken by surprise, frowned and half-rose. "Mrs Hall . . . "

"No, sit down, Rosa. It's time we had a talk, you and I, and I'm no good at beating about the bush. Now you can tell me it's none of my business—most likely you will behind my back if not to my face—but it's my boys involved, so that's a risk I'm prepared to take."

Rosa's eyes narrowed, but she sat down again, straight-backed and composed. *"Boys*, Mrs Hall? It's only one of them I'm marrying."

"Yes, but you're in love with the other," Charlotte said. She saw the flicker of hurt in the dark eyes and knew she had hit upon the truth. "I've got eyes in my head," she went on. "I've seen you with Ted, and I've seen you with Jack, and I know which one it is you really want. And he wouldn't have you, would he? So you turned to Jack. For spite, Rosa, or for consolation? Not that it matters much. Either way, I won't stand by and see him hurt."

Rosa's face had turned quite white, apart from two spots of dark colour burning her cheeks.

"I don't know what you mean . . . "

"Oh, yes, you do, Rosa," Charlotte told her. "You know as well as I do you've had eyes for nobody but our Ted since you were just a little mite. You've chased after him for years. And now he's gone away, you've started on Jack. But not because you care for him, Rosa. He's just a stand-in. And he deserves better than that."

Rosa put down her cup with hands that trembled and got to her feet.

"I think I'd better go, Mrs Hall. I don't want to quarrel with you, but, like you said, it really isn't your business, is it? It's between me and Jack. He wants to marry me, and I'll make him a good wife. That's all that matters."

"It is not all that matters," Charlotte managed to position herself between Rosa and the door. "What do you think it'll do to him when he finds out it's not him you wanted but his brother?"

"He won't find out," Rosa said, and Charlotte threw up her hands.

"I gave you credit for more sense, Rosa. How can you keep a thing like that to yourself for thirty years—if it lasts that long. For on second thoughts, I can't imagine that it will."

Rosa stopped, her brows coming together.

"What do you mean?"

"I mean he'll get tired of you, Rosa. He won't have it at the moment, of course. He's too taken with the idea of making love to you. But how do you think you can keep up with him, and the life he's going to lead, eh?"

Rosa tossed her head. She was back on familiar ground.

"I don't see the difficulty, Mrs Hall. We were brought up next door to one another. Our fathers are both down the pit. Only mine is going to be a deputy."

Her tone, implying that Walter was a better man than James, infuriated Charlotte. She had one card left up her sleeve, and she hadn't been sure whether to play it or not. Now, by her own words, Rosa had forced her hand.

"You think so, eh, Rosa?" she asked, her voice rising. "Well, let me tell you something. Your father and Jack's have nothing in common at all. Nothing. You know who your father really was, eh?"

She saw a shudder run through the girl's body. The arrogance had gone now, leaving only fear, a fear that had lurked at the back of her mind all her life. She shook her head, trying to back away from Charlotte, but somehow she was unable to move.

"All right, I'll tell you, Rosa, whether you want to know or not. Walter Clements isn't your father. He just happened to marry your mother. Your father was one of the men on the fun fair—a gypsy, you know? One of the ones whose children come to the school in winter with their feet hanging out of their shoes and their noses running. The children who can't even read or write . . . "

She broke off at the sight of Rosa's face, her anger suddenly dissolving into remorse.

She shouldn't have said it, she knew. All her life she'd told her family that people who lived in glasshouses shouldn't throw stones, and now, in the heat of the moment, she'd done it herself. Shame filled her, and she took a step towards the girl, holding out her arms.

"I'm sorry, Rosa, I'm upset. Take no notice of what I just said. I'm out of my mind with worry about you marrying Jack, or I'd never have told you. But it doesn't alter anything . . . "

"You're right, Mrs Hall, it doesn't." Rosa had recovered her composure. She stood, straight-backed and beautiful, so that for a moment Charlotte saw clearly what it was about her that entranced Jack. "I'm going to marry him, and there's nothing you can say, however cruel, that's going to change that. Good afternoon, Mrs Hall, and thank you for the tea."

She crossed the room with such determination that Charlotte had no choice but to move out of her way. As the door closed after her, Charlotte collapsed on to a chair.

Well, she'd done it now and no mistake. She'd said things she should never have said, and when Jack got to hear about it, he'd most likely want nothing more to do with her. And who could blame him?

I've lost him, she thought, and it's all my own doing. But even if it comes to that, if I have done the smallest thing to break up the match, it will have been worth it.

ROSA'S composure lasted until she was out of sight of the house. Then she felt her knees go weak and her head spin with unshed tears.

She wanted to cry. She wanted to be alone and undisturbed. And there was only one place she could think of that would do.

Stopping only to fetch her coat, Rosa made for the woods.

As soon as she was in sight of the trees, she let the tears come, choking out of her in great, body-shaking bursts, and when she could cry no more she leaned against a tree trunk, her head sunk on to her chest, her arms wrapped about herself.

A gypsy. That was what she was then. The dreams she had woven about who she might be could hide the truth from her no longer. The only surprising thing was that no one had told her before. She stared, unseeing, at the tracery of new green, and her heart seemed to burst inside her, sending shivers of pain through every part of her body.

A gypsy. One of the fair folk. A wanderer, dirty and illiterate. No wonder Mrs Hall had not wanted her to marry Jack. Only one thing puzzled her. She had not seemed so opposed to her being with Ted. Or was that because in her heart of hearts she knew they belonged together?

Yes, it was Ted with her. It always had been, and it always would be. She'd tried to put him out of her mind and replace him with his brother—the very thing Charlotte had accused her of. But in reality she had not changed a thing. Jack had never been more than a substitute.

Oh, she'd been proud to be seen with him, it was true. He was clever and a bit of a hero into the bargain. And he seemed a cut above the rest, how she was not quite sure, but he was, all the same.

Perhaps Charlotte had been right in that, too. She and Jack weren't suited. She had attracted him, yes, but how long could she have held him? How long would it have been before he wanted more than she could give him?

Rosa shivered. She had known all the time all the things Charlotte had said to her. She just hadn't wanted to face them, pretending to herself that it didn't matter that she was marrying Jack for all the wrong reasons.

But it did matter, all the more now that she knew the truth about herself for certain—conceived because Ada, her mother, had gone with one of the fair folk, that despised breed. No wonder her mother had never quite been able to forgive Rosa for having been born! No wonder she had hated to look at the dark cause of her shame!

And how many other people in Hillsbridge knew the truth? A good many, Rosa guessed. It explained the whispers and the sniggers and the pointing fingers that had warned other children away from her. She had pretended to herself it was because she might be a witch, but it wasn't that at all. It had been because she was a gypsy's bastard.

I should have known, she thought. They only treated me the way they treated the children from the fair, but I was too proud to see it. And if I married Jack, it would begin all over again. And the fingers would point at him, too, and his children. If I loved him, maybe it wouldn't matter. But I don't love him, and so it wouldn't be fair to either of us.

She stood in the wood, weeping, but gradually even as she wept she became aware of the sweep of the trees and expanse of sky above her, and a sort of wonder began to run through her veins like shivers of hope.

The gypsies might be all the things people said of them, but they were something else besides. They were free. They moved where the fancy took them, they were not confined by the four walls of a house or tied to a job they hated. They had the very thing that Rosa had always prized most in life, next to Ted. Their freedom.

It came to her then that she had been granted a most miraculous escape. Willingly she would have traded her freedom for Ted's love. And Ted, being Ted, and almost as wild as she, would not have asked it. But Jack was different, and he would not have been the only one who was unhappy when the novelty wore off.

There and then, Rosa made up her mind. She would go away again, quickly and quietly before anyone could try to persuade her otherwise. Her father and the boys would be all right. They had Molly Hamblin now. And a clean break would be best for Jack, who still thought, mistakenly, that he loved her. She would go tonight, or tomorrow. And she would go not to Bristol, the city that could cage her, but to the countryside. Somewhere, she would find the space and freedom she loved, and then maybe she could discover at last who she really was.

Her face alight with a strange, new-found excitement, Rosa walked back through the woods for the last time. Tomorrow, Jack would find her gone. He would miss her for a little while, but not for long. She had been a crutch to him, proof to him that he was still a man in spite of his disability. Now, he no longer needed her.

As she passed Charlotte's house, she looked towards the window with mixed feelings. She would never forget Charlotte's cruelty, never forgive her for her destructive outburst. But in a strange way, she could not help admiring her.

You got your way, Mrs Hall. But God help us both if I ever get you as a mother-in-law, she thought—and knew that even now her hope of winning Ted would not die. It was, after all, the root of all her plans.

26

IN SEPTEMBER, rationing was stepped up—a result of the railwaymen's strike.

"Only an ounce of butter each a week!" Charlotte complained, unloading her shopping basket one wet autumn afternoon. "And an eighth of a pound worth of butcher's meat. That'll go nowhere at all!"

"They're blaming the miners, too, aren't they?" asked Dolly, who had come down for the afternoon. "Captain Fish had some visitors the other day, and they were talking about something called The Triple Alliance, and saying the miners should be on strike as well, by rights, and the transport workers, whoever they are."

"That's a lot of nonsense!" Charlotte said shortly. "Strikes never did anybody any good. And who wants the coal mines owned by the nation anyway? I can't see Lloyd George making a better boss than Hal, can you?"

Dolly shook her head.

"Senseless, that's what it is. Senseless!" Charlotte pronounced. And then, as she took a wedge of Jack's favourite Cheddar cheese out of her basket, she went on, "I wonder how they're feeding our Jack at that hostel place?"

Jack had left Hillsbridge for Bristol and was living in a hostel near to the University where he was studying. To Charlotte, it seemed he had recovered from Rosa's departure much better than she had dared hope. He had been upset to begin with, of course, and Charlotte salved her conscience by telling herself that he most likely realized it had all been for the best.

"I'm in hopes he'll meet that O'Halloran girl when he gets settled in," she confided to Dolly. "She was sweet on him, all right, you could see that, and they'd make a lovely couple."

"Don't you ever stop matchmaking, Mam?" Dolly teased. She was engaged again, to Victor Colman, the young man from Bath.

Amy, too, seemed fairly settled with Arthur Packer, the bookmaker's clerk, back now from the war and doing quite well for himself.

"Well, he always seems to have plenty to spend on our Amy, anyway," Dolly had remarked, and Charlotte suggested she should repeat the piece of information to Ted next time he came home.

"He's too keen on horse-racing for my liking," she said tartly. "And if he sees what Arthur Packer has to spend, perhaps it'll make him realize the bookie always wins in the end."

Since he had left home in the spring, Ted had done a variety of things, and none of them had really met with Charlotte's approval. He had gone to London first and got a job at the Alexandra Palace, cleaning windows. Then, when that had palled, he had worked his way around the south-east. By September, he had been a labourer in Harrow, stacked deck-chairs in Margate, and picked hops in Kent, and before the year was out, he was back in London, cleaning more windows at Somerset House.

But whatever he did, he was driven by restlessness. The only way to assuage his grief and pain was to constantly be moving on. Over two years in a prison camp would have been unsettling enough. To come home and find the girl he had loved so much dead had left him completely bereft and with no sense of direction.

The months went by, and the seasons, and still Ted drifted. And when summer came again, he took another job as a deck-chair attendant, this time at Weymouth, on the south coast.

As work went, it was one of his better jobs. He liked the feeling of sand between his toes and sun beating down on his face when it was fine. When it was not, there was some of the old comradeship of the trenches, squeezing under the canvas awning of the tea-stall, sharing a plate of cockles and a cigarette with the other beach attendants.

One summer afternoon, he was leaning against his pile of deck-chairs when he saw a party of four coming along the beach. He glanced at them idly, the two men in their blazers and straw boaters, the girls giggling and holding on to one another as they tried to walk on the soft sand. Then he pulled himself upright, staring in surprise.

Surely that was Marjorie Downs! He hadn't seen her since he had gone off to join the Somersets, but his mother had written in one of her letters that Marjie had gone off to marry a Canadian officer. Now, here she was in Weymouth, hurrying towards him, and looking as pleased to see him as if they had been the closest of friends.

"Ted!" she greeted him. "What are you doing here?"

"Working!" he rejoined. "That's more than you're doing."

"Nobody can work all the time. I'm on holiday."

"So I see!"

"You're looking well, Ted, and no mistake!" Marjorie was taking in his golden tan and sun-bleached hair. "And at one time we thought you were dead!"

The irony of her words struck them both at the same time, and her eyes fell away from his. "Oh, Ted, I'm so sorry."

Her companions were standing a little way off, watching impatiently. She half-turned as if to leave, but Ted caught at her arm. He couldn't let her go like this. She was his one last link with Becky.

"Were you there, Marjie, when she . . . ?"

"In Hillsbridge, you mean?" There was an expression in her eyes he could not read—evasive, perhaps. "Yes."

"What happened to her, Marjie? I've never been able to find out the rights of it."

"Oh, Ted, it's a long time ago . . . " Again the evasion.

386

"Come on, Marjie!" one of her friends called, and she looked over her shoulder.

"All right. I'm coming."

"Please, Marjie! I must know!"

She hesitated. "I can't tell you now, Ted. It's a long story, and you've got customers and my friends are waiting."

"Can I see you some other time, then? Your husband . . . "

"He's not my husband. Just a friend. Oh, oh all right. I'll see you at the entrance to the pier tonight. Say half past eight? Wait for me if I'm late." Then she had gone, giggling with the others as they went off along the sands.

AS THE DAY wore on, he began to wonder if Marjorie would keep the appointment, and somehow it seemed increasingly unlikely, so that by the time he had bolted down his supper at his lodgings and changed from the casual clothes he wore on the beach into a more respectable jacket and trousers, he was almost certain she would not. But a few minutes after eight-thirty he saw her coming along the promenade alone.

He walked to meet her, and she caught at his arm, smiling at him mischievously. "Did you think I wouldn't get away? You don't know how crafty I can be, Ted. Or else you've forgotten!"

He ignored this. The last thing he wanted now was intrigue. "Shall we go on the pier?" he suggested. "We ought to be able to talk quietly there."

"Yes, all right. It's a nice night," she agreed, though not very enthusiastically, he thought.

"I thought you got married, Marjie," he said, putting off the moment when he would ask her again about Becky. "What happened to your husband?"

She pulled a face. "I didn't like him much. Uniform does a lot to hide the real man, don't you think? In it, he seemed very strong and masterful. Out of it . . . well, he was just a bully. And nobody's going to bully *me*, thank you very much."

"No," he said, but the same thought had occurred to both of them, and they fell silent. Then, when they had passed through the turnstile and the crush of people around the first bank of fun machines, he turned to her again.

"I'm grateful to you coming to meet me like this, Marjie. I know it can't have been easy for you. But like I said to you this afternoon,

I've never really been able to find out the truth about Becky. Her father was dead too by the time I got home from the war, and her mother in the asylum. And Mam didn't seem to know anything—or if she did, she wasn't saying."

Marjorie looked puzzled. "But she went to see your Mam," she said.

"What?"

"Rosa Clements saw her coming out of your house a few days before she died. We were talking about it at the shop . . . "

"But Mam never said anything to me! She just said Becky was home from Wycherley."

Marjorie looked embarrassed. "Perhaps I've put my foot in it then. But you're asking me about Becky, and you'd do better not to, Ted, honestly."

"Why?"

"Because you won't like it. Look, she's been dead a long time, now. Why don't you just leave it?"

"You can't back out of it now, Marjie," Ted said. "I want to know what's going on—and what people have been keeping back from me."

"All right." She took a deep breath, leaning against the pier balustrade and looking out to sea. "They'd moved house, of course, before all this happened. But she used to write to me when she could, and sometimes, if she was in Hillsbridge with her mother, shopping, she'd come into Fords to see me. That was how I found out about Rupert Thorne."

"Who's Rupert Thorne?"

"A relation of Becky's. Her father always wanted them to make a match of it. Didn't she tell you about him?"

"Yes, she did mention him. I'd just forgotten his name. But she couldn't stand him."

"I know. But Alfred wanted it, and when Alfred wanted something . . . Anyway, I think that's why he got her home from Wycherley—so that Rupert could court her."

"You mean he was going out with her?" Ted asked, shocked.

"Yes, but . . . she was able to take a rise out of him at first. He'd broken his arm, you see, and was in plaster, and she told me once it was almost funny seeing him trying to . . . " She broke off, sudden tears filling her eyes. "That was just Becky being brave, of course. If she hadn't laughed about it, she'd have gone raving mad."

"Go on," Ted said grimly into the small silence.

"Well, I don't really know any more for certain," Marjorie explained hesitantly. "Suddenly there was this . . . silence. She didn't write, or come into the shop, although Rosa said she'd seen her coming out of your house. I couldn't understand it at the time. But afterwards . . . " She broke off again.

"Afterwards?" Ted pressed her. "After what?"

"Well, it was something I overheard at the funeral, and I started putting two and two together. Rupert was there, but not with the family mourners as you'd expect. And Alfred got in one of his rages when he saw him. There was quite a scene—they almost came to blows. And Alfred was talking about something Rupert had given to Becky, asking where he'd got it, and saying Dr Froster wanted to know, too."

"Dr Froster?" Ted said, puzzled. "What's he got to do with it?"

"Well . . . " She bit her lip, her eyes flickering to Ted's face and away again. "This really is conjecture, of course. But I think she was going to have a baby, and he'd given her something to get rid of it."

Ted stood rigid with amazement and horror. "A *baby? Becky?*"

"I know. It doesn't sound like her. But it's the only thing that fits. I think when his arm was out of plaster, he started molesting her and things got out of hand. Then, when he realized what he'd done, he got the wind up and gave her something to get rid of it. Perhaps she took more than she was supposed to, I don't know. All I keep thinking is . . . if only she'd told me! But then, I can understand, really. She was ashamed, I suppose."

Ted stood stunned. Beneath him the boards of the pier seemed to rock; the sway of the waves nauseated him; and the sea wind took his breath away. At last he said, "Do you think that's why she went to see my mother?"

"To get in touch with you. I think so."

"But Mam said she died just after they heard I was missing . . . Oh God!" he stopped, horrified, as a new thought struck him. "You don't think she took too much of whatever it was on purpose, do you?"

Marjorie bowed her head. "I don't know."

"Oh, Becky—Becky!" It was an anguished cry torn from deep inside him, and for a moment they stood in silence staring out to sea. Then, with a suddenness that almost frightened her, his grief had turned to anger, white-hot, searing, cauterizing.

389

"Rupert Thorne—the bastard! She didn't just die, I knew it! Oh let him wait—I'll kill him, Marjie, I will!"

"Ted, Ted, don't do anything silly . . . " She was trembling now. "It's over. Even Dr Froster's dead, isn't he? They're all dead . . . "

"Rupert Thorne's not dead." Ted's eyes were grey and steely. "And I'll get to the bottom of this if it's the last thing I do. I owe her that much, Marjie."

She nodded. She, too, had lost her friend.

"What will you do?" she asked.

"I don't know yet. But I'll tell you one thing. The first train home, I'll be on it. And that bastard Rupert Thorne is going to wish he'd never been born!"

CHARLOTTE was startled when Ted arrived home the following day without so much as a word of warning. And the look of him alarmed her still more. She had seen him tense before, but never had she seen him quite like this—no, not even when she had told him Rebecca was dead. There was a hardness about his mouth that had not been there before, an expression in his eyes that defied description. And when Nipper rushed up to him, trying to jump up for a pat, he pushed him aside with only an impatient, "Down, boy!"

"Well, this is a surprise!" she said, trying to hide her misgivings. "I never expected you today. If I'd known you were coming . . . "

"I didn't know myself until last night," he said, shortly. "Mam, I want to talk to you."

"Well, give me a chance to put the kettle on first," she said, but he was in no mood to wait.

"I've been told Becky came to see you just before she died. Is that right?"

The kettle slipped out of her hand, landing on the hob with a thud, so that water splashed out of the spout. Dear Lord, who could have told him? she thought, but aloud she said, "For goodness sake, Ted, what is all this?"

"Did she come, Mam?"

Charlotte sighed then, straightening up. "Well, yes, she did. But . . . "

"Then why didn't you tell me?"

"Because, oh, I don't know, I didn't want to upset you, I suppose."

"You didn't want to upset me! She was dead, my girl, and you didn't want to upset me!"

"It wasn't like that, Ted . . . "

"Why did she come, Mam?"

"*Why?*" She hadn't expected that question. "I don't know, Ted. I've often asked myself the same."

"What do you mean?"

"It was funny, really. When she came to the door, I thought it was because she'd heard about you, being missing, I mean. But I was wrong. She didn't know. I could tell that by her reaction. And then, well, she went again. I never saw her again."

"You let her go?" Ted said. "Without finding out why she'd come?"

"Oh, Ted," Charlotte spread her hands helplessly. "Don't you think I've blamed myself a hundred times for what happened? But you must understand how it was. I was upset . . . I didn't know what I was doing. I thought you'd been killed, and . . . " She broke off, pressing her hands to her face. "Look, I'm sorry, son, I should have told you, but I didn't want you to think . . . "

"Think what?"

"That she'd . . . done away with herself when she heard you'd been killed." She turned away from him. "That's what I keep tormenting myself with, you see, that if I hadn't told her you were dead . . . Oh, Ted, I wouldn't have had this happen for anything in the world, and now . . . "

"Oh, Mam." He was no longer angry at her, but all the more certain of what he had to do. "You can stop blaming yourself. I don't think she took her life intentionally. Not Becky. She was too religious for that—and she'd never have given up that easily. I think there was far more to it than that."

"What do you mean?" she asked. Slowly Ted related to her what Marjorie had told him. As he spoke, his anger mounted again, and the need for revenge boiled up in him.

"I'm going to Bristol," he said. "There'll be a bus, won't there?"

"Yes, but . . . "

"I'm going to see that bastard Thorne. And I'm going to smash his bloody face in."

"Ted, wait a minute . . . stop . . . think!"

"I've thought enough. It's time now for a bit of action." He gesticulated at the kettle. "Have that on the boil when I get back, Mam. I shall probably need it."

He went out. Helplessly Charlotte watched from the doorway as he passed out of sight along the rank. She was shaking now, terrified of what he might do. Perhaps if she went with him . . . But that wouldn't do any good. He'd never let her. But he needed somebody with him, somebody to stop him from doing something stupid . . .

Jack. Jack was the one, of course. He was already in Bristol, and if she could get hold of him, perhaps he could meet Ted off the bus and talk to him. If he'd listen to anyone, he'd listen to Jack. But how was she going to get in touch with him? She couldn't send a telegram, there wouldn't be any way to explain what she wanted, and it might not reach him in time. The answer was to telephone—there would sure to be a telephone at the university—but Charlotte had never used a telephone in her life.

She stood for a moment with her hand over her mouth, thinking. There was an 'attended call office' in the centre of town, but she didn't know how it worked. Perhaps if she ran up the hill to Captain Fish's, they would let her telephone from there. Come to think of it, Dolly could get through for her. She knew how to use the contraption. Since it had been installed she used it to ring through orders to the shops.

Yes, that was the thing to do. And without further delay, she went.

RUPERT THORNE'S office in Bristol looked out across a pleasant, tree-lined square, and from the sash window he was able to watch the motors and the horse-drawn wagons visiting the other premises in the square.

On that summer afternoon, he stood at his window, hands in pockets, gazing out idly as he toyed with a delicate problem of litigation on behalf of one of his clients. But his concentration was momentarily broken when he saw a figure walking urgently towards his offices. He noted the jaunty cap and cheaply cut suit and half-turned away with distaste. What was King James' Square coming to that people of that type could patronize it? If it was slipping down the social scale, he would have to mention to his senior partners that he thought it was time they looked for new, more exclusive, premises.

Since qualifying as a solicitor, Rupert Thorne had been moderately successful. He had been absorbed into the firm where he had taken his articles, and although he was not much liked, the other partners had found him useful for taking the brunt of the cases they did not want.

No matter was too trivial for Rupert if the client had sufficient social standing, and many was the time he had burnt the midnight oil in an effort to find a loop-hole that might serve the purpose of some greedy, overbearing bully or his rich and spoiled lady. By a curiously clever juggling act, Rupert managed to combine an overweening desire for social advancement with a streak that was almost cruel in its ruthlessness, and he somehow managed to command a respect that was a constant surprise to those who knew him.

Rupert had married soon after the end of the war, and with typical craftiness he had chosen a wife who could help him further his career —the daughter of a much-respected accountant in the city. Unfortunately, she was not the prettiest of girls, and when Rupert was alone and a little the worse for port wine, he sometimes found himself comparing her with his image of a frightened horse—all nose and long teeth. Occasionally he even thought of Becky Church with genuine regret. But he accepted that in this life it was just not possible to have everything. And on the whole, he could not grumble at the way things had turned out.

That afternoon, however, he was thinking not of Rebecca, but of the pert little stenographer who had started working for the firm, delighted that most of the boring male clerks had been replaced by ladies since the war. The stenographer looked as if she might give a man the pleasure his wife did not.

A smile curved his thick lips as he turned away from the window, reaching regretfully for the file he should be working on. It wasn't a day for work. It was a day for going for a nice motor-car ride with a pretty girl and a well-stocked picnic hamper. The sort of day . . .

A tap on the door interrupted his thoughts and there she was— the stenographer.

"Mr Thorne . . . "

"Ah, come in, Miss . . . ah . . . "

"There's a gentleman to see you Mr Thorne. He doesn't have an appointment, but he says it is most urgent . . . "

"Ask his name and tell him to wait . . . " He broke off in surprise as the door was flung open and a man entered the room—the same man he just had seen crossing the square. "Just a moment!" he demanded. "Where do you think you are going?"

Ted faced him across the desk. "I've come to see you. My name is Ted Hall."

"Ted Hall!" Recognition flashed across his flaccid features. With a wave of his hand, he dismissed the girl. "Well, you'd better come in, I suppose. What do you want?"

"To talk to you about Becky."

A nerve jumped in Rupert's cheek. "Becky," he repeated woodenly.

"Yes. I want to know why she died."

"Now how should I know?" Rupert blustered.

"Because I think you were the cause of it!" Ted flung at him.

Rupert was brick-red now. "That's a serious accusation, Hall."

"It's a serious matter. What did you give her, eh?" Ted demanded. "What was it her father was asking about at her funeral —and the doctor wanted to know about too? Was it . . . "

He was interrupted by a commotion on the stairs outside, footsteps, and the stenographer's voice raised in protest. Then the door opened again, and to his surprise Jack came into the room.

"What are you doing here?" Ted asked, startled, and Rupert Thorne seized his opportunity.

"Get out of my office, the pair of you! I have no wish to talk to either of you! And if you don't leave at once, my girl will call the police . . . "

"The police, is it?" Ted went around the desk to him, pushing Jack aside. "Oh, I'd like to see you call the police, I would. If you call the police, there's a thing or two *I* should like to say to them, and after that, they'll be asking you some very awkward questions!"

The colour drained from Rupert's face. For a moment he stared at Ted, his eyes bright with fear and hatred, then he stabbed the air with a trembling finger. "Don't you threaten me! If you stir up trouble, it'll be Becky who will suffer. I shall tell them what she was really like—crazy for a man, any man—throwing herself at whoever came her way until she got what was coming to her. And then begging me for something to get rid of her bastard. I should never have helped her. I should have left her to rot . . . "

At that point, Ted hit him. His fist connected square with his jaw. "You bastard!" he spat at him, and would have hit him again if Jack had not intervened, catching at his arm.

"Ted, no!"

Rupert Thorne sat down heavily in his padded chair, one hand coming up to caress his bruised jaw bone, and his eyes, wide and shocked, stared at Ted strangely.

"Leave him!" Jack said again.

Ted jerked his arm free, a tremor running through his body. Then he leaned forward so that he towered over the hunched figure of Rupert.

"I hope you rot in hell, you filthy bastard!" he said.

Then he swung round and marched out of the office, with Jack following, past the fluttering stenographer, down the stairs, and out into the undisturbed peace of King James' Square.

SERGEANT EYLES came knocking at the front door of number eleven, Greenslade Terrace, soon after Charlotte had cleared away the breakfast things next morning.

Bluff and unsmiling he stood there on the path, waiting while she fetched Ted to the door. He knew the Halls, had known them for years, and didn't like what he had to do.

Ted, who had slept the clock round, came downstairs at his mother's insistent calling.

"Morning, Sergeant. You'd better come in. Mam says you want a word with me."

The sergeant stepped into the doorway, his bulk shutting out the morning sunshine.

"From what I've been told, you went to Bristol yesterday afternoon, to the office of a solicitor, a Mr Rupert Thorne."

Ted groaned. The bugger had actually had the gall to go to the police about it, then, just because he'd taken a swing at him.

"Yes, Sergeant, I was there. But if he's making accusations, there's a thing or two I'd like looked into myself. If he says . . . "

"Hang about, hang about!" the sergeant interrupted. "Mr Thorne isn't saying anything."

"Oh!" Ted was nonplussed. "Then what . . . "

The sergeant rolled his lips together slowly until little globules of saliva appeared.

"Mr Thorne's saying nothing," he said at last, "because he's dead."

"Dead? Rupert Thorne?" Ted repeated, his expression more puzzled than shocked.

"That's right, dead," the sergeant repeated. "And from what I can make of it, you caused his death by striking him in the face, Ted. I shall have to ask you to come along down to the police station with me—right away if you please."

Ted stood silent, too stunned to argue, but Charlotte, who had overheard, came to the door, wiping her hands on her apron.

"What's this? What's going on, Sergeant?"

"A man is dead, Mrs Hall," the sergeant told her, grim-faced. "Your Ted is believed to have caused his death. That's murder. And unless I'm much mistaken, that's what he'll be charged with. Now come on, young feller-me-lad, let's get going."

"Wait!" Charlotte caught at his sleeve. "Are you going to keep him there?"

"Not for long, I shouldn't think. He'll be detained until our inquiries are complete, then he'll be released on bail I shouldn't wonder, until the quarter sessions or assizes. Now, if you're ready, young Hall . . . "

He stepped back out into the sunshine, and Charlotte could only watch helplessly as a subdued and shaken Ted was led away down the hill.

27

SERGEANT EYLES was wrong. There was no bail for Ted. After he had been up before the magistrates to be charged, he was taken off in the Black Maria to Stack Norton Prison, ten miles away.

There would be a post-mortem straight away, and the inquest would be opened 'for purposes of identification only'. But after that it could be weeks, or even months, before the workings of justice lurched their way through a resumed inquest to an assize or quarter session. And until that happened, they were going to keep Ted locked up between weekly court appearances, as Charlotte was told when she called at the police station for the fourth time in two days.

"Best thing you can do for him is fix him up with a solicitor," Sergeant Eyles advised in his slow drawl.

"I see. Well, p'raps we should."

They had discussed it last night, sitting around the kitchen table in a family council of war, and Jack, who had come home immediately when he had heard the news, had said much the same thing.

"Look, Mam, he's got to have a solicitor. Somebody to look after his interests."

"I admit I'm beat when it comes to something like this," James said. "But you've had a good education, Jack. You're well up with it all."

"Not with anything to do with the law, Dad," Jack told him. "This is a serious thing. It's not like going to court for getting rowdy after a few too many on a Saturday night. It's murder he's charged with. If you ask me, he ought to have somebody there even when they open the inquest, to make sure everything's done as it should be."

They sat in silence for a moment or two, digesting it. Then James asked, "What's it going to cost?"

"Oh, never mind the money!" Charlotte said impatiently. "Our Jack's right. We shall have to ask Mr Clarence. He can give us advice, and if somebody has to go along to the court, he can go. That'll save our Jack getting involved."

"But, Mam, I am involved," Jack put in. "I think you should get Mr Clarence in, of course I do, and the sooner the better, but that's not going to let me out. I was there. I saw what happened. They'll want me to give evidence to the coroner, at any rate. They told me that when they took my statement."

"Well, of course you'll want to get up and say what happened, whether they want you to or not," James put in. "It's a good job you were there, Jack."

Charlotte said nothing. Privately, she was not sure she agreed, and in the last twenty-four hours she had found herself regretting that she had summoned Jack to the scene. Being involved in something like this wouldn't do him any good at all, either at college or when he came to look for a job. As far as helping Ted, she couldn't see that Jack's evidence was either here or there. For surely anyone with a grain of sense must know there had been some kind of mistake. Ted was slightly built; Rupert Thorne had been a bull of a man. It was madness to say Ted could have killed him with one blow.

As if echoing her thoughts, Jack said musingly, "I can't understand it. I've gone over and over it, and I still can't. It didn't look as if our Ted had even hurt him. He looked more surprised than anything. Then he just sat down in his chair and stared at us. It was a strange look, vacant almost. But I tell you this, and I'll swear to it in any court in the land. Rupert Thorne was alive when we left him."

"Could somebody else have gone in after you left?" Charlotte asked.

Jack shook his head. "Well, that I wouldn't know. I suppose if there was more than one blow, it'll come out at the post-mortem. But I don't see how one blow could kill a man of his size, anyway. I'd have thought it would take a bullet or a hatchet to do that. It isn't even as though he fell. No, he just sat there."

The group around the table fell silent. There was nothing more to say, yet they were unwilling to leave one another, unwilling to move out of the bright pool of light thrown by the lamp.

At last, Charlotte got up, stirring the dying embers of the fire and swivelling the kettle on to the hob.

"How would we get by without a cup of tea? What this old pot has seen us through is nobody's business."

James got up then, stretching. "Ah, and it'll see us through again. It's not the end of the world you know, not yet."

"Oh, how you manage to take everything so calm, I'll never know!" Charlotte exploded. "You'll be telling us next, worse things happen at sea!"

"Well, so they do," James said philosophically. "It don't do a bit of good, getting in a state, Lotty. Not one bit."

Charlotte snorted impatiently.

"Dad's right, you know," Jack told her, taking the teapot out of her hand and spooning tea from the caddy into it. "It doesn't help anybody. But what will help our Ted is a good solicitor."

Charlotte snatched the pot back again, irritated to have the task taken from her.

"Give that here, Jack. P'raps you're right about that solicitor. We'll have to see."

"P'RAPS you're right," she said again next morning to Sergeant Eyles, and did not add that, to her, the calling in of a solicitor seemed like admitting the seriousness of what was happening.

Besides that, she had an inbred distrust of professional people, whom she considered looked down their noses at ordinary working folk. But what both Jack and Sergeant Eyles had said was true. Ted was in serious trouble, and perhaps it was time Arthur Clarence, the one and only solicitor in Hillsbridge, was called in.

She turned it over in her mind as she walked along the street, but even preoccupied as she was, she could hardly avoid noticing the way heads turned as she passed.

She knew what they were saying, of course—that they had always known Ted would come to no good—and the knowledge hurt. She had always been so proud of her family's reputation, and the fact that none of them had ever been in trouble with the police. Now, she guessed there would always be somebody who would be ready to exaggerate out of spite or jealousy, the story becoming more distorted with each telling.

By the time she reached Mr Clarence's office, her mind was made up. She would go and see him, and she would do it now, before her courage failed her.

The office was on the first floor, above a row of shops on the main street. For some reason it had always intrigued her, the impressive brass plaque on the wall, the steep flight of stairs leading to a murky unknown, the patterned glass windows bearing the legend Willoughby & Clarence—although only the oldest people in the town could remember a time when there had been a Mr Willoughby. Now it overawed her too, but with a quick, determined movement, she rang the bell beside the brass plate, pushed open the door, and started up the steep staircase.

Josia Horler, Arthur Clarence's stooped and balding clerk, met her at the top, motioning her into the glorified cupboard that did duty as a waiting room. "You've come to see Mr Clarence, I dare say," he said gravely, and she could tell he knew exactly why she was here.

He left her, and after a few minutes returned to show her into Arthur Clarence's office, a small, frowsty room, cluttered with piles of musty, pink-ribboned documents. Behind the large, leather-topped desk sat Arthur Clarence. He rose to greet her, then sat down once more, pressing his fingertips together beneath his chin and regarding her solemnly from behind owlish spectacles.

"You want me to represent your son, Mrs Hall. Is that it?"

"Yes . . . well . . . we thought . . . "

"I'm not at all sure I'm the person to help you," he said seriously. "Murder is a grave charge, and it's not something I've had many dealings with. In many ways, Hillsbridge is a backwater, you know."

"But we only want someone to keep an eye on his interests, Mr Clarence," she explained. "It was an accident—it wasn't murder."

Mr Clarence tapped his fingers together lightly. "But to prove it, that's the difficulty. When it comes to something like this, I don't think I'm the person you require."

"Are you saying you won't take the case on, Mr Clarence?" she ventured.

"No, but I feel there may be someone else better able to help you than I."

399

"In Hillsbridge?"

The fingers tapped together again. "I do see the problem. Anticipated it almost, you could say. I even took the liberty of making a few enquiries as to who is a good criminal lawyer . . . "

"Criminal!" Charlotte was on her feet, indignation making her bold. "Ted is no criminal!"

"Mrs Hall, please don't misunderstand me . . . "

"I don't think I do, Mr Clarence! You won't help because you've already made up your mind our Ted is guilty, and you won't soil your hands with him. Maybe you're even against him because Rupert Thorne was one of your own. Well, we can manage without grudging help of that sort. I'm sorry to have taken up your time!"

"Mrs Hall, please, don't take it like this . . . " he protested.

"How else am I supposed to take it, Mr Clarence? No, don't bother to see me out. I can find my own way."

"But Mrs Hall . . . "

She hardly heard him. The blood was singing too loudly in her ears. The cheek of the man! The barefaced cheek, to call Ted a criminal like that! Oh, she'd show him they could manage without the likes of him, just as they always had. And when Ted's innocence was proved, she'd tell everybody about the way that stuffed shirt Clarence had treated her!

She clattered down the stairs and into the street. It was a sultry day, and before she had gone far the sweat was prickling on her forehead, but her indignation drove her on. Even in the steepest part of the hill she did not falter, and it was only when she reached the corner of the rank that the mist before her eyes and the drumming in her ears made her slow down. As she did so, she realized she was trembling all over, and her legs felt as heavy as lead. Her own weakness only added to her impatience, and she drove herself on, throwing open the scullery door and going into the house.

"Jack—James!" she called, but the effort of finding her voice on top of all the other efforts seemed suddenly too much. The room swam around her, and she groped her way along the stone sink and cupboard.

"James!" she called again. But there was no reply, and in the doorway her knees buckled. She clung to the frame, gasping. The settle was so close, yet it looked far away. Without much hope she took a step towards it. Then the ground came up to meet her with a rush, and the mists closed in around her.

CHARLOTTE WAS ILL.

She 'hadn't been right' as James put it, since the day she fainted in the kitchen, although as soon as she came round, she had insisted on taking charge once more.

Try as James might to persuade her to go up to bed, she had refused to leave the settle in the kitchen, saying it would finish her to be cut off from the family at a time like this.

But clearly she was not well. Although it was high summer, she kept having bouts of shivering, and it hurt her to breathe too deeply.

She didn't look well, either. Most of the time, her skin was too pallid, moist and lifeless, except when she seemed to burn up into a scarlet flush.

"It's nothing," she insisted. "Just my time of life."

James, knowing her as he did, was certain it was more than that. He had seen the pain in her face when she drew a deep breath; he'd seen her stop when she thought no one was looking, head down, hands splayed against the upper part of her chest. And he had heard her cough too when she exerted herself—a rasping cough that seemed to leave her breathless and shaken.

He told her she should pay a visit to the doctor, but she dismissed that suggestion as if it were the silliest thing she had ever heard.

"Doctor? We can't afford a doctor's bills at a time like this!"

"But Lotty, your health comes first . . . "

"I'll be all right," she said shortly, and he sighed with resignation. It was a waste of breath trying to tell Lotty what to do.

For more than two weeks she soldiered on, up one day, down the next, but on the day of the resumed inquest, her temperature suddenly shot up, her breathing became worse, and although she still stayed stubbornly downstairs for as long as she could, huddled over the fire while icy waves rippled over her burning skin each time she moved, at last there was nothing for it but to give in and go to bed.

"It's my own fault," she told James through chattering teeth. "This all started the day I came rushing up the hill in a temper. My vest was wringing wet, and I let it go cold on me. I've caught a chill, that's all."

"Ah, I expect you'm right," James said stoically, not bothering to voice his own opinion as to the cause of her illness—that this time events had simply been too much for her.

"Try not to think about it, Lotty," he told her. "T'won't do no good. If I know our Ted, he'll be as chirpy as a sparrow. If the Germans couldn't break him, I'm darned sure Stack Norton isn't going to."

She tried to answer, but her breath was short and hard, and he went on, "Now look. Our Jack's gone off to the inquest, and when he gets home, he'll be able to tell us all about it. You get some rest now. I don't like the look of you at all."

Get some rest! As if she could, knowing her boys were both in Bristol being looked on as common criminals. Ted and Jack, two of the finest boys that ever were.

She wished now she hadn't been so hasty with Mr Clarence, for she couldn't get it out of her head that if he had been able to represent Ted, there would have been no need for Jack to be mixed up in the business at all.

And although it was Ted who was accused of the murder, nevertheless it was Jack she was worried about. So convinced was she of Ted's innocence, she simply could not conceive of anyone doubting his story. And once it was over, that would be the end of it as far as he was concerned. He would treat it with the same stoic resignation as James, putting it down to experience. What was more, it might even help him to get over Becky Church—the only thing that had really ever touched him deeply. This nasty business could very well be the way to cauterize that wound.

But Jack was a different matter. In spite of his wartime experiences, she still thought of Jack as too gentle for this kind of brush with vulgarity, and she couldn't stop thinking it could damage his career.

It was as if all her life she had been working towards the moment when he would achieve his ambition and step away from the trap of a miner's life and into the world where he belonged. And that now, by her own actions in sending him after Ted that day, and refusing legal advice when the whole horrible business had exploded around them, she had brought it all tumbling down.

The worst can't happen, she thought. If there's any justice, it can't.

But in the corner of her mind, a small persistent devil seemed to taunt her. "You got rid of Rosa Clements. You were needlessly cruel. Maybe this is your punishment, to see him back where he started, or worse, and all through your own doing."

With a touch of her old impatience she shifted herself on the pillows, telling herself not to be so stupid. But the devil was still there, mocking her from every corner of the room. Wherever she looked, he was there, his small, ugly face forming part of the pattern on the wallpaper and somehow working its way into the array of bottles on the dressing-table.

Sleep began to overcome her, weighing down her eyelids and wafting her back and forth like the waves of the incoming tide, but the devil did not go away. His nagging became more insistent, so that her whole mind, waking and sleeping, was full of it.

If things went wrong for Jack now, it would be more than a misfortune—it would be a betrayal of his birthright. But she was the only one who knew that, the only one who could tell him he must not sacrifice his due, but be true to himself and the blood that was in him.

The secret she had kept for more than twenty years was sharp and clear again, just as it had been that day in the Rector's study when she had asked for his help to educate Jack. The smell of the early summer afternoon was in her nostrils, and she felt again the potent mixture of grief and desire that had made her ache with a strange restlessness and a need for . . . what? She did not know. She had never known, any more than she had known where the attraction lay between a miner's wife, twenty-two years old, who had borne four children, and the Rector's nephew, a college boy, and four years her junior. She had not known then, and in the years afterwards she had sometimes wondered how it could have been.

Now, she did not stop to wonder. It was all so real—much more real than the bedroom where she lay sick with fever—and she felt as if she could reach out across the years and touch him, his hair, fairer even than James's, long, straight and thick, his finely chiselled cheekbones, his dreaming eyes, his wide, sensitive mouth.

Oh, Jack was so much like him! So much like him she had never ceased to wonder that James could not see it. Sometimes the look of him had been a knife-thrust in her heart. She had learned to ignore it, to push the memory to the back of her mind. But now it was here, real and vivid, and she was too weak . . . too weak . . .

She had met him in the churchyard. She had been on her knees in the sweet-smelling grass, putting her finger into the pot of flowers that stood on the small, fresh mound to test the level of the water. She heard his footsteps on the path, but she was too lost in her thoughts to take much notice.

"Excuse me, but if you want a jug to refill the vase, there's one in the vestry."

She looked up, startled, seeing him through a haze of tears, and unable to speak for the knot in her throat.

"I . . . I'm sorry . . . " He was confused now, guilty at having intruded on her grief.

"It's all right." With an effort she swallowed the tears. "This is . . . my little girl's grave, you see."

"I'm sorry," he said again, and suddenly she was almost as full of pity for him as for herself. He had only meant to be helpful. He couldn't have known Florrie had been dead just a few weeks. There was no stone yet to mark her grave, and Charlotte didn't know if there ever would be. James's money hardly went around to cover necessities, and they were still struggling after the expense of the funeral.

It was only after the young man had gone and she had left the churchyard on her way to meet Jim and Dolly from school that she wondered who he was and how he had known about the jug in the vestry. She wasn't a churchgoer, her family had been Baptists, and when she had married James she had gone along to the Methodist Chapel with him. But in a town the size of Hillsbridge, she knew most people by sight if not by name, and she was curious about him.

She mentioned him to Peggy when she collected Fred—Peggy looked after him when Charlotte went to tend the grave because she was afraid people would object to him running about in the church-yard—and Peggy thought she knew who the young man was.

"That's Rector Archer's nephew, I expect, here for a holiday. His people are out abroad somewhere, but he had to come home with one of those tropical illnesses, I heard." Peggy seemed to know everything!

Charlotte did not give much thought to the Rector's nephew. There was not much time in her life for thinking. But a few days later, when she went to the churchyard with some fresh flowers for Florrie's grave, he was there again, sitting under the tree with an artist's easel and painting.

They nodded to one another, shyly, and as she crossed the grass to the tap to fill her vase with water, her heart was thudding and there was a strange expectancy in her mingled with her sadness for her child.

On the way back she glanced at his painting. It was quite good, the trees in blossom above the deep, gravestone-sprinkled grass and the occasional splash of colour from a bank of flowers. But she said nothing.

While she was arranging the flowers, he came over and stood behind her, and this time she knew he was there. There was a fine-honed, tingling awareness in her that she could not place, except that it was bound up, somehow, with this young man, and it seemed a lifetime before he spoke.

"You come here a lot."

"Yes," she said. "I'd stay here all the time if I could. But I've got other children at home."

"Have you?" He sounded surprised.

"Three," she told him. "I love them all, but . . . "

"They don't make up for losing her," he said, and his words seemed to touch the heart of her pain.

She looked back at the small, flower-decked mound. There were no tears in her eyes now, only the dry ache. "She was fifteen months old, and so pretty! She could talk . . . well, say a few words, anyway . . . She broke off, embarrassed suddenly. "But you don't want to hear my troubles."

"I don't mind," he said. "I've got plenty of time."

She looked at him in surprise. Plenty of time? Who in the world had plenty of time? As if he had read her mind, he smiled unexpectedly, his face lighting up. "I've been in India since I left school. My father's with the diplomatic corps. But I had this fever, and I had to come home. I'm going to Oxford in the autumn, so I've got the summer to kill."

She nodded, and as their eyes met, it was there again, the spark of sympathy, the fusion of two personalities that transcends age and class.

At once she felt alarm. "I must go."

"I may see you again. I'm not much of an artist. It'll take me a long while to finish this painting."

It was a week before she dared go to the churchyard again, a week when she could not get him out of her thoughts. But Florrie's grave had to be tended, and besides . . . If she was truthful, she wanted to see him again, very much.

She had never thought, never stopped to think for a moment that there could ever be any man in her life but James. He had been her first love, and she had assumed, naïvely, that it would go on forever.

The first glow faded with the babies and the endless round of work, but she was almost too tired to notice it had gone. Sometimes, she listened to James snoring softly beside her when their love making was done and wondered why she no longer felt the restless desire of their early times. But the sense of loss was only a vague, sad ache, nothing more.

It was only after Florrie died that the dissatisfaction was fanned to something close to hatred. Grief, then, was new to her, raw and terrifying in its intensity, and it took her in a hundred different ways. Sometimes she wished she could be alone and do nothing but think about Florrie, at other times she threw herself into everything she did with a vigour that almost disgusted her. And sometimes she wanted to talk about the baby she had lost, remembering all her little ways, until the tears came hot and searing, to heal for a little while at least. But James was curiously reluctant to talk about Florrie. When she began to reminisce and weep, he would get up and leave her, going out into the garden to dig, or hoe, or just wander, and it seemed to Charlotte he simply did not care.

Years afterwards, she realized she had been wrong—he cared very much, and it was displays of emotion he could not deal with. But at the time she was too young and too hurt to understand, and it seemed to her that she was alone just when she most needed support. And it was into this mood of grief and desperate loneliness that he came—John, nephew of the Rector.

To her, he was everything James was not, gentle with the gentleness of breeding, sensitive and caring, yet somehow removed from the brutal reality of her own life. If tragedy touched his world, it would wear velvet gloves—or so she thought—and she yearned towards the illusion, just as she tingled with awareness at the unexplainable chemistry that sparked between them.

Why did he find her attractive? She did not know. She was too bemused to know what he saw when he looked at her—her face pale but proud with chin held high, thick honey-coloured hair above the high collared black of her blouse. Suffering had given her a fine edge of poignancy that was somehow highlighted by her dignity, and in her he saw all the knowledge and experience he lacked. To him, the fact that she had borne four children and lost one gave to her the same aura of romance that his rosy world lent him in her eyes, and the fact that she came from a different, unfamiliar background, lent spice to the association. If she had been plain, with a thickened body, he would have given her pity and nothing more. But she was

406

pretty in a compelling and unusual way, and the initial attraction blossomed into obsession.

Week after week they met, and talked, and the meetings warmed them both. They had no intention of letting it go further. But they reckoned without the strength of their feelings.

It happened on an afternoon in June when the air was heavy with the scent of the roses that grew wild along the churchyard wall. They walked up the path between the graves towards the wicket gate that led to the meadow beyond, talking all the time to cover their awareness of one another and delay the moment when it would be too late to turn back.

At the gate they stopped for a moment, glancing back with conscious embarrassment to the churchyard. There was no one there to see them, and they stood quite still, looking at one another. Then they moved slowly through the gate and into the meadow as if drawn by invisible strings.

The first touch was like flint on flint, burning and sending shivers of anticipation rippling through them. As their hands fumbled for one another, gentle at first, and afraid, the breath caught in Charlotte's throat. But the hiatus was brief, and she sobbed softly as he pulled her to him. As one, they sank into the deep grass. Kneeling, their eager lips sought and found each other, exploring with tenderness, then urgency. Desire mounted, sweetened by the sense of the unreal. The grass was prickly behind Charlotte's neck, but she scarcely noticed.

It was there, the excitement she had thought to find only with James, the elusive, wonderful excitement. And a feeling of the lost mingling with the forbidden, pain and sadness and wonder. His body was young and hard, his sun-warmed flesh was good against hers. And in her nostrils was the heady scent of the roses, wafting her away to another place and another time where there was no heartbreak, no endless work and worry, no small coffin beneath a mound of cold earth . . .

When it was over, the shame began. Even before she had straightened her clothes it was there, spoiling what had been so perfect, embarrassing and frightening her. And she knew it was the same for him. He was embarrassed, too, and in awe of what he had done to her, a married woman and a miner's wife. The closeness that had been between them since they had met was gone, evaporated as if it had never been, and in its place was guilt, ugly and disfiguring.

She knew she would never see him again. He had no need to tell her, or to explain. And she was glad, glad that the madness was over, wanting only to get back to normality.

But normality was out of reach forever—or so it seemed. For she was pregnant, and she knew, almost from the outset, that it was his baby she was carrying.

Strangely the knowledge brought her closer to James. Now she wanted only to be with him as she had used to be with him. She still wept, but now it was for this thing that was between them. She longed to tell him what she had done, laying her head on his shoulder and unburdening her guilt, but she knew she never could. The look that would come into his eyes would be more than she could bear. And he would never forgive her—never!

Jack was born, and she treated him exactly as she treated the others, although as he grew the difference was there, too plainly for her peace of mind.

John, she never saw again. He went to Oxford, as he had told her he would, but he left Hillsbridge to stay with friends while he was waiting. Afterwards, she heard that he had followed his uncle into the church, and some years later, she heard that he had married. She wished him only happiness, although just to think of him could start an ache of regret inside her. As time passed, she thought of him less and less often, until in the end she hardly thought of him at all. He was like a figure in a dream who had never been quite real. And she changed, too, until she found it hard to believe that the grief-stricken young woman had really been herself.

But that summer's afternoon in 1920 as she lay tossing with fever he seemed to be with her as surely as he had been then, sometimes closer, sometimes farther away, and when the door opened and she saw the fair hair and fine features, she spoke his name wonderingly: "John!"

"Mam?" He came into the room, his face puzzled, and stood beside her bed. "Mam? Are you all right?"

Her bleary eyes focused on his face, and she shifted herself with an effort. What was she thinking of?

It was Jack. Of course, it was. Why had she called him John? She never had—not since he was a baby. What had come over her?

"How did it go, Jack?" she asked.

His face creased into a grin. He crossed to the bed, sitting down on the edge and taking her hands in his.

"It's going to be all right, Mam. I'm sure it is."

"You mean they've let him off? Then where is he?"

"No, this wasn't the court, Mam," he said patiently. "This was the inquest. They couldn't let him off. But after what happened today, it's almost certain they'll reduce the charge from murder to manslaughter."

Her brain was foggy with fever, but she struggled to understand. "What do you mean?"

"Because of what came out at the post-mortem."

She closed her eyes. Court, inquest, post-mortem, she couldn't tell one from the other. Jack, understanding, leaned forward.

"Listen, Mam, first they have the post-mortem. That's when the doctors have a look at the body to find out the cause of death. Then they send all their findings along to the inquest. That's what we had today, a sort of inquiry into what happened."

She jerked her head impatiently. "All right, Jack, I'm not stupid."

"I know that. I just didn't think you understood."

"I understand they're saying our Ted killed that Rupert Thorne. And now you're telling me he didn't."

"No, not exactly." Jack rubbed his jaw. "Listen now. When they opened Thorne up, they found he was suffering from a very rare condition—something they call *status lymphaticus*. Now don't ask me to explain that, but it's to do with a gland, the thymus gland, and because it's the way it is, the most trifling thing—a blow or a shock—can prove fatal. They found no other injuries on him at all, no marks of violence, no broken bones, nothing—and they reckon it was the shock of our Ted hitting him that killed him."

"But they said he was in perfect health!" Charlotte murmured.

"That's nothing to go by, it seems," Jack told her. "There's no way you can tell if a person is suffering from this complaint while they're alive. Nobody could have known."

"Well, well, well!" Inwardly Charlotte was jubilant, but she felt too ill to do more than smile weakly. "So they know now it wasn't our Ted's fault. They know he didn't murder him."

"Oh, they know that. But . . . " He broke off, wondering how he could explain to her that murder or not, Ted was still technically responsible for Rupert Thorne's death. "If an unlawful blow is struck, the striker must take the risk of the condition of health of the person struck," the coroner had said.

But Mam looked so poorly he didn't want to worry her more than he could help.

"There's another piece of good news, too," he said. "I've got a barrister for Ted—a first-class chap. He came up to me after the inquest and offered his services, just like that. It seems he knew Rupert Thorne and had no time for him, and he told me that considering the way he treated folk, it's only surprising no one had taken a swing at him before."

"Oh, Jack, that is good. But what's it going to cost?"

"Come on, Mam, you were the one who said money was no object."

"Yes, but now they've found out about this . . . this . . . "

"Status lymphaticus. Yes, I know, but Ted still needs someone to represent him, and I think this chap will be more than reasonable. From how he spoke, he'd do it for nothing if he could. So you see, Mam, things don't look quite so black after all, do they?"

"No," Charlotte said, but already she was drifting again. The effort of understanding what Jack had been saying had exhausted her, but as she lay back against the pillows she was aware of the most tremendous sense of relief.

"So at least you won't be involved, Jack," she said.

"What do you mean, Mam?"

She closed her eyes and opened them again with difficulty, seeing him through a red mist. How like John he was! Strange how she should have refused to acknowledge it all these years!

"You won't have to get up in court, Jack, and give evidence. There won't be any need for your name to be brought into it."

"Oh no, Mam, it won't change that. I'm still a witness."

"But . . . " The sweat began to run down her face. Some went into her eyes, or so it seemed, so that they blurred again.

"Don't worry, Mam, it'll be all right."

"No!" she said.

The devil was back, mocking her from the corner. Why couldn't he leave her alone? That evil, monkey-like face, challenging all her plans, and laughing, laughing . . .

"No, Jack, I won't let you."

He started at the hysterical note in her voice, easing her back against the pillows with soothing words, but she struggled into a sitting position again as soon as he released her, her eyes fiery in her flushed face, and the rasp of her laboured breathing filling the room.

"You can't, Jack. I won't let you," she said again.

"But why, Mam?"

The fever was singing in her ears. Why? Why? The reasons clamoured around inside her head.

Because you're about to become a teacher, she thought. Because you mustn't drag your name in the gutter, or folk won't want to employ you. Because I've worked all my life to bring you to this—the future you were robbed of, the future you deserve. You can't risk it now. You can't!

Her lips were cracking, her throat and mouth parched, and she was unsure whether or not she had spoken aloud. Through the red mist, she saw Jack's anxious face as he leaned over her, and his voice, when it came, sounded a long way off, and distorted, as it had been when she'd spoken to him on the telephone in Bristol.

"Mam, come on now. It'll be all right. Don't worry yourself. Only I must speak up for Ted. He is my brother, after all."

"But he's not . . . he's not . . . " She was babbling now, all the wanderings of the afternoon uppermost in her foggy mind. "You don't understand, Jack. He's not your father. He's not . . . your father . . . "

As the words left her lips, the coughing began again, racking her body, burning her lungs. She gasped for breath, the room spun around her, and the last thing she saw, before the fire enveloped her, was Jack's face, pale, tight-drawn with anxiety—and so much like his father's that again his name rose unbidden to her lips.

"John! John!"

WHEN the fever subsided, the conversation with Jack was the first thing she thought of.

She opened her eyes to see the fair head silhouetted against the window, and it all came back to her like a vivid dream.

For a moment she lay quite still, fighting a sense of panic and trying to sort out the dream from reality.

Jack's worried face—that had been real enough. And the doctor, he'd been here, too, mumbling over her and putting his cold hands all over her. But the things she had said, had they been real, too? Dear God, surely she hadn't actually told Jack the truth after all these years? Surely not!

She gazed at him, afraid of the moment when he would turn around and she would see his eyes. It would be there, all right, if he knew the truth. There would be no hiding it. Ever again.

As if sensing that she was awake and watching him, he moved.

She cringed away, trying to take refuge in a pretence of sleep, but he was too quick for her.

"Mam!"

She swallowed, afraid, still so afraid.

"You worried us to death, did you know that? Fancy getting pneumonia in the middle of the summer! But you're looking better now, and no mistake. I'll call Dad and tell him you're awake."

"Jack!" she said, and he stopped at the sharpness of her tone.

"Yes?"

Her eyes fell from his. How could she ask the question that was tormenting her? If she had said something, to mention it now would be to give it importance. But the need to know was overwhelming.

"Was I . . . was I really bad?" she asked hesitantly.

"You were, Mam. Now lie still. I'm going to get Dad."

She lay still, but her mind raced. He seemed the same—so did James, when he came in and sat on the edge of the bed—but how could she be sure? How could she ever be sure? If she had told Jack, she would never forgive herself. Never. It would be terrible for him, and it would be a double betrayal of James, into the bargain.

James. She looked at him as he sat beside her, his leathery face still lined with the anxiety of the last few days, and a tenderness filled her.

That boy, John, what had he been but a passing fancy? A madness that had lasted a short time only? Maybe she had long since forgotten what it had been like to love James with the crazy intensity of youth, but they were still together, nearly thirty years on from the day they had first met. And what was that, if not love of the most enduring kind?

Could she have withstood thirty years with John? She very much doubted it. That fiery passion would soon have burned itself out, and she wouldn't have wanted what was left.

As for Jack . . . Looking at the two faces beside her bed, she smiled. They might have nothing in common, but what did that matter? There were plenty of blood relations just as different as they were. And the family bond was there—the living together and sharing good times and bad, and that counted for more, far more.

She would go to her grave wondering if James had ever suspected, but she was almost certain he had not. His lack of imagination had served him well in this instance as in many others. It simply would not have occurred to him that Jack might not be his son.

And Jack himself had never suspected. Of that she was positive.

The only other people who had known the truth were Rector Archer and possibly Caroline. But he was dead, and it was unlikely she would ever admit to such a scandalous liaison between her husband's nephew and a miner's wife.

James leaned forward over the bed, loosening the neck of her nightgown to free a long end of hair that was caught. In the light of the afternoon sun, she noticed his own hair was almost white, and it shocked her. Strange, the way fair people turn white almost overnight.

"Thank the Lord you'm better, Lotty," he said, and the emotion in his voice humbled her.

"Delirious you were at one time," Jack added, and she looked at him sharply.

"Delirious? What was I saying?"

He laughed. "Oh, Mam, I don't know. Just a lot of nonsense. I didn't take much notice."

She nodded, tired again, and relieved in a way that was almost an anticlimax. Of course she hadn't said anything. Why in the world should she have ever have imagined for a moment that she might have done? And if she had, he would have written it off as delirium —wouldn't he?

As if from a long way off she heard their voices soothing her, urging her to sleep again. But in the instant before it claimed her, she had one piercingly frightening moment when she wondered if she would ever feel her secret was safe again, and the enormity of having been able to keep it all these years filled her with panic. Yet at the same time, she felt lonelier than she had ever done in her life, and with a small, fumbling movement she reached for James' hand.

She was still holding it when she fell asleep.

28

IN ALL her life, Charlotte thought she had never seen anything quite so grand as the assize court.

Worried though she was about Ted, she could hardly fail to be impressed by the majesty of it all: the vaulted stone walls and carved and polished woodwork, the uniformed policeman at the entrance, the dramatic legal figures who walked the corridors with easy arrogance, fussily curled wigs sitting on their heads, gowns streaming out behind them like broken blackbird's wings.

"Are they the judges?" she asked Jack in a loud whisper.

He shook his head, wishing he had been able to persuade her to stay at home. Although it was two months since her attack of pneumonia, she had never really recovered her strength, and he didn't think the long journey and the strain of seeing Ted in court would do her any good at all.

But Charlotte had been adamant. If the worst happened and Ted was sent to prison, she preferred to hear it for herself, rather than have someone else tell her.

"I can go with you, Jack," she insisted, and no one, not even James, could move her.

"You're going to have to go in by yourself, Mam," Jack told her as they approached the enormous doors with the small glass panels that gave a restricted view of the court room. "I'm a witness, so I'll have to stay out here until I'm called."

She nodded. "I know that." And away she walked across the polished floor to take her place on one of the public benches.

Jack turned away, going along the corridor and into one of the ante-rooms to light a cigarette. He'd never been much of a smoker, not like Ted, but just now he felt the need to calm his nerves.

He didn't really know why he was quite so nervous. He'd been in grand places before—Buckingham Palace, no less, when he'd been awarded his decoration—but there was something about the atmosphere here that set the blood pumping through his veins and turned his bowels to water.

Perhaps it was because he was no longer confident as to the outcome of the trial. A few weeks ago, when the post-mortem had disclosed Rupert's condition, he'd felt jubilantly certain that no jury would find Ted guilty of manslaughter, much less murder. Now, he was not so sure.

After talking to Winston Walker, the barrister who had offered his services, he realized there was a possibility they might not see Ted as innocent. Thorne had died as a direct result of Ted striking him, and the blow had been an unlawful one. Added to that, Rupert Thorne had been a highly respected citizen—a professional man— while Ted's mottled career was far less likely to impress.

Ted was still refusing to explain in court the reason behind him hitting Rupert, too, saying that to drag Becky into it now would do no good and would just defile her memory, for there would certainly be those who would say she had got what she asked for, and this was adding to the worries of the defence.

"We shall have to talk him into explaining his reasons," Winston Walker told Jack. "That way, if he's found guilty, the judge will be more likely to be lenient with him."

But so far, nothing either of them had been able to say had done a thing to change Ted's mind. He was as determined as ever to keep Rebecca out of it, and Jack was seriously worried.

Didn't Ted realize he could end up in prison for a very long time over this? Didn't he even care? After the years he had spent in a prison camp, during the war, one might think he would go out of his way to avoid further incarceration, but he seemed mulishly indifferent, threatening to break Winston Walker's neck if he so much as mentioned Rebecca's name.

The sound of footsteps and voices in the corridor attracted Jack's attention, and he glanced up. Through the open door he saw a group being ushered into the court and guessed that they must be the jury.

Twelve good men, he thought, except that there were a few more than twelve, and at the back, trailing along as if she didn't belong, was a woman . . .

Rosa Clements! It hit him like a ball of icy water, and he stood quite still, the cigarette dangling dangerously from his fingers.

Then he took a step towards her, and at the same moment she turned and saw him. The defences came up in her sloe-dark eyes, veiling any emotion, and her whole frame tightened.

"Rosa!" he said before he could stop himself. "What are you doing here?"

She stopped, detaching herself from the others, and he realized she was not with them at all, but held up by them.

"Jack! I . . . I heard about the case. I had to come. Is he . . . "

She gesticulated helplessly towards the court, and Jack swallowed at the constriction in his throat. It was the first time he had seen her since she had gone away, leaving him and his proposal of marriage, but he knew without asking that the reason she was here today had nothing to do with him.

It never had been him with Rosa, he knew that now, but surprisingly it didn't bother him any more. His passion for her had come and gone, and he had had time to realize how ill-matched they would have been. But he was glad to see her.

415

For a moment they looked at one another, then, as the doorway cleared, she moved uncertainly.

"I'd better go in. Will I be able to see you later?"

He nodded, grinding out his cigarette into a tin receptacle that looked almost out of place, and following her to the door. As Jack had told Charlotte, he couldn't go into the court himself yet, but there seemed to be nothing stopping him from looking through the small glass panel in the door.

Yes, they were all assembeled now—counsel, police, jury. And above them all the judge, looking as if he had fallen asleep already. From where he was standing, the dock was outside his line of vision, but he knew Ted would be there, and he wondered how he would be feeling.

The public benches were immediately opposite the door, and he saw his mother and Rosa sitting there among the handful of other folk who had come in to listen to the case. They were at opposite ends of the seat, both stiff and still, not looking at one another. Funny how his mother had turned against Rosa. She'd always been such a one for standing up for Ada Clements when others ran her down and called her names.

Through the glass panel in the door, Jack saw the prosecuting counsel rise. He was a dark, whiskery man with a booming voice, but the thick door effectively muffled his words, and Jack could not make out what he was saying.

In the adjournment for lunch, he and Winston Walker took Charlotte to a small café nearby the courts for something to eat, but the barrister was the only one with any appetite.

"The things they're saying!" Charlotte exclaimed angrily. "Awful things, making our Ted out to be a real lout! It's all I can do to sit there and hold my tongue, Jack!"

"Don't worry, Mrs Hall, we'll get our turn later," Winston soothed her, but his calm manner only seemed to irritate her more.

"It's all very well for you. It's not your son they're on about!"

"Mam!" Jack said sharply. "Mr Walker's doing his best for us and don't you forget it."

"Yes, yes, I know." Charlotte mopped her face with a handkerchief. "And how that Rosa Clements has the cheek to come and listen to every word, I don't know. Sitting there like that! I've never seen anything so brazen!"

Jack said nothing. He thought that Rosa looked more lonely than brazen, but perhaps the proud determination in her bearing could be taken for that. To say so now would only upset Mam more, and he didn't want that. But he made up his mind to try and see Rosa when the court adjourned for the day.

He was called to give evidence half-way through the afternoon. Christ, but it was as bad as taking off for a bombing raid in Belgium, he thought, as he went through the now-open door into the large, yet airless, court. It would have been bad enough if he had been going into the witness box on Ted's behalf, but he wasn't. He was there because he had seen the blow struck, and the prosecution would be doing all they could to make it as damning as possible.

Struggling to keep his limp to a minimum, he crossed the court to the witness box. In the dock, Ted was pale but calm, and the two exchanged a quick, brotherly glance. Then Jack was asked to take the oath, and prosecuting counsel rose, bowing and scraping in the direction of the judge.

"Your honour, I ask that I may be allowed to treat this witness as hostile. As brother of the accused, I fear he may be less than helpful."

Jack stiffened. What the hell did they expect?

"I'm not given to lying, sir. I shall tell you exactly what happened that day."

The judge peered at him narrowly over his spectacles, then cleared his throat.

"Hmm. I see. Proceed, Mr Scales. I shall decide how much leading of the witness can be permitted as we go along."

"Thank you, your honour," the prosecuting counsel paused for a moment, then went on, "Perhaps this would be an opportune moment for me to say I am not questioning for one moment the honesty of Mr Jack Hall. It will doubtless be raised at some stage that he has a most distinguished war record. But I would remind you it is not he who is on trial here, but his brother, a much more colourful character, as I believe I have already shown . . . "

Jack did not dare look at Charlotte, but he guessed it was all she could do to restrain herself from leaping to her feet and interrupting.

"Mr Hall," the prosecuting counsel turned his attention to Jack once more. "A previous witness, an employee of the late Mr Thorne, has already told us how you and your brother came bursting into his office looking for trouble. You did not arrive at the same time as your brother, however. Is that correct?"

Jack nodded. "I arrived a few minutes after him."

"Why?"

The short sharpness of the question took Jack by surprise.

"I . . . I'm sorry, I don't understand . . . "

"You arrived at Mr Thorne's office a few minutes after your brother had forced his way in, and you, too, charged up the stairs without further ado. I simply ask, why? What was in your mind as you pushed past Mr Thorne's young lady and ran into the room where your brother was attacking him?"

"He wasn't attacking him," Jack protested.

"No?" Prosecuting Counsel asked smoothly. "Then why were you in such a hurry?"

"Because . . . " Jack broke off, realizing the trap that had been laid for him, but not knowing how to avoid it, and the prosecuting counsel followed up his advantage.

"Dare I suggest, Mr Hall, that it was because you suspected your brother was likely to commit some violence on the deceased, and you wished to avert this if at all possible? Come now, you told us just now you are not given to lying. I'm sure in this small point we can expect the truth from a man of your integrity."

Helplessly Jack glanced towards the dock and saw his own futile anger mirrored in Ted's face.

"An answer if you please, Mr Hall," Counsel pressed him. "You went to the office, did you not, in the expectation of trouble? Further, you went at the request of your mother, who was also afraid of the violence your brother might perpetrate . . . "

"Objection!" Winston Walker was on his feet, but the prosecuting counsel was not to be put off.

"If necessary, Your honour, I can call witnesses who will say the mother of the accused telephoned Bristol University, where Mr Jack Hall is a student, to ask him to intervene. But I am sure the *truthful* Mr Hall will verify this for us."

Jack nodded warily. "Yes, it's true. Ted had a bone to pick with him."

"A bone? A bone to pick with him? Surely, Mr Hall, that is the most ludicrous of understatements? Isn't it true that your brother was madly jealous of the deceased because he had become engaged to a young lady your brother fancied himself?"

So that was the way they were going to make it look! Anger flooded Jack's veins, and he looked at Ted again. Surely, now, he

418

would have to come out with the reasons behind what had happened! He questioned him with his eyes, seeking permission to say more, but Ted's mulish expression told him nothing that had been said had changed his mind. If anyone raised the true circumstances of Rebecca's death, he would never forgive him.

"Well, Mr Hall?" the barrister persisted, and Jack gesticulated wearily.

"It wasn't the way you're making it sound."

"Oh, really? Then perhaps you would tell us how it was? Or perhaps his honour would prefer it if I steered you back towards the only thing you can really know about—what happened in Rupert Thorne's office that fateful day. When you arrived, Mr Hall, when you pushed your way in, what was happening?"

"They . . . they were arguing."'

"Arguing—or quarrelling?"

"Oh, I don't know," Jack snapped. "What's the difference?"

The barrister smirked. "All the difference in the world, Mr Hall. An argument smacks of a friendly disagreement, while a quarrel—a quarrel is far more likely to end in violence, wouldn't you say? Just as this one did! Now, as the argument—as you call it—progressed, did you hear the deceased threaten your brother at all?"

"No, he . . . he just . . . "

"Yes?"

"He said he'd call the police if we didn't get out."

"Hardly surprising, I'd have said. And did he attempt to throw you out himself? Use any violence on either of you?"

"No, he . . . "

"But you saw your brother use violence on him. In a completely unprovoked attack."

"Unprovoked!" Jack exclaimed, remembering all too clearly the insults to Rebecca's memory which Rupert had used to taunt Ted. But under his brother's warning gaze, he said nothing.

"He only hit him once," he said lamely.

"And once, it seems, was more than enough!" Counsel turned dramatically to the listening jury, arms outstretched. "Gentlemen of the jury, how much clearer does it need to be? With one blow, the defendant murdered an innocent and respected man, a man who had had the misfortune to fall in love with a girl the accused thought of as his own—quite mistakenly, as it happens. For some insane reason, he . . . "

The judge stirred restlessly.

"Thank you, Mr Scales, we will hear your summing up later, no doubt. Now, Mr . . . ah . . . Walker, do you have any questions to ask of this witness?"

Winston Walker rose, doing his best to set the balance to rights, but with Ted's insistence on keeping silent, it was a hopeless task. With all the skill of his profession, the barrister had succeeded in making Ted into a dangerous lout, and the jury, used to stories of the drunken rowdyism of the Hillsbridge miners, were all too ready to believe every word, particularly when the victim was a highly respected professional man like Rupert Thorne.

When, at the end of Jack's evidence, the court adjourned for the day, Winston Walker said as much, standing in the same corridor where Jack had waited this morning.

"It's hopeless," he admitted. "Unless we can persuade Ted to tell them the truth behind what happened, they'll not only find him guilty—which they're pretty well bound to do anyway—but the judge is going to be damned hard on him. When I think of a bounder like Thorne it makes me furious, but if Ted won't help himself, there's not much I can do."

Jack nodded. After his grilling in the dock, he hardly felt like disagreeing.

Out of the corner of his eye he saw Rosa Clements standing uncertainly by the door, and excusing himself from the others, he went over to her.

"Rosa, don't run away. I'll buy you a cup of tea."

As he said it, he wondered briefly if she might think he was trying to resurrect old relationships, but clearly she was too worried and too preoccupied for such a thought even to enter her head.

"Oh, Jack, what are they doing?" she asked. "They're making it sound all wrong. I know Ted's got a temper when he's roused, but there must have been more to it than that."

"There was," Jack said. "Becky died because of an abortion that went wrong."

He heard the quick intake of her breath, and saw the stark pain in her eyes. "You mean she was . . . "

"Having a baby. Yes."

"I saw her, coming out of your house! She'd been to tell your Mam, had she? Was it Ted's?"

Jack shook his head. "It was Thorne's."

"*Thorne's?* But she . . . she wasn't that sort of girl."

"Exactly. That's why Ted went mad when he found out . . . that, and the rest."

"What rest?"

"He gave her the stuff that killed her, something to get rid of the baby, only it went wrong. He admitted it to us when we went to see him. It's no wonder Ted hit him. He just sat there, smug as you like, saying things . . . " Words failed him.

Rosa's hand was over her mouth, and her eyes were closed. After a moment she said, "He must tell them."

"He won't. He's too concerned about protecting Becky's memory. He says he knows she would never have gone with that bastard willingly, but who else would believe it?"

Rosa's eyebrows made a fine dark line on her pale oval face.

"I would."

"Why, did you know him?"

"No, but I knew her. She was too much of a prig ever to . . . " She broke off, reddening. "I'm sorry. I shouldn't have said that. But I . . . "

"I know," he said softly.

"It just makes me so angry. What's the point of keeping quiet about something like that? The dead are gone. It can't hurt them. But Ted . . . they can't lock him up again! Not after what he's been through! Oh Jack, I won't let them . . . "

Her voice tailed away, but before Jack could wonder what she meant, he was aware of Charlotte standing beside them, her eyes cold with dislike as they rested on Rosa.

"Good afternoon, Rosa. Jack, are you going to take me back to the train, or shall we go and have a cup of tea somewhere first? Mr Walker has some work to do preparing for tomorrow."

He nodded. "All right, Mam, we'll go for a cup of tea. Rosa . . . "

But the sloe-dark eyes were veiled again.

"No, thank you, Jack."

Then, without another word, she turned and walked away.

"What did she want?" Charlotte asked suspiciously.

For a moment Jack did not reply. Then, "You always knew the way things were with Rosa, Mam," he said quietly.

JACK SLEPT little that night. He tossed and turned in the narrow bed at his digs, the happenings of the day jostling in his mind.

Ted was going to be sent to prison, there was no doubt of it, and he personally was aching to stand up and denounce the saintly

Rupert Thorne to the entire court. It was more than infuriating to see the jury left ignorant in this way—it was a travesty of justice. But he was helpless to do anything about it. If Ted wouldn't have the truth brought up, it was not for him to do it, and in a way he respected his brother's reasons.

What Mam was going to do if Ted was sent to prison was something else that worried him. She was upset, of course, by the whole proceedings, but still touchingly confident that in the end justice would prevail. If Ted was found guilty—as Jack was becoming convinced he would be—she was going to take it very hard indeed. The thought of her son being branded a common criminal, and locked away, would push her to the limits, and Jack was not sure her health could take it any more. Once, maybe, but not now. Not since the pneumonia . . .

Incensed by a feeling of helplessness, he pushed back the bedclothes, sitting up against the pillows, and for some reason he found himself thinking of his sleepless nights in hospital during the war.

Musing, he found himself going back to those days, and in particular to Stella O'Halloran, with her sound common sense and the cheerful brand of good humour that had helped so many men through a crisis in their lives. In different circumstances, he thought, I believe we could have made a go of it, but it had all seemed so thoroughly impossible then. He'd been too busy feeling sorry for himself, and she'd probably never seen him as anything other than another patient.

Where was she nowadays, he wondered. Maybe she had stayed abroad, married some other patient who had had the sense to sweep her off her feet.

Jack shifted the stump that she had helped him to accept, and asked himself why he minded the thought of that so much now, when he'd scarcely given her a thought in two years. Because of the similarity of the situation, he supposed. Because of the way lying awake and worrying had brought it all back.

The first soft light of dawn began to creep through the curtains and he got up, reaching for his leg and strapping it on. He'd go for a walk—anything rather than lie here thinking. He'd watch the city waking up, and then, maybe, things would come into perspective a little, and he would find some fresh resource of courage with which to face whatever the day brought.

WHEN THE court reassembled for the day, later than the previous day, because of some legal tangle nobody seemed anxious to explain, the whole atmosphere seemed hostile, and Jack, looking at the faces of the jury, felt sure that they had already made up their minds. Even the judge, sitting hunched in his throne-like seat above the well of the court, looked as if he deemed the result a foregone conclusion.

Jack, having given his evidence, had been able to go in with Charlotte today, and Amy too had joined them to show family solidarity. Rosa was there again too, still sitting at the opposite side of the gallery, and not exchanging so much as a glance with any of the Halls except Jack.

The morning began with the conductor of the omnibus which had brought Ted to Bristol that fateful afternoon giving evidence as to how he had sat stony-faced the whole journey and given the impression of being in a bad temper when buying his ticket. Winston Walker, who intimated to Jack that the prosecution had probably not realized Ted would be legally represented when they had decided to put the bus conductor in the box, managed to demolish his evidence fairly satisfactorily, but when the prosecution barrister came back for his re-examination the questions he put were so sharply slanted and so pertinent that Jack felt he had undone any good Winston Walker might have done.

By the time the prosecuting counsel had finished, the case he had presented seemed so rational that it was almost impossible to believe that events could have happened any way other than that he described, and when he sat down, Jack was convinced that any last doubt that may have lingered in a juror's mind would have been well and truly dispelled.

Then it was Winston Walker's turn, but it was clear that whatever he said, and however well he said it, without disclosing the mitigating circumstances there was no way in which he could defend Ted against the destructive case that had been built up against him.

Jack felt his spirits sink lower and lower, and when they adjourned for lunch it was a dejected party who crossed the road for a bite to eat. Charlotte, for once, seemed to have nothing to say, and both Jack and Amy felt things were too serious for any trivial small talk.

But, when they made their way back to the courthouse, Jack was surprised to find Rosa Clements deep in conversation with Winston Walker. There was a great deal of shaking of heads and waving of hands, but Jack could not hear what was going on, and at last the barrister came over to him, his pleasant face pink with anxiety.

"That young lady—Miss Clements—was asking me if she could give evidence on Ted's behalf. I've told her . . . "

"What!" Charlotte demanded, finding her voice and using it to interrupt him. "Rosa Clements give evidence for our Ted? I've never heard of such a thing!"

"What's she going to say?" Jack asked.

"It's a character reference of some kind, I believe. She won't say exactly what."

"You can't let her!" Charlotte said sharply.

Winston Walker spread his hands on the wooden dividing bar, pressing down until the knuckles turned white.

"It's unusual, I admit. I'm not even sure if the judge will allow me to introduce an extra witness at this late stage. But if he will, I believe we should let her do it. Our case is so thin, we need all the sympathy we can get."

"Hah!" Charlotte exploded. "She's looking for a chance to twist the knife, if you ask me. And she'd have cause. There's trouble between her and me—and the boys, too. There's no telling what she'd say to get her own back."

"Oh, dear, and I was hoping . . . " Winston Walker began, and Jack laid a hand on his arm. Like the others, he was unsure of what Rosa was going to say, but unlike them, he was quite certain it would be nothing to harm Ted. He remembered her anxiety yesterday, and the expression in her eyes when she had said, "They can't lock him up—I won't let them." Then, there was the fact that she was here. Charlotte might think she had come to gloat. Jack knew she had not.

And lastly, there was her appearance. To Charlotte and Amy, she was still Rosa, the skinny urchin of doubtful parentage, looked down on by most folk in Hillsbridge. But Jack could see her as the jury would see her—and he knew they would be impressed. She was not only beautiful, she had an air of self-possession that would lend credence to anything she might say.

"Let her go into the witness box, Mr Walker," Jack said. "No, don't look at me like that, Mam, I haven't taken leave of my senses. Mr Walker's right. Unless we do something drastic our Ted is going to go to prison, maybe for a long time. Do you want that?"

"No, of course not, but . . . "

"Then let Rosa go in the box. If she can."

THERE WERE consultations and wranglings, but clearly the prosecuting counsel was so sure of having made out his case that at last he gave way, and it was agreed to let Rosa go into the witness box. She stood there, a slight, proud figure, chin held high, dark eyes challenging all those who looked at her with curious gazes. She took the oath in a voice that was low but firm. But she never so much as glanced in Ted's direction.

"Miss Clements, you have gone into the witness box to tell this court what you know of Ted Hall. Is that correct?" Winston Walker began, somewhat tentatively.

"Yes, I have."

"You have known him a long while?"

"All my life. He's a very fine man."

"You sound very fond of him, Miss Clements. So as to put the record straight, I'd like to establish right away what is your relationship with the accused."

A muscle tightened in her cheek. "None. We were friends for a time. Nothing more."

"But you believe Ted Hall to be incapable of the kind of violence he is accused of?"

"Not incapable. He has never denied hitting Rupert Thorne. But he wouldn't have done it without a good reason."

"But we have heard it suggested that the reason was that he was insanely jealous—that Rupert Thorne had stolen his lady friend."

"That's not true," Rosa said quietly. "He was in love with her, yes, and he's in love with her now. That's why the full story has been kept from this court. You see, she was in love with him, too. And it wasn't jealousy that drove Ted to see Rupert Thorne that day. It was anger for what Thorne did to her."

A murmur began to ripple around the court, but it was quickly silenced as Ted leaped to his feet, leaning forward over the dock.

"No, Rosa! Don't you dare! Keep quiet, do you hear?"

In almost the same instant, the prosecuting counsel realized something was very amiss, and he too rose in haste.

"Objection! Objection, your honour! This witness is trying to muddy the waters. Her evidence is not admissable. How can she possibly know . . . "

"Just a moment, Mr Scales," the judge had woken up now, leaning forward to peer at the court, his eyes beady with anticipation. "Just a moment. I think I would like to hear what this witness has to say. I've felt throughout the case that something has been kept back. Proceed, Mr Walker."

Winston Walker cast an agonized look towards the Hall family. "Your honour . . . " he began.

"Proceed, Mr Walker, if you please! You have put the young lady into the witness box. I want to hear what she has to say."

"No!" Ted cried again. The judge turned to silence him.

"Any more interruptions from you, Hall, and you'll be answering an additional charge of contempt of court. Now proceed, please, Mr Walker."

Winston gesticulated helplessly, searching for words, but Rosa did not wait for him.

"There's no need for him to question me. I'll tell you what I'm here to tell you, and why it's me that's got to do it. It's because Ted Hall is too much of a gentleman to tell the truth, and he's told his family he'll break their necks if they do. But he's got no such hold over me, and I won't stand by and see you send him to prison when he did what any decent man would have done, given the circumstances."

"Circumstances?" the judge roared. "What circumstances?"

Rosa swallowed once, keeping her eyes straight ahead of her.

"Rupert Thorne killed Becky Church. He gave her something to get rid of his baby, and it killed her," she blurted.

At her words, the court erupted. Above the gasps and the cries, the prosecuting counsel's voice rose shrilly. "Objection, your honour! Objection!"

"Order! The court will come to order!" The gavel banged and slowly the hubbub became a murmur gradually subsiding into shocked silence.

"Mr Walker, does your witness realize what she is saying?" The judge was leaning forward now. "These are very serious charges . . . "

"Your honour . . . " Winston Walker turned anguished eyes on the small figure in the witness box.

"It's true!" Rosa burst out again, as if realizing the forces of law were marshalling themselves to silence her. "I saw Rebecca Church just a few days before she died. She was in a terrible way—she would be. Her people were religious maniacs . . . "

"Objection! Objection! This has nothing whatever to do with the case . . . "

"I think you may safely leave me to be the judge of that," Mr Justice Hayburn retorted. "I have already said I feel that there is more to this case than meets the eye, and I would like to hear what this young lady has to say." He turned to Rosa. "Proceed!"

Rosa hesitated. She had caught sight of Ted's white face, and it had horrified her. "There's nothing more to say, really, except that Ted—Mr Hall—was a prisoner of war when it happened, and it's only now he's found out about it. You can't blame him for doing what he did. It was just his bad luck that Rupert Thorne had this . . . this funny gland thing. And I thought you ought to know!"

"How do you know all this, Miss . . . ah . . . Clements?" the judge asked.

"Jack told me. But they won't say because . . ."

"You mean it's hearsay."

She looked at him, puzzled.

"Hearsay evidence, Miss Clements, means that you are repeating something you have been told, rather than something you knew from your own experience. I cannot allow that, I am afraid."

"But . . ."

"It's a matter, of course, which the police may wish to investigate further. But for the present . . . do you have any further questions to put to this witness, Mr Walker?"

"No, your honour."

"Mr Scales?"

The prosecuting counsel was on his feet in an instant. "I most certainly have, your honour. This story, I am sure, is entirely without foundation, a slur on the memory of a fine young man. It would be entertaining if it were not so wickedly scandalous. And how this witness can possibly ask the court to accept her story is beyond me. She speaks of matters of which she can know nothing. First, she accuses the deceased of giving an unfortunate girl a child, then, blithely, she talks of 'something to get rid of it.' As an innocent young girl, have you the slightest idea of what that might mean, Miss Clements?"

"Well, of course, I have!" Rosa scoffed. "It's some concoction mixed up by a quack, herbs and things."

"And you know of places where you can get such things?"

"No, but I could find out easily enough if I had a mind to."

"But you don't know yourself."

"No, but . . ."

"Thank you, Miss Clements, that's good enough for me, and for this court, too, I suspect. Now, supposing we turn our attention to the scandalous slurs you have made on the deceased, Mr Thorne. To all who knew him, he was highly respectable, a man of fine qualities. I suggest that you are taking advantage of the fact that he is dead and no longer able to defend himself to imply all manner of things you cannot possibly prove."

"I'd say the same if I were face to face with him. But that's not likely, is it? If he weren't dead, we wouldn't be here."

"The point Mr Scales is making, Miss Clements, if I am not mistaken, is that what you are saying is completely unsubstantiated speculation. Not one member of the family of the accused has even hinted that Mr Thorne was in any way connected with the unfortunate girl's death—or, in fact, that she died anything but naturally. As for the slurs on Mr Thorne's character, I take it they too are hearsay. You did not know him personally, did you?"

Rosa swallowed. Her chin came up and she looked at him defiantly.

"You're wrong, sir. I knew him only too well."

The judge's jaw dropped visibly. "You did? How?"

There was just the slightest hesitation as Rosa composed herself. But when she spoke, her voice was quite level. "I worked in Bristol during the war—on the trams. Mr Thorne's office was on my route. I met him then. He asked me to have dinner with him. I was very flattered, and I accepted. Afterwards, I regretted it. He wasn't a very nice man to know. He could be very persuasive. And he told me that if anything went wrong, there were ways and means of putting them right again."

The judge, who must have heard plenty of similar—and worse—facts outlined during his career, managed to look suitably shocked.

"You are saying, Miss Clements, that the deceased actually tried to seduce you by offering you the means to . . . ah . . . "

"Get rid of a baby if I got one. Yes. That's why I wasn't surprised when I heard what he'd done to Rebecca Church. I knew such things could be dangerous. She wouldn't. She was too innocent."

"But why have you not said this before?"

"I wasn't very proud of myself. I didn't want to admit to having known Mr Thorne as well as I did. But I don't want to see Ted Hall go to gaol for something any man would have done in the circumstances. I happen to think it's important that the truth should come out. Much more important than my reputation." And in spite of lengthy cross-examination, Rosa remained adamant. She had known Rupert Thorne, and he was an out-and-out bounder. Nothing could move her on that point.

Finally, the judge put an end to the examination. "Mr Scales, have you any more questions of this witness?"

"None, Your honour."

"Mr Walker?"

"None."

Rosa left the witness box.

"Mr Walker, I presume you intend to put your client into the witness box," Mr Justice Hayburn said when she had reached her seat, and then it was Ted's turn.

Ted was clearly shaken by Rosa's evidence and stood facing Winston Walker with eyes that were full of reproach. But there was nothing the barrister could do now but question him about the background to his assault on Rupert Thorne, and nothing Ted could do but admit it.

In a low voice, he told the court how he had come to hear of the reasons for Rebecca's death.

"I was wrong to take the law into my own hands, I suppose, but I'd do the same again," he said quietly. "To do that to her, and then threaten to tell people she'd asked for it—Becky, my Becky . . . " His voice cracked, and his fists clenched on the wooden surround of the witness box. Winston Walker, although he, too, was shaken by Rosa's disclosures, knew that he had gained the sympathy of most people in court.

After the closing speeches Mr Justice Hayburn had his turn. "This is," he said, peering over his spectacles at the jury, "a very good illustration of the variety that can be found in cases of manslaughter —more varied, in all probability, than any other crime known to law. In some cases manslaughter is tantamount to murder, in others it can be almost accident. But in the case now before this court, you, the jury, have two questions to answer. The first—was the blow struck by the defendant an unlawful blow? The second—did it cause the death of the deceased? On this point you must take into account the excellent medical evidence which has been placed before you. If, after consideration, you decide that the answer to both these questions is 'yes', then the defendant is technically guilty of manslaughter, and it is your duty to find him so.

"You may be feeling, with justification, a certain amount of sympathy for the accused, but you must not let this sway you in reaching a fair verdict. Rather, you must trust in me to exercise the discretion vested in me as regards punishment. This is a matter which is entirely within my discretion, and you must trust me to exercise it."

Jack glanced at Rosa, sitting expressionlessly in her place. Her evidence was Ted's only hope now, and though he doubted his brother would thank her for it, he himself was more than grateful for what she had done.

Although the jury were out for only an hour, it seemed like a lifetime. And when they returned, and Mr Justice Hayburn took his place again, Jack found himself searching their faces for a clue as to their decision. There was none. With the rest of the hushed court, he could do nothing but wait for their verdict.

The foreman rose, and the clerk of the court asked him if they had agreed.

"Yes, we 'ave." His voice seemed to echo around the four walls.

"Do you find the defendant, Edward Hall, guilty or not guilty?"

"Guilty."

Their breath came out as one so that the whole court seemed to have sighed. Jack looked from Ted's white face to Charlotte's impassive one, on to Amy, who was taking no trouble to hide her emotion, and Rosa, who was staring straight ahead, as if she had removed herself from the court and all the proceedings.

"Edward Hall." Mr Justice Hayburn turned towards him, his gimlet eyes looking more like black beads than ever. "You have been found guilty, quite rightly in my opinion, of the manslaughter of Rupert Thorne. There are, however, certain mitigating circumstances in this case, and I am prepared to take these into account. You were, I believe, provoked and pushed beyond the limits of your endurance, and when you struck the deceased, I do not believe it was your intention to do him any lasting harm.

"You should not, of course, have struck him. We cannot have people like you taking the law into their own hands. But in passing sentence I have taken into account your previous good character, your war record, and the fact that you have already served several months' imprisonment for what you did. I intend, therefore, to bind you over for a period of twelve months on condition that you are of good behaviour and commit no further breaches of the peace. I trust you will not behave in such a rash and foolish way again."

Ted stared at him, as if unable to take in what he had said.

"You mean—I can go home?"

"Yes."

"Court will rise." That was the clerk, and as the judge and his entourage left, hubbub broke out. Ted, coming down from the dock, was surrounded, and half-laughing, half-crying, the family took him in their arms.

Only Rosa stood alone, and seeing her, Jack left the others and crossed to her.

"Thank you, Rosa," he said quietly. "If you hadn't said what you did . . ."

She shrugged her slight shoulders. "I did what I could."

"But I thought you said you didn't know Rupert Thorne?"

She glanced around her, as if afraid she might be overheard. Then she smiled faintly. "I didn't."

"You *didn't?* But you said . . . "

"It was only the truth, wasn't it? But nobody was going to believe me. So I just added to it a bit."

"On oath! Rosa, for goodness sake!"

"It worked, didn't it? Ted's free—and so he should be. And it was time the truth came out. There's too much covering things up for fear of what folk will think or say. It isn't good."

"Oh, Rosa!"

"Jack, come on! Mr Walker's waiting," Charlotte called.

He put his hand under Rosa's elbow.

"You come, too. There'll be some kind of a celebration."

She shook her head. "No. I know where I'm not wanted."

"But after what you've done . . . "

"You're a fool, Jack," she said, smiling sadly. "After what I've done, they hate me more than ever."

"Oh no, they'll want to thank you . . . "

"Jack!" Charlotte said again, and there was no mistaking the icy aggression in her tone.

Rosa turned, sliding her elbow from his grasp and walking towards the door. She did not look at the Hall family as she passed them, and although their eyes, as of one accord, followed her, none of them made any move towards her.

Then, head held high, she passed through the swing doors and out of sight.

"HE SHOULD never have let her go in the witness box. He should never have let her!" Ted said vehemently.

It was the next day. The family were gathered in the kitchen, and naturally the only topic of conversation was the trial, and its dramatic ending, but all those present seemed to be looking at what had happened from different points of view.

"Winston Walker was only doing what he thought best," Amy said. "I think he's a wonderful man, and you should be jolly grateful to him for getting you off."

"I've no doubt you'll show him how grateful we are," Ted snapped, referring to the way Amy seemed to have forgotten Arthur Packer since she had clapped eyes on Winston Walker. "He's far too old for you, and the way you were flirting was downright disgusting."

"Well, I like that!" Amy pouted. "You get yourself found guilty of manslaughter, and you have the nerve to accuse me of being disgusting! That's a funny set of values, I must say!"

"For the Lord's sake, stop it you two," Charlotte intervened. "Amy's right, Ted, you should be very grateful to Mr Walker."

"I told him I wouldn't have it brought out," Ted said stubbornly. "I told him I wanted Becky protected whatever the cost. Now it's been blown up into a proper scandal, thanks to Rosa Clements."

"But it had to come out, Ted," Jack said reasonably. "Can't you see, you'd be in gaol now if it hadn't been for her bringing out the truth."

"I'd have rather that than have Becky's good name dragged through the mud," Ted replied, lighting a Gold Flake. "You all knew how I felt about it. So why did Winston Walker give her the chance to let it all out?"

Charlotte turned away impatiently, reaching for her hat to go out to the shops.

"Jack's right, Ted. It'll all be a nine days wonder, and it can't hurt Becky now. I just wish I'd had the courage to stand up and say it myself, instead of leaving it to the likes of her."

"She doesn't care about anything, does she?" Amy put in. "Fancy, in front of all those people, admitting . . . well!" She broke off, giggling and biting her lip.

"Like her mother, if you ask me," Charlotte said shortly. "I hope you can see her now for what she is, Jack, a common little hussy."

For a moment there was a complete hush in the kitchen, for the sight of Jack's face silenced them all, and as he got to his feet they shrank before the fury of his gaze.

"I don't think you realize, any of you, what that 'little hussy,' as Mam calls her, did for our Ted. Well, it's about time you did. It wasn't just that she had the courage to stand up and tell the truth —and believe me, in a place like that to call it 'courage' is an understatement. No, it went much further than that."

"What do you mean, Jack?" Charlotte asked.

"You really don't know, do you, Mam?" Jack's eyes held hers, then moved slowly to Ted. "And nor do you, though you bloody well ought to. She perjured herself for you, Ted. Before God and the law, she perjured herself."

"What?" Charlotte said sharply, and Jack turned back to her.

"She didn't know Rupert Thorne, Mam. She never had. But she knew the only way to make her evidence of any importance was to say she did. That's how much she cared about getting our Ted off. And all you lot can do is run her into the ground!"

The silence seemed timeless. Into it the clock ticked and the fire crackled, but none of them noticed.

"Dear Lord," Charlotte said at last.

"You see, Ted?" Jack turned to him, ignoring her. "That's how much she thinks of you. I was ashamed at the way you all treated her yesterday. And I should think the least you could do is give her credit for what she did."

"I didn't know! I had no idea!" Ted was almost as white and shocked as he had been yesterday.

"Well, there you are," Jack said flatly. "While you were buggering on about Becky's reputation, she gave up hers without a murmur to keep you out of gaol. And it's about time you all realized that and treated her with the respect that's due to her."

They couldn't look at one another. They were too shamefaced. But when at last Charlotte turned to Amy, her old brisk manner had returned as if nothing were wrong.

"Go round next door and find out if Rosa's there, Amy," she instructed. "She'll no doubt be off again before long, back to wherever it is she's been, but I think I saw her go into the house last night. And ask if she'll come around and have a drink with us. I think we've all got something to say to her."

Jack knew that was the closest Mam was ever likely to come to admitting she had been wrong.

433

29

By OCTOBER, discontent was stirring once more amongst the miners, and the Ted Hall affair was forgotten as the call to strike grew louder.

"We'll show 'em what's what this time," James said, confident in the support of the railwaymen and transport workers, and in no time at all, it seemed, he was proved right, for Lloyd George quickly agreed to settle on their terms, with money on the table and the promise of a National Wages Board to look into things later.

It was only the sharpest and most pessimistic among them who noticed that he had chosen the very same time to bring in the Emergency Powers Act, and some of those who did notice dismissed it as being unimportant. After all, it was only an extension of the powers the Government had had during the war, and that didn't seem to be harming anybody. So with a bit of extra cash in their pockets, who was going to complain about that?

The trouble was, as autumn turned to winter, things began to look black for every working family in the land. Post-war elation began to flag as prices soared and wages fell, and more and more men found themselves in the dole queue.

In the Miners Arms, where the chief topic of conversation over the last months had been the Guss Committee that was going to be set up to investigate the continued use of the old guss and crook carting method, the talk turned once more to wages, conditions of work and the state of the country as a whole.

"A land fit for heroes!" Hubert Freke observed drily one night early in the New Year. "That's a joke if ever I heard one. Why, there's more out of work now than ever there was."

"And with so many killed in the war, you'd reckon there'd be more than enough to go round. Leastways, that's what they tried to put over on us," Walter Clements agreed. Stanley Bristow snorted loudly into his beer.

"I don't know what 'tis coming to! All o' my best horses, they had, and told me it was for the good of the country. Good of the country, my foot! It's all gone to pot, if you ask me."

The others murmured their agreement. They didn't like what was going on. It made them feel cheated, somehow. Too many men had given their life's blood, and the ones who had come back had found a world changed almost beyond recognition.

"The working man has got to get together," Walter Clements said in his quiet way. "All we want is to be able to get on with the job and take home a decent wage packet at the end of the week. Leastways, that's how I look at it. And I cassn't see that's too much to ask."

"It shouldn't be. Especially when you look at what we've got to put up with—and how many's getting killed down the pit all the time," Ewart Brixey put in. "There was a bloke got his lot over at Beechleigh last week, weren't there? Suffocated when the floor caved in. And the week after Christmas, too."

The others nodded their agreement, and not one of them passed comment, as a stranger might have done, on the oddity of a "floor fall" causing the man's death.

Each and every one of them knew that in the topsy-turvy seams at Beechleigh colliery, roof was floor and floor was roof and had been ever since some huge geological disturbance had up-ended the rocks and crushed them into strange angles and disjointed arcs.

Working beneath soft, shored-up sand was just one of the hazards of being a miner, and sometimes it resulted in a death, along with the dangers of fire and flood, bad air and explosion, although here in Somerset an explosion was more likely to be caused by a badly laid shot than anything else, and many of the accidents were due to carelessness.

Still there were far too many deaths for a man's peace of mind, and it didn't stop there. There was the dust in the lungs that most miners suffered from after only a few years down the pit, and the hernias and groin injuries caused by carting putts of coal, not to mention the broken ribs and sprained backs from a hundred and one minor accidents and the general loss of health from simply being underground for so much of the time.

But far from being compensated, as they had hoped, the men were finding themselves worse and worse off. Why, already most of the collieries were working only four days a week, and future prospects were far from bright.

"There'll be another strike. No doubt about that," Stanley Bristow said, voicing all their thoughts. "Stands to reason. People just won't put up with it. Not nowadays. And so long as we all stick together, we'm bound to get something done."

"Ah, just so long as we do stick together," Ewart Brixey said with a rare flash of insight. "Trouble is, I've got a feeling it's going to end up this time with every man for himself."

The others laughed at the idea, but had they known it, the events of the spring would prove that his words were not so very far from the truth.

IN MARCH, Jack undertook the first stint of teaching practice his university course demanded. He had known it would be expected of him as part of his second year's training, and he had been looking forward to getting back into the classroom. But when he was sent to a primary school in the poorest part of the city, he found things very different from the way they had been in Hillsbridge.

The buildings themselves were in a poor state of repair. The walls of the cloak-rooms were running with water, so that often the pupils went home in coats that were wetter than when they had arrived, and all members of the staff shared one tiny privy on the far side of the playground.

But more than the actual bricks and mortar of the school, it was the general air of poverty and deprivation that really upset Jack. Whether the area had been particularly affected by the depression, or whether it had always been this way, he had no real way of knowing, but he was shocked by the condition of some of the children.

There had been poor families in Hillsbridge, of course. There had been the fair-ground children, and the Higgins family from Eight Houses and the Pollocks from under the batch. They'd had lice in their cropped hair and holes in their shoes, stuffed up with cardboard. Sometimes they'd arrived at school with a piece of bread and jam in their hands, and Lord knows what tucked up the leg of their knickers. But compared with the children here, they were like kings and queens.

The children here didn't arrive with their breakfast in their hands. They had no breakfast, and sometimes had not eaten a tea the previous day either. They were scrawny and pinched, old before their time like wizened little men and women; some were aggressive and bullying, others cowed and miserable.

Congregating with the other teachers around the ancient coke stove one chilly playtime, Jack asked Hugh Eastment, the head teacher, why something wasn't done for them.

Hugh Eastment shrugged wearily. He was used to eager young students and new members of staff raising the point, and even going away to write lengthy reports on it, and it seemed almost criminal to disillusion them so soon. But they'd have to learn sometime. They couldn't go on in cloud cuckoo-land forever.

"There's nothing you can do," he explained. "Do you think we haven't tried, each and every one of us? When I first came here, I used to bring in a cake of soap to scrub the dirtiest, a bag of buns to feed the hungriest, and any good second-hand shoes I could find to put on the feet of those that needed them. And what happened? The buns were wolfed down by those who could eat the fastest, the children I washed with soap came in next morning dirtier than ever and the shoes found their way down to the pawn shop. It's a losing battle, I can tell you."

"But surely they're not all the same," Jack argued. "If you could do something for just one of them, it would be worth it. They can't all be idiots underneath all that grime. There must be one or two who could do well if only they were given the chance."

"I dare say, and we do our best. But it's no good coming here and expecting to work miracles. If you do, you'll only be disappointed," the headmaster said flatly, and the other teachers nodded their agreement.

"He's right, more's the pity," one of the younger ones told Jack. "It's the way people look at things round here that's to blame. They think all that matters is getting out and earning some money. The trouble is, with things as they are, there's not much chance of that at the moment."

"Most of them consider education a waste of time anyway," Hugh Eastment added. "Haven't you noticed—or did you put the lack of attention down to your own inexperience?"

Jack bristled. He had thought he'd held their attention pretty well considering a student was usually seen as fair game for any horseplay going, and he thought, too, that the others were wrong to give up so easily.

Perhaps many of the boys would grow up to be layabouts and louts, and the girls would be saddled with long families of their own almost before they had hung up their pinafores, but he felt sure there must be some eager to learn, given the opportunity and protected from the ridicule of their fellows.

One child in the class he was taking came to mind immediately, a boy whose face was bright beneath his pudding-basin haircut and who generally sat, fingers stuffed in his mouth, listening attentively to the lessons he had prepared.

"Take that boy Walter Heath," he said, drinking his tea. "You know the one I mean? He's quick and clever. I've noticed him particularly."

"He was asleep in my class this morning," the young teacher told Jack triumphantly. "Clean away, with his head down on his desk. You see, it's the parents I blame. If a child is overtired, he can't learn any more than if he's hungry. But they don't seem to know that— or care much if they do."

Jack grimaced, surprised to hear Walter had been so inattentive, but not ready yet to give up the argument. But Hugh Eastment was checking his watch and reaching for the bell-rope to summon the children back to classes, and discussion was at an end.

He did not forget, however, and that evening, making up his notes, he gave a lot of thought to how he could include a mention of established teachers' attitudes to boys like Walter Heath.

Note-making was a very important part of teaching practice. Jack had been told to provide himself with a good stout notebook, and in it he had to report on everything about the school where he was practising, from lighting to discipline, administration to toilet facilities. He was expected to draw detailed plans of the classrooms and playground, and to make suggestions as to how he would like to see things improved.

It was hard work and time consuming, but he enjoyed it, gaining great satisfaction from the neatly planned pages and meticulous detail. But tonight as he wrote, it was Walter Heath who was on his mind.

He was the one who could break out of the run if any of them could, Jack was sure of it. But why had he been so inattentive today? After the other teacher had mentioned it, Jack had noticed it himself. Was he just tired, as the teacher had suggested, or was he unwell? And if it was tiredness, was there nothing anyone could do —a word here or there—to insure he was fit to concentrate on the lessons that clearly interested him so much?

At last, sighing, Jack packed up his notebook and writing materials. Tomorrow was another day. And he would try to put some of his ideals into practice. If he didn't, he'd never be able to face his tutor at college again, no matter what Hugh Eastment and the other, more hardbitten teachers might say.

Next morning, he was disturbed, however, to see his star pupil was clearly no more able to concentrate than he had been the day before.

"Are you all right, Walter?" he asked once, and although the boy replied, "Yessir," his tone was such that Jack was sure he was not.

"Are you ill, or just tired?" he pressed him, very conscious of Hugh Eastment sitting at the back of the class and listening to him.

The boy rubbed a grubby hand across his rather flushed face.

"I'm a bit achy, that's all. And I can't keep warm."

"I believe you've got a temperature," Jack said, but the boy denied it, and after Jack had sent him to fetch his overcoat he settled back quite unobtrusively.

Later in the day, Hugh Eastment called him out of the room for a few minutes to discuss a teaching point, and when he returned the class was, as he had expected, in uproar.

"Back to your places at once!" Jack said sharply, hoping to impress Hugh Eastment, who was waiting on the other side of the door to see how he coped with the situation.

In the face of his authoritative tone, most of the pupils obeyed promptly, but he was surprised to see young Walter Heath still on his knees beside his chair.

"Well, Heath, and what do you think you are doing down there?" he asked sternly.

"I dropped me rubber, sir."

"Never mind that now. Get up at once."

The boy put a hand on the desk, appearing to try to pull himself up.

"Please, sir, I can't, sir," he whimpered.

The rest of the class erupted into laughter, and Jack unreasonably felt more annoyed than if the offender had been any of the others.

"What do you mean, Walter, you can't get up?" he demanded.

"I just can't. Me bloomin' legs won't work." Tears were filling the boy's eyes, and Jack realized that this was no prank.

Giving him his hand, he pulled him up, and as he did so, he noticed that the boy's hands were hot and sticky though he was still shivering.

"I don't think you should be in school, Walter," he said with decision. "You'd better go home and get your mother to call the doctor in to have a look at you,"

His words were greeted by another hoot of derision from the pupils.

"We don't have no doctor! We gets better by ourselves!"

Behind him the door opened and the class jumped to attention as they saw their headmaster standing in the doorway.

"Standard Five! Are you behaving for Mr Hall? There'll be three strokes of the cane for the first one I see trying to be too clever. And you, Walter Heath, in your place at once!"

"Wait. He's ill," Jack said and went on to explain to the headmaster. "I suggested the doctor," he finished. "That's what they were laughing at."

Hugh Eastment nodded sharply. "They would. Come here, Walter, and let me have a look at you."

The boy moved with difficulty and the headmaster sighed.

"You'd better get your cap and go home."

Jack was somewhat shocked.

"He ought to have medical attention. I don't care for the look of him."

The headmaster shrugged irritably. "Maybe. But this is a school, not a hospital, though what with fumigations and inspections for head lice, I sometimes wonder. No, if he's sick enough, his mother will have to call the doctor, whether she wants to spend the money or not. His sister can take him home. She's in Standard Seven—quite a big girl."

Jack was far from satisfied, but he knew there was little he could do. Hugh Eastment was right. It was a school, and with another forty children in this class alone to teach, there was no time or scope to do anything for Walter Heath, apart from sending him home. But all the same, it was far from the concept of teaching as he visualized it, and he decided that somehow, sometime, he would try to influence someone to accept his view that it should go much further than simply imparting knowledge of the three R's within four damp walls.

Walter Heath's sister, Lillian, did not return that day, and the next morning Jack sought her out.

"He's in hospital, mister," she said when he asked after Walter. "He fell down on the way home, and he couldn't get up again. We was going to carry him, but a man came along in a motor and took him off to the hospital."

"Good gracious! Well, what's the matter with him?" Jack asked.

The girl wriggled up her nose in an effort to remember. "Rheuma-ticky fever," she said at last.

"Rheumatic fever! Oh dear, dear," Jack repeated.

He should have known, he supposed. The stiff, aching joints, and the high temperature. Poor little lad! He'd be well looked after if he was in hospital, of course. But you never knew with rheumatic fever. It could leave you with a weak heart.

For the rest of the day, he couldn't forget Walter. Even reading in the newspapers that another miners' strike was imminent only took his mind off the child for a short while. It was as if, in some strange way, he had become responsible for him.

When he had finished his tea, Jack made up his mind to go over to the hospital to see the child. It was a Friday, so he did not have a lesson to prepare for the morning, and he set out, stopping on the way to buy some oranges and apples and a few books that he thought might interest Walter. Whether he would be able to see him or not, he did not know, but at least he would be showing an interest.

He had chosen his time well. It was visiting hour. He established which ward Walter was in and pushed open the swing doors, won-dering how he would be received if any of the boy's family were visiting. There were people sitting beside most of the children's beds, but Jack could not see Walter anywhere.

"I'm looking for Walter Heath," he said to the nursing sister, a tall, kindly-looking woman.

"Over in the corner. He'll be pleased to see you, I should think. He hasn't had anyone in to visit him today, poor lad."

Jack walked in the direction she had pointed. Walter was almost hidden behind a crate that covered the bottom half of the bed. But what surprised Jack even more was the cotton wool type of wadding that covered his body.

"Walter!" he said, shocked, and the boy looked up in surprise. "Sir!"

"How are you, Walter?"

"Not so good if I tries to move, sir. It bloomin' well hurts."

"Dear me!" Jack sat down beside his bed, noticing that the wad-ding extended even to the boy's fingers, holding them apart. "I brought you some books and a comic or two, but I can see you aren't going to be able to read them yet. Never mind, at least I can tell you what we've been doing at school today."

Beneath the fever, the boy's face brightened.

"Yes, sir. Thank you, sir."

For twenty minutes or so, Jack sat talking. Then, when it seemed to him the boy had had enough, he got up, stacking the reading materials on the locker beside his bed.

"I'll be going then, Walter."

"But you'll come again?" the boy asked eagerly.

Jack smiled. "I'll see what I can do. Just you concentrate on getting better, young man."

Leaving the boy, he went back into the corridor, following the signs for the main entrance. He was not really taking much notice of the people he passed, and when a nurse came towards him pushing a trolley he stepped aside automatically. Then, as she stopped, staring at him, he looked up into a welcome familiar face.

"Stella!" he said. "I don't believe it!"

"Jack! What are you doing here?"

"I'm visiting. And you're working. I didn't know you were back in this country, let alone in Bristol."

"Didn't you? But . . . " she looked puzzled, then shrugged. "Oh, never mind. Are you teaching yet?"

"Not officially. I'm still supposed to be training. At the university."

"Oh, yes. Well, you're looking very fit, Jack."

"You too."

"I always was disgustingly healthy. How's your leg?"

"I almost forget it's not mine."

"Hah! There speaks a veteran! And married life, how does that suit you?"

"Married life?" he repeated, surprised.

"Yes. Didn't you get married?"

"No. Why?"

"Oh, I thought you were engaged."

He shuffled. "Oh, that. It all fell through."

An authoritative figure appeared at the end of the corridor, and Stella made a face.

"Oh cripes, that's Sister. I shall have to go. One of these days I'm going to see if I can't pass my exams so I can be the one to do the bossing around for a change."

He laughed. She hadn't changed.

"Nice to see you, Stella."

"You too."

When she'd gone, he felt elated. It *had* been nice to see her. What was it about her that could make him feel like this, warm through and through? She'd had the same effect on him in London and he'd put it down to the fact that he was just recovering from the most traumatic experience of his life. But it was nothing like that now.

He couldn't get her out of his mind all night, and before long he was wishing he'd tried to make some arrangement to see her again. She might have refused, of course. A girl like Stella wouldn't be short of company. At least she wasn't married, for he'd carefully noticed the absence of a wedding ring.

The thought reminded him of the remark she'd made about him being married. Odd, that, to have half a story. It wasn't as if the Rosa affair had ended only yesterday. It was a long time ago now. And yet, why should she know? Why should he imagine for even a moment she might be interested in him, or anything to do with him?

But he hoped, all the same, that he would see her again, and the hope gave him an extra reason for going back to the hospital to visit Walter. He went the very next evening, but as he walked through the grounds and endless corridors, there was no sign of Stella.

When he entered Walter's ward, there was already a visitor beside the boy's bed, a fat, pasty-faced woman who appeared to be bursting out of her tightly buttoned coat.

She must be Walter's mother, Jack assumed. He went towards her, holding out his hand, but she merely sniffed, eyeing him with narrow suspicion.

"I'm Jack Hall," he began. "I don't know if Walter had told you about me . . . "

"Indeed he has!" The woman's chins were quivering. "I'm pleased to meet you, Mr Hall."

"And I'm pleased to meet you, Mrs Heath."

But there was no answering smile on her face.

"I'm pleased to meet you so as I can tell you what I think of you, bothering my boy. Don't you know how ill he is? And you come in here, pushing books under his nose. Why, you're as bad as that interfering bugger who brought him in here—poking into things that don't concern you."

"I'm sorry you see it like that, Mrs Heath. I was concerned about Walter. He was in my class when he was taken ill, and . . . "

443

"Yes, an' all the work you expect him to do, it's not surprising! Enough to give him a fever of the brain, if you ask me!"

"Oh really!" Jack exclaimed. "You don't seem to realize, Walter is a bright boy."

"I'll thank you to leave my boy alone, and not go putting ideas in his head!" Mrs Heath said indignantly. "He's got enough of them without the likes of you making him ten times worse." She stood up, gathering the books and comics Jack had brought the previous evening and thrust them into his arms. "Now take these with you, and don't come here bothering him no more!"

"But Mrs Heath . . . "

"Go on!"

Her raised voice had attracted the attention of the ward sister. She came bustling up, and Jack, deciding this was a case where discretion might usefully be the better part of valour, apologized, bid goodnight to the round-eyed Walter, and beat a hasty retreat, pushing the pile of comics into the arms of the surprised sister as he went.

He was beginning to see what Hugh Eastment had meant when he talked about the difficulties of educating these people. And although he felt he had failed Walter badly, he could not help being glad that by the time he left hospital and took his place once more at school, he, Jack, would be safely back at university. For he couldn't see what credibility he could possibly have after being chased out of a hospital ward by the boy's irate mother.

It was only when he was out in the road that he remembered he had not seen Stella again and knew there was no way, now, that he could go back into the hospital to look for her. But he wouldn't let it rest, he decided. As soon as he could, he would look her up again. And unless she had some very good reason for not going out with him, he'd do his best not to take no for an answer.

FOR THE next few days, the newspapers were full of the imminent miners' strike.

Jack had always been against militant action, but as he studied both fact and comment he began to see there was little else the men could do.

Since their agreement with Lloyd George in the autumn their meagre pay award had been whittled away bit by bit by inflation; and in any case most of the pits were on short time. They had pinned their hopes on the promises of the National Wages Board, only to be disappointed when quite suddenly, in the middle of March, Lloyd George announced that he intended de-controlling the mines.

That precipitated the crisis. The owners had no intention of being held to any rash promise made on their behalf by the Government. They huffed, puffed and fudged the issue, and the miners' representatives saw only too clearly what would happen in the long run. There would be more men out of work and a devalued wage packet for those lucky enough to have one at all.

Thinking they had the so-called Triple Alliance behind them, they stopped work at midnight on 31st March.

Within days Hillsbridge was like a ghost town. Without the hooters and sirens, without the turning pit wheels, without the coal carts grinding through the streets everything was unnaturally quiet, and not even the groups of men, gathered on the street corners at unusual hours, could lift the air of unreality.

"Strikes—I can't abide them!" Charlotte said crossly as she did her weekend baking. "They don't do no good—more harm if you ask me. You just end up worse than you started."

"But there comes a time when a man's got to take a stand," James argued.

She snorted again. "That's all very well—if you can afford to do it. I'm not so worried about us—we'll get by—but take our Jim. How's he going to manage? No work, no pay. That's the way it is."

"Don't worry, they'll see him all right," James told her. "Tom Heron, the agent, is going to find out if we'm entitled to unemployment pay and there's bound to be a relief fund opened up sooner or later to help them with young'uns."

Charlotte ignored this, pounding at the dough with unnecessary vigour.

"It don't do no good," she said again. "They say the pump men are coming out too, and the engine winders and the ventilation men. What's going to happen, I should like to know? The seams will get flooded and then where will you be? I even heard a story today that the poor ponies over at Grieve Bottom might be drowned."

"That's rubbish, Lotty," James said mildly. "They'll make sure the ponies be safe. You needn't worry your head about that."

"Well, all the same, I don't hold with it!" Charlotte went on. "If they've got any sense, they'll go back before May Day. That's all I've got to say."

But they did not go back before May Day. When the townsfolk

gathered in the recreation ground for the big Labour Gala, the pit gates were still locked, and the speeches made by the leaders from the wagons that had been loaned for the purpose were mostly all concerned with the struggle that was going on in the coal-field.

They had to stick it out, that was the message. If they didn't, they'd be right back where they started—and most likely even worse. The miners cheered, their spirits refreshed by the stirring music of the four bands, and the feeling of comradeship that came from being determined to see this thing through together, even though they had been betrayed by their allies.

But they had no way of knowing that before the strike was over, they would be stirred to a mood of violence worse than any of those present had seen in their lifetime.

JACK KEPT his promise to himself to see Stella O'Halloran again as soon as his teaching practice was over, by finding out what hours she was working at the hospital and waiting for her one evening outside the gates.

He was prepared for her rejection when he suggested he should take her out, but she appeared quite willing, and they arranged to have dinner together to talk over old times, on the following Friday.

Jack was ridiculously anxious that it should turn out well, thinking at first it was because it was so long since he had taken a girl out. But as the day drew nearer, he realized it was more than that. It was important for it to be successful because he wanted to impress Stella, not just as any girl, but as herself.

He need not have worried. From the time he collected her from the hostel where she had a room, they were comfortable with each other. The meal was a success, Jack handling the menus with impressive authority.

Stella, however, was not overawed as some girls would have been.

"You're really spoiling me," she said, pulling a face as she saw the prices on the menu. "And on a student's grant, too!"

Jack laughed. "Losing a leg in the service of one's country does have certain compensations, especially if one happened to be an officer," he commented drily.

She nodded. "There are plenty of poor Tommies as badly off as you and worse, trying to scrape a living now, and you treat me to a meal like this."

"It's a special occasion," he told her. "But don't expect such a lavish outing next time, will you?"

"All right, I won't," she laughed, and he noted with a sense of elated surprise that she had not denied that there would be a next time.

Over a meal of roast lamb, washed down with wine, they brought each other up to date on what had happened since the long-ago London days, Stella describing with brevity and humour what must have been hell, France in the last weeks of the war, and Jack explaining the method of teacher training he was now undergoing and his reasons for deciding on the university course.

But he made no mention of Rosa.

Although meeting her again had convinced him their engagement would indeed have been a disaster, the pain of rejection was still there. Just why he was so sensitive about it he was not sure, but he thought it might be because at the back of his mind he believed the loss of his leg had been responsible in some way for her change of heart and sudden flight.

He knew this was unreasonable—he had already lost his leg when she exchanged Ted's company for his. But he wondered if that might actually have been some kind of morbid attraction for her in the first place, before she realized she couldn't after all go through with it.

That night when he left Stella at the door to her hostel, they made arrangements to meet again the following week, and Jack, although tired, was pleased with the way the evening had gone. The pleasant, warm feeling was back, surrounding him as it always seemed to when Stella was around, and he felt exhilarated as he took a taxi back to his lodgings.

Why hadn't he looked her up before? he asked himself. Why had he just let her go? There was no answer to that, but he was determined not to let her go so easily again.

APRIL came and went, and May, and the warm sunshine mirrored Jack's happiness.

For the first time in his life, everything seemed to have come together just as he wanted it. He was busily engaged day by day in the sort of study he found most fascinating, and soon he would be embarking properly on the career he had always wanted. His personal life too was rewarding — not the wild, passionate elation he had known with Rosa, but something which was just as good in its own way, warmer, safer and more comfortable. He took pleasure in the way Stella looked, the tone of her voice, her cool touch. When they were together, he felt happy and strangely complete, and when they were not, he missed her, storing up every amusing or interesting experience to share with her.

But after a while, he noticed another reaction, one he thought of as very odd. If he began to think about how things might be if he and Stella remained together, a tight, choking feeling he could not explain began inside him, closing in like a straight jacket, until he found some way of channelling his thoughts into a different direction.

It was the same when they were alone together. He kissed her and held her with tenderness, but if ever he felt the stirrings of breathless desire, a shutter came down almost at once, blocking off feeling and producing the same sense of inexplicable claustrophobia.

At first, he did not worry about it. But as the weeks passed and the days became longer and warmer, he began to realize he could not go on like this forever, shutting himself off from extremes of emotion and refusing to plan beyond the next few casual meetings.

Already, people were beginning to look on them as a couple. Stella was always included in invitations from his friends, and he from hers, and his landlady had commented on one occasion that he should look for a teaching post with a house to go with it. At the moment, he thought Stella was quite happy with things as they were, but it might very well be that before long she would be thinking along the same lines as his landlady. Sooner or later she was almost bound to look for some commitment, and the thought of that made his stomach knot in panic and everything in him cry out in silent protest.

Why? he asked himself. Why should he feel like this? He was so fond of Stella, he had begun to think he was in love with her, yet the very thought of telling her so made him feel physically sick, and he would almost rather not see her than have her expect more from him than a transitory love.

But why . . . why? She was a nice girl, a wonderful girl, and plenty of men would give their eye-teeth to be in his position. So what was the matter with him that he should feel like this?

It was Charlotte who gave him a glimpse of the truth.

He had come home, as he so often did, for a cup of tea and a couple of her delicious home-made johnny-cakes, and he was sitting in the kitchen with her and Harry when she suddenly raised the subject of Stella.

"When are we going to meet this girl of yours?" she asked bluntly.

448

"But you know her, Mam," he said. "You've known the O'Hallorans for years."

"You know what I mean, Jack," she said impatiently. "If you don't want to lose her, you ought to do something about it. I know there's a shortage of men, thanks to the damn war, but you can't expect a girl like her to wait for ever."

Oh no! he thought. Not Mam, too!

"Give me a chance," he retorted. "We've only been going out together a couple of months."

"Long enough to be fixing up some kind of an understanding," Charlotte told him tartly. "Don't you know there's talk of Hal retiring soon? If he goes back up North where he came from, like as not she'll go, too, and that'll be the last you'll see of her."

Although annoyed, Jack said nothing. Mam was biased of course. She'd always wanted him to marry someone to suit her ideals, and she no doubt thought Stella was a good match. But it wasn't knowing that that made him turn away silently. It was hearing her put his own thoughts into words.

"You know what I think?" Charlotte went on, ignoring his stony response. "I think you're afraid she'll let you down like Rosa Clements did. Well, you're wrong, Jack. She's a very different girl. I know that Rosa business hurt you more than you ever let on, but it was all for the best, and you mustn't let what happened mar your life."

"Oh, don't be so silly, Mam," he said irritably, but in his heart of hearts he knew she'd struck pretty close to the truth and when he was alone in his room, he mulled it over again, looking squarely for the first time at the facts he had refused to face.

Once before he'd told a girl he loved her, and asked her to marry him. He'd bared his soul to her, and pinned all his hopes and dreams on the future they would share. And she'd gone—disappeared without so much as seeing him to explain. And he hadn't needed her explanation. He had known why. Deep in the part of him that was hidden even from himself, he had known.

He was only half a man, and it was too much to expect any girl to take on a cripple . . .

Now that it was out, it should have been better, but it was not. For in spite of himself, in spite of all the contradictory emotions, he knew he was in love with Stella, more deeply and lastingly than he had ever been with Rosa. But at the same time, he knew it would

449

be no good. It would end in misery for them both. What she felt for him could only be based on pity, and one day she was certain to realize that. Perhaps she did already. Perhaps she had only accepted his invitations so as not to hurt his feelings. That would be like Stella. She was a nurse, and the most generous of people. And he could not put her in the position of testing her kindness to the limits.

Yet, he wanted desperately to know the truth, even if it meant the end of everything between them. The strain began to tell, added to by the worry of his examinations and knowing he would soon have to find a job. Tension crept into their meetings, where before there had been only warmth, and he became distant, moody and irritable.

One day in June, she lost patience with him.

"What's the matter with you these days?" she asked. "You used to be full of fun, but not any more. Now it's an obstacle course not to say the wrong thing."

His heart sank. So she was getting tired of him, just as he had known she would. He sought a defence in bad temper. "You'd better find someone else to spend your time with then, hadn't you?"

"Oh, Jack, there are times I could hit you!" she said in exasperation. "I don't want someone else. Don't you know that by now?"

He looked at her, wondering if he dare believe her. But once before he had been stupid enough to think a girl had forgotten his disability. He could not take the risk of making the same mistake again.

"You can do better than me, Stella," he said. "You don't want to be landed with a cripple."

"I don't think of you as a cripple. And neither should you. For goodness sake, stop pitying yourself."

"I'm not pitying myself. I'm pitying you, stuck with me when you could do so much better."

"Oh!" she exclaimed. "With all these exams you're just impossible, Jack Hall. You're absolutely infuriating!"

"Maybe. Maybe it would be better if we didn't see one another until they're over." As soon as he had said it, he was hoping she would tell him again not to be stupid. But she didn't. This time she, too, had been pushed to her limits.

"Maybe that would be best," she said.

AFTER she had gone, the darkness seemed to close in around him, shutting out the sun.

He had thought that, by pretending he had not committed himself, it would hurt less. He had thought that this time he would be prepared. Not so.

She had gone, and the rejection was as sharp as when Rosa had left—sharper, for this time he knew he really cared. Depression was like a stormy sea. He felt he was drowning in it. Although he had prepared himself, although he knew he had brought it upon himself, he still was shocked. Despite his tormenting self-doubt, he had expected her to stay.

His final days at college meant nothing to him now. Without her, even the things he had worked for seemed meaningless. When it was all over, he packed his things and went back to Hillsbridge in a daze of misery. He had interviews to attend, but he had no enthusiasm for them.

So sunk in self-pity was he, the depression of Hillsbridge hardly affected him at all. It was merely an extension of his own depression, another example of the wretched black world he found himself in.

Had he but noticed, he would have seen that the mood of the men had changed now, hardened with the passing weeks, with the poverty and the hunger. Their meetings were more bitter, although still peaceful, and when groups of them gathered on the bridge, the hopelessness was etched into the leathery lines of their faces.

They had had support from their own, it was true. A Welsh male voice choir had toured the area, giving concerts in aid of the relief fund, and there had been parades when those with money or food to spare had given it for those whose long families had quickly eaten away what little they had. But quiet though they might be, they were also stubborn, and already they had twice voted against acceptance of the owners' offer.

Now, it was coming to the vote again, and hardship was driving a wedge between those who wanted acceptance and those who were determined to see the struggle through to the bitter end. Whereas before there had been unanimity, now there were arguments, with vociferous factions arising on either side.

Stepping off the train that day in early July, Jack felt the tension in the air, but cared little for it. He had not seen Stella for three weeks now, but she still occupied his mind as much, if not more, than before. And he wondered, too, what his mother would have to

451

say when she heard it was all over. She wouldn't be at all pleased, he knew, but perhaps he could keep it from her for the time being at least.

That hope was short lived.

Almost as soon as he got into the house, Charlotte raised the subject, turning from the fire that was making the sweat run in rivers down her cheeks. "Well, Jack, and what have you done about Stella?"

"Nothing, Mam," he said, hoping his tight tone would stop her, but he should have known better than that.

"I thought as much," she said, brushing a strand of greying hair behind her ear. "She's home, you know. The woman who goes up there to clean told me. Home for a holiday and then going back to London, she said. I knew straight away there must be something wrong between you."

Jack felt sick with shock, but he hid his dismay. If Stella was going back to London, it could mean only one thing, that she had decided to wash her hands of the whole affair and start afresh.

"Jack, you're a fool," Charlotte said, and he bridled.

"Mam, I wish you wouldn't interfere in things you know nothing about."

He would have had his answer when Charlotte had recovered from her surprise, but at that moment, the door opened and James came in calling, "Cheerio," to Walter Clements over his shoulder.

"Can we have tea a bit earlier tonight, Mother?" he said to Charlotte. "There's a meeting down in the square to talk about this 'ere offer."

She nodded brusquely. "If you must. And I hope you'll have the good sense to call it all off this time."

"Be you coming down to hear what they've got to say?" James asked Jack.

Jack shook his head. "No thanks, Dad. I've got some applications to write out. I'm going upstairs where it's quiet."

"Ah, well, at least our Jim's coming," James said resignedly, and for the first time, Jack saw that his father actually minded that he had not followed him into the pit. Not wanting to be buried there himself, he had seen only Charlotte's eagerness for him to be free of it. He hadn't realized that James felt, deep down, that what had been good enough for him should be good enough for his sons. Even in troubled times, as these were.

Jack left his mother washing up the tea plates and went up to his room. The window had been thrown open to the summer's day, and through it he could hear the sound of music floating up from the valley below.

They must have got the band together for the meeting, he supposed. That didn't bode well for those who wanted a vote to end the strike. The band was always good for stirring up a fighting spirit.

He sat down on the window-sill, his writing pad beside him, and remembered how he had sat here as a child. How long ago it seemed now, and yet, in some ways, how close! Nostalgia brought the misery flooding back again, and impatiently he took the top off his pen and began to write.

When he had finished, he looked out of the window again. The band had stopped playing now, but from time to time he heard the distant roar of a hundred and more voices, raised in a unanimous shout, and he wondered just what was going on. Perhaps he'd wander down the hill and find out after all. The sweet evening air was making him restless, and anything would be better than facing his mother's questions again.

He could hear the hubbub more clearly as he reached the foot of the hill, but it seemed to be closer than the town square. The wind must be blowing this way. But as he rounded the corner, he stopped, unable to believe his eyes.

The road, as it curved away again up South Hill, was a seething mass of men. And as he listened, the band began to play again, ragged now, as if half the instruments were missing, but still belting out a defiant 'Men of Harlech.'

Puzzled and a little alarmed without really knowing why, he hurried across the bridge and saw a small group of men who had broken away from the main procession smoking and spitting as they watched the tail end disappear round the bend of the hill. Among them were James, Jim, and Walter Clements.

"What in the world is going on?" he asked when he reached them.

"Trouble," James said shortly. "I've never knowed them so mad. We'd just took a vote on the strike and decided we was going to carry on when the news came through."

"What news?" Jack asked.

"The strike's over." Jim spat deliberately at the kerb. "At least it's supposed to be. We've been sold down the river again, and we'm fighting mad about it. But we don't want nothing to do with that lot and what they'm going to do."

Jack stared up the hill. Only a few men were visible now, but he could still hear the noise, the shouts and the ragged band music.

"Where are they going?" he asked. But in his heart of hearts, he already knew.

"They'm off up to the big house to get O'Halloran," James told him. "They'm going to tar and feather him—or so they say. Well, we don't want no part of anything like that."

"But why?" Jack asked. "What's he done?"

They shook their heads. "Nothing really. Though there was talk of him retiring on all the money he's made out of the pits. But I don't envy him. I wouldn't want to be in his shoes, the mood they'm in."

"No, t'won't do no good him hiding inside his fine house," Walter Clements put in. "They'll break the door down soon as look at it, and have him out of it."

Jack said nothing. Slow horror was filling him, driving out all his fears and resentment. The men's patience had finally been exhausted, and this last straw had somehow turned them into a howling mob, crazy for revenge. They were marching up the hill to Hal's house with violence in mind. He didn't care much what they did to Hal. He was old enough to take care of himself. But Stella was there, if his mother was to be believed, and he couldn't leave her to their mercy.

Without a word he began to hobble along the street after them.

"Where d'you think you're going?" James called after him.

He hesitated, knowing that if he admitted to what was in his mind, they'd stop him. "To see what happens," he said over his shoulder.

"Don't be so daft. You don't want to get mixed up in it," James called, but he took no notice.

He hurried on, cursing his leg for the way it was slowing him down, and wishing for the moment that he had his crutches back. He'd really been able to swing along on those.

The evening had become close, and before he had gone far, sweat was running down his neck and soaking his shirt, But he kept going. Half-way up the hill he caught the tail-end of the marchers, and the wild atmosphere struck him with the same fearful apprehension that he had felt on sighting an enemy aircraft in the war.

454

"For Christ's sake, where do you think you're going?" he asked one of the marchers.

"Don't you know? We'm going to tar and feather old Hal. He's bloody well asked for it."

"Why?" Jack panted.

"Living it up while we're starving. Making out to be our friend, while all the time . . . We'll show him, don't you worry."

The hill began to flatten out and O'Halloran's house came in sight, a big, stone-built dwelling set back in its own grounds.

The leading marchers were in the garden already, trampling plants and small bushes underfoot as they surged forward, chanting now at the tops of their voices:

"We want Hal! We want Hal!"

"Come out, you yellow bellied coward, or we'll come in and get you!" one man yelled above the uproar, and Jack saw the curtains of one of the bedrooms move.

He was not the only one.

"We know you're there, you bugger. Come on out!"

Jack looked around him in disbelief. They were mostly men he knew, men he'd known all his life as peaceable and slow to anger. But now some madness had taken hold of them, and driven by hunger and despair, they were seeking revenge upon the person who was to them the bosses' figure-head, Hal, the man who stood between them and the hated owners.

As he watched, one man ran forward, hammering on the door, and others picked up stones and clods of earth. It was a riot, the most dangerous situation Jack had seen in peacetime, and his only thought was to get to Stella.

Looking around to make sure no one was watching him, he found a path at the side of the house. There, by the greenhouses, he saw one lad about to put a stone through the glass and catching him by surprise he hit him so squarely on the jaw that the boy lost his footing and fell backwards into a cucumber frame. Not waiting for him to pick himself out, Jack went on.

The back door was locked. He had expected it would be. And he had little hope that they would answer his knocking. But someone must have been in the kitchen and heard the glass cucumber frame smash, for he saw a face peeping anxiously from behind the curtains, and he ran forward, knocking on the window.

"Stella! Is Stella there?"

The face, that of a timid maidservant, disappeared, and moments later the inside door opened and he saw Stella come into the porch. She was pale and frightened, but when she saw Jack she opened the glass door quickly, pulling him inside and locking it after him.

"Jack! Thank God, you're here! They've gone mad!"

He took her arm, and it was as if their separation had never been.

"Let me get you out of here, Stella. If we slip out this way and up the garden, we can go down over the fields and along the bottom of the batch."

She shook her head. "No, Jack, I can't."

"No one will see. They're all round at the front."

"I can't leave Mummy and Daddy. I just can't do it."

"But they're violent, Stella. They want to tar and feather your father, and God only knows what they'll do if they get in here. I couldn't stop them."

"I'm not leaving, Jack," she said stubbornly. "Mummy and Daddy are in the bedroom. You'd better come up."

He followed her up the stairs, and she clung to his arm all the way. He thought he had never seen her so frightened, and when they reached the landing looking out over the front garden he could see why. From up here, the mob looked even more menacing, a sea of snarling upturned faces. Someone, looking up, must have seen them move, and a clod of earth struck the window.

Jack drew Stella away, up the last flight of stairs to the top floor. In the front bedroom, Hal and his wife were having some kind of argument, and Mrs O'Halloran turned to Stella with, "Stella, for goodness sake, tell him . . . " before realizing she was not alone and stopping in mid-sentence.

"This is Jack," Stella said briefly. "You've heard me talk of him."

"Oh, yes." Mrs O'Halloran smiled vaguely from a social habit too strong to be broken even in circumstances like these, then the mask dropped and she ran to Stella, catching at her arm.

"Stop your father, dear, do! Tell him he can't do it!"

"Do what?" she asked.

"I'm going out on that balcony to talk to the men," Hal thundered, pointing to the French windows that gave on to a small stone balcony. "They'll see sense. They're bound to. I just don't know what all the fuss is about."

"You can't go out there, dear!" Mrs O'Halloran cried in real distress. "Oh, tell him he can't do it, Stella!"

"She's right, Mr O'Halloran," Jack said. "The mood they're in they'll be right up here and get you."

"Well, we've got to do something!" O'Halloran roared. "Look at them out there—all over my fuchsias!"

"Never mind your fuchsias, Daddy . . . "

"Hal, you can't go out there! I won't let you!"

O'Halloran ignored them both. A lifetime of living in a houseful of women had given him plenty of practice in doing just that. He crossed to the wardrobe, pulling up an ottoman and standing on it to reach on top.

"Where's that gun of mine? If they don't mind themselves, I'll blast a few rounds off at them. That'll cool 'em off!"

"Let me talk to them," Jack said suddenly.

They all stopped talking and looked at him.

"*You?*" O'Halloran boomed, echoing the thoughts of the others.

"Yes, me," Jack said. "I'm a miner's son. They know that. At least let me try."

As they hesitated, looking at one another, there was another roar from below, and taking the decision, Jack moved purposefully.

"Go on out of this room, all of you, and barricade the door," he told them. "Then if they do come up after me, they won't get any further. Go on!" he said again when they made no move.

Stella was the first to recover her wits. She put a hand on each of their arms. "Mummy, Daddy, do as he says." Then, in spite of their protests, she led them firmly out of the room.

Jack followed them, locking the door after them and pushing the key into one of his inside pockets. Then, pausing only to summon his courage, he crossed to the window.

It was exactly like flying an operation, he thought. He'd done that over and over again. He had to do this only once. And it wasn't a matter of life and death—at least, he hoped it wasn't!

As soon as they saw him at the window, the roar went up again, but he did not let it deter him. He lifted the catch on the French windows, pushed them open and stepped out on to the balcony.

For a moment the roar seemed to rise up and swallow him, but he went forward until he was at the very edge of the stone balcony, his hands resting on the balustrade. Beneath him, the faces were no longer familiar and he wondered if he had been wrong to think he could influence them. These weren't the men he had known since boyhood. They were a hungry, crazy mob. They wouldn't listen to him. It had been stupid and presumptuous of him to think they would.

Slowly, very slowly, he raised his hands, motioning them, without much hope, to silence. At first, among the shouts, he heard his name. Then, to his enormous relief, the roar seemed to lessen until he thought he could risk shouting above it.

"For Christ's sake, what do you all think you're doing? You're like a lot of animals, gone crazy. What good do you think this will do?"

"We want Hal!" came back the shout, a hundred voices almost as one.

"What for?" Jack shouted back. "What's he done?"

"He's sold us down the river. That's what. Sold us down the river!"

"That's not true," Jack yelled above the hubbub. "And even if it were, what the hell do you think you're going to achieve this way? You ought to stand back and look at yourselves. I can't believe you're the men I've grown up with. Take you, Mr Presley, what are you going to tell your wife when you get home? That you've been up at the manager's house throwing stones at his window and trampling all over his garden? And as for you, Ewart Brixey, I shouldn't want to face your mother if I was you. I should be too bloody ashamed of myself!"

The roar became an uneasy muttering. Above it, someone shouted, "Who d'you think you bloody are?"

"I'm a miner's son and proud of it," Jack yelled back. "But I'm not feeling very proud at the moment, standing here and looking at you. You've got a grievance, of course, you have. But this isn't the way to put it right. It's nothing to do with Hal. It was Lloyd George who betrayed you. He's the one to get at if you can."

"What, march to bloody London?" called one wag.

"If you want. That would make folk sit up and take notice. But if you don't think your feet would stand it, there are other ways, civilized ways, not making fools of yourselves like this."

"How then?" somebody called.

"You get a vote, don't you? Use it. Kick Lloyd George so far out of office he can never get back. Oh, there's ways if you look for them. But it's not like this. This way you're a disgrace to Hillsbridge and a disgrace to the coal mines. And the lot of you should be ashamed of yourselves!"

He paused, pressing down hard on the stone balustrade. He was shaking from head to foot, and he had no idea whether or not he had done any good. To him, the men looked as angry and dangerous as ever, twisting and turning this way and that, looking to their mates for a lead. Then, to his amazement, he heard one voice louder than all the others.

"He's right, lads. He's right!"

Jack held his breath, afraid almost to hope that the tide might be turning. Then the muttering became a murmur of agreement, and he realized the crowd was gradually diminishing—those at the back had already drifted away. He remained on the balcony, and beneath him they turned in twos and threes, casting furtive, shamefaced looks back towards the house as they sidled away.

"Back to the square, lads," someone shouted in an effort to muster something of the previous spirit, but it was all over, and they knew it. As Jack watched them go, he felt not only relief, but sadness that a proud and responsible body of men should have been brought to this.

Damn Lloyd George, he thought. Damn the owners. Damn everyone who thought he could exploit the miner and drive him to the limits of his endurance. It would be a long time before the men of Hillsbridge forgot the shame of having been goaded beyond that endurance, a long time before they forgot the glimpse they had had into a world where law and order had been pushed over the knife-edge on which it balanced and mob rule had reigned, if only for a short time.

And Jack thought he would never forgive those who, by their complacence, had stripped the dignity from men he had known and respected all his life.

As the last of them drifted through the gates, Jack heard the door handle rattle, and taking the key from his pocket with fingers that shook, he unlocked the door.

Stella ran to him, catching at his arm and almost sobbing with relief.

"Jack, they're going! What did you say to them? What did you do?"

Suddenly he was more embarrassed than anything.

"I don't know really . . . "

Mrs O'Halloran took his other hand, holding it tightly between hers.

"Oh, thank you, Mr Hall! Thank you!"

Only Hal himself stood by the window, looking almost as shame-faced as the men had done.

"Look what they've done to my garden!" he grumbled loudly. "What the hell did they think they were playing at? Those fuchsias are ruined—ruined—and they were just at their best, too!"

Mrs O'Halloran shook her head to express her exasperation with him, but she was smiling all the same.

"Mr Hall, how can we ever repay you?" she asked.

Jack grinned at Stella.

"For a start you can give me a large glass of whisky," he said.

"I DON'T KNOW another man in Hillsbridge who'd do what you did today, Jack," Stella said. "You were very brave."

It was an hour later and they were sitting in the back garden in the fading golden light. From here, it was impossible to see the havoc the mob had wreaked on the front garden. Above them, the apple trees were heavy with foliage and young growing fruit, and around them the air seemed to be alive with a haze of gnats—all the peace of an English summer evening that made it difficult to believe that the events of the day had really happened at all.

"Oh, I don't know," Jack began modestly, then laughed. "If you knew how frightened I was, you wouldn't say that."

Her eyes held his.

"What's that got to do with it? Only idiots are never frightened. It's much braver to be scared out of your wits and still do what you have to. Isn't it?"

He shrugged. "I don't know. Let's change the subject, shall we?"

"To what?" she asked playfully.

"Us," he said. "Stella, I've missed you like hell."

Her face had gone solemn. "And I've missed you."

"What's all this nonsense about you going to London?" he asked her.

She looked away. "I didn't want to stay around here any more. Not after you . . . Well, there didn't seem any point."

"Why?" he asked tentatively.

"Because . . . oh, Jack, what do you want from me? A declaration of undying love?"

He grinned, wishing it were just a joke. "Yes."

"Well, you won't get it! It's up to the man to take the risk of being turned down. Or so I've always heard. And to think I said you were brave!"

He smiled briefly. She was right, of course. There was nothing to be gained by sitting back in case he got hurt again, any more than there would have been by shrinking from facing the mob, or chickening out when an enemy aircraft was on his tail. Playing it carefully didn't make it any easier. He'd learned that during the last few weeks, but he should have known it anyway.

He leaned over, touching her hand.

"Are you calling me a coward?" he teased.

"Maybe," she teased back.

"No woman is going to do that and get away with it. I can see I'll just have to take the bull by the horns and ask you to marry me."

"Go on then. I dare you."

"All right. Will you marry me, Stella?"

"Oh, Jack," she said. "I thought you'd never ask."

The teasing had gone from her eyes now, and he could see them only as a mirror for his own feelings.

What the hell had he been worried about? he wondered. Why should he have thought she would be in the least like Rosa? Love swelled in him, drowning all doubts as if they had never been.

30

NEXT DAY, the very old carts, laden with coal, were trundling along in the streets of Hillsbridge, and the pit wheels were turning once more.

The strike was over. But the town would never be quite the same again. Too many jobs had been lost, and the economic climate in the country was such that there could be no regaining them. The depression that had begun in the disillusioned days that followed the war to end all wars would go on until yet another war, another holocaust, rocked the world.

James was among those laid off when the pits went back to work.

"It's about time you had a bit of a rest," Charlotte said, but beneath the forced cheerfulness, her heart was heavy. With a chest like his, she knew it was unlikely he would ever work again, and the thought was a miserable one. It made her feel the way she did every autumn, watching the green leaves turn to brown and drift down to the gutters, leaving the branches bare and forlorn, the sadness that grew sharper as the sun lost its strength. She had always hated autumn.

"At least our Jim's been taken on again," she said, determined to look on the bright side. "What he'd have done with the children to bring up if he'd been out of work for long, I don't know."

"Talking of children, I suppose we shall have to be thinking about our Harry soon, and what he's going to do," James said, and Charlotte looked at him in surprise. It was so unlike James to be the one to do any planning for the future it made her a little uneasy.

"We've no need to worry just yet," she said briskly. "He's bound to stay on at school for another three years now they've changed the law. But perhaps it would be a good idea if I was to go and see Mr Davies to see if he can get him a scholarship. I shouldn't like him to think we'd done less for him than we did for Jack. He might not be so clever, but he's no fool for all that."

"No, he's a sharper, though he tries hard to pretend he's not," James said, and Charlotte nodded. He was right, Harry was a sharper —he would do well. And so might they all, if they'd had the chance . . .

She shivered. Would it never be completely exorcised, that guilt? Would it be with her to the end of her days?

"I still can't get over our Jack, though," James went on, shaking his head.

It had been the talk of Hillsbridge when Jack had announced his engagement to Stella O'Halloran, and no one had been more surprised than James. It was hard enough to believe that he was going to be related by marriage to Hal—the boss—and when he stopped to think that he would be related to Dr Oliver Scott as well it made his mind boggle. And Jack had fixed himself up with a job, too. In September he would be taking up a position at a school in Bath, and he and Stella were busy looking for a house.

"What I can't understand is why the boys are settled, and the girls still on the shelf!" he went on.

Charlotte smiled. "They aren't on the shelf. I think our Dolly will make up her mind for this one. And Amy—well, it wouldn't surprise me if she didn't marry up the scale, too. Mr Walker, who defended Ted, was very taken with her, you know."

James spat impatiently into the fire. "Our Dolly's been engaged quite long enough. It's time she got on with it. And as for Mr

Walker, he's far too old for Amy. He must be thirty, if he's a day."

"You can't pick their husbands and wives for them," Charlotte said. "I've learned that. Although ... " She broke off, a small smile playing around her mouth as she remembered how she had broken up Jack's affair with Rosa. "Maybe sometimes you can give things a bit of a helping hand, or otherwise!"

Outside the scullery door, Nipper began to scratch and whine, and she got up to let him in. He was getting old now and couldn't see too well, but he was contented enough, and always managed to find the energy to greet Ted enthusiastically when he came home, which, these days, seemed to be more and more often. Three weeks ago, he'd been home, and he was coming again this weekend, and from the tone of the letter she'd had from him this week, Charlotte thought it sounded as if he might be going to stay for longer than usual. She supposed the difficulty in getting a job could be a reason, for although Ted would be no more likely to find employment here than anywhere else, at least he would have a roof over his head that he didn't have to pay rent for, and three meals a day placed on the table in front of him.

As she came back into the kitchen with Nipper padding softly at her heels, James rose, re-tying the silk muffler in the neck of his shirt.

"Well, Mother, I think I'll just walk down to the pub for half an hour. Our Jim said he might look in, and I've got a few cabbage plants I want to give him."

Charlotte smiled. Some things never changed.

"Get off with you then," she said.

As the door closed after him, she went to the cupboard, and took out the Royal scrap-book Jack had kept for her when he was a boy. Then she carried it over to the window where it was light, and sitting down on the hard-backed chair, began lovingly to turn the pages. It was all there, the story of an age, between the dog-eared covers. And although she knew it almost by heart, it never palled. There was the picture of the King and Queen in their coronation robes, and one of the king and the Prince of Wales reviewing the fleet just before the war. And even a picture of King Albert of the Belgians, who had fought with his people in the trenches when his country was invaded, had been included.

In the failing light, Charlotte sat poring over the book. These were her memories. Nobody could take them away from her.

463

IT WAS a warm Sunday afternoon in August, and Rosa Clements was singing to herself as she crossed the field behind the post office and general stores at Withydown.

Six months ago she had moved in here, helping in the store and sharing the flat above with Mrs Cray, the elderly widowed owner, and she was happier than she had ever been in her life. She had a certain status here that she had never had before, and the people who came into the shop treated her as they found her, instead of looking down their noses at her as the people of Hillsbridge had done. Three miles was far enough to leave a reputation behind, and Rosa was attractive enough in both looks and manner for her new acquaintances to give her the benefit of the doubt.

As for her living quarters, Rosa had never known such luxury. She had a room of her own, filled with furniture that had always been treated with respect, instead of the battered junk she had been used to. The jug and basin that stood on her wash-stand did not have a single crack in them, and the design of pale pink rosebuds and darker, fully blown roses pleased her. Even the mirror was still perfect, so that when she looked at her face, it did not impose blemishes that were not really there. Without doubt, the greatest luxury of all was the inside privy, or W.C. as Mrs Cray called it. Sharing the flat posed no problems. Mrs Cray was good-natured and easy-going, and she liked Rosa. Best of all, she never questioned her as to where she was going in her own time. If she had, Rosa would have forgotten all the other advantages and left, because to her, nothing in the world was more important than her freedom.

Most evenings, when the shop had been tidied and she and Mrs Cray had eaten and cleared away their evening meal, she went for a walk along the lanes or across the fields, and it was the same at weekends, too.

Yes, she was happy, and her only aching regret, still, was Ted.

She had done her best for him in court, and she had expected nothing in return. But the day after the trial, when the Halls had invited her around for a cup of tea, she had thought for a minute that things might be different. There had been something in the way Ted had looked at her that had given her the idea, a brief glance that had set her heart singing and the blood pumping through her veins in an excited torrent. And a feeling of closeness, too, as if he, like her, was remembering some of the things they had shared. Afterwards, when he had gone away again, she had told herself it was

464

nothing but wishful thinking. It was a long time since she had been so sure that he would one day be hers, and looking back it seemed just a dream, wonderful, but childish.

But for all that, she still clung to the conviction that no one but Ted would do for her. She had tried to forget him with Jack, and that had been disastrous. Now, if she could not have Ted, she was determined to make a life without a man.

Briefly, that August afternoon, her mind went back to the days when she had first learned for sure the truth about her father and run away—from Jack, from Hillsbridge, and everyone who had known her. She had gone, for a while, with the fair, thinking that if they were really her people, she belonged with them and the roving life. But it had not worked out as she had hoped. She had found the close-knit family atmosphere even more claustrophobic than the four walls of a house, and in spite of what she knew about herself, she had almost looked down on the gypsies who might, or might not, be her blood-related kinfolk. She left them even before the court case, finding work as a live-in maid, and when on one of her visits to see her father and brothers, she had decided to apply for the job in the post office at Withydown, it had been like coming home in more senses than one.

Now that she was only three miles away, it seemed she went back to Greenslade Terrace less often. Walter was married again, to Molly Hamblin, and he never seemed as pleased to see her as she would have liked. Perhaps because he knows he's not my father, she thought, with the extra sensitivity that the knowledge had brought to her.

They no longer needed her, and now that she was back in the countryside that had the familiar smell of Somerset—that indefinable combination of corn and coal-dust, green grass and pit-chimney smoke—she needed them less, too.

And so she hardly ever saw Ted. He was away, too, still getting the wanderlust out of his blood, and their visits rarely coincided. But the last time she had been in the rank she had seen him, and she had turned away, as shy as if she were a young girl again. That was the result of thinking about him too much!

But that summer afternoon, as she climbed the stile into the lane, he was still on her mind, and as the front of the post office and general stores came into view, she started. The man standing on the pavement in front of the shuttered window might almost have been

Ted! His back was towards her, but the set of his shoulders and his thick, fair hair . . .

"Don't be so silly," she told herself. "Why in the world should it be Ted?"

But her heart was thumping, shyness making her hot—as if I were thirteen again, not twenty-one, she thought. And when he turned around, and she saw his face, all the use seemed to go out of her legs.

The similarity had not been in her imagination. It *was* Ted.

Colour flooded her cheeks, and she wished she could turn and run. What was he *doing* here? He couldn't have come to see her, could he? She mustn't even think such a thing!

She walked towards him slowly, eyeing him warily.

"Hello, Rosa," he said, and she somehow knew the casual manner hid an embarrassment as acute as hers. "How are you doing?"

"All right. How are you?"

"Oh, all right. There's no work to be had now, that's the trouble. Serves me right, I suppose. I should have took a job and stuck to it."

She laughed, a little falsely. "I can't say anything about that. It would be the pot calling the kettle black."

"Yes. But you've landed on your feet, haven't you?"

"I've been lucky."

There was an awkward silence, and taking her courage in both hands, she added: "What are you doing in Withydown?"

He looked embarrassed again. "I came home last week, and I'm at a loose end. I've been for a walk, and when I found myself at the top of the hill, I thought I'd stroll down and see if you were about."

Suddenly the old hurt was back, and she was remembering how he had once told her she was just a substitute for Rebecca Church. "So I'm only good for when you're at a loose end," she said tartly.

"No, I didn't mean that . . . "

She sighed. "It's all right. I know what you meant. But I won't be used twice, Ted. Once was more than enough."

For a moment he did not answer, and she was about to turn away when he stopped her. "Have you got to go back in now—or do you fancy a walk?"

"I've just been for a walk, but . . . it's a nice day, I suppose. Which way?"

"You're the one who knows it around here. I'll follow you."

"There's a lane across there that leads up to the railway line. It's steep, but there's a nice view from the top."

They set off, but the awkwardness was still there like a wall between them, and they did not speak until they reached the V-gate at the top of the lane. They went through it, Rosa first, then Ted, and sat down on the slope of the railway embankment. Beneath them, the valley spread out green and peaceful, but they hardly noticed it. Rosa began picking wiry blades of grass, plaiting them together, and Ted watched her for a moment. Then he said, "I wasn't fair with you. I know that now. But it was too soon."

Breath caught in her throat. She hardly dared hope there might be anything more behind his words. She went on plaiting grass, not looking at him.

"Becky was very special to me." He might almost have been talking to himself. "But now it's more as if she was a dream. Sometimes I can hardly believe it ever happened—any of it. It's more like a picture I'd seen at the Palace, or a book I'd read. And now . . ." He glanced along at her. "I can't help thinking about you, Rosa. I have done ever since the trial, really. You saved my neck—and all that after I'd treated you so badly."

"I thought you were angry with me, saying what I did," she said quietly.

"At the time I was," he admitted. "But I wasn't seeing things very straight then. Now . . . well, I'm grateful."

"You don't have to be," she said. "That wasn't why I did it."

"No, but I am, all the same. And it's not only that. I shan't be surprised if you refuse after the way I let you down, but I'd like to see you again, Rosa."

"Not as a substitute," she said.

"Not as a substitute."

For a long moment they looked at one another, the blue eyes and the dark meeting. Then his hand slid across the wiry grass until their fingers touched. Happiness burst in her like a Roman candle on firework night, so that there was suddenly brilliance and beauty where before there had been only darkness. And still in the grass, their fingers twined, tentative, but outstretched and seeking.

It was a beginning.

JACK and Stella were married in September, in one of the grandest ceremonies ever seen in Hillsbridge. Neither had really wanted it to be that way, but the rumours about Hal had proved to be true. He was retiring and going back to his native North Country, and Mrs

O'Halloran was determined not only to make up for the austerity of Grace's war-time wedding to Dr Scott, but also to leave an indelible impression on the town where she had spent most of her married life.

Instead of horses and traps, there were motors to carry the guests to and from the church, where the Reverend Reuben Clarke officiated. Dolly and Amy were among the six bridesmaids, in dresses of figured silk, and Alex was a pageboy, looking very grown-up and important as he led Oliver and Grace Scott's toddler, Frances, up the aisle to strew rose petals from her little basket in front of the bridal pair.

The wedding breakfast was held in a marquee on the lawn of the O'Halloran house, and there were a hundred and fifty guests. All the important people of Hillsbridge were there, even, to Charlotte's discomfort, Caroline Archer, but she managed to hide behind her hat every time she saw the former Rector's wife looking in her direction. And Peggy, of course, had been invited. No family celebration would be quite complete without her.

When things quieted down a bit, Charlotte and James found a corner where they could sit down in peace to have something to eat —small, dainty sandwiches and some sort of meat paste that Jack said was called paté—and catch their breath after the excitement.

"Fancy our Jack marrying into all this," Charlotte said, but as she caught sight of him, standing beside Stella and talking with ease to the most important of the guests, she knew that he would fit in much better than he ever would have done with his father's pit cronies. It was the way he was made, and that was all there was to it. But it could never be her way. She would never feel anything but an outsider with grand people like these.

Beside her, James was slurping a little as he tried to drink his tea with unaccustomed delicacy, and she knew he was probably longing to undo the top button of his trousers and lie back, handkerchief over his face, to enjoy the warm September sunshine.

A smile played around her mouth, and she found herself remembering her own wedding, so many years ago now.

It hadn't been a grand do like this, of course. But she'd been happy, just as happy as Stella looked today. She had felt quite sure she was doing the right thing, and so she had been. Maybe the batches hadn't been the romantic black mountains she had imagined them, protecting their magical hidden valley. Maybe James hadn't been her Prince Charming on a dashing white charger. But then, in the end, who is? We are all, after all, only human.

And in spite of the hard times and the tragedies, in spite of the bone-aching work and the small graves in the churchyard, it hadn't been such a bad life. There'd been plenty of laughter and love, plenty of happy memories to warm the autumn of her life. If Jack and Stella were as lucky as she and James had been, they wouldn't do too badly.

But in the end, it's all what you make it, thought Charlotte. Whatever they do, they have to learn that for themselves. I cannot do it for them. Nor should I.

In spite of the warm sunshine, a feeling of loneliness touched her momentarily. None of them needed her any more, except Harry, and he was growing up fast. Soon they'd all be gone and the house would be empty.

No—not empty. It would be simply her and James as it had been in the beginning. Smiling, she reached out and tucked her arm through his, knowing how he would be hating all this.

"We'll go home soon, don't worry," she said.

I

Tanner, Janet.
The hours of light

PORTVILLE FREE LIBRARY

PORTVILLE, N. Y.

Member Of
Chautauqua-Cattaraugus Library System